WORLD WALKERS

By Neal Asher

Agent Cormac series
Gridlinked • The Line of Polity
Brass Man • Polity Agent • Line War

Spatterjay trilogy
The Skinner
The Voyage of the Sable Keech
Orbus

Standalone Polity novels
Prador Moon • Hilldiggers
Shadow of the Scorpion • The Technician
Jack Four • Weaponized • War Bodies

The Owner series
The Departure • Zero Point • Jupiter War
World Walkers

Transformation trilogy
Dark Intelligence • War Factory
Infinity Engine

Rise of the Jain trilogy
The Soldier • The Warship
The Human

Cowl

Novellas
The Parasite • Mindgames: Fool's Mate

Short-story collections
Runcible Tales • The Engineer
The Gabble

NEAL
ASHER
WORLD WALKERS

Published 2024 by Pyr®

Cover illustration © Shutterstock/Vezdehod
Cover design by Jennifer Do
Cover design © Start Science Fiction

Inquiries should be addressed to

Start Science Fiction
221 Reiver Street, 9th Floor
Hoboken, New Jersey 07030
Phone: 212-431-5455
www.pyrsf.com

10 9 8 7 6 5 4 3 2 1

ISBN 978-1-64506-088-8 (pbk.)
ISBN 978-1-64560-098-7 (ebook)

Printed in the United States of America

I seem to be running out of things to write on this page. The well of Oscar speeches about whom I would like to thank or dedicate this to has run dry. I've talked about all those wonderful writers I read in the past, the scientists and science article writers, the podcasters and others – all those sources of inspiration and suppliers of the grist to my mill. But let me talk about them generally. As well as being useful to me, all are positive forces – much needed in a world seemingly laden with doom. The crazy thing about this is that, by every metric, human existence has never been better than it is now. But then it is a human survival mechanism to think the worst. He who always runs from movement in the bushes thinking it's a sabre-toothed tiger may get it wrong a hundred times, while he who thinks it is not and doesn't run will only be wrong once. A version of thinking the worst, for me in writing, has been the dystopia of the Owner future, with its totalitarian Committee Earth. It's a possible horrible future that would require utter totalitarian oppression to slow technological development to a crawl and drive humanity into a Malthusian nightmare. It's a shaking bush we perhaps should not ignore. Here I return to that future, but from a different angle. I've done utopia, dystopia and time travel, so now it's time to look at parallel worlds.

Enjoy!

Acknowledgements

Thanks to the staff at Pan Macmillan, and elsewhere, who have helped bring this novel to your e-reader, smartphone, computer screen and that old-fashioned mass of wood pulp called a book. These include: Bella Pagan (publisher), Michael Beale (editor), Melissa Bond (editorial manager), Neil Lang (jacket designer) and the Pan Mac marketing team; freelancers Claire Baldwin (structural editor), Jessica Cuthbert-Smith (copy-editor), Robert Clark (proofreader), Steve Stone (jacket illustrator) and Olivia-Savannah Roach (publicity); and others whose names I simply don't know.

1

The Fenris – Past

The Fenris awoke with a surge of excitement. Curled up in gel, with pipes and data feeds entering his body at numerous points, he opened violet eyes and gained only a blurred impression of his surroundings. But then, engaging other receptors in his long skull, he found himself in a maternal cyst, in one of the long halls that must be a birthing facility – according to the knowledge already loading to his brain. This knowledge, a dry factual cataloguing of reality, swiftly laid down strata of scientific understanding and told him of his race and something of their history. Birth, millennia ago, had been an organic matter of gestation inside a female fenris. But nowadays, with their science so advanced, the optimization of a new addition to their race could be much better controlled outside the womb.

His skull continued to fill. Data was laid down in semi-organic substrates, of which so much of his body consisted, added throughout a million years of biotechnology and controlled evolution. But the data was just a lens through which he looked at the world, with the excitement of a child. Grasping his power and huge breadth of understanding, he became eager to take his place in the world. The loading continued to fill in detail about his kind, finishing with the Great Project. The audacity and high aims of this astounded him. Only on his world could something so ambitious have been attempted. Then, on checking timescales and his inception date, he realized that the experiment must have already concluded. He waited, anxious to be born into his new life to see the results.

Nothing happened.

Hours and hours passed, during which he kept pushing his concentration back to the feed to learn more, and it became clear he should not have been conscious for so long inside the cyst. Using his enhanced senses, he gazed beyond the birthing cyst as far as possible, but could detect no movement. Something was wrong. He began to squirm in the gel, to flex his limbs and stretch out one arm to the wall of the cyst, but still nothing out there responded. Finally, examining himself through the lens of that knowledge, he saw that he was way beyond the point when all his tubes and wires should have automatically disconnected. He had to do something more. Now knowing the extreme durability of his body, he began pulling out tubes. The sudden pain had him frantically searching internal control until he could shut it down and concentrate on healing processes that for him could be conscious. The gel darkened with a network of his black blood. He closed off broken capillaries, sealed entry points to his gut and other organs, closed up splits through dense muscle, and then switched over the detail to autonomics. Soon he had freed himself of all but the data and neurochem feeds into his skull. As yet, he didn't feel confident enough to remove them, but the pipes and wires had plenty of slack, so he could free himself further in another way.

He reached out with one long arm – still far from attaining its full growth – and prodded the cyst wall again. It was tough stuff but not resistant to the sharpness of the claw he extruded from the end of his finger. With a jerk, he stabbed through it, feeling guilty about damaging the cyst. He then drew the claw down, slicing through the membrane. The gel bulged out, and the whole bubble of it, with him at the centre, slid out of the cyst, as he would have done in a natural birth. He hit the floor in a squat, the gel splashing around him then blobbing up with the pseudo-life of a Newtonian fluid. He squeezed out tears, blinked, and cleared the stuff from his eyes, then looked up at the flaccid cyst above, with the connections to his skull running up into it. He next snorted gel from his nostrils and, in a series of convulsions, expelled it from his lungs. He took his first breath.

The air had a strange taint and seemed overly warm, but how could he be sure of what it should be, with these being his first breaths? Looking along the row of cysts, his among them, he saw that all the others hung like figs dried out on their tree, yet with angular structures caught inside. Much of their gel contents had pooled on the floor below and dried out to turn crusty like scabs. Amid these lay thousands of small objects of a regular shape. Focusing his superb vision on the nearest, he recognized red insect chrysalises. Now he realized that something was *very* wrong. He sniffed, raised analysis through his implanted database and attached the chemical signatures to a word: putrefaction. Then he heard a droning sound. A black mist arose at the far end of the birthing chamber, and he felt the first flies landing on his skin and biting.

The Fenris brushed them away. He understood their biotech purpose was to update the biology of his kind, to inoculate him against new threats, but the dry factuality of his upload told him he couldn't trust them to be functioning correctly. He came unsteadily to his feet, seeing the larger cloud of flies boiling towards him, and he feared how their programming might be defective. They might all want to impart their information, and thousands upon thousands of bites and the ensuing updates could very well kill him. With little choice now, he reached up and pulled the connections out of his skull. Intense pain hit. He closed this off, and then the blood vessels spilled their contents down his face. Leaving the wounds to autonomics again, he headed away from the swarm towards the clean lock door at the other end of the chamber. A touch to the central pad opened it for him – like all the devices of his world, it responded to his DNA – and he entered the lock. As the first door closed behind him, he belligerently crushed every fly he could find before opening the next door. Stepping out, his foot crunched on something and he moved aside, peering down. It was a skeleton.

He recognized the bone structure of a female of his kind. As an adult, she had of course been three times his height and her bones had a bluish cast, glinting with the nacre of inlaid bio-electrics. The oddity of her presence here was no more baffling than finding that the inocular flies had managed to penetrate the layers of security into the birthing chamber. He recognized other oddities too. Nothing remained of her but bones. Besides the death of a fenris being an improbability, the decay of a fenris body would take an age due to all the protective biotech. That the body had remained here indicated no one else had been around to clear it up either. And now he looked more closely, he could see that some of the bone had turned to powder. Horrifying speculations arose about what he might find beyond this place, and then a flash of anger. He kicked a bone, skittering it across the floor. How unfair to be faced with this as a newborn!

The dry factual drone of his knowledge, stifling his youthful mind, did not allow the anger to last. He scanned around him. This circular room had semi-organic ducts, for data and materials, growing up the walls as well as branching across the domed ceiling. The trunks and branches were dull and flaking in places, and the technology here appeared to be dead. Yet the clean lock behind had worked smoothly. Fenris technology rarely broke down; when it did, other tech swiftly repaired it – it wasn't often that a fenris had to intervene. Returning his attention to the skeleton, he now understood the breakdown here was the reason it had been left, since cleaning biomechs should have removed it, for submission to the requisite authorities or disposal. But why was this corpse so decayed, while the decay in the birthing chamber had been more recent? Just a moment's thought rendered the answer. Fenris were not born regularly. He'd mistakenly applied the label of 'birthing chamber' to the hall beyond that lock, when it was in fact a storage chamber for pre-birth fenris. The place should have been kept at absolute zero, with the likes of himself removed to another place for defrosting and birth. The system had obviously failed a long time after the death of the fenris here, letting in the flies and allowing the temperature to rise. He had survived the thawing process, while thousands of others had not. The fact the system had retained enough integrity to provide his mental loading must have been a matter of luck. His whole existence was.

The Fenris abruptly headed for the next door and found it did not react to him. Undoing its manual lock helped, but the door was stuck to its seal, so he dug his claws into the edge of that and heaved. The thing resisted until his arms were burning, then it finally opened with a tearing sound. Had he been an adult, it wouldn't have challenged him at all. He stepped out into a long tube curling up to his left and right, oblate and twisted, with the walls lichen patterned. A map of his world arose for his inspection and, with his other senses also giving him the shape of his surroundings in a sphere a kilometre across, he perfectly located himself.

He turned right and began walking, carefully studying his immediate surroundings. There was no sign of any other dead fenris but, a few hundred metres along, blue beetle cleaner bots crawled along the walls. If there had been remains here, they'd long since been removed. He needed to know what had happened, and that need boiled up into a surge of energy. He broke into a run and felt the joy of that movement, with the map and dry knowledge providing a destination where he might find answers. After branching numerous times, the tube eventually came out onto the surface of his world, and there opened a transparent band, with a view of the outside. He slowed to a walk, annoyed by the childish exuberance that had driven him to run, and annoyed by the adult knowledge implanted in his mind. The tube ran across a metallic landscape, seemingly assembled out of numerous blocks. This was what he had expected to see, but not the great scar of wreckage before him, with collapsed structures and skeletal frameworks slewing in from the right and converging ahead.

He kept walking, until he came to a safety door and looked through its window. The tube had been severed and more tangled wreckage lay beyond. Scanning further ahead with his inner senses, he saw the continuation of the tube after a hundred metres and pressed a hand against the opening pad. He received a warning straight into his biotech, though, and quickly withdrew it. The mix of air out there was lacking in oxygen, and he didn't know why. Another thing he really needed to find out. He hyperventilated, understanding this would be all he'd need, since the distance wasn't too far; he had no reason to switch his body over to hypoxic. He opened the door. A blast of equalizing air pressure hit him and it was freezing cold. Breath held, he walked along the bonelike beams and slabs that were like dragon scales. A building had fallen here, collapsing the tube, while deep pits delved down into a mass of fenris structure. It had the appearance of some titanic creature twisted through hard technological wreckage, and long decayed. He paused and scanned around, lost in the intensity of this new input.

Cirrus clouds frosted the deep blue sky – white above, then darkened to yellows and browns over the sunset. He walked out to the edge of a slab and leapt onto another, peering ahead to his destination. There he saw the five-kilometre black thorn of a tower rising from a spread of giant, nodular, fungal masses. At least that still stood. Just like the tube he'd walked along, and everything that lay below, the thing had grown, guided by harder technologies. Similar biotechnology covered the entire surface of the world – an ecosystem turned to fenris utility, and only scraps of old evolved biology left. But now he had no idea how much of it remained intact.

Finally, reaching the continuation of the tube and a second safety door, he entered and breathed again. Dry knowledge raised a wave of dread, for the lack of oxygen out there seemed unlikely to be a local phenomenon. The child walked on, absorbing the wonder of a world that was new to him.

The tube finally turned up into the tower, acquiring slab steps suitable for the long stride of his kind. The Fenris climbed them, made aware again of his diminutive size, but also of the growing hunger that would feed his growth. On the way up, he passed entrances into globular chambers whose outer faces were transparent to the sky, almost like eyeballs. A few of these were shattered and closed off by doors, while others somewhere in the tower lay open, with frequent frigid breezes blowing through. He found himself panting at the lack of oxygen as the biotech in the building struggled to keep it to the optimum. The chambers grew smaller as he climbed higher, and the circumference of the tower tightened. Finally he came out into the data transmission peak.

The tall room, with its ceiling closing to a vanishing point, seemed wholly occupied by standing sheets of glass and filmier substances too, all bound together with hard, fleshy biotech. The transparent walls gave him a view across his world, where the scars of wreckage formed curious, regular curves. Here and there he saw the glint of powered lights, but also fires that must be fed by biotech-generated oxygen. Up above, stars speckled the now night-time sky, a backdrop to the giant orbital structures also hanging there. One, like an ancient combustion engine a hundred kilometres across, he recognized. It was one of the engines that had driven the Great Project. The moon rose like a city dome on the horizon, with its ring system hooked up above it.

He walked through the room, the glass sheets sliding out of his path, until he reached a console. This doughnut of material held a pseudo-matter interface at its centre, which seemed to shimmer in and out of reality, but the hand-shaped imprint in the middle of it remained perfectly stable. The Fenris reached down, painfully aware of how his small hand wouldn't fit it. Now he'd find out what had happened to his world, and to his people. And about the Great Project.

In the far past, his kind had gone to their moon and explored it thoroughly. They went on to explore their solar system and took their shots at the stars. Interstellar exploration continued, but their race then divided into two factions: those who had their eyes on the stars, and those who began to examine, and gain access to, the seeming infinitude of worlds parallel to their own. They discovered the multiverse. The latter remained in the vicinity of their world and retained much of their biological and mental history, in their forms and their technology. The former changed beyond easy conception, adapting to vacuum and the vast reaches of time that interstellar travel involved. The Fenris was of the multiverse kind.

In the multiverse, the fenris explored worlds that seemed to be shadows of theirs – or reflections in mirrors, facing in towards their own world. These stretched into infinity, with infinitesimal differences between each accumulating, until they became utterly alien places, occupied by alien cultures or no cultures at all. Oddly, those on the nearest reflections had also discovered the multiverse, but no effort had been made to explore it beyond that. His kind made contact with their mirrored kind on those closest worlds and began technological and material exchanges. Some conflicts ensued too, but his kind always seemed to come out on top. Their shadows appeared to lack substance, will and energy.

So they held dominion over many worlds and discovered flaws in the reflecting, shadow world model too. Drastic changes, or twists, in their laws of physics became apparent, and the symmetry of it all seemed to have broken. Overall it was as if, stretching out from their world, reality steadily degraded. Dirty mirrors, one researcher called it. Their growing understanding of the multiverse and these worlds then raised something concerning, and ultimately depressing: reality returned to its original form.

If they made changes in closer worlds, over periods of months and years those changes dissolved, swept away. The world concerned would return to being a weak reflection of their own. The theoreticians got to work on this, while the mathematicians and other scientists shaped and proved their model. Their own world they described as nodal; it was the only one on which drastic changes could be enacted, then *these* would be reflected. Any drastic changes on shadow worlds eventually came to nothing. Their 'nodal' world was, in essence, the only one where true free will existed. Why? There was no 'why', just the reality. To test this, they caused an atomic blast on a shadow world, destroying an island. Much was the furore on that world about

9

the incident. Then the fenris tracked the changes over the ensuing months: the disappearance of information about it, the rapid drop of radioactivity on the island, and the return of its life and shape. Five years later, no one on that world had any memory of the incident. During this time the nodal fenris also brought shadow fenris to their world and it soon became evident they were sickening, growing increasingly confused and *thin*, until they started dying and fading completely. It seemed at first that they couldn't exist in the harsh clarity of the nodal world. Only later did the nodal fenris discover these individuals alive again, back on their shadow worlds, some with vague memories of travelling and others with none at all.

The shadow worlds weren't real and nobody there had any choices or ability to decide their future. The nodal world stood as the central model they followed poorly. This stabbed at something deep within the fenris concerning free will. It had arisen a million years in their past, during tens of thousands of years of authoritarian rule, when they'd lived under regimes with every thought and action monitored and controlled. Hideous wars and slaughter, and the adaptation of their own biology, had arisen to release them from that. Now it seemed they were the unwilling autocrats, and their every action dictated those of an infinitude of shadows. And so, because they were the ones who could bring about change, the Great Project was conceived, becoming the focus of their race.

What if the shadow, reflected worlds could be unlinked from their nodal world? What if they could be freed to navigate their own course? The fenris turned their powerful science to the task of severing these chains. Making engines that would feed off the power of their sun, and a million other suns, they aimed to dice up the parallels in their multiverse network. They would fold reality around those other worlds and free their brethren from this unintentional dominion. Some raised concerns and pointed to those places in the multiverse where parallel worlds ceased to be reflections, and where the laws of physics appeared broken. Could these be the detritus of previous attempts to do the same? Their concerns were ignored by the bulk of the race, though, and the objectors took what they needed and headed out to their interstellar kin. The great engines were rigged for this task, while a particular fenris was gestated in a womb cyst, and grew to the point where he could be stored. This was where he'd been just before the engines were turned on. And now he was born.

I am the Fenris.

The truth of that statement tore at his insides, while his second-hand knowledge didn't give him the experience to know how to grieve, as he watched the rest of the history play out. The engines came on, and he saw their sun, as well as the many others, wink out of their existence. The sky turned black but the fenris survived with their technology intact. They found themselves caught in their own cyst of reality, much like the cyst he'd been frozen inside, even as their atmosphere itself froze and snowed down over them. Survival for perhaps millions of years remained assured, for they could burn the matter of their world to that end. But what then? With an expiration point to their existence in sight, and their world closed off from the greater multiverse, they fell into despair. Many began to die – mostly through choice and deliberate neglect. However, a small clique of scientists worked on something radical that would require sacrificing a massive amount of energy to entropy. They began to alter the engines in orbit to create a pseudo-matter tool that would be able to penetrate their enclosed reality.

Fenris continued to die, with many now sacrificing their resources to this new project. Four thousand years passed, while much of the life, biotech and even atmosphere of their world expired, and the race diminished. Finally, the engines were ready for the next step. But remaining fenris, clinging to life, baulked at turning the things on again. Autocracy arrived in the form of a science council, an echo of their despised history of societal repression. War ensued in an agreed form but, as the council began to lose, it acted independently and turned the engines on anyway. It was sacrificial and suicidal, because the plan had been to put the remaining population into hibernation. The Fenris observed the engines reach out a claw to penetrate the reality cyst around his world, and he shuddered at how this reflected his own birth. The massive drain sucked life and energy out of the world, freezing fenris where they stood, or fought, and dropped them to the ground dead. Massive feedback loops wrought destruction, as did the fall of some of the engines, with world technology failing. Then, like a wonder, the sun rose, but it was over the death of a race. Remaining technology, and the world, absorbed energy from this new continuum and began to rebuild, with many failures along the way. It was one of those failures that had allowed him to be born.

'I am Fenris,' he said out loud. And this was indeed the case. He could find no trace of any other living member of his kind on his world. He was now the entirety of his race.

Irene – Present

As Irene arrived in the sprawl, the stink immediately hit her: excrement, body odour, the putrefaction leaking from ill-named macerators and composting tanks, which mainly functioned to grind down human corpses. The disgust wrinkling her nostrils fled in seconds, to be replaced by a weird nostalgia for her childhood spent here in the New York Sprawl. She paused to touch her right ear and inspect the blood on her finger. She felt tired in ways that went beyond the physical, drained of the energy it had taken to get her here, and slightly nauseated. She could do it again, this journey between worlds, but knew that afterwards she'd be even more drained, with more blood leaking out of her, and biological alerts she only understood on a visceral level rising to her inner perception. But had it been easier this time? Was it getting any better? Further thought was cut off as someone bumped into her, reminding her that the people all around were no longer shadows.

Her hand snapped down, grabbing another that had already undone the Velcro sealing of one pocket in her long coat. She held it tightly and gazed down on the thief.

'You weren't here. Then you were!' the girl exclaimed.

Irene studied her: clothing part paperwear, but with nigh-indestructible monofilament trousers, jacket and slippers that had probably been passed down over generations. The girl looked healthy and surprisingly clean, her black hair cropped close to her head and lightly dusted with the purple of louse powder. She gazed at Irene with startlingly blue eyes. It reminded Irene of a time when she had been put out to thieve, quickly losing all innocence.

'And your first instinct was to see what you could steal?' Irene asked.

'You're a mutant,' the girl said, by way of delaying the expected beating, or killing. Human life had become cheap in the sprawls, with policing focused on being a barrier between Zero Assets like this girl, and the more important Societal Assets, who contributed to this sick society. It was a social model the USA had adopted years ago under the direction of the international Committee. One consequence was that the deaths of ZAs were now simply viewed as a sanitary problem by those above them.

The streets did have their own enforcement, but usually at the level of family, criminal gangs and the very occasional attempts by some to form a charitable and altruistic network.

Irene scanned around her. A few of those in the milling crowds had halted to watch, something interesting in their dull struggle for survival. Others were beginning to gather; they'd seen a thief being caught and expected some bloody entertainment. More importantly, the one who'd caught her seemed to be an unusual mutant. Irene stood exceedingly tall, at nigh-on two metres, and her features were extended on a long face. Upon checking herself in a mirror, Irene had also discovered she'd acquired strikingly violet eyes. Her clothing bespoke some degree of wealth, for the military long coat was a rare acquisition, while the baggy camo monofilament trousers were tucked into boots that looked not in the slightest bit worn. She must be a crime lord, a family matriarch or one of those slumming SAs of the more violent kind who sought out prey amid the horde.

'Go.' She released the girl's hand and pushed her away, then pulled up the hood of her coat for concealment and headed off with a long, vigorous stride. Occasionally glancing back, she saw some people following but, being tired, hungry and weak, they soon lost interest. Scanning her surroundings again, she took in the high tenements, the armoured blocks of distribution centres and the composting silos. There were no shops here, since no one in the middle of a ZA area had the social credit to buy anything. However, she did see some market stalls for the trade of second-hand goods and occasional produce grown on the tops of the tenements.

Cams were in evidence, usually on thin, unbreakable posts, or high up on buildings. These ran with just low-level crowd-control AI, and only a few had readerguns, which was why she had chosen this point of arrival. Such areas, interlinked throughout the sprawl here, were effectively internment camps. The smarter AI watched the SA areas and the monolithic buildings of the Federal Bureaucracy. Most of the readerguns, razorbirds, police, Inspectorate and other mechanisms of control resided in and around there too. Strategically positioned to keep out the dross.

Irene moved into an alley just as crowded as the main streets, then backed up against a wall. She raised one long hand on which the fingernails seemed to be turning into claws, and pulled up her sleeve. This revealed the Chinese military-grade, bullet-proof padding beneath, going over her forearm and down to the wrist. Her partner Chenghu, using equipment stolen in China from his previous place of employment, had reprogrammed the ID chip in her forearm, since – with her recent physical changes – she wouldn't have matched its original stored profile. Any return here would have become very difficult for her otherwise, as soon as one of those smarter AIs spotted the disparity. Not that she was adverse to difficulty, of course.

Now the chip confirmed her biometric identity, a readergun wouldn't automatically slam its usual three mercury slugs into her chest. She turned her arm over and studied the screen inset in the padding. A map had already established, along with a locator dot for her target, but she didn't need it. The weird internal sense her biotech had given her was like having holographic vision of her surroundings in a sphere half a kilometre across, and she recognized her location. She set out again, pushing through crowds and slapping away seeking hands.

'Why shouldn't I just jump straight in there?' she'd asked Chenghu when she had first proposed this. He had demurred.

'Because we don't want them to know anything about us. It has to look just like a normal resistance attack.' He'd grimaced, rubbing at his arm where she'd dug out a bullet, the wound now swiftly healing. His last visit to China for the equipment had not been without cost. 'AIs would see your arrival, analyse the threat, and strategies would be prepared. That'd be dangerous for us the next time, should we have any reason to go back there.'

It made sense, but she didn't particularly believe him. She reckoned this had been another of his not-so-subtle moves to try to dissuade her from going altogether. She could have argued him down, asserting her dominance. But in the end, she'd agreed because she relished the prospect of testing herself alone, and the other way also seemed too easy to be satisfying.

In yet another alley, she noted two large men coming in behind her and felt a surge of anxiety. Then the realization hit her, one that had been coming more and more often now. She was no longer a young woman who needed to be fearful of masculine strength. Her travels across the multiverse had certainly made her recognize *that*. And her internal perception of the changes she'd undergone took this even further. She knew how fast she was, and she had a physical confidence she'd never felt before. No normal man was a match for her – the only one she might have had something to fear from in that respect was the similarly biotech-advanced Chenghu. She'd found other ways to control him. She turned to face the two amid the crowd here, but they just moved on past her, talking low. It seemed her enhanced senses also brought some degree of paranoia. Watching them go, she felt a momentary disappointment before moving on.

The crowds began to thin as she strode from the tenements into a slightly more salubrious area. This was still in ZA territory but exchanges with SAs had raised some ZAs to a higher, though not government-recognized, status. She frowned at that. The ZAs here improved their lives by providing services to the SAs. This usually entailed the only thing they had any ownership of, or at least nominal control over: their bodies. And too often the bodies of their children. She suppressed a stab of anger, knowing that her loving family had been preparing a place for her here, to become an SA whore.

She surveyed the better buildings, with windows still in place, reinforced doors and security systems. She even saw a street-cleaning robot, which, a mile back, would soon have ended up in pieces to be traded. The people here were better dressed too, with some SA clothing in evidence. Thugs lingered about the entrances to many buildings, lit signs above them flickering to advertise the wares within. Occasionally she identified someone who looked too clean and healthy, despite the downgrade of their clothing. Usually heavyset individuals walked around them, with suspicious bulges under their coats. SAs out on the town for entertainment.

Irene paused to study the scene. Using her enhanced senses – her holosense – she glimpsed those wares in action behind the doors, and then withdrew. So much was broken here that it all appeared beyond repair. Eighteen billion people lived on this Earth, most of them in utter poverty because of the political system becoming entrenched in ever more countries. This system took away reasons to strive, to be better, and considered the majority of the populace an infestation that needed to be controlled, or exterminated. Scum floated to the top in countries like this too and seemed to be coagulating into a whole across the world. The state bureaucracies were the worst of it – now nepotistic and almost on a different course of evolution from those below them. She could kill one piece of that scum, but the rest would just flow into the space it occupied. So why bother? She was, as Chenghu had argued, out of it now.

She almost turned away then, but Garrick came to her mind once more. The man had been an SA street political officer who'd risen through the ranks in the New York Sprawl. He had been in control – a city sector governor – when Irene was brought in. She raised a hand and touched the faded scars on her face.

He'd taken a special interest in her and had been there watching, and directing, her *treatment*. To her he represented everything that was wrong with this world. She felt she had to do something about him – not so much because it would improve things here, but just because she needed it. She continued on her way.

The dividing line between ZA sprawl and SA territory soon became evident. The street widened and the buildings on either side could be characterized as apartment blocks rather than tenements. Scattered outside them, beside the pavements, were actual personal transport vehicles. And, mostly well dressed, the people moved along those uncrowded pavements with a purposeful air, stopping to peer into shopfronts. Flashes of green in side streets seemed to pull at the eyes, for trees and even some patches of grass grew here from exposed soil.

However, tension was laced throughout this place. SAs, though wealthier than ZAs, with social credit to spend and luxuries available to them, still didn't live anywhere near the level of their forebears before the Committee began imposing its will across the world. Also, precisely because they were 'societal assets', the state kept an even closer eye on them. A lot of the human watchers – armed security or Inspectorate officers – patrolled here because of its proximity to the ZA sprawl but, up on the buildings and posts, the usual cams now protruded predominantly over the barrels of readerguns. Higher still, Irene could see what looked like rows of roosting metal seagulls. These razorbirds could fly down at any moment and punish infractions. Generally there was only one punishment.

As she moved in, Irene pulled back her hood, since concealing one's face was one of those infractions. She noted some ZAs in the area being checked out by two Inspectorate officers in impact armour and carrying squat machine guns. The ZAs were then turned away. Glancing at her arm screen, she saw it indicate the cams were checking her out too. Like the Inspectorate officers, she wouldn't die from any readergun shots, for her riot gear lay concealed under her bulky clothing, as did her weapons. The cams, ranging across parts of the human spectrum beyond standard vision, would have detected these. But since Chenghu had given her the identity of a ZA Inspectorate officer, as well as matching her chip to her biometrics, they should be accepted. She'd know soon enough if his reprogramming was any good. Quite likely anomalies about her would eventually bring her to the attention of an AI. But she intended to be close enough to her target for that not to matter.

She continued through the streets, following the memorized course, then checking it as she drew closer. Ahead lay even heavier security, since within this SA area stood the monolithic towers of the Bureaucracy. No visible barrier blocked her progress except for a red line across the road. Beyond this point no ZAs were permitted, and only SAs who worked there or had received special permissions in their ID chips were allowed in. Readerguns and flocks of razorbirds had multiplied. She halted and scanned around, finally fixed on a suitable vehicle and walked over to it.

The four-person Lectromax ran on plastic grip wheels and its shape resembled a cut-out tongue. Walking over, she reached into her pocket and took out a chipstick, pressing the button on the end of it. Another thing courtesy of the resources Chenghu had managed to steal. It seemed that Chinese military, inducted into the Inspectorate, knew all the holes in security. She checked her arm screen, seeing the chipstick connecting there, all the routines coming up, then touched a simple car icon. By the time she'd reached the vehicle, the locks had already clicked open. She casually took off her coat and climbed inside as if she owned the car, dumping the coat on the seat beside her. Inserting the stick brought the dashboard alive in front of her. Now things

19

were going to start getting gnarly, as Chenghu was fond of saying.

She pulled on her armoured gloves and attached them to the suit at her wrists. A glance down at the weapon on its stick pad on her front, then at her sidearm, as well as her collection of grenades, gave her a reassurance she didn't need. She hesitated, then with a nod to Chenghu's caution, detached the collapsed helmet from above her belt, expanded it on its sliders, and put it on too.

She grabbed the wheel and floored the accelerator. The software of the chipstick had already removed all limiters and any possibility of surrounding computer systems seizing control of the car. Its purpose was to provide officers with transport when they needed it. She pulled away from the kerb in a cloud of road composite dust and plastic fragments, grip wheels shrieking. It would have been more sensible to drive away sedately until reaching her destination, or until security forces reacted, but her adrenalin and aggression were up, something that seemed to have become a feature of her life since her change. As she approached the red line, she belatedly remembered to lock her helmet down onto her riot gear.

A hundred metres beyond the line, the security forces finally reacted. Readergun slugs began to slap into the car. The low-impact ammunition – designed to kill just the target and not anyone standing nearby – only put passing dents in the composite bodywork, though, or splashed then fell away from the toughened glass windows. In that moment Irene remembered Chenghu telling her of a new policy that'd been instituted: in China mercury slugs were being phased out as environmentally unfriendly, to be replaced by high-penetration rounds. What did it matter if they killed more than the intended targets? Earth was over-supplied with human beings.

She screeched around one corner, a crowd of SAs jumping

out of her path. Two didn't quite make it and with leaden thuds went cartwheeling through the air. She felt a stab of guilt, quickly ameliorated by the fact they were part of the system. Two more corners and something flashed in front of her. The apparently chromed seagull hit the screen and punched through it, spreading cracks across all that remained. It clipped her shoulder, tearing up the impact fibres of her riot suit, and landed on the back seat. Steering one-handed again, she drew her sidearm, remembering perfectly Chenghu's instruction on how to use it, and shot the razorbird, three slugs punching through its body. But the thing had been wrecked anyway.

Next to come: solid rounds. Probably from some Inspectorate weapon mounted on the building ahead. These took out the rest of the screen, shredded the passenger seat and thumped into her chest. The impacts failed to penetrate her armour but their force tore the seat back out of its mountings. Lucky her arms were so long. She steered towards the building's lobby, heading for the steps leading up to the glass front. As the car hit them, it shuddered, losing its front end underneath, but this served to bounce it up so it hit the armoured glass frontage. The glass, perfectly designed to stop most rounds, didn't break, but sheets of it did crash out of their frames, which bent and broke under the impact. She was in, at least partially.

Part of the frames blocked the car door, so she threw herself out through where the front screen had been, conveniently blasted clear by the Inspectorate. Forward-rolling off the bonnet, she came down on her feet, snapping marble smoke grenades from her bandolier and scattering them, while delighting in her physical competence. They began to detonate and rapidly filled the place with thick white smoke. This had no effect on her; with her visor closed and her holosense it might well have not been there at all. She next tossed some of her other grenades, blowing craters in the tiled floor, fragmenting a desk and tearing out the side of a security-scanning arch. Two officers appeared in the spreading smoke, their shots wild but still dangerous. She ran at them, and in one smooth motion pulled her machine pistol from its stick pad, then fired a full clip at them. They spun away in blooms of impact fibre and she crashed into them, knocking them sprawling. As Chenghu had instructed, she put in a new clip. She fired a short burst at one of them, shattering his unprotected head, then came down on the other with one knee and pushed the weapon into his face.

'Where is Garrick?'

He stared at her in bewilderment, so she shoved the barrel in his right eye. He shrieked and babbled, 'Third floor!' She backed off, then smashed the weapon across his head. Still not accustomed to her own strength, she realized as she stepped away that she'd broken his skull. No matter, he was Inspectorate. She focused upwards on the third floor, everything becoming clear and her target located. Across the lobby lay the stairs and she dashed up them, knowing the lifts would be shut down. She'd already known Garrick's apartment was on the third floor, but hadn't been certain whether he'd even be here. A gamble Chenghu had been quite critical about.

Three floors up, she exited the stairs into a corridor. Inspectorate were ahead. She rolled some grenades and crashed through a door as the floor splintered upwards. An office filled with bureaucrats at desks and consoles faced her – grey and insipid creatures of another race. She tossed a grenade at a wall and followed it, crashing through the remaining old plasterboard and expanded-plastic beams. Another room was the same, then another. Here she ignored the wall and went out through the door, corpses scattered in the corridor before her. No more resistance now; she'd come in too fast for them. She began kicking open doors, firing bursts at anyone in the corridors, scattering grenades and chaos. A decorated private door loomed ahead and she ran straight at it, shoulder first. It burst open and she staggered on entering, then focused immediately on the single individual in there.

'Garrick,' she said.

The man was turned towards a wall, an arms cache open before him, his finger up against the fone in his ear. He looked both startled and offended, and Irene could see little to distinguish him from those in the offices she'd passed through. Yet still the memories were there, and the old pain. She strode across as the man grabbed for a gun. Garrick managed three shots before Irene had him up off the floor by the throat, his gun thumping to the carpet. He could now see her through her visor.

'You,' he said, eyes growing wide. Did he even remember her name?

'Yes, me.'

She felt the sharp anticipation of imminent vengeance, but would there be satisfaction? She wondered about her justifications to Chenghu too. Would there be justice either? No, she'd be breaking just one cog in a machine overly supplied with them. With a feeling of disgust, she turned and threw him at the window. Garrick hit hard, horizontally, then peeled off and dropped to the floor. He continued moving weakly, with blood running out of his nostrils and staining his suit elsewhere. His skull had acquired a flat spot on one side. Irene stared, dumbfounded by her strength, but then realizing the adrenalin had ramped it up even further. She shrugged herself into motion and walked over, picking him up and angrily slamming him against the window again, until the armoured glass popped out. She then dropped him down towards where Inspectorate trucks had pulled up below, with soldiers spilling out of them. She didn't dare linger,

23

so she headed straight for the door and out.

'The sewerage system,' Chenghu had said, when they'd discussed her strategy for escape. Irene grimaced as she ran for the lift, hearing shouts from the stairs below of 'Clear!' Now certain of her strength, she tore open the doors, grabbed the lift runners and went down so fast she could almost have been falling. She then blew her way through the lift on the ground floor, dropping through human debris, and ripped open further doors into the basement. Her exact perception of her surroundings led her to an inspection hatch amid the laminar power storage stacks. At the next hatch below it, she undid the catch and, bracing herself, pushed her feet down against the thing. Sewer water, laden with ground-up remains, rose up and engulfed her. She forced herself inside the sewer and swam with the diminished flow beyond, understanding that she'd now reached a suitable jaunting location to make her escape from this world.

She had accomplished her vengeance and she had accomplished nothing. It all felt empty. As she swam on, she acknowledged some small satisfaction that the bureaucratic enclave above would soon be flooded with shit, but even that soon diminished on realizing it was just one of millions of such places.

Chenghu – Present

Irene stood with one foot up on the low wall that rimmed the top of the building they were on. Like Chenghu, she had comfortable clothes on – in her case jeans, a white vest top, leather biker boots and jacket. She should have appeared sexy, but having grown nearly as tall and long-boned as him, she did not have so much sexual appeal now. Anyway, the sex hadn't been so frequent after he argued against her returning to this place, and his need for it seemed to be diminishing too, though he acknowledged that her hold on him remained.

She gazed at him with violet up-slanting eyes in a long face, below a shiny cap of black hair tied into a thick plait at the back. Her hand was raised, pointing out across the sprawl with one clawed finger.

'It's amazing they have the energy,' she said drily.

'They always have the energy,' he replied. 'Believe me, I've been down in that enough times.' *And haven't you?* he wanted to ask.

She nodded contemplatively. 'Usually the starved and down-trodden are easily controlled, herded and led to the slaughter. Historically this has always been what happened. Maybe ZA and SA evolution *has* diverged, with the ZAs selected towards strength.'

'Indeed,' he replied, knowing she was trying to be all intel-lectual to cover her discomfort. And detaching herself from the ZAs, as though she hadn't once been one of them.

They were on the roof of a tenement. No one else was here, for the guards below had locked the hatches and were standing ready to fend off any interlopers from the streets. The roof was a precious place, with its greenhouses and walled vegetable plots. Here lay the kind of wealth ZAs could well understand. And, of course, no one *normal* could get to the roof without going through the guards . . .

From this position they were able to see numerous streets branching away, crammed with people. The handwritten placards bobbing around made events below seem out of another age. Except everything had been scaled up. Millions of people, all across the sprawl, were converging on the wide street called Laagerstrass, heading towards the major SA and bureaucratic enclave at the far end. Irene knew it all too well, of course, since she'd walked along it two weeks ago to find, as she said, unsatisfactory vengeance. And she wanted to do more.

'Why did you suggest we come here?' she asked.

'Because you say you want to cut off the head of the snake, but you need to see why that might not be such a good idea,' Chenghu replied.

She shot him a hard look. 'You've got the data still? It's confirmed.'

'Yes, it's confirmed: a major meeting of all the heads of state under the aegis of the Multinational Development Committee early next year. All those involved in the global transition will be there.'

'A boot stamping on humanity's face forever,' said Irene bitterly, looking over the crowds. After a moment she turned back to him. 'Not a good idea?' she said disbelievingly.

'The Bureaucracy here, just like in China, is an end in itself,' said Chenghu. 'Its only purpose, and efficiency, is in the employment of bureaucrats and their protection.'

'I'm aware of that.'

Chenghu had prepared himself for a predictably angry reaction from her. It had surprised him how deeply he'd thought on all this, and the things he'd researched via gang resources in China. But what surprised him more was the ruthlessness with which he was now applying this knowledge. He had known what would happen here, gathering information on it too, and now it was playing out. It was so useful to be able to go just about anywhere, as he and Irene could.

'You killed Garrick, who was a major sprawl sector governor,' he said. 'And you killed others there who were key workers. By breaking the sewerage system and flooding the place with shit, you also rendered it unusable and effectively made one node in the bureaucratic network defunct. Other nodes could have taken up the slack if the attitude of the Bureaucracy wasn't so "not

26

my problem".' He paused and pointed at the riot. 'Look. We have the herd – or perhaps flock would be more apposite in this case – and now come the shepherds.'

Chenghu shuddered as he studied the crowds. Yes, there they were. The robots strode along on spider legs but with a body form that resembled mechanical Cthulhus. Initial manufacture of the things had started only last year in his home territory, in big automated factories, and the design had been sent to all countries who were bending their knee to the Committee. They moved ahead of armoured vans coming in from some side streets, and they grabbed up rioters in sticky tentacles, dropping them into large net bags. Each of these, when full, they then deposited on the road, where Inspectorate officers from the vans decohered the nets and used shock sticks to force the captives into the vans. The shepherds strode on, extruding new bags.

'Not in shredding mode yet,' said Irene harshly, 'but it's inevitable.'

He'd hoped for a different reaction to this horror.

'Get to the point,' she added snappily.

Chenghu sighed and continued: 'This system failure because of one bureaucratic node being knocked out meant others began snatching food supplies that had been under Garrick's control. Personnel fled the disaster here too, and a scum of corruption moved in. The food ran out just four hours after you killed Garrick, and the water supply shut down two days ago.'

'Hence this riot.'

'This is a fragile place. Whatever you do has severe consequences.'

'And that's your point?' Irene enquired. 'Lesson learned.'

Chenghu felt his insides sinking. He really didn't want to do this, but it was time for him to be brave with her at last.

'No,' he said, stepping in closer to her. 'You have not.'

He reached out to the world around him, as well as those lying beyond. He'd had more time to understand the biotechnology inside him and his powers to move from world to world. She was catching up with him quickly, though, so perhaps this was his one opportunity. With an effort of will, he mentally took hold of her material form and grounded it in place here, with him. While he maintained the link she could go nowhere. She sensed it, looking puzzled as she took her foot off the building's rim, then became angry as she turned towards him.

'Neat trick,' she said.

'You need to see this,' he said, 'and with the senses you now have, you can see it all.'

She shrugged, as if it didn't matter, put her foot back on the rim and returned her attention to the food riot. He wasn't fooled; he knew he'd pay for this later. As he returned his attention to the riot too, he could feel the strain of maintaining his mental grip on her, sweat breaking out on his forehead. He wouldn't be able to hold this for long.

Far ahead he could just see the entrance into the SA area. Inspectorate troops gathered there behind armoured cars slowly rolling out. These vehicles raised flat matt squares across their front ends as the first protesters came into range. The effect was immediate, with the crowd shuddering to a halt and then melting back like wax under a blowtorch. The analogy was apposite, since the pain inducers would make the people feel as if they were burning. The sound reached Irene and Chenghu a moment later – an odd composite hissing, like the buzzing from a wasps' nest tuned up a notch or two to a higher frequency. This was what the concerted screaming of tens of thousands of people sounded like. Rioters surged into side streets, to then be confronted by shepherds and more inducers.

'Only the small side streets are open,' Irene said flatly. 'As I'm sure you'll be aware from your role as a riot cop, the crush will kill hundreds of thousands. And it'll take some time for what the Federal government see as a human abscess to drain.'

'Nice analogy,' said Chenghu bitterly. It seemed he just wasn't getting through to her.

They watched the crowds surging and the continued arrests for an hour. Chenghu said nothing more, but Irene was relentless in detailing what was happening down there. It was as if she was saying the things he should be saying, and simply didn't care. Another change in the riot came when a surge overran an Inspectorate position – the human mass so unstoppable there it even turned over a heavy armoured car. Chenghu winced at that, knowing those closest to the car must have been turned to a slurry of broken bones and torn flesh. The order was given, and armoured cars in other streets began to fold out guns either side of their inducers. Firing commenced, pushing the millions there into an even tighter crush and mounding up the dead and dying. When a sufficient 'space' had been made, the Inspectorate cars and personnel finally began to withdraw. Meanwhile, the shepherds strode in, now switched to shredding mode. They snatched people up, pulling them apart like soft fruit and discarding the remains. Thereafter, with the larger streets clear of Inspectorate, the crowds dispersed rapidly.

Chenghu watched it all with leaden horror. He understood perfectly that under Committee *advice* the Federal government had passed a law classifying street protest as insurrection, punishable by death. That all those millions down there had not been exterminated wasn't because of any merciful motives but simple logistics. Clearing up and disposing of millions of corpses would have been a formidable task. He had little doubt that this response had been carefully calculated so the death toll wouldn't go beyond the processing capacity of the macerators in the area. This

29

processing had to be done within a set decay time, to ensure the stink wouldn't reach any SA areas.

'Are we done now?' Irene finally asked.

'Yes, I think so,' Chenghu replied.

'You made your point,' she continued, waving a hand at the scene. 'This cannot continue and, if it cannot be stopped, better that it all burn.'

Chenghu slumped, defeated, releasing his hold on her.

2

The Fenris – Past

He had spent enough time in the data transmission tower reviewing history, searching his world, the moon and the orbitals above for some sign he wasn't alone, yet found nothing. In the few birthing and storage chambers, he uncovered only decay and inocular flies. The technology of the world was at least steadily repairing itself, though. Those areas where entropy had killed the biotech were large but steadily shrinking wounds scattered around the planet, along with the remains of his kind. So what now for him? He couldn't decide. His existence seemed to have become pointless; the exuberance of the child had shrunk under the dry load of knowledge. He felt lost and desperately alone under this weight.

And what of the other fenris in the multiverse?

This nodal world had been denuded of his kind, so surely that would be reflected in the parallels of it? Unless, of course, the Great Project had been a success and those other worlds had attained independent existence, evolving on their own terms. Or had all those worlds ended up in cysts, as had his own? Perhaps with the differences and the degradation of reflections, those

31

worlds had escaped their cysts in a similar manner and fenris still existed there. His optimism grew.

He'd only be able to find answers to these questions through the big engines that lay above, in orbit. Though he possessed the full genetic inheritance of his kind in his biology and biotech, and as such would be a world walker, he couldn't yet travel to other parallel worlds. This ability would only occur once he was fully grown, sometime after puberty, a hundred or more years from now.

He sighed out a breath as the reality grounded him. He was still an organic, growing creature and the demands of his body began to make themselves known. He was tired, hungry and thirsty, and the need to act on these raised him out of all this grey history.

He sent final instructions to the machinery around him, removed his hand from the interface and turned, having initiated full-contact sensory armour. He would continue to gather information, monitor ongoing repairs and intervene where necessary, but for now he had to move. Though his kind might be dead, he still existed. He *was* his kind! He stepped away, towards one of the glass sheets, now rippling in anticipation. As he moved into it, it folded around him, forming glassy armour. This segmented and adjusted to his body and issued sensory spikes. Once settled in it, he finally walked out of the upper peak of the tower, making his way steadily back down, noting as he went the crunch of dry and long-dead inocular flies under his feet.

His new route took him close to the birthing and storage halls from which he'd issued and he paused, reviewing the programming around him and searching for actions to take. The entropic surge had killed organic connections between the halls, and other surrounding biotech, but hard technological links remained. They'd managed to maintain integrity, which was why data had downloaded to him, and why the clean lock had worked. It was the dead organic seals finally failing that had allowed the flies in and the temperature to rise. Incorporating further stored data, he learned the sad fate of sixteen fenris along the line he'd occupied in the storage chamber. The horror of those closest to him scraping at the walls of their cysts with claws not yet grown sharp enough to penetrate, then the hard technology making a logical, mechanistic decision to redirect limited resources to him – to save only what was possible. He swallowed drily, feeling bitter at this unwanted load of further knowledge.

Next, searching his surroundings for what else still worked, he ordered tendrils of growth from the surrounding biotech, so he could make reconnections. Then he ordered in flying cleaners to remove the population of inocular flies, slapping at one that landed on his face. They seemed to be everywhere.

He moved on.

The nearest food hub was dead, as were the thousands of flies that crunched under his feet as he walked through. He tracked repairs around him and made further adjustments, then checked the hard memory as he walked. The entropic effects had killed off nearly all the biotech of this world a thousand years ago. And it had taken that time for the few functional cells and patches to spread out again, restoring what he now saw. Sixty per cent of it had returned, but laden with faults, and with some iterations of the technology completely missing. He paused and then, before heading to the next food hub, took a new course to bring himself to the door of an abode.

The door resisted him – still set to private for the individual who'd lived within. Via his armour, he accessed coding to rub out the lock, then, as an afterthought, encoded that as a viral instruction to retransmit around the world. Now no further doors, unless broken, would resist him. A touch to the tilted ellipsoid opened it, its surface sliding into the wall like a nictitating membrane. Beyond lay a series of interconnected chambers spread in a volume half a kilometre across. Snakelike manipulators coiled out from the walls to observe him, with interfaces closely resembling fenris eyes, for much of the biotech around him contained the genetics of the past resident here. On realizing this, he grasped the possibility of resurrection. Obviously some small part of the erstwhile residents had survived the entropy wave. But that was something for the future.

In a small room resembling the insides of a mammal blown out like a balloon, he tugged a slick pipe from one wall and waited. After a moment, water began to pour out. He held it to his mouth and took in a little but didn't swallow. Using his sophisticated sense of taste that extended almost to the point of being a laboratory, he detected the various minerals, salts and trace organics. Nothing raised an alert, so he gulped it down greedily, filling himself up. His whole dehydrated body responded to the point where his armour had to expand to incorporate it. Afterwards he went on to a cuplike growth from another wall and urinated copiously, with a penis whose design had never been changed. He looked down at the undeveloped thing, knowing that though procreation might have changed drastically, sexual recreation among his kind had not. This was something that wouldn't affect him for a hundred and fifty years anyway, so he put thoughts of it aside. His dark green urine stank and he detected the accumulated toxins leaving him. His body could reprocess them should there be a need, but expelling them was still the easiest method. He drank again and again, then relieved himself again and again, until the urine ran clear.

Moving on from the abode, his thoughts felt much clearer and he had a surge of optimism about the future. He would never know his kin, for they were gone and he must accept that, but around him at least some of them remained, in the form of information both genetic and hard stored. There was also the genetics of his own body. Through birthing facilities, and alteration of stored databases, he'd be able to raise clones with a suitable variety. The possibilities began opening up as a landscape before him, as endless as they'd been before the cyst enclosed this world – he felt powerful, effective. He broke into a run again, burning up a burst of energy and enthusiasm.

When he reached the next food hub, he slowed to a walk, weariness returning, his mood dampened and his world vast and empty around him once more.

He could have tried some of the biotech mechanisms in the abode to produce food for him, but this hub was the destination he'd decided on. The spherical chamber had entrances all around. Its walls seemed to be a jungle of trees and apparently fungal forms. Had gravity tech been working here, they would have grown inwards to the central light. But with the effects of planetary gravity having dropped the radiation sphere to the lower cusp a hundred metres away from him, where it lay cracked and emitting only a dull glow, the plants now grew downwards. Their colours were still riotous, however, and he could see food was available here.

The rings of communal eating areas sat amid all this growth, and one lay nearby. He ignored it and walked down a slope, coming to some tilted-over grey trees offering sprays of red nodules the size of his fist. He plucked the ripest and sniffed it, then touched his tongue to it. Detecting no toxins, he took a bite and chewed with an almost painful rush of saliva. Meat: densely woven proteins in their huge variety. The fruit dripped liquid, like red blood of a past fenris age. Unable to stop himself, he consumed ten of the things in quick succession. Further along, he next pulled down long beans from a vine and took a lot more time inspecting them, even linking to surrounding scanning systems for further data and history about them. Finally reassured, he crunched them up, filling with fibre and a variety of substances his fenris biotech needed. Old biology then reasserted itself as his newly born digestive system rebelled.

It took him some days, marked by the rise and fall of light, which was broadcast through pipes all around him, before he could eat again without ill effect. He left the mess to the cleaning robots and the ever-seeking plant roots in this food hub.

The space elevator, which he needed to go up in to get to the great engines in orbit, first revealed itself as a line scoring up from the horizon. But it was only visible when the sun glinted off it, so, as the day progressed, it disappeared. The Fenris, having run all the way, breathed a sigh of excitement and relief on seeing it still standing, then felt a stab of annoyance at the data for being correct. From first consciousness, the data loading to his mind had presented him with harsh, unpleasant realities that stifled and suppressed him, but he shouldn't be angry at it. This was an easy observation to make; not so easy to adhere to, though.

Now exploring this *knowledge*, he understood that even though the elevator was still there, it didn't mean it would be working properly. He searched out options and realized he could test the ground-based version of it beforehand. This train would also take him to the entrance of the elevator more quickly than walking or running.

Tubes spiralled down through the massed biotech city, into the underlying rock. He tracked one of these steadily down, until it opened out into a cavern kilometres long and wide. A larger tube ran through the centre of this cavern, with ribbon walkways snaking up to it. The thing looked like the hollow stem of some giant plant, eaten away in long oval sections to expose a silvered interior. The various walkways joined up to the lips of these hollows. He scanned along to find the red bullet of the hypertrain stretched across three of the openings, then chose the corresponding walkway and headed up. On reaching the lip, he turned to look, in awe, at the vastness of it all. Though he had no memory of this place, he imagined how it would have been when the world was populated. Gravity technology, which seemed to be working only in some places now, would have been in operation here. The walkways were just a matter of choice, and the air would have been filled with people floating to their destinations or in general-purpose transports too, which could travel under the sea, in the open air and out in space. But those he now saw smashed and mounded up at the bottom of the cavern. He turned away from this bitter reality, walked across twenty metres of floor that was like polished wood – in fact it *was* polished wood of a kind – and came to the skin of the train.

He reached out a hand and pressed the red surface. After a brief hesitation, it parted from his point of contact to let him inside. He kept checking on the systems around him as he stepped in, gleaning diagnostics and looking out for any signs of danger. Gravity tech still seemed functional in the enclosing stem. This was of course the case for the space elevator ahead too, because without such tech it would have become millions of tonnes of coiled-up dead biotech, crashed into the world city. He wondered about the living systems in the tech around him. They seemed to have re-established well, which could have been because the entropy effect, coming in from space, had been blunted by all the material lying above this cavern. But that didn't account for the elevator still standing. He sent a signal for the train to get moving, while also probing data ahead, trying to understand what had happened here.

'Dead biotech,' he said out loud as he sorted through this data. The transport system, though it contained biotech, mostly consisted of what it *had* grown already. Like the woody floor he'd walked over, and the continuing substance of this one stem, stretching for thousands of kilometres through the rock. Perhaps he needed to spend some time at the place ahead checking things, initiating regrowth and repairs, running maintenance checks and more besides before he took the elevator to the stars. The idea held zero appeal.

The train surged into motion. It too was a general-purpose vehicle, which, if removed from its tubes, could travel independently in any environment. But it ran faster here, and more energy-efficiently. He moved over to one of the rests, sat back with his legs out at an angle, and his back sinking into the support. It closed around him and he fought it reflexively, until he understood its purpose. The thing was a safety measure, for the remote possibility the inertial damping fields failed within. A moment later he realized how much he needed this feature.

The surge of acceleration pressed him back hard, the support closing round him further. His breath went out and he could feel his torso crushing down, almost to the point of breaking. His vision grew dark and he consciously closed up his veins and arteries to keep the blood supply to his skull. The train took a turn, which, without the support, would have put him through the side of the thing. A subsequent four alterations of course had the same effect and, at one point, he felt a rib crack and his spine crunch. He began to suffocate and slid organ support over to full hypoxic function, still maintaining consciousness. Deceleration finally ensued, the stuff wrapped around him stretching out and out until it snapped and he tumbled forwards, slamming into the support positions ahead. The quarter-hour journey had seemed much longer. The train halted and he dropped to the floor, took a breath and dilated those veins and arteries not ripped, then assessed his broken bones.

'Inertial damping does not seem to be working,' he said out loud.

There was no one to hear what he felt to be quite a good attempt at humour. The void into which he'd spoken remained so, and might never change . . .

He stood up, angry at himself as he shut off afferent nerves. Running a program through the muscles of his back, he straightened up his spine too. He directed healing blood, laden with organic tech, to the numerous cracks in his bones. The only full break he had was his left ulna. Grabbing his wrist, he pulled and twisted, aligning the break, then sent the arm's muscle into a solid spasm around it. Autonomously, his body also redirected a vein to bring more blood to the damage. With that arm hanging stiff, he went over to the door and out. This had been a salutary reminder of the extent of the malfunctions around him. If he didn't take care, they could kill him.

Walking slowly and cautiously, checking all around with his enhanced senses and running diagnostics in the surrounding systems, he headed through oblate tunnels. These led into the base station. Here he entered a vast pyramidal space where the giant ligaments of the elevator, which were rooted deep down in the bedrock, extended up to the peak. At the centre stood a conglomeration of stems, like those of the transport system that'd tried to kill him. He moved along one of the ribbons threading through all this, still constantly checking for faults. Inertial damping was down here, too. Running the coding through his mind, he tried to ascertain why it had failed, since it was a hard system and not something organic that had been killed off by entropy and was now regrowing. He went so deep that he halted and sat down, concentrating fully on the data and excluding the outside world. He eventually began to get answers.

Many of the hard tech systems had survived but were not unaffected by entropy. It had sucked out their energy too, crashing electron-stored data. Much had been restored afterwards from hard storage, but it was not all back, and this was the case with the computers controlling inertial damping. Why was this the case? He realized another of those mechanistic choices had been made by the computing – like the one that had directed resources to help him live when those beside him died in the storage hall. All of this steady restoration, which had been going on for a thousand years, took energy. And the constant, massive drain on the zero-point collectors scattered about the planet meant the systems only dealt with essentials first. Inertial damping, since it simply hadn't been used in that time, had been ignored. But then he noticed that systems were responding to him, for even now it had started to be brought back up to function in the transport network.

'So you know I'm here now,' he muttered. He looked at the emptiness around him and grimaced at his need to talk aloud.

The whole planetary complexity was too difficult for him to parse, so he focused instead on his immediate vicinity and pushed over some virtual switches. The restoration immediately extended to the space elevator, and it felt as if his surroundings had grown taut. A buzzing sound, like the inocular flies, reached his ears. Coming partially back to his senses, he saw light tubes opening and shifting to bring more clarity here. He watched hemispherical robots climbing the ligaments and an orbital train coming down in the stem of the elevator. Focusing in again, he studied the diagnostics being offered, and the levers of control. He nodded, stood up and walked back, then jumped down a couple of metres to another ribbon. There he winced at his impetuousness, for he'd forgotten about his broken bones; cracks half-healed opened up again. He turned his afferent nervous system back on and suffered the pain, since its evolutionary purpose was to be a reminder of such damage.

He headed over to the elevator's train. Once more, he pressed his hand against a red surface and it parted before him. He paused and stepped back. He wanted to go up above, and could control the ascent now, but without inertial damping it would have to be a slow acceleration and an easy deceleration. This meant it would take many hours to reach the Geostation, his first stop before going on to an engine. He turned away to go and find a food hub, and any other supplies he might need. As much as it often ran contrary to his emotions, he couldn't ignore the second-hand knowledge loaded to his mind.

Ottanger

Ottanger had known there was a high chance of it happening at some point. It didn't matter how much he kept himself prepared and alert, what contacts and resources he had available, plain dumb bad luck would surely screw him over. However, in this case, he realized he hadn't been as alert as usual. The operation to restore his face to how it had been before he'd left here, the New York Sprawl, hadn't been too bad – returning the slight points to his ears and adjusting other facial features had been simple cosmetics. In fact, the gang surgeon had told him it was almost as if he'd been relieving stresses, with his face pushing to go back to its previous shape. Ottanger had nodded agreement to that. This return to his initial form had nearly led to his arrest over the other side of the sprawl. Removing his stolen chip and implanting his old one just stung a bit. However,

41

the chemicals used to deactivate the dyes in his skin and his eyes had left him feeling sick and very much out of sorts. Perhaps, if he'd felt otherwise, he would've spotted the signs and not have let himself be caught up in the flood of protesting humanity rapidly turning into a riot.

The internment camp they were being taken to sat within the city, since the mayor had decided croplands too valuable to be cleared to accommodate the camp. Ottanger recognized the gates as the van drew to a halt and reversed towards them. He still had hopes of survival, of some game to run, but they diminished as those gates opened and the van went inside. The guards, clad in combat suits and wielding shock sticks, pulled open the van doors and shouted at them.

'Out! Out now! Form a line and move to the door!'

Like them all, he couldn't move very fast. His clothing was gummed with shepherd glue and his body bruised head to foot. He should consider himself lucky to be among the first to be captured during the riot, since the shepherds went into shredding mode just minutes later, grabbing up rioters and turning them into broken offal. Stavanger, a gang enforcer sprawled next to him in the temporary compound, had wondered why they didn't do that right from the start.

'Interrogation,' he'd replied. 'And shredding leaves a mess that has to be cleaned up. In the camp, that mess goes straight into the sewers or composters.'

With his hands zip-tied behind his back, he staggered from the van after the others, but obviously too slowly. A shock stick caught him on the side of his neck. The surge felt as if it broke vertebrae, then pain filled his skull and one side of his body. He fell, managing to turn a little so he didn't smash his face straight into the concrete, but it felt as if he'd cracked his shoulder bone. He knew at once why he'd been chosen. He was bigger than the average ZA and his mutation singled him out too. When the guard proceeded to kick him, he just wanted to curl up into a ball, but he knew the kicking wouldn't stop. He either got up or died here on the concrete. Or, even worse, he lay here until incapable of moving and the guard got bored, whereupon he'd be dragged off, still alive, for processing. Here, final processing for prisoners was through a macerator, with the resultant mess going into the sewers or composting tanks, as he'd told Stavanger.

He lurched to his feet, his body a slab of pain, and staggered through the door after the others. And the brutality didn't let up. It was calculated, of course: keep them scared, weak and hurting, and all they did was try to be the one who received the least punishment. No thoughts of rebelling, of turning on the guards. Eventually the guards lined them up facing the doors into cells – the luxury here being one cell each – prior to interrogation. A guard walked down, detaching their zip-ties, then with a clonk the door locks disengaged. The guard walked back, shoving them into their cells in turn. Ottanger fell through onto his knees as the cell door closed and locked behind him. When he finally tried to stand up, he realized he'd been lucky to fall in here, else he would have smacked his head on the lintel on the way in. He could only stand with his head cricked over.

He studied his surroundings.

The cell was two metres square and less than that high. A stinking drain hole sat in one corner. Of course, the whole thing was tiled in white, and of course he could see it all clearly because of the bright lights inset in the ceiling, walls and floor. He went over to the drain hole and, with shaking fingers, managed to undo his trousers. When he pissed it didn't surprise him to see blood in his urine. He knew he wouldn't be taking a shit in the hole, since the recent lack of food had affected him just as much as those who'd been rioting about it. After urinating, he walked over to the nearest light and inspected it. It had small black squares either side of it and the same, when he looked, for all the others. Cams, of course – they wouldn't want to go to all the trouble of capturing him only for him to find some way of killing himself in here.

He sat with his back against the wall, then after a moment lay on his side, wincing. Fight or flight slowly unclenched its fist from around his guts, and a wash of terrible weariness came over him. His eyes began to close and with that, the lights began to dim around him. A fraction of a moment later a siren sounded and it seemed that some knackered engine had started up behind the wall, then the lights came on, painfully bright. He pulled himself upright and the lights dimmed back to their original intensity, while the sounds died. He grimaced, aware some low-level AI system was monitoring him, or a guard. It wouldn't stop, he knew. Every time he drifted into sleep the noise and the lights would come on – they always started with sleep deprivation.

How long it lasted he had no idea; he ceased counting the times they woke him. He felt sick and so very, very weary when the door finally opened and two guards came in. He tried to stand but they shocked him until he lay shuddering, then they dragged him out. The floor of the corridor beyond was purposely designed with rough serrations to tear off a prisoner's shirt and lacerate the skin on his back. They dragged him into a larger room, sat him in a chair bolted to the floor, strapping his arms and legs in place. Ahead of him was a desk and behind it a 'crat clad in a grey suit, with a narrow red tie. He thought this person a man, but realized when she spoke she was a mannish woman, with a barrel body and short-cropped grey hair. The former confirmed her status as an SA – a Societal Asset. No one in the ZA class – the Zero Assets like himself – would have found enough to eat to actually build up a layer of fat.

44

'You will answer my questions succinctly and politely,' she said, lifting a tablet, glancing at it, then putting it aside. It doubtless had the questions on the screen per bureaucratic diktat, but she probably knew them by heart now. 'Failure to answer will be punished.'

He looked around. The guards were gone so it wouldn't be a beating, and they hadn't attached power leads so it wouldn't be that. He then looked up at the matt square inset in the ceiling directly above him. A pain inducer, then.

'Why did you take part in the civil disorder on —' she paused in bored irritation to check the tablet, then continued — 'on Laagerstrass?'

'I didn't take part,' he said. 'The riot started and I couldn't get out through the crush.'

The pain hit him in a wave, travelling down from the top of his head to his feet. It felt as if he had been set on fire. He screamed and found his bowels were not as empty as he'd supposed. When it faded, he sat there rigid, the heat draining away to leave him shivering.

'Answer the question,' she said.

His guilt was already a given and he had no doubt his disposal scheduled. The horror of this so-called interrogation was its pointless bureaucratic box-ticking. They didn't expect to learn anything important from him, and he'd been sure he could be strong enough so they wouldn't. But he had never actually experienced an inducer outside of a protest, and that was bad enough. This was pain of a higher order, and he knew he would do all he could to avoid it. He really hoped they asked no truly pertinent questions.

'I took part in the riot because I was hungry. We hadn't had our rations for two weeks,' he replied, and then flinched.

'Who else took part in the riot that you know?' she asked. 'You must list at least ten names.'

He stared at her. He didn't know ten people who had taken part. He'd been there with only two others. Stavanger and Cross, the two gang enforcers accompanying him to his stash of smuggled ammo, which was to pay for his surgery. They hadn't escaped – he'd seen Cross being shredded and Stavanger was in the temporary compound with him before here. Those two names he could give, but there were simply no more.

'I was there alone,' he said. Lack of fairness and justice were simply a reality of life and the reason he'd joined the resistance to do what he could to fight. Here they raised a sick feeling inside, and his sudden bravery in such circumstances utterly baffled him.

The pain hit again and this time it went on for longer. He came out of it with a further bowel movement and then vomited a mouthful of sour bile. He couldn't close his mouth, nor spit the stuff out, and began to choke until he brought his chin down on his chest and it ran out. He coughed as his head came back upright, then couldn't stop coughing. She watched him in irritation.

'Names!' she demanded.

He gave the two he knew and then, utterly disgusted with himself and in terror of the inducer coming on again, scrabbled for more. He told her the names of neighbours who had caused his sister Jane problems – a family of four. Then, hating himself for that, and in a fit of stupid rebellion, pronounced the names of local bureaucrats and a street political officer. She took a brief moment to check her pad, the names doubtless having been entered by his voice and files automatically coming up.

'Well, aren't you a foolish ZA?' she commented.

Again, the pain. He came out of it after a nightmare age, feeling sucked of all moisture and somewhat of sanity. He couldn't scream any more because it felt as if something had broken in his throat. The 'crat stared at him, shook her head and pursed her lips. She glanced at the tablet and sighed. Something suddenly occurred to him. Though he had access to information outside of public knowledge, he didn't know how things actually ran inside such places as this – few came out to tell the tale. He didn't know how he would be killed and wondered about the length of her list. Quite likely he would die in this chair. That was probably how everyone brought here for interrogation died.

'Now I want you to tell me of any knowledge you have of dissident activity,' she said.

Terror rose up in him. They'd used a cell set up in his resistance group and switched identities. He didn't necessarily know any names, but he did know locations, activities. He gritted his teeth and delved deep inside for reserves of will. *I want you to kill me now,* he thought. But on top of that came the dry, horrible knowledge that he would break – everyone did.

'You will give me details and names, and more questions will—' She stopped and looked up, frowning. A red light had come on up on the wall. Picking up her tablet, she banished the questions and then checked something. Her face turned pale and she abruptly stood up.

'This interrogation is terminated.' Tucking her tablet under her arm, she rounded the desk and headed out.

Ottanger slumped there, baffled. The abrupt termination of the interrogation must have come from an order higher up. This meant he'd somehow come to the attention of that person higher up, which was normally a bad thing. Panic tried to clench his guts but just couldn't get a grip and waned away. How could things be any worse than they'd already been here, and with what was inevitably to come afterwards?

The door opened and one of the guards came in. He unstrapped Ottanger's left arm, handed him a bottle of water, then held out a couple of pills. *That's it*, he thought, they'd been trying to give him hope by apparently ending the interrogation, and now intended to break that hope with drugs and sickness. But he wanted the water really badly, so he drank it, then turned his head away from the pills.

'Fucking take them,' said the guard.

'What are they?'

'They'll make you feel better,' the guard replied.

'Yeah, right.'

The first guard stared at him in surprise as another came in. They strapped his arm down again, forced his head back and his mouth open and put the pills into it, followed by water. They were obviously long experienced with this kind of thing and he eventually swallowed. One of the guards moved to unstrap his arm again.

'No,' said the other. 'He'll try to make himself puke.'

They departed and he sat there waiting for the horrible, inevitable effects, but instead a bit of a buzz gradually came and his aches and pains faded. He found himself welling up and tried to clamp down on that. They really were giving him hope, almost certainly with the intent of subsequently destroying it.

Much later the door opened again, and the first guard returned with a bowl and spoon. He unstrapped Ottanger's left arm once more and dumped the bowl in his lap. As the smell hit his nostrils, his mouth filled with saliva. He stared down at the steaming bowl of porridge and the tears welled again. This was so unfair. Why couldn't they just torture him to death and be done with it? He couldn't stop himself, despite fears the food might be laced with an emetic, and probably something to burn his insides. Anyway, he had long ago learned that his mutation enabled him to handle the most severe food poisoning, so perhaps he'd be okay. Grabbing the spoon, he scooped up a mouthful;

the pleasure of it was better than some drugs he'd been able to obtain. He swallowed, but the stuff felt like lead and he gagged a little. Experienced with hunger, he then ate very slowly, only small portions at a time. By the time he looked up from the empty bowl, another 'crat was sitting at the desk. He hadn't even seen the man come in.

'Your name is Ottanger Smith?'

He nodded mutely.

'You have been difficult to track down,' the man said blandly.

Ottanger did the mute nod again, but his mind started racing. His sister Jane had told him about some SA department, involved in genomic testing, seeking them out. He'd dismissed it as related to the sampling and tests they'd undergone periodically because of their odd mutation. Now he wondered if there was something more sinister behind it – if they knew about his allegiances.

'Your parents were Ruth Ansen and Simael Smith?'

Again the nod.

'You were born on 1 February 2249 in . . .' The questions went on and on. He couldn't see the point of them because surely all this was on record and, of course, detailed in the chip implanted in his forearm. At one point he didn't want to answer, and instinctively looked up at the square in the ceiling above him.

'The pain inducer has been turned off,' said the man. 'We seek confirmation of who you are.' The man gestured to someone behind Ottanger, and a lab-coated technician moved in beside him, rolled up his sleeve and stabbed a needle into his arm. Ottanger eyed the device attached to the man's fone. It was a genetic tester. They were making absolutely sure he was Ottanger Smith because they knew dissidents could swap out their chips with others, sometimes with those of murdered 'crats so they could access Federal systems. Had they done this just twenty hours ago, they'd have found his DNA didn't match his chip profile, which had been that of a mulching-site manager who unfortunately fell into one of his own machines. The technician studied his fone for a moment, then nodded at the man behind the desk.

'Very well,' said the 'crat. 'You can take him.'

Another man moved forwards, clad in the same kind of white coat as the technician. But the coat hung open to reveal, poking out of the pockets, various implements that didn't look at all 'regulation'. Ottanger recognized 'senior researcher' at once. The man bent over him as the technician now came back in, pushing a wheelchair.

'Who are you? What do you want?' he asked, amazed at his temerity.

'I am Savarack and you are going to have such adventures,' the man replied.

They'd fitted a docilator before moving him, to keep him compliant. A guard had held his head steady and he'd felt an injection go into the back of his neck while Savarack had talked. His neck had gone numb, and he watched the technician sliding the object out of a packet and bending it into a rough curve. It then slotted onto the back of his neck with a crunch and the feeling of something penetrating. Next they'd unstrapped him and lifted him out of the chair, for he couldn't move his limbs, and dumped him in the wheelchair. They wheeled him through the nightmare realm of the camp into a small courtyard, then up into the back of a van.

In the back sat two guards, but their combat suits were khaki and their weapons of the rather more lethal kind. They studied him for a moment, then continued their conversation as the van drove away from the internment camp. They were military,

Ottanger realized, soldiers he'd never seen anywhere other than on a screen. He didn't pay attention to what they were saying. Though he felt numb and beaten, he was just glad to be leaving the camp by road, rather than through the sewer.

Time passed in irregular segments between dozes, and an acknowledgement of feeling returning to his limbs. The van stopping for a short time brought him back, and he glimpsed wild land and trees out of the back, then one set, and another, of security gates closing in a double fence. When they wheeled him out of the van, he looked back beyond the fence, astounded to see so much open land not being used for crops. Inside they took him to a room, but there were no white tiles in sight.

'Food will arrive shortly,' said Savarack, looming in and out of focus in front of him. 'Get yourself cleaned up and well again. The first trial will begin in three days.'

The man and all the others then left him alone. He looked around and saw the kind of space a family would be lucky to occupy. After testing his limbs and finally gathering the will, he managed to ease himself out of the wheelchair. He tottered over to the single bed and sat on it, studying the two comfortable chairs either side of a coffee table, then the chair and small desk with fold-down console by the wall, below a screen set to mirror function. He couldn't quite believe it all, and that feeling increased as strength returned and he managed to explore further, opening a single door to find a shower room.

The doctor arrived pushing a trolley, a guard accompanying her, just after he had finished washing. He'd dried himself and was staring at the clean clothing and underwear in the cupboard. The woman gave him an assessing look as the guard took away the wheelchair, then pulled the computer chair into the middle of the floor.

'Sit here,' she said.

He felt no inclination to disobey, and with that sensed a hint of the docilator's capabilities. She ran a scanner over him, then gave him a series of injections, dressed his wounds, bound up his shoulder and ribs, treated the fungal infection on his feet, and finally squirted something into his ear, which had been leaking a steady stream of pus for many months.

'That will do for now,' she said. 'You mostly need food and rest – I'll check in on you tomorrow.'

'What do they want me for?' he asked.

She just gave him a look and departed.

Food arrived next on another trolley, the smell hitting him even as the door opened. It consisted of boiled vegetables and fruit juice, but he wondered if his stomach could handle even that. He ate very slowly, experiencing flavours and textures that were a rare treat in the ZA world. He did manage to eat it all, but his stomach started up its concert of groans even as he finished, and he spent much of the ensuing time sitting on the toilet, shitting fluid. While there, he reached up and touched the device attached to the back of his neck.

He'd been informed by Senior Researcher Savarack, as they had pressed it in place, that nanowires connected it to his spine, so it wouldn't be a good idea to try pulling it off. That had been a lie, of course, since they worked by induction, but Ottanger wasn't supposed to know that. Not that he'd felt any inclination to pull it off once they turned it on. He'd expected it to continue making him feel stupid, hazy – like someone on the drugs they sometimes put into ZA rations – but now he had a feeling of clarity. Though perhaps that came from the rest in the van, medications and food.

He thought about fighting and escaping, and dismissed the idea. Why would he want to fight against his situation now, when it made him better off than the billions of ZAs on the planet?

His thoughts then segued into his time with the rebels, and how he had grown tired of the fight, returning to his original identity for a reason. Every action the rebels took, every blow against the government, just seemed to end up with innocents being hurt and the screw wound tighter. The very idea of rebellion had come to seem risible, with the Committee now all but ruling the entire world. No one had a way out, there was no halcyon place, and they truly lived in the time of a boot stamping on a face forever. Or was all of this a rationalization for giving up, for cowardice?

The three days passed. The doctor gave him a drink to settle a stomach that had never been so full. She also gave him a course of treatments to rid his body of various parasites he didn't even know he had, as well as numerous supplements to make up for a severe lack in him. She became more talkative during the subsequent visits.

'You're picking up very quickly,' she said. 'I take it as proof of the Morlock theory.'

This was apparently a joke, but he didn't understand it and gazed at her in bafflement.

'It's from an old science fiction book by a writer called H. G. Wells. He visualized future humanity as diverging into two different species. And some theorize that this is actually happening. ZA lifestyle is harsh, with little food and little in the way of medical treatments. For a hundred and fifty years ZAs have been dying young, quite often before producing offspring, while SAs have much softer lifestyles, with medical treatments, and live longer. It's also the case that the offspring of SAs usually end up as SAs themselves through nepotism in the Bureaucracy and nurture in other parts of society – like mine.' She shrugged.

'I still don't understand,' he said.

She grimaced at him. 'Your education is lacking. Can you read?'

He suddenly felt just a little sharper, and annoyed. 'All ZAs can read the warning signs and government instructions. It would be a bad survival characteristic not to be able to.'

A hint of a smirk appeared on her face. She continued, 'The upshot is simply this: even though ZAs still die young, it's proposed that they are now physically and mentally tougher due to plain selection pressure.'

'All the weak ones have died before reproducing,' he said. 'Equally, all the weak SAs get to breed.'

'Precisely.'

He frowned, remembering things from screentime deemed safe and educational. 'But surely a century and a half is not enough time for evolution?'

'One wouldn't think so, but the theory is predicated on the basis of the entire world being overloaded with more muta-gens than was ever the case in prehistory. Cancers are still the main cause of ZA deaths, and then of course there are the mutations.'

'Like me,' he said.

'Like you and more besides.'

He nodded. Extra fingers and toes were never unexpected, but he specifically remembered Double-eye on their block, before the police took the man away. Double-eye had had skin like a lizard and his eye sockets each held two eyes, one above the other.

'Cancer is really the main cause of death?' he asked.

'Yes, it is.'

'I thought it was the Committee.'

This ended the conversation abruptly and he watched her head out of the door. An odd smile twisted his mouth, as he realized the docilator didn't have so strong a grip on him now as when they'd first put it on. Resistance had returned to being an option.

They fetched him on the third day and he found himself walking to the laboratory between the two soldiers who'd been in the van with him. He knew his comment to the doctor had been a bad slip-up, and one he didn't want to make again, though he acknowledged his mouth would probably overrule him. He had it good here, and other possibilities might open out from it, though he kept suppressing the thought. Damn it, he would keep his mouth shut, only opening it in such a way as might be of benefit. At least that was what he told himself. He studied the lab.

The huge room had work surfaces around the edges loaded with equipment. More benches with computers and further kit stood in from these, while in the centre, on a raised platform, stood a glass sphere three metres across. A door opened into this, and inside was a chair that made his skin creep. It was padded, but also had straps and a variety of devices attached. It looked like sophisticated torture to him. He noted numerous leads running from the chair to the computers on the inner benches, while in front of the sphere were two rows of four chairs. Whatever happened to the individual in the chair would have an audience. He didn't need to speculate much about who would be in the chair.

'You can go,' said Savarack to the guards.

'You behave yourself,' said one of them to Ottanger, before they both departed.

Savarack sat at one of his workbenches, hands inserted into gloves, into an isolation booth – the kind of thing seen in thrillers about lethal viruses spreading into the world. Ottanger

walked up quietly and stood at his shoulder to watch. Inside
the booth were two bowls, one containing black objects and
the other white. Peering closer, he saw they were the empty
halves of pill capsules. With great care, Savarack picked up a
black end in his right hand, then with tweezers in the other,
took something out of one glass tube and inserted it in the
capsule end. Next, putting down the tweezers, he picked up a
white capsule half and pressed it into the black, finally placing
the finished pill in a tray on one side. Ottanger peered closer
as Savarack assembled another capsule.

'They're flies,' Ottanger said.

Savarack glanced round. 'Yes, we call them bot flies, though
that's decidedly wrong and there's already a fly with that name.
These are related to the tsetse fly, though only vaguely so. The
biotech they hold is extreme, and the hard nanotechnology occu-
pies much of their bodies. In our terms, they seem half-machine.'
He grinned and added, 'Cyborg flies!'

'Okay,' said Ottanger. He didn't know what to say, but he felt
sure biotech and nanotech hadn't been so advanced the last time
he read about it. But then, the likelihood of government broadcasts keeping the ZA population up to date with such things was
remote.

'You make them?' he asked.

'If only that were the case,' Savarack replied. 'Someone released
them into the world.' He shrugged. 'We don't know who. But
we do know that something in them keys into particular genes,
which is why we have to use them only with the people who
carry those genes.'

Ottanger just stood there with questions buzzing around his
mind. He simply had no idea what the man was talking about,
but he also didn't know what questions might be safe to ask.
Savarack might seem quite mild and talkative, but Ottanger

knew well enough that asking the wrong question could result in him in a punishment cell, or even back at the internment camp.

'Particular genes?' he dared.

Now other people were coming into the lab: white-coated technicians taking chairs in front of computer screens, a group of heavily armed soldiers spreading themselves strategically around the room, as well as military officers and a variety of 'crats in groups, heading to the audience chairs while they talked.

'Like the genes of both your paternal grandparents and, unusually, your father's wife,' Savarack replied. 'Which is why we have high hopes for you.' He retracted his hands from the gloves and stood up. 'Come with me.'

Ottanger followed him over to what he presumed were the brass and the bigwigs, and stood back, trying to look as inoffensive as possible.

'Here is Ottanger Smith, our latest candidate – Subject Zeta,' said Savarack.

'Well, let's hope you have better luck with him than with Epsilon,' said an attractive and lush but prim-looking woman. She had black hair tied back tightly and a sensible 'crat jacket and skirt that struggled to conceal something primal. 'Though interesting, that incident was disastrous.'

Ottanger absorbed this information and thought about his own place in the Greek alphabet here. He really wanted to know about those other subjects, and he especially wanted to know what had been 'interesting' and 'disastrous' about what had happened to Subject Epsilon. But, as ever, he was in no position to ask.

'Dangers of translocation,' said an army officer. 'I do hope you're sure of your parameters, Savarack.'

'As sure as I can be,' the researcher replied. 'There are dangers inherent here. You could, of course, all be safely in your offices or elsewhere.'

'Screw you, Savarack,' said a short, balding man.

The officer grunted in annoyance, looked around at the others, then said, 'The nearer to power the nearer the danger.'

Somebody else laughed as the small crowd moved in around Ottanger. He noted that no comments had been directed actually towards him, and few of them looked him in the eye. The balding man prodded his arm, then took his finger away and inspected it as if it might be dirty. 'Much the same as the others. Are there any notable differences otherwise?'

'It's mostly at the genetic level,' Savarack told him. 'And not much of it is active until the nanites and organelles key into that. However, his speed of recovery from his previous life is similar to that of the others, so I'm hopeful.'

Compared to you Morlocks, Ottanger thought.

Others touched him too, as if this was somehow necessary, and he was a lucky charm. The lush woman put her hand on his chest and, as she turned to speak to Savarack, kept it there and gently rubbed. She seemed unaware of doing it – like someone idly petting a cat.

'But in this case I understand the genetics are stronger?' she enquired.

'Yes, his grandparents through to his father, obviously, and his mother also carried the genes.' Savarack frowned. 'Or at least the visible characteristics.'

'Like the ears,' someone interjected, to which another responded with a giggle.

The woman took her hand away and was then one of the few, along with Savarack and the military officer, who looked him in the eyes. She stepped back.

'Will you be using the suit?' she asked next.

Savarack shook his head. 'It's not quite ready yet and, anyway, we need this translocation assessment before I'm prepared to risk wrecking it.' He looked around then continued, 'Now, if you would take your seats. It's time to get him ready.' He beckoned and two technicians came over, one taking Ottanger by the arm and leading him to the sphere.

'Doesn't say much, does he?' said the woman behind him.

'But I gather he listens very well,' said Savarack.

They guided him into the sphere and made him strip down to his underpants. Once he was seated in the chair, he expected them to secure the straps, but they didn't. Instead they began sticking monitor patches on him, and placed on his head a skullcap containing a complicated mass of wiring, as well as inserting needles into various veins. Other items of computer and scanning hardware attached to his skin. He felt his scalp going numb, but not enough that he couldn't feel the hundreds of needles penetrating. By the time they'd finished, he had gone from feeling naked to overdressed in technology. The two then headed out, still without securing those straps, which he judged must be a good sign. Savarack stepped inside next.

'Put this in your ear.' The man held out a small fone. Careful not to dislodge the equipment, Ottanger raised his hand, took the thing and inserted it. From his pocket, Savarack then brought out another device, which looked like a piece of a harmonica. Only now did Ottanger notice he was wearing surgical gloves.

Savarack clicked open a lid on the device, placed one of the black and white pills inside it, the white facing outwards, then closed the lid again with another click.

'When I tell you, you press this button on the side to puncture the end of the capsule. There's no need for more than one puncture because the . . . substance is exceedingly strong. Next you put this inhalator to your mouth, take one long and hard deep breath, and hold that in your lungs for twenty seconds.'

'Okay,' said Ottanger, not wanting to nod and spill the skullcap. Savarack handed the device over. As Ottanger took it, he couldn't stop himself asking, 'And then what happens?'

'That, dear boy, is precisely what we are trying to find out.'

Savarack turned away and headed out of the sphere, going over to take a seat behind an array of consoles and screens on one of the benches. He put on a com headset as the technicians closed the door to the sphere.

'System check,' said Savarack, his voice coming through Ottanger's fone. 'Are we all online?'

Ottanger didn't hear the replies but saw the nods, so presumably they were. The lights dimmed then came back up again. The wiring on his body produced a subliminal fizzing and he wondered about his chances of being electrocuted.

'Okay, Smith, use the inhalator now.' Ottanger just looked at it, warily.

3

The Fenris – Past

The ascent in the space elevator took eight hours, during which the Fenris ate from a stock of food and drank from a spherical bottle of water, while gazing out with renewed wonder at his world. The elevator car had a toilet, but he concentrated on switching his body to a higher energy state, utilizing what it had previously designated as waste. Slow deceleration reoriented the floor, giving him a false perception of gravity until the last few kilometres, during which it steadily waned. Before leaving the car, he finished all the food and water, not knowing what he would find in the Geostation. As he consumed the last morsels, it gladdened him to find all the cracks in his bones had healed, while the ulna break had stabilized. He'd also grown slightly, his sensory armour having to adjust its fit.

He took a long, slow breath, enthusiasm building, then propelled himself over to the door. When he probed ahead, he detected activity now reaching up here from the computing of the world. A great deal wasn't online, however, and the Geostation sat cold and airless. Turning quickly to head to the other end of the car, he found a compartment, and there pulled out a long black cylinder.

61

He touched it to the front of his armour. A request appeared as luminous icons in his visual cortex and he granted it. The cylinder then opened out, revealing screwed-up metallic black fabric that began to crawl out and across his chest. This emergency spacesuit engaged with his armour, blending with it, and continued to spread, providing him with gloves and boots, and a covering over his face and skull that ballooned out and grew transparent. He checked its status and found it firm. Its nodules contained metallized oxygen he could use for a hundred hours, while in that time it could recycle at least fifty per cent of his carbon dioxide. It should be more than enough for his explorations here.

He pushed against the car wall and it hesitated before parting. A safety protocol was apparently checking he was suited up first. When it finally opened, the pressure differential blew him forwards, and he had to catch the edge of the door to stop sailing into the arrivals sphere. After pausing there for a second, he initiated controls. He directed his attention towards one of the numerous tunnel entrances around the sphere, and the suit used some of his already stored carbon dioxide to propel him that way.

Entering the maze of tunnels, cyst rooms, gantry work and halls, he found areas where grav still worked, but he tended to avoid them because they held up his progress. He did slow when he saw the corpses, though. Fenris in armoured spacesuits, with edged and spiked weapons scattered around them. Most had decayed down to their bones, but some had mummified. Here then were remains of that long-ago war between them all, over whether to fire up the engines again to escape their enclosed universe. Looking at them, he felt torn. Through the lens of his inherited knowledge, it seemed inconceivable to him that they had come to this. Yet the eyes of the child saw the sacrifice of people fighting and dying for what they believed in – it was foolish to think this inconceivable with the evidence before him.

That inherited knowledge drily informed him that for evil to prevail, the first step was denial of its possibility, and this seemed a concession. He nodded an acknowledgement as he gazed upon one mummified form, but refused to accept what had happened here as evil. He turned away from the unresolved internal conflict and looked beyond, to the future, telling the system to store viable DNA from these corpses before recycling them. He then copied the instruction and routed it down the space elevator to spread on the planet below.

He moved on.

Finally, he came to some viewing blisters positioned in the circumference of the Geostation. But he was still troubled. The knowledge loaded to his mind had given him a black and white division between right and wrong, which, if he'd been born normally into his culture, would perhaps have served him well. Yet here he'd seen where things had become grey. This perception felt very adult to him as he gazed down the length of the elevator, to where it seemed to turn into a needle point, spearing down like an inoculation into the planet lying below. He then put the conflict aside once more and studied his world, with its landmasses seemingly formed of millions of opalescent squares. He saw the blurred edges where those same city slabs dipped into the oceans and covered most of what lay below. He could make out other objects scattered across the oceans in a variety of shapes: sea farms and harvesters of the biotech life there. Here in its totality was a world that could easily and comfortably support billions, and he suddenly felt certain it was his job to ensure its resurrection. Was this arrogance? No. A fenris child he might be, but he was powerful and controlled an immense technology and its resources!

He transferred his attention to the great engines sitting in a higher orbit from the Geostation, his mood rising and shadows dispersing from his mind. The even distribution of the engines around the world had been disrupted, and some of them had simply gone missing. He still couldn't access their data as yet, so he checked via the long route, to telescope arrays down on the planet. This showed him that of the original eight hundred and twenty engines, just over six hundred remained. He eyed the nearest one, then turned to the controls of the blister he was in. A simple mental instruction had the back hemisphere sliding up and mating with the front hemisphere of the blister. It then detached from the station easily and drifted out into vacuum. Like most fenris technology, this was general-purpose and could serve as a vehicle to travel through any environment. A blast from invisible thrusters, for the thing was made for all-round view, sent it out towards that engine.

He surveyed the engine as he approached. It resembled the kind that the fenris had put in their transport in ancient, pre-biotech ages, with its long block to contain pistons, driven by organic fuel, and its fatter section below to hold the linking and driving mechanisms from those pistons. A variety of pipes and other attachments were tangled over its surface too. But it was also eight kilometres long and had an entirely different function. This engine could open holes through the interfaces between parallel worlds, allowing the transport of massive materials through them, as well as the inspection of those worlds. It had functions that went beyond that too: manipulation of space–time in other ways, the creation of wormholes and even the compression of matter to create singularities. These engines had been a bulwark of fenris science for hundreds of thousands of years. And yet, one key part of their function, which had been incredibly energy hungry, had eventually been transferred into fenris DNA and related biotech. What had once been a massive project to open up paths to the parallel worlds, he would be able to do simply with an effort of will . . . once he was fully grown and at last became a world walker.

The blister drifted to the engine, then planed along above its hull, over a series of other observation blisters, until it found a recess. It dropped down into this and attached. After a pause for another safety check, the rear hemisphere of the blister sank down to allow his exit. A pressure differential hit him once more, but this time with gas blasting inwards. Via sensory spikes, he detected inert gases that had been flooded throughout the engine for its preservation. He moved inside, straight onto the floor of a corridor that was running grav. He still maintained connections to the Geostation, but though he could detect massive data shifts ahead of him, he couldn't link into them. It was dark, so he ramped up his vision, also noting that his other senses, based on emitted radiations beyond the visual spectrum, were failing to penetrate. So what now? There would be a control deck, which, checking into external views of the engine from the Geostation, he saw were to his left and up. He hesitated, anxious to be on the move, but with that dry, factual part of his mind considering what danger he might be walking into yet again.

There had been a war here between those who wanted to break the cyst enclosing the world and those against it. They'd allowed ritualized combat to settle the matter, yet in the end someone had activated these engines anyway, to claw the isolated world back out into the multiverse. It seemed highly likely that whoever had done this had been prepared for the combat to return to the use of serious weaponry, and so might have put defences in place here. How could he prepare for that?

As he stood pondering, lights abruptly came on and he had to adjust his vision rapidly back to normal. He stepped back towards the blister, unsure of what to make of this. The interference went down and his other senses kicked in, now able to penetrate some way into the engine's data. He viewed the machinery packed inside it, with corridors and cyst rooms throughout, just as some data feed also probed for connection through his sensory armour. Was this an automated system responding to the presence of one of his kind? He feared it would demand a code, or a form of identification and, upon his failure to respond correctly, would activate weapons against him. He stood frozen, his mind at war with itself, until he came to the conclusion it had been an immature idea to come here without properly preparing. But youthful optimism then put his thoughts on a new course. He now wondered if the bodies he'd seen, and that 'conception of evil', had influenced his thinking – made him cowardly. Abruptly he opened to the connection.

Via the armour, a demand opened in his skull for a DNA key. This was a shock to his previous rationalizations, until he studied the data structure of the demand more closely. It seemed any fenris DNA would do. The data feed then twisted and changed, folding into a 3D shape, and he realized he was looking at a map of the engine corridors. A bright line scribed into it, obviously sketching out a route for him to take. It was towards where he'd been heading anyway. He smiled, shrugged and continued walking, feeling victorious.

Deeper into the engine, he began to see the remains of biotech everywhere. Jointed arms and tentacles, terminating in a variety of tools, were coiled or folded into various niches. Bloated curved surfaces had shed scales, like oyster shells, on the floors. Other surfaces had decayed right down to reveal structural bones. He paused to grab the wrist of one jointed arm, below a spread hand of ten fingers, and tried to turn it towards him. He recoiled as the thing snapped off, as brittle as charcoal, and in the centre of the hand he saw a single shrivelled eye. From this he began to formulate some understanding of what might be going on here. Like the fenris abode he'd gone into below, the biotech here had been genetically linked to an individual, or perhaps many. Those individuals, or individual, were long dead, as was most of the biotech. But some hard system remained. Still following orders, this system had sent him the demand for DNA verification but, because the original was gone, the demand had been open, and then dismissed.

The Fenris strode on with jaunty confidence, then stuttered when he encountered something ahead. A single tentacle shifted in a recess and slowly began to reach out towards him. *Live* biotech. As it stretched out like a spring he decided to circumvent it quickly and moved on. So some biotech remained alive here, but was probably now disconnected from the hard system that had sent the demand. What this would mean for him he had yet to ascertain. He decided to try something, and spoke, broadcasting his words to his surroundings.

'Are you capable of speech?' he asked.

The image of a formula arrived, which took him a moment to decipher. It turned out to be part of the formulae covering 'temporal entropy'. What did that mean? Perhaps, since all its values were negative, the system was trying to indicate the negative, and the fact it couldn't speak. Though, having provided the formula, it could – after a fashion. He decided to leave this exchange until he knew more.

The closer he came to the control deck, the more living biotech he saw. One arm folded out to observe him with its pale, colourless eye. This baffled him. More live biotech here, closer to such a control deck, surely meant a higher likelihood of the hard system still being connected to, and able to access, the original fenris's DNA. But he was in this now and fully intended to reach his destination.

The next corridor opened onto a gangway running above convoluted machines, with tall energy pylons rearing over him.

No gravity here, so he towed himself across, until he came down onto another grav floor. A space remained open around him, walled in by great cylinders. These were covered with pipes and optic feeds. The floor extended to a ribbon pathway, and this then wound up around a mechanism he recognized as a gravity press for making singularities. And amid all this, biotech shifted and worked diligently, further raising his fears about their DNA connection to the hard system here.

Up at the top of the pathway, via a transparent tube, he finally came to a circular blast door. He pressed a hand against the soft reader at the centre of it and got no reaction. With an instruction to his suit, he retracted the glove on that hand and tried again. Through the inert gases around him, he heard the clonks of locks, just as he felt them through his hand, but then pincers suddenly shot out around the skin reader and dug into his hand, trapping it in place.

Pain surged and he denied it. The things had punched through his skin and into his hand, and he couldn't tear it away without losing much of his flesh. Panic rose, but he fought for rationality. The pincers were translucent at first, but then darkened, and a quick check inside revealed the thing was drawing blood. He sensed movement behind . . .

When he glanced back, he saw a biotech horror filling the end of the tube – a great mass of silvery grey tentacles and manipulators. The thing surged down the tube and engulfed him. He beat at it with his free arm but to no avail. He then saw its thin tentacles engaging with the spikes of his sensory armour. Information began to roll in. He also felt the thing copying from him, then linking back through his armour to the Geostation, and thence to the systems of the world below. Reality slid aside for a short period as he tried to parse the informational exchanges. Then, all at once, he fell free and staggered into the control deck, the tentacles pulling on the door and slamming it shut behind him.

Something informed him, without words but directly through his biotech, that atmosphere was available. He looked around. The control deck bore some resemblance to the transmission peak he'd been in down on the planet. The floor was transparent, and all the surfaces around were veined with fleshy biotech, as well as above, in some complex geometric form that kept sliding from his perception. When he looked back at the blast door, it had receded to a dot, while ahead of him floated the chrome sphere of a console. He checked through his suit and soon saw the place did indeed have breathable air. A brief instruction retracted his helmet and the other glove. He inspected his hand, seeing the scabbed-over holes the pincers had made.

'Can you speak now?' he asked.

The affirmative that arrived in his biotech was again without words.

'What just happened?' he asked.

The reply this time was a logical construction that took him a few moments to understand. A past individual had eradicated his DNA in the surrounding biotech, then set a protocol to be activated by the presence of a live body, whenever it may come here – which had been him. He guessed this past individual must have been whoever activated the engines to break out their world from the cyst too.

He delved deeper, checking recent data history. The system here had been much degraded, but by grabbing his DNA and connecting to him, it had now routed to the outside system again and was recovering function.

The Fenris felt a flash of anger. So much more could have been left for him. In fact, the fenris who had broken the cyst could have recorded much of his life and knowledge to AI levels.

But fenris had turned away from such intelligences due to the way they'd been used for control in past regimes, so perhaps his benefactor had made the right choice.

He stepped over to the console's sphere. It contained no handprint like the console on the planet below, but he understood its function nonetheless and reached out to press his hand onto it. All around him the surfaces shifted in response, giving brief glimpses into something that twisted the mind. Hundreds of data streams, connected to the spikes of his sensory armour, filled in context and opened up perceptions. But the main contact ran through his hand straight into the biotechnology growing inside him. His body denied much of the data and access, simply because he and his biotech were far from fully grown, while the exterior biotech had yet to grow enough to be part of him. He fined things back so he could at least perceive his connection status to this engine.

Already his DNA, extracted from his blood taken at the door, was being shifted into unoccupied slots. Meanwhile, the engine's hard system, routing through his suit to the Geostation and thence to the world, continued to update its database and recover all it had lost. One almost immediate result of this was the re-establishment of nutrient feeds and power supplies to the dead biotech of the engine. Fluids carrying living cells, and the rapidly proliferating technology of his blood, had begun to flow through their dry arteries. Fragments of the old biotech still remaining provided contextual format and mated with his biology in the systems all around. Already, in the closer sections where more of the previous biotech survived, he could feel himself falling into the places vacated by the previous fenris's DNA. And with this came an expansion of self beyond his body. Becoming fully established here would take some time, however. He'd then need to send organic missives to the other engines and establish on those too. For now, though, he first wanted to take a look beyond this world. With a surge of excitement, he instructed the engine's hard tech to open up holes in reality that had long been closed.

At once the engine struggled to follow his instructions, bringing zero-point collectors online and sucking on giant capacitors as the demand for power increased. As he understood it, just this one engine should have been enough to open things up, to gather enough photons to give him a view of the parallel worlds. All he could see, however, was darkness. Glimmers only began to arrive after he diverted the power that had been supplying biotech regrowth. But the computers still couldn't gather enough data to start constructing a picture. He paused, thinking hard, then started diverting power to diagnostics throughout the engine. As these gathered information and routed it to him, he felt stupid. As with the train before, his eagerness to progress had overridden checking the technology sensibly. This engine, although in the process of repair, was still badly damaged. Its function ran below ten per cent, and this wasn't enough to open more than nanofractures in the space–time continuum.

He made contact with the other engines still left and assessed them. Many lay in pieces amid the wreckage on the planet below, and those that remained in orbit had all sustained the same damage as this one. In many cases they were barely functional. Still, by running a number of them in parallel, he might just be able to achieve the penetration of the multiverse he needed. He made the required links to them through the hard technology, then melded them to run subordinate to the engine he was in. Control remained slippery, until such a time as he could fully establish his biotech in all the engines, but he managed to set four nearby to this task.

Glimmers turned to flashes, and blocks of data slid into a preformed matrix. He finally glimpsed continental masses, cloudy and clear skies, bare bald moons, and some worlds with technology spreading around them like new metallized skin. He pushed harder, trying to bring other engines into the task, but found his lack of control over them caused disruption and they hindered more than helped. He eventually decided on patience and the slow accrual of data. The massive landscape of the future lay ahead of him and, while it was a hard admission to make, he was still just a child.

It took hours before he began to understand the full representation of the multiverse before him. Numberless worlds were reflected and shadowed across dimensions beyond simple evolved perception. The Fenris soon realized that this multiverse was not the one his world had departed. In that, his world had been the central one, which created the shadows and reflections. Yes, there had been flaws and disruption to that symmetry, but always just the one nodal world. In this, his world simply had no parallels, while greater flaws and disruptions had proliferated around it. These formed a pattern that intersected with a multiverse, which had, apparently, been first generated by another nodal world. Where the two symmetries intersected, however – where those disruptions lay – other nodal and semi-nodal worlds had appeared too.

Did we cause this? Is this the consequence of the Great Project?

The disruptions, patterned around his world, seemed to be the result of his world somehow crashing into the multiverse of this other primary nodal world. He struggled under the complexities of all this, knowing that – still being so young – he didn't have the breadth of experience to understand fully what had happened here. In time he would, but for now he turned his attention to that other primary world.

The thing rose up out of the representation, and it seemed as though he was hanging in vacuum to observe it. He gazed upon it from near and far, vaguely as a whole but also in detail, across swathes that could overload his mind with their data. First he saw the satellites, and the big ring-shaped space station with an asteroid as its hub. Next he saw a space plane rising up through its atmosphere – a flying vehicle with actual wings. Down on the planet, he surveyed massive sprawls of habitations, ocean farms clogging the coasts, fenced agricultural areas patrolled by robots. He sampled the air filled with pollutants, and he sieved their data realm. Then he finally pulled back in bafflement.

He seemed to have fallen into some ancient history virtuality. Here was a world of the fenris past, a million years gone. A society on the cliff edge of falling into complete totalitarianism, if it hadn't already done so. These were the humans of his race's far past – the form of the fenris before they'd started altering their biology. The whole thing felt like a huge open sore to him as he perceived the sheer scale of the suffering there. Pulling further back, he saw it all reflected in the parallels of this world, but then noticed a further anomaly. There were so few of them. And a severance point in their propagation seemed to be marked by a dead version of their *Earth*, as cold and airless as his own world had become. Some odd disruption lay in that region too – a dark manifold and tangle of the plenum between worlds. It was only one of the endless anomalies in this multiverse, so he dismissed it.

What had happened then? How had his world come here?

Entropy.

He would understand it all properly in time, but for the present all he needed to grasp was that his world had apparently fallen back in time, a million years, to its earlier iteration. And in so falling, it had disrupted the pattern of this past multiverse, putting

NEAL ASHER

it on a new course in many places – though not, unfortunately, in the case of this hideous old version of Earth. And then again, no . . .

As he gazed upon the thing, he felt a sudden surge of confidence in the powers he now controlled, and would come to control. He had the technology of a million years behind him and could change things in this past. He could halt or limit the ten thousand years of totalitarianism here, during which the majority of the human race became slaves and toys of the ruling elite. He could end those thousands of years of suffering before they even started and switch this nodal world to the fenris model!

Later, the thought came to him that this was the naive enthusiasm of a child whose reach at that moment was limited to merely gazing upon that place in indignation. He dismissed this as he pulled back to observe the overall model of the multiverse, while the engines laboured to keep the microfractures open and the data coming in. Finally accepting that he couldn't do much for the present, he was about to shut it all down when the system got there first, diverting power away from maintaining the fractures to dump data in through his biotech. He struggled to understand what he was being told, until a moment later, via the system, he saw a weapons turret out on the hull activating and tracking. The limited energy had been diverted by a defence protocol.

The fenris history hadn't been all about peace and scientific exploration, and they had taken precautions to protect their technology, and their world. The weapons on the engines and other satellites had never been used, but now they were activating. Something out there had broken through, and he had no idea what it was.

He froze, overloaded and suddenly experiencing real fear

74

for the first time. Despite all the powerful technology around him, he sensed the emptiness of its spaces and the reality that he was a mere speck of biological matter that controlled this alone. He suddenly wanted to be back down on the surface and stepping out into the old, populated fenris world. Or, at least, stepping out into this one with more caution. But dry knowledge informed him he couldn't change *his* past, and whoever, or whatever, the interloper might be, only he faced it.

Before giving himself time for further thought, he dived into the data streams to gather full-spectrum imagery from the sensors all about his world. The incursion lay far out. Though of course it was nothing he had ever seen before, it was also nothing identifiable from his acquired knowledge and was definitely alien to the system. A dark patch, a hole, was traversing vacuum and steadily drawing closer. The systems next alerted him to heavy scanning, and massive, power-hungry shielding blossomed out from every engine. In response the hole closed, but then just a moment later opened again, over one of the deep-space satellites. He observed the feed from there as the thing engulfed the satellite, then closed again.

Over the next few hours, the protocol remained in place while the Fenris studied the data and fretted. He realized that by activating the engines to penetrate the multiverse, he'd alerted something to his presence, and it had come to take a look. Blocked from gathering data via scanning, it had snatched the satellite for further examination. He looked to his defences. It was all very well contemplating interference on other worlds, but now he knew there was something out there capable of doing the same. It wasn't just a humbling experience, it was a terrifying one.

Chenghu – Past

How much more can I stand? Chenghu wondered, as he scratched at the crusty lump on the side of his neck, peeling off an oddly glistening scab and discarding it. He peered at himself in the mirror, turned his head and looked at the lump to see that it had shrunk a little. At least there was that. But he didn't like what else he saw. His eyes were bloodshot, his skin seemed to have taken on a greyish blue cast and he simply didn't look right. His features were strange to him, having further elongated, as the rest of his body. It seemed that the visible elements of his mutation had become more pronounced recently, but that was often the case when he became stressed by some swiftly passing malady or hard training.

When the fly had bitten him two weeks ago, he'd slapped at the thing, then examined it stuck to his gauntlet. There had been something odd about it – the ichor squeezed out of its body looked nacreous, almost metallic. Then the surge hit him. His meagre apartment multiplied in every direction, and the whole world seemed to turn ephemeral. He felt as he had once when eating some dried mushrooms offered as a bribe by the Hsu street gang. What happened next he couldn't get clear in his mind – weird nightmares of suffocation and strange landscapes. Then he'd found himself naked, down in the basement of the apartment complex. Returning to his room, he discovered his riot rig where he had apparently stripped it off, lying in a heap on the floor. He found the fly and put it in a sample bottle, sure it must be some form of drug-delivery biotech. He'd wanted to get it tested, but feared where that might have led. He was army, seconded to riot duty and, though an SA, he knew that drawing Inspectorate attention would be unhelpful.

Perhaps the Hsu gang could take a look for him in one of their labs? He glanced at the sample bottle, still standing on the table below the mirror, and grimaced. Perhaps it was better to bin the thing. He felt sure the other changes since the bite had little to do with its initial hallucinatory effect. If the Hsu gang found something very unusual, he had no doubt they'd sell the information to the Inspectorate, and he didn't much like the idea of ending up in one of *their* labs.

Chenghu now stepped back and checked his rig. The readout on his wrist console told him his riot gear had lost twenty per cent efficiency, with the fibres clumping, while the inlaid chain mesh had some breaks in it. His helmet efficiency was down too, being overdue for service by six months. This last was of most concern. The chain mesh protecting him from stabbing had breaks at his knees and elbows, but what were the chances of anyone trying to knife him there? Eighty per cent bullet-proofing was more than enough to stop a readergun slug. The ZAs with guns tended to use them to maintain their criminal organizations – like the Hsus – which the Inspectorate avoided. No, his greatest danger was being knocked over then trampled underfoot. And, anyway, he really didn't want to draw attention to his rig.

The breaks had occurred when he opened up the expansion points of his riot gear, for his arms and legs had grown and he now stood four centimetres taller than he had before. He had also put on five kilos, and not around his waist as usual, but muscle. He didn't want the helmet examined for damage and fit either, because the shape of his skull had also changed so much. He used packing insulation up the sides instead, to stop it rattling around.

Further checks revealed his shock stick losing its charge again, but his handheld inducer was fine, while his Glock, in its safety holster, remained as reliable as ever. He shrugged. He was as ready as he would ever be. He turned and headed out of the door.

They're going to kill us.

The riot had spread like a cancer from deep in the Kiakong Sprawl and no one really knew what had instigated it. No one really cared – it didn't seem to take much nowadays anyway. His unit, his brothers, stood guard on Chsing Street, behind the inducer wagon, with its machine guns already folded out for deployment.

'Containment,' said Dreyson sarcastically and patted at the machine gun hung on a strap at his front.

Chenghu looked down at the weapon he'd also been issued. He considered the five one-hundred-round clips he had, and the further ammo boxes behind, noting that this street required at least three inducer wagons, while they had one. They had no shepherds here either. Also notable was the lack of Inspectorate personnel – all the crew here were on secondment from the army. In his mind, he visualized the map of the area he'd glimpsed from right at the back of the briefing room, and it remained perfectly clear.

'They just want us to kill,' Dreyson added. He glanced aside at some ZAs coming through their line, heads dipped and scuttling in the familiar 'please don't notice me' way. The street ahead still had many people in it, as anywhere in the sprawl, but seeing Chenghu's line of troops, and hearing the distant riot roar, they were dispersing as quickly as possible. There would still be people in the way when it kicked off, though – with sprawl population density, the idea of 'clearing a street' was risible.

Everything about this operation seemed utterly wrong to Chenghu and played into a lot he'd been thinking about recently.

He now perfectly understood why he had chosen to join the army rather than the Inspectorate, despite its lack of career advancement. The world was shit. The political system was shit. The Party was shit and, like governments across the world, too heavily influenced by the Multinational Development Committee, which seemed more intent on developing its own interests than anything else. He grimaced, for he could do little about that. But he could look after his own interests. He had joined the army because before it hadn't seemed so much part of Party apparatus. In the forces, he could learn the skills to keep safe, protect those he cared about – though few remained since his family had died in the sprawl firestorm of five years back. And, eventually, he'd be an effective part of rebellion that would come . . . surely? All of this thinking had been on a subliminal level then, but now lay as clear in his mind as everything else. The MDC-initiated Inspectorate was steadily absorbing the army, rooting out the 'agitators', and soon nothing would remain of a force whose purpose had once been to protect the public from foreign threats. It was defunct now, since the greatest threat to the public came from the Committee itself, while 'foreign' was a fading concept.

'This is not what I signed up for,' Dreyson prodded, giving Chenghu a concerned look. 'You okay? You look a bit . . . odd.'

Chenghu smiled at him, closed-mouthed, aware from looking in the mirror that attempting a wide grin now just looked frightening. He turned and peered down the street. He could hear the roar down there but as yet could see no sign of the rioters. Reaching up, he touched the ring around his helmet containing cams and other recording gear. Everything around them would be inspected, everything they said, too. Sensors in their suits also collected physiological data. This constant observation had been happening ever since they'd been seconded. He had no doubt the Inspectorate watchers fully understood his unit to be traditional, hard army, with its contempt for them. And he had no doubt now about the sacrificial purpose of him and those in his unit. He raised his machine gun and fired a burst of three shots into the air to draw their attention, then waved everyone in.

The twenty men and women of his unit came over at a trot and gathered round. He studied their concerned faces and noted an excitement in some that he didn't like. But in their cases, it didn't matter that they might well have fitted into the Inspectorate – what would happen to them next would happen whatever their loyalties or inclinations.

'Listen up,' he said. 'We've got one inducer wagon and it's a robot, and Inspectorate controlled. We've been given a shitload of ammunition and there are no shepherds here.'

'This isn't containment,' said Dreyson.

'Precisely,' Chenghu continued. 'We weren't invited to the briefing. I managed to catch some of it before Inspectorate guards threw me out. I've seen the deployment. Army units are in eight streets, with similar armament and a similar lack of inducer wagons and shepherds.'

'Shepherds aren't as effective as this,' said one, grinning nastily and slapping his weapon.

'Depends what your aim is. Shepherds scare the shit out of everyone. Their function is to herd the crowd and they do that very well. Inducers serve that function too.'

'So what's this all about, and why the hell are you talking about it so openly?' asked another.

'I'm talking about it openly because it's a done deal. The army units aren't expected to survive this. The Inspectorate has heavy deployment of shepherds and inducers in their streets only. Their aim is to drive the riot towards the army units.'

'And then?' asked Dreyson, though it was evident he knew.

'When that inevitably fails –' Chenghu stabbed a finger at the inducer wagon – 'we'll have thousands upon thousands heading straight towards us, with nothing to stop them but live ammunition.'

'Then we'll stop them,' said the grinner.

'No, we won't. We'll kill thousands and eventually be overrun, ending up as smears on the pavement. Meanwhile, the Inspectorate will claim that army units on secondment acted against orders, and with extreme violence against the citizens. It'll be a political hammer for the Inspectorate against the army.'

'That makes no sense,' said another. 'Insurrectionists are under death sentence anyway, and the Inspectorate would be no less violent in the same situation. An investigation will find out about the deployment, the weapons, inducer failure . . .'

'You're correct, but the fact you are doesn't matter at all.'

'Tell them why it doesn't matter,' said Dreyson flatly.

'Because any investigation will be conducted by the Inspectorate, of course. All news and reports will be shaped by them.'

'It makes no sense,' the man protested again weakly, then shook his head at his own naivety. They had all grown up under the Party and understood.

Chenghu ignored him and continued, 'We have limited choices: we stay here, kill thousands and then die, or we run, get hunted down, and die.'

'Or we survive this.' The woman, Itzen, pointed to the buildings on either side. 'We do what we can to contain the riot, then get inside and fortify.'

'Yes, that seems like a plan,' said Chenghu. He shrugged. There seemed no point in going on, and now he could see the rioters boiling towards them at the end of the street. What could they achieve by discussing this further? Why tell them that surviving here, even in the buildings, was impossible, since their

81

ammo would still run out? And even if they did make it, they wouldn't survive any Inspectorate questioning afterwards. Not that there'd be any questioning after his little speech – just a bullet in the back of the head.

'Get back to your positions. I won't be watching what you do thereafter, at all.' He faced forwards as they moved away.

Dreyson lingered. 'What are *you* going to do?'

'I don't know yet,' Chenghu replied. He studied the man. 'Whatever decision I make shouldn't necessarily be yours. Do what you want to.'

Dreyson frowned and moved away.

The street filled up as if with the flood of a tsunami. Running and screaming people boiled towards them and he saw many going down, to then be trampled. Some were naked because, thinking they were burning under the inducer, people often tore off their clothing. Subliminally – his hearing seemed to have become very good lately too – he heard a series of clonks. Glancing round, he saw three of his soldiers heading away, their helmets rolling on the street. They'd kept their weapons, which was stupid since they'd contain trackers.

Turning back, he captured the entire diorama in his mind, frozen. It was as if he had stepped aside from time. The crowd ahead roared. The Inspectorate stood behind it, behind him, and he sensed it lurking all around virtually. He and his men were in a pincer – already crushed and squeezed out of the world, before the mass of humanity steamrollered over them. It was all so pointless and just a thin skin over reality – a page to be torn away to go on to the next.

So what for Chenghu now? If he survived this he knew, with the odd physical changes he'd undergone, that he'd come under intense scrutiny. Vivisection would not be out of the question. But did he want to survive? The horror of it all, of this world he inhabited, and all the hideous choices he must make to survive, had felt too much for a long time. As he watched the approaching horde, he recognized the strange unreal moment as similar to when he'd first been bitten by that fly. Pushing with some sense that resembled imagination, he suddenly saw the street empty, but with weird buildings, like tall worm casts, rising on either side. He also saw a ringed moon in the sky, soon supplanted by another that had regular structures all over its surface. The world continued to slide, as if into meaninglessness.

The riot drew closer still, whirlpools and currents of human beings bouncing from the walls on each side. He could see doors going down in the buildings, relieving some of the surge, and the buildings filled up. The pressurized flow seemed to make the structures groan, but this arose from the masses of humanity packing inside them. Soon many people were falling screaming from windows. He shrugged, knowing just how much more he could stand. Perhaps better just to step into the flood and let it take him, to fall into this thinly strung world and allow himself to fade . . .

The inducer fired up, snapping him back to his reality – he could feel a slight backwash from it that set his skin tingling and then turning hot, as if from sunburn. That wasn't right, since he was standing well back from it and there shouldn't have been so much spill. Screaming ahead increased. Street people who'd not been part of the surge went down thrashing, trying to put out invisible flames. The centre of the approaching mass shuddered to a halt and melted back, but the rest flowed round on either side of that centre. Only now did Chenghu notice that many in the crowd were armed with makeshift clubs and various tools to serve as weapons. Instinct brought up his machine gun, then morality lowered it again. Some of his unit opened fire without any need to select targets. Others fled like the first three.

NEAL ASHER

He saw Dreyson looking across at him. The man discarded his helmet, gave Chenghu a nod and headed away, dropping his weapon and steadily stripping off his riot gear. Perhaps he'd survive for a while, if he stayed clear of readerguns, but eventually the Inspectorate would track him down. They lived in a society in which there simply was no place to hide.

Inevitably, an explosion bucked the inducer wagon, blowing out part of its armour and skittering it sideways. It then shifted and reoriented, its machine guns opening up to carve into the mass. The heavy fifty-millimetre rounds turned human beings into explosions of disconnected body parts. This inclined more soldiers to abandon their stations. Itzen and five others headed over to a nearby door, blew it off its hinges, and entered. Their choice. They would die in there. Those remaining looked to him for guidance as they loaded and then emptied clip after clip. He returned their glances, feeling just plain shitty that he could do nothing for them. He raised his machine gun and walked up to the wagon. He put a whole clip into the left heavy machine gun, shattering its workings. It stalled, something cracked, and it began spewing a snake of ammo out onto the road. By the time he'd walked round to the other gun, his remaining soldiers were already running. When the second heavy weapon died, he sent his own skittering away from him, then turned back to the surging crowd.

Chenghu took off his helmet and cast it aside as he walked. He undid his belt, dropping his Glock and shock stick with it, and held out his arms to the side. This was it. Let them take him. In the thousands rolling down on him, he could see no hint of recognition of what he'd done. Expressions were animalistic – driven mad by inducers and the shepherds in shredding mode. A man crashed into him, others packed in close behind, falling over him and crushing him to the ground. It was all men at the forefront – the reality of body mass and strength already having left the women behind, dead or disabled. They washed over like a hellish tide, with feet thumping down on him and others. It seemed he'd entered a world of tangled body forms in some Gigeresque artwork. It amazed him that he hadn't felt anything break, and he found himself further amazed when he managed to heave himself up to his feet.

His head rose above most of those around him, and he gazed across the flesh-scape as it towed him along. It took on the appearance of a sea, with the buildings on either side like rocks. He pushed towards them in no physical manner but with something else – that enhanced sense like imagination. The whole scene tilted and slid away, the sky turning dark. A shepherd rose up nearby, successively munching up human beings and leaving a red mist behind it – a bloody spectre from a Lovecraft universe of death and evil. The crowd tipped him over again and he fell, rolling on something gritty. He gasped for breath and reached out to fend off the stamping feet, yet encountered nothing. Air continued to evade him. He rolled, searching for relief, and realized he was naked.

'Not enough energy . . . Push!' said the voice of a monster, fading in and out of existence at the edge of his perception. He pushed and the world jerked sideways, rolling him out onto contorted stone, and he gasped in clean air.

'You'll do,' said the monster, as it receded and winked out.

4

The Fenris – Past

Spheres, each the size of a head and carrying the Fenris's blood, launched one after the other from the engine he'd first visited. These were fielded by all the other engines, which drew them inside, cracked them open and extracted their contents. Just as with his inoculation of the first engine, his blood spread throughout these engines' own meagre biotech. The systems of all of them gradually upgraded and connected, their functionality increasing as their biotech began to grow. He gave it direction, concentrating on bringing all defences up to maximum first. Because altruism, he felt, started at home.

It took five years, during which no further incursions occurred. He returned to the surface to establish a base in a city slab. There, by using the same method, he began incorporating all the planetary biotech, while also upgrading and complementing defences. Steadily, he became at one with his world, and the technology of his race. As it grew, he grew too, enough to know that this work kept him from the introspection that emptied the world around him and took him to dark places in his mind. And enough to understand that his loading of fenris knowledge was but a grounding on which he must build. For his world was not the old one – the paradigm had changed.

With energy generation and storage levels increasing, he finally took the risk of reopening the microfractures, to gaze out upon the multiverse once more. This time he paid close attention to detectors, and to the shield generators that could block material attack. The mechanism used to penetrate the multiverse could also be inverted to block the arrival of anyone from elsewhere. Though he had no idea if it would work against the thing that had snatched a satellite. He ensured every weapons turret was fully loaded and powered too.

But nothing happened for a further three years. He assumed that whatever came had seen his world as a high-tech one but unoccupied, so dismissed it as not a threat. He increasingly turned his attention to other matters.

His perception and knowledge continued to expand. He dredged up and codified records about the years between the initiation of the Great Project until now and came to understand how his people, while so advanced, had slid back into the rule of a few. In essence this kind of order lay written in their old DNA and needed to be constantly suppressed. Strength, his grounding told him, lay in the capacity to do evil but resisting it. He saw where this approach had failed, though, and where perhaps the old biology response, which built hierarchies and rulers, was the correct one. As he absorbed these contradictions, his focus increasingly returned to data coming in via the engines.

He viewed numberless worlds and varieties of civilizations in the multiverse, searching them for the kind of technology that had penetrated his own world. But they were all mostly at the level of the nodal Earth he'd first viewed. They had been parallels of it after all. And, while they had been sheared off to take wildly different courses, becoming nodal themselves, they still tracked the same timeline. None of them were a million years ahead.

Since he could gather and transmit information through the fractures, he contacted some and conducted exchanges, though they were primitive and the exchanges one-sided, for they had little to teach him. But the contact was established and eased his feeling of moving through empty spaces. Increasingly, he studied the main nodal Earth, and recognized it had not yet fallen into its nightmare age, for nation states continued to exist. Complete totalitarianism lay in the future, though not a distant one. Still it irked him, coming from the impulse for freedom that had been the core driver of his race up to the Great Project. Yet it was also a perspective he questioned now.

The suffering amid those designated ZAs under the Multinational Development Committee – the MDC – model was immense. They lived meagre lives, without direction, and died young by design. The ruling SAs blamed all the world's problems on overpopulation and pollution. Yet, as he understood the history of his own world, freer virtual utopias with much higher populations had come after this long and evil time. Their problems were really due to the inefficiencies of autocratic rule, politicized science and the belief that the answers lay in reducing the consumption of resources. Because of this, the whole regime had begun to zero in on tightening control and likely extermination, and he calculated that the latter would come soon after total rule. Already MDC diktats, applied by national governments, were in place, such as resource control, population strictures and suppression of insurrections. And these meant starvation and disease, chemical suppression of fertility applied haphazardly and dangerously, and the lawful killing of anyone who might object. What could he do? Every time he asked himself this question, the answer came back: biotech.

General technology, and latterly biotechnology, had been the fenris's escape from their human past. Though authoritarian regimes had hampered technological development, it continued nonetheless. For thousands of years elites had used technology such as AI to subjugate the majority of the human race, but they couldn't stop it steadily disseminating. This process gradually distributed power too, so those previously subjugated found more and more ways out of their chains. There were revolutions – many that failed and some that simply resulted in a new regime aping the old – but freedom gradually came, as those who would rule found themselves less and less able to impose their will on others. And the biggest driver of this was biotech.

Controlling people via resources ceased to be an option as resources became plentiful. Violent suppression and other methods began to fail against a population of increasingly durable, capable, intelligent individuals, aware of their evolutionary drives and perfectly in command of themselves. The horrors beforehand had been driven by the need for power, to create safety and secure resources, and the games of mating strategies, but that need went away as the rulers changed too. What became the fenris went beyond these old drives, as each became powerful and secure in their own right. In rising above their own evolution, they had broken the hold of the autocrats. And, by and by, they created their society of free individuals, working towards goals that were, for the first real time in all human history, *not* about power and the subjugation of others.

Biotechnology.

If the biotech of his kind could be established on that nodal Earth, it would short circuit ten thousand years of horror. Certainly there would be problems – especially on such a fragile world, always teetering on the edge of major resource or environmental disaster. But still, the ten thousand years could be shortened to mere centuries. And, of course, this was also a quick and dirty way to resolve another issue.

The Fenris didn't like where his mind had taken him on that other issue. He saw it had arisen from old biology, and perhaps the effect on him of empathizing with those on the nodal Earth. Obviously, out in this multiverse, there was another race, civilization or entity with capabilities similar to his. Though he controlled vast and powerful technology, he was just one fenris alone. However, if he established his biology and biotech on the nodal Earth, it would result in others of his kind, or beings similar to him. They were, after all, humans, and fenris ancestors. He'd be able to garner allies. Another thought made him wince, arising as it did from the need for safety and the inevitable rule of the few this engendered: they could be soldiers. This was utterly contrary to his dry founding knowledge, but it was there nonetheless.

The problem of access remained, however. Walking out of his abode in his city slab and into the next one, near the space elevator, the Fenris now stood half again the height he'd been when born, and three times the bulk. He still hadn't attained sufficient growth for his biotech to enable him to travel between parallels, though. He could not be a world walker yet. Meanwhile the engines, growing ever more efficient as they slewed away the dregs of their damage, still couldn't open a fracture for a creature of his size. But he was not the only form of life . . .

The laboratory he went into in the next slab consisted of a series of interlinked spherical chambers, filled with biotech utterly controlled by him – an extension of him. This meant he could do everything at a distance, but he preferred to be present during the work. Entering one chamber, he sat down in an organic throne, and snakes of optical fibre rose up around him to connect into the spikes of his much-expanded sensory armour. With palms down on organic interfaces, and eyes closed, he entered a virtuality. Here he gazed upon the project that had been occupying him over the last two years: a virus. The thing hung before him – a spiral of vast molecular complexity.

It was still far too big to pass through the rift he could open into the multiverse, but he now felt he had the solution. Working the coding with his mind, he watched the spiral divide into five separate spirals, and then it began shifting around molecular components. The first contained fenris DNA, as a substrate for additional biotech in the others. Its viral infectivity was zero, until the addition of the remaining four, since he wanted to test the DNA substrate, which was the only part of the overall consolidated virus that he had doubts about. The other four would thereafter create infectivity, allowing the virus to spread. Those infected would then pass the changes on to their children. These would cause little of note at first, beyond increased toughness and resilience and some visible changes. The consolidated virus was just a foundation for the rest. Interestingly, due to the population differences and the immunological programmes employed by the SAs, this virus would mainly spread among the ZAs. The Fenris frowned. It would then take hundreds of millions of different, follow-up viruses to establish his full biotech amid these past humans. But it was a start at least.

After many hours of work, he decided he'd been tinkering for long enough and could not improve on what he had. He dropped the design of the five viruses into the lab's system, and thence to the engines floating in orbit. Finally opening his eyes, he observed the optic snakes detaching from his armour. He would go up to that first engine, to be there as he triggered this first of many interventions into the multiverse. Yet again he had no need to go, for he could look upon any of his projects without changing from one location to another. But he winced at the thought. That had been a problem for some fenris when they became static creatures wrapped in biotech – somewhat like their interstellar travelling kin.

The elevator trip up to the Geostation was fast, at just over an hour, with his train travelling slowly through atmosphere, then accelerating to almost fifty thousand kilometres an hour in natural vacuum. And once in the control deck of the engine, he issued instructions mentally and with gestures. In some cases he didn't have to give instruction at all, as the now perfectly melded hard and biotech system here anticipated him. Filmy screens and surfaces filled with imagery. Within this engine and others, huge energies worked to open microscopic holes in space–time and adjusted to his selected area. Finally he gazed into the city sprawl of the first nodal Earth.

Here ragged tenements stood hunched together – structures flung up with foamed stone and composites, with the minimum aesthetics and often the minimum of functionality. Three crowded street levels ran evenly alongside the first nine floors of these buildings. It was evident that full authoritarian rule had yet to be imposed here in New York, because people could still spend their dole on a selection of goods in these streets. Elsewhere the future was showing itself, with distribution centres and money being phased out. Cams, up on poles, were everywhere. Some cops watched from balconies designated for them only, while down on the streets amid the crowds riot-control robots sat folded up in alcoves, or under metal covers. The Fenris observed the scene briefly – little needing to be reminded – then made adjustments to focus his perspective inside one building.

A large family occupied a series of rooms, each individual keeping to their own little castle of a cushion or two, a ratty blanket and some other belongings gathered in close. They didn't move about much because they simply didn't have the room.

This set-up was reflected throughout the building, throughout the sprawl it occupied, and around the world. Here was as good a place as any to start.

Meanwhile, in another view from his biotech manipulators working deep within the engine, he observed a bulge growing in one scaled surface, then opening like some great boil and oozing out a translucent egg. He picked this up with his manipulators, which then rose up around a tall metal cylinder hazed with purple energy. A hexagon opened on the cylinder's surface and he moved the egg to it.

In the other view, he fell down on a healthy-looking girl of about fifteen. Though, with the lack of nutrition, she had the appearance of one five years younger from a previous age. His perspective slid right down inside her, to a haze of red. Within the engine's mechanism, the egg dropped into a small press, its contents squeezed through biotech chips and sieves, finally to pass through a needle injecting into a wall of light. Thence it arrived in that girl's internal redness.

The program ran on, shifting to another human target, and then another and another. All around him, he felt the massive energy draw of the operation. Ongoing repairs and maintenance ground to a halt. When the operation itself slowed, he searched for options and found the largest remaining energy reserve for the weapons and defences.

He hesitated, after all this time still wary of that previous incursion and what it might mean. Finally, in irritation he shut down weapons and defences. There would be a delay now before they activated, should another incursion occur, but decades had passed since the last one, and what he was doing now shouldn't take long. He returned his focus to the operation, gazing upon the girl, his first viral recipient, as if he hoped to see some response to his gift. He saw only indifference.

With the one egg drained of the first iteration of the virus, the program switched over, ready to produce the next, and awaited his prompt to continue. But he halted the process there. Not because he couldn't send the other four components of the virus, but because he needed the remaining energy to observe the effects of the first one closely. Generation and storage began to come up. Repairs and maintenance restarted, and now he considered routing observations to his sensory armour and returning to the surface. Then, at his instigation, the weapons and defences came back on. He breathed a sigh of relief at that as he stood and headed for the elevator.

He watched the inoculated continue about their bleak and difficult lives as he returned to the surface.

It wasn't until two weeks later that the effects started to kick in. Signs of infection were similar to one of the many kinds of flu that regularly spread through the sprawls. This resulted in others clearing as much of a space as they could around the infected. He felt the horrible slam of guilt when a man expired, his lungs filling with fluid. Many of these people were weak and without defences, so he rationalized that some deaths were to be expected. He had to take the long view on the balance scales of life and death, but he didn't find that easy. After the twentieth death, he could no longer justify what he'd done and looked on in horror as more deaths ensued. How different was he from the damned Multinational Development Committee, with its ill-considered experiments in population control?

Over many months the deaths continued, while he tried to distract himself with any work he could do to facilitate continued regeneration of his world's technology. He garnered all the information he could from the deaths. His instinct to shut down emotional responses he clamped down on, forcing himself to suffer, though his was a meagre reflection of what he'd created.

The fenris DNA was too alien and caused wild cytokine storms and fast immunological diseases. And then, at last, it was done. Of the hundred subjects he had infected, seventy-one had died. He noted the girl had survived, and that the remaining twenty-eight mostly consisted of her extended family. Some quirk of their DNA had obviously enabled this, but it was something too rare to pursue.

The Fenris sank into guilt, recognizing that in his eagerness to bring about a change for good, he'd brought only tragedy. Historically this was a cliché that the road to Hell was paved with good intentions, and precisely what had created the horrific regime on that Earth. Allowing his emotions, and the pressure of outside events, to influence him, he'd acted prematurely. He turned off the feed to his armour, setting the tech in orbit to alert him only should any incursions occur up there. Then he travelled around his world, busying himself with what could be described as domestic chores.

He brought a general-purpose vehicle out of storage. It was like a giant rice grain, with multiple drive systems, and could protect its occupant from any environment. He used this to venture under the sea, into atmosphere, up to his engines, and even once to the moon, to ensure everything was working as it should there. He worked and he grew, and years slid by, in a life that could continue endlessly. He was the Fenris, and his perception of time was an utterly different thing to that of conventional humans. He thought deeply and played out scenarios in his mind. He continued to gather knowledge from databases, adding the relevant parts to his own, and honing his mind. Finally, while aboard an ocean harvester transporting its load to feed the world's biotech, he came to realize he'd grieved for long enough, and procrastinated ever since. And so he returned to his base on the surface. He had done material good on his world at least – spurring regeneration so now planetary functionality was up to over fifty per cent. But increasing his resources and power was make-work, not his final objective. He'd also done well mentally, feeling a degree of maturity now and some emotional distance. He reconnected to the feeds from the engines.

Gazing on the nodal Earth, he updated on that first virus. The family was now three generations on, while the girl he'd first observed had died surprisingly old for a ZA, at seventy-five years. He winced at the disparity between his perception of time and what had actually passed, while his dry knowledge reminded him that as a fenris he was the equivalent of a teenager to one of them. The family had expanded by dint of their ruggedness, passing on their much-altered DNA to their proliferating kin. In them, the changes had done some good, but it was far from what had been his objective in driving change on that world, and further still from his secondary aim of garnering allies. Or, he allowed himself the hard reality, soldiers. He needed to get back to this, and now.

On the surface, he called up his viral models and began the long task of making adjustments. He reformed the biotech in the remaining four viruses so they didn't need a fenris DNA substrate and could meld to its more ancient form – human DNA. He then ran thousands of virtual tests, until finally realizing he'd explored every possible danger and was procrastinating again. Then he returned to orbit.

Power generation and storage had increased over the years, but it still wasn't enough to send more than viruses. Back in the control deck of his favoured engine, he began the process again. He selected an island population and sent the first virus, observed it, then sent another, continuing to observe and send, and gather data. During this process some of the recipients died, but from a higher point of perception he hardened himself and kept his end goals in sight. He learned strategies and application that lay beyond all his modelling, and saw the route to success. Once more shutting down everything extraneous to his task, including defences, he began to prepare for larger transmissions. And that was when they came again.

The alert jolted him to his feet, and then he just stood there, stunned by the data streams coming in through his biotech. Visuals showed three black holes open in vacuum, and one down on the planet traversing a fenris street. Massive scanning then ensued. His pure visceral fear had him reaching to turn weapons and defences back on, but then he stopped himself. He needed to think with maturity and intelligence. He must not simply react!

No attack was coming through these incursions, and he needed to put himself into the mind, or minds, that lay behind them. Obviously they detected when he penetrated the multiverse. The previous incursion had come when he first did that, and they'd seen defences activated, then snatched a satellite, undoubtedly to assess the technology here. He paused his train of thought there and reactivated defences, ensuring they were at the level they had been the last time. Down on the surface, the incursion there wavered and turned, somehow ripping up surrounding technology in a whirlwind, then it snapped out of existence. Those out in vacuum, however, started to move in.

Think!

These incursions hadn't occurred when he sent the first virus containing his DNA, and they hadn't returned while he continued his observations of the nodal Earth. So why now? What had they seen, and what might they be thinking? Previously he'd guessed their driving intelligence had perceived a high-tech world, but an unpopulated one, and not considered it a threat. Now they had come because of an increased multiverse penetration. What should he do? He ran hundreds of scenarios through his mind but, in the end, decided that doing nothing was the best option. They might snatch some of the deep-space satellites but would learn no more from those than they probably had already. And yes, they'd seen an unpopulated, high-tech world but had to be aware it was steadily regenerating, and that this could account for the further multiverse penetration. Perhaps that was why they hadn't reacted to the first virus. He felt sure, however, that if they learned a living intelligence controlled all this, their reaction might be very different indeed.

The holes drew closer and scanning ramped up higher and higher, now beginning to penetrate shields. The Fenris gave instructions that resulted in his immediate surroundings seeming to drop behind thick distorting glass, concealing him. The defence system meanwhile went to a higher level of alert as a single ship flew out of one of the holes. The thing was a strange mess of laminated materials, shot through with holes, and he desperately wanted to direct more scanning at it than the defences' simple reactive kind. It drew closer and closer, coming within range of his weapons, and his system broadcast its demands to the vessel. He continued to do nothing, while also noting there was no reply from the interloper on any band. Then a weapons turret on one of the engines fired.

A bright yellow beam of phase-shifted plasma stabbed out into vacuum, whipping past the ship and passing between two of the holes. If the demands in thousands of languages, computer codes and graphical illustrations had not been enough, then surely this was. No intelligence could ignore such a warning. The ship abruptly slowed, then turned around, with seemingly quite primitive ion drives stuttering white flame. It was only halfway back to the holes when something blew out of its side. One of the holes immediately began to advance on it, then winked out like the one on the planet. The other two holes brightened like Catherine wheels, and the Fenris soon understood he was seeing the drives of hundreds of rockets. The things arced out past the ship, and set themselves on course for his world. He didn't need system information to tell him this was a massed attack, and those missiles likely contained fusion warheads, if not something else even worse.

What should he do now?

He watched as one of the remaining two holes tried to advance on the ship again, now drifting away from them, but again it winked out. A moment later, bright light flared, annihilating the ship in a hot fusion conflagration. This was enough to ramp his defence system even higher. Bright yellow beams stabbed out from numerous engines and satellites. Incoming missiles puffed to vapour in vacuum as the Fenris now shut down the shield immediately around him and increased scanning of everything out there. Bursts of radioactivity from the destruction of each missile revealed they were fusion devices, with yields in the megatonnes. If they reached the engines, and the planet, it would be disaster for him. But they wouldn't. Scanning where the ship had exploded revealed little of value. It didn't all quite make sense, and this fact set his mind back into motion.

High-tech multiverse incursions had been made, yet what looked like a low-tech spaceship had come through, malfunctioned and then exploded. It seemed likely it had been detonated by whatever lay behind those incursions, when they failed to scoop it back up. Next, low-tech missiles had been fired, and now he watched as the last of them glowed and turned to vapour. He could only speculate. This could be a high-tech civilization sinking back into primitivism, or a primitive society with its hands on some high-tech tools, or perhaps the former rising out of primitivism after some catastrophe, like war. Whatever they were, they'd come here to assess a threat, found it to be a little beyond them, then chucked an arsenal at it while retreating. He could be arrogant and simply dismiss them, but that might be fatal, because whatever their circumstances were, they could develop.

Days passed with no further incursions. Knowing he could elicit nothing further from the collected data, the Fenris returned power to his penetration of the nodal Earth. Whatever threats he faced from the interlopers, part of the solution lay there, because the idea of soldiers or allies had rooted deeper in his mind.

Should he mass distribute all four viruses now? Yes. With these alien incursions evidently hostile, this had gone beyond merely short circuiting the nodal Earth's route to hell. Driven by a sense of urgency, he queued up the four viral forms ready for mass transmission, then started that process and routed feeds to his sensory armour so he could observe. If the viruses established their tech firmly, as his tests had shown, the recipients would be rugged enough to take a lot more than the previous targets had. However, to send this, as well as protect himself from the exigent threat of those incursions, he needed something else.

He needed more power.

With a thought, he called up new images from satellite cross-spectrum telescopes around his world, and stretching beyond. He gazed then at a structural framework in orbit, which had only some components in place, and immense robots long frozen in the middle of their tasks. The thing had hung there unchanged from before his birth, and he knew it had been an attempt by those before him to rebuild the destroyed engines. He sent instructions and observed the robots beginning to ease into motion. Bringing the number of working engines up to its original amount would certainly help, but would only raise available energy in line with their number. So that would give him twenty-five per cent extra. And with energy levels as they were, it would take the best part of a century. His urgency required another answer.

He gazed next upon the ringed moon of his world, and all the machinery he knew to be there. He'd already inoculated the place with his blood, and the biotech had begun restoring. But the moon's machines, and the artificial ring system with its energy scoop fields, served no purpose. The massive energy source that had fed this, and thence his engines, as well as supplied previous fenris efforts – including the Great Project – had been cut off. He now transferred his gaze to another image.

Here the sun glared as brightly as it could without damaging his eyes – a curved surface raising its hellish fusion tornados. Set out from this, and small in comparison, but still as large as the moon of his world, was a sun tap. This bloated device resembled a great mass of clumped and tangled organs, bound in place by golden bands. Giant glassy spines speared out from it, while on its inner and outer faces sat huge dishes. The thing looked burned, as it was, and though he'd sent it an inoculation of his blood, as he had done for all other available fenris biotech, there had as yet been no response.

'It is time,' he said. 'I need to go out there.'

Ottanger

On Savarack's instruction, Ottanger raised the inhalator device and looked at it. He was reluctant and, as his docilator weakly prodded him to obey, he felt for a moment that he should have asked more questions. Then he dismissed that stupidity. His choices were either his involvement in whatever they were doing here, or the interrogation cell. He also had no doubt that here, should he no longer be useful, he'd be disposed of, or worse. If he understood correctly what Savarack had been saying about the genetics of his father and great-grandmother, then he would probably be subject to examinations. And, as a disposable Zero Asset, he wouldn't put vivisection past any of those in authority.

He clicked the button on the side of the device, raised it to his lips and took a long hard breath as instructed. Holding his breath for twenty seconds became a struggle, as he fought the urge to cough out the dusty and oily feeling at the back of his throat. Everyone outside the sphere he was sitting in was watching him intently now, and he felt what he could only describe as performance anxiety. What if nothing happened? What if he didn't react as predicted, or do what he was supposed to? And really, he had no idea what they were expecting.

Finally breathing out, he tried to relax as he took another breath. His lungs felt tight, just as they did when he sucked stims from a vaporizer, but then they began to loosen and a strangely clear euphoria spread through his body. Whatever he'd breathed in had to be some weird-shit drug, because now things seemed to be shifting about outside the sphere. The spectators appeared to him as translucent images painted on glass, while beyond them, in some way he couldn't parse, it seemed giant curved surfaces were turning, like the cogs in some vast machine. He glimpsed landscapes like those of the past, which he'd only seen on a screen. Odd buildings, skies of a thousand different hues. And, in a way he couldn't focus on properly, he felt something alien watching him. It seemed to be speaking, but he couldn't hear the words.

Next he smelled something raw, metallic and salty, as the ceiling above became translucent, bringing a weird iridescent sky in over him. The inhalator lost substance between his fingers and fell away from him. The technology cladding him felt loose, the chair underneath insubstantial. The whole world seemed to be losing coherence. Suddenly he fell backwards, the chair disappearing out from under him. He landed on gritty soil and immediately pushed back up into a sitting position. Looking down, he saw only his naked body – all the wiring and devices were gone. With blurry vision, he tried to blink back into focus, in air that seemed to be sucking moisture from his eyes. A whaleback bank of orange grit lay underneath him. Similar humps extended to the far horizon, on flat hard ground yellow as old lemons, scattered with cacti like pale green roses. The iridescent sky then passed by, revealing deep blue-black scattered with stars. Illusion, he felt, surely . . . He turned, breathing the metallic air. Black mountains extended across the horizon behind and above them . . . above them. . .

Was it a planet or a moon? The distinction seemed important. It loomed much larger in the sky than Luna, and its face simply couldn't be natural – he knew that at once. It was as if cities covered the thing, etched into its surface like the electronics of an integrated chip. He took a panicked breath, and then another. The sight was scaring him? No, he realized that though he could breathe the air here, it didn't give him what he needed. He struggled to his feet, looking around, but where could he go to find some good air? In that moment, his gaze fell upon other shapes lying beyond the next drift. The hundreds of naked corpses were dry and shrivelled, and extended to the horizon. He knew his fate if he didn't get away from here.

'Move . . .' The voice drifted into his mind, coming in and out of audibility like voices on the wind. '. . . you can . . . here.' Along with the voice came patterns that settled through him, into some hot network laced through his body. And with that came a species of understanding, beyond expression through human language. The world tilted under him, then back again.

He shifted something, like his centre of gravity, but definitely not that. Looking down, he saw the orange gritty soil was leaching out its colour to pale beige, strewn with knobbly dark brown objects as the light brightened. He felt as if he was clawing up a slope, out of a pit. Then with a further tilt of the world, he tumbled across a plain of fractured rock – the channels between the slabs worn smooth. Bruised and aching, he took another breath, which satisfied his lungs but brought the stink of putrefaction to his nostrils. He looked at a cloudy but seemingly normal sky. A rushing, hissing sound came from behind him and, his panic yet to die, he turned quickly and crouched. Waves. Ahead of him they rolled in on a sandy beach. He'd never stood beside the sea before, and frankly there wasn't much of it left like this on his world.

And there it was, the thought had arrived: *on his world.*

He suddenly felt warm, despite his nakedness, and sweat began to sheen his skin. Looking along the beach, he easily located the source of the smell. *A whale?* The partially deflated corpse looked the right size for one of the extinct creatures, but no. This thing had two great long flippers sticking out from the side, and at the back end a long tail extended and coiled, rotted away in places to expose vertebrae. He walked from the rock to the sand, then along the beach, until he could see where the dead creature's head protruded into the surf. Most of the flesh had rotted away from the thing, leaving a huge skull with long jaws packed with a carnivore's teeth. Perhaps whales did look like that when the flesh rotted away? But he thought not.

So what now? Although this world appeared real and solid, it felt like a skin over emptiness. The feeling inside him, like balance but not, seemed precarious, and he realized he could tip out of this place in an instant. It was almost as if something within him was groping for familiarity, to restore that balance. The thought that this drive might put him in another airless place frightened him, though, and gave him a firmer grip on the strange network within himself. The world stabilized around him and, taking a series of shaky breaths, he focused once more on those remains. The vertebrae of the neck extended too far for this thing to be a whale, he realized, and he mentally fleshed the thing out in his mind, finally recognizing something prehistoric. For a moment he thought he had no idea what it might be called, because his supposedly comprehensive, government-sanctioned schooling had been full of politics, but a memory then came crystal clear: a mosasaurus.

Ottanger shook his head, turned away and walked back up onto the rock. He had no idea what he should do now. He wandered aimlessly, an odd opening of perception seeming to intrude from a direction he couldn't point to. Through this, as if from deep in a cave, he heard a hollow muttering voice but couldn't make out the words. Then in a flash, this perception rushed in on him and something appeared. Iridescence shimmered around a tall form, floating towards him. It looked vaguely human at first, but then he saw how its proportions were all wrong: the skull extended vertically and jutted forwards on a long neck, ears pointed, eyes squinted half-closed under a heavy brow, so they looked almost non-existent and narrowed into a line. On its tall thin body, it seemed to be wearing armour, but with odd crystalline protrusions and devices that might have been weapons attached all over it. He backed away from the thing. But, not properly paying attention to his surroundings, his bare foot slipped down into a crevice and he bashed his knee painfully as he sprawled forwards.

'Fuck! Fuck!' He hauled his leg out of the crevice, rolled over and began to push himself to his feet again. The creature reached towards him with one long-fingered hand, or perhaps claw, palm up.

'What do you think you are doing?' it enquired.

Ottanger felt abruptly foolish, as the words helped him bring the image into context. It wasn't here in the real world, or in *this* real world, but in his mind. He straightened up and looked around. The image of the thing remained in place, and didn't affect his perception of his surroundings. It was as if he'd acquired a new eye looking into the place this creature occupied, with the image being processed through another part of his mind.

'What the hell are you?' he asked.

'I am the Fenris, but what is more pertinent is what are you?'

He shrugged. 'Ottanger.'

The creature acknowledged this with a dip of its head. 'The DNA has complemented the process – the energy I require to get through to you is minimized. Your perception is wider and more detailed than the others' is, so in this sense you're closer to the ideal of the world walker. But your ability has not refined. Something is missing . . .' It contemplated this matter for a moment, then said, 'I see – not enough primary biotech.'

The thing began to recede, its further words becoming a hollow mutter again, which he couldn't extract any sense from. He felt the emptiness underlying this world coagulating and closing. Panic rose in his throat as everything tilted yet again. He fell with his arms windmilling in blackness, grabbing for some hold on familiar reality, then felt the network inside him flash like a faulty light.

A tiled floor came up and hit his shoulder but, travelling horizontally to it, he slid along it, finally slamming into a door. He lay there utterly stunned and wondering what this place might be. Then he recognized the institutional green and grey of the paintwork, and the light squares in the ceiling, with their tell-tale smaller black squares of cams in one corner. Tilting his head up, he rubbed at the side of it, then the back of his neck, feeling the absence of the docilator there. A confirmation of the lie Savarack had told him about its connections. Sound began to impinge, and a bolt of fear struck through him at the blaring of a klaxon. Out on the streets, this usually meant the security forces and shepherds were on their way. A door at the end of the corridor banged open, then someone shoved at the door he was lying against. He rolled away as soldiers burst in through the far end of the corridor, and then another door nearby. One of them immediately hit him with a shock stick and held it in place. He convulsed, feeling the world tightening around him, wrapped around a core of pain, then his consciousness fled.

Ottanger woke up, quivering and jerking. His body ached from the excessive application of the shock stick. He felt the tingling pressure of a drug patch applied to his neck, and it quickly washed away the pain, as well as stilling the quivering. Now he could see. He'd actually been able to see before, but the visual information hadn't reached his mind. He kind of caught up now, seeing himself waking and the doctor applying the patch.

She stood back, arms folded, nodded once, then turned to her trolley to pick up a syringe and prep it. He held out his arm meekly but she shook her head, swabbing the base of his throat instead and gave him a quite painful injection there. Two more injections followed, but those were into his arm, then she made him sit upright. He swung his legs off the bed and sat there looking at the dressing on his knee, and the yellow stain of disinfectant on the grazes on his foot. Had that really happened, then? He squinted at his surroundings. They seemed unreal, odd, dislocated.

'Savarack is very pleased,' said the doctor. 'Initial translocations are usually brief and not so spectacular.'

He stared at her, feeling utterly stoned. 'What's your name?'

She stared back. 'It's not necessary for you to know that.'

He nodded. He was Subject Zeta, and so he would remain until no longer of use to them. He sat there numb and stupidly cheerful while she took blood, and then swabs from his mouth and his sinuses. Glancing over at the trolley, he saw numerous sample bags and bottles with swabs inside them. On one he could read the label, which said 'Ankle Contusions'. Retrospectively, he realized his skin felt dry, and overall he felt very clean. He guessed she'd worked on him for a while before he woke up too, swabbing him from head to foot.

'Are you steady enough to dress yourself?' she asked.

He managed to stand and walk over to the cupboard, but she supported him while he put on the clothes and slippers. He then shuffled after her as she led the way out, past two guards at his door, and down various corridors in the Complex. The testing and sampling continued, and it all blurred together in a strange medical mash. They took urine and shit from him when he needed the toilet, and they ran him through a variety of scanners, one of which raised him to sweating redness. He puked afterwards and they collected that too. Finally she led him back to his room.

'You will sleep for a while now,' she told him.

She was right.

Food and drink arrived on a trolley shortly after he woke. A man in a grey paperwear suit, with a docilator on the back of his neck, pushed the trolley. He had no teeth and scars covered his face, while each of his hands was missing two fingers. He walked painfully, his feet twisted and lumpish. With the drugs departing his system, Ottanger realized that here was another ZA who'd somehow come to the attention of the Inspectorate, survived that, and now served. It was a timely reminder of his status. Yet, even with the drugs leaving him, the feeling of unreality lingered.

He reached up to the back of his neck, but felt a weird reluctance to touch there. His docilator was back in place.

After the man had left, Ottanger ate just some of the food, then took a shower – not because he needed to clean himself, but because he could. He then ate all the rest, drank the juices provided and worked his way through the luxury of a pot of coffee. Quite probably they'd been watching him, because as he finished the last cup and sat back in the comfortable chair, the door opened and two guards came in. Feeling cheerful after such an astounding amount of quality food, he had to stamp down on the urge to ask them if they ever knocked. He didn't think they'd appreciate the humour.

'Up,' said one of the guards. Something else now impinged, sweeping away his good humour. He didn't recognize these guards and they weren't military; they wore the black and grey of street police. He stood and followed the first, the other falling in behind him. Though he'd been confused when the doctor took him for medical tests and scans, he still recognized they weren't heading towards that part of the Complex now.

They took him to an area where the corridors looked less salubrious. The paintwork was old and chipped, and some suspicious stains marred the floors. Ahead someone stepped out of a door and he recognized the bald man who'd been part of the audience outside the sphere. This individual gave him a nasty smile, then turned and headed away. The soldier pushed him through a thick, soundproofed door, of a kind he'd seen once before, and into a horribly familiar room. Three 'crats sat behind a long desk facing a chair bolted to the floor. The latter had straps too and when he looked up, he saw the matt square of the pain inducer in the ceiling.

'Sit.'

He wanted to turn and run, but obeyed, not because of the

increasingly weak prodding of the docilator, but because he had nowhere to flee to. The guards strapped him in place, then rolled over a machine from which they took a rubber skullcap full of monitor nodes and pulled it tightly over his head. This was a new addition. One of the guards then gave him an injection, and he wasn't as gentle as the doctor.

They interrogated him. The docilator pushed him to answer as precisely as he could, even if the presence of the inducer above did not, and he went with it. He was also very voluble – making all sorts of additions – which he put down to the injection, whatever it was. They wanted to know everything about his 'translocation'. Every detail, even down to the colour of the sand he'd first arrived on. They even brought out a colour chart so he could select the correct one. When he described the plants, a screen-painted wall activated behind them, and they showed him pictures of similar plants until he selected one. This seemed to go on interminably, because he couldn't find an exact match. He learned that the nearest to what he'd seen had been something called 'echeverialola GM234'.

When he told them about the mosasaurus, they wanted to know how he could possibly know that name, and seemed suspicious when he told them about the educational broadcast. The questioning became more intense. It then reached the shouting stage – two of them coming out from behind the desk and yelling in his face. This escalated to slaps and then punches. He tried not to tell them about the Fenris, but it just came out of his loose mouth.

After a period of quiet, two of them tilted their heads and left the room, listening to the fones in their ears, while the other continued hunting for detail. The two then came back in with new questions, checking tablets doubtless for updates from elsewhere – he suspected from that bald man. One of them skimmed a hand across his tablet to throw up a picture on the screen. Ottanger peered at it in puzzlement.

'Did it look like this?' one of them asked.

The body stretched out on the slab looked vaguely human and, at first, he thought it was headless. He then recognized the head was there but was the same diameter as the neck, and it did possess features. The nose was a small protrusion without nostrils, the eyes round beads, and the mouth a circular orifice. He next noticed how the proportions elsewhere looked wrong. The body was long, while the arms and legs were the same length as each other. And all four limbs terminated in hands, with what looked like three fingers and two opposable thumbs. Its colour was odd too, though he assumed he was looking at a corpse. It was yellow-orange and covered with dark red thread veins.

'No – nothing like that,' he replied.

'Or this,' asked another, skimming a picture from his tablet.

Another creature appeared, hanging in some sort of frame. Arm and leg length were much as his own, the body a fat cylinder. It appeared ribbed and layered with muscle, but the configuration seemed odd, looking more like segments under tough wrinkled grey skin. As in the figure before, he recognized a distorted human form. The head was wildly different too. It was almost like a set of organic binoculars poised on a muscular neck, with some sign of an upward 'V', a sharkish mouth below, and long ears folded back.

'No, it wasn't that either,' he said. 'What are they?' he then asked, trying to engage.

'None of your concern. Now describe this . . . vision in detail. And tell us exactly what it said.'

He followed their instructions to the letter concerning the appearance of the Fenris. When he started to leave out detail of their brief conversation, he guessed the effects of the injection must be fading, though. He instinctively didn't tell them about the mention of DNA, or those 'others', or his own supposed lack of 'primary biotech'. Finally, they seemed satisfied with that. But then the questions started to stray into different and equally dangerous territory. They asked him about how it had felt to be free and in another place. They segued into ones about whether he thought some escape lay that way, and whether he thought to bring something, or someone, back with him.

He screamed when they finally, inevitably, resorted to the inducer, though he'd told himself he wouldn't. By now the three had stripped off their jackets. Their yellowish shirts were soaked with sweat, and the stink of body odour permeated the room, along with the smell of shit in his trousers and the urine pooled under his chair. At last, after another hit from the inducer, it all seemed to be coming to an end. The three picked up their tablets and departed. He sat there, wishing to die, when the next three came in.

At some point in a nightmare age, after he'd lost track of just about everything and thought he was back in the internment camp, he heard a clattering sound outside, then the door behind burst open. Two soldiers came in, fast. In response, one of the three 'crats before him brought his hand down on a horribly familiar control on the desk. Pain washed through him and he screamed again, subliminally aware that one of the soldiers was yelling and staggering away, having caught some of the inducer beam. Gunshots clattered again, and the pain went away as pieces of the inducer fell onto him – meta-material flakes like lizard scales. There was shouting, but he couldn't quite understand what was being said. He saw the attractive 'crat woman stride in, peer at him with a worried expression, then turn on the three behind the desk, beginning to shout at them too. One of them stood up and yelled back, gesticulating wildly. A soldier moved up quickly and smashed him in the face with his machine gun. He went down, spitting blood and teeth. Ottanger couldn't help but feel happy about that.

The other two leaned back, hands held up, and the woman questioned them. They answered willingly, and she glanced up at the cams in the ceiling. Ottanger now quite distinctly heard her say, 'Following fucking orders.' She then pointed to him and stabbed a thumb at the door. The soldier who'd taken some of the inducer beam stepped over and unstrapped him. The man appeared quite ill and, looking Ottanger in the eye, shook his head almost in disbelief. Perhaps he'd never experienced an inducer. It was a learning experience.

The two soldiers heaved him up, his arms over their shoulders, and took him out. He managed to walk a little but mostly they carried him. Outside, he saw the two police on the floor in spreading pools of blood. When they arrived at his room, the doctor was waiting there. She even had some sympathy in her expression as she gave him an injection to send the world away.

5

The Fenris – Past

Before he could set out on his journey to deal with the sun tap, there were preparations to make. By slow degrees, the Fenris transferred responsibility for the virus transmission from the engine under his feet over to another. That engine began manufacturing the virus. Then, drawing on the power network, it initiated the constant transferral of the four viruses into unknowing ZAs scattered around the nodal Earth. The tests he'd run, with a viral deactivator on standby, had been a partial success. More than two of the viruses together caused life-threatening reactions. However, a delay between virus infections allowed enough recovery for implantation of the next. Feeling no need to work a database, he'd mentally constructed what he perceived to be the correct strategy. This was to transmit the different viruses to widely separate populations. Gradually, as the viruses spread, there would be overlap. It wasn't ideal, but it was the best he could do for now.

Next he turned to readying his transport for getting out to the sun tap. As his engine extracted itself from the main network, he switched its zero-point collectors over to filling up its immense capacitors. His gaze then wandered to huge old ion drives scattered over its hull, as they ignited blue glows deep inside. He felt the drag, despite grav, and a surge of excitement. Though these drives were a complement and subsidiary to the main method of moving the engine a long distance, he now felt he was on his way. As he'd learned, action rather than introspection was what cheered him. He then set in motion the processes for *really* travelling.

Giant gravity presses shifted and aligned. The tech that clawed at space–time, to give him access to the multiverse, now turned to a new purpose. Within a hyper-collider ring, strange superfluids began spiralling round and accelerating. Instead of creating microfractures, these energies behaved as a huge gravity motor, acting against the world behind. The immense push came at once, flinging the engine out, and it hurtled away from the fenris world. It would now be some months before he'd need to change the gravity alignment of it on course to the sun. The Fenris had time on his hands during the start of his journey. And inevitably fell into introspection again.

It seemed a foolish move to leave his world and its defences while they were under threat, but he'd calculated it to the nth degree. What had attacked him had been dangerous, but not sufficiently effective to penetrate his defences, whether he was there or not. Civilizations advanced and regressed, though, and if the former, it might very soon become more dangerous. His best option to counter this threat was a firm and plentiful supply of energy, to bring his world and its defences back up to their optimum state. To engender allies (which always came with the subtext 'soldiers' now) required that energy too.

Over the ensuing month, he concentrated on make-work to ensure everything in the engine was operating at optimum. This also kept him from straying into inner darkness. He thought a lot about his interstellar kin and wondered if they'd managed to find a faster way to cross the gulf between stars – whether they'd ever managed to travel faster than light. He wondered too about multiverse effects over those long distances. Did the changes his kind had wrought around their world extend out there? He had to admit he didn't, and couldn't, know. Occasionally he tried to make contact with the biotech of the sun tap, but every time only picked up a muttering, drowned by the output of the sun.

After the requisite period, the Fenris counted and observed, then when the time was right, gave the instructions for the change. The engine's grav-presses shifted out of alignment and the superfluids abruptly slowed. The entire structure jerked, as if slapped by some giant hand. Transition took a further week, before he brought the presses to a different alignment and wound the superfluids up to speed again. Acceleration continued, with the grav-motor now aimed at drawing itself to the star, rather than pushing against the world. Then at a midpoint, it began to wind down.

He spent his journey time studying, firmly imbedding knowledge, taking updates from his home planet behind, and sending instructions back. Heat began to become an issue. He switched ion drives on for a steady deceleration and observed internal changes, as convertors shifted and relocated some of the heat. Stores of plain water were diverted through the drives, adding to their impetus, but also draining away some of that heat. The convertors also loaded heat into the superfluids, raising their temperature and changing them to something more conventional. Diverters then took those out of the ring and ejected them as plasma, to lower the engine's overall temperature. Meanwhile the skin of the engine, at first black as it absorbed energy, faded to green, then switched over to near-perfect reflection, bouncing the radiation away. But still the temperature continued to rise, as the engine headed towards a growing black dot at the centre of the solar disc.

That black dot, the sun tap, expanded in the remaining weeks, and being closer, without so much interference, the Fenris was able to study it in greater detail. He still felt no sense of connection to the slow-growing ceramic biotech in the thing. At length, the engine touched the tip of its shadow cone – the sun tap expanded to blot out the solar disc, and then moved into complete shadow. Here the engine's systems managed to stabilize its temperature, switching over from the material expulsion of heat to wide-spectrum lasers. Meta-material layers dulled the conduction and spread. Convertors turned heat into electricity to feed the lasers, but this had limitations, as the entirety of the engine began to gain a negative charge.

The vacuum ahead hazed with ionization, drawn in from the surrounding solar storm. Meanwhile the Fenris's temporary vessel descended towards the crater of a giant emitter dish, in a landscape of technology. He breathed a sigh of relief when, a mile up, lightning streaked down massively from the engine into the dish, to shed the negative charge. Systems rebalanced as he slowed the thing and finally brought it in to land, with a crash, at the centre of the dish. The exterior of the dish rose up like golden cliffs all around.

'I can feel you,' he said.

Yes, he could now sense the biotech on a subliminal level, which had more to do with quantum weirdness than any direct electromagnetic communication. He also sensed biotech he didn't directly control, so this might have had nothing to do with his attempt to reclaim it. Yet EM connection should be available if the hard system had survived, so he suspected it hadn't, and began to gather some hint of future difficulties. He grimaced and strode out of the engine's control deck, pausing to wipe the novelty of sweat from his face. His mood was rising at the prospect of action, though. He made his way to an observation blister. Before entering it, he opened a compartment and took out a silvered biofabric spacesuit. The thing crawled over him, joining to his sensory armour, expanding cooling veins and testing heat-emission fans, before highlighting its requirements. He moved over to the side of the room and found a spigot, then connected a pipe from the suit and waited while it filled up. The suit compressed this mix of cooling gases to solidity.

Back in the blister, he gazed at a point on the edge of the dish – at the top of those golden cliffs – as the other hemisphere of the blister closed up behind him. The blister eased out and wafted up through vacuum, with the cliff illusion dying as it sped up the long curve of the dish. Coming out over the top, he gazed across the technological landscape before him, with its silo capacitors and quantum foam wave guides looking like a polished brass maze. Flying over this, he noted the temperature in the blister rising, but nowhere near enough to affect its tech, or him. Beyond an outer ring, he came down on a structure resembling a flute and sent his bubble inside it. It descended through hot darkness, into ovenlike internal spaces.

Now, within the skin of the thing, and out of the radiation storm swirling around outside, he probed hard via his sensory armour. In a vast internally polished pipe, he detected nothing. The silence seemed eerie. Flying between quadrate structures, which seemed ready to mesh and close into a whole and crush him, he still had no EM connection with the hard computer tech of the sun tap. However, deeper inside, the feeling he got from the biotech there grew intense. He decided to at least search that out.

He found it around a vast spill of silvered tubes, connected to an even larger pipe. Here he could see more evident damage caused by some explosion of the molten cooling lead from these pipes. It had spattered all around, and greyed on the surfaces of superconduction strips, while a great glob of it had lodged between two gravity presses the size of hundred-storey buildings. The biotech hung out from the spill of tubes like a giant dandelion head, and a further extension of it spread over the pipes in blue lichen patterns. The thing was making repairs, but at the slow rate dictated by its ceramic form, and the necessity of retaining integrity in such high temperatures. The task would take it hundreds of years. Without the hard systems operating here, it was like a human trying to repair an old combustion engine using only soft fingers and hands.

Now, being close to the thing, the Fenris found connection and gained a brief overview of similar growth throughout the sun tap, springing from a surviving central source. But he also discovered something else: the biotech was making a generalized response to one of his kind and not something shaped to him. The packages he'd sent out this way had obviously not impacted on it. He travelled on, deeper and deeper inside, and soon found the biotech source. It was sprung like a giant epiphyte on a trunk sixteen kilometres wide, and seemingly formed of alternating diamonds of silver and gold. He drew his blister in amid its blue lichen branches and felt the willingness of connection, but little detail, little information. Now he knew what he had to do. It seemed his journey out here hadn't been enough; sacrifices would have to be made. He felt adult and utterly knowing of this vast technology as he came to the decision. He would have to make a physical connection to it.

After checking his suit, he opened the blister with a thought and went out. His suit immediately raised its fans and began spitting out streams of vaporizing coolant. He directed this, and used it as motive power, driving him down onto one branch.

The biotech consisted of palm-sized scales, shifting slowly, occasionally revealing threads and the turning of bionic cog wheels. This thing, though alive, seemed to resemble the internal workings of a giant clock. He peered closer, the illusion of blue disappearing in the nacreous effect. The scales would be enough, he decided, seeing they were laden with bioelectrics and organo-ceramic processing. Now he had to prepare himself.

He raised a gloved hand and gazed at it, and into it. Routing through his sensory armour gave him more detail as he took full control of his biotech. Growing layers of it compressed the skin cells in his palm, while the nerve trunk up his arm, into his spine and to his brain thickened. Nerves opened through these layers of his biotech, creating neural beads on his skin. Running through the centre of those beads, he wound his DNA around nanofila-ments to ensure fast delivery, and sheathed it in a ceramic that could mirror its pattern to the organism lying below him. A thousand other alterations also occurred, including veins and capillaries closing down as he extracted liquid from his hand. Otherwise, turning to steam, it would interfere with contact.

Meanwhile, he collated data, instructions and a list of queries to make, and shaped them to the biotech here. The response would necessarily have to be fast, so he simplified it as best he could. When he finally reached the point of readiness, he suddenly felt a great reluctance. He understood the process perfectly, and that he'd be able to recover from it quickly, but he also knew that since he was using them to send and receive data, he couldn't shut down his nerves. Finally, with a thought command that his suit contested, he pulled his glove off.

There was no pain at first, but it was as if he'd thrust his hand straight into an oven. The burning then started to grow, with blisters rising and vapour slewing away, as he quickly dipped and pressed his palm down against a scale of the biotech. The agony of contact surprised and appalled him, bringing with it firm realization of his vulnerability here. Knowing that the sound he heard was his own keening, he felt connection through the fire and sent his data and his DNA. Utter concentration on this task pushed him aside from his pain into an awful clarity, as he saw the flames issuing from the back of his hand, like those of a stuttering candle wick.

All around him the biotech scales, moving much faster than before, turned and oriented on his point of contact. He had the satisfaction of feeling his DNA hit home, dispelling the illusory contact he'd had before and assuring him that the biotech below would soon be his. It responded to his queries with a massive error-report file it already had ready, and he took it in, even as his nerves started to burn out. He absorbed this to a file in his mind. The pain grew dim, transitioning to his wrist and disappearing from the hand as the biotech sent more, and as the flow of information steadily died. He made a brief assessment through the surviving organics in his hand and knew what he must do next. He brought his boot across and pressed it down hard on his hand, viciously twisting his arm to snap the brittle wrist bones and break the dried and charring flesh. He stood upright, the suit now flowing over the stump of his wrist, and staggered back to the observation blister, then stumbled inside.

During the journey back to the engine, the Fenris started to have doubts and thought of other strategies he could have used to seize control of the biotech. Why had the sacrifice seemed so necessary? Did it somehow ameliorate the guilt he felt about his intervention on that nodal Earth, and the deaths he'd caused there? Though he could control so much inside him, he felt sick and struggled to dispel the effects of shock, the phantom pains from his missing hand, and the real pain from his wrist. He sat on the floor and concentrated, shunting control of the blister over to a subprogram. Finally running his black blood in, and capping off nerves, gave some relief, and soon he managed to turn off their constant broadcast of damage. Scar tissue formed like hyperglue hardening, and he began to shed dead matter from the stump – a clump of it shifted under the suit when he touched it. One more thing . . .

Next, delving into his biological programming, he selected out protocols that had long been refined and handed them over to his autonomics. For a brief while, he watched as blood supply increased, as nanofilms began growing, and a coiled shape started to etch out in the end of the stump. The new hand would take some months to grow, and in the process slow down his overall growth too. He tried not to resent this as he turned his attention to the data the biotech here had transmitted to him.

The blister finally thunked down in a recess in the engine. He stepped inside and walked shakily back up to the control deck. There he ordered the system to bring the temperature down and down, to the point where ice began to appear on some surfaces, and he retracted the heat-resistant vacuum suit. He shivered. There'd been no need for this beyond a psychological one. Then, as he began to understand the shape of things here at the sun tap, he saw that even more sacrifice would be required.

The main biotech growth had been lodged on the sun tap's extended system that contained the hard tech core. During the Great Project, the vast amount of energy routed through here had burned that core to oblivion. Rebuilding it was possible, but starting from what survived here would take centuries. However, there was an alternative.

Firing up the engine's ion drives, the Fenris raised it out of the dish and took it across the landscape he'd previously traversed. He directed it on, around a curve, to where the horizon ahead burned, and brought it down towards the intersection of two curved structures, into what looked like some mechanoid river valley. Here, just a little further on, lay a long split running down inside the sun tap. He'd only learned about this from the data provided. That past energy surge had created gaps like this in a surface that should have been perfectly sealed, but they were convenient for his purposes. After three kilometres down, the engine could go no further – progress was blocked by a series of capacitors like a giant bandolier. The Fenris finally landed it in an arched alcove resembling some huge church, and set to work.

Within the engine, he woke large maintenance robots and observed them peeling out of walls. They were monstrous multi-limbed things, like the by-blows of mechanical spiders and living squid, with great triangular sensory heads. He set the majority of them to disassembling the engine, for the sun tap was in sore need of its components. More specifically, it needed the hard tech core – to use the intelligence of this machine as a basis on which to build and grow a new one in itself.

Other robots he tasked with equipping the empty shell of a giant capacitor. They installed a zero-point collector and an ion drive, swiftly upgraded to fusion, as well as fuel and steering thrusters. One fragment of the engine's core was added for control, and there was a central chamber, to be maintained at a temperature just a little above the freezing point of water. And so his vessel for the return journey came together.

The engine began to come apart around him. The robots towed off components as their biotech smoked and cracked, and they devolved to running on hard tech only. He then watched them finally pulling out the hard computer core, spraying on insulating foam to protect it, and towing this away too. Even as this occurred, the control deck began to fade away around him. He moved out and installed himself in an observation blister again, now experiencing a weird species of grief as the biotech in the engine began to die. This mirrored his feelings about his hand, for it was as much an extension of him. As it all died, he issued a final instruction for it to gather elements of itself in a globular protrusion – a yolk.

He moved the blister out and observed the engine breaking up further, its components strewing from the alcove along the route of the capacitors. Mentally he tracked the hard tech core as the robots brought it to the place in the sun tap where he'd found the main growth of biotech. The core spoke to him in code about its preparations, as robots peeled up a series of those diamonds, pulled out chunks of blackened sapphire and inserted the thing into position. They stripped off its insulation as they installed it, while bathing it in cooling gases. Finally they put everything back into place. And then, denuded of their own cooling, they just hung on the surface, dying in the heat. The Fenris nodded to himself, took the blister out and round, and headed towards the capacitor shell with its installed drive.

As the blister slid into the shell, he felt as if reality had stuttered, and he quickly blocked input. Once inside, he opened the blister again, while closing up his suit, and went out. Precisely where he'd detailed, he found the yolk. The thing contained a great liquid mass of organics collected from the dying biotech. He lugged this back inside the blister, closed it, then watched as the larger sphere closed around it and him. With this done, and the cooling system kicking in, he removed his silvered suit. He sat down, detached a pipe from the biotech yolk and, with its organic pump pulsing, began drinking its glutinous contents. This took some while, during which he continued to feel probes from outside. His guts steadily expanded, then held stable as he pushed his body to absorb the nutritious fluid into muscle and fat stores. His sensory armour meanwhile adjusted to his larger bloated form. Once finished, he fixed the yolk down, then lay on his back with its pipe in his mouth. Making some further adjustments to his biology, he next issued sticky threads from his bare skin and through his sensory armour to stick himself in place. Now, as the temperature steadily dropped, he finally allowed the input.

The hard tech core had made connections and was already making further ones. As the engine robots died, those of the sun tap went into motion. These ceramic and composite entities were a whole ecology of robot forms, from the microscopic to behemoth segmented worms. They began making repairs straight away, and already he could see a giant beetle-like thing at the spill of silvered pipes, steadily inserting them back into place and printing in new sections. Meanwhile the new core grew into the burned remains of the old core, converting its materials to use. With absolutely no shortage of energy, this was happening at an increasingly accelerated rate.

He concentrated back on the large beetle and watched it, as around him ice began to form on the blister walls. At length, a chunk of the sun tap's biotech growth broke away and dropped down towards the beetle. It reached out with one long gnarled limb and snared it, drawing it down to where outer layers folded out to receive it, and drew it inside. This started happening elsewhere too, as the system healed – biotech and hard tech mated up again and fused in perfect synergy. The Fenris felt this to be enough – there was no more he could do here now.

He instructed the chunk of hard tech core in the converted capacitor and it fired up thrusters. The capacitor rose, out of the remains of the engine and of the sun tap. It left the flute structure and drifted over to the dish, upon whose surface he could see mechanisms like starfish spreading out from maintenance holes. His new vessel oriented upright and then fired its fusion drive. Acceleration pressed him down into the floor. He needed a lot of speed away from the sun, to take him on a course that would arc out of the sun tap shadow cone and put him in that of one of the hot worlds in orbit three million kilometres further out. Deceleration, closer to his world, would then be a lengthy affair, with the engine needing to switch over from fusion to ion drive again.

The Fenris closed his eyes and stopped his body fighting the steady drop in temperature around him. Hibernation would kick in soon enough, though it would never be total, because he wanted to use the five years of this journey productively. By the time he reached his destination, his body would have utilized all he had drunk, and all that remained in the yolk, as well as repurposed much else. And he would have taken a large step closer to adulthood.

Irene – Past

As she crawled in a place that couldn't exist, the nightmare cycled in her mind. After they'd strapped her in the chair, she'd been utterly shocked to look up and see Sector Governor Garrick sitting behind the table. The interrogation had commenced, as ever, with questions she couldn't answer. How had she ended up right in the SA area, past the readerguns, the birds and the guards? Who was she working for? Who were her associates? A wave of inducer agony followed every babbling reply, until a doctor came in to check her. With a nod to Garrick, he had given her a series of painful injections. The guards would come then and drag her off to her cell, giving her more food than she had ever been accustomed to eating.

'You are going to be okay,' said a voice, the statement seem-ingly dopplering in and out of audibility.

No, no she wasn't.

For the next interrogations, the questions changed as she began to change. And always ahead of her was Garrick, smiling as he hit the button to turn on the inducer.

'We think it's puberty, but the changes are so radical,' the doctor had said.

This seemed to please Garrick immensely, and she only found out why later when the guards came for her. Instead of taking her for interrogation, they led her up and up, and deliv-ered her to Garrick's apartment. There they left her manacled on the floor, and that's where she remained, until Garrick picked her up, bent her over his sofa and raped her. After the horror of that first time, she later learned to submit, then feigned participation, because this seemed to offer her some control and leavened the brutality of it. However much she was sickened by doing this, anything was better than facing the inducer again.

'. . . hallucinating,' said the voice, '. . . need more power.'

Of course she was, because the monster was speaking to her again. This had to be a hallucination brought on by the pain and sickness. She now gazed around at cropland like none she'd ever seen before, and she crawled on a little further. Hard growth coiled up from the ground ahead and, raising watery eyes, she gazed up at a massive tree. Not cropland, then – some Committee park, fenced off from the ZA population, and probably most of the lower echelons of the SA population too. The monster wasn't here, but she could hear it in her skull as it rose into perception. With a little concentration in those moments, she could see it there too.

'You are on another world,' said the monster, its voice clearer

127

now, with a wash of something through her that seemed to illuminate a structure inside, like the filament of an ancient light bulb.

'I don't know what you mean,' she replied. The words rose out of the chatter in her mind but didn't reach her dry mouth, broken teeth, or the stapled-together split in her cheek.

'Yes, you do.'

'What are you?' she managed, dragging herself up against the bole of the tree and turning over so her back was against it. This gave her a bit more height to look around. The nightmares of interrogation receded and she suddenly felt better than she had any right to be.

'I'm the Fenris,' it replied.

'You're a fenris?'

'I am *the* Fenris,' the creature said patiently.

She could understand the distinction it was trying to make, but the word was meaningless to her.

'Where are you? How are you speaking to me?'

'I am elsewhere, and speaking to you via the biotech that has grown inside you. And it continues to grow.'

This seemed logical because, yes, she had undergone some serious, unnatural changes. But she didn't want to deal with that, or its implications right now.

'Another world,' she managed.

'Consider what happened to you.'

It had never been far from her consideration at any time. She'd been just one of the masses, struggling to get enough to eat and find some comfort in the world, before inevitably expiring. Like most of the women of her family, she'd spent a great deal of time trying to avoid pregnancy, because the birth-control chem in the water didn't work on them. Then the strange dreams and sense of dislocation had started. She'd often found herself wandering in areas of the sprawl she didn't recognize, running from gang members and hiding in strange abandoned rooms. There was one horrible episode when she'd found herself lying in some barren deserted place, struggling for breath, consciousness fading. She then returned to find herself in the grip of an Inspectorate cop, his hand on her arm, and the man demanding an explanation.

'Drugs,' she said. 'Someone gave me drugs.'

'No, not drugs. What happened to you was as real as the reality you are in right now.'

Concentrating, she studied the creature's face. It looked like one of the extreme mutants who'd been a feature of her family over four generations. In fact, it looked a bit like her great-uncle Zak who, legendarily, managed to disable a shepherd during a riot, before he became one of the disappeared. As she thought further on that, another comparison arose, for the face also reminded her of those stone heads on Easter Island. She blinked at the memory, which had come from just a glimpse at a screen showing some documentary before she'd even learned how to walk. It astounded her that something so obscure and forgotten had now returned to her so clearly.

'Okay, suppose I accept this is real – what about that other place?'

'So many were pulled there and died. Others never even got that far. You are one of appallingly few I've been able to contact . . . able to help.'

She wanted to say again that she had no idea what he was talking about, but now she was discovering that, despite her injuries, her thinking had begun to gain a pellucid clarity. She could see the shape of something potentially fantastic and didn't want to admit it – especially as it seemed it might be falling into the grasp of Committee scientists, with their bloody hands and filthy minds.

This clicked in her skull. Yes, they knew something.

'On your first jaunt off-world, you nearly suffocated. There is no oxygen in the air of that place,' the Fenris stated.

She'd fallen back, gasping for breath, and then screaming at the intensity of the hallucination. How she'd ended up in that airless place she had no idea. That'd been the first of . . . what, more than three others? She remembered one time being in the cell after Garrick had finished with her for the day, and then finding herself just outside the building itself, lying on a meagre patch of grass. She hit one of the soldiers who came for her and knocked him sprawling, much to her surprise and the chagrin of the others. Before they beat and shocked her into unconsciousness and threw her back into a cell.

They'd fed her for a while in there, and water was available from the spigot that washed her faeces down the hole in the corner. Then this stopped. Was it because they didn't want to provide nutrients to drive the changes they were seeing? If so, it had been a foolish move, because the lack of food only seemed to accelerate them. Fragments of biological understanding arose for her inspection. Of course: starve a human and the body will clean house, recycle and reprocess . . . There was no mirror in the small cell, but she could see how her fingers were growing long and her nails folding into claws. She also felt the elongation of her face, and could measure her body against the dimensions of the floor.

'They're handing this over to the military,' said Garrick.

The cell door had stood open, Garrick and some others looking in. When she looked up, they slammed the door shut as if they might be afraid of her, which was ridiculous. She lay there having hallucinations again, and they seemed to be gaining traction around her. Sometimes the walls of the cell *felt* paper-thin, as though she could just step through them or, in some way she couldn't quite grasp, around them.

'Out!'

The light glaring in from the corridor made her realize there had been none in the cell, but she'd been able to see everything quite clearly in there. She came out into the light and stood upright, now seeing that she loomed over the four guards. They looked frightened and that, as ever, made them vicious. The shock sticks went in, bringing her to her knees, and then down on her face, vomiting water bile and pissing her Government-issue disposerall. They pulled her arms behind her back and fitted a heavy bar cuff. They clamped manacles around her ankles, linked by a wire that could be wound closed to drop her on her face. They put a collar around her neck that contained similar motors to those of the manacles, for it was a strangulation collar. And finally, a white-coated medic injected her with something that made her passive, obedient and uninterested.

'I don't want to jaunt again,' she said to the Fenris, as she stopped the replay of memories, not wanting to go any further.

'Without this ability, you would not be alive now. You are a world walker. Consider that surgery room,' the creature replied.

How could he know about that? He must be a part of her own mind, talking to her. And yet, behind the words, she sensed energy shifts and seemingly desperate activity, as if this creature was trying to hang on to her. Like gripping the slippery wrist of someone hanging off a cliff. She wanted to explain that this thing she had, this ability, just meant hallucinations and agony, rape and humiliation, and people trying to kill her, but this segued into remembering what had happened in horrible, agonizing detail.

The journey in the van was vague to her, but she knew it had been long. When the doors opened, it had seemed painfully bright outside. Guards in uniform she recognized as military undid her manacle chain from a hoop in the floor. They dragged

NEAL ASHER

her in through a door and, at some point, she saw two men standing before her – one obviously high-up military and the other looking like a researcher out of a movie. This latter man stepped close and inspected her with keen curiosity.

'– the fuck you want,' she managed.

He smiled widely and replied, 'Welcome to the Complex, Subject Alpha.' Then he waved her guards on.

As they dragged her on, she quite clearly heard the military guy say, 'Was that necessary?'

The researcher replied, 'One must maintain the social niceties.'

'Fuck you, Savarack,' the other replied.

They dragged her through the Complex to a room all aseptic white and chrome. Still drugged and out of it, she observed the table with its heavy straps and clamps, the surgeons all robed and masked, the trays of glittering instruments, surgical robot arms depending from the ceiling, and the various empty containers on wheeled trolleys. The soldiers hit her with shock sticks a few more times, then dragged her onto the table, quickly securing her.

'Remove that,' said one surgeon, pointing at the strangulation collar.

'We were ordered,' said a guard.

'We do not want some idiot pressing the panic button and ending this before we've begun. And anyway, I'll want to cut there at some point.'

They removed the collar.

They used gas first, and then an intravenous anaesthesia when she woke struggling after they'd sliced open her left thigh where she'd once had a badly infected fly bite. The cutting continued as she sank back into unconsciousness, but then she began rising out of it again. She managed to tilt her head and look down, seeing various scopes directed at the open bleeding flesh. A glance

132

aside revealed her left arm and hand were opened up too, like something in a Da Vinci drawing. Her face felt painful, and she didn't then know how they'd opened up things there for inspection, then stapled and glued them back together again. But it was the drill that pierced her fog, just as it pierced her thigh bone. She screamed.

'How the fuck is she still awake?'

She struggled once more and her pain dredged up anger from deep inside – the two bouncing off each other and creating a kind of synergy that cleared her mind. Her body went into spasms, jerking against the restraints, the surgeons stepping back because they couldn't continue their *work* while she was moving like this. The utter, total injustice of her circumstances turned anger to rage, which banished the pain. She had fallen into the hands of these people through no fault of her own, and they'd tortured her, experimented on her with weird hallucinogens, while abusing her into compliance. Now, as a culmination to this utter weirdness, they were vivisecting her. She had to escape!

Irene pushed at the world around her, seeing it as lacking in substance, just like her cell was before. It seemed her only escape from here must be into hallucination and madness. Reality was heavy composite straps that simply couldn't be broken, and cutting that would only end when she'd been distributed into those various sample containers. Yes, while she was jerking about like this, they'd had to stop. But it wouldn't be long before they tried something else to steady her under their knives. And if drugs continued to fail, next would be an incision into her spine, since their purpose here was not to fix something but take it apart.

With the horror of her circumstances continuing to grow, she pushed further into a tissue-thin world, in which the surgeons grew doll-like around her. Then, as if the illusions had grown too burdensome for it, the world tilted, slewing them away. Irene hit the floor and rolled, completely naked and smearing her blood. She lay there for a second, baffled. And, in the ensuing stunned silence, her ankle manacles clattered to the floor from the end of the surgical table. Though bafflement remained, her rage brought her up fast to her feet. She wouldn't end up on a table like that again. She would never relinquish power over her body to the Inspectorate again – she would rather die.

She turned to the nearest surgeon – the dumpy woman who'd been opening up her arm. The woman stood there holding up a scalpel. Irene stared at her, not sure what to do, for she'd never really hit anyone in a calculated way before. She knew the dangers of lashing out. When she'd done that once with one of the persistent men in the sprawl, nursing a broken hand afterwards had shown her that punching someone wasn't as easy as the films portrayed. But memory came to her assistance of another man, trying the nice guy route into her underwear, showing her how she should have hit her attacker.

She changed her stance and drove her bloody skinless palm hard into the woman's nose, then gaped at the effect. The blow had turned the woman's face into a cavity. Time also seemed to have slowed as Irene snatched the scalpel out of her hand, while she dropped bonelessly. Irene turned, memories of fight scenes and the real thing seeming to form up in her mind as a logical whole. She sliced the scalpel down the back of one man who was trying to escape. As he lurched forwards in his rubber boots, she kicked his legs away, came down on him, and drove the scalpel deep into the back of his neck.

Two more headed for the door over the other side. She leapt up onto the surgical table, then down behind them. Her reach incredibly wide, she grabbed their heads and slammed them together. Hard. Turning, she wiped pink matter from her face and realized it had been a spray of brain. A sideswipe sent an assistant into a wall, and she felt a horrible, almost guilty, delight in her power. Ahead, two surgical nurses stood frozen, terrified. Irene probed her face after wiping away the brains, and felt staples there. She looked around, found the surgical staple gun and picked it up. A blow with the machine caved in a temple. She then held the device out to the other nurse remaining.

'Fix me,' she said.

Irene flinched through the memories: the nurse stapling together her thigh while she pushed back flaps of skin over her arm. The staples in her arm were enough that the nurse had had to refill the device with shaking hands. And then the door crashed open.

The soldiers simply sprayed the room. The nurse staggered backwards under multiple impacts, as Irene leapt the surgical table and rolled. She felt bullets slap into her lower back and she searched for escape. There was none that seemed viable, but maybe that back wall was just some expanded foam creation? She jumped up and forwards, hurling herself to shoulder into the wall, utterly intent on escape. She then found how to go around the wall, and was suddenly rolling into the place of suffocation and bones. Clawing through the debris of life, the urge to escape had grown stronger, and she'd rolled on and down, and through and around, to finally end up in this place she was now. This garden, cropland, forest or whatever, but certainly her graveyard.

'How can I be on another world?' she finally asked the Fenris. There seemed no harm in asking questions. She was in a strange and alien place. She had been sliced up quite badly and, as far as she could gather, had three bullets in her lower back. That she was going to die seemed certain, so she might as well not die ignorant.

'You jaunted, as I said before – you walked from world to world,' the Fenris replied, hardening in her mind.

'Yes, you've used that word and so have I,' she replied, 'but that still gets me no closer to knowing what exactly it means.'

'So you are stupid?' the Fenris enquired.

The jibe hit home because, ever since she'd found herself in SA territory, it seemed her mind had been working at an accelerated pace. And her recall strayed into memory she should reasonably have expected not to have retained. The only times her mind had been crappy had been under drugs and the shock stick. She delved more deeply into it.

'It's some mental method of travel to . . . to walk to another world, though the distances . . . no, not other worlds in my universe, but parallels. I can move my physical body from one to the other with just a thought – an act of will. I haven't been hallucinating.' She said it firmly and now truly believed it. 'Some kind of technology inside me gives me the ability to do this – the biotech you mentioned. I doubt it was something developed on my world and, since an alien creature is talking to me in my skull, I reckon its source is you.' Her logic pleased her.

'Very good.' The Fenris gave a tight smile, then talked fast: 'Now you are out of the denial phase, we can see to your survival. Over to your left, you will find a slope leading down. At the bottom of that, you'll find a stream. This will obviously supply your water. If you dig in the bottom of it, you will find large freshwater clams too. They'll provide the nutrients your body sorely needs.'

'Survival?' she said out loud, and laughed hoarsely. She wanted to point out that she had been starved, beaten, shocked, vivisected and shot, and really should be dead now. However, it was evident that she'd undergone some extreme physical and mental changes. She didn't feel quite as feeble and human as she had been before.

'No power or time left,' said the Fenris, and contact abruptly winked out in her skull.

Irene sat there trying to sense the creature again, to find it in that place in her mind. But though the place remained, no monster occupied it. Evidently there was some energy limitation on its ability to communicate with her. She speculated on that, considering her comment about parallel worlds, which it hadn't denied. But this was pointless. Though it seemed every scrap of knowledge throughout her life had become available to her, she got no further than fictional stuff about machines for that purpose, intrepid adventurers, and the usual load of government propaganda.

Abruptly she pushed herself away from the tree bole. Sure, everything hurt and things in her lower back felt as if they might be about to snap, but the pain seemed within her tolerance. Taking little in the way of care, she stood and looked down at her naked body. The split down her thigh looked dry and crusty. The slices in her arm were much the same, and skin the surgeon had peeled now appeared firmly back in place. Something then drew her notice. She'd 'jaunted' a short distance at first, from that surgical table, dropping the remains of her disposerall and those manacles. Yet in jaunting here, she'd retained all the staples holding her together. Was this because the staples were an organic plastic set to dissolve over time? No, disposeralls were organic and made to degrade too. Was it because they actually penetrated her body? She reached up and probed inside her mouth, finding the tooth implant it had cost her two weeks of rations to have put in. So yes, maybe that.

Next, she properly surveyed her surroundings. An astounding variety of other tree trunks were visible through the thick foliage. Vines hung across between them, clamouring for space among the tree branches, jigsaw masses of leaves and oddly shaped seeds, fruits and pods. Above she could see only a few patches of sky dotted with stars, for it seemed the branches and foliage grew even thicker up there. She had only seen things like this in historical documentaries on the screens – usually with some political message about disgusting and destructive humanity. On her world, there were no natural environments left, and variety had been whittled down into monocultures to feed the massive world population. Was that the truth? Like many, she dismissed much of what the government produced in the way of education and entertainment, but accepted many of the basic tenets. Now she found herself questioning those too.

Turning, and forcing herself to walk proudly upright, she headed for the slope. Here the greenery thinned a little to reveal more tree trunks and boulders rising from tangled undergrowth. Pushing aside vines, then through the tall stalks of plants like bamboo, she began to make her way down. Going was tough at first and she didn't trust her body. Then, gaining more confidence, she picked up her pace. Moments later she stumbled in thorny growth and went down on one knee. Coming up again, she leaned against a tree, peering down at large bright white toadstools poking up through the leaf litter. Her body reacted with a surge of hunger that set her salivating, but she moved on, not knowing whether the things might be poisonous. The image of clams fixed in her mind – again from screentime – and she kept going.

Soon low, flat leaves and stands of reeds displaced the trees, and she came in sight of the stream. It was a couple of metres wide and ran slowly over plants like underwater cabbages. Amid the wide leaves, her feet began sinking into mud, but she stumbled on quickly and then threw herself forwards, face down in the flow, and began drinking, only realizing the extent of her thirst just then. She gulped down water that had an odd but pleasant taste – nothing like that supplied in the sprawls, with its chemical components that changed monthly. In some sense, she seemed to be able to distinguish components of that taste, but then this perception faded as she tried to focus in on it. Her face eased, as if it was sucking in water too.

Finally replete, she pushed right into the stream. The water sat just half a metre deep and she got up onto her knees, rubbing at the chill in her arms, and dislodging a few staples from the damaged one. She began scooping randomly at the bottom, first coming up with some stones and then, when she dug in a small hollow, finally coming up with a clam. She recognized it as such, though it looked little like those she'd seen before. It was longer, and white, with the shell frilled where the foot had retracted inside. How could she eat a thing like this? She'd never eaten any kind of unprocessed food before in her life. But her body, crying for food, and her stomach knotted into a solid lump, dictated her actions.

She brought the thing up to her mouth and bit down on the shell but to no avail. And her face hurt abominably. She searched the bottom again, until finding a stone and holding the clam in her palm, bashed it until it broke. Slimy flesh squirmed as she peeled away the shell. She used a piece of broken shell to scoop out the body of the thing, and bit down on it. It moved as she chewed and an intense, unrecognizable taste filled her mouth. Again, as with the water, she seemed to get some sense of the components of that taste. They appeared to fall into categories and, focusing on these, she glimpsed odd geometric shapes in the place where she'd seen the Fenris. She swallowed and wasn't sure if she liked it, until she found herself searching the bottom for more of the creatures.

She ate twenty clams before the chill water drove her out. Shivering, she crossed the mud to squat under a tree, arms wrapped around her legs as she tried not to feel so cold. Her stomach bubbled and boiled and, even having fed, she now felt sick with hunger. She didn't want to go back into the water, so finally stood up and went to have a look at those toadstools. She picked one, sniffed it, and received sensory data in the same way as from the water and the clams. This really meant something, and she considered the biotech inside her again. Perhaps she had conscious access to it, and perhaps it delivered data to her beyond her normal human senses? She concentrated on those geometric shapes as she brought the thing up to her mouth and nibbled a piece. Another flood of data arrived, and one set of shapes diverged, coiled and turned inside out. Adrenalin surged and numerous other shapes appeared in her mind, as if requesting acknowledgement. But the sense of danger was enough, and she spat out the piece of toadstool and discarded the thing itself. It was now evident to her that she could detect whether something might be poisonous or not, and it seemed she also had the option to do something about that, but didn't really know how.

Irene searched her surroundings, pulling leaves from vines and branches, finding many she could eat but few that were palatable. She found berries that gave her such a caution response she dropped them immediately and went to wash her hands. She found bitter quinces and ate as many as she could stomach, then she crunched down many rosehips too. She was investigating a bracket fungus on a tree when she noticed brightness to her left. Heading in that direction, which tracked the stream, she came out into the open and saw the flare of sunrise over distant mountains. She only now realized she'd arrived on this world at night and, as in her cell, had hardly noticed the darkness. Then, out in that open area, she saw squat grouse-like birds pecking at long thick pods on the ground, and on a low bush. Protein hunger surged again, and she went down on hands and knees, beginning to creep through increasingly long grass and weeds. If she could grab one of them, she'd feel full at last. And if not, she could always try those pods.

Closer and closer she drew, until peering past a low bromeliad at the birds, which thus far had been oblivious to her presence. She chose one and slowly shuffled up into a crouch, ready to leap. She felt utterly carnivorous, a hunter and ready to kill. Something spooked the birds, and they ran clattering and cheeping away from the bush. One of them ran straight towards her, and hardly thinking about it, she snapped out a hand and caught it around the neck. As she'd seen on pictures and documentaries, she spun its thick meaty body once, snapping its neck. The thing died, shuddering and kicking in her grasp, and now her predatory part died along with it. Sadness and shame arose, but she knew she couldn't abandon this valuable source of protein. Then a shadow loomed over her, and something made an odd whickering sound. She looked up.

6

The Fenris – Past

His awareness remained, but low key and disconnected from the passage of time on the long journey back. The Fenris, although in complete conservation mode and discarding nothing, still grew. A fist, like some strange nodule, folded out from his damaged wrist, then steadily expanded and opened out fingers, spider-thin. These slowly filled and the bones hardened. With that business out of the way, the rest of his body began growing again. His bones, steadily destroying themselves and rebuilding, grew longer – muscles, skin and connective tissue multiplying to match. Cells died and were cannibalized, and neither bladder nor intestine took any waste. Closed pores prevented water loss, but still it evaporated from his skin, and during the long, slow breaths he took every few weeks.

When his vessel for the journey decelerated, and the blister around him reoriented, he was jolted to a brief higher awareness. In that awareness, he noted starvation, and growth winding down. He had already made calculations but checked them again. This was about right: he would be at maximal growth possible by the time he returned, with reserves enough for the required movement. In chagrin, he then made adjustments for this unnecessary use of his energy-hungry brain and shut himself down to low ebb again.

Further decelerations prodded at him, but he stubbornly refused to do more than acknowledge them. Only as the temperature began to rise again, and accelerate his biological developments, did he finally allow higher awareness to return. He lay starving and thirsty, but found some relief as his body absorbed the threads sticking him to the floor, and eagerly distributed their amino acids and fibre within. Keeping energy usage to a minimum, he didn't allow his larger internal sensorium to kick in, but merely opened dry eyes and blinked, then searched passively for connection elsewhere. Data from a nearby engine came via his sensory armour and located his vessel in orbit. He was back around his home world at last. His vessel steadily swung in towards the nearest dock, which was on that engine. Creaking like old leather, he sat upright, breaking final adhesion, then removed the pipe to the shrivelled yolk from his mouth, and with a push against the floor, floated up. He snared the cylinder of the spacesuit and pressed it against himself. The suit spread over him and engaged with his sensory armour, which, he noted, had acquired large gaps to accommodate his growth. It too required materials for expansion, but his internal biology had refused it. He now stood two-thirds the height of an adult Fenris, but thin from famine, and as lacking in substance and density as a thing made of tissue and sticks. He moved with care, sensed with care, and thought with care, using as little energy as possible.

All around him, following its program, the enclosing sphere unlocked its jigsaw components and folded away. The blister shifted, then started to restore internal gravity. He rose to even higher awareness in panic, lashing out and forcing this to shut down again. He wasn't perfect, for he hadn't foreseen this standard procedure that would have collapsed him broken to the floor. He retained higher function, with internal senses giving him a view of his surroundings out beyond the usual kilometre, since vacuum lay out there. Best he stay alert to other faults in his reasoning, like neglecting to account for the grav. And almost at once another arose, as the blister detached and headed to where the end of the vessel was opening. The route he'd programmed in had been to the nearest engine, but he would more likely find what he urgently needed right now aboard the Geostation. He made the course change.

The blister slid out into bright sunlight, painfully reminding him of the sun tap. He looked down at his new hand, noting it to be completely white, unlike the silvery grey of the rest of his skin. This was another sign of his body lacking some of the things it needed – in this case, certain metals that made up the rugged durability of his meta-material hide. The blister fired up thrusters to decelerate, as his vessel sped on past him, and then past the Geostation lying ahead. Finally, after an hour, the blister swung in around the station, slowing further and cruising in towards one of the recesses. As it did so, he reached out into the system, brain feeling slow and tired, to see what he could find out.

Yes, biotech under his command had become firmly established here, running in synergy with the hard system. All repairs and rebuilding had been completed, and the station was now just running a maintenance schedule. He probed, searching, and at length found the four garden spheres inside, each one up to maximal growth. Mapping a course to the nearest, he shut down all the grav along that route. He was ready.

The blister mated in its recess and automatically folded down its rear hemisphere. The pressure differential dragged him forwards to where he weakly grabbed an edge to stop himself sailing on in. The effect then was astounding, as air swirled and mixed around him. He smelled, tasted and otherwise sensed oxygen, and his body immediately kicked out of hypoxic function. The slow cycle of his lungs, of which he'd hardly been aware, switched to deep, fast breathing. Starved of oxygen for so long, his body took it in hungrily. His temperature jumped up, and then hunger and thirst overrode his control of them. He propelled himself from the blister along a tunnel, and then at a junction forced himself to halt what would have become a headlong rush towards the garden. He slowed his breathing and forced hypoxic function back. If he continued like this, he'd burn through his remaining resources in moments. His skeletal muscle, thin and drawn, was almost at the point of failure even now. He then moved on, slowly and carefully.

It seemed to take a nightmare age to go through the tunnels, for his time sense was at its maximum in survival mode. When he finally reached an area where organic pipes lay coiled against the walls, it seemed unreal – as if he must be hallucinating. With waning strength, he took hold of a pipe and pulled it free, then put the soft end of it in his mouth and gave a suck to get the flow started. Cool water, loaded with minerals, flowed into his mouth. He suppressed the survival option of shutting down his reaction to it and simply enjoyed the most wonderful thing he'd ever tasted. The water flowed down into him as if into sun-baked earth, filling his stomach, and at once leaching out into the rest of his body. It freed up remaining nutrients, locked in place by dehydration, and boosted him out of what had become a hallucinatory state. With more perception opening up, he observed it spreading into the rest of his body, and it seemed he took another breath as his pores opened. Clarity arrived and with it the almost physical impact of a smell. For ahead lay the garden.

Full of water and sloshing like a filled gourd, he propelled himself along another length of corridor. A door thumped open ahead at his mental command. The smell increased to unbelievable intensity as he passed through it. The light sphere hung centrally in the chamber, sun bright, and threw black shadows from the plants on the surrounding walls. With a shove, he fell through white branches – their fruits around him like bloodshot eyes – then put himself in a cradle of those branches. The urge to grab and stuff the fruits into his mouth was almost overwhelming. But he showed restraint, remembering his initial reaction to food on leaving the storage hall, now many decades ago. He bit into one fruit and, with saliva flooding his mouth, chewed with long deliberation before swallowing. It felt almost as if he'd swallowed fog, as the proteins and fats simply dissolved into his system. He waited to see how his body would react, desperate to take another bite. When no ill effects became evident, he bit again and again. Finally, acknowledging that his new body had everything aligned, he spent hours eating, moving from growth to growth to satisfy his different needs. Here the red nodes, there the beans, out of loose soil gnarled roots, then other fruits in a variety of colours and loaded with sugars, as well as a fungus that made a whistling sound when he plucked and ate it. When he was done at last, he pulled himself into one of the communal rings and fell into deep sleep.

With wakefulness came the return of what at first seemed a hallucinatory state. The Fenris moved from the garden and on through the Geostation, baffled by how the world around him seemed to have grown ephemeral but also acquired depth. It was an odd disparity. Objects initially appeared to be coatings on reality, but when he concentrated on them, they seemed to penetrate down, repeating in some manner. As if what he saw at first was the cap over a long, deep tunnel. Realization came with a flicker when he glimpsed the station around him changing form, and the ghostly shapes of *humans* moving past him. He was an adolescent and the biotech in his body, properly fed at last, was closer to attaining its full function. Maybe now he'd be able to do what it took the engines vast amounts of energy and hard technology to. Maybe at last he'd be a world walker!

He concentrated on the biotech laced thick through his bones and splintering into billions of nanomachines in the soft matter of his body. He then pushed at reality and tried to step into those shadows and reflections. Reality resisted him, however. For a moment, his surroundings blurred but then the Geostation snapped back into solidity around him. He went out through an airlock and, standing on the skin of the station, tried again. This time he concentrated on that nodal Earth – specifically the area where he'd first started distributing his virus. He could feel that other place, but it lay just out of reach – some meniscus sitting between him and it. Now he didn't understand why he'd earlier glimpsed humans around him. Squatting down on the hull, he turned his focus on the systems within and began to elucidate them, going deep and ensuring he understood their function. Finally, he opened his eyes, disappointed. Again, he came back to the disparity between the dry knowledge loaded to his mind and the exuberant, unrealistic perspective of youth. But perhaps, just perhaps, he had acquired *one* of the abilities of his engines.

The action required effort and concentration to a high degree, while his body burned through material resources and biologically stored energy. Finally, with an effort that nauseated him, he found himself gazing into various tenements on the nodal Earth. He travelled through them, but only mentally, and found the descendants of the girl who'd been the first recipient of his DNA. They were widely scattered, and the family much larger. He recognized some from the last time he'd looked, now grown old but still vigorous. He also saw just how many of the females seemed to be pregnant. Brief analysis revealed that these, or their parents, had encountered the later iterations of the virus and it had an unforeseen effect. It negated the birth-control chemicals in the diet and water supply. He would have liked to have known more, and perhaps taken samples for physical analysis, but he needed to use his engines for that. He accepted, after his brief euphoria, that even though he'd acquired the ability to gaze into the parallels, he still wasn't an adult. It would be years yet before he could actually walk to other worlds and personally take samples.

The power, now beamed from the sun to his world's moon and thence to the engines, began to arrive. The difference caught the Fenris by surprise, as feedback through his biotech increased, to the point where he needed to filter it. Previously the engines had conserved power by winding down various functions, or putting them in rotation, but more and more of those began to come online. Operations that had been on hold also kicked in. The first of these he noticed was regular orbital drops, and ensuing launches back to orbit. The engines were a bulwark of the technology, and also included huge orbital manufacturing. Now they started to supply long-missing necessities for the tech down on the planet, with the result that grav, and other complex systems, could finally be brought up to power. It was very satisfying, in the sense of seeing machines work well, but it all felt so utterly pointless too, while the only fenris alive now resided alone in one of the engines.

With the increase in available power came a heightening of his ability to view, and otherwise penetrate, the multiverse via the engines. He transmitted more viruses to the nodal Earth and found that, with each, he could increase their size and content. Meanwhile, he watched the family. The descendants of the girl encountered many others with high viral load beyond the tenements, so they were continuously reinfected with further iterations of the virus. In them, the fenris DNA made the visible signs of their changes more pronounced than in those who just had the biotech installed virally. They grew tall and long-boned, their skin taking on a slightly purple hue and their eyes shading to the same end of the spectrum.

As energy from the sun tap steadily increased over the years, so did data gathering from the nodal Earth and other parts of the multiverse. And he realized this would now also allow him to send something much larger than the viruses.

The Fenris walked his world as he considered his next moves. Many people on Earth were now loaded with viral changes, which were sockets waiting to be filled with the mechanisms of the biotech. How could he deliver that, and *should* he deliver it yet? Already the changes there were having mutagenic effects that the scientific elites and government bureaucracies were putting down to pollution, and natural selection, amid short-lived ZAs. But if those changes began enhancing people further, it might elicit a response the Fenris didn't want to see. They might start examining those changes more closely, and quite likely see them as a threat, then begin hunting down those changed. There was a high danger this could push them down the usual totalitarian path towards extermination camps.

Did he need to wait until he could finally travel the parallels to that nodal Earth and get a firmer grip on the situation? No, he must have confidence in the changes he was aiming for, and the beings they would produce. He needed to create people who'd be able to carry through his plans to divert that world from its authoritarian course. And he needed ally soldiers to counter the threat of the incursions, as yet not fully understood. At least there'd been no repeat of them in a long while, and none while he had been away. In another year, hundreds of thousands of people there would reach a point where the changes had become more radical. Gradually building up to that with viruses would result in the authorities being alerted to the mutagenic enhancements. And, though it would take time for the bureaucratic behemoths to react, the result would be highly destructive. However, if he could transmit the full gamut of the additional biotech over there in one hit, the effects would allow those enhanced people to escape their world quickly, and into his hands – before they could be killed. Well, at least a good number of them. He looked down, his feet as ever finding some of those crunching remains still scattered here and there after all this time. Looking at them, he realized he had a suitable delivery vehicle: inocular flies.

It all seemed so perfect.

Ottanger

His recovery took two days. The doctor commented, 'Remarkably fast, even for a Morlock,' and he realized that previously he'd had things the wrong way round. ZAs were Morlocks and SAs were the Eloi. He felt the analogy didn't really work, but enjoyed the idea of his kind feeding on theirs.

'That will not happen again,' said Savarack, referring to the interrogation. 'Murcheson is now languishing in one of his own cells awaiting lengthy questioning.'

Feeling that maybe he could now ask some questions, Ottanger tried, 'Why *did* that happen? I was cooperating.' But even as he asked this, a dry cynical part of his mind called him stupid and reminded him that cooperation didn't matter. Nothing mattered. He was an asset and that was all – there would be no justice or fairness for him.

They were in a large office. Savarack was standing, often pacing, agitated. The man behind the desk, who had been introduced as Colonel Jones, appeared phlegmatic and mildly amused.

'Politics,' said Savarack, waving a dismissive hand.

'I think we can go into more detail than that,' said Jones.

Savarack gave him a puzzled look.

Jones leaned forwards and, putting his elbows on the desk, steepled his hands. 'This project, right from the beginning, has been a military one,' he explained. 'As you no doubt understand, national militaries are not as powerful as they once were.'

'Nobody to fight,' said Ottanger, then wished he'd kept his mouth shut.

Jones shrugged, neither agreeing nor disagreeing. 'Some countries do stray out from under MDC *guidance*, but usually resource restrictions pull them back into line. It can be argued that the military should be used in cases of civil unrest – against rebellion. But the Inspectorate, as an international force following the MDC world security model, has taken on that role. There has always been contention between Inspectorate and military in every nation.'

'Inspectorate,' said Savarack sourly.

Ottanger nodded dumbly, as if he was an ignorant ZA hearing this stuff for the first time. He could have added that the Inspectorate, though supposedly serving the national governments in each country, and having all but absorbed police forces, was ultimately and deliberately shaped to be loyal only to the MDC. It was one of the many organizations aimed at displacing those governments, to finally bring in the utopian, one-world government under the MDC, the *Committee*. He was also aware that, as an ignorant ZA, he shouldn't be hearing this stuff. It was the kind of talk that could take him right back to a room like the one he'd been in two days ago.

Jones continued, 'The project here, and its potential, means power. The Inspectorate of course doesn't like the idea of that power being in the hands of the US military and has tried many times to take it away from us. Until now, it has mostly been political manoeuvring. However, the very successful recent trial with you resulted in elements within their ranks trying what they tried . . .'

'And what exactly was that?' Ottanger asked, noting Savarack wincing at the question.

'The intention had been to turn what should have been a simple debriefing into an interrogation, and for, unfortunately, the subject to die during that interrogation.'

Ottanger nodded. He now understood some of what he remembered. Those behind the desk had been under orders to kill him, and when interrupted, had tried to follow through on that. This was why one of them had hit the inducer at the end. If the soldier hadn't shot it out, he would not have been sitting here. But that raised interesting speculations. Why had the Inspectorate been prepared to kill a major asset to this project, this means to power, merely to undermine the military? Surely they considered this work of prime importance too? And surely they wanted to take it from the military intact? Could it be that the Inspectorate knew a damned sight more about all this than so far supposed?

'Some senators were most displeased, which buys us time,' Jones added.

'Why are you telling me this?' Ottanger asked.

Jones looked over to Savarack, now leaning against the wall with his arms folded. The researcher pushed himself forwards. 'Because we require more than just obedience from you – we require cooperation. These experiments have a great many unknowns. To this end, I have proposed that, due to your importance in them, you should be raised to Societal Asset status.'

By his expression, Savarack had expected Ottanger to be filled with joy at the prospect. All it did was shift the ground under him. He'd played the role of SA briefly in a rebel operation that had again resulted in innocents being killed – precisely why he'd opted out of the cause. Or at least that's how he rationalized it. But at heart he was ZA and couldn't put aside a lifetime of 'us and them'. He liked being a Morlock. He also knew that, while everyone who wasn't a ZA was an SA, even including those mentioned senators, they still had their hierarchy. SAs not in the Bureaucracy, the Inspectorate, and presumably the military, were even more closely watched than the useless and dispensable ZAs. The status did not negate the possibility of ending up in an interrogation room.

'That seems sensible,' he said. 'Since I do now apparently have value.'

It was the best he could offer for the moment. He understood the political infighting that had occurred, just as he understood the military to be weaker than the Inspectorate. They could end up taking over here. It didn't matter what label they gave him, he would always be at risk of torture and death.

'What does that mean for me?' he finally asked, trying to ameliorate the disappointment in Savarack's expression.

'You will now be included,' the researcher told him. 'You will have access to information about the project. You can ask questions.' The man searched around for other things to add. 'You will have state basic income, which may rise, and you'll be able to obtain luxuries.'

Ottanger nodded again. 'When do I become a Societal Asset?'

Savarack waved his hands in the air. Jones replied, 'The status change is going through, but as of now you can consider yourself such.'

'Then I would like to ask a question.'

'Fire away!' Savarack had rediscovered his enthusiasm.

'What happened to Subject Epsilon?'

The silence that followed was telling.

One of the soldiers was called Yorgos, and the doctor's name was Alison. He found this out as they relocated him to another room.

'Your new home,' said Dr Alison, turning to where her trolley awaited, just inside the door, on the *carpet*.

Ottanger went over to the sofa, kicked off his slippers and tried the sensation of soft flooring against his feet. Some ZAs managed to obtain woven rugs via barter, but why get something like that? Food was more important. Also, once the mites and lice got in, they were almost impossible to dislodge without a particularly powerful insecticide, which cost almost a week's rations in barter, if it could even be obtained.

Next he turned to the window – yes, he had a window now. The view, across a shingled area, and then concrete to a security fence, he found astounding, despite his cynicism. Scrubby land extended out there, and trees, surrounding the Complex, just as he'd first glimpsed on the way in. ZAs, and most SAs, didn't usually see these anywhere but on a screen. Buildings and infrastructure crammed all available ground, or it was cropland, which they could only see at a distance, through high fences punctuated by readergun towers. Thousands of ZAs did often try to get into croplands, to grab something to supplement their meagre diet, but most died on the fences, and very few of those who made it inside returned. The agribots, which spent their time laser-zapping or spraying, also included ZAs on their kill list of pests. Come time for soil preparation, which Ottanger had once seen, the robot machines preparing the soil and planting seeds also had attachments for grinding up bones or half-decayed corpses.

'Roll up your sleeve,' said Dr Alison.

He went to do it automatically, but then found he had to undo a cuff stick-seam, which none of his clothing had ever possessed before. They'd given him different, though worn, clothes, and apparently he could purchase further clothes and other items. She gave him a series of injections and it never occurred to him until later to ask what they were – that he *could* ask.

'These are your supplements – the instructions are on the bottles,' she said, carrying a bunch of plastic bottles over and dumping them on the table. She then came back and handed him a leaflet. 'And this is your exercise regimen. Just ask Yorgos the way to the gym.' She took hold of her trolley handle and pushed it towards the door. 'Oh.' She looked back over her shoulder. 'He can also direct you to the refectory, or the shop – your food will no longer be delivered. And, of course, your meals will be charged against your account.'

He turned, remembering there were things he was supposed not to know. 'How is that done?'

She pointed towards his forearm. 'Straight read of your chip.'

She moved to leave but he quickly said, 'And this?' She looked back and grimaced as he dipped his head and pointed to the docilator on the back of his neck.

'Attached to your spinal nerves,' she said flatly. 'Removing it can cause problems and we don't want to risk that – you're important to the project.' She finally left.

Ottanger stared at the closed door. Apparently his SA status didn't mean he would not still be lied to, but then he'd known that. He turned away and explored the apartment. Behind a counter lay a small kitchen area with a sink, microwave oven, fridge and water boiler. It all looked so incredibly clean, but old and worn too, like most things here. The bed sat against one wall and he tried it. It didn't feel any softer than the other one, but it did have sheets and a blanket, and no plastic cover over the mattress. The shower room looked pretty much the same as the one he'd had before, but he noted it lacked the bar of cheap soap, electric toothbrush and single disposable razor. He shook his head and grimaced, then erased the expression on remembering the cam up above, attached to the light fitting. He knew how some things were going to go, but wasn't supposed to know. He would have to be careful with his reactions. The 'wage' he'd be paid would only just cover the things he needed to buy. Still, he was of course used to living frugally. And being in this place, with all that he could probably obtain, he'd have been looked on as royalty by his ZA compatriots.

Expression now blank, he was utterly aware he was being bought. Despite his past and his understanding of the situation, it concerned him that it might go to his head. It *did* matter how much better his circumstances were now, but he had to keep in mind that they could change in an instant. Justice did not exist here. They gave him SA status easily, and could just as easily take it away. There were no rules he could rely on. He needed a way out . . . Ottanger frowned at the thought, which felt so odd occurring to him in these circumstances. Yes, he'd shrieked for a way out when under interrogation, or on the way to the internment camp, but it seemed ridiculous here. Another result, he felt sure, of better nutrition and health, this thinking the impossible.

Savarack and Colonel Jones led the way out of the Complex to what Savarack called the Northern Gate Tunnel – the two guards walking close behind. It ran between two security fences, where dardogs patrolled the space between. As they went through the tunnel, Ottanger studied one of the dogs. Sure, out in the world they'd been given heads in which to position their sensors, and overall their appearance was made more doglike, but those were toys for high-status SAs. Here they retained the flat, slablike bodies of their ancient forebears, and were headless. Security units didn't need to look nice, and he rather suspected retaining their original menacing look had been deliberate. Their bite wasn't evident at a glance, but apparently, Jones relished telling him, they sported tasers. And, if that wasn't enough, they carried a machine gun in their bodies too.

He'd asked where they were taking him, because he could, because he was an SA. Jones had just looked at him in irritation and turned away. Savarack patted him on the shoulder in a way that was supposed to be reassuring.

'It's a surprise,' he'd said, and Ottanger didn't push it.

They exited through the outer gate, into the 'Wild'. The Complex's security did not end here, because a mile ahead stood the final perimeter wall. From that, watchtowers reared up, their readerguns and cameras controlled by the Complex AI. They followed a well-trodden path, across open grassy ground becoming occupied by vicious hook-thorn brambles – a modified plant often grown up the walls of government buildings. Then, coming under trees, Ottanger looked out for the cams that littered this place but knew he wouldn't see them. They were called pin cams, but that only applied to the lens. With their thermal-gradient power supplies, the whole devices were larger, but still no larger than a shirt button, and camouflaged too. However, he did see one of the razorbirds roosting in the branches of an oak, plugged into a power supply that had been positioned up there for it, and for the rest of its kind.

The trees grew closer together for a while, then finally they came out into the open again. Here a trench had been carved through the ground. It started over to the left towards the Complex – just a shallow double cut through the sandy soil – and then got deeper and wider. Turf and earth were peeled up on either side of it, and the sandy ground took on a darker burned hue.

'Subject Epsilon,' said Colonel Jones.

'As you can see,' said Savarack, pointing back towards the Complex, 'he did not begin rematerializing after his translocation until he was beyond the inner fence.' He walked over to the start of the trench, where the double cut lay, and the rest duly followed. He pointed. 'These grooves were made by his feet, before he began to come apart. Our estimations put him as travelling at well over fifteen hundred kilometres an hour at this point. And we speculate this was during transition, before Einsteinian physics fully got a grip on him. Beyond this point –' he gestured up the length of the trench – 'he was accelerating and transitioning into photonic matter – a particle beam in essence. Though somewhat more powerful than those your people are working on, Colonel.'

'Part of the reason this project remains in our hands here,' said Jones.

Savarack turned to Ottanger and almost confidingly said, 'Besides the Inspectorate, some senators wanted to close us down – mostly those without much of a science background. They admitted that the strange flies people have been bitten by were something almost otherworldly, and the tech in them difficult to explain, but they couldn't see the point of my research until this.' He gestured to the trench.

Ottanger looked along the length of the trench. It occurred to him that some of the darkness of the soil could actually be Subject Epsilon while, further along, he could see where the sandy soil had turned to dirty glass. At the far end, it widened out to reveal part of a similarly glassy and burned crater. He knew he should be afraid, but he wasn't. Perhaps something had changed within him.

★ ★ ★

Checking his screen – it immediately read the code of his implanted chip – a menu gave him a number of options. Ottanger studied his account and saw, as expected, it went right back through the twenty-eight years of his life. He started at zero, then every day thereafter a fractional SC or 'social credit' charge went against him. The charge was for RC, and when he tapped it, the screen revealed 'ration charge'. His life had put him thousands of social credits in debt. Upon his arrest things changed, for he went even deeper into debt. He stared at this, thinking about the bureaucratic motivation to charge ZAs for their own arrest and imprisonment. The very few ZAs who were released afterwards stopped receiving rations. The accounts could never be squared, and they usually died of starvation.

After his arrival at the Complex, he'd gone even further into debt. Apparently they had been charging him for food, medical treatment and accommodation. Over the last few days, he had been receiving payments of two hundred and fifty SCs a day, followed by an immediate withdrawal of two hundred and ten for 'FT', which turned out to be 'federal tax'. The remainder hardly made a dent.

He sat back, pondering as he had before on all this Byzantine accounting. His account wasn't unusual, because everyone was in debt, and in debt to the state, of course, which gave the economic justification for everyone being labelled 'assets'. Every country on the planet was like this, since all of them applied the same MDC economic model. Somewhere in the grey monoliths of the Bureaucracy, all this negative accounting was perpetually assessed and shitty decisions made on its basis. Like cutting rations, increasing ZA arrests and disposals. But he had to ignore it and think only of what he could obtain for himself now. Allowed to roam the Complex freely, he stood up and headed for the door. Down at the end of the corridor, the soldier Yorgos sat behind a combined console and desk, a handgun before him and other weapons, including assault rifle, stubby machine gun and shock stick, racked behind him. Ottanger eyed these then quickly dropped his gaze when Yorgos looked up.

'I want to find the shop and the refectory,' Ottanger said.

Yorgos peered at him. 'You're going to spend some credit?'

'It will be a novelty,' Ottanger replied.

'And you've never done this before?'

'No,' Ottanger lied.

'Take some advice, then: get food in the shop and prepare it in your room. The refectory is for SA12s or above. Go in there and eat, and before you know it you'll be minus 10K and restricted.'

'What does that mean?' he asked innocently.

'You don't know?' Yorgos shook his head. 'Once you go 10K, you're restricted on what you can buy from anywhere, and that includes medical treatment. And the restrictions get tighter the deeper you go. Everyone tries to hang on to Medical for later – y'know?'

'I see, thank you for the warning.'

Yorgos gave him directions and he set off. As a ZA, he had never really thought about how things worked for SAs, until his brief role pretending to be one. Social credit was irrelevant to a Zero. Medical treatments were what SAs got. For his kind, survival was simply getting enough to eat and avoiding those who would take it from you. And avoiding the attention of the Inspectorate. Before joining the resistance, it had always been his idea that the state owned everything, and distributed it on the basis of your usefulness to society. It had never really occurred to him that there had to be a method of apportioning, or counting, social credit. And that, in the end, it was little different from old-style money.

He passed the row of refectory windows down one side of the corridor and, peering inside, saw people sitting at tables. Savarack was in there with Colonel Jones. There were a few other military officers but most of the rest were 'crats. This was no surprise since, whether money or social credit, those in power always got more of it than their contribution deserved.

The shop looked like others he'd seen on streets he'd passed through quickly, if there weren't checkpoints in place to stop ZAs entering. Even working for the resistance in the role of an SA, he'd avoided such high-security places, because his stolen identity was a precarious one.

Two large windows displayed goods either side of the doorway. Food and drink were arrayed in one window, but these were luxury goods with prices that had a lot of zeros. He felt growing uncertainty at venturing into this new territory. Sure, he knew a lot more than the average ZA, but in this world he was beginning to realize just how meagre that extra knowledge was. The other window displayed electrical goods: roll-up screens and tins of screen paint, kitchen appliances, tablets and fones. Again, far too many zeros. He entered the shop, now feeling on edge.

By the door a trolley detached itself from the rest and trundled over. He looked around for people and saw a woman in paperwear, stacking goods from a mobile pallet onto a shelf. Recognizing one of his own kind, he felt a need for contact. When he walked over to her, the trolley followed him and, as he approached, she turned away, concentrating on her work.

'Excuse me,' he said, then had to say it again before she turned to him, looking frightened.

No teeth, scars on the face, and one missing finger. Just like the ZA who'd brought him food, here was another who had encountered the Inspectorate.

'I've come to buy some things, but I don't know how.'

She looked as if she wanted to run away – as if this must be some sort of ploy to trap her into saying or doing something wrong. She wouldn't meet his eyes.

'I was a ZA but I've just had my status raised,' he said. 'I don't know how to shop.'

She stared at his chest. 'Read your chip when you came in. Just pick up what you want.' She turned back to her work.

Ottanger wanted to say more, but now knew it wasn't the right thing to do. Engaging in conversation with her here, with all the cams above, could be dangerous for him, and probably more dangerous for her. The idea disgusted him as he headed off to walk the shop aisles. It soon became apparent that the section where all the goods had the same dull green packaging was the one for him – not so many zeros. He found a toothbrush, a shaver, soap, and each time he put an item into the trolley, a screen on it showed him total cost. He found food: cheap bread, meat paste, margarine, ratty vegetables, salt and something very cheap called probiscuits.

Ottanger wanted to buy more but, despite his earlier thoughts about just getting whatever he could for himself now, he didn't like the way the numbers were stacking up. When he departed, he was charged for a compressed fibre bag, and then 'FT' appeared, knocking up the overall cost of his goods by half again. He felt a flash of anger at that, and at himself for buying cheaply earlier. As he lugged his acquisitions back to his rooms, he decided that next time he *would* just take what he wanted. He understood that it didn't matter how careful you were, or whether you were ZA or SA, in the end you were the loser. He didn't want to play this game.

They allowed Ottanger into the laboratory.

'I'm to accompany you while you're in there,' Yorgos told him. 'Savarack says you can ask questions, but only so long as they don't interfere with the work.' The soldier then warned, 'And you'll be searched on your way out.'

He soon discovered that all his questions interfered with the work of the various technicians and scientists in the room. And, beyond their particular specialisms, they didn't know much more than him. Hands behind his back, he walked over at last to inspect the suit two technicians were working on.

The thing stood supported by a framework and looked like medieval armour made out of white plastic. One of the techs had the chest plate off to reveal complicated electronics and wiring underneath. A skein of wiring came out of the back of the thing, to be wound in a coil hanging from the framework. The man turned and picked up the chest plate to secure it again, giving him a mild nod as he did so. This was the most pleasant interaction he'd had from anyone in the lab thus far – they all seemed busy, harried, and just a little bit scared.

'Why a suit?' Ottanger asked. 'What does it do?'

The man gestured at it. 'It engages with the meshwear you'll put on, so we'll receive much better sensor readings. The other stuff it does is a bit out of my remit.' He looked briefly puzzled. 'New technology.'

'The other stuff it does?'

The tech seemed willing to continue. 'You generate some kind of electromagnetic field when you translocate. It's patterned, and somehow related to your biological aura.' He shrugged dismissively – he didn't know what that was all about. 'Somehow the suit keys off that and mirrors the field, giving a negative pole to a positive. This might, I'm told, result in you rematerializing back inside it, rather than ploughing up the ground outside like that other guy.' He went pale suddenly, glanced to Yorgos, then around the lab. 'Don't ask me how it works – I just do sensor webs.' He abruptly turned away.

163

'Thank you,' said Ottanger.

'It's nothing,' the tech said.

Ottanger moved off, understanding the man had scared himself by talking too much. He looked around, finally focusing back on Savarack, who had dismissed him with a 'not now' when he first came in. And he thought about the suit.

He'd visited other worlds, and those who had tortured him had questioned if he'd thought about escaping to one of them. He hadn't, even during and immediately after they'd asked him that, because he had never been accustomed to thinking that way. It was all such an unknown still, out there. He had, of course, been quite resolute about trying to change *his* world, but even that had faded, with too many disappointments and a growing understanding of just how solid the regime was. But now he'd begun considering the . . . possibilities.

First he had explored the idea of how he'd return. Maybe he could come back somewhere else in the world and escape to the resistance, get a new identity. No, new identities never worked for long, the resistance was ineffectual and there was no escape on this world. Anywhere he returned to, he would be a lot worse off than now. Until such a time as readers and cams detected him, and an AI worked out how he didn't quite fit in. Once that happened, he would be lucky to end up back here, because the Inspectorate would get hold of him first, and likely he'd die under interrogation. Perhaps this was why Savarack wanted something that, as far as he gathered, would pull him back here.

Anyway, he felt that merely escaping the Complex, as well as being a stupid idea, simply wasn't ambitious enough. He'd seen and walked on two other worlds, and interacted with a creature claiming to be the Fenris. Could there be a world out there better than this one? When he thought about it, even one with dinosaurs would be better. At least there'd be something to eat and, most importantly, no Committee. Perhaps he could even reach worlds with human populations under more benevolent rule? But then, how would he stay there? Would he be drawn back here? How did he assert control over the process? And finally, could he do what he'd done without the bot flies? In some manner he was tethered here, and the suit would strengthen that tether. He needed to learn more, a lot more. He headed over to Savarack.

The researcher was gazing at a recording on one of his screens. The words 'Subject Zeta T1' were up in the top corner. Looking over Savarack's shoulder, Ottanger saw himself sitting in the chair within the sphere, clad in the monitoring gear, with the skein of wires leading from that into the system. At the bottom of the screen a time display clicked down. For a short period things within the sphere looked confused, as if seen through a fractured lens. Then an iridescent fog surrounded Ottanger and he simply disappeared – all the monitoring equipment collapsing into the chair.

Savarack stopped the recording, took it back until before Ottanger disappeared, then ran it through again, much slower. When the disruption came, he brought it down to one slow frame at a time. Before Ottanger disappeared, a blurred figure appeared beside him, seated in a chair. As the frames continued, the figure faded in and out of existence, as if clouds were passing before it. Then an even more blurred figure appeared over to the side of the first, then another and another in a line curving round, through the wall of the sphere and stretching off-frame. Ottanger thought it must be some kind of refraction of him, though he couldn't truly tell. He might be seeing any of the other subjects prior to him, for all he knew.

'Quantum fluctuations?' Savarack muttered.

Ottanger stepped closer and decided to risk a question.

'So what does all this mean?' he asked. 'Have you not seen this before?'

'I'm working on that,' said Savarack, distractedly. 'It's crazy – if you take a look at this recording another time, the figure isn't there. I've layered the recordings, and in some it appears, in others it doesn't.'

'That's impossible.'

Savarack waved a hand. 'That's the territory we're in.'

He turned back and brought up all the frames on the screen. Even on the still images, the other figures were changing – some were fading into existence, and others fading out. Ottanger looked at the impossibility here and oddly it cheered him.

'AI,' Savarack said. 'Search for pattern matches over the time series and relate to . . . just search for patterns.'

'Found,' replied the flat voice of AI a moment later.

'Display on second screen.' Savarack swivelled his chair to face another screen, as graphs and bar charts blinked into being around the edges. Something then appeared in the middle that made no sense to Ottanger. Savarack reached over to the screen, grabbed and pulled. A hologram moved out from the surface, and now Ottanger could see it more clearly. But it still made no sense to him.

'What is that?' he asked.

Savarack glanced round at him, a flash of annoyance coming through his intense concentration. Ottanger realized the man hadn't been aware who he'd been talking to before.

'It's a 3D representation of five dimensions,' said Savarack, his tone indicating that he didn't expect Ottanger to understand that.

Behind the hologram, on the screen, a single word displayed: *Calculating* . . . Ottanger asked no more, not wanting to be sent away. By the researcher's stooped and rigid pose, he knew the

AI must be working out something important. After a short time, the AI replaced the word with others: *Pattern Match at 96%*. The hologram then changed shape, as did the graphs and bar charts. Savarack studied these, shook his head, sighed and sat back, rubbing at his eyes.

'It's a fucking time crystal,' he muttered.

Ottanger nodded to himself. He didn't understand and that didn't matter. What did matter was that Savarack didn't understand either.

7

The Fenris – Present

The inocular flies *had* seemed perfect. For those on the nodal Earth who had high levels of the biotech installed by the virus, the fly bites would turn them into humans capable of crossing the parallels. They'd become world walkers. And they would be freed from Committee Earth, to assist in his efforts to divert that place from dystopia. A positive force in the multiverse, whose members might also serve as allies to him. But from the first fly bite, the nightmare began.

The Fenris sat rooted to his sensory throne as the data began to come in. The first ever jaunter took a leap of just a hundred metres, but smacked into the side of a sprawl building at over ten metres per second. With growing horror, he saw more people failing to match physical velocity to their arrival point. They jaunted into objects, or deep into the ground, or high in the sky only to fall to their death. Each death juddered through his body, expanding a malaise of dark guilt and grief that left him unable to do more than watch in dismay. Over a hundred of them died in the first day. The number had increased by an order of magnitude on the second, and that was when he hit a threshold. He lashed out mentally, sending power surges through all his engines. Transmission of viruses ceased, in sterilizing fire that burned biotech, melted metals and charred composite. And, refusing to disconnect, he allowed the pain of this to flood through him. His next blow shattered storage and blew plumes of fire out of four engines, as he incinerated the inocular flies. He then sat gasping and wincing with guilt, which couldn't be washed away by what he now saw as a destructive, childish tantrum.

He'd stopped those transmissions, but he hadn't stopped the deaths. He needed to turn back into this, to understand, and as time passed he was at least able to make some sense of the data. Most of the deaths were a result of a failure in the safety homing feature of the biotech. They couldn't control where they would end up. However, others, in whom it functioned correctly, failed to get away from the nodal Earth, mostly ending up prey to readerguns, or Inspectorate interrogation rooms. Still others suffered similar fates on the two close parallels of that world. But the worst death toll came about on the airless Earth that had somehow broken the pattern. Thousands slid down some wrinkle in the multiverse network to die there. He remained rooted to his throne and watched, aware that he was punishing himself, and he did this for months.

On many occasions, he simply lost track when his power supplies were low, but the death toll just kept going up. Meanwhile, even under this load, he started to come out of his shock. Though he couldn't dispel the darkness that had risen inside, he delved deeper into analysis of all he'd done, and its effects. The biotech establishing in the majority was still not entirely compatible with their biology, despite his alterations. The horrible reality here was that the recipients of the biotech needed more of the requisite substrate, which was fenris DNA. And, as he had discovered, that killed most of them. Fenris DNA had, in the far past, been human DNA, but natural and controlled evolution, as well as interactions with their similarly evolving biotech over a million years, had wrought major changes.

No amount of analysis allowed him to escape the disaster, however. Too often he wanted to shut down his consciousness and curl up in darkness. But a stubborn part of his soul wouldn't allow that, so he turned his analytical mind on himself. Soon he decided that it had been the result of his godlike position controlling vast technology, and omniscient perception of the multiverse, exacerbated by the arrogance of youth. With this new perspective, he had a decision to make. And then he realized he'd already made it during his tantrum. He had ceased to think in terms of intervention, or accruing allies closer to his biology. So he turned to rescuing whoever he could, for amid all this death, there were some successes. Like the lovers.

Their story was almost Shakespearean. He was an enforcer in one ZA gang, while she was the daughter of the boss of another gang. Hack Chancel, who went only by his second name, had risen to the position of enforcer not because he was brutal, as was usually the case, but because he was smart. He could get things done without breaking limbs or killing anyone. Adriana Chester lived a protected existence in a ZA area that was a step up the social ladder. It abutted an SA enclave, and her father's gang provided entertainment for those SAs going *out on the town*. Both Chancel and Adriana were advanced mutants, whom the Fenris had his feeds tracking. As seemed the case for all of their kind, they felt a mutual attraction, which he knew arose from a blend of their primitive drives and the quantum entanglement of their biotech. They became lovers, much to the annoyance of their respective gangs. It was the cause of a great deal of negotiation, then bickering, and finally the possibility of street war. Chancel had been ordered to drop Adriana, while she'd ended up in semi-imprisonment by her father. She escaped, and they met up in one of the whore rooms of her father's business. This was going to be their last time together. And then a fly came in through the window and bit them both, one after the other.

The Fenris missed their jaunt at first, because it was so quick, and his reserves of energy were so low after his childish destruction of virus and fly transmissions. What happened next came as much of a surprise to him as it did to them, when he finally went through the recorded data. Subsequent analysis revealed that their individual biotech was an interlocking whole – what one lacked, the other had. Their connection, which they called love, went very deep. They hardly noticed the fly bites during yet another marathon sex session, just as they hardly noticed their bodies exchanging so much more than the usual bodily fluids. The bites initiated their ability to jaunt at once, while they were locked together in mental and biological synergy.

They fell out of the world of Committee Earth while orgasming simultaneously, and into a crowded tenement of the first parallel world, still naked and entangled in more ways than one. They dropped a couple of metres to the floor, which soon snapped them out of their exultant haze.

'What the fuck?' said Chancel, pulling away from Adriana. He leapt to his feet and then looked up, perhaps trying to find the hole in the ceiling they must have fallen through. Belatedly watching all this, the Fenris was frustrated to only have the recording.

'It's another place,' said Adriana, standing up too and rubbing at her backside.

He turned to her and nodded. 'Yes, I see it now.'

Around them ZAs had scrambled back – one limping because

171

Chancel had landed on his legs. Now they were recovering, and a look of callous estimation came into the expressions of some of them. Chancel scanned them, noting someone picking up a heavy bar stock club, and another drawing a knife. Strangers unprotected in the middle of such a tenement tended to have bad experiences, usually involving being handed over to organ traders or brothel keepers. Chancel knew that.

'And perhaps we need to be in another place,' Adriana added, moving closer to him.

'Yeah, seems that way.' He reached out and grabbed her biceps, pulling her in. Their synergy was still something formidable, which had enabled them to grasp what they'd done, if only on an instinctive level. He pulled her in even closer and, with a shrug, kissed her hard on the mouth. They then both turned, balletically, and slid from that parallel into the next.

'That was harder,' said Adriana, collapsing to the street.

This time, the Fenris noted, they'd managed to come in at ground level. And had made an almost perfect jaunt. But their initial impetus and biotech energy reserves, as he'd seen in too many other tragic cases, was putting a damaging strain on their conventional human biology. Chancel clutched at his face, fingertips coming away red from the blood leaking out of his tear ducts. Around them crowds parted, but then halted their progress along the street to stand and gawp. Chancel warily scanned their surroundings once more. He had to know they were no safer here than they'd been in the tenement before.

The Fenris scrabbled to analyse the meagre information he had available from a feed. This had strayed along with them, as if they'd been dragging it. Their synergy, and their immediate grasp of what they were doing, was something unique and precious. Though sufficient data were not available, he came to some conclusions: DNA and history. Those on the nodal

Committee Earth were the ancestors of the Fenris. Although it was a debatable point – since his arrival in this time was now changing their future – this meant many of them possessed those elements of human DNA that the Fenris had retained, and therefore meshed better with the fenris biotech, some more than others. These two were by no stretch as close to the fenris optimum as the girl and her family who'd survived the input of his DNA. But what they had still gave them the visceral, instinctive, and now intellectual, understanding of what they were doing.

'We can't stay here,' said Chancel.

The Fenris desperately wanted to communicate with them, even though all he was seeing lay some hours in the past. He wanted to tell them to run, to find somewhere to rest up and recoup their resources, before their next jaunt. Because the pit trap of an airless Earth awaited, and it could kill them, as it had others.

'Oh I agree,' said Adriana, pushing herself upright, then backing up to Chancel, as she watched the steadily growing crowd too.

He put his arms around her, winced, and closed his eyes, then they jaunted again.

In the recording, the Fenris tracked them through the high dimensional surfaces of the local multiverse and saw them hit the slope that would take them down onto the airless Earth. He dreaded what he would see next – what he'd seen a thousand times as jaunters arrived there and died. But they disappeared.

The Fenris switched away from the recording to focus on that hostile planet, scouring the surface for them. Just so he could close their brief story and torture himself with their tragic end. The odd interdimensional and regular disturbance of the place interfered with his search there, as always. He continued for another half an hour, searching meticulously. There was no sign, though, and he could only surmise that they'd ended up deep in the ground, or had failed to align their exit speed and evaporated. But the way they'd disappeared niggled at him.

He withdrew his attention from that world and focused back on the surfaces and patterns of the local multiverse where they had, apparently, disappeared. He began to map the volume of it much more carefully. By this time the feed from the repaired sun tap had brought up engine energy to the point where he could have communicated with the two of them, if they'd been alive. Greater available energy also allowed him to push his examination of the surfaces to the limit, and that's when he saw the twisted off-shoots and breaks. It was as if this airless Earth had disrupted the in-between spaces of the multiverse, as his own world had. This bore investigation, but right then the disruption gave him hope. He tracked through a break where the two had disappeared, and thence to a tube, through to a cystlike dent in the continuum. That's where he found another Earth, and picked up a direct link to their biotech.

'This is weird,' Chancel was saying, as they walked hand in hand along a street with tenements on either side. The place looked much like any other on Committee Earth but for one exception: no people. The Fenris watched them for a while, tempted to communicate, but decided to save energy and let the engine's zero-point collectors and the sun tap ramp up storage while he examined this world.

'It stinks of death here,' Adriana replied.

The street along which they walked was empty because the corpses had been cleaned up there. Plenty of them occupied the surrounding buildings, though. Other streets were scattered with them, and still others had mounds of them dozed up and ready to go into macerators. This hadn't happened yet because there was no one around to drive the machines, or guide the clear-up robots. The same scene repeated out and out, across this sprawl, which was in India – the Kerala Sprawl. The Fenris detected pockets of humans still alive all around the world, living comparably richly on the remains of a crashed civilization.

This world was evidently a parallel of the nodal Committee Earth, but not a direct one, in the sense of the other two close to it in multiverse terms. He studied patterns and saw that the airless Earth, seemingly displaced from somewhere else by the catastrophic arrival of his own world, had sheared this one away from the others, then dropped it into an interdimensional cul-de-sac. But what the hell had happened to everyone? Penetrating databases was as easy here as on the nodal Earth, and soon he had the general story of the plague. Deeper penetration of Committee databases revealed the truth, and he realized the horror of it. A virus had been put into the implants of a vast swathe of ZAs, ready to be initiated by radio signal in targeted exterminations. That process had commenced, killing millions here and there, so they wouldn't overload the system and could be disposed of in a sanitary manner. Then the virus had mutated and become transmissible.

The plague had leapt from targeted populations to other ZAs, and SAs too. Emergency measures were introduced that involved readerguns. These were the installation of what one official called 'firebreaks', exterminating millions in the path of the virus. But it made no difference, because the thing was in the air. It had, fortunately, saved Chancel and Adriana's lives, though. The readerguns around them were receiving instructions to shoot, but simply had no ammo left. This area of Kerala, containing the residence of a high Committee bureaucrat, had been one of those firebreaks.

The Fenris now fined down his feeds to examine some human

remains, and anything he could find of the virus. Meanwhile, the two lovers ventured into one building and came out again clothed. He was relieved to discover that their biotech would prevent the virus killing them. Further analysis of the survivors elsewhere in the world revealed humans who possessed a parallel, reflected form of the biotech in them, which is what had saved them too. He pulled back and assessed, then decided it was time to start talking. He hardened his link to their biotech in preparation, noting power levels dropping the moment he did so. He would have a little time, not much, but enough.

'Hello Chancel and Adriana,' he said.

They halted and Chancel glanced at his companion.

'Now that doesn't look human at all,' he said.

The Fenris winced. His connection wasn't just voice but bleeding through some of his own appearance too.

'Hello to you,' said Adriana. 'What are you, and what the fuck is going on?'

The Fenris decided not to go the route of lengthy explanations and confirmations. These were two smart people and their biotech, in reaching the point that had enabled them to jaunt, would have pushed up their intelligence to a point beyond the conventionally human. This was a natural upshot of their ability to map and travel in more dimensions than four. They also had the instinctive understanding of their biotech, which would be turning into something intellectual.

'This parallel has been all but denuded of human life by a plague installed in ID chips,' he said.

'Parallel,' Chancel repeated, but said no more – he never really spoke much, he just acted.

'Are we safe?' Adriana asked.

'Your biotech protects you.'

'Biotech that you put into us somehow,' said Adriana, then

after a pause, 'or rather put into our ancestors, going back a few generations. What activated it? And what are you?'

'Flies did, and I am the Fenris,' he replied. He then launched into an explanation but Adriana kept anticipating what he would say next. Her perspicacity pleased him, but it also annoyed him when she started asking deeper questions about his origin, the multiverse and its present state, and the reasons for what he'd done.

'Enough now,' he said eventually. 'I am running out of power here and will not be able to keep this communication link open.'

'So what do we do now?'

'See the hill ahead of you?'

'Yes.'

'The residence on top was that of a high Kerala bureaucrat. In English it's called Caprock. I've just shut down its defences – the readerguns there do still have ammo. Inside you'll find all you need. It has power and water, and the owner stored up other resources there too.'

'And then what?' Adriana asked.

'You will be safe and comfortable there. I suggest you don't jaunt elsewhere just yet. I warned you about the airless Earth, and there are other dangers too.'

'That doesn't really answer her question,' said Chancel.

'There will be others like you – other world walkers,' said the Fenris. And yet once the words were out, he felt depression looming again. Would there be others?

'And what do we and these world walkers do?'

The questions, he realized, would continue.

'Energy low – I can speak no more,' he said and, feeling sour and guilty, cut the link.

There *were* other survivors, because their DNA was incrementally closer to his own. But the appallingly few successes in no way justified what he had done, or helped to raise the Fenris out of the dark place in his mind. One fleeting light was that the number of flies had diminished, because of the nodal Earth extermination aimed at the burgeoning version of the tsetse fly. It had been fine while it spread yellow fever amid the ZA population, but when it began to spread to the SAs they'd acted.

Is this the reality of adulthood? the Fenris wondered. It certainly wasn't the confidence, optimism and naivety of youth, or its arrogance. The darkness began to diminish, but the guilt would always remain. He couldn't track the flies because that granularity took far too much power, but he did maintain feeds to all likely candidates. This was when he discovered that Earth authorities now knew about the flies. The numerous on-camera disappearances, people reappearing half-sunk into solid objects, or obliterating themselves messily against the same, had not escaped the notice of national governments, or the increasingly powerful MDC – now mostly referred to as the *Committee*. AIs, which had been tasked with analysing this phenomenon in millions of hours of cam data, had made the connection. These strange events occurred shortly after the people had been bitten by flies. Only an AI could have made this connection. Flies were then collected and studied. And now that biotech was in the hands of researchers there.

He watched them delving into the technology, their first jaunt experiments, and lashed himself with this further consequence of his arrogance and naivety. There would be more jaunters, there would be more deaths. This was limited to the amount of biotech they'd collected, for they simply didn't have the level of technology to reproduce it. But still, further thousands would die. It was a situation he could only ameliorate, and then minimally. So he turned to what statistically had become the greatest killer of neophyte jaunters: the airless Earth.

There was a storm of darkness and distortions in the area between multiverse worlds adjacent to the airless one. It had at first seemed utterly chaotic, and similar to other mid-parallel storms his kind had observed before. He'd classified it as a natural phenomenon. This storm thing was moving like an amoeba, and shooting out threads of its non-substance to various worlds. And yet, while in this state of flux, it still consistently routed jaunters out of Committee Earth down onto the airless one. There was something very odd about the place.

Humans existed, or had existed, on the greatly enlarged moon, where their cities or machines had changed its face. Signs of their previous occupancy showed up throughout their solar system. Details on that were hard to acquire, because the storm had been disrupting his penetration right from the start, when he'd tracked the first jaunters arriving . . . and dying there. He'd picked up transmissions around the moon, but with nothing outside of the pragmatic, he couldn't tell if they arose from a living population, or some system run by AI. Whether whatever existed on that moon was relevant, he couldn't know. But in the end, the pit trap on the planet below it remained constant. He needed a harder link to that place, so he could learn more. And so he'd be able to do more for the jaunters arriving there than just watch them die. He initiated the production of a seed – one that would be filled with his biotech. A part of himself he could use to establish a foothold on that world. The only problem would be the massive energy required to send such a thing through . . .

The Fenris could see in the dark, but such was the profligacy of energy networked across the engines, and coming in from the sun tap, that the engine he'd made his base was full of light. This he now understood to be an anachronism, and a comfort for that part of him that was still related to the world he was now observing. The seed, picking up its programming for a new and hostile environment as it ran through a network of glassy pipes, finally arrived at the engine's interface with the multiverse – ready to go. It was as if all the engines gathered around him, and his world, took a deep breath. And then it went through. The Fenris felt the massive exhale, and noted the lights going out, as the system shut down its inessential functions. His engine connections died a moment later, and only he remained, with his sense of his immediate surroundings, and the multiverse – the oxygen-free world and its moon – retreated to points in the massive tapestry.

Then the lights came back on, and the ancient human in him felt relief, thinly distributed as it was throughout the biotech that made up most of his being. Through the engines, his suit quickly reacquired its direct feed from the seed itself. It had appeared a kilometre above ground level of the airless Earth, falling through an atmosphere that consisted mostly of carbon dioxide and nitrogen. It hit a rocky surface and bounced on to lodge itself in a pile of fine granular gravel. The fall had disrupted the feed and caused some damage, which it was in the process of correcting. He would've liked to have dropped it on, or much closer to, the surface, but the extra energy draw necessary for such accuracy would have added another six months to the recharging time from the sun tap.

Lying in the gravel, the seed activated, and with that his perception of its surroundings began to clarify. He realized how, until this moment, he'd been seeing this place through a glass darkly. Small splits developed in the seed's surface, and out of these it began issuing its mycelia roots. The process was long and slow because of a lack of moisture at the location, but having detected a source, the mycelia began to head in that direction. The Fenris frowned when he saw what the source was. Lying half-buried in the gravel was the partially mummified corpse of a woman. Here was one of the failed jaunters from the nodal Earth. Accessing stored data on all of them, he found her. She had jaunted once in her sprawl, putting her straight into a restricted SA area where readerguns had yet to be installed. There she'd appeared out of thin air, travelling fast and slamming into a wall. Local police had grabbed her and, since they had recorded video of her appearance, she was hospitalized rather than thrown into a macerator. When she was conscious again, the questions began. When those doing the questioning didn't get the answers they wanted, hospital treatment transitioned into psychoactive drugs. She was half-mad by the time they put her under an inducer. She had jaunted then, and arrived on this airless version of Earth, still unable to control her exit velocity. She'd hit the ground travelling at tens of kilometres an hour. Having reviewed the data, the Fenris felt bitter and angry in a way he never had before. This woman's experience so closely matched Irene's story, and there had been hundreds more like them. What cost his morality, or his need?

The corpse was a compacted, misshapen lump, full of shattered bones, but it contained the moisture the seed needed. The Fenris felt there was something both poetic and dreadful about her body enabling his biotech to grow here. He checked himself on that and wondered, not for the first time, if his interactions with the jaunters were raising old human characteristics in him. Then he focused completely on the seed as it finally reached the corpse.

The mycelia penetrated leathery skin and slowly crept inside. When they hit moisture that had yet to evaporate, they abruptly fattened and started pushing out sideshoots. Over the ensuing hours, the mycelia completely occupied the corpse, sucking up any moisture and nutrients. Brief further spurts of growth

181

occurred as they hit fenris biotech in the body and incorporated it. The corpse gradually deflated, the skin disappearing and the skull collapsing, while the threads spread all over the pile of gravel. The corpse had all but disappeared as it finally put a thread out across bare stone. There it found one of the odd succulent plants slowly growing in this environment, and put out a series of shoots from that to seek out other plants. By then, the Fenris had seen enough and he withdrew.

The seed would grow slowly, so it'd be a while before its product rendered useful data. The delivery was at least a success. He thought back to the other seeds he'd sent before, too. The first, which he'd put so much hope in using, and spent so much time and energy sending, had reached Chenghu, as he intended. But the thing still remained in the man's pocket, as yet unactivated. One other seed he'd sent to the nodal Earth had, ridiculously, landed on the deck of a massive oil tanker in the Atlantic Ocean, where a bureaucrat aboard had picked it up and now kept it as an ornament in his office. The Fenris dared not activate it, because this would be seen and no doubt the technology of the thing recognized. He didn't want to exacerbate further the dangers of the rapidly growing research project on Committee Earth.

Turning his attention back to that, the Fenris focused on a brother and sister with whom he felt kinship. They were of the family line he'd been watching since his first installation of biotech in that girl in the tenement. He'd honed the virus down in further transmissions since that first one, which had contained not only initializing biotech but his own DNA, and had nearly killed her. But its effect on her family line thereafter had been a positive thing, apart from those who'd been killed after they were bitten by the inocular flies. The survivors had developed fenris mental characteristics, an inherent morality and fierce intelligence. The brother, now with researchers and being provided with the tech of an inocular fly, was developing his powers fast. Probably faster than the lovers, or even the woman Ektian. Maybe *he* would survive?

Ektian

The world had changed. It felt thin and unsubstantial, while the people around her seemed weak and ghostly. She was sure the suffocation had damaged her brain. She had no idea how she'd ended up here, naked in this unfamiliar sprawl, where they spoke a language she didn't know. Just previously, after a long illness in the Paris Sprawl, she'd been shivering in all her clothes, and wrapped in her one blanket, sure she was dying. And now. . . She looked at the three men lying on the ground before her. Two of them were still alive. With senses that seemed unbearably keen, she could detect their breathing and, if she concentrated, the beat of their hearts. The third was dead – his neck twisted off at an odd angle and the stink of shit rising from him.

Someone yelled in what she now recognized as German from one end of the alley. She'd been asked a hostile question, probably concerning her appearance, so turned towards the voice, and locked eyes with a woman who had pushed to the front of the crowd there. The woman's face fell, and she abruptly retreated. In fact the whole crowd did a little. Ektian glanced down at herself. She still looked enough of a woman for her nakedness to have attracted the three now on the ground, whose intent had been obvious. But her mutation, which she'd had since birth, had progressed in some way. She'd glimpsed her reflection in a window while moving away from the crowds and she seemed taller, much more long-boned, and her features elongated. She looked skinny too, as did most ZAs, but with muscles sharply defined rather than withered. Her eyes, when she peered close at herself in the glass, had turned deep violet. But it wasn't just that. She looked dangerous, as if there might be something of a beast within her. Now she'd found out she really *was* dangerous.

She couldn't just stand here, but she also couldn't walk around the streets naked, attracting the kind of attention she just had. Stepping over to the largest man of those still alive, she began stripping off his clothing. She took his trousers, jacket and shirt, but left the filthy undergarments as a home for the lice crawling all over his body. As she dressed he grunted and looked up at her, bewildered. He'd been the first to grab her arm and try to sweep out her feet. She'd simply turned and gone to push him away. But much to her surprise, he'd seemed light and weak, and she'd ended up launching him into a nearby wall. The one with the broken neck she'd hit with a flailing blow, cringing to feel bones break under the impact. The third man had been charging her at that point. She'd fallen over, with him on top of her, trying to pin down her arms, seemingly unaware that his companions were no longer capable of the help he doubtless requested. He'd felt flimsy to her too, and she knew she could break his grip. As she struggled to get out from under him, her forehead smashed into his face. She'd pushed him away, feeling nauseated. But as she rose from the ground and saw what she'd done, this transformed into a guilty delight.

By the time she had dressed, having discarded his footwear as too foul, and too small, to put on, the crowds at both ends of the alley were pushing in, driven by the curious behind them. She stared at the wall of people from where the woman had questioned her. She just wanted to hide, but there was nowhere, and if she stayed here she'd be in trouble. She forced herself towards them and, as she approached, people struggled to get out of her path. She pushed into them, shrugging them aside like tissue figures, picking up one man by the scruff and tossing him from her path. Why did she feel so solid and real, and they so insubstantial? Why did everything, in fact, all around her, feel like some tapestry, rippling in the wind? And why, oh why, had she become this dangerous being?

She moved on through the crowd, going faster where it thinned, and then into areas beyond the commotion she'd caused. Still people gave her odd looks, as they always had because of her mutation. But now being clothed, and with her head stooped, those gazes glanced off her. People moved back to their own concerns, which would as ever be food, comfort and safety.

Why was she like this, and in this position? She'd been odd-looking when younger but never particularly physical. In fact she had a reputation as a nerd. Her time had mostly been spent studying code and technology, and garnering what work she could from the street gangs. Like when they brought something stolen from EU infrastructure to be disassembled, reprogrammed and turned to useful tasks. The change, it seemed, had come when they brought her the shepherd. Had she somehow picked up her sickness from it?

Like all ZAs, she'd felt an immediate abhorrence and fear of the thing. The Condors gang had given her space and provided tools. They wanted all the information she could glean from the machine, and some way to access its programming. She had gazed at it, down on the floor, with its legs up around it like a spider, and its body nested in sticky tentacles smelling of putre-fied blood. She'd taken the thing apart, got deep into its hardware, and managed to copy its software to a DNA drive, then began decoding it on three ancient linked laptops. And that was when she felt something jerk inside her, and had vomited. The fits that followed had her biting her tongue. She shit herself and felt as if she was burning. Skin began peeling from her face. Condor enforcers found her, searched her, checked her work and shot questions at her that she only just managed to answer. Then they just threw her out on the streets. They probably saw no reason to pay her for what she'd done, since they expected she had one of the many killing maladies sweeping the sprawl. Her brother had found her, carried her back to their tenement, and there she had fallen into hallucinations of other worlds, with reality stretched thin and taut and penetrable.

And now she was here.

Ektian assessed what had happened to her. In the alley, while naked, she'd noticed the swell of breasts, and hair between her legs. Not having had these features before, she realized she must have gone rapidly into her long-delayed puberty, for she was nineteen already. And this seemed to have somehow kicked her mutation into motion. Since her first growth spurt, she'd always been tall, with an odd, slightly purplish shade to her skin, a long face and long dextrous fingers. She'd been just far enough away from the norm to be recognized as a mutation, like others in her family before her. But still near enough to the norm to be accepted by most people. So how did she feel, now her mutation was much more pronounced?

Ektian wasn't sure.

Her changes had burned all the dross out of her system, sharpened her senses and made her strong. She should feel great but actually felt uncomfortable, displaced, unnatural and *wrong*. She paused, inspecting those emotions closely and analysing them in a way she had never done with her feelings before. In a moment, she understood that her sense of being out of place seemed more to do with *where* she was, rather than *who* or what she was. She looked around.

The wide street here was not as crowded as back where she'd come from, and it seemed everyone was heading in that direction. She grabbed the arm of a passing woman.

'Where are they going?'

The woman babbled in German and oddly Ektian found herself understanding more, but she said, 'I don't understand.'

The woman winced and looked down at her grip. Suddenly feeling ashamed, Ektian let go of her. The woman stepped back a pace, frowned and rubbed her arm, looking thoughtful for a second. Then she made a motion, as if putting something in her mouth.

'Food,' she said with a thick accent, and hurried away.

Ektian guessed there must be some sort of food distribution, or market, that way. She herself felt ravenously hungry, in a way she had never experienced before – the reality of hunger in the sprawls was shrunken bellies, and appetite always taking some time to restore. Perhaps she should head back that way and see if she could get something to eat? No, logic dictated otherwise. They were speaking German here. How she'd got here she didn't know, but could only surmise that organ traders had drugged her and transported her. The drugging would account for her faulty memory. She winced at that because it just didn't seem right. She'd been very sick, while organ traders grabbed healthy ZAs to go into the SA transplant clinics. Whatever. If the crowd was heading for a food distribution centre, then the chip in her forearm would be read before she received a ration. The watching AI would then refuse her ration and notify the Inspectorate of her being out of her designated area – *way* out of it. She'd be arrested, questioned and likely end up in a macerator.

Thinking on this, Ektian abruptly snapped her head up and looked straight at the cam up on a nearby pole, then around at others on various buildings. Since she was deep in a sprawl, none of these had readerguns, but they would have the chip-querying software. She didn't need to go to a distribution centre to be spotted. And now she had looked directly at a cam. First alerted by her presence out of her zone, the AI would run other checks. It would see that her face no longer matched a previous scan of her. In fact, it had probably already done so. Dropping her gaze, she felt a weary inevitability when she heard the screams and saw the people running.

What looked like a drain cover rose from the street just ten metres away, a frame below it holding a neatly packed and folded shepherd. As the structure locked in place above the tarmac, the crowd-control robot activated, stretching out one, then two, thick spider limbs. With a clattering sound, it pulled out of the framework. There it stood on four limbs, with its head section coming up and thorax dropping. The head bore the appearance of a large hood, out of which spilled numerous tentacles. It turned, focused the glitter of optical plates on her, and lurched into motion.

For Ektian, time seemed to slow while the world around her took on the quality of old film – unreal, drained of colour and a distortion of what she knew. Even though she hadn't looked in that direction, she sensed in some unknowable way that the Inspectorate were behind her, and then she heard the thrum of air fans. With a glance back, she saw the car, with its crew of riot police dropping into the street there and heading towards her. She ran into the space the panicking crowds had cleared, going to the right of the shepherd, intent on circumventing it and getting out of this trap. The shepherd swivelled and then came after her.

It seemed strange to her how quickly she got past and round it. Then, passing one of the crowd sprinting in the same direction as her, she realized how fast she was moving. A side street revealed itself, but was packed with people drawing back from hers. She just kept going, looking for gaps and shunting people aside where necessary. With a thud, something struck someone nearby, lifting him off his feet and sprawling him. An object clattered away and began whining with vapour trails rising from it. They were using knockout gas, and she saw the canisters landing far ahead of her, sketching lines in the air as they released their load. She just stopped breathing and kept running, since that was one technique to evade the effects if you could maintain it for long enough. People began dropping ahead, and all around her. She leapt convulsing bodies, foam bubbling from their mouths. Then, with an ability that seemed to give her sight all around, she sensed the shepherd bearing down on her.

Its shadow loomed ahead, and a tentacle slapped down on her shoulder, instantly bonding there. Turning sharply, she ripped fabric from her jacket and ran for a nearby building. A flimsy aluminium door lay ahead and she fully intended to shoulder into it and crash through – the shepherd would be slower in the confines within. She had to get away! The door loomed up and she did force through it, though her shoulder didn't touch metal. The world grew even thinner around her, with people misting out and the shepherd receding behind, as if down a long tunnel. She felt herself dragging out of her clothing and, in some way, trying to hang on to her dignity, grasping at it and pulling it back in around her. Then she was through and rolling on packed earth.

Ektian had no doubts now, didn't feel she had suffered some hallucination, but knew with absolute certainty that she had pushed aside a veil of reality and passed through to another place. She felt the hard burning activation of it through her body as she came up into a squat and looked around. The crowds were back, and the shepherd too, as she found herself in waste ground between two buildings. She took a deep breath of metallic air but this felt somehow unsatisfying. The shepherd was out on the street, beyond a fence and Inspectorate riot police closing in. She gazed up at an orange sky, scattered with black stars and scarred with red cloud, as the shepherd crushed the fence and skittered towards her. The thing had six legs now, while its tentacles were metallic, segmented and lined with hooks. No glue here, it seemed. Standing fully upright, she gazed at the thing, then at the police beyond, in their cream uniforms. They fired weapons that seemed to fill the air with angry hornets. Then she stepped away again.

Her surroundings misted and she sensed the readiness of them to transform into some other version of the two places before. But this next distortion of reality seemed to be fighting against a rip tide through the ether, and she found herself seemingly falling down a long slope. She came down feet first on gravel, and the sky had transformed yet again. She looked upon a moon with structures spread across its face, then down at drifts of gravel and strange plants stretched across a flat plain. A breath told her she could not survive here, as did a skeleton half-covered by one drift, and a corpse crawling with green threads. She shifted again and again, from place to place, realities flicking past like a slide show, some related to each other and some utterly different where she hit the rip tides. Slowly the boiling adrenalin and hard bright activation in her died, and she felt tired and bruised inside. She chose a place to rest.

She staggered onto a mountainside, below a pure blue sky, and went down on one knee. Liquid ran from her nose and one ear; wiping at it revealed blood decidedly darker than usual. The sun sat hot and bright above thorny scrub and plants, which appeared to be a combination of cactus and spreading fungus that seemed to have flowed between the rocks like syrup and then frozen there. From this position, she could see down into a forested valley, and what looked vaguely like villages scattered here and there on the mountains opposite. It all looked a bit like something she'd seen on a screen once, of villages in mountain locations before the sprawls, and before such land had been developed. Most mountains now had massive greenhouses, solar plants and SA enclaves. A nearer one, off down the mountainside to her right, revealed dwellings like nothing she'd seen before. The houses were domed and linked by connections above ground, coralline loops and flat surfaces like landing pads. She could see people there too. Now utterly sure she could leave any place behind if she so wished, and knowing a sense of power and control that had been absent all her life, she felt little fear. But glancing at the blood on her sleeve, she realized there was a cost she didn't want to pay again just yet.

Nearby she could see a track cutting through rocks and thorn scrub. Feet still bare, she stood up and carefully made her way over to it. It seemed to wind down towards those dwellings, so she followed it there, noting the packed creamy surface of the track consisted of a wide variety of strange fossils under a glassy film. After she'd gone a few hundred metres, she saw three children just off the track levering up chunks of the cactus fungus and putting them into a wheelbarrow. They saw her and one of them waved hesitantly. She focused in on them, with her vision and that other odd all-around sense sharp. Yes, they seemed to be children but, just like the village, they were nothing like she'd seen before. They were squat and wide but certainly not fat. Their skin had a yellow, almost jaundiced, look while their fingers were webbed. She studied the face of the one who'd waved, noting big round eyes with wide pupils, nose blending into mouth and a bald head with no ears.

As she drew close enough for them to get a better look at her, they moved out of the rocks and onto the track, then abruptly started heading away, glancing back at her. She raised a hand to wave at them, and perhaps seeing the lack of webs between her fingers was enough. They abandoned their wheelbarrow and ran. Ektian kept to the same pace, only pausing to peer into the barrow at the fungus, wondering if it was edible. Hunger was a hard tight clench in her guts. Just past the barrow, she looked to her right and saw the blue glitter of the sea at the end of the valley. There was a road running down there, to a larger settlement now coming into sight. Would she be safe here, she wondered? What kind of world was this?

And there it was: *world*.

Once more, as with her ability to step away from that strange version of Committee Earth, she was utterly sure. She had travelled to another world, and the ability to do this sat within her. She speculated on what this might mean, and immediately dismissed the idea that she had somehow mentally propelled herself across the gulfs between stars. Her education, such as it was, didn't allow for the possibility of that, what with the distances and energies that would have to be involved. That left something from the endless multiworld fictions. The differences between the two Committee Earths she'd been on indicated parallel worlds. However, should they not be only slightly at variance to each other in an infinite series? The last world had been a major variation from the one before. Which, now she thought about it, might not have been her own world. And this place was something completely different, with a different form of humanity. She just shrugged at that – she didn't know what she didn't know.

The adults weren't at all like the children, who were there amid the crowd. Their heads jutted forwards from their bodies, with a wide flare of flesh back to their shoulders. They were also more definitely yellow, shading to green, and their mouths were much larger. Two to the fore wore something that resembled

Inspectorate riot gear but with a nacreous, organic look. It seemed to consist of oyster-shell plates fixed to underlying fabric. In fact, reassessing, she realized it looked more like medieval armour. One carried a heavy weapon that protruded a barbed spike from the single barrel and had a long magazine on the side. It looked like a repeat-firing spear gun. The other one carried a trident, and this confirmed the impression she was getting that these were some aquatic form of humanity. One of them, opening splits on their neck flare, confirmed this further. Gill breathers?

Ektian concentrated on her surroundings and pushed. The world turned thin again, confirming her ability to step away from this place if she wanted to. Then she eased back and continued walking, watching the two carefully. The reaction here was understandable, but she had yet to confirm any straight hostility, while she was also tired and hungry. As she drew closer, the one with the trident stepped forwards and said something, his words blurring into a sound that throbbed in her ears. Underwater communication, she surmised. She halted and held her hands out to her sides.

'I don't understand you,' she said. 'I'm from another world.'

The two policemen, or whatever they were, looked at each other in puzzlement. She moved closer and the lead one lowered his trident, pointing it at her. She held out her hands again, palms upwards, then brought her hand in to rub it in a circular motion on her stomach. With her other she mimed putting food in her mouth.

'I am fucking starving,' she said.

The one with the trident watched her for a moment, then turned and gave orders. Some members of the crowd ran off. He gestured for her to walk past him and ahead, meanwhile taking a clam-shaped device from his hip. He pointed this at her and rubbed a thumb across the back of it, held it there for a moment, then attached it at his shoulder. When he spoke into it briefly, a high-pitched chattering replied. As Ektian stepped past him, she took a closer look at the thing and saw a squid eye in it, tracking her. Was it some kind of advanced biotechnology, or perhaps a mutualistic creature? The thoughts as they occurred to Ektian seemed strange.

They guided her in between the buildings, following a track under arching tunnels, to what looked like it might be a town square. Under an overhanging roof, either made in the shape of, or actually, a giant scallop shell, rested a collection of rocky slabs. Like some artistic representation of a section of seashore. The trident bearer indicated a rock beside one of the slabs and, understanding, she went over and sat down. He then seemed to get annoyed and spoke to all the gawpers. Many of them departed, but reluctantly; others sat down to watch the show. A short while later, an even wider version of their kind, a male even further removed from the humanity she knew, came out carrying a wooden platter. On it rested a large whole fish, raw and neatly sliced, with piles of what looked like seaweed around it. Small bowls contained tiny squid in dark liquid, moving sluggishly. He put down a clear glass bottle full of water too, and a double-handled cup beside it. Ektian just grabbed up the bottle and drank, gulping the cool liquid down and noting the slight taste of mushrooms. The trident bearer sat down on a nearby rock, detached the device from his shoulder and rested it on the slab.

'Greetings, world walker. You have been a surprise to me,' a voice from the clam device said in perfect French. 'After the fly bite, I thought you a failure, until the biotech mutated when you hit puberty. I then expected you to end up in the usual place, but your abilities developed fast.'

The surprise at hearing this didn't stop her eating, as she stabbed up slices of fish on a two-pronged fork and shoved them into her mouth. She didn't reply, instead abandoning the fork as her hunger took over and grabbing up handfuls of the fish and seaweed, cramming them in. She ate one of the squid, the liquid burning her mouth and the thing writhing as she chewed it up then swallowed. The trident bearer held out a hand in protest when she picked up the fish head, then withdrew it as she bit a chunk out of the bony thing, crunching it down.

'Where you are is another nodal world in this multiverse, but I was able to make a link through to the inhabitants' biotech and have been talking to them for seventy years,' said the voice, sounding impatient, perhaps because she hadn't replied. 'They are one of the few I managed to contact without massive energy expenditures. They understand what I am, and I have given them knowledge to advance their technology. Perhaps, through that technology, I can gain a better foothold here.'

Ektian consumed the head, the gritty backbone and the next layer of flesh. Another bottle of water arrived and she drank half of it. She emptied all the bowls, feeling slightly ashamed as she ate the rest of the squid. And then, like a switch clicking over, her body told her it was full, and a wave of weariness washed over her.

'It's good you managed to make it there rather than end up dead on one of the two direct parallels of Committee Earth. Or suffocating to death in the trap,' the voice said morosely. 'The sea people are at peace and now know what you are. Stay there. Others will come.'

'And what am I?' she asked.

The weariness had her head dipping towards the table, but then she felt a surge spread out from her guts, while her surroundings came back into sharp focus.

'If you require an explanation then you are not what I assume,' the voice replied sniffily.

'I was a mutated girl and now I'm an adult with biotech growing inside me, likely from you, enabling me to travel between parallel worlds.'

'That will do.'

'So what are you?'

'I am the Fenris,' the voice replied.

Ektian gave a nod of acknowledgement, then reached out and picked up the device from the slab. It had the weight of hard technology, while the eye sat under a glassy film, with golden wires spreading away from it, which had the regularity she'd seen in more-familiar electronics. She wanted to take it apart, but supposed that wouldn't be the right thing to do now. And anyway, she didn't yet have the required tools. She put it down again.

'What others will come?' she asked.

'Just like you,' the Fenris replied.

8

The Fenris

The biotech growing on the airless version of Earth had reached another two corpses. This had given it sufficient resources to develop mycelia roots to where it then found groundwater. Growth thereafter had been massive, and the thing had begun to consolidate neural masses and larger manipulators. Over the original drift of gravel, the biotech had mounded up into a great sluglike object, protruding long, partially jointed tentacles that terminated in star-shaped hands. It was now turning into something the Fenris could command, and so he sent instructions, then waited . . . and waited longer. Finally, annoyed at the lack of response, he probed the thing, only to discover extremely limited access. Just like the biotech all around him in the engine, the biotech there had incorporated command DNA. But from where? It didn't seem to be using his own, which had been in the seed . . . A moment of analysis rendered the answer: the corpses it had digested.

It took the Fenris days to circumvent that, only managing to do so when the neural mass passed a perception threshold and he could deliver data, convincing it that it couldn't take instruction from the dead. It then quickly incorporated his DNA from the seed again, and fell under his control. From within it, he turned his attention to its various meta-material detectors and directed their focus towards the moon. He could see it more clearly now, but still the effect of the storm seemed to block any penetration via multiverse routes. He accepted that and concentrated on the data he could acquire. Many structures on the moon's surface had thick domed coverings, seemingly formed of sintered regolith, with reflective lamination. This indicated they were human habitations – the exterior made to protect those within from solar radiation. Many more structures were machines, which were active, since they distorted EMR around them, and studying them was as difficult as looking through a faulty fractured lens. A survey of cosmic radiation indicated low density throughout the orb of the moon, and he reckoned on a large portion of it being filled with tunnels and other subsurface spaces. The mutter over radio bands he'd detected earlier was more intense, and he began recording this, then running it through his systems for a translation of something akin to computer code. Still, he could see nothing to show that human life actually existed there. And, as always, to obtain more data he needed more power, and for that he needed his biotech here to be stronger.

Having surveyed the area, he ordered the larger clump of biotech to detach itself physically from the rest of the growing mass and get into motion. The thing moved slowly, like the slug it resembled. He focused next on the target. The biotech was gathering plenty of materials, but a much richer source lay some sixteen kilometres away. Stuck to the hard rock over there was a limpet. Or the thing, which stood three metres tall, at least had that mollusc in its ancestry. Having glimpsed into it before, and ascertaining it to be laden with rare earths and organics, he now focused on it more closely.

The rare earths were inlaid in its pyramid shell, which, by slow degrees, the thing flaked off in pieces packed with distinct elements. The organics were mollusc, but highly altered to enable its growth to such a size, to withstand its environment and to feed off the meagre plant life. All while extracting those rare elements from deep within the rock, using tendrils that resembled the mycelia of his own biotech. Its metabolism was incredibly slow, and further analysis revealed the thing to be over a thousand years old. He also saw that it was in motion – steadily progressing across the surface at a pace that made his slug form look rocket propelled. It was a biotech mining machine, surviving from some previous age, and probably put here by whatever occupied, or had occupied, the much-enlarged moon. It could feed his biotech, and perhaps he'd be able to learn something about those who'd made it.

His slug form slowly drew closer and, after eight kilometres, began to encounter pieces of shell that the mining mollusc had shed. It snatched these up, digested them, and distributed materials. It then passed back an instruction to the main mass of biotech produced by the seed, which extended out a feeler towards remaining processed lumps of material the mollusc had dropped behind it, like gleaming round turds.

Eventually the slug form reached the mining mollusc and partially engulfed it. It then began splintering up shell to process further, until the Fenris sent a correction and it just discarded the shell, ripping a hole into the interior instead. Water vapour rose as it broke through an internal membrane, and the slug form flowed over that to contain the precious moisture. It reached in with two of its tentacles and began pulling out and hoovering up the soft matter within, though 'soft' was a relative term, as the thing's flesh and organs were as tough as old wood. Another growth spurt ensued for his biotech, and the slug speared out a feeler back towards one approaching from the main mass. As the two connected up, they fattened, and the slug began transferring useful material back through it. Everything was going as the Fenris wanted, and he lost himself in the detail of acquisition and growth. But then, as if to remind him of his purpose here, the man arrived.

The Fenris felt the dislocation, signalling the materialization of another jaunter. The man arrived naked, as they all did, staggering from a drift of gravel right in the middle of the main biotech mass. His foot hooked up a braid of mycelia and he fell hard, smacking his head against the rock. Now linked through the biotech, the Fenris had much easier penetration here than he'd had with any of the others and sent a pulse straight into the man's growing internal network. Meanwhile, comparing his DNA to the massive database of the same, he recognized the man to be Pranjab Hussain.

'Use this, here, take yourself from this place,' he said, but then realized he was speaking to a mind unable to respond. For Pranjab had knocked himself unconscious.

The sheer universal bastardy of the situation brought a sudden surge of anger. He had put the biotech here to gather information, and to have a vehicle through which to help people just like this. Now the man had tripped over the stuff and knocked himself out. He was going to die.

The Fenris checked his record on the man at high speed, in an eye-blink. In the Mumbai Sprawl, Pranjab had been treated with a respect for his evident mutation that was lacking in other cultures. They'd seen him as something more than human, not a distortion of humanity, and in that they'd been correct. He'd grown to adulthood hungry for education, which was cultural too, and had become a doctor in the sprawl, doing what he could for his ZA fellows. Now linking to his biotech revealed that the additions to raise him to jaunter status had come in through his gut, so he must have somehow swallowed an inocular fly. He would be a useful addition as, with his biotech activated, his intelligence had skyrocketed, mostly keying off his chosen profession.

The Fenris's anger grew. He couldn't allow this, for he had seen too many die. With the man unconscious, the mental shunt he would normally have used wouldn't work, as that went in through the consciousness, so a more direct approach would be required. He seized full control of all the surrounding biotech, opening the bandwidth. This resulted in all his other connections, to other worlds and people, closing down due to the energy draw required. He snapped mycelia threads and guided their raw ends towards the man's head, towards the bleeding wound there, as he gasped for breath, not knowing he was dying. The threads went in, through the wound, and through his skull, then began nesting around his brain. Through these, the Fenris fed in oxygen to the man, while tweaking neurons and synaptic junctions in his brain – seeking out the biological safety system that had rendered him unconscious. Thirty seconds later, Pranjab rolled over and sat upright, gasping, eyes watering, blood still flowing from the wound.

'Go here,' the Fenris instructed, forcing data into the man's internal network. He then hesitated over doing something else, since it would be an infringement on the man's right to choose. But he did it anyway. Since he had such deep access to Pranjab's biotech, he made a tweak that would, he hoped, and for a while, limit the man's jaunt to the next destination only. He'd done the same with Irene, to keep her safe. After he did it with Pranjab, the Fenris felt as ashamed this time as he had before. How easy it was to limit the freedoms of others 'for their own good'.

Pranjab abruptly jerked to his feet and groped ahead of him

for something the Fenris couldn't see. Then he seemed to slide into a pocket in the universe, disappearing. The Fenris snapped away from the biotech, diverting energy into other feeds again, and watched as Pranjab bounced through the twists and nooks of the multiverse and then fell out on the soft ground of a river valley. He looked around, bewildered, and the Fenris spoke to him for a while, calming him and apprising him of his reality. When it seemed he'd finally got it, the Fenris sighed out a breath and diverted his now meagre energy again, returning his full attention to that airless world.

He was satisfied with the way things had played out. His biotech had established well, and he had saved a life. Now, with his perception ranging wide on that airless place, he understood his guess about the mining mollusc had been correct. It seemed likely it had broadcast its situation, for he'd seen the flash on the surface of the moon. And now he watched a ship departing the surface there, to head this way.

Irene – Past

Irene looked up at the man looming above her, then a second later reassessed her first impression and wondered if this was a man at all. He stood upright like a man, and seemed to be wearing metallic clothing that reminded her of the mesh some people had worn to protect themselves from sharks before they became extinct. Containers were attached to various straps crossing his body. His torso was cylindrical, and what she could see of that, under the odd iridescent sheen of the fabric, looked both heavily muscled and as if plates had been inserted underneath the skin. And that skin was the colour of a drowned man. His hands were big and clawed, and when he flexed one it looked symmetrical, with three fingers and two opposing thumbs. But it was the top of him that seemed to have discarded any last vestige of humanity. On a long muscular neck sat a head that resembled a large pair of binoculars. Two dark eyes observed her and blinked, then cowlike ears flicked out at the side and shifted like radar dishes.

'Hello,' she said, pushing herself up into a squat.

Now she saw something else: this man-thing had been through the wars. Parts of his clothing and equipment looked charred, as did some areas of his skin. Dried blood had soaked his right forearm, where split skin revealed one of those underlying plates. It resembled bone. Blood had also run from one of his ears. He emitted a strange gobbling sound, and made a grasping motion at her with one hand. She then saw the 'V' shape of his mouth below that binocular head, and the array of sharp glassy teeth. She backed up, coming to her feet still holding the bird she'd just caught. Did he want her catch? He struggled to reach back with his damaged arm, grabbing something on his back and pulling it over his shoulder. Irene recognized the butt of a weapon, so turned and ran.

The creature made that gobbling sound behind her again. Glancing back, she saw him coming after her, still struggling with the weapon. His loping run was imbalanced, for there seemed to be something wrong with one foot, but still he was fast. He finally got his weapon free. She dodged for a tree as the weapon made a slapping thwack like none she'd heard before. Something whipped past her and hit the ground far ahead. It looked like a long grey fibrous rope, which swiftly balled up, drawing in a great clump of leaf litter. She ran on, trying to keep trees between her and her pursuer, it being evident the weapon was firing some kind of lariat for capture.

'Left turn! Turn left!'

For a moment she thought the Fenris had returned to her mind, but this voice had a different quality, as if its owner was struggling with the words. She then realized that, though she had a sense of the voice in her inner space, as with the Fenris, it had also been a distant shout. She turned left, heading back in towards where the trees grew even thicker, not sure this was such a good idea. She didn't think she'd be any more nimble between them than the creature behind.

With another gobbling sound, her pursuer fired again. This time the fibrous rope hit a sapling and crushed up its branches. The thing looked horribly alive. She dodged into the trees, leaping masses of bramble.

'More left!' the voice shouted, closer now.

She realized she felt this voice in her mind, and sensed the meaning conveyed, rather than the words – that came with the shout. She also sensed the position of someone moving fast towards her. She veered towards the approaching figure, sure he must be somewhere near where she'd first arrived in this place . . . on this world. She also surmised that English wasn't his main language, else he would have said, 'Bear left'. Glancing back, she saw her pursuer enter the trees, surging towards her. Then, ridiculously, his feet were caught in the brambles she'd just leapt over, and he sprawled. She concentrated ahead, jumped a log, veered off the course she'd chosen, and weaved her way between more of the thorny growths. Another look back showed the man-thing struggling to his feet, tearing away brambles. He then began hunting for the weapon he had obviously dropped.

She jumped another fallen tree and saw a long, potentially lethal stretch of open ground ahead of her, covered only with leaves. Why was this thing pursuing her? Perhaps it was all about the bird she'd caught? She brought it up to her chest and raked her claw fingernails across it, then shoved in deeper and raked again. Blood spattered her front and its smell issued a thousand geometric shapes in her skull. She looked back, seeing her pursuer coming on once more, and held up the bird, then tossed it behind, quickly changing course as another of those lariats sped towards her. The thing clipped her arm, abrading it and leaving a sticky smear, at once reminding her of the tentacles of a shepherd. Back on track towards that other figure she'd sensed, she swung around a tree, seeing her pursuer just run past the bird and keep coming. She hit a slope, feeling close to exhaustion and knowing he would be on her in a moment. As if the proximity to where she'd arrived reminded her, she pushed at the world around her and it did, thankfully, grow thin. But then it was as if the walls of reality had gained elasticity. She could push at them but not through them, and it seemed they folded around her, offering no route past.

'Fuck,' she said.

She ran down the slope, bouncing off trees and her injuries protesting. Blood was running down her arm and her thigh where those wounds had reopened. As the initial surge of adrenalin faded, it brought home that she was probably in worse condition than her pursuer. It now seemed, however, that in having pushed at reality, she'd opened up another sense of her surroundings. She could see the man-thing bearing down on her, but without needing her eyes. She dodged, just taking her away from a black line writhing through the air, then with that other sense, saw him toss the weapon aside. Slinging out projectiles so large and cumbersome, it would only have had a few shots. Ahead the stream came into view, but what use was it to her? Running into it would only slow her, and her pursuer would catch her in the water. She dodged right at the sight of those low, flat leaves, realizing he would have her long before she reached the stream if she ran into the mud there. A surge of hopelessness overcame her as he drew even closer, nearly upon her, and with that came a change in the set paradigm of her mind. By running, she'd designated herself prey and this weird-looking human, if that's what he was, the hunter. But now he no longer had his weapon . . . She caught hold of a nearby tree to spin herself on a different course. Even as she released her hold, one of his big hands swiped at her, curved nails cutting slices through the bark. Slightly upslope stood a larger, wider tree, with dead wood scattered all around it.

Irene reached the bigger tree, anger rising now. She ran around it, and her pursuer skidded on past, kicking up leaves. This gave her time to snatch up a branch as thick as her arm, winnowed of bark and solid looking. She turned and faced the man-thing as he came back towards her, and she swung with all her strength at his head. The branch hit home, hard, smacking his head aside. Eyes clenched shut, he skidded with one foot, going forwards and down into a partial fall. In that position, he slowly raised his head again, blinking, as Irene stared at the short, broken-off length of branch she still held. The man-thing rose, hands clenching and unclenching, spat blood out of his mouth, then reached down to unclip a cylindrical object from one strap of his garment. Irene threw the piece of wood at him and ran again, around the tree, looking up for handholds, thinking madly about maybe leaping on his back and biting his neck. Or perhaps her fingernail claws were hard and sharp enough to rip into his flesh.

'Drop and roll. Now!' the voice shouted, loud and close.

Time seemed to slow as her thinking accelerated. She glimpsed the figure coming through the trees, but also felt him there, as a presence in her mind. She knew her chances of winning against this weird pursuer were doubtful – especially as he now seemed to have another weapon to hand. She also began to understand, though, that with the changes her body and mind were under-going, perhaps she *did* stand a chance. But someone was here, helping her, and had now given her this instruction. If that someone meant her ill, dropping to the ground would make her easy prey. However, if they did, all they needed to do was stand back and watch. She dropped and rolled.

A vicious snapping crackle broke the air and, on top of that, the thwacking of fleshy impacts. These she recognized from when she'd caught those bullets in her back. She rolled again, seeing the man-thing staggering with chunks of his garment, and of him, flying from his torso. He turned, raising that cylinder. Another vicious crackling ensued, and his head came up as bullets ripped into his neck. He staggered and turned, pointing the cylinder waveringly at her. The object made an odd crackling sound, and an electric discharge shorted up his own arm as a third fusillade hit him in the back. She scrambled up and jumped back in towards the tree, as he crashed down into the leaves, jerking and shivering, blood spurting rhythmically from his neck. As he finally died, she saw the shots had ripped up and shattered those bone plates under his skin. She then switched her attention to the man approaching.

'I am Chenghu,' he said, fixing the weapon he'd used to a pad on the front of his armoured suit, and taking off his helmet.

Irene sat with her back against the tree, her knees up to her chest, and just studied the man. He was tall and muscular, and his general appearance, name and handle on English indicated he was Asiatic. But she recognized the same lengthened features as her own, as her great-uncle Zak and as the Fenris. His eyes were pink, she noticed, taking on a pronounced slant, while his ears had points. He was definitely one of her kind.

'What the fuck *was* that?' she finally asked, pointing shakily to where he'd dragged and dumped the corpse.

'Don't know,' he said.

'It had weapons, tools . . .' she said, not sure where to take this.

He gazed over at the corpse, then he pointed off to his left. 'More . . . there.' He turned and grimaced at her, obviously having trouble finding the words. 'Fight maybe. Explosion maybe. Burned and broken.'

'Maybe warring tribes,' she suggested, though she wasn't sure why she chose the word 'tribes'.

He nodded. 'Maybe.' And just looked at her.

'What now?' she asked, now very aware of her nakedness.

'Your wounds,' he said, dropping his gaze and taking off a pack, then squatting before her to open it.

She recognized the riot gear he wore. It was just like that of Inspectorate cops, though not the black they favoured, but khaki instead. Before, her understanding and perception of these things had always been vague, now her mind remained sharp. She put together fleeting memories of screentime, and glimpses of things that'd been of no interest to her in those years. She noted the pictographic writing on his sleeve, on the side of his pack and on the side of his helmet.

'You're Chinese military,' she said.

'Good you quick,' he said, taking various items out of his pack. 'Arm.'

She held out her arm. Sore splits had opened along it and around her hand. She reached across and pulled out some loose staples, as he uncapped a spray bottle. He batted her hand away and sprayed the arm with synthetic skin. It stung at first, but then the analgesic kicked in. He peered down next at the split in her leg, still leaking blood and filthy with soil and leaf mould. She half expected him to clean it for her and then spray it, though such kindnesses had always been a rarity in her life. Instead he shook his head and pointed.

'Stream. Go wash. Come back here.'

Irene stared at him, wanting to rebel, wanting to swear at him, but her logic wouldn't allow that. This man had saved her life and obviously knew a lot more about her situation than she did. She stood up, gave him a nod of acknowledgement and headed off, really feeling her aches, pains and injuries now the adrenalin was all but gone. When she came to the stream, she rinsed the filth out of her wound. Then, in a fit of obduracy, she used balled-up green leaves, plucked from the bank, to clean it out properly, as well as scrub her body all over. When she climbed out again shivering, she bunched up some of those flat leaves against her leg, pressing to quell the bleeding, and limped back towards him. As she did this, she probed around her back, finding the bullet holes there and her fingers coming away bloody.

Chenghu had piled up dead wood by the time she returned, and had somehow found and retrieved the bird she'd killed. His pack and weapon were against the tree, and he'd stripped off his jacket too to reveal a white T-shirt stretched taut over a muscular chest and arms. Looking at him further raised her awareness of her nakedness – she needed to find some clothes, sharpish. He glanced at her and pointed to where she'd been sitting before. She went over and lowered herself down beside his pack. He came over and took out some more items, frowned at them for a moment and shrugged. The disinfectant stung enough to make her yell. The spray he used next dulled the pain but didn't completely block it out as he poured wound glue into the bleeding split in her thigh, then pinched it shut using both hands. After gazing at a watch for a while, he took his hands away and the wound remained closed.

'There.' He pointed ahead of her at the ground, and made a gesture turning over his hand, palm to the ground. She understood and crawled out to lie face down. Peering back at him, she saw him take a pair of long-nosed pliers out of his pack. The pain that came next had her burying her face in the leaf matter to stifle her screams. After the rooting around in her back wounds, disinfectant and skin spray were applied. When he was done with that, he turned her over gently and held out his bloody palm, showing her the bullets before he tossed them away. Next he took out a roll of thin film bandage, bound up her leg, and indicated that she should sit up and put bindings around her waist to cover her lower back too. He finally grunted satisfaction, put all the medical stuff away and took out a packet, which he tossed in her lap.

'We need to talk,' she said.

'We will talk,' he replied. 'Still remembering English.' He pointed at his skull.

She shrugged, her busy mind going to work. Meanwhile he lit the pile of dry wood with a block of something that burned hot and bright, once he set it going. She knew he was like her. And, like her, he was probably remembering so much that he'd thought was irrelevant, and discarded. Childhood language lessons, words and phrases picked up from screens, and even labels on food or other items. But she also felt it extended beyond that, because of the odd sense of connection she felt with him. She knew he'd known about her wounds through that sense. It seemed almost like telepathy, but wasn't that. She felt sure that her own understanding of English was somehow bleeding over to him, facilitating his 'remembering' of it.

She opened the packet to find combat trousers and a jacket, underwear, socks and folded-down, tough monomesh footwear. She dressed gratefully as he cut lengths of wood, sharpened them with a heavy sheath knife and laid them down beside the fire. His occasional glances at her didn't escape her notice. He then sat with his back against the tree and began plucking the bird. Now dressed, Irene stepped over and sat down beside him. He glanced at her again.

'I was bitten by a fly,' he said, and then told his story, choosing his words carefully, and his vocabulary growing noticeably as he spoke.

He was Chinese military and he'd undergone the same changes as her. The Fenris had contacted him in the same way it had her, and guided him through the initial stages of how to jaunt from world to world. He'd learned how to extend his powers to items around him too. And, because it was comfortable, he'd returned to their home for the supplies he needed, including what he wore and carried in his pack. Apparently he'd been travelling from world to world for some time.

'It dangerous there now,' he told her, almost viciously pulling the guts out of the bird as he said it.

'Surely it's always been that way,' she opined.

'I mean . . . they know about us kind. They can detect. AIs are alert for us.' He stood up and spitted the bird on one of the sharpened sticks. Then, jabbing the other two into the ground either side of the fire, he set up the spit over the flames.

'Us,' she said. 'And what exactly are we?'

'Don't know more than you,' said Chenghu, sitting back down beside her again. 'Fenris cannot talk much. Energy problems.'

'But it must have spoken to you again to send you here?'

'Have a place,' he said. 'Safe place. Keep things there. It speaks to me there sometimes.'

The most recent time the Fenris had contacted him had been in his 'safe place' and it had sent him a map, though she couldn't quite understand what he meant by that.

'I think you still know more than me. So tell me,' she said, and found herself pushing him on another level.

He looked uncomfortable, but he spoke anyway. 'Is a far-advanced human, I think. It cannot reach the worlds we can. Energy. It can only send and gather information and some small things. It sent the biotech to us in viruses, then in flies eventually. We have it inside us. We are becoming fenris.'

This was the longest statement he'd made without interruption, and she noted the exactitude of his words, and the speed of his grasp of the language. Analytically, she noticed how he was picking up the words she used and using them himself. Checking her own memory, she thought about Mandarin Chinese, and words in that language instantly started coming into her grasp. Some were without context in memory, and she felt sure they were bleeding over from him.

'How many of us are there?' she asked.

'I'm not sure. Just you and me at the moment, that I know of.'

'We have power,' she said, now distracted by the smell of roasting meat. 'We can do things. We could do something about the Committee, about our home.'

'I don't think the Fenris wants us to,' said Chenghu. 'Committee Earth is unstable and any . . .' He frowned deeply, searching for the word, then continued, 'Any intervention make can cause more bad than good.'

She turned to him. 'Why should we do what it wants us to? Must we bow to this creature because, for reasons that still remain unclear, it has inserted its biotechnology or biology into us? We lived under totalitarian rule at home, do we have to obey another now we've escaped from there?'

He nodded. 'You make a valid point.'

She studied him, sensing a weakness there, or perhaps simply that he'd not thought beyond survival and understanding his powers. She felt abruptly superior and began to think angrily on the things she must do. She'd been a pawn, living in misery and filth, experimented on and tortured, and ultimately disposable to those who'd had power over her. Just as she'd decided in that vivisection room, she would never let herself be so vulnerable again. She'd learn everything she could from those who had knowledge she didn't, and she would seize a position of control. And then she would deal with those who had hurt her . . . Garrick's face came to her mind, sparking an even stronger stab of anger. That man could not be allowed to get away with what he did.

Chenghu stood up, took a kettle out of his pack and headed off. Irene heaved herself to her feet as he went and walked over to the fire. The smell of roasting meat had become almost unbearable now and, though pin feathers had burned away from the bird, it was hardly cooked. It didn't matter – even the thought of uncooked meat had her salivating. It passed briefly through her mind that she should wait, because he'd put this here to cook, then she grabbed the spit angrily. She didn't need his approval. She had after all caught the thing herself.

The bird fell off the spit, bounced off the burning wood and into the leaf litter. She used handfuls of leaves to pick it up and tested it against her mouth. Despite the heat, she couldn't stop herself biting. It burned her lips, but she sank her teeth in and worried at the tough sinewy flesh, blood and other fluids running down her chin. Tearing out a lump, she hardly chewed it before swallowing. She bit again and again, and every lump felt wonderful as it went down easily.

'Our bodies know our needs more than they did before,' said Chenghu as he returned. He squatted by the fire, placing the kettle on the coals. 'It's the biotech. I found myself . . . hungry for rust on the bodywork of a car one time.'

She nodded, but was too intent on eating to talk. Already she'd made a substantial hole in the raw breast meat. She consumed a leg next, and then, after a hesitation, even crunched down exposed bone. Chenghu put out a couple of cups and a box of tea bags. That he had two cups raised a wave of shame in her. If she was to achieve the things she wanted to, a little thought for others would be required – she needed not to be a bitch. She abruptly stopped eating, stabbed the bird back onto the spit, over the fire again, and sat back. Her insides gurgled and seemed to be writhing, but the rest of her body was fizzing, as if the nutrients were already arriving there, while her wounds throbbed and itched.

'You have much you can teach me,' she said.

'Difficult . . . difficult to teach what outside of . . . conventional senses. You will learn.'

'I need to know how to travel between worlds.'

'You did.'

'By chance, accident . . . I need to know how to do it consciously. To control it.'

'You will learn,' he repeated.

'How do I contact the Fenris?'

'You cannot. He contacts us when wants . . . has power. Not very often. But I think that will change.'

'What do you mean?'

He reached out to snare his pack and pulled something out, holding it on the palm of his hand. The flat white ellipsoid had metallic orange frills around its edges and veins of a similar hue across its surface. It vaguely reminded Irene of the clams she'd eaten, or some other shellfish sans its shell.

'What's that?'

'A seed the Fenris sent to me . . . It is a biotech . . . and can become a transporter cage . . . for helping me move large items from world to world. It told me also it will be able to send me . . . us . . . larger items of biotech.'

214

'And?'

'I think about that,' said Chenghu, frowning at her.

It took her a moment, so loud was the function of her body with her gut full of meat, but she began to see the implications. For whatever reasons, the Fenris couldn't travel the worlds as they could. It had first sent viruses to implant its biotech in them, and then flies. And more recently, it had sent Chenghu this item. Was its ability to send things increasing?

'Larger items of biotech,' she said. 'So at some point, maybe the Fenris himself will come?'

Chenghu nodded.

Chenghu – Past

'I have a map in my mind,' Chenghu told her at one point during their travels, visualizing the thing, but getting a slight stab of a headache when he tried to see it in a way that related to the reality he knew. 'But it's not something I can describe to you.' He paused and looked around. He felt proud of himself – feeling sure his English had been nigh perfect. He remembered every unfamiliar word she used and, it seemed, the weird connection between them provided context for those words. She'd also spoken a few words of Mandarin, to demonstrate her depth of memory during one discussion. It sort of bothered him that she hadn't continued with that but, for reasons he cynically under-stood, he didn't want to press her.

The jaunts they made together from world to world, with the necessary rests between, had been illuminating too. On the first occasion, his grip on her had been firm. But even then he'd felt her adapting and somehow assisting. She healed quickly, strip-ping off bandages after the second jaunt to expose crusted, solidly scabbed wounds. Those went away quickly too as they returned to his base, rested there for some weeks, and then travelled on so he could show her the worlds he had seen. She healed mentally too, growing stronger all the while and a lot more assertive.

This time there'd been no gulf to cross, but a transition from one reality to another, as if they blurred into each other. But what a transition it had been. The next world had a green sky and purple vegetation. Distantly, a city stood on a plain, with roads and fields all around it and airplane contrails cutting up the sky. The city reminded him of Beijing as it had been once, before it swelled into the massive coastal sprawl it was now and acquired new levels. And certainly, after that, there hadn't been so many planes in the sky. The variety of the worlds he'd seen still amazed and awed him, and he wondered if he would ever grow tired of it. Thoughts of returning to his home world now seemed irrelevant, and he hoped to impart a similar view to Irene. This hadn't seemed to be the case thus far. But if she decided to go he would not be able to stop her now. He hoped she wouldn't do that, since the Fenris seemed to want all of their kind to stay together. And for Chenghu, that creature was the only point of stability in all this, albeit a risky one.

As was usual after a jaunt, Chenghu felt the sick hunger and depressive malaise that used to come over him while in military training. It was getting better, but still he knew the time had come to take a break.

'Why does it do this to us?' she asked as she mopped up the blood leaking from her ear. She had asked many questions in their time together and he felt sure he had answered this one before.

He shrugged, rubbed at his aching forehead, then dabbed at the blood in one nostril.

'The biotech,' was all he said, since something of their previous conversations about fenris came back to him. Many had jaunted and not survived. The biotech didn't mesh well with all humans. There was a mismatch, and it didn't always function correctly – probably because they weren't fenris. But still he felt some confusion about that, because the biotech was also making them fenris. He hadn't had a cogent answer for her before and did not have one now.

Here, in the place they'd landed, the sky was a more conventional colour, as the sun set and the day darkened into twilight. Again they'd arrived in wild land, because he'd pushed for that, though it seemed a damned sight easier on worlds away from Committee Earth, for obvious reasons. Coming out of the transition, they dropped a few feet to churned-up ground, just out from a forest of trees. These weren't quite pines. The needles were as long as porcupine quills, and the cones looked like suspended beehives. Rolling hills ran away from them, with wooden fences and stretches of stone wall dividing them up into fields. Nearby, creatures like goats but with three horns bleated and made popping sounds, before running away as one down the slope. Chenghu considered their meat, then dismissed the idea – he still had a good load of meat in his pack from a deer-like creature he'd brought down on another world.

'You are tired,' said Irene.

He nodded agreement and quashed the urge to point out that she was stating the obvious or noting that she was tired too. They were tired after every jaunt.

'Then we'll rest here and perhaps continue in the morning,' she said.

Chenghu turned away, slightly annoyed at her attitude, for she somehow seemed to be taking ownership of their travels. He led the way alongside the trees and down a slope, the geometry of this place firmly in his mind. Irene moved ahead to climb over one of the fences, demonstrating that she knew where they were going. They finally reached a stream filled with cress. Chenghu turned in under the pines and found a clear area, scattered with dead wood.

'This should do,' said Irene.

She moved over to help him as he struggled to take off his pack, and with that his further stab of annoyance dissolved. Yes, he was tired after each jaunt, and the weariness had built up cumulatively in other ways too. In reality, he was weary of thinking about how his life had changed, and what it all meant. It helped to have someone to share all this with, and it was comfortable and easy to let her take control for a little while.

They gathered up wood for a fire. Chenghu put on the pot to boil for tea, while Irene took his knife and sharpened some sticks to spear a chunk of *maybe* deer over the flames. It was already partially cooked, but he supposed giving it another sizzle would make it more appetizing. He took out two thin blankets and handed one to her. They weren't necessary, since it was warm here. The riot suits they both now wore, which he had obtained and kept at his base, were well insulated anyway.

'I need to wash,' she said, peering down at the stream.

Without further ado she began stripping off her clothing. Chenghu watched her for a moment then realized what he was doing and turned away, just as she glanced round at him. He caught a knowing smile from her and didn't like what that meant. The tension had been there between them for a while now, with her teasing and him fighting not to respond, knowing what she'd been through.

'Don't worry,' she said. 'You've seen me naked.'

He had indeed, a couple of times now as they had travelled and it'd been somewhat painful to him. Even back on Earth, before he left, it had been months since he'd paid for a ZA prostitute, for he'd feared the changes he'd undergone might be reported, while those changes if anything had made his sex drive stronger. Also, though the naked Irene had revealed changes, she remained very definitely female. He didn't know what she'd looked like before, but now she had the build of an SA clothing model.

'I won't be long – I don't suppose the water is that warm,' she said.

He looked back as she walked down to the stream, hips very definitely swaying. She glanced back at him once more, her look unreadable, and he stubbornly kept his eyes on her. Reaching the water, she bent over to test it with her hand. It was so utterly obvious but still it had the required effect. Chenghu snorted and checked the kettle. It wasn't boiling yet. He prodded at the meat, noting she hadn't done a very good job of setting it up over the fire, so corrected that.

Finally she returned, shivering, and sat down beside him, pulling her blanket around her, but not enough to conceal very much. Chenghu deliberately studied her.

'You're completely healed now and can handle jaunting nearly as well as me,' he said.

She responded by pulling the blanket back from her thigh, and ran a finger along the dark red line of scar tissue. He distracted himself by thinking about the injury when he'd first seen it. He'd seen many injured people during his service and knew the difference. Those he'd seen did not have blood as dark as hers, and perhaps his own, while the scar tissue, which took ten times longer to form, was not so dark either.

'It seems fenris biotech is very good,' he said, because he could think of nothing else.

'We have to return to Earth,' she said – a conversation they'd had before.

He waved a stick at their surroundings. 'Why?'

'We have this technology inside us. It has given us fantastic powers. Do we just excuse ourselves from responsibility for what happens on our home world? What else do we do? Just exist? We need a purpose.'

'Perhaps we should wait and see what the Fenris has in mind?' he said, as he prepared some tea, then handed her a cup.

As she took it the blanket slipped from her shoulder, exposing one breast. She seemed oblivious to that, but he knew she wasn't.

'That creature has helped us, but who's to know what it really wants? We need to do what we can. We need to make decisions for ourselves.'

Chenghu nodded, not so much because he agreed but because he really didn't want this discussion. It seemed to him that she'd like to be the one making the decisions.

'Or are you reluctant for another reason?'

'Like what?'

'Well, you were no ZA. You were part of the oppression back there.'

He reached out and pulled the meat from the fire. It was sizzling and would keep. He gulped his tea and put the cup aside.

'Look, Irene, I'm too tired for this now.'

She watched him for a long moment without speaking, then said, 'Then lie back and relax.' She moved towards him and he knew what was coming.

She had told him of Garrick's abuse, and how she'd then submitted to the man. He was saddened that all she seemed to have taken from her experience was that sex could be used as a tool of manipulation – a power play. And yet, that seemed less important to him than what he wanted now. Almost without conscious volition, he lay back and sighed out a tight breath.

She moved quickly astride him and opened his belt and then his trousers, pulling them down enough to free his penis. She grabbed it then leaned forward to kiss him on the mouth. She tasted slightly foul and then good, but with something that seemed alien to him.

'Relax, let go,' she said, leaning back again.

As she inserted him inside her, he did relax and let go. It seemed pointless and ephemeral to disagree with her and she did have some valid points. The future right then did not matter to him, for all that seemed important was the slow gyration of her hips.

9

The Fenris

The ship coming from the moon was a confirmation. It looked like an irregular chunk of slate as it sped closer, but it very much resembled the one that had come through the incursion before, into the space around his own world. Lines of light brightened between its layers, as a drive, definitely not a simple reaction drive, slowed it towards the airless Earth's atmosphere. It then settled into a descent like a falling leaf. This indicated gravity technology, and perhaps inertial dampers, which bespoke sufficient advancement to be of concern. Even more concerning was how much of an upgrade the ship had had from that previous one. It then slid sideways, through low atmosphere, to come in over the location of the miner mollusc, before shifting through the sky over the main spread of fenris biotech. It finally descended and landed off to one side of it.

He focused scanning on the ship, making confirmations and feeling a surge of an old biology adrenal response. He remembered his fear when the incursions had first come, tried to deny it now with anger, then segued into intellectualism. The technology evident here, in this vessel, threw what he'd observed on

222

the surface of the moon into a different light. He turned half of the now increased biotech scanning in that direction again. With new interpretation of their design, the sensors and telescopes seemed likely to be able to view the entire electromagnetic spectrum. But he now surmised that other visible machines, by their shape and their emissions, could be precursors of what resided in the engine around him, while still others remained opaque. It suddenly became obvious that whatever lay on, and inside, the moon, which had been capable of creating the incursions to his world, must also have created the tangled disruption, this dark manifold between the airless Earth and other worlds – the trap that dragged his jaunters here. Anger rumbled back. He had an enemy.

Now the Fenris hurriedly switched over computing in his engines, and down on his world, to sort data already collected, and still being collected. His initially long, slow view of how events might go had been shattered by the catastrophe of the jaunters, his world walkers, dying in their hundreds. But that had also distracted him too much from investigating the mystery incursions. He needed to know things now! His biotechnology crunched data and made comparisons with the same competence as those AIs on the nodal Earth that had discovered the fly connection, but on a much larger and more intricate scale. This crunching was part of him, because of course the biotech was too, and its results rose up as his own thoughts and acquisition of knowledge. The minerals on the moon's surface showed that asteroids had been brought in to add to its material. But these were not the reason it loomed so large in the sky. He and his system theorized that the civilization settled in the moon had expanded the thing itself, like open cell foam.

Data and extrapolation steadily accrued, and he made further connections as results hit the upslope of an exponential curve. He, the Fenris entire, began building a model of the moon, from cosmic and other highly penetrating radiations. He observed cysts and tunnels running down hundreds of kilometres, resembling the structure of an ant's nest. And, in the process, the signatures for organic life came in. If there were humans there, they could number in the billions. Confirmations now appeared hard and fast – each a shock to his organics, as the system filled in detail like a subfunction of his mind. Light collectors on the surface of this moon ran sunlight into larger chambers for growing crops, while fusion power ran all the rest. Flow patterns indicated a static society, neither expanding nor contracting, and one in which everything was perfectly recycled. Meshing observation with electromagnetic communications showed that it consisted merely of information about the processes of existence. It was lacking in individuality and devoid of any forms of entertainment, news or distraction – human language fined down to something akin to computer code. However, the fact they had those outward-facing instruments on the surface indicated some direction or purpose to their society, as did the presence of the mining mollusc down on the planet, since that lay outside their cycle of existence.

He analysed their communications further, diving deeper, with translation building to a logical whole. The similarity of the underground structures to an ant's nest indicated this to be a society modelled on that of social insects. However, as far as he could see, there was no singular guiding intelligence, neither human nor AI. This didn't mean it was *not* controlled by AI, since AI itself could be a distributed hive form. But he decided to label them hive humans in the interim. And they repulsed him. The hive was, in fact, the epitome of what the fenris had escaped in their past. Such a society was also the destiny of Committee Earth, if humans couldn't find a way to change their course, or he couldn't change it for them.

He fought down his visceral revulsion of what he was finding here and tried to confine himself to intellectual analysis. Next, fining out hints of their external purpose, extrapolated from communications with that ship, he ascertained that this, and other technologies and actions at the interface between the hive and *everything else* in the multiverse, were all slanted towards threat response. The hive must continue to exist – the purpose of its existence *was* continuing to exist. And in that respect, threats from the surrounding universe, and multiverse, must be countered. Tracing one informational thread that related to something other than the landed ship, he obtained a location at a distant Lagrange. He directed sensors there, which found mothballed ships waiting out in space. These were tugs, with huge engines and other mechanisms for diverting any comets or asteroids that might come in from the Oort Cloud or the Asteroid Belt. He then ascertained that the mining mollusc on the airless Earth's surface was not the only one. Rare earths were being acquired to rebuild technologies that would better detect and counter other possible threats. He tried to track that 'rebuilding' and received the impression that the hive had been damaged and was slowly recouping losses. Wreckage on the surface of the moon confirmed that. But, since the cause of this lay in the past and the hive lived in the now, he could garner no more information on the matter.

Their telescopes were directed outwards, to watch for the remote possibility of interstellar travellers, and other instruments were for the detection of interdimensional ones. And the chatter was all about that now. Those instruments, much like the ones in the Fenris's engines, had been detecting a large anomaly down on the surface of this Earth, while the mollusc's alert had confirmed it.

And then there were the people, now having reached the Earth's surface and leaving their ship.

Gazing upon this strange diversion from humanity confirmed his contention that they were hive humans, and he scanned them from the biotech. The ship had opened along one of its layers, the top half rising up on rods to reveal hundreds of cell compartments inside. The humans packed in these cells oozed up and unfolded, triggered into action and purpose. They scuttled on all fours along the paths between the cells, to pour down the side of the ship and swarm onto the surface. There they moved sometimes on all fours, sometimes standing upright to look towards the Fenris's spreading biotech. They were small – not one of them much more than a metre tall – and their bodies were encrusted with odd-looking instruments, as well as what seemed likely to be weapons. Ascertaining that they had no difficulty moving in the gravity here, the Fenris realized they must have been specially bred for the purpose of coming here, and probably stored in their cells until that necessity arose.

Their legs and arms were the same length, both terminating in hands with three fingers and two thumbs. Their bodies were barrels laden with fat and, probing into them, the Fenris saw they had no digestive system, and only limited organ capacity elsewhere. They were for one use and once they'd burned off all their fat, they'd die. Their heads seemed just extensions of their necks, like simple pillars. They had eyes, and that was about it. Taking another look within them, he saw oxygen bottles attached to their fronts, running pipes to static gill-form lungs inside, while their brains were small, with an addition that was simply a bioradio. A networked subsidiary intelligence linked back, via their vessel, to the overall intelligence on the moon.

Seeing the hard tech melded with their bodies, without thought to how they could *live* with it, confirmed his assessment that they were simply disposable components. He observed where limbs had been lopped off here and there to incorporate it, internal organs displaced or removed, and open wounds that would never have a chance to heal. He tried very hard to stay rational, but his repulsion grew to utter detestation of a society that would evolve into this.

They moved out, into his biotech, and began unlimbering a variety of scientific devices – some actually holstered in their flesh – to inspect and sample it. He'd expected some kind of attack on it, but now divined a more intelligent and worrying reaction. Should he allow them to gather such information? *No!* The answer rose out of anger and aggression just as much as logic. Though he judged from what he'd seen of their technology that his biotech lay far in advance of their ability to reproduce it, he was also aware he might be prey to arrogance in that respect. He'd already seen on Committee Earth how his tech could be adapted to the purpose of lesser cultures. And, though he suspected this was all part of a threat assessment that would eventually lead to them trying to destroy his biotech, other possibilities existed too.

They'd detected him opening a rift into the parallels and come to inspect his world as a result. Seeing it unpopulated, they'd deemed it no threat. They'd then returned when his activity increased, and thrown a nuclear arsenal at it. When they had also detected travellers through the multiverse continuum – and this was speculation – they'd set their artefact to catch them here, and doubtless watched each of them die. Now, seeing an even greater incursion into their trap, they would surely move to negate the threat. Thus far, it seemed they'd opened routes between worlds, just as the fenris had in the past – transport systems – and this matched hive psychology. But they were at a disadvantage in that area still, and he couldn't allow them to get their hands on his technology and reverse engineer it. The very idea of these creatures easily slipping from world to world was anathema. He needed to do something!

As his visceral reaction ebbed, the urge to *do* fell into the light of all the things he *had* done. Doing something meant more interventions, and thus far those had been disastrous. Then again, wasn't he responding to a threat to himself and the world walkers he was trying to save? And there he stopped, running into a mental morass, with the morality of his acquired fenris knowledge conflicting with who he was right now. He had been premature in trying to change Committee Earth – that was the child in him. But the fact he'd wanted to had been a moral duty, arising out of that knowledge loaded to his mind. He'd moved into grey areas, driven by fear when he thought about soldiers and their implications of command, and the rule of the few. Now it wasn't just fear driving him into the grey, but loathing too. It hurt him to realize that the paradigm here, in this multiverse, had changed too much for the old fenris way to apply.

He *had* to do something.

The Fenris set a number of reactions in motion in his biotech. The first spread throughout it at the speed of photons, along connecting nanotubes. This instruction switched clumps of enzymes over to activation, should they become disconnected from the whole. The hive creatures already had some samples in the cellular packs they'd opened for that purpose, so he also translated the instruction into a radio burst. This triggered the enzymes in those samples already taken and began to dissolve them. Henceforth, any new samples they collected would dissolve too. But this wasn't enough.

The Fenris focused on those biotech threads injected deep into the ground to a layer of water, and had them thicken out, ceasing to transport water up but instead to draw biotech from the surface down. He knew there'd be a response to the stuff slowly disappearing and dissolving, however, so he needed to move faster than this. Scanning with terahertz waves, he mapped the ground below the spread of biotech, and beyond it. The perfect solution lay out below the slug form, and he speculated on some connection with the mining mollusc being at that location too. Tracking the thing's own threads down, he saw a concentration of rare earth elements around what appeared to be a version of the excavations in the moon.

This underground complex resembled the structure of an ant's nest even more, with its tubes and branches into individual cysts. There was heavily degraded technology down there too, and other items in its various cysts and chambers. But his scanning couldn't display all that clearly. The technology showed no sign of activity, however, while he also couldn't detect any physical movement down there. It seemed an old, long-abandoned place that slotted into the ancient history of those strange humans now ranging about the surface.

The Fenris sent down a braid of biotech mycelia, tracking along faults to the partially collapsed cave of an underground river, then from this along bored tubes to the nest itself. Running micro machine rings along this braid, he began to carve out wider access, following this up with a steady tubular expansion of the braids. Meanwhile the hive people on the surface had discovered what was happening to their samples and had frozen in place, doubtless receiving further instruction. The Fenris reacted by increasing the transfer of biotech from the surface to down below. Around the hive people, the tech visibly began to collapse, dissolving away. This state of affairs lasted for an hour, as the Fenris opened a tube to the nest and rapidly expanded it, while drawing down more and more biotech. The hive people finally set in motion again, heading for the slug form, which was now the largest clump of his tech left on the surface. He sent another instruction, strengthening the skin of the slug so it wouldn't collapse as he drew out biotech from inside it.

Within the underground nest, his mycelia spread, building up clumps of material, in which it connected up nodular sensors. The place was full of old technology, as well as the dried-out husks of a past iteration of the hive people. Nodules expanded into larger puffball growths, which then began to grow jointed tentacles and hands. Up above, the hive people reached the slug form and, using molecular sharp knives, started cutting away chunks and inserting them into their cellular packaging. Radio chatter increased and, analysing it, the Fenris saw they were gathering data even as the tech dissolved, transmitting it to their ship and thence to the moon.

Time to get proactive there too.

Penetrating the communication, he began sowing viruses, and other computer life, to eat up and destroy data. In moments it transmitted and, via feedback, he felt the link between the moon and the ship break. This lasted for a full minute, until a response came a few seconds later, with a complex signal down to the ship and to the people, before the link broke again. Discarding their tools, they turned as one towards their vessel and raised their hands to cover their faces – this was an automatic protocol and irrelevant in this case as the ship disappeared in an immense flash. The Fenris felt sensory data disappearing as the biotech on the surface died in the flash. The blast ball ate up a square kilometre of ground and a wave of heat rolled up, burning the surface, incinerating the hive people, the slug form and the miner mollusc. The neutron pulse, penetrating the ground, disrupted and killed biotech there too, curling it up like grass in a fire. Again it was clear the collective hive was all, and its individual humans disposable components. Seeing danger, it had sterilized the area.

The Fenris watched data acquisition on the surface diminish

and die, while his perception of it, and the moon, otherwise returned to what he could snare directly via his engines. At once he realized something had changed. Communications spill had tightened, moved to a higher frequency, and now consisted of complex packets he couldn't read. At the same time, instruments on the moon's surface were on the move, while his perception below that surface was diminishing, darkening, as if some large shadow were expanding out from the moon's core. Then, with a thump that felt physical, the moon slipped from his grasp. This had all happened very fast, and he'd been cut off with worrying efficiency. He now recognized precisely the same kind of shielding he used for his world, and this came as further confirmation of the fact the hive had sent those incursions before.

He withdrew and leaned back in the sensory throne he'd been occupying throughout this confrontation, angry and humiliated. He would, he decided, weigh his decisions with more intelligence in future, and then winced because he'd already made that assertion more than once. And anyway, he had a sense that here, just as on Committee Earth, he'd made mistakes he could neither correct nor recall. The hive was alert and active and, he had no doubt, would be quickly building a threat response. He grimaced at that, accepting the paradigm truly had changed. His long view was gone and the dry whispering voice of fenris morality seemed like the prating of some ancient religion. He had uncovered his enemy, and he too needed to respond to threat.

Ektian

Ektian saw at once that the two figures walking down the track were not sea people. They were too tall, and wore what looked like police gear of Committee Earth, along with its bulletproof

231

layers. They also carried weapons. She cast aside the half-disassembled remote control, from which the Fenris had spoken to her, and put her tools back into their roll. She'd come to understand quite a lot of its general function, but detail would require studying it under the scope in the blood-testing laboratory they had in the coastal town here. It was all purely her curiosity; the technology she really wanted to get her hands on was of a harder nature – preferably in shepherds, Committee systems and AIs. She was on a rock, outside the accommodation dome where the sea people had given her a room, and quickly jumped off it to go back inside. By the time she came outside again, carrying the repeating harpoon gun she'd persuaded them to give her, the two strangers had entered the village.

She didn't like this at all. The Fenris, in one of his infrequent communications via the biotech here, had told her two people of her kind would come to collect her. It had said no more than that, and she'd received no response to further queries she'd made over the last month. What the Fenris hadn't told her was that these two looked like Inspectorate thugs.

She stepped out and turned in towards the centre of the village. Darkle and Green – the two local cops – were already heading out to meet the incomers, with the usual crowd drifting there to see what was happening. Ektian caught the arm of one of those on the way over.

'Tell them I'm at the Shell,' she said in her best effort at their language, stabbing a finger to the place where she'd first eaten here, which was essentially the local pub.

'Okay, Ektian,' said the woman, her voice shrieking to an ultrasonic Ektian couldn't manage, making her wince.

Over at the bar, she chose a rock that put one of the table slabs between her and anyone approaching. She then rested the weapon next to it, out of sight. As the two drew closer, she studied the gear they were wearing. The guy looked dangerous and she wondered whether the best option would be to put a harpoon round in his face the moment he came close enough. The woman was taller than usual too, and seemed no pushover either. She then noticed the khaki colour of their gear and eased back on that idea. Their clothing was military, which was better than Inspectorate, though not exactly good.

The cops shouted at the milling crowd and waved people away. As was usual, some obeyed, while others moved in ahead, to grab seats so they could keep watching. As they drew even closer, the woman reached out and touched the man's shoulder, catching his attention, and they both halted. She said something and the man nodded, then she handed over her machine pistol. He remained where he was, as she moved ahead of him and strode into the seating area, eyes fixed on Ektian. She walked around the table slab and stood next to her, gaze falling to the weapon, then coming back up again. Ektian found herself drawing back a little under its intensity.

'The Fenris told me where to find you, and informed the people here I was coming. I'm Irene.' She held out a hand.

English, then.

Ektian shook it and felt a shock of connection. This expanded into a weird awareness of both Irene and her companion, and an odd feeling of subservience she didn't like. Irene turned away and went to sit down on a nearby rock. The guy remained where he was, inspecting those around him suspiciously, one hand on the weapon fixed to the front of his torso. Irene's one he held loosely at his side. Ektian was given the instant impression of a hierarchical relationship – he was the muscle and Irene the brains, and she liked that. What she didn't like was the growing feeling that she fitted into this hierarchy below Irene too.

'We've been travelling for a long time,' said Irene. 'We've seen so much.'

Ektian shrugged and felt slightly ashamed. She had the ability to jaunt but hadn't used it since her arrival here. It had been too comfortable and easy, with a lifestyle way above anything she had experienced before. Food was plentiful. They provided her with a place to live, with facilities akin to those of a high-ranking SA. She'd learned the language fast and found a source of revenue in being employed by their government, writing, sketching and recording her knowledge of the technology on her erstwhile home. Also, because of the Fenris's special interest in her, and their almost worshipful attitude towards that creature, they treated her with great respect.

'I've had no desire to travel,' Ektian felt the need to reply, her English halting at first and then somehow switching into place in her mind. This facility with languages, in fact with everything, sometimes frightened her. She'd never been this intelligent and capable before. And she realized her fear was that it might all go away again.

The fleeting expression on Irene's face made her feel uncomfortable with her choices.

'We have a place where we rest up and keep our stuff.' Irene gestured to what she wore. 'Chenghu knows the Chinese military and we've been grabbing all we need. Useful to go wherever we want.'

'I have all I need,' Ektian replied, gesturing around her and feeling guilty once more.

Irene nodded, as if she understood such choices of ease. 'Apparently the Fenris wants us all together now, and I see no reason that's a bad idea. We have a kind of mental map to guide us to another two of our kind, who've established a base on a world with a great deal of resources.'

'I know,' Ektian replied quickly. 'They're on a parallel of Committee Earth that's somehow broken away from the rest – it's sitting in a niche in the multiverse.'

'A parallel Earth depopulated by its Committee,' said Irene, watching her.

'Indeed,' said Ektian, feeling something about their strange connection driving her. She looked around at the bar, at the homes and at the people here. She felt as if, like some complex computer interface, she'd just unplugged from them.

'And something that could happen on our Earth,' Irene added.

'Should we care about that?' Ektian asked. The question until just a moment ago would have been a pertinent one, yet now it seemed somehow rhetorical. The injustice of the place in which she'd grown up came into sharp focus, and everything she'd done here seemed to be an ephemeral waiting game.

'Or maybe it might not happen,' Irene continued, 'if the national governments of our Earth no longer follow the diktats of the Committee.'

'And how might that be achieved?' Ektian asked.

Irene smiled.

Pranjab

Something about the curry had been decidedly odd, Pranjab felt, but then he was used to that, with the gifts of food he received for his work. The shepherd had made a real mess of the Patel boy's leg, its tentacles having been in shredding mode and cutting a deep slice down into the muscle. The boy had also bashed his head when the thing discarded him and continued on for larger prey. Why it had done this Pranjab had no idea, though he wondered if some humanity remained in those who programmed the things. He disinfected and sewed up the leg wound, checked for concussion and left it at that. He also provided some anti-biotics just to reassure the Patels, since few of them had any effect any more, and didn't bother with the painkillers since the boy seemed bored with the whole procedure and just wanted to go and play. He would make it. He showed signs of being one of Pranjab's kind, with his odd pinkish eyes, high forehead and the touch of a point to his ears. In payment, the Patels had given Pranjab the curry.

It had been fish, he recollected – highly spiced and with a good portion of rice. Not having eaten for a couple of days, Pranjab took his time over it, only wolfing down the last half of the meal. He'd felt a clench in his guts shortly afterwards, and then a weird hot flush spreading out from that, as if highlighting the network of his veins. He'd grimaced, expecting food poisoning, though hadn't been too worried about that. Those of his kind didn't suffer the malady in quite the same way as others. There would be stomach cramps and diarrhoea, then it would pass, with his rugged body extracting nutrients despite the poisoning. But this time it took a different course.

Pranjab grew hot and fevered, and it just didn't go away, day after day. He was always hungry and, fortunately, seemed full of energy, so took on a lot more work than usual. Payment was usually in food, to complement the irregular government dole or items he could barter for the same. He didn't sleep much, and hallucinations began to invade his waking moments. Sometimes the sky appeared to change colour, star patterns to shift, and something other than the moon hung up there. One time he seemed to be wandering in a part of the sprawl he simply didn't recognize, and when he looked up, the bright daylight sky had filled with machines. People changed too, and their altered skin colour was the least disconcerting thing about it. He saw creatures that seemed to be out of the Hindu pantheon, and others straight out of gaming and VR visors. But he was a doctor, a rational man, and knew these to simply be waking dreams, as he moved on about his work.

After a couple of weeks, he noted his customers looking at him oddly and asking him if he was okay. When the questions later turned to queries about cosmetic surgery, he went back to his garret and decided to look more closely at what he'd been denying for a while.

Over the last week, the lump of fat over his belly, from a poor diet of processed carbs from the distribution centre, had disappeared and he'd been glad about – sure the fever had burned it away. But he'd ignored the fact his trousers were higher up his ankles now, and his sleeves higher up his arms, while his jacket had grown tighter across his shoulders. His face also felt strange when he ran the electric shaver over it in the morning.

In his garret, he looked at his screen. It was always on, spewing out government propaganda about their incredible successes in agriculture and production. Like most in the sprawl, he ignored it and had had Mustafa round to disconnect the sound. This was of course illegal, but few worried about inspections that'd become increasingly rare years ago and had come to a stop completely in recent times. Home inspectors and street political officers didn't do so well around here. Usually everyone was alerted the moment they appeared, so they found nothing. And they quite often suffered unfortunate accidents while on their rounds, like having rubble falling on them from a couple of storeys up.

The cam was still in place, of course, and he received regular alerts, and a warning on the screen, if he inadvertently hung his jacket on it. Today he tossed his jacket over a chair and, with a swipe across the screen, called up the menu. It took him a little while to find what he wanted, because he'd ignored the thing for so long. When he finally did, the cycle of propaganda flickered for a long time before bringing up the image from the cam. He would've preferred to use a mirror, but they were as rare in the sprawl as most commodities. Standing back, he inspected the image of himself. It couldn't be denied: he was taller and his arms and legs had grown longer. But his face? This had grown longer too. It looked cruel and bony, the eyes slanting, the points to his ears more pronounced, while the ageing grey seemed to be growing out of his hair, returning it to its youthful black. He held up a hand and inspected another thing he'd been ignoring: his fingers had grown longer, and his nails seemed to be folding in to produce points. His skin colour too. It had darkened and taken on a purplish hue. It seemed that the mutation he'd been born with, which had separated him out from the herd and made him almost revered in Mumbai ZA culture, was becoming more pronounced.

The screen flickered once more and various squares appeared over his features, framing details and shifting around. These then blinked out, and the tone of the image background began cycling to orange and black. He recognized an alert, and knew that if the speaker had still been connected, he'd have been hearing it too. Then text came up along the bottom telling him to remain where he was and await inspection. He understood in a second. They didn't much bother with the data from millions of cams in the sprawl but, in using this function and showing unexpected behaviour, he'd alerted the constantly monitoring AI. It must have done a chip read and compared the data there to his recorded facial features, and found the disparity.

Pranjab stared at the message as panic rose and his situation properly began to impinge. He felt abruptly nauseated with fear, and the world around him grew thin, as it had in his waking dreams. It was oddly as if the harsh reality of what would certainly come next had become unreal, for it was too intense, too horrible. He had done nothing wrong, but knew that wouldn't matter. It wouldn't be the bureaucratic slugs of inspectors coming here but Inspectorate officers. He'd be dragged off for the standard interrogation, which would include beating, physical torture and finally an inducer. In the unlikely event they let him go, he would return physically and mentally crippled to die in the sprawl. People would try to help, of course, but they struggled hard enough to help themselves. He abruptly lashed out at this injustice and, obviously misjudging his strength and his aim, tore the screen and its cam from the wall, then sent them crashing to the floor. He paused, contemplated the act, then grabbed a bag and began stuffing it with food, his medical supplies and anything else he could think of in that moment, as *his* reality seemed on the point of collapse. He had to get out of here, and yet, he had nowhere to run. He turned and headed for the door, the knowledge that he could never return here being a fader switch on his mental grasp of what had been his home. Then the whole of it tilted, and he slid down into what he took to be another waking dream.

He abruptly found himself away from there, but naked in a suffocating place. He staggered, glimpsing a weird land of flat rock and drifts of grit, then something snared his foot and he went over. It all seemed so unreal and inconveniently irrelevant that he failed to respond in a natural manner, not putting his hands out – almost like a drunk going over. But the flat rock against his head was all too real and his consciousness flashed out.

Something else happened then, and he felt it on a visceral level. Something had entered his body. Stars flashed in his skull as he raised his head.

239

'Go there,' said a voice, and he caught a hint of something monstrous gazing at him.

There was a location arising out of a hot pattern in his body, which he now knew didn't track his vasculature but something else. He stood up and staggered towards that location, groping for the promise of survival, and found himself tumbling through hidden corridors, beyond reality, and then out onto soft ground, where he took a panicked breath. Cool calming oxygen suffused him and, as if pursuing him, the monster came back – just a large stern face and a hint of a gesturing, clawed hand. At first it seemed to loom over him, but as he sat up and looked around it drifted with his perception, and oddly didn't interfere with it. It was as if he was seeing it with the third eye inside his skull.

'You'll survive,' it said. 'This valley is isolated from the human civilization on this version of Earth, who only have steam technology, and you'll find food all around you.'

'What the fuck?' he managed, his voice hoarse. But it seemed that recent events had clarified his mind, for he absorbed the creature's words and understood at once that he had somehow travelled to a parallel Earth.

'I have to make this brief this time. I am the Fenris. I spread a biotechnology on your world that enables its recipients to cross the parallels, and you are one such. There are others like you, and I will send someone to collect you. Stay where you are.'

'What? What are you? . . . Why did you do this to me? What the hell is going on?' Pranjab babbled and then, even as the head drifted out of his perception. 'And fuck you!'

The thing was firmly and utterly gone from his mind, and he now sat cross-legged on the ground, analysing what had happened to him, and what he'd learned. The hot network igniting inside him had to be that biotech the Fenris spoke of. The first place he'd landed had been airless and would have killed him if the

Fenris hadn't intervened in some way, driving him on. He now inspected the mental image of the creature, noting how the characteristics of his own mutation matched it. But then he could go no further. Abruptly he stood up, and thirst drove him across the soft ground, pushing through reeds, to the bank of a river. He squatted, cupping his hands and drinking his fill, feeling with an odd intensity he'd never known before as the water suffused his body. When he finally stood up again, he felt a surge of excitement and interest in his body and his surroundings.

He'd always seen himself as an oddity, despite the reverence others held for him, which he knew arose out of the dregs of the Hindu religion and its pantheon. He had seen his mutation rationally, as something inherited from past generations of his family who'd been subjected to a massive toxin load in the environment. He'd considered it a matter of luck that it hadn't proved detrimental, but in fact the opposite. Now he'd been told it was the result of biotechnology, and he really, really wanted to explore that. He looked down at his naked body. He had grown tall, thin and tough, and felt great too. His senses seemed incredibly keen. In fact, when he focused first on his hand, and then on nearby mountains, he realized his vision had improved markedly. He also had an amazing ability to focus: first on the pores and hairs in the back of his hand, and then on a group of odd-looking animals coming down the mountainside ahead. But it went beyond that, for he seemed to have some sense of what lay behind him too, as well as to the sides. When he turned to look, natural vision confirmed what he'd sensed. He started walking into the deciduous forest occupying this side of the valley, and next focused on hearing. That too had improved, and when he tried to concentrate on the sound of a nearby cricket, he felt his ears move, and the sound becoming more intense. Smell? Yes, he could smell the reeds separate from water, and from the odour of this tree, that plant, and the toadstools at the base of another tree.

'I'm testing my superpowers,' he said happily to his surroundings. He jumped up and grabbed a branch, hung there for a moment, then dropped. He'd just leapt a couple of metres straight up! His excitement mixed in with astonishment, and he knew there was still much more to explore. Those smells, for example, had raised images of complex formations in his mind, which, he guessed, might be their molecular structure, or icons representing the same.

Hunger now began to impinge more keenly and he searched the branches as he walked. The walnut tree was immediately recognizable, since one still survived in the sprawl, fenced off and protected by a gang, with its few nuts sold at the high cost of favours to be collected. Only this tree was immense, standing two storeys tall. No search was required thereafter, because hundreds of nuts lay on the ground, and hung from the lower branches. They were solid, unlike the nuts from the tree in the sprawl, but he didn't require a nut cracker, for the strength in his hands had increased too. He sat down beneath the tree, cracking and eating the nuts, then shifting every now and again to bring more in reach. Eventually he began to feel full in one sense, but also had a craving for either meat, specifically organ meat, or something green. There'd been more low plants near the river, so he stood up and returned there.

The sun, far to the end of the valley over a flat plain, had now dropped to the horizon. He searched the ground before losing the light, and found wild onions and garlic that he had no problem identifying. Yet he noted, as he sniffed these, the molecular patterns arising in his mind again, and some sense that it was okay to eat them. The taste was intense and, concentrating on it, he saw more of those patterns. He tried something else that looked like it might be edible, and sensed it was okay too, though it tasted as bitter as lettuce root. Another small bush yielded fat berries, which were nice and sweet. But a low vine, with what looked like a gourd, triggered other patterns and he discarded the fruit, knowing it would poison him. So what other senses did he have? The sun had sunk now and the light gone with it, yet he could still see his surroundings clearly, albeit in a different palette. So he had night vision too. And there was something else, because now he felt utterly sure he was being watched.

They had gathered on the far bank of the river, and he recognized the animals he'd noticed up on the mountainside earlier. Eight of them stood there, and they were like nothing he'd seen in documentaries on the past natural world, now destroyed by men, or in any fantasy VR games or entertainments.

He was given the impression of pale, sickly yellow, hairless skin, and areas of hide covered in metallic fur, though that might have been a result of his night vision. Down on all fours, they seemed to be walking on what looked like hands, and had all sorts of objects stuck to their bodies. But their heads were the most disconcerting. At first, it appeared as if their heads had been removed, and all that remained was the long pillar of a neck. But on closer inspection, he saw some features on the upper part of that pillar. They had dark bulbous eyes, small round mouth holes and a slight protrusion that corresponded to a nose. A curiosity, then. That was until two of them stood up on what he had taken to be hind legs.

Their resemblance to humans now brought them into firmer focus. The torso structure was much the same, bellies loaded with slabs of fat. Narrow shoulders led to arms, then hands, with three fingers and two thumbs. Their legs, which were the same length, terminated in foot hands of the same design. What he'd taken to be fur was in fact some garment fashioned in a tight chain mesh of golden wires. When one of them reached down to its side – he couldn't tell whether it was a he or a she – he abruptly realized the objects stuck to, and sometimes penetrating, their bodies were items of technology. Meanwhile, the action itself, so utterly the same as an Inspectorate officer reaching for his sidearm, had Pranjab diving behind a tree. The shot flashed through the air – what looked like a small nub of ball lightning zipping across the river. It hit the tree with a snap and disappeared, splintering up bark. Pranjab jerked his hand away from the trunk as a shock slammed up through his elbow to his shoulder. Inspecting his hand and arm, he saw an odd luminescence there, travelling in waves as it faded. As it did so, the arm felt slightly numb, but also tired, as if after heavy exercise.

Were these the people of this world the Fenris had mentioned? No, Pranjab immediately knew that was wrong. The items on, and in, their bodies were too technological, while also possessing a strange organic look. The weapon the shooter held did have an antique look, with its funnel-shaped barrel, but no way was it the product of 'steam technology'.

'Now that was unkind!' he shouted at them.

The response was a series of further shots sizzling the undergrowth and spreading mists of static electricity. As Pranjab scuttled back for more cover, he noted that some of the shots had come from weapons seemingly incorporated into the arms of the creatures. He grimaced, knowing he'd shouted like that because he felt strong, potent and confident in his newfound abilities. Arrogant too. If he wasn't careful that could get him killed. He then reassessed and thought about what had happened to his arm – the effect was fading now. Killing wasn't the intention here, for they'd used a stun weapon similar to an Inspectorate shock stick, or the effect of an inducer.

'What do you want me for?' he called, then damned himself for doing so when another fusillade ensued. He next heard splashing and knew they'd entered the river to come after him. He turned and headed back through the trees, wondering what the hell to do now beyond running away.

'Fenris?' he enquired, directly to the place in his mind where the creature had appeared before. But he received no response. He considered his ability to travel between parallels but dismissed that for now. The Fenris had told him to remain here, for someone would come to collect him.

He heard sounds behind, and in, the forest on either side, so broke into a run. Trying to see them with his night vision got him no further than the trees lying between him and them, as with any conventional vision. But when he concentrated with that other sense of his surroundings, the world expanded. His perception encompassed an area maybe a hundred metres wide, and in it he could 'see' stuff on the other side of trees, and one or two rocky ridges. The creatures were moving quickly, down on all fours, to encircle him. He decided to push himself harder and accelerated, delighting in his strength and speed. He dodged past trees, stepped onto, and jumped over, a boulder, neatly rolled on, hitting the ground on the other side, then leapt up to keep running. Soon outdistancing those that had tried to get ahead of him, he abruptly turned to the right, thinking to lose them. As the trees thinned out, to be displaced by shrub that slowed him, he realized he'd reached the top of the valley.

He paused, lungs cycling easily, and saw that beyond the shrub lay heathery hillside sloping down. That would put him in the open and make him an easy target for their weapons. Meanwhile the creatures, now fifty metres behind him, were all closing in on his position swiftly, even though they weren't within human sight. Perhaps they possessed similar senses to his. A stab of anxiety rose up through the adrenalin. What the hell could he do now? He remembered the leaps he'd made. Anxiety switched to an anger and aggression he'd never really experienced before. And he turned to run back towards them.

Pranjab chose a point where there were fewer of them and just went at full speed. A glowing shot, drawing a streak across his night vision, came in at him from the side. He threw himself down and rolled up out of it, running still. One of the creatures rose up ahead of him and he launched himself straight at it, feet first, as it tried to zero its weapon on him. With his perception and reactions heightened, it was as if time slowed, or rather he could do more in the time available. He thumped hard into its chest and felt the ribs breaking under his bare feet. A shot speared off to one side, setting foliage sizzling to red embers as the thing slammed down. He rolled beyond it, putting a foot down hard, and leapt back, snatching up the weapon that had fallen from its grasp. Shame clenched his chest when he saw it lying there making choking sounds, little spurts of blood coming from its circular mouth.

The butt of the weapon felt small in his hand, but he did find a soft trigger and turned it to fire at another of the creatures that was drawing into view. Nothing happened. Pranjab threw the weapon at the nearest pursuer, and himself into another roll, then into a dodging run. A shot hit his shoulder, sending him staggering. Its effect numbed and slowed him, and a wave of weariness passed through him. Yet inside, it seemed the biotech responded, with its network flashing like a faulty light and a searing pain spreading out to banish the numbness. He felt terrible, but his speed picked up again and he was functional once more.

Dodging down through trees again, leaping rocks, he became tangled briefly in briars and felt them ripping his skin. The things still relentlessly pursued and were close – shots zipping through and splashing on the trees. The ambush revealed itself ahead, with the things rising up out of thick leaf matter. Three shots converged on him, but he managed to dodge enough for only one to hit. Again the pain, and this time a horrible sick feeling went through him, but it didn't reduce his speed. He swiped one of them and, just like with the screen and cam in his garret, he didn't fully realize his strength. He sent it through the air to crash into a tree, after which it dropped soggily to the ground. He noted the weapon in its arm had the same barrel as the one he'd tried to fire, but the rest of its mechanism bulked under its skin, all the way up to its shoulder. He'd obviously damaged it because it was sizzling in places – cooking that skin from inside. The creature showed no reaction to that and again he felt shame, certain that he'd killed it, as the other. As he ran on, he realized that the knowledge that he could simply leave this place whenever he wanted to had made him overconfident.

It was time to go, so he pushed in the direction of that waking dream. The network flashed into being inside his head, and the walls of reality grew thin. But then something bounced up out of that network into his mind. He felt a surge of fear and the stark memory of suffocation actually stopped him breathing for a moment. His ability to leave now felt blocked, just as he wouldn't have thrust his hand into a fire, and the world around him juddered back into solidity. The blowback from this was a return of aggression, and he wondered if his best tactic would be to turn back against his pursuers again, because death felt certain anywhere else. Then he saw the river once more ahead of him. Breath stuttering back, he began hyperventilating. The manner of those weapons was a form of electrical discharge, though what they delivered, much like inducers, was more compli-cated than that. Might they be negated by water? It seemed highly likely. Reaching the edge of the reeds, he threw himself into a flat dive, hit the water and swam down – memories of swimming as a child in Mumbai cisterns came to him.

Pranjab's hand touched underwater plants and sank into soft mud. He readied himself to sigh out his breath rather than fight full lungs to stay down, but felt no pull to the surface. It seemed his body had grown a lot heavier than before. Opening his eyes gave him a clear view of his surroundings, except where he'd stirred up the mud. His other sense extended this still further. The plants scattered along the bottom reminded him of cabbage fields in an agricultural area, though without the fences and readerguns. Long-legged, crablike creatures perambulating across these reminded him of agricultural mechs. He swam hard and strong to get as much distance as possible before he ran out of breath. And then, as something shifted inside him, he discovered another superpower: he seemed not to be running out of air. Some hypoxic function of the biotech?

Finally, because he knew his pursuers could swim too, he headed for the far bank and carefully crawled out through the reeds. He'd just done at least a hundred metres under water. He eased upright, looking for a sign of the creatures. And then he felt something twisting inside as that network came alive, along with some sense of the world diminishing, like it had before, when he travelled, only it felt wrong and oddly centred now. This swung his head round, so he could focus on a black macula hole that had appeared on the mountainside where he'd first seen the creatures. They were there again, gathered before this opening, and then stepping into it and disappearing – two of them were being carried by the others. The hole next winked out of existence, and the world stabilized. Pranjab breathed a sigh of relief and moved back into forest.

Morning came with the singing of birds. Senses attuned,

Pranjab finished up the raw remains of the rabbit he'd caught, then went to the river to wash his hands and face. He next headed towards where he had sensed something similar to that black hole in the night, the tunnel or portal the creatures had used. He suddenly saw a Chinese man walking along the river-bank towards him and felt a flash of fear at the combat gear the man had on. But he also recognized the mutations of his *own* kind.

'You took your time,' he said.

'If you speak English, use that,' Chenghu replied. 'We've decided on it as our common language.'

Pranjab raised an eyebrow at that, repeating his comment in English, then added, 'I've not been having a good time here.'

The man tossed him a pack of clothing and said, 'Not as warm as you're accustomed to? Or the wildlife bothering you?'

'Something more than that,' Pranjab replied.

10

Adriana

Carrying a beaker of coffee, Adriana walked outside their residence, along the path to the viewpoint, and gazed down at the massive Kerala Sprawl below. The centre – the old city – could just be made out due to the gap around it, loaded with security, while spreading out from that lay the neatly quadrate streets of the massive ZA sectors. The SA population had mainly been in the central old city, obviously well protected. But it hadn't helped them much in the end, and their status hadn't given them immunity from inclusion in the 'firebreak'. Chancel was walking up from below, lugging a heavy backpack. She felt him coming even before he was in sight, and her usual stomach-twisting surge of emotion had diminished. She knew better now than to describe it as love. He spotted her and walked over, taking off the pack and depositing it on the ground.

'Anything interesting?' she asked, indicating the pack with a nod.

He shrugged. 'Just a few bits and pieces.'

Though not as strong now, the twisting in her stomach still drove her forwards, and she threw her arms around his neck, pulling him

250

into a kiss. It lasted a while, their connection reaffirming. When they parted and she caught his expression, she knew this would be continued later. But for now they had other concerns, and she locked down on the urge just to take his hand and lead him back to their room. Instead she gestured back to the domed residence they'd occupied. 'There's not very much more we need on top of what's here.'

The official, high up in the Committee of this Earth, who'd lived in this place, Caprock, had obviously expected severe problems. He'd ensured his home was a fortress, and that he and his family would be assured of all the luxuries they required. A fission reactor down in the rock below supplied power, pumps delivered deep groundwater, and the caves below were filled with supplies and defences, including readerguns and mines. Missile launchers had also been installed on the mountainsides all around the house. Adriana had even found a link to a military satellite geostable above, capable of lasering to ash anything human-sized down here. Fortunately, the Fenris had turned off all those defences before they arrived.

Chancel shrugged again. 'Like I said, just a few bits and pieces. I wanted to take a look and thought it'd be a good idea not to come back empty handed.'

'You should have taken the flier,' she said, indicating the large fan-driven vehicle sitting on a nearby air pad.

'I considered that, but we don't know what's still active down there.' He waved at the house. 'This guy was just one member of the Committee ensuring his survival; there were others.'

'He wasn't very successful,' Adriana opined.

'Nobody here was.'

The corpses had been scattered throughout Caprock and, upon their arrival, they'd dragged the dried-out husks to the house macerator and fed them in. Adriana could still smell something a bit off in some areas and felt sure they hadn't found them all. The odour sometimes arrived on the wind too. Though it had been many months since the extermination, the decay was still ongoing.

The Fenris, during a later terse communication, had explained to them what had happened here. They'd then researched and confirmed it via the still-working computer systems in the house, which were in contact with AIs scattered all over the planet. This had taken a little while, as the screen interface was in Hindi. But they'd soon realized their memories were eidetic, and they could learn things at a phenomenal rate. Even the street signs and graffiti they'd seen upon arrival helped, while all Earth languages now incorporated English, which the Committee mainly used, so this gave them an advantage too. They found a lexicon and learned Hindi, not because there was any need to, once they switched the interface over to English, but because they could. From the distributed AIs, they came to understand that, of a world population of twenty billion, less than a billion remained. They were mainly over in Europe, where a shadow of fenris biotech ensured their survival, though some pockets were here in India – the nearest almost a thousand kilometres away. Adriana and Chancel were, by dint of their biotech, immune too, according to the Fenris. Thus far that seemed to be true.

'So what did you find down there?' Adriana asked.

'Corpses, burned-out areas, a big crater that still seems to be hot.' He pointed at his head. 'I actually felt the radiation . . . Readerguns are still in operation down there, but without ammo. I took care not to go beyond the firebreak.'

They turned, Chancel picking up his pack, and Adriana hung on his arm as they headed back towards the Caprock residence.

'What's the situation with our new arrivals, then?' Chancel asked.

'Pranjab is settling in now, and the same as before – fascinated by what we've become. It seems our interests and traits have been emphasized by the biotech, which is somehow reassuring.'

She held up her arm and looked at it – the scar was gone now. That had been a watershed for them all, when Pranjab had emerged from his exploration of the medical area, with a chromed surgical device and blood on his arm. He'd then removed the ID chips from them all. It had felt a profound moment.

She added, 'It means that perhaps it isn't changing us into something we weren't, rather enhancing.'

'Obviously it's enhanced your optimism,' said Chancel drily.

Adriana winced, then continued, 'We know he was a doctor before and is now raiding the database regularly. Our ability to retain information and process it is . . . phenomenal. Now he's trying out other equipment in the medical area. He's studying the biotech inside himself.'

'We are *all* extremely smart now, it seems. Let's hope our intelligence is ours to control. I still have my doubts about the apparently altruistic motives of the Fenris.'

'If it was twisting us to its purpose, maybe it would have prevented your pessimism from being enhanced,' she said.

Chancel grinned. 'And how are the other three?'

'Chenghu still seems like a good guy – I think our initial assessment about him is the same as when he first arrived. He didn't hesitate when the Fenris told him to go and get Pranjab.' Adriana pondered on that. The Fenris's message had been brief, just telling them another of their kind had jaunted and survived, then presenting a map of where to find him. When she thought about that message now, she couldn't remember any actual words. Chenghu had immediately grabbed up his gear, though it seemed he required a nod of agreement from Irene before he stepped out of their world.

253

She continued, 'With Ektian it's hard to know – she hasn't been away from the computer system much since she arrived. Irene is . . .' She grimaced. 'Still Irene.'

'And her plans?'

She waved a hand at their surroundings. 'We've seen the horrors of our world's possible future here, and we both felt we should do something. The Fenris is no help. Perhaps trying to sell the idea of his non-interference in our decision-making with his reluctance to advise us. I can't fault her aims, I just don't much like her attitude.'

'Irene is Irene, as you say.'

They entered the house and went through to the large and luxurious living room. Irene and Chenghu were there, back from the central area and sitting behind Ektian at the main house console. Irene saw them and stood up, briefly patting Chenghu on the shoulder and stroking her hand across Ektian's back. Adriana took note of this, the sense of ownership Irene seemed to have over them, and felt an oddly uncharacteristic jealousy.

Without greeting, Irene went straight into it.

'The infrastructure here is much the same as it is back on our Earth. Pranjab gave us what he could about the area, though he'd never been here, while Chenghu has located a military base, and even now Ektian is shutting down its AI. We should be able to walk straight in there with no problem and take what we need,' she said.

'And what do we need from there?' Chancel asked, as he dropped his pack on the sofa.

'Something that'll offer a way to stop what's happening on our home world,' Irene replied, a fierceness to her expression. 'And a way to prevent what has happened here.'

Adriana, who had some idea what that method might be,

jumped in to ask, 'So what did you find out on your last trip back to our home world?'

Irene moved out into the central area and Adriana took a step back. The woman had a presence that brooked no denial. The scars on her face were fading, but her anger at injustice hadn't lessened at all. She seemed to dominate every interaction.

'I found out there's a meeting due in Dublansk – most of the world leaders, if they can be called such, corporate heads, and the usual complement of billionaires.'

'And you intend to cut the head off the snake.'

Irene held her hands out in plea. 'Do you have any better ideas?'

'Not really,' Adriana admitted.

They were powerful and they could travel between worlds. World walkers, as the Fenris described them. They had a base to work from now, and they could obtain anything they wanted. Were they then to just sit back and do nothing about the world they'd came from? Let it fall into ruination?

'So again, what's in that military base?' Chancel asked patiently.

'Tactical nuclear warheads,' Irene replied.

Irene

The stink was intense and Irene initially thought it came from the sea. But, looking out across the water, she saw clouds of gulls and other darker birds circling and landing on structures that lay some kilometres out from the further edge of the sea farms.

Something's there.

Now more accustomed to expanding her senses, she focused out there as if looking through a telescope and saw the source of the smell. The broken-off stubs of wind turbines jutted up from the sea like rotten teeth in diseased gums. Moored to these was a series of barges, piled high with human corpses in seriously advanced decay. The birds were feeding, though whether on the corpses or on the great swarms of crabs that had crawled out of the sea onto the dead, she didn't know.

'I wonder what the purpose was of that,' she said.

Chenghu shrugged. 'Maybe a temporary measure to keep the sprawls clear. The macerators were probably over capacity.'

She looked at him. Of course he'd know this from his previous position in the system of oppression, as she liked to remind him. 'You think they cared enough about those in the sprawls?'

He waved a dismissive hand at the barges and looked annoyed.

'This should be good enough,' he said, gesturing at their surroundings.

The barrier edge of the nearest sea farm lay a hundred metres out. Between it and mudflats lay clear water. The mudflats' only purpose seemed to be to bind together rubbish consisting of shreds of forever fabrics, composites and human bones. And the clear water was only clear in the metaphorical sense, being sheened with oil between floating debris. Irene assumed that here, just as on her home Earth, the oil came from sunken wind turbine generators, still leaking after their demise decades ago, just as most of the chunks of composite were from their shattered blades.

The two of them stood on a sea wall running above these mudflats. Immediately below them, a small outlet led through the shiny mud from a drain. Directly behind them lay huge warehouses, cranes and a park for the mega trucks that had supplied the Indian sprawls. This area lay sixteen kilometres from the port where the cargoes were delivered. Sixteen kilometres of dockyards – now completely inactive.

'It would be best to drop it down there,' Chenghu pointed at the outlet.

'You would know. The Fenris hasn't seen fit to give me any information on the seed.'

'He told me seawater was best to activate it, as you know, preferably in a place where lots of nutrients are available.' That was the verbal explanation, but Chenghu had had a more holistic sense of what was required. It'd arrived as a construct in his mind when, as he'd described it to her, the fabric of reality had ripped ahead of him, giving him a glimpse of organic weirdness, before the seed dropped through. He now took the thing out of his pocket and held it on the palm of his hand.

'You sure about this?' he asked.

'We need a stable container to move the device.' She grimaced.

Transporting the nuclear warhead physically wasn't a problem, since two of them could carry it between them using the handles provided. However, when they'd tried to jaunt the thing, they'd struggled with it and left it where it was. Irene had vaguely understood why, and Chenghu had confirmed that the problem lay in the plutonium it contained. It felt slippery in their grip, and heavy in a way that it wasn't in the real world. Irene had concluded throughout their travels that they could only jaunt things they could physically carry in the real world, but now it seemed that wasn't the only limitation. Perhaps this had something to do with density? No, other metals were nearly as dense and they'd had no problems with them. It had to be the radioactivity somehow interfering with the process. Perhaps all six of them could have jaunted it, but then they'd have struggled with the weapons they wanted to take too.

'So it needs blood,' she said.

He shrugged. 'We discussed this. The biotech in the seed requires the DNA as an identifier. The one controlling it then receives a link to his internal biotech – it becomes an extension of the same.'

She noted his use of the word 'his' and held out her hand.

He grimaced, probably more annoyed at his own weakness than her presumption. Her sexual hold over him had diminished, yet still she managed to bend him to her will. She didn't like what she had done to manipulate him, but at the time, with her body recovered and the surprising return of sexual feeling, it had seemed a necessary response. She realized now that her misandry and need for control had risen not so much out of Garrick's abuse of her, but from her submission to the man. It had been a way for her to regain power. Chenghu weighed the seed in his hand for a moment then tossed it to her.

Irene caught it, and it felt slick and odd in her hand. She stooped to draw the combat knife from her boot. Pulling up her sleeve, she clenched her hand on the seed to raise the veins in her arm and drew the tip of the knife along one. She winced, not expecting it to hurt so much, and watched as blood oozed out – much darker than human and almost purple. It ran down her arm a little way, then the bleeding stopped. Focusing in with her enhanced senses, she saw that the wound had already closed. It would have to be enough. Putting away the knife, she rubbed the seed in her blood, smearing it over every surface.

'And now?' she asked.

He just shrugged. They'd talked about this on many occasions, as they'd flipped from world to world, taking the grand tour, as he put it. While Irene had looked for what she could use, her purpose firming in her mind. And no, the riots after she'd killed Garrick had done nothing to change her course, nor had Chenghu's unsubtle attempts to make her see the 'bigger picture'.

Irene flung the blood-soaked seed down into the oily water. It sank to the bottom and lodged in the mud. If she'd possessed only human senses, she wouldn't have been able to see it, but in fact she could make it out clearly, just as she could see the warehouses behind, and their flier down in a yard surrounded by mega trucks. It was a weird perception of the world, which had taken her some time to get used to. It wasn't three-sixty vision, but something beyond that; she could see behind and inside things within her range, and in radiation bands outside the human spectrum. Searching for a suitable label, the jaunters had settled on calling it holosense, since that covered both the 3D aspect and its holism. She watched the seed closely.

It did nothing visible for a minute or two, then abruptly expanded, opening numerous splits in its surface. Out of these, it extruded nubs, which seemed to hesitate, as if the thing couldn't quite believe where it had found itself. In fact, she felt some sense of that drifting up from it to her. A second after that, the mud disrupted for metres all around it, and the seawater clouded. Eager growth then ensued, and a link to it firmly established in her mind. Focusing in, she perceived mycelia, which the Fenris had described to Chenghu, streaming out at an incredible rate. The mud around the thing then hollowed out, sinking the seed lower as its mycelia sucked up materials and converted them into further mycelia. She knew this because the steadily expanding growth had *told* her, feeding her progress data. The things thickened to become visible to the human eye as a black web. This spread along the outlet's channel and then out of the water.

'I'm in it,' she told Chenghu, with a touch of wonder, even for her. 'It's detailing its progress to me, and I can see its surroundings through it. It's an extension of me.'

The threads climbed over the sides of the outlet coming from the sea wall and spread across the mudflats, while also extending out across the seabed. Running through spiky grey grass and anaemic shrubs, it gathered materials. She saw it, inside and out, grabbing crab carapaces, rubbish, the plants themselves, and hollows appeared around every thread as it absorbed the mud.

259

She watched one thread hit a chunk of protruding iron and form a net over it. The iron began to steam and dissolve. The biotech could apparently use and digest just about anything, which was something of a concern when it then began to climb the sea wall towards them.

'Maybe see if you can exert some control,' said Chenghu, taking a step back.

She puzzled over the data stream coming from it as it changed, depending on where she took her perception. Close focus along the sea wall gave her a richer and richer feed, so she could perceive it eating up microbes and soil laden with cadmium and other nasty toxins, which, of course, it found very useful. But she didn't know how to stop the thing continuing towards them, until she did. It turned out to be simply like flexing a limb – no particular thought involved, just the action itself. The growth ahead of them stopped. But then, perhaps because of those useful toxins left behind from all the cargo that'd come through this place, it circumvented them and continued spreading behind. After closer inspection, Irene discovered that she and Chenghu were already excluded from its materials gathering because of the biotech inside them. She added in the flier too, but excluded nothing else. Though perhaps, she acknowledged, she would have to keep a wary eye on its progress.

'Growing quite large just to generate this transport cage we need,' Chenghu noted.

Irene peered deeper, trying to understand what she was seeing. She could decipher the basic mechanism that would produce the transport cage, for it was simply that of a plant, or a fungus producing its fruit. But huge data stores were accumulating in the growing biotech, and in a moment she realized that the thing could produce more than just this one fruit – much, much more. Then her logic floundered on that accumulation of data. It was far more than could possibly have been contained in the seed, and yet it seemed still to be expanding and making connections that simply couldn't have resulted from any of the initial schematic. She also started to sense something of intelligence in the thing spreading before her. Perhaps it was gathering information from material reality all around it, as well as from elsewhere.

'It's a multipurpose tool,' she said. 'It has a program to grow the cage as we require it, but it can also grow much else besides. I still don't understand a lot of what I'm seeing.'

'It's good that you can control it, then,' said Chenghu flatly.

Irene reached out. The biotech was spreading under the sea farms now, flinging up fishing line mycelia to snare GM salmon, cod and pollack, and reeling them in. She made the effort of will to halt the thing, but it simply had no effect. Her perception remained within and throughout it, but it seemed to have strayed out of her control, having grown enough and accrued enough data. She wondered if the way she felt now was the way her parents had felt when she strayed from their control, into the gangs.

'Yes, it's good that I can,' she said, admitting nothing, a slight flicker of panic within.

Before them the mycelia had braided, thickened out and created other structures. They now looked like a thick mass of vines, trailing out from expanding puffball growths, as white as that same fungus but with a metallic hue. It then threw up a stalk, growing visibly, as thick as a lamp post. Irene found her focus much more drawn to this than the rest of the thing. Why? She pushed the data for explanations, her perception sliding into the microscopic and below. As her sense of connection fined down, through the system of the biotech, it became clear: this was where her DNA resided. Where her real control resided. And, even now, it was oozing into a growing bud on the end of that stalk. But this then begged the question of her DNA throughout the rest of it and her supposed control. She explored and found DNA elsewhere, splitting and spreading out as the biotech grew, but this was something more complex, and definitely not her own. She didn't need to go any deeper, she knew in the pit of her stomach what this was about. Yes, the thing would give them a transport cage that she could control, but the rest of it lay at the command of another: the Fenris.

The stalk's bud resembled that of a tulip as it kept on expanding. Meanwhile, still having her perception of the whole, if not any control over it, Irene observed the rest of the biotech reaching the rafts out there. It thrust up tentacles, like hugely long lampreys. These thrashed over the barges, dragging corpses down or feeding on them in situ. One even speared high, going after seagulls, but missed as the birds rapidly departed. They snatched up crabs and broke them down their length, chomping and digesting them too. By the time the remains of these creatures had reached the main mass of the biotech below, they were reduced to amino acids, lipid particles and other small molecules of material. One of the barges tilted. Focusing in, Irene saw a larger jointed tentacle with something on the end of it that looked very much like a human hand. It had grabbed the edge of the barge, then, as she watched, sank it.

'How fucking big is this thing going to get?' Chenghu asked.

'As large as required,' Irene replied, declining to add *by the Fenris*. She concentrated on the bud again, sensing the transport cage forming inside it. A few minutes later, spiral splits had developed down its sides, giving a glimpse of yellow material inside. The splits connected at the top of the thing, then it opened, the outer skin of the bud peeling back precisely the same way as a flower. This revealed a yellow object inside, like a grass seed, standing a metre tall. It grew steadily taller, and with that Irene felt a greater sense of connection to the thing, and its readiness. Functions like three-dimensional pictographs fell into her mind. She had a visceral sense of what they would do, although in many cases it was not something she could translate. However, some she did understand and, with a thought, she initiated one of them. A soft popping sounded, and the seed detached, drifting towards them, coming to a halt just a few metres out from the sea wall.

'Transport cage?' Chenghu wondered.

Irene initiated another pictograph and the thing sprang open in strips down its length, then expanded into a spherical cage two metres across. Another one opened the top of the cage and folded its ribs out. Now they'd fattened, they did resemble bony ribs. Yet another thought separated these ribs at the base, and opened them out across the air, in a neat circle. When one of them hung within touching distance, she reached out to rest a hand on it. The thing felt like warm metal, and her sense of connection increased. The cage was indeed an extension of herself, and anything within it she'd be able transport across the parallels with the same effort of will as just herself. She waved a hand and the thing snapped back into a seed form.

'Let's go,' she said.

'What about that?' Chenghu gestured at the biotech down below the sea wall, as the stalk sank rapidly back down into it.

'It can produce other things,' said Irene, as she sensed it rumbling out across the ocean floor, now spread across twenty-five square kilometres. 'It will be useful to us later.'

Chenghu looked doubtful, but he followed without a word as she returned to the flier. The closed-up cage bobbed through the air behind her. They stepped over vinelike growths as they went, for the tech had spread inland here too, and through the clay below the concrete ahead, eating its way to the nearby sprawl.

The Fenris

His ability to understand what was going on with the hive people was now curtailed. Instead, the Fenris concentrated on his biotech spreading in the old underground nest, down on this airless Earth. The few corpses that weren't reduced to bones, or just drifts of dust on the floor, rendered interesting data. They presented a variety of different forms. Some resembled those above, with two thumbs on their hands and feet hands, but also one extra finger. The skulls of these particular corpses were bigger, to accommodate a larger brain, and connected to eyes that, judging by some desiccated remains, could be pushed out onto telescopic protrusions. The size of the nerve running back from these was twice that found in a conventional human. A scan and extrapolation from other remains revealed a nose on one that would have been a highly complex sensory device. And most whole corpses of that kind possessed mouths with teeth, as well as evident remains of a digestive system. Were they engineers, he wondered bitterly? Perhaps they were the forebears of those the hive had incinerated above.

Others of a different design, with long spiked fingers on their hands and flat fingers on their feet, were clustered in and around a chamber that contained the remains of plant life. Horticulturalists perhaps? There was also a heavier form, similar to the engineers and the gardeners, which he labelled builders, or diggers, since their spatula toes could lock together in what were quite obviously shovels. Then there were two he found below the collapsed shaft leading up above. It took him very little time to identify and label these. They were big, obviously having carried a heavy musculature, though this had shrunk to mummified threads below the chitin plates of their armour, under their dried-out skin. Their fingers also bore scythe claws and spikes protruding from the knuckles. Their brains were small, with their heads turned almost wholly to vision and hearing. The withered remains of directional ears spiked up on either side of a skull, which resembled two tubes positioned side by side, rather than something human. He identified these as warriors, even before finding the weapons lying nearby – assault weapons with a variety of ammo feeds, and ugly saw-toothed bayonets.

The biotech spread, examining each find down to the molecular level and cataloguing as it absorbed its materials. In light of what had happened above, the Fenris needed more data than just the shadow of what had once been a human society here – now dehumanized and converted into something resembling that of social insects. He set the biotech to explore the remaining hard technology down here. He found food-transfer tubes running from the garden, and throughout the nest. Tracking these, he discovered a long hall, filled with cylindrical glass tanks and a lot of support equipment. He spent some time closely examining it all, expecting this to be the place where the hive *creatures* had been gestated. Eventually he realized, after studying dried-out remains in one tank, that these cylinders had only been for growing protein and fat food sources. Turning back to the data he'd gathered on the corpses, he noted they possessed sexual reproductive organs. Since these were energy-hungry things, which would have been removed if unnecessary, he could be fairly sure that reproduction had continued here in the conventional way, after the radical alteration of these . . . people. Perhaps the ability to alter themselves was something they'd lost. The hard tech here was at a level not much higher than that of Committee Earth, while he had yet to find any remains of biotech, beyond those food tanks and the bodies themselves. He then hit the jackpot in his explorations. Even as something else shouted for his attention, back where his body and its senses resided in the engine orbiting the fenris world.

The Fenris ignored this call as he focused intently on the ancient piece of computing and the trails of dust, which were all that remained of some optical fibres spearing off to the rest of the nest. An examination of their various termini mostly revealed the remains of optical plugs. Again referencing data on the corpses, he found the sockets in their skulls, and dusty remains of optics there too. This then was how these creatures were maintained as a hive: optogenic alterations to make their minds responsive to light impulses, and connection to a central core for reprogramming, upload and download. While disconnected, they carried out their tasks; whenever connected, they received their programming. In this they varied from what he'd seen of those above, who hadn't had hard connections, but had advanced to wifi. Both forms were little more than organic robots. As much as he tried to intellectualize what they were, he still felt the same repulsion. They looked like an evolutionary dead end, as far as he was concerned – humanity reduced to its base function of survival and procreation, with nothing beyond that. Not really human at all.

But was this a consensus intelligence – a true hive intelligence – or had there been an overall mind in charge? He might be able to find answers to these questions in the memory-storage rods in that central core of ancient computing – along with much else besides, with any luck – and start to understand that thing in the moon. He carefully made connections to those rods.

Next he instructed the biotech to alert him once it began to obtain data, or if anything else of interest arose, then steadily withdrew from this connection, which had run far too deep. The alarm shouting for his attention had grown stronger now. He fell back and out, regaining a sense of self in his own body, sitting in a cupped chair and gazing at the tangled biotech around him. He realized he'd spent much too long connected. He didn't want to become one of those fenris who lived vicariously through their tech, eventually merging with it. But he had to see what was trying to attract his attention, so, losing sense of his immediate surroundings again, he returned into it once more.

Chenghu had activated his seed.

No, that wasn't right: Irene had activated the seed. He focused into, and through, the growing biotech. It had produced a transport cage, as he'd programmed, and confined the initiator's – Irene's – DNA connection to the thing. Meanwhile his own DNA had been maintained throughout the rest of its, at present, unlimited growth. He saw the biotech had spread across thirty square kilometres of seabed, and twelve square kilometres inland. It was thickening and consolidating, building neural nodes and stacks, producing limbs and more complex systems for absorbing the materials it needed to grow. Already it was bigger than the one on that airless Earth. He observed it with satisfaction, knowing it could expand still further to cover most of the planet and provide massive resources beyond his world. But then, noting his own reaction, he began to feel increasing puzzlement.

The biotech, wherever established, gave him greater access. And he'd given the seed to Chenghu to activate once he established a base somewhere, so this would provide him with this greater access to what he'd hoped would be a rapidly increasing population of jaunters. Why was it relevant now? Brief self-examination gave him the answer: he'd gone from altruistic acts to non-intervention, and now to a form of intervention truly outside of his traditional fenris morality. But this was a new multiverse, with a new paradigm, and he had to change to encompass it. He was now thinking of the world walkers as the core of a force to stand against the hive, rather than just allies, and the problems of Committee Earth as secondary. He could speculate that his constant interaction with more primitive people had instigated this, for he'd had no contemporaries to keep him in line, but he felt it was actually something else. This was the *right* thing to do. He felt righteous, sure and driven. The hive went against everything his kind stood for, whether or not he slid into the morally debatable. He had to use whatever means to counter it and, if necessary, eliminate it.

However, a handful of walkers, though powerful and effective, were no answer to countering something as immense as the hive. He needed more of them; he needed an army of them. Must he therefore begin dispatching inocular flies to Earth again? Hollowness grew as he imagined the disaster of another intervention there. He could see no clear way to the future, so for the moment put all that aside. Whatever he did in the present would have to be through the agency of the walkers, for he still couldn't travel where they did. As much as the older, uploaded part of him reacted with moral outrage to the idea, he had to maintain his links to them, and push them to his purpose. The biotech would enable that.

He returned his attention to it. So why had Irene initiated the seed now? The Fenris focused attention back through the rift, and through the growing biotech, to listen in on their conversations. The spill from six minds now all came through at the same location, on the split-away parallel world. Over the ensuing hour, he observed Chenghu and Irene enter a military facility and carry out an easily identifiable device: a tactical warhead, yield of kilotonnes. Meanwhile, the others had been elsewhere in the facility and were coming out with crates of weapons and ammo. Obviously they were planning something drastic, and the Fenris needed to know what that was.

His previous distaste for being a perpetual voyeur had become irrelevant. Now he needed to guide the six of them to the correct target. His old morality would have preferred that they make the right decisions based on the right information, as they slowly understood the facts for themselves. But besides that being naive, his new sense of urgency dismissed the idea. Anyway, with their hierarchical organization, and other upshots of their old biological drives, they were, in essence, becoming what he required.

He'd already noticed a delight of violence in Ektian, as she slowly transitioned from the vulnerable person she'd been, into having strength beyond anything she'd thought humanly possible. The situation had been similar with Irene, and he'd seen how the shape of her mind grew, knowing what she was becoming capable of. Chenghu, already accustomed to fighting, hadn't taken any particular delight in that aspect of his increased strength and ability. As a military man, he was good at taking orders, be they from the Fenris or Irene. Adriana seemed a calmer, more collected person, as did Pranjab. Their past existences had been relatively sheltered in comparison to Ektian's and Irene's, with less core bitterness on which to build. Chancel was as yet an unknown quantity – something of a loner, as he waited and watched, silently making his decisions, as he had been in the sprawl where he'd lived. Adriana was the only one who seemed to understand a little of what he was thinking. Whatever their hopes, hang-ups and agendas, all of them were powerful, dangerous and effective.

So what had happened here, and what were their plans?

With less reluctance than previously, the Fenris turned to recorded data from his permanent feed at Caprock. He scanned their computer usage, conversations, and social interactions. The six lacked the internal direction that should have arisen after they became accustomed to their powers and intelligence. Instead of taking the fenris route, however, they'd fallen back on their human driving daemons. This had allowed Irene, strong and vengeful after her experiences at the hands of Garrick and the Committee scientists, to assert dominance over them. In presenting her plan, she'd given them at least a choice of direction and leadership they felt they needed. And what a plan it was. She intended to cut off the head of the snake, as she saw it, by assassinating all the world leaders who formed and received guidance from the Committee – people who, in themselves, were just a symptom of a systemic problem.

They had no subtlety.

The biotech gave them great power over their own biology, as well as over their existence and existence around them, but the fenris mental component was missing. They were primitives who were still functioning as such in their application of this great power they'd acquired. Meanwhile, the split-away parallel Earth on which they'd established themselves gave Irene the justification she wanted. Maybe their home, nodal Committee Earth, didn't have time for them to be subtle, because a virus might well be sitting in the ID chips of millions even now, waiting for activation. The Fenris tended to agree. But he also understood that killing off those heads of state wouldn't stop that outcome either. In fact, it might instigate it, and would certainly drive that world further and faster along the path of totalitarianism. What could he do?

He could simply tell them his predictions for the result of their act. However, his understanding of their social dynamic killed that idea. Due to his physical distance from them, and their primitive biology, they already didn't trust him. Sure, he could have convinced some of them, but Irene would go ahead with her plan anyway, and was quite capable of carrying it out alone. There was another way, though. Taking a medium-term view, the Fenris saw that allowing them to carry this through would provide him with leverage. He could use their inevitable failure to turn them away from Committee Earth, and direct them towards where they were truly needed, for the benefit of humanity as a whole: countering that loathsome subhuman culture, the hive.

But still there was Irene, who, with her history, wouldn't respond well to leverage. Perhaps there was a solution to that dilemma. The Fenris now turned his attention to the people captured by the two jaunt research teams on Committee Earth. Some there were the product of the family line on which the Fenris had used the initial virus, carrying his own DNA. They were fiercely intelligent and held within them some element of fenris morality. Any of those would be much stronger than the present six, and would be able to take charge, displacing Irene. All one of them had to do was survive the experimenters and find a way to escape . . .

Ottanger

When he arrived, he saw the suit laid out in pieces on a table in front of the sphere. The technicians were already in place at their consoles, and Savarack was over by the suit with two more of them. Yorgos patted Ottanger once on the shoulder of his mesh undersuit.

'Good luck,' he said, then walked to where more of his kind were coming through another door. As Ottanger headed over to Savarack, it occurred to him to wonder about the heavy security here, with so many armed men scattered about the room. Had subjects before him seen the Fenris too? Did the researchers fear they might be opening some doorway to something? Perhaps this related to those autopsy pictures of strange humanlike figures his interrogators had shown him.

'Ah, you're here,' said Savarack. He stared at the undersuit technicians had put on Ottanger in his room. The thing had the appearance of a full bodysuit, made of fine golden chainmail, and went on over a series of round sensor patches they'd stuck all over his body. It pinched a bit in places, but at least felt light. 'Perfect fit. Dr Alison got your measurements just right.' He turned to the technician. 'Suit him up,' he said, and headed for his consoles.

Ottanger moved forwards and the technicians began to clad him in the white plastic armour. On the inner faces of every segment he could see complex electronics, and each piece stuck like Velcro. As they dressed him in this, he watched some of those who'd been in his previous audience coming in. The same black-haired woman was there, Colonel Jones, another officer and a couple of 'crats. They were talking, and the woman was obviously agitated as she spoke to Jones. Then, looking grim, they took their seats. What did this mean, he wondered – was the Inspectorate making a further attempt to take over? Likely he was being para-noid but it seemed a good idea to keep that possibility in mind.

When the technicians pulled up the mesh hood of his inner suit, then put on the helmet, he saw the fly-pill inhalator positioned just in front of his mouth. He stared at the thing, feeling a tug inside that he recognized. He *wanted* to suck the dry but seemingly oily dust of that fly into his lungs. He filed this feeling away for later inspection as they next directed him towards the door into the sphere, which he now saw no longer contained a chair. As he stood inside, they began connecting up the skeins of wires to the surrounding system.

'Not many of them today,' he said as a tech worked behind him.

The tech looked around – it was the one he'd spoken to on his visit before.

'Spectators?'

'Yes.'

'Many of them want to be associated with this, but don't have much interest in the science. They know you're wearing the suit today so won't be able to see you disappear.'

'I see.'

'But I'm sure they have other important work to do,' the tech hurriedly added.

Ottanger frowned: always fear everywhere.

The suit was restrictive. When they attached mechanical components between the sections, he'd expected them to hinge, but then found that the elbows and knees didn't bend. The gauntlets were like solid mittens too, and rigid. As they finished connecting up the wiring, they fixed clamps across the lower foot coverings, securing him to the floor of the sphere. He understood now that the audience wouldn't even be able to see the suit collapsing as he departed it. Finally, one tech flipped up the lid of the inhalator, inserted one of the black and white pills into the device and snapped the plastic lid home again. The two techs then retreated out of the sphere door, closing it behind them.

'You can hear me?' Savarack asked, voice close to his ear.

'I can hear you,' Ottanger replied.

'Do not use the inhalator until I specifically tell you to do so, understood? The suit will puncture the pill upon my instruction – you'll hear it.'

'I understand.'

'Larson, power up the monitorware.'

'Powering now,' Larson, whoever he was, replied. It seemed

that Ottanger could hear the other side of Savarack's exchanges with his staff too. Was this because he was now an SA and 'included' in the project?

A slight tingling impinged, but then faded away.

'Feed is good,' said Larson.

Other voices then began to speak, running through checklists. He only understood the stuff about his physical state – heart rate and suchlike. This all went on a lot longer than had been his perception of it last time, and he started to feel bored and uncomfortable. Then his nose started itching, and this became the focus of his world until the next words:

'Andrews, fire up the snare field,' said Savarack.

The suit jerked and he felt the dangerous hum of power around him. A high-pitched whine started right inside his head, and he abruptly felt constricted. Yet, when he tested his movement within the suit, it hadn't changed from before. Something happened to his perception too. The laboratory, the equipment and the people seemed to solidify, taking on more substance for a second, and then, as if they had taken on too much substance, it spilled. Every object and person cast out iridescent striations, or interference patterns, from their surfaces, yet somehow, none of these interfered with each other. All appeared to extend off in a direction he couldn't point to.

'Okay, can you still hear me Ottanger?'

Savarack's voice was strangely distorted, as if it too was throwing off interference patterns in the sound spectrum.

'I can hear you.'

'Use the inhalator now.'

Ottanger dipped his head forwards eagerly. The inhalator made a crunching sound, as some electronic actuator punctured the pill. He gladly huffed out, closed his mouth around the thing, and took a deep breath. Again, as he held his breath, he struggled not to cough from the dusty oily feeling in his throat. But now he felt something else too.

It was like gulping a cold drink when thirsty – that feeling of liquid entering the stomach and permeating the rest of the body. In this case, it was in the lungs and spread out from there. There was a hint of something else too. Tobacco had once been obtainable for ZAs, and favoured because it helped kill hunger. He'd been addicted to it for a while, until demand utterly outweighed meagre supply and it became too expensive in rations and difficult to obtain. This also felt like the quelling of a nicotine craving, though a craving he hadn't known he had until now.

Next, around him, iridescent striations centred on him like the rays of the sun, and the world felt ready to fade away. This too was not the same as before. He felt poised on the brink, yet to make the choice to jump. He remembered orange sand underneath him, and it gained reality, then he collapsed down onto his knees.

The place didn't look quite the same as before, and didn't feel the same either. The gritty drifts were a different shape, and the plants down on the yellow solid ground between them had a purplish cast. Perhaps he'd arrived at a different location? Fighting panic because of the lack of air, he studied his surroundings more intently. He noticed that the plants looked burned on one side, and powdery ash striated the ground in some areas, while the drift looked as if it had been seared too. He couldn't see any human remains like before. Perhaps a different location, or had there been a fire at the same one? No, the atmosphere lacked oxygen, so more likely some kind of blast. Next, peering down at himself, he saw that he was still wearing the mesh suit. On the one hand, he felt glad to have clothing, but on the other it was restrictive, which he also understood to be its function. *Snare field*, Savarack had said. Ottanger knew what a snare was.

He finally huffed out the breath he'd been holding and breathed in the unsatisfying air, thinking fast. What could he learn here? What advantage could he gain? And most importantly, would the Fenris speak to him again? Whatever, he needed to breathe.

Closing his eyes, he visualized that previous beach, with its rotting mosasaurus, but this didn't seem to help. He opened his eyes and visualized again, but visualization became looking, and he saw the place over *there* . . . but in a direction he couldn't point to. He stepped towards it, physically and in another way. Blackness briefly enveloped him and then, out of that, something snaked in and connected. He felt a network grow hot inside himself as he stumbled out onto rock. Relieved to hear the sound of the sea, he glanced over at the mosasaurus and saw that some of its bones had been scattered.

'Gotcha,' said the Fenris. 'Been sniffing fly pills, have we?'

11

Ottanger

Ottanger turned, then felt foolish because his perception of the creature lay inside his mind. Gazing upon it, he saw hints of weird surroundings: flat surfaces seemingly meshed into a mass similar to intestines. And a strange jointed tentacle, with a hand on its end that looked decidedly human, was moving an object. Something shifted then, and those surroundings retreated, depositing the Fenris on a stone slab at the top of the beach, just a few metres away from him. He turned his head and the creature remained in place. He didn't know whether he, or it, had done this, but it felt more natural for the creature to be in one place. More convenient, though it wasn't actually here. Holding up one long-fingered hand – in fact more of a claw – the Fenris made a strange swivelling gesture.

'Take off the garment,' it said.

He stared at the creature. It frightened him and, though he understood that the suit strengthened his tether to a world he hated, he felt a species of rebellion. Here was where people didn't tell him what to do.

'Fuck you,' he replied.

The Fenris's eyes opened wider, giving its narrow face a more human look, until their deep violet colour impinged. He studied it further, taking in the body shape and connecting it to his own mutation, as well as to that of others in his family. It was the source of information he needed, and had shown no hostility towards him. He should stop regarding it as some impossible monster. He then made the conscious decision to stop seeing a creature here, but a 'him'. Because the Fenris, despite being so radically different, bore all the characteristics of a man.

'I am trying to help you remain here, in place, but we can only do this for a little while,' the Fenris said. 'They will pull you back.' Something about *his* expression puzzled Ottanger . . . something there . . . Then he read the creature's amusement.

Abruptly he came to a decision. Going back to the Complex meant dangers he knew, and no chance there of escaping to anything. Back could also mean an eventual power shift, and for him probably interrogation and death. Here perhaps he could really learn something to his advantage, because this creature obviously had some understanding of what was happening to him. He pulled off the hood and suddenly it seemed easier to breathe. He then undid the seams down the front, and began the laborious task of pulling the suit off. Red lines mottled his skin underneath, between the circular monitoring patches. The more of the suit he took off, the freer he felt. Yet he could still feel something linked to him, pulling him back. It occurred to him that the patches might not be what he thought. He began to peel one of them off.

'The suit is enough,' the Fenris said quickly.

'I don't want this shit on me,' Ottanger replied. He then reached up to the back of his neck and touched the docilator there, as if for permission. The Fenris sighed.

'You will have to put the suit back on soon and go back. If you take off anything else, they'll know you removed the suit.'

'I don't want to go back,' said Ottanger, feeling like a protesting child.

'You have no choice in the matter.' The Fenris huffed, perhaps realizing he had to give an explanation. 'A safety measure, amplified by that suit, draws you back to the location of your first jaunts. Only your own incomplete abilities, complemented by my own, are holding you here. You're not fully transitioned yet, though; you're not fully a world walker. When I stop helping, you'll fall back anyway. And if you're not wearing the suit, you'll probably end up splattered over the landscape.'

'Then I need to be fully transitioned.'

The Fenris nodded. 'A woman, who was the first taken into the research there, on your world, and later designated Subject Alpha, changed very fast while they *examined* her.' The Fenris winced and Ottanger guessed those examinations hadn't been pleasant. 'They were killing her when she jaunted, and I found her. It was from the research on her that Savarack learned to limit the amount of material he gives you from the flies. To slow down the changes and study the subject more effectively.' The Fenris pointed to the undersuit. 'And now he's learning how to control the subject.'

'Then get me one of your flies,' he said, feeling the need tighten his guts.

'That's not possible, unfortunately. But if you want your freedom, you need more of the fly nanotech in your system – more of those fly pills. I hope you can get it before they kill you.'

Ottanger hesitated, then lowered his hand and finally pulled the suit off his feet and left it on the sand.

'That's better now, isn't it?' said the Fenris.

He gazed at the creature. He now felt very warm, and his

mind seemed to be going into overdrive, throwing up scenarios connecting this individual with his world. For surely he must be connected in some way.

'The flies are yours, aren't they?' he said, his reasoning flashing all over the place, but certainty there.

'I see the genetic changes are having their effect,' the Fenris said. 'Yes, I sent the flies, just as I sent a virus beforehand to install biotech in your ancestors.'

The next flash of insight arrived: 'I have something of you in me.'

The Fenris gave a tight smile. 'Very good. You are, in essence, a relation. But don't try to work that out – there will be far too much use of the word "removed" in it, and in the completely human respect it would be incorrect.'

'There are others like me. There have been others like me,' said Ottanger.

'Too few, unfortunately.' The Fenris's face clenched with pain. 'You saw many of them back in the place you were in before. I am attempting to ameliorate that problem, but a further problem has arisen there.' He frowned off to one side, then focused back on Ottanger.

Ottanger's mind continued its buzzing. As he made plausible connections, and some implausible ones, he couldn't yet see the shape of it all. But one question occurred.

'Why are you doing this?' he asked.

The Fenris made an odd gesture with his hand, or perhaps claw, and answered bitterly, 'I felt a need to intervene in the nightmare that is your world, and I made some severe errors in doing so. Now I am simply trying to help those I've changed.'

'Please, I don't understand. You need to be clearer.'

The Fenris peered in at him. 'You're new. The biotech transformation is not fully rooted, and you remain dull.'

He wanted to swear at the creature, but clamped down on it, aware he was being prodded to think.

'But not too stupid to learn,' he said.

The Fenris looked off to one side and pursed his lips, then, turning back, continued, 'I found a dystopian and terrible world and thought to change it by imparting some of my abilities to the people there. A hundred and fifty years ago I sent a virus, infecting numerous subjects far and wide, enough for it to propagate. It implanted foundational biotech. In more recent times, I then sent through the remainder.'

'The flies.'

'Quite.'

'And something in the flies activates the biotech, so we become capable of travelling to parallel worlds?'

'That is the essence of it, but not all . . .'

Ottanger tried to ignore his bafflement, because he needed to keep the creature talking.

'Why is the situation as it is now?' he asked, trying to sound logical, exact, but not quite sure what situation he was referring to.

'Most of you humans don't adapt well to the biotech, and it killed many. My flies were also destroyed on your world by an insecticide programme, and I will send no more.' The Fenris again looked off to one side, then added, 'For the present.'

'But the Complex . . . the experiments.'

'Ah, ingenious and surprising.' The Fenris looked distracted, as if bored now, yet it seemed to Ottanger to be an act. 'Your world is of course closely surveiled, and one of the numerous AIs with that job made the connection. It saw people disappearing, on camera, and connected that to them earlier having been bitten by a fly of some kind. A human would never have made the connection. Some of the disappeared reappeared, many dying in the process, others were captured and killed.'

'I heard nothing of that,' Ottanger said, then realized it had been a very stupid thing to say when the Fenris gave him an irritated look. He'd just felt the need to interject something, assert his presence.

The Fenris continued, 'By then, various investigators were in serious overdrive after realizing that people had simply disappeared, and some of those captured on their return managed to escape their cells. Corpses of those who died, or fragments of them, were handed over to researchers for thorough investigation. They found the oddities in their DNA – the extraneous genetic material. They'd also collected dead flies and examined them. And that was when things got really serious.'

'Savarack called them cyborg flies,' he said. 'But why would you use such a Byzantine method to . . . to try to do something about Earth?'

The Fenris shook his head, looking bitter. 'Should I have gone there to kill the heads of state, perhaps?'

'Seems like a start.'

'Your world is a fragile system, and that would result in disruption and mass death. Others would simply replace them anyway, and use the deaths as an excuse for further clampdowns. Presently your world still has some national divisions. They would dissolve, and totalitarianism would become fully established, and long lasting.'

Ottanger absorbed this, and saw how it correlated with his own thinking on the resistance, and why he'd left. But he also had the strong sense they weren't just talking about something speculative. He was about to question this when the Fenris continued, 'I don't yet have the ability to jaunt between the parallels as you do.'

'So how the hell was your plan supposed to pan out?'

The Fenris focused on him hard, as if looking deep inside him. 'With the power of biotechnology to raise you out of evolutionary drives. The massive increase in intelligence, which is a by-product of the ability to map and travel in five dimensions. You will understand eventually, if you survive.'

Ottanger tracked back through their discussion and saw that a lot didn't make sense. Big interventions, like assassinations, would be destabilizing. But how could he think that giving people such abilities wasn't such an intervention? It seemed to be an open-ended thing, like a solution from academia, with all its lack of understanding of human realities. The thought then came to him, an almost risqué questioning of authority: did the Fenris actually know what he was doing?

The Fenris held up a hand and waved it to one side. 'Time for you to put that back on.' He pointed to the undersuit.

Ottanger stared at the thing resentfully, then stooped to pick it up and reluctantly put it on. He had so many more questions, about the 'Subject Alpha', for example, and still he didn't understand what the Fenris had been trying to achieve. But it seemed he'd run out of time, as he closed the suit's front seam.

'I sincerely hope we will talk again,' said the Fenris.

I have to lie now, Ottanger thought as he woke up, and then reminded himself that in some sense he'd been lying all along.

Dr Alison had made her initial examinations, and more intensive examinations had followed. They'd been very attentive, and even gave him painkillers when they took samples from just about every part of his body. He strongly suspected that the change in attitude – this attempt to recruit him – starting with him being made an SA, had been designed by psychologists. They were steadily treating him better, giving him more rewards. The basket of foods and some wine, all exotic to him, left by Savarack. And the '*rest of the team*' confirmed this when, weary and aching, he returned to his apartment. On checking his account, he'd been completely unsurprised to see that his daily social credit had doubled.

He understood perfectly that if he'd really been a simple ZA, this tactic would have worked very well. He wasn't, though, of course, and he'd also found himself thinking with painfully clear precision. His recall had very much improved too, and he could remember his interrogations in detail, as well as his life before them. He felt sure the Fenris would be happy about him ceasing to be 'dull'. He paused then and considered one thing it had said, which he hadn't understood at the time. But now he did: *The massive increase in intelligence, which is a by-product of the ability to map and travel in five dimensions.* His thoughts then segued to the Fenris telling him it couldn't travel as he could. Perhaps it didn't have that facility of mind? Certainly, some of the things it had apparently done seemed, as he'd said, 'Byzantine'. And, from his own understanding, even before his present clarity, when things were overly complicated it was because someone smart hadn't thought of a simple solution. He pondered on that, then returned to thoughts on manipulation.

Along with using straightforward carrot-and-stick behavioural techniques to control him, they'd also lied to him here. The docilator was an example of the latter, since they'd repeatedly lied about it being permanently connected to his spinal nerves. As he showered, he contemplated what he must do next, fitting together scraps of knowledge garnered throughout his life, and of which he now seemed to have almost eidetic recall. As he dressed and reached up to touch the docilator, he felt the strong impulse to keep his hand away from it – confirmation if any were needed that it *did* come off. He fought the impulse to take his hand away and felt it grow stronger, but not unbearable. He nodded to himself. Even though the thing's influence over him was growing weaker, it was a hindrance to the necessity of him telling lies. He needed to do something about it, as with much else.

Yes, he had to be proactive rather than reactive soon because something else had changed too, he realized. Since his return from the last jaunt, the need inside him for that unpleasant dry oiliness in the back of his throat hadn't gone away. This addiction, if that's what it was, also related to how *precarious* the world around him now felt. Briefly he'd thought this just to be the after-effects of his jaunt – a feeling of unreality engendered by having done something so extraordinary. But it confirmed precisely what the Fenris had told him regarding what was in the flies, and his need for more of it. Now, alone at last, he tried to pursue it by *leaning* or *pushing* in that direction he couldn't point to, and for a moment the world felt like a skin over another reality. But that was all. This world maintained its grip on him. He grimaced and started probing at the docilator again, when someone knocked on the door.

Ottanger stared at the door, accepting this as part of the psychological programme – someone was actually knocking rather than just walking in. However, he dreaded what would surely ensue. They'd come to take him for 'debriefing'. He stepped over and opened the door to find *her*, the lush woman, there.

'I thought it about time I got to know you,' she said, holding out a hand. 'My name is Jillian.'

He found himself staring at her body. Yes, she wore a 'crat skirt and jacket, but the skirt was cut high and the jacket over her white shirt pushed her cleavage into prominence. She also wore make-up, and had studs in her ears, when the Bureaucracy generally frowned on such ornament. Notably, she didn't have that strict bullish look of most female 'crats he'd encountered. Abruptly aware that too long had passed, he reached out and grasped her hand.

'Hello . . . Jillian,' he said, but could think of nothing else.

'Aren't you going to invite me in?'

'Oh, sorry.' He stepped back and gestured into the apartment.

She flounced in, closing the door firmly behind her. Even as she went over to the sofa, she unbuttoned and took off her jacket. As she sat down he noticed that more buttons were undone on her shirt than had been apparent at first.

'I see you received the gift,' she said. 'That was my idea. We're not Inspectorate here, and we treat our essential staff as they should be treated.' She took off a hairband and shook out her black hair.

He walked over and sat down on the other end of the sofa. She immediately moved closer, swinging her knees towards him.

'But I might have had an ulterior motive,' she added. 'The wine is one of my favourites and a rare treat on my credit.' She gave him an arch look while casually putting a hand down on his knee.

Hollow, cynical amusement rose up inside him. He began to see the lengths they were prepared to go to in order to gain his loyalty, keep him onside. They didn't want him disappearing like this Subject Alpha had. He also wondered what had happened to the other three, between that woman and Epsilon. Perhaps they'd been steadily perfecting their technique on them. Then he wondered what other subjects they had lined up. In a flash he knew there'd be many. He had no doubt that his sister Jane was in their sights, probably captured and in a cell somewhere even now. He would have to do something about that, if he could. No. He *would* do something about that.

'I wish you'd included glasses,' he said, thinking, *Why not?* His previous sexual encounters had been with female ZAs, who would fuck for a day's rations. It had become risk-free regarding pregnancy in his sector, because the cross-sex contraceptive chemicals in the water supply never waned as elsewhere. Though the danger of STDs remained, unless you could afford prophylactics. Anyway, he'd eaten well and was healthy, and he couldn't deny the smell and look of her was stirring a response.

'Whatever you have will be fine.' She smiled at him knowingly.

He reluctantly stood up and went to his kitchen area. He had two ceramic cups, which he brought back. She raised an eyebrow at them but said nothing. Picking up the bottle, he was glad to see a screw-top rather than a cork – a method of closing bottles he'd only ever seen on a screen. He opened it and poured. She picked up one of the cups and took a sip.

'Ah, perfect,' she said.

When he tried the wine, he found it dry and strange. He obviously knew about red wine but had never drunk it in his life before. His only access to alcohol had been the product of illegal stills, mixed with ersatz fruit juices. Once, alcohol had been all but impossible to obtain for ZAs, but some change of policy allowed those who operated stills to get away with it. Now, with his mind working differently and having a new perspective, he realized someone had probably looked at the figures and seen that cheap alcohol helped keep them docile. And, with the frequent poisonings, it would kill some off earlier too.

'What do you think?' she asked.

'It's new to me, but I guess I could get used to it, like with a lot of things here,' he replied. 'My life has certainly improved.'

'And it will keep on improving,' she said, leaning forwards.

He put his hand on her leg. 'I certainly hope so.'

She smiled, something quite smug and victorious in that, then placed her hand on his, while putting her cup down on the table. She slid closer, guiding his hand up her skirt as she did so, leaned in, and kissed him on the mouth. He realized his hand had slid up past stockings onto bare inner thigh, then against the knickers over her vagina, which felt hot. He put his drink aside too and already she had both her hands at the front of his trousers, undoing them. Still kissing him, she pulled out his penis and began slowly rubbing it.

'Ah, fuck,' he said, knowing he wouldn't last long at all.

Apparently she read this, and pushed away from him, lying back on the sofa, pulling her skirt up to her waist, then opening her legs wide, one foot down on the floor and the other up on the back of the sofa. She reached down to pink knickers, hitched the fabric to one side of her vagina. No hair there, just an equally pink, wet opening. He gazed at her for a long moment. He'd only ever seen a woman naked, with this amount of flesh on her, on a screen. Pulling his trousers down to his hips, he hurriedly shifted over on top of her, sliding easily inside. She groaned and shuddered, as though having an orgasm almost immediately but, knowing her purpose here, he doubted it. He went slowly, propped up on one arm, trying to stop himself coming. She looked up at him and only one word described her expression: dirty. Still looking at him, she undid the remaining buttons on her shirt, then pulled her bra down below large breasts. He got both his hands on them, and the feel was just too much. His pace increased as he tried to bury as much of himself inside her as he could, thighs slapping hard against hers, and when he came it felt like it'd issued from the base of his spine. She groaned in response, pushing up against him. He kept shuddering afterwards, further small orgasms following. And then he was lying on her, gasping.

After a short while, she took hold of his hair and turned his face to hers, then kissed him again, long and soft. Even so soon afterwards, he could feel himself starting to respond again, but she pulled her lips away and pushed at him.

'We have some wine to drink,' she told him.

He slid off her and retreated to the other end of the sofa. Of course – just the one time, to keep him eager. Swinging her legs off the sofa, and with her skirt still hitched up, she walked to the bathroom, spunk dripping down her leg.

'I think you were saving that up,' she said, reaching down and smearing it.

While she was in there, he pulled up his trousers again and took another sip of his wine. It tasted better now, but he felt he shouldn't drink too much of it – he should not allow himself to become too relaxed. The thought that it would be nice to let things ride for a while, with her coming to visit, arose just for a second, as if for examination. It was then drowned in a sea of cold logic. He was an asset they were trying to hang on to. The spectators came because here lay power and it attracted them. She'd either been instructed to fuck him, or had done so because it would bring her even closer to that power.

When she returned from the bathroom, her state of undress evinced surprise. He'd expected her to be fully clothed, to drink some more wine, and then to leave with promises of dalliances in the future. But she came back carrying her jacket, skirt and shirt, wearing only pink knickers and bra, black stockings and suspenders. He began to get up but she tossed her hair, then rounded the table to sit down. Facing him, she topped up her wine and picked up the cup.

'When I finish this,' she said. 'We'll try that again, and this time I expect you to last longer.'

The Fenris

The data-storage rods were highly corrupted, but from them the Fenris was able to sketch out at least some of the history of how the hive creatures had come to be. It had started with their Earth falling under totalitarian control. And in this it diverged from the history of Committee Earth, as well as its few parallels, and what the Fenris understood of the history of his own kind. On Committee Earth, when world powers had been poised on the brink of nuclear destruction, they'd stepped back from that. Here they'd come to it much earlier and didn't.

The nuclear exchange had annihilated cities, irradiated populations, smashed infrastructure, and seemed to be throwing them back to the Stone Age. Except, despite the dire warnings of utter annihilation such a conflict would bring about, it wasn't as bad as predicted. Yes, it was horrific – of a population of four billion, one-quarter died – but there had been no ensuing nuclear winter. Radiation diminished quickly, as did deaths from cancer after an initial spike. At that time, they hadn't comprehended that the malady resulted from constant exposure, and not so much from exposure to a burst of it. Meanwhile, enough technology and infrastructure remained intact, like agriculture and food, which hadn't really been a target so hardly suffered at all. Seeing all this, the Fenris understood human hubris. They had utterly overestimated their ability to destroy themselves.

The political zeitgeist that arose out of this war was cultish in its determination for this to *never happen again*. Very swiftly, previous political leaders who'd been involved in the destruction were found and put on trial, if they even managed to come to that point, and then executed. The new politicians arising linked up rapidly to form a world government. Remaining armed forces were used in this task to suppress those who wanted to retain nation states, or otherwise some independence. It was a brutal time of short wars, usually ended by the deployment of remaining tactical nukes – whole populations being wiped out because of their 'aberration'. And out of this evolved a new World Council, controlling everything. Its similarity to the Committee didn't escape the Fenris, though it came into being nominally a century and a half beforehand.

Under this Council, a technocratic class of scientists were the SAs, working to be the saviours of the future. Research advanced at an astounding rate, because wealth was concentrated on it, with there no longer being a military–industrial complex to feed. As seemed standard, computer technology was first superseded by biotechnology. And, considering those past 'aberrant' populations, eugenics raised its ugly head. However, though the sciences advanced, the world outside of these cliques fell into the same model as Committee Earth. Having rid the world of the burden of money, and instituted a social order based on corruptly applied status, industrial and food production suffered. At the same time, their version of the ZA population burgeoned, and infrastructure steadily broke down. They hadn't learned that people without hope took a genetic shot at the future by having more children. It was a biological imperative in all life. Plants, subjected to harsh conditions, tended to produce more seeds.

The scientists, of course, had the solutions, even when they didn't. Experts, whenever given the power to speak and act, find they very much like it, and never want to give up speaking, acting, or power. The first of these solutions was that smaller humans wouldn't use up so much in the way of resources. Genetic changes were made via vaccination programmes, and the resulting humans did indeed use fewer resources – usually by dying young. Riots and civil disorder ensued, and the experts had the answers to this too. These came from the area of computer science, with devices installed to people's heads to punish, suppress and instruct. Again the parallels with Committee Earth: very much like the docilator that supposedly made Ottanger malleable and docile.

Here the record became disrupted and the Fenris put the rest together by inference.

The leaders of the older regime either died, or were displaced, and the world government turned into a technocracy, without restraint or morals. The main population became a testing bed for numerous hypotheses to 'better humanity' and often ended up twisted and grotesque, when not dying in their millions. These mistakes rendered data, and the technocrats learned how to form people for particular tasks and niches, and to control them, like swarms of insects. Yet, while standing separate and elite from this, the technocrats hadn't realized that they themselves weren't immune to what they'd set in motion. It took many generations for society to evolve down the route of social insects, falling into swarms and nests, both large and small, and for the elites to be subsumed into what became consensus intelligences. But being more 'social', just as with the insects, didn't negate violence. In fact, it increased its likelihood, as distinct nest ideologies clashed. Wars ensued, with many nests being wiped out and others subsumed, until just two hive cultures remained at each other's throats.

The Fenris finally took a breather from all this history, questioning his basic premise in letting biotech loose on Committee Earth. He'd seen it as leading to individual power and freedom, as had been the history of his kind. But now he saw how it could take a completely different course. Whether technology was good or bad, as ever, depended on its application. He came to a conclusion in that moment: sending his biotech had been a mistake not because of his intentions, or the catastrophic failure, but because the increasingly totalitarian regime of the nodal Earth was now studying it. And they would find ways to apply it to their own political ends. He needed to go through and put a stop to that, then institute a better, more subtle, plan to make the corrections he wanted. But then other doubts occurred – so much that turned sour had been done for the 'good of humanity'. Anyway, he needed his focus on the greater danger right now: the hive.

There was something utterly wrong in this hive history, which he had yet to plumb fully because of the disruption to the recording. He needed to know it all. The most glaring oddity was the timeline. Yes, this alternative route for history had begun well in the past of this Earth. But all the events, changes and technological advancements that had led to this state of two hive cultures at war must have taken centuries. This would put the hive well in advance of all the other worlds across the multiverse. Something really didn't add up here.

The two hives fought with increasingly sophisticated weapons, and populations turned into multifarious iterations of the warrior. They created artificial intelligences they integrated with their hives, and went from atomic weapons to shielding technology and energy weapons. They started to crack dimensional barriers, to route lethal plagues and bombs around their present reality, and into their opponents' hive. They built vast machines and played with energies that the Fenris, until that moment, had thought the territory only of his own kind. One hive pulled all its resources from the world to gain advantage over the other. And . . . there the record ended completely.

The Fenris went through it a few more times and ran the extrapolations. The two hive cultures would have created ever more powerful weapons and sophisticated defences. But he surmised one had begun to gain an advantage, while the other built an escape route, based on technology far too familiar to the Fenris. Almost certainly, they'd encountered the same problems as his kind, and an entropy wave had sucked out every erg of energy from those on the planet, denuding it of life and oxygen producers, with the result as he'd seen it now. Those on the moon had somehow survived, and it didn't really matter which hive they arose from.

So there then was the reality: the Fenris wasn't the only interloper in this particular multiverse. The hive had come from somewhere else too. Now understanding this, he accessed data and built models, then ran them while making intensely complicated calculations. Soon he came to some conclusions: in the timeline of this universe, the hive had arrived at about the same time as the fenris world had. This seemed likely due to a confluence of energy flows. Or, in other terms, they'd both been swept up on the same tide. The hive had been highly advanced but had arrived here damaged, to begin the long process of rebuilding. It perfectly matched him and his world in that respect. Detecting the presence of jaunt technology had accelerated its rebuilding, raising it to a state of threat assessment and negation.

Things were, as Chenghu often said, starting to get gnarly.

Ottanger

It was night time – something he hadn't noticed in the other apartment, but here required the closing of blinds because of the actinic lights outside. It seemed they weren't going to question him today – or at least that's what Jillian had told him when she departed, leaving him exhausted on the bed.

In darkness, with the covers up over his head, he explored the docilator on the back of his neck. Like a large dry slug, the soft thing clung there horizontally. He pulled at an edge and felt it peel up. Yes: skin-stick layer. This confirmed what he'd felt when Jillian had been here – how the thing had shifted on his neck, lubricated by sweat. Considering his options, he thought about how, when questioned, it took away any inclination for him not to answer, rather than impelled him to do so. But then he hadn't yet been in any situation while wearing it when he hadn't wanted to answer. Should he try to fight it? He decided no, because it would be too easy to slip into the truth. Then he realized he had a perfect excuse in the form of Jillian. Their sex had gone on for a long time, involving the table and the kitchen area, the floor and finally here. It had got quite rough, as the scratches on his body attested, until she hinted that perhaps she needed to be punished for hurting him. His palms still felt warm from that.

He rehearsed in his mind what he would say later on, perhaps with a hint of embarrassment, or pride, as he now peeled up one end of the device and probed into a point that felt like the sore spot under a scab. Then he tore the thing off. He had expected pain, but it did just feel like a large scab coming away from a wound already healed. And it also seemed to release his mind, which felt like some elastic mass springing open from it. Thinking abruptly became easier than before. And, despite his weariness from his recent activities, he suddenly felt very awake. A new scenario was now, he realized, abandoning the docilator in the bed. He wouldn't even notice its absence until someone pointed it out to him. Then he'd just have to hope they didn't react too severely and would accept his explanation.

But there would be other problems too. He felt that this time they probably wouldn't use drugs or the pain inducer, since they were trying to bring him onside. However, when they questioned him, he had no doubt they would monitor his reactions on many levels. How could he beat that? Pulling the covers down off his face, he lay on his back and reached down to feel his own pulse. Even as he did so, the beat of his heart became evident on another level. He certainly hadn't been able to feel it before as he did now, so could he also control it? He concentrated on the fast beat and tried to slow it down. It slowed, instantly. He speeded it up again, pushing it higher and higher until he broke into a sweat and his chest felt tight, then brought it down again.

Next he turned to his adrenal response. He pushed himself to fear and panic, and felt the surge of it tightening his guts, though it wasn't fear he felt but excitement. He pulled it down again to a point of meditative calm. Tiredness then washed over him. He finally decided to sleep and experiment further in the morning.

'Take a seat, Ottanger,' said the man facing him across the table.

The room wasn't the expected interrogation cell. It had carpet and no square in the ceiling above. In fact, the chair he'd been directed to sat close to this side of the desk, where an inducer couldn't have been used without the interrogator catching some of the backwash. He sat down quickly, as if under the influence of his docilator, which still lay in his rumpled bed. Nobody had made any comment about it being missing – they probably hadn't noticed. He suspected that when someone finally spotted its absence, Yorgos and other guards would be in trouble. Not for him to worry about. His problem now was the need to tell lies.

'I'm Axel,' said the man, reaching a hand across the table.

Ottanger shook it, cynicism arising, which he closely monitored within himself. 'Pleased to meet you.' Ottanger inspected his internal reactions to that lie too, finding that through his practising earlier, he seemed to have obtained a sense of his body's operations well beyond the conventional, as well as control.

'Now, I would like you to describe to me, in as much detail as you can, your recent jaunt. Bore me with detail if you will – I'm a good listener.'

Axel was thin, with cropped white hair. He looked old but fit, and wore a dark suit that didn't really shout 'bureaucrat'. His appearance bespoke a worrying professionalism. He leaned forwards a little to look down at Ottanger's hands.

'Put your palms down on the arms of the chair, if you would,' he added.

'Oh, sorry,' said Ottanger, then enquired, 'Lie detector?'

The arms of the chair had some rough white material – a meta-material, he suspected.

Axel waved a dismissive hand. 'That's the regime we live under. I've sat in a chair like that many times. Now, your jaunt?'

Ottanger nodded, and then spoke about his initial arrival point and what he'd done there. He told no lies, all the time monitoring the beat of his heart, and his adrenal responses – then, because he'd only just thought of it, how much his palms were sweating too. The room, his responses, the man's minute changes of expression, in fact everything in his vicinity, appeared in bright, almost terrible, clarity. The exactitude of his mind, as he memorized every change in himself, in consonance with his words, amazed him. There seemed no barrier to recall, or to layers and layers of his understanding, expanding out from every word and connected responses outside and within him.

Yet, along with this excess of control, the feeling of unreality had returned stronger. Axel and the whole situation seemed like a play, a drama, while the room and its contents had become tawdry set dressing. He tried to keep this feeling at a distance

297

and to apply even more exactitude. He could see the risk of becoming dislocated and not seeing the danger here.

'So, when you began to experience anoxia, what did you do next?' Axel asked.

'I closed my eyes and visualized the beach I went to before, but that didn't seem to work. I then visualized it with my eyes open, and it was as if I could see it. And in that way I tried to describe during my last . . . debriefing –' he increased his heart rate, allowed some adrenalin and sweat – 'I shifted there.' Speaking the words seemed to tilt his surroundings a little, and he quickly locked down on that.

Axel nodded. 'And this time?'

'When I arrived there, a person began speaking to me. . .'

'This was the creature you saw the last time?'

As he continued, he could see Axel's interest increasing, and obviously that of others who were watching and speaking into Axel's fone, or sending messages to his tablet. After describing how the Fenris had appeared to him, Ottanger came to the conversation they'd had.

'At first it seemed curious about me, then it seemed to become bored – I'm only guessing here, because its expression was difficult to read.'

His first lie was neglecting to mention that it had instructed him to remove his suit. As he told further lies, he allowed some adrenalin and sweat to come through, because of course he'd be excited or scared recounting all this. As he continued, he permitted this to die down, and his internal reactions to segue into his state when he'd been concentrating on recalling detail.

He wove in some of the things the Fenris had told him about the flies, and how it had considered its intervention a mistake. He expressed his own genuine bafflement about what it had hoped to achieve. He managed to convey its increasing boredom and irritation with him and how, in the end, it had become dismissive, finally releasing its hold so he was dragged back to the Complex.

The questions continued, of course, as Axel kept exploring detail, going back over things again and again. Ottanger remained firmly in control, and briefly worried that maybe he had too much control of his reactions, so threw in some more variance. Yet even with such internal focus, he found his mind straying to other things. To what degree were they measuring his responses? He had much larger control over his physiology than most people, but he didn't control it all, yet. It concerned him, in this cold, detached logical world, that all his responses would be, or were at that moment, subject to scrutiny by AI. An AI that could make connections a human never would, such as the one between the fly bites and people disappearing, as the Fenris had said. And then what if they did suspect he was lying? Would they interrogate him using drugs and the inducer?

Ottanger contemplated this prospect, of course not happy about the idea, but suspecting he could beat such an interrogation now. Anyway, he had leeway, because they wanted him onside. It also struck him as likely that previous subjects had undergone physical and mental changes that made their responses aberrant. He surmised that they hadn't seen enough of this to plumb it completely.

Finally, the questioning came to an end as Axel turned off his tablet and leaned back.

'Thank you for your cooperation,' he said.

'It's becoming apparent to me that cooperation has its benefits,' he replied, allowing a brief surge in his body related to sex. 'Is this over now?'

'Yes, we are done – you can go.'

Ottanger had half expected Axel to finish and go away, and then another questioner to come in. He stood hesitantly, taking his hands from the chair arms. Axel had his fingers up to the fone in his ear and appeared distracted, but then looked up and waved to the door, nodding and giving an encouraging smile. Ottanger headed for the door.

'Wait,' said Axel, just as he reached for the handle.

Here it comes, Ottanger thought. He turned.

'I've just noticed that your docilator is missing,' said Axel.

Certain that the monitoring extended beyond the chair arms, Ottanger reached up to the back of his neck. As his fingers touched the interface pad, he allowed a surge of surprise and shock, quickly followed by a growing fear reaction.

'It can't come off,' he said, putting just the right amount of pleading in his voice. 'They told me.' And now a hint of desperation.

Axel nodded, grim and suspicious. He reached up and touched his fone, probably receiving hurried instructions, then said, 'They were half right. The fibres entering your spinal cord and the interface pad cannot come off, but the docilator itself can – for maintenance or reprogramming.' He paused for a long moment, studying Ottanger, then asked, 'Did it come off, or did you take it off when this Fenris was questioning you?'

'No!' Ottanger protested at once, but then hesitantly added, 'It couldn't have – my suit. . .'

Axel grimaced for a second, then said, 'It's not important. It should have been removed anyway since you are now an SA and cooperating. You can go.' He waved a dismissive hand.

The relief Ottanger allowed himself to feel was half the real thing. As he closed the door behind him, his rigid control relaxed and he staggered, suddenly dizzy, the world tilting again. He put a hand against the wall and fought for stability, pushing himself upright and walking forwards rigidly, aware that the cams and other monitors were out here too.

★　★　★

Guards and other staff were moving about the Complex as Ottanger neared his room. Some of them were carrying wand detectors. When he reached the end of the hall leading to that room, Yorgos halted him.

'You can't go in there for the moment,' said the soldier.

Ottanger noted his pale and worried look, and knew precisely what was occurring. They were looking for the docilator, and of course would find it.

'Why not? What's the problem?' he asked.

If anything Yorgos turned paler. 'Security sweep.'

'Oh, I see. Has something happened?'

'Just routine.'

Ottanger swallowed, dipped his head, and made himself look afraid. 'It's the docilator, isn't it?'

Yorgos stared at him blankly, now looking as if he wanted to throw up. Ottanger felt a brief flash of pity for the man but quickly suppressed it. He waved a hand at the back of his neck. 'It came off, I don't know when.'

A worried and annoyed Jillian, accompanied by a soldier carrying one of those detection wands, saved Yorgos from replying. She saw Ottanger and her expression changed, as if she'd clicked a switch inside. She became amused, in control and apparently sure of herself. She waved the soldier on – Ottanger noticed he had a sample bag with the docilator inside.

'It seems,' she said, walking up close to him, 'docilators aren't made to withstand vigorous physical activity.' She smiled suggestively. 'Not that it really matters, beyond it being equipment whose loss can get us into tangled bureaucratic trouble – you have no need of one now.'

'I'm sorry,' he said, meek, apparently terrified of repercussions.

'Don't worry.' She patted his shoulder. 'And I'll see you later?'

'I have no wine left.' Poor erstwhile ZA managing some humour through his fear.

'I'll bring some.' She headed off.

Yorgos gestured wordlessly down the corridor. He could return to his room now.

12

The Fenris

As he strode along the intestinal tube of a corridor, the Fenris now thought about weapons. He hadn't wanted to consider these in any depth previously, preferring as he did to use subtle manipulation and persuasion. The ideal of people doing what was best for them and their kind applied to everyone, including the hive. But what was best for that entity simply wasn't best for humanity in general, and he told himself he had to accept realities.

His effort to change the course of Committee Earth by sending his biotech there had been the impulsive, ill-thought-out action of a child. Then seeing the disaster he'd caused, and swearing never to intervene again, he now viewed as the reaction of a child too. Sure, he'd done what he could to rescue those who survived his biotech, but that wasn't enough either, for his own safety or that of others. He had great power, which came with responsibilities, and he'd been reneging on them, reacting emotionally and not taking the long view. He needed to accept that losses couldn't be avoided and that, sometimes, if you wanted to do some good, you had to fight for it.

Reaching the end of the corridor, he turned into a series of wide open sphincters and stepped through, into the space beyond. The memory storage of his world contained all the technology of the bloody history prior to the fenris age, and he could access that here, as elsewhere. He gazed down long halls crammed with bio and hard tech, with the loops of complex conveyance tubes running between them. Here was where the fenris had made their smaller tools for scientific investigation, exploration of their world and of themselves. And here they made art of a technological nature too.

He took a position over beside a curved translucent surface, below which objects shifted like foetuses in an egg. There he reached out through his sensory armour and demanded connection. A new opaque surface slid down over the one below and sprouted glassy optics, which writhed through the air to connect to the sensory spikes of his armour. With the further expansion of perception, he then entered the realm of weapons technology, sorting through the endless options and making some selections. All around him, the technology shifted and writhed, as if his demands caused it pain, or perhaps he was just sublimating. He felt a small portion of it switch over from its constant chore of maintaining the tech of his world, to his immediate demands. Ahead of him, a circular part of the pale green floor folded up some edges, like those of a lily pad, and then within those edges, tubes opened, down into the machinery lying below. One of the tubes spat out an egg. Trailing optic links like sticky lines of glue, he walked over to pick it up, as around him other tubes squeezed out similar items too.

The glossy surface of the egg dissolved back as he held it. The thing inside then opened out to reveal a gauntlet of a similar glassy material to that of his sensory armour, though slightly darker and shot through with red veins. He slipped it onto his hand and attached it at his wrist to the main armour. A sense of its function immediately fell into his mind. With a thought, he retracted it, the thing splitting and rolling back off his hand, to form a ring around his wrist. He didn't need its protection right now. The other eggs contained other items of armour, which required him to detach his optic links and then discard those parts of his present armour they replaced. Jointed tentacle arms reached out to snatch up the discards and cart them off for recycling.

Actual weapons came next in the form of a pair of pistols. These, but for their glassy material, resembled muzzle-loaded duelling pistols from another age. They slid into rings at his waist, long barrels pointing inwards, while flat connections in the rings immediately fed them initiation charges, from the power segments that now ran down his back. The weapons themselves, once powered up, drew their destructive energies from the parallels. Other items arrived, which had their equivalents in the armament of the jaunters: explosives of multiple function, wrapped into cylinders so he could peel off strips of precisely what he required. And a larger weapon that slid into a holster on his back – a thing he hoped he'd never have to use. Once fully kitted out, he viewed himself via the surrounding biotech and saw something larger, command-ready and dangerous. And this reminded him of the fenris corpses he'd found and disposed of, both up in orbit and down here. The comparison made him uncomfortable as he next turned his attention to the needs of the jaunters, the world walkers, his soldiers.

The machines around him sorted back through the recorded history for armour and weapons designs that would be suitable for them. Too much power would heighten the arrogance arising from their old biology, but he also didn't want them to be too vulnerable. The combat suits the machines produced were state-of-the-art, perhaps fifty years beyond those on Committee Earth. The weapons he limited to the projectile variety, but still beyond that of an Inspectorate officer. And he gave them software and computer systems edging into AI territory. As the machinery around him went about producing his requirements, he detached the optic feeds, even as he headed out. The things retreated, snaking across the floor behind him, and snapping back into their curved surface.

As the elevator took the Fenris back up to orbit, he mentally tracked his orders from the factory, seeing them being loaded onto a train behind him as he arrived in the Geostation. He took a blister over to his primary engine, as the Geostation dispatched a cargo pod after him. Once there, he went deep inside the engine, to where energy stacks loomed, and locked singularities still seemed to pull at something inside him. Again, he found a sensory throne and sat down in it to connect up. But this time, rather than directing all this massed technology outwards, he pointed it within. Sitting on the throne, he flung his vision out to other worlds, leaping from one to the other. He stopped in on the aquatic humans, who were running multiverse experiments the fenris had done millennia ago. Then he dropped in on Committee Earth's Complexes, to view the trainee jaunters there. Finally, he focused on one place – the depopulated parallel of Committee Earth, where his world walkers were – and pushed. Everything in the engine grew thin as that place seemed to sweep in around him. Apparently poised on the brink, he monitored his own internals, and then he closed it down.

His surrounding biotech confirmed in detail what he'd sensed, and his disappointment gnawed at his insides. He still hadn't made that final formative step to adulthood, for he had yet to attain the ability to walk to other worlds. He wondered if this had informed the other changes in him. Could it be that what he saw as his increased aggression and hard pragmatism were arising because he approached full fenris adulthood? Was all this like the hormonal surge of a human teenager? And could it be that the altruism and empathy he'd felt before were fancies only a child could afford? It didn't matter. He must do what he must do.

From the throne, he observed the arrival of the cargo pod and then, with a gesture, he summoned an outgrowth from the biotech surrounding him. A snake of it, the thickness of his leg, extended out. The hand on its end folded in over its eye, and then the whole fist retreated inside itself. Seconds later, with pressure fed from behind, a bud grew out of it perfectly, matching the one Irene and Chenghu had seen from the biotech they activated. It turned upwards and then sprang open, exposing the grass seed form of a transport cage. The Fenris stared at it, while at the same time opening his ability and once again gazing upon worlds he no longer needed his instrumentation to see. The urge to jaunt grew painful in its intensity. Because this was as much a function of his being as reproduction was for conventional humans, and his frustration at not being able to do so grew equally, as his body developed.

He was anxious for action, and that didn't diminish, as tentacles with hands and eyes matching his own hauled the cargo pod up through the engine, and finally into view. The thing looked like a huge segmented grub. With a thought, he expanded the transport cage, opening it out into its spherical form. With another thought, he separated the cage into its individual ribs and sent them swirling in around the cargo pod. This meant the cargo would now be included as part of him, and he could take it wherever he wanted to jaunt. And yet he still couldn't go! He paused there, seeing the cargo, and the endless worlds and people he knew, and he snarled at the multiverse.

Another harsh instruction closed up the pieces of the cage into its grass seed form again, and he dispatched it to stick on one wall. He then sat back to chafe and rationalize. It was all very well having a sense of urgency, but even better to maintain a sense of perspective. Even if he could jaunt, he was being premature, allowing either pre-adult or old biology to govern him. Events out there on Committee Earth had to reach a natural conclusion before he acted. He just hoped he would be ready when they did.

Irene

They stood in one of the many basement rooms of Caprock, where crates of supplies were stacked around the walls. Everyone now wore the best combat suits Chenghu had been able to obtain, and they were all loaded with weapons. No one but Chenghu and Irene had used them before. But with their intelligence, enhanced senses and degree of physical control, they quickly mastered what was, in essence, a simple art. Irene inspected them briefly, then turned her attention to the transport cage.

The cylinder within the cage stood half a metre tall and was as thick as a torso. A lot of its weight came from the shielding and the cooling jacket, which had previously been linked into a system within the military compound. It also had a touch console attached, and an optical socket for the initiation device, which presently resided in Chenghu's backpack. The thing still felt heavy in her jaunting mind, but more in the manner of a weight on a wheeled cart, for she could move it between worlds now. The transport cage and its load definitely felt like an extension of her, but also a tool. She looked around at the others.

'Are we ready?' she asked.

Ektian was certainly ready, as she clutched her machine pistol close to her body in one hand and fingered the grenades hanging from a bandolier with the other. Chenghu was ready in his way, with his reluctant acceptance that this was something they must do, because they had to do something. Irene felt this was the attitude of the others as well, to an extent. They'd been gifted with, as Pranjab put it, 'superpowers' and now felt beholden to *do* something about their home world. But there was nuance to this. Chancel agreed verbally, but as ever seemed to be holding something back, and contemplating matters. He would bear watching. Adriana had finally angrily and reluctantly agreed. She'd talked about targeted assassination until Irene argued her down. That route would have put them in danger on every occasion. And, since there were so few of them with these powers, they could afford to lose no one. The nuclear blast would take out a chunk of the conference city, in which the majority of the population would be SAs and bureaucrats. People utterly in agreement with diktats from the increasingly powerful Committee. Yes, there would be innocents there, certainly no protesters, but this would be a blow to take out a large portion of those who wanted to lead Earth further into nightmarish totalitarianism. That was the essence of Irene's argument. But she'd also researched and found the statistics to back it up. The blast would kill in the region of a hundred thousand people. The last Committee diktat, which had directed that agricultural land should be switched over to fallow for regeneration it neither needed nor was any longer capable of, had caused mass starvation and riots, killing millions.

'Well, I'm ready,' said Chenghu.

'Me too,' said Ektian eagerly.

Chancel gave a cool nod of acknowledgement, while the

other two remained silent, just waiting. And it was then the Fenris came.

Irene felt the creature drop into her mind. But she also felt that he'd appeared to the others, perhaps through some subliminal connection they had, related to them preparing to jaunt together, and *seeing* their destination *over there*. He shifted with their vision for a second, then stabilized like a hologram, just to one side of the transport cage.

'Greetings, world walkers,' he said, then after a tight pause continued, 'So you are all in agreement to carry out this act.'

Irene focused on him, because she'd never seen him so clearly before. Making the assumption that how he appeared here matched his actual size, she realized he stood half a metre taller than the biggest of them, which was Chenghu. The glassy armour he wore was different this time, bulkier and shot through with red veins, and now looked as functional as actual armour, whereas it hadn't before. She could also see a hint of lines coiling away from the armour's spikes, along with other devices either attached or inset, and she assumed that body protection wasn't its main function. She could see all their own physical alterations, which at one time they'd believed to be mutations, taken to their extreme in him. He was long limbed, with somewhat of the ectomorphic physique of a high jumper, though with unnaturally wide chest and shoulders. Again, as she'd noted before, his head resembled an Easter Island stone sculpture, with a jutting nose, wide chin, high tapering forehead and deep-set eyes. He was hairless, she now noted, and his skin a grey-mauve hue. At a glance, he did look like something carved out of rock, but as he made eloquent gestures with his clawed hands, shifting as if to study each of them, and as his expression changed too, he seemed to possess an excess of life and energy. And that wasn't all. Something was different, and she sensed it on the level of her connection to the others. The Fenris seemed angry and uncomfortable, *conflicted*.

'Yes, we are all agreed,' she said. 'Unless you have something to add. Though it seems you're somewhat lacking in suggestions for those who managed to survive what you did to them.' She grimaced, wishing she hadn't said so much. Firstly, she didn't want any suggestions from this creature, for she guessed it didn't much like what they were about to do, and she certainly didn't want him asserting any control here. But also, she knew she'd been unfair. He *had* saved their lives and given them this transport cage.

The Fenris glanced at her with what seemed like dismissive irritation, and that annoyed her further. 'I have nothing to add. You must make your own choices and accept the consequences of them.' He scanned around them all. 'It's not my business to interfere in your learning process.'

'And what's that supposed to mean?' Irene shot back.

'I wish you the best of luck in your endeavour, though that is hardly required.' The Fenris paused, gaze going distant. 'And beyond wishing you well, I'm also here to give you a warning. Be on your guard when you transition through the airless Earth.'

'We are quite capable of holding our breaths,' said Ektian.

'We can do more than that,' Pranjab added.

He'd told them all about his swim underwater, and had been studying his own body and theirs, surmising that they did have a high hypoxic function.

'Indeed,' the Fenris continued. 'The moon of that airless Earth, as some of you saw, is occupied. The occupants are creatures that were once human, and now form a hive. The hive has advanced technology. It is aware of you, and it has the capability of crossing the parallels.'

'Fuck,' said Pranjab.

Irene glanced at him, and the rest of his story came into sharp focus in her, as well as in them all. The creatures on the world the Fenris had shunted Pranjab to, which had chased him, had almost certainly been these hive humans. That they'd tried to grab him implied they wanted something from him. And, since they were capable of crossing parallels, that something almost certainly concerned his ability, and theirs. She suddenly felt a stab of realization. The creature that had attacked her had seemed an unlikely denizen of the place she'd ended up in. Might it be connected too? She glanced at Chenghu and felt his consonance with the thought. Then she closed her eyes and forced dismissal of where all this was taking her. Focus on the now, and what they intended to do.

'This is something we can get into after we've dealt with the Committee,' she said.

'Yes, this is something we must discuss further in person,' said the Fenris ominously. 'Again: I wish you well.' With that, he blinked out of their perception.

'So we're ready,' Irene said after a long silence.

The only response this time was a few guarded nods.

Chenghu had partly shown her the way to do it, during their first jaunts. And, as with them all, her ability and perception of the multiverse had grown phenomenally since then. She sighed out a breath and reached out to harden her connection to them, feeling the network inside herself flash into life. Now she looked upon the multiverse as a great twisting glassy manifold, dotted with nodal worlds and their reflections. She recognized the Earth she'd called home, but not by any physical features she could describe in human language, and she found herself stretching for it. Just as on other occasions, it felt slippery and distant – out of reach. Chenghu now fed them his planned route there, taking in two nodal worlds. The networks inside them lit up and connected, then Irene *pushed*.

The residence's basement grew transparent around them, and for a moment their conventional senses showed them sliding sideways, through the packing crates, and the wall, and then through the packed earth and rock. In their holosense, they tracked along the course Chenghu had laid out. This, if it could be compared to something in the world, seemed like passing down a great glassy tube, in a mass of the same – an almost organic thing, like some vast worm cast. Except the tubes went beyond three dimensions, into the territory of Klein bottles, tesseracts and hyperplanes.

They surfaced through earth, with landscapes and cityscapes folding past them, which might or might not have been real, as well as skies of different colours flickering above. They glimpsed strange forms of humanity, and of the fauna and flora of multiple Earths. As the strain began to tell – as if a charge were draining out of them – Irene gazed upon it all with some perplexity. The physical universe had its laws, and distributed its worlds and stars in a regular and understandable manner, yet all this seemed so chaotic. Why, for example, was there Committee Earth with its parallels, then the airless version of Earth inserted as a nodal world too? And how had this separated out the depopulated version of their home world, which they'd just come from, and dropped it a *relative* distance away? This kind of disorderliness repeated across the portion of the multiverse she could perceive. It was as if the multiverse had once had regularity, but had then later been smashed and reassembled haphazardly. She noted some patterns in the disruption, not least around the airless Earth, where there seemed to be a great deal of disruption in general. But this waned over a relative distance from that place. She finally dismissed these thoughts as they arrived at their first stopping point.

Sky stabilized to lavender, streaked with orange cloud, and stars blinked through at twilight. A landscape tilted up at them, fled along underneath, then slowed. They fell through a ghost jungle of purple-green, and then felt the tug of material matter as they slowed. Irene allowed Chenghu to take the wheel at this point, since he was still better at this. They drifted out of jungle to its edge, where sandy ground lay, scattered with the tumbled pebbles of a river that spread wide and shallow ahead. A cold wind whipped against them at first, then their final transition came. Irene dropped a few metres to the ground, still travelling at some speed, coiled into a roll. She jounced off Ektian, who was doing the same, and finally came up into a crouch. The others compensated similarly, quickly coming to their feet. But the transport sphere hit and rolled, sliding out of her grasp, then sprang open, spilling its load, and abruptly snapped closed into its grass seed form. It came down with one end stabbed into the ground.

'For fuck's sake!' said Irene, standing up.

She looked at the nuclear device. The thing had bounced a couple of times and come down to rest on its side. Its jacket was dented. She saw that the console lay a short distance away too, and glared at Chenghu, who looked chagrined.

'Check that.' She pointed.

As he went over to the bomb, she concentrated on the transport cage, firming her grip on the thing. She pulled it from the ground and directed it to float across to her, standing upright, until it settled before her. She checked its function as best she could and found nothing wrong, then opened it back out into a cage and left it there, ready to receive the bomb again. She turned to the others.

'That could have gone better,' she said. 'But this is, after all, only the third time we've tried this. We'll do better next time.' She felt angry and resentful, but clamped down on that. She wanted to blame Chenghu, and had suspicions that this might have been deliberate, but at least recognized her own paranoia. And anyway, she also had a distinct suspicion that the sphere crashing like that, despite their fast arrival, might have been her own fault. She'd allowed her concentration to lapse as they travelled and, as she'd learned before, that wasn't a good idea. The safety function of the biotech, which operated on the level of instinct, diminished when doing joint jaunts, and while transporting things. The slightest error could put your arrival point inside a rock or, as this arrival had illustrated, travelling at high speed into the side of that same rock. It wouldn't happen again, though.

'Maybe shorter jaunts would have been a good idea,' said Adriana. 'I feel somewhat tired after that.'

'We'll shake that off quickly,' Chancel offered.

'I love that we can feel it happening – the changes in our bodies as we recuperate,' said Pranjab. 'Such an apparently simple function, and yet it cannot possibly be so.'

Irene nodded an acknowledgement to him as she shrugged off her pack and found a place to sit down. She took out some food and water. Pranjab was right. On the rare occasions they exhausted themselves, all that was required was food, drink and a brief period of rest, sometimes sleep. They could feel the nutrients spreading within their bodies and establishing where needed, with the drink lubricating the process. They could also feel the healing process as they rested, or as they drifted in and out of sleep. And, as Pranjab had said some time before, it was different with *normal* humans. Food created weariness through the digestive process, thirst signals were confused with hunger, and brief sleep left people feeling worse afterwards – they didn't have this inner perception of the function of their bodies.

They all sprawled out on the ground and made inroads into the food and drink they'd brought. Chancel stood up and collected their water bottles to head over to the river and refill them, while Ektian and Adriana lay back to snooze. Pranjab sat with his legs crossed and eyes closed, perhaps in a meditative state, which he said allowed him to perceive even more of his internal workings. Chenghu came over to Irene.

'What's it looking like?' she asked, nodding towards the bomb.

He sat down, dropping his pack beside him, taking out his food and drink. 'Just a little bit of rewiring. External damage to the detonation control, but nothing to the actual bomb inside. I'll have to run a diagnostic when it's ready to go.'

'Can't you do that now?'

'I did, but another one will be a good idea. Jaunting does some funny things to the electrics.' He waved a hand at their surroundings. 'Some of these places have slightly different physical laws.'

'How long will that take?'

'Just a few minutes, ten at most.'

'That could be a dangerous delay where we intend to end up.'

He tapped the weapon at his side. 'We knew that.' He paused, looking slightly pained, then continued, 'Perhaps I should handle the whole transit while you concentrate on the transport cage?'

Irene felt angry at him being so careful with her, as if she was someone who couldn't control her emotions. But she acknowledged that, though she had more control over them now, she hadn't previously. This was also the upshot of the changed dynamic between them. She could feel the sexual tension waning between them now, evolving into something else, but he might still retain the residue of male sexual angst.

'Agreed,' she said, overcoming the irrational urge to argue back.

He looked relieved, and then puzzled by his relief. Irene understood that in all of them the grip of their human biological drives was fading.

On the next version of Earth, Chenghu deposited them, with just a slight drop, on the place's version of concrete, and this time Irene's grip on the transport sphere remained firm. They looked around at what seemed to be a partially empty car park, with a building over to one side, and a wide road running alongside both. Beyond it lay a forest of plants resembling banana trees, with weird flower spikes of black nodules spearing out between yellow leaves. The sky was a natural blue, and high overhead an airship was slowly crossing.

'Let's move,' said Irene, eyeing the glass front of the building where people were peering out. On the road, a truck running on fat white tyres sped past, as they headed over to a similar vehicle parked in a state of collapse.

'I've passed here before,' said Chenghu. 'Over in a city nearby.' He pointed. 'There was a strange lack of reaction to me, but a cheerful wave or two. It's almost like they knew what I was.'

Irene shifted the transport sphere out of sight of the building, and they took their rest, though with one of them on watch all the time. Gawkers came out into the car park – odd people with long coats, heavy boots and enormous ears, but they didn't draw close.

The next few worlds were equally uneventful, until finally they were ready to make the last two jumps, which included the airless Earth.

'Stay alert,' Irene warned, and then they went.

The transition this time felt abrupt and precipitous, but Chenghu brought them out of it perfectly, above the flat rocky ground. Once they'd landed safely, Irene slowly let the air out of her nostrils as she looked around. It all appeared much the same as before, with its drifts and odd plants, though lacking in dried-out corpses now. Only half the moon, with its hive-fashioned face, showed on the horizon. And within their vicinity she could see nothing to concern them.

'Again,' she said, her voice tinny in the oxygen-free atmosphere.

Chenghu finally guided them through the short transition to Committee Earth. The landscape reared up at them, and they slid over the globe. They flicked over an ocean crossed by huge cargo ships, over a patchwork of sea farms, and then straight into the endless buildings of a sprawl, sliding through those same buildings and glimpsing the packed humanity there. Irene was sure she could smell it all, but that wasn't possible just yet. They came out over a sprawl that crawled up mountains, like some giant technological slime mould, then in over rare forest, punctured by wide roads all around. The sky was full of air-fan vehicles and helicopters, while high above a formation of jets was passing, ranked out behind a huge black space plane. Then the city reared ahead.

Here lay a concentration of the wealth of the world, and a concentration of the power, fed by national governments. Skyscrapers clustered at the centre, while the rest consisted of neat, clean buildings, ranging from ground level to three or four storeys. Here she saw the luxury of gardens and parks, broad roads occupied by ground cars, and boulevards that wealthy, healthy SAs strolled down. But it was no paradise. Even here the readerguns watched and the razorbirds roosted, while shepherds crouched in their cylinders under the streets, waiting. They all dropped down towards a complex, which might have been a university out of a past age, as Chenghu refined their approach. They fell through a tiled roof overseen by gargoyles from another roof nearby, then through halls, and rooms. As the map tightened, they finally closed in on one huge auditorium, crammed with people.

'Here at last,' said Irene, into the no-space between worlds that they still inhabited.

Chenghu refined further, exploring the area around and below the auditorium, then finally settled on a room filled with racks of book-thin servers, and skeins of optics running up to the ceiling between the cooling ducts. People worked here, but then there was nowhere in this world without people.

Irene replayed the debate they'd had on where to position themselves. The weapon didn't need to be right inside this building to do what she required of it. They could have used a rooftop, or a cellar, nearby in the city. But further from the centre would result in higher ZA casualties, and she'd insisted they ram the thing right down the Committee's throat. All had finally agreed and, in retrospect, she understood why. They wanted to risk themselves, because any other way would have seemed like cowardice and a circumvention of responsibility.

In the server room, they had to adjust their formation. Chenghu and Irene were set to arrive, with the bomb, in the middle of the aisle, between the racks. Chancel and Ektian placed themselves to come down on the other side of a rack from the aisle. Finally, Pranjab and Adriana were on the other side of the opposite rack. Chenghu refined again, and the world rose up, firming around them. Then, with a thump, they were out. Their connection for the jaunt dissolved, but still something remained. They had a sense of each other – location, actions and mood. It wasn't quite telepathy but felt uncomfortably close to that.

Irene heard and felt the transport sphere crunch down as she too dropped a couple of inches to the floor. Her breath was visible in front of her face in the cool room, and a plastic electrical smell filled her nostrils. With rehearsed precision, she grabbed the machine pistol from the front of her suit, turned, then fired at the startled man who was pulling a series of servers out on their sliding trays. He wore a clean white shirt and black trousers, which she'd seen on others as they arrived, and seemed to be a uniform in this place. He spun away in a red mist, tearing out a couple of the thin servers as he collapsed, white shirt steadily turning red. Beyond and around him, electrical shorts sizzled and sprayed sparks.

Irene felt a tug inside as she stared at the corpse. All of this had been so easy and factual in the planning, but now the reality of killing human beings had arrived, for no reason other than them being in the way. She felt regret, even though the man was part of the hierarchy of oppression, and none of the satisfaction she'd expected. She forced herself to view the act in an utterly pragmatic fashion. The man was a product of that oppression. And, though trying to do the best for himself, he and all the others in this city stood between her and her objective. It was necessary he die for the greater good.

In the aisle to her left, Ektian dropped two more of the workers, while to her right Pranjab shot into the floor in front of a woman to send her running. Adriana then shot the woman in the back, sending her sprawling at the end of the aisle.

'Squeamish, Pranjab?' Irene asked over their suit radio connection – more to raise her own bravado than criticize.

'A little,' he replied. 'And yes, I know they're all going to die anyway.'

He looked directly towards her, though the rack stood in the way. They could all see like this – their holosense covering an area a hundred metres across, and even extending outside the server room.

Irene turned and stepped over to the transport cage where Chenghu waited. Via her connection, she opened the thing at the top, so it rested on the floor like a claw cupping its load. She and Chenghu reached inside, grabbed the two carry handles and deposited the bomb on the floor. Shrugging off his pack, Chenghu squatted beside it, taking out his tools while Irene turned her attention to the cage. She closed it up into its grass seed form and raised it from the floor. Now using a greater nuance of control, she applied a new technique and pushed it away from her with a dismissive gesture. The thing faded out of existence, to occupy some space neither in this world nor another.

'Okay, Adriana, Pranjab, you go in here with Chenghu. Chancel – take the south door.'

'I see them,' Chancel replied. Two Inspectorate guards had come in through that door. She watched him move off, machine pistol casually resting over one shoulder. Were they too arrogant, she wondered? No, not really. They could perceive so much more than the conventional humans around them, and they were stronger, tougher and faster. It was well to remember, however, that they could still die like normal humans. She should stay here to ensure the bomb was in place, and then jaunt out to the rendezvous just prior to the thing detonating. She hadn't wanted to do that, though – she'd wanted to engage with this place and these people here, for vengeance on a personal level. And, because she'd been a ZA, with no view into such places as this but the propaganda glimpses on the screen, she also felt some curiosity. Those wants didn't seem so important now.

The other two came around the end of the aisle and into human sight. At a gesture from Adriana, Pranjab lingered at the end there. Adriana then came down, looking grim.

'Still going for a look around?' she enquired.

Irene nodded and glanced over to Ektian, who gave a sharp nod of agreement too.

'We cannot allow any of them to escape,' she said flatly.

That had been another discussion, verging on argument. With cams everywhere, their arrival had certainly been noted, with human and AI watchers analysing them. Without a doubt, someone would recognize the bomb, and that would alert the most important people to flee quickly to their vehicles and escape. Irene had stressed that they must stop that happening. Chenghu had countered that there were no jets here, and even the fastest flier would have no time to get clear of the blast. When she'd pushed him, he conceded that perhaps some might escape it. Everyone had recognized his concession as a lie, driven by Irene's dominance over him. They'd finally settled on the agreement that those who wanted to try stopping delegates escaping could do so. In the end, it had been only Irene and Ektian who did.

Adriana snorted and moved on to take a guard position at the other end of the aisle. Meanwhile, the sound of machine-pistol fire stuttered, paused, then came on again with a full burst. Through her holosense, Irene saw the two guards down at the south door, and struggling to rise. Their protective gear sprouted blooms of impact fibre, while Chancel kept firing as he ran towards them. He kicked one of them back down, concentrating fire on the other as he drew his sidearm. Next he leaned in close, jammed the second weapon in the armpit of the one he'd knocked down, and fired. The man slumped. Chancel turned to the other again, machine-pistol clip empty, and stepped over. This man was already dead.

'We have to remember their armour is as good as our own,' he observed over radio.

Chancel next moved to the door. He closed and locked it, then attached grenades by their sticky pads, activating motion sensors in them as he stepped away. He took a position back from the door, squatted down to take off his pack, then laid out further weapons and ammo clips. As he did this, he glanced to one side, picked up a weapon and fired a short burst. One of the white shirts spun back into a server rack and slumped.

'How long?' Irene asked Chenghu.

Using a plug-in optic, he was running a diagnostic of the bomb via the detached screen.

'I'll give you a mark at five minutes,' he replied without looking up. 'I suggest we all get out a minute before, if not earlier.'

'Okay.' Irene gestured to Ektian, and they headed for the remaining door.

'Are we amoral or immoral?' Ektian asked as they moved down between the server stacks. 'The others seem . . . reluctant.'

'Yes, seems that way,' said Irene, trying not to reveal her own growing reluctance. 'They've never been as powerless as we have, though, or suffered as we did.'

'As women or ZAs?' Ektian asked.

'Both.'

Chenghu had made the dry observation that men such as him, a trained soldier, possessed a greater sense of physicality and dominance over their environment, and so, having acquired the powers they all had, were more reserved in their use. Irene had instinctively and vehemently denied this. But she'd then begun to wonder, having found her thinking arising from logic rather than emotion. Could once being a physically weak woman in a society without protections for the same, make her more likely to be vengeful upon acquiring power? The thought had made her uncomfortable. She now wondered how Ektian really felt. The woman had shown the same relish Irene initially had for this venture, and still seemed to be showing it, while her own continued to wane. Perhaps it was something inherent in them. No matter; right now she dismissed such thoughts to concentrate on the task in hand.

They reached the door and Irene took hold of the handle, already using her holosense to see the four guards running down the corridor outside, towards the door. She stripped some grenades off her bandolier, set them one by one, then pulled open the door and tossed them out. Swiftly closing the door again, she and Ektian stepped over to either side of it.

Multiple blasts bulged the wall panels and sent the door crashing into a server rack. They stepped out into the human ruin. Two guards had survived and were crawling bloodily and noisily. As she and Ektian worked their way through, Irene paused to release bursts of fire at where body armour had shredded. The remaining two ceased to make any noise. Moving on, with the map clear in her mind, she understood Chancel, and Adriana and herself. Emotion might be there, distaste or abhorrence, but that didn't stop their high functioning or their perfect understanding of the weapons they carried. She broke into a run towards a stairwell, Ektian behind. They climbed this fast, their perception of the server room fading, but holosense extending into the building around them. Two floors up, they took another corridor, and then another, finally arriving at a door. Irene did her grenade trick again, and they walked into an observation room to the screams of those who'd survived the blast.

The place was now a wreckage of desks, computers and people. Irene stepped carefully through it all, firing short bursts at some still managing to crawl or howl. Her mind tried to offer her vicious delight in this chore, but she brushed this away and felt a moment of shame, followed by hard pragmatism once more. Pausing halfway across, she took off her pack and picked out a further three machine pistols from it. Ektian glanced at her and nodded, taking off her pack to do the same. In only a minute, they'd interlocked them in pairs, since they were made to be used this way. The function usually also came with dampening arm braces, though, as Chenghu had told them.

The far wall contained a long window of safety glass, now crazed and sagging. Irene stepped up to it and swiped across with one of her paired weapons, collapsing the whole thing, then gazed down into the conference chamber below.

This place resembled so many such chambers throughout history, with its tiered rings of seats rising up from a central floor. Hundreds of delegates had been seated here, with their computer access and translator feeds. Now all was chaos, as they swarmed out of their seats, with security personnel guiding them towards the exits. She recognized some familiar faces of world leaders, usually surrounded by men in dark bulky suits holding machine pistols. Many of these were now looking up to the source of the explosions.

'Like you said,' said Ektian. 'They know what's coming.'

'The cam system,' Irene shrugged. 'I would guess Inspectorate are now heading down below.' She paused then conceded, 'I hope Chenghu gets a move on.'

'But as he said, these still won't have time to get away.' Ektian gestured with her weapon at the people below.

Irene turned to her, searching her face. 'Do we care?'

'Not really.'

Ektian showed a hint of the vicious anger they'd both felt before, but it seemed to have muted now. They stared at each other for a moment longer, then turned simultaneously to open fire on the conference chamber. Then they pulled back and crouched, as those below returned fire, filling the viewing and translation adjunct with flying debris. Ektian unstrapped her bandolier, primed a series of grenades on it, then in one hard motion hurled it all through the window. Irene contemplated how nasty it would shortly get down there and, seeking out some vengeful response, was unsurprised when it didn't arrive. Chenghu had been right: no one would have time to get away. Coming here and risking their lives like this, ostensibly to stop delegates escaping but really to get some personal payback, had been a foolish thing to do.

'Five minutes,' he now said over radio.

'You okay down there?' she asked.

The grenades detonated below, like firecrackers going off. The shouting and chaos increased, with a great deal of high-pitched screaming. Did that satisfy her?

'We're holding them,' Chenghu replied. 'They're bringing down some heavy tripod shrapnel guns, but we'll be out of here before they're able to use them. Seems they haven't been apprised of what we're doing and think they have time.'

'The bomb?'

'We pulled up some floor panels and put it there, then dropped a server rack on it – no way they can stop it now.'

'Okay, get out.'

She turned to Ektian, who pointed upwards and said, 'They'll be up there – the fliers.'

'Okay,' Irene agreed. This had been the plan, and now they were following it through like automata. They headed out and up. People were crowding the stairs, and into the elevators. Nobody seemed to realize she and Ektian were the attackers, for they looked little different to the Inspectorate officers in the chaos. Ektian raised one of her twinned weapons, pointing it at a crowd trying to squeeze into an elevator, but Irene reached out her hand and pushed it down. Ektian shrugged.

'Save it for the roof,' Irene advised.

They worked their way up, to find similar scenes of chaos on the roof. Too many people were trying to get into the fliers and helicopters. A helicopter launched with people clinging to the runners – one falling several metres to the roof edge, hitting it and bouncing over, out of sight. Ektian's weapons crackled and the helicopter slewed sideways, then down, after the person who'd fallen. Irene ran through the crowd, firing bursts into vehicles to cripple them, one after another, with Ektian behind, covering her by taking shots at any of the Inspectorate who showed their faces. They reached an air-fan vehicle, which was spewing smoke and chunks of blade from one of its fans, as firing converged on them. Irene staggered back as a shot carved a groove across her chest, while Ektian dodged to one side with impact fibres sprouting from her shoulder.

'This is pointless,' said Irene.

'I agree,' Ektian replied flatly.

Irene reached out and grabbed her shoulder, then together they pushed the world into ghostly overlay and slid away through it.

Chenghu

Chenghu dropped a couple of metres onto a roof, rolled, then came up sideswiping with his weapon and dropping the guard. He gazed down at the thin man, who was now clutching at his bloody head, picked him up by the scruff, dragged him to the door into the stairwell and tossed him down it. The man recovered enough to come up into a crouch on the stairs and look up. Chenghu pointed his weapon, then took a grenade off his bandolier and weighed it in one hand. The man turned and ran down, out of sight. Chenghu sighed and pulled the door closed, sliding across the locking bars, then looked around.

The rooftop, just like most in the sprawls of Committee Earth, was owned by a gang; it looked little different from the one from which he and Irene had watched the riot that her assassination of Garrick had triggered. They had greenhouses up here to catch the precious sunlight, and some gardens whose sides had been constructed out of expanded foam plastic blocks. With a good harvest here, the guard would at some point return with other gang members. But they wouldn't be hurrying back. The man would've assumed Chenghu was Inspectorate and therefore bad news. Chenghu turned.

Chancel, Adriana and Pranjab came out of the transition separately, as if stepping individually through the menisci of bubbles. They looked around, grim faced. Adriana and Chancel turned as one and headed over to the roof edge, looking back towards the conference city. It was just visible in the distant mountains, marked out by a green barrier lying between it and the sprawl below. Pranjab simply sauntered over to a walled garden, sat on the edge of it, and pulled up a carrot for inspection.

'How long?' he asked.

'One minute twenty,' Chenghu replied.

No way could the Inspectorate soldiers make it into that server room, move the fallen rack and disarm the bomb in that time. He tilted his head, sensing another approach, then Irene and Ektian fell through, staggering. They'd been hit a few times, as had they all, but he sensed no injuries, just as he could also distinguish their change of demeanour. He nodded, understanding as they all did that their biotech was wiping out their base drives, and now only the grim chore of coming to completion remained. Irene gestured, and she and Ektian went over to join the other two at the edge. Chenghu followed, Pranjab falling in at his side while munching on the carrot he'd picked.

'So we'll be safe here,' Pranjab commented.

'Just so long as we don't look at the flash,' said Chenghu. 'And even then.' He shrugged.

'Probably okay to do that,' said Pranjab. 'Our eyes are no longer human.'

The words kept playing in Chenghu's mind as he reached the edge, and then checked his watch.

'One minute,' he said.

They just stood in silence, surveying the sprawl, seeing gang members far down in the street below looking up – one had a pair of binoculars. Some copters and fans glittered in the sky above the distant city. It seemed Irene and Ektian hadn't managed to stop them completely. He sensed they'd lost their enthusiasm for that particular needless task.

'Twenty seconds.'

'It's been a while since this Earth has seen such fireworks,' Chancel commented.

It seemed a strange thing to say, but Chenghu noted the emphasis on 'this Earth' and tracked the implications. Why, he wondered, should this place be so much a focus of their attention? And how could they ever call it home when they returned with such reluctance?

'Ten seconds,' he said, and bowed his head.

The ten seconds dragged, but then, precisely on time, a giant flash bulb ignited out there. Chenghu kept his head bowed a moment longer, then raised it as a glaring ball of light wiped out most of the view.

'As I thought,' said Pranjab. 'These eyes have a filter function – feels like a nictitating membrane coming down.'

Chenghu glanced at him and saw that the man's eyes had now become a glossy black.

The glow died down to a ball of fire, as a blast wave sped towards them. The city was effectively gone, as were those escaping fliers, but then he saw sprawl buildings shredding as the wave hit them and felt a growing horror. Many nearer the blast were already burning as they fragmented. It tracked along streets, throwing up a wave of oily burning debris that was almost certainly human beings. But slowly, as it advanced towards them, the damage it caused diminished. The crackling roar of the explosion finally reached them and, shortly after, the dregs of the wave. It still knocked them staggering backwards from the edge and shattered two of the greenhouses behind them.

'Bigger than expected,' said Pranjab tightly.

As he recovered his balance and moved back, Chenghu saw that the bomb had done what was required of it. But he couldn't ignore those fires in the surrounding sprawl, and even now some buildings there were collapsing. Struggling to put aside the horror, he reviewed his data. The weapon should have taken out the centre of the conference city, the blast wave destroying the rest, and then dying in the surrounding forested area. Minimal damage to the sprawl, he had said.

'The data were wrong,' was all he could say.

He sensed with all the others, as in himself, the internal debates, the guilt and the questioning.

'There, it's done,' said Irene, turning from the view, expression haunted.

'Along with thousands of ZAs,' said Chancel, 'but I guess they're not important.'

Irene moved fast and they didn't anticipate what she was going to do till she did it. She slapped him hard, lifting him off his feet and sending him to the ground.

'Do you think I enjoyed this?' she shouted at him, as he flipped into a crouch, looking decidedly dangerous. 'We didn't have a perfect selection of weapons, and the surgical excision of this cancer was out of our reach.'

Chancel just stared at her, fingering his machine pistol.

Chenghu looked at Irene in surprise. It would have been easy to blame him for what had happened here and yet in essence she had defended him. He'd selected the tactical nuke based on its yield, which supposedly resulted in a blast area covering only the conference city, though the others had reviewed his data too.

She turned a circle, taking them all in, then pointed to the blast as it rose into the sky on its smoky stem. 'They were making decisions there that would kill millions, and just keep on killing them. We did what we had to do, and had no choice in this, if we're to consider ourselves moral beings.'

Chancel waved one finger at her. 'You get that one for free. Don't try it again.'

Irene threw her hands up, turned, and then, stepping away, she disappeared.

'We need to be more considered in our decision-making,' said Adriana, only because she seemed to feel the need to say something. Ektian snorted in derision.

Chenghu kept his mouth clamped shut, sensing the cracks.

'We can hash this out back at Caprock,' he finally said. 'We need more information to make more informed decisions, and we also need to talk to the Fenris. Let's not fly apart right now. We're stronger together, and there are these hive humans to consider now.'

Chancel dipped his head in acknowledgement of that, and Chenghu felt a breath of relief. Chancel next looked to Adriana, who nodded reluctant agreement, then the both of them turned away and were swiftly gone from the roof top. Chenghu breathed into the silent space, even as chaos reigned without. He glanced over the sprawl, keenly aware of the suffering there now, and for some time to come. He thought of all those other sprawls everywhere, and knew that though there were many other better worlds he could go to, he'd accepted a responsibility to this one now.

'Moral beings?' Pranjab enquired.

Chancel looked at him. The man's eyes were still black.

13

The Fenris

The Fenris watched things running entirely as expected on Committee Earth, and had to instruct his body, via his internal biotech, to lock down his frustration. The world walkers were also assessing the results of incinerating eight out of ten world leaders, a substratum of politicians and bureaucrats, and five million citizens, whether SA or ZA. They didn't have his access to that world, however, so weren't getting the whole picture. He collected data to be used when the time was right, and busied himself about other tasks in the interim.

The steady expansion of his ability to penetrate the multiverse personally, or by growing his biotech on other worlds, brought him key information in a series of confirmations. What he'd earlier labelled a storm and manifold now clarified as a spreading wormish network that penetrated the parallels and resembled the tunnels of a nest in its structure. And its ultimate source: the hive moon. Only now, after contacting Pranjab alone, and getting a precise description of the things that'd chased him, had he recognized them as hive creatures. Next, hearing Pranjab relay the description of what had also hunted Irene, which Chenghu had killed, he realized this creature closely resembled the remains of the warrior he'd found in the abandoned nest, on the airless Earth.

So the hive had its method of travel between worlds – this wormish network, or manifold – and was trying to grab his world walkers wherever they appeared. It had recognized a technology superior to its own and wanted to acquire it. Which meant he must prevent it doing so. He had to admit that the thought of such power in the hands of the hive both sickened and frightened him. The fact it had failed to capture either Pranjab or Irene he saw as the errors, inefficiencies and plain inertia of such a culture, still damaged by war and an entropy wave. It had sent multiple warriors after Irene, yet all but one of them had been killed, almost certainly by some malfunction in their method of travel. It had then sent the creatures he thought of as post-heads after Pranjab, when warriors would have been better. It was a large, interlocked self-referential thing, without the facility to delegate. However, as it got up to speed, he knew it would become increasingly efficient, single-minded and dangerous.

With this in mind, the Fenris abruptly focused in on the airless Earth. Then, via threads to the surface, which sported microscopic sensors, he scanned. At the edge of his reach on the surface, where his biotech hadn't explored and fed, and the ground hadn't been seared by the nuclear blast, he saw the usual scattering of corpses. Raising one thread into a tall sensory spike, he surveyed further and saw the swathe of corpses trailing out, like the tail of a comma, across the barren landscape. Here was a resource for the hive to study. For, though much degraded by whatever processes of decay existed here, they still contained fenris biotech. Had any of them been grabbed already?

He'd kept data on all potential, and actual, jaunters in his system, though in many cases he'd updated this after the fact.

With those who'd died here, the records simply ended, but he'd retained them. Now he steadily matched those records to corpses here – excluding those who'd interred themselves underground – and found all accounted for. But next, tracking back to data stored before the nuclear strike the hive had used to destroy its ship and creatures here, he found that corpses had been missing in the burned-up area, though he could only estimate their number as between one and five. There were no scavengers on this world, so the hive must have taken them for study, he thought bitterly. He could do nothing about that, but decided to do whatever he could to prevent the hive having any more opportunities with the dead, or the living.

Dipping into his biotech on that airless Earth, he tracked its spread underground, and assessed its resources. It was gathering the energy and materials it required, but expanding nowhere near as fast as it usually did elsewhere. After making his assessment, he began withdrawing growth to four points of the compass, and concentrating resources. He then pushed for fast growth in the remaining direction: underneath the slew of corpses. It took some hours before he'd developed enough tendrils below a scattering of corpses, beyond the burn of the hive's nuclear explosion. He raised a thread to the surface, braiding it with others as it pushed open a crack, to come up underneath the corpse of a woman. He inspected her history. Once a resident of a sprawl that covered Okinawa. She had, inevitably, fallen foul of the authorities when they'd found her clinging to a barrier around one of the sea farms, utterly bewildered about how she'd got there. It hadn't come to interrogation and inducer torture with her, for she'd jaunted again while Inspectorate guards were beating her. She'd then ended up here to suffocate.

With a bitter taste in his mouth, the Fenris raised his threads below her dried-out corpse and penetrated it. Shutting down their programmed inclination to feed on this resource, he directed them in towards her bones, and in particular the biotech inlaid in them like lichen on rock. From there, his threads reached out into the biotech skein running through her muscles, along nerve channels and up to her brain and senses. There he allowed his threads to feed, scooping up the biotech and ingesting it whole, or in parts. He scraped her out, cored her of his technology. And then he allowed the threads to feed slowly, but only on those materials that wouldn't cause the collapse of her body down to nothing, and thus alert any watchers on the moon who might be looking this way. The biotech reached two further corpses by the time it had finished destroying her viability as a subject of study for the hive. He estimated it would take weeks before it reached them all. And in retaining a foothold here, he intended to ensure, as he'd done with Pranjab, there'd be no more.

This was all good necessary work, but still the Fenris waited.

Ottanger

Where were the flies? The question cycled in his mind as he prepared something to eat, having returned from the shop with new, more expensive foods. He wanted those flies; he *needed* those flies. Their biotech was the key to his development, as the Fenris had said.

They'd collected them from the areas around where people had disappeared. There would surely have been a lot of them, if the Fenris had wanted a breeding population to establish. But how many the Committee searchers had managed to gather was debatable. He imagined a lot, since after establishing their importance, they would have used AI cam searches and hosts of mini-drones, as well as insect robots and other high-tech methods to collect them. But, on the other hand, the things might have been eaten by the ever-growing rodent population, or other creatures, or have decayed away quickly. It occurred to him, as he ate a meal of chips cooked in his new fryer, peas and something that might have been fish, that the only ones now available were those in that isolation booth he'd seen Savarack operating.

He needed more of their biotech inside him. Contemplating the idea that a large number of the flies might be stored somewhere else in the Complex, he saw difficulties anyway. Cams were everywhere, and the AI along with others were always watching. If such a place existed, it would almost certainly be under heavy security – an armoured room or safe, with DNA code access. He had to dismiss the idea of getting to those, if there actually were any. That left the laboratory and those fly pills they provided when he jaunted.

He finished his main meal, washed down with tea and some water, then started grazing on other food. He emptied the gift basket, eating the cardboard probiscuits, and all of his last loaf of bread smeared with margarine, then had to stop himself from starting on a new loaf, as well as the other items he'd recently bought. Was this hunger due to recent stress, and last night's sex? Partially, he surmised, though it had become evident the biotech was changing him. He thought about the Fenris and wondered if he himself would end up looking like that. The thought didn't appeal.

In his bathroom, he studied himself in the mirror, and with his new clarity saw quite plainly that his reflection peered back at him from higher up than before. His face had also taken on a gaunter look, which he recognized from those times when the rations had been in short supply, though he knew it had nothing to do with lack of food now. His eyes, at a glance, appeared bloodshot, but when he studied them more closely, he saw a darkening of the iris, while the white didn't look veined, but had taken on a slight mauve hue. Next he studied his hands. Did the fingers look longer? He thought so, but felt he might be sliding into confirmation bias there. Certainly the sleeves of his shirt didn't reach as far down his wrists as they had before.

The laboratory, he decided impulsively. The flies would be there in that isolation booth. He used the toilet, washed his face and sweaty arm pits, put on another shirt recently purchased, and larger, then headed out of the door. Yorgos wasn't at his station, but another soldier, a thickset brute with receding hair and bad teeth, had taken his place. The guard stood up as he approached and Ottanger hesitated. This man wore a military jacket but underneath he also had on darker Inspectorate gear. Had Yorgos lost his job because of the docilator?

'I want to go to the laboratory,' Ottanger finally said.

The man held up one finger. 'He wants to go to the laboratory,' he said, then dipped his head, listening to his fone. After a moment he looked up. 'I'm told the lab is closed up today for fullclean. Another time.'

'Ah damn – I wanted to talk to Savarack. Something is changing about me and I'm concerned.'

While the guard relayed this over the fone, Ottanger looked along the corridor towards the laboratory and saw someone crossing. The man there, with two Inspectorate guards behind him, halted abruptly and turned to look towards him. Sick recognition hit him. Though thinner and his suit wrinkled, it was Murcheson – the man who'd wanted him interrogated to death. Murcheson's expression gave nothing away and he moved on, the two Inspectorate guards following him. He didn't look like a prisoner.

'Dr Alison will be along directly,' the Guard said. 'You can wait for her in your room.'

Now Ottanger felt a sense of something wrong, beyond the new guard here and the sight of Murcheson. It was almost as if he could see hurrying, worried figures throughout the Complex, social shifts and power shifts going on.

'Has something happened?' he asked.

'Why do you ask that?' the guard asked, studying him suspiciously.

Ottanger shrugged and pointed. 'I saw Murcheson. I thought he was in a cell.'

'Yes, something happened.' The guard abruptly sat. 'But it's not your concern. Return to your room.'

Ottanger hesitated, worry writ in his expression and somewhat in his heart, but he knew he would get no more here. He turned around and headed back. That he was undergoing physical changes had to be evident to them anyway, so he hadn't given anything away. However, he doubted the lab was undergoing cleaning. They didn't want him there. They were worried and paranoid and, though not necessarily about him, it could affect him. As he stepped into his room, he realized that even if he could control his internal reactions under lie detector, that didn't, in any way, make him safe.

Dr Alison looked haunted as she pushed her trolley into his room. He studied her and, beyond her and this room, he still had a sense of urgent activity and danger.

'So what's happened?' he asked.

She paused and looked at him, then glanced up at the camera on the light fitting, until finally dipping her head. He caught the look of fear – he'd never seen that in her before.

'A terrorist incident,' she said. 'Terrorists have detonated a tactical nuclear weapon killing many national leaders and MDC serving members.'

'That's terrible,' said Ottanger, trying to sound like he meant it.

'Thankfully,' she said, 'the Inspectorate is acting quickly to suppress rogue elements and we are grateful that they're also taking charge here.'

Ottanger winced internally, but didn't let it show on his face. She too had spoken the words with a conviction that didn't reach her eyes. That was the horror of totalitarianism. You not only had to follow the rules and say the correct words, but you also had to behave as if all of it was fine and correct, and you utterly believed it was for your good, and the good of others. Dr Alison evidently didn't believe.

'Inspectorate in charge here,' he repeated flatly.

'Yes,' she said, and he knew not to push her further on the subject. 'Now I must examine you,' she added.

'I'm all yours,' he said holding his arms out at his sides.

After giving him a lengthy examination, Dr Alison took him for scans and sampling again. Now he saw more Inspectorate uniforms in the Complex. Even as she did her work, two blank-faced guards arrived to stand at the door, with hands on shock sticks at their belts. The two then followed as they returned to his room and remained outside, either side of the door.

'I'm presuming you have questions?' she asked, after following him into his room and giving him a brief warning look, before adding, 'About your condition.'

He turned to her, managing a worried expression. 'What's happening to me?'

'Do you really need me to explain that?' she asked. 'I've seen your debriefing.'

He shook himself, as if irritated that he'd asked the question, then closed his eyes as if to get his thoughts in order, when really they were already perfectly clear and precise. 'I know this implanted biotech is changing me somehow, but *how* is it changing me? What do the scans and the samples tell you?'

'To a limited extent, the biotech has pulled you back to a childhood state, and you are growing again, very rapidly – faster than a teenager, for example. This is why, right now, you are five centimetres taller than you were when you arrived here.'

'Fuck,' he said, and he wasn't pretending. He knew he'd grown but hadn't realized how much.

'It's making other changes too, which are more interesting. It has increased vascularity throughout your body, your musculature is changing to that of an athlete – specifically a marathon runner – your intestinal system and its biota are transforming, and we are still speculating on why . . .' She paused, shook her head in irritation, then continued, 'I said earlier that growth has started again, but it's not quite the growth one would see in an adolescent. There are some extreme differences, which again we cannot parse, though can speculate on.'

'Those speculations?'

'Physically you're becoming more formidable, and durable, while there have also been changes to your nerves. Quite a lot of what we're seeing is similar to something that was tried well over a hundred years ago, during an attempt to genetically modify people to make better soldiers.' She waved a hand dismissively. 'Unfortunately, the data on that are limited.'

'Limited?' he enquired.

She looked decidedly shifty and said, 'A great many military projects are now out of the hands of the military and controlled, for our safety, by the Inspectorate.' She then turned a little pale and glanced up at the camera. Ottanger considered briefly how as an SA one could almost be less free than a ZA. Zero Assets were starved, killed and generally treated like a plague upon the Earth, but at least in their tenements they could, for the most part, think and talk as they wished.

'But that's not as interesting as other alterations,' she hurried

341

on. 'Your brain is changing shape, developing structures we've never seen before, which also relate to your senses. Some nerves are thickening and branching out further, and we think this indicates greater conscious control over your autonomous nervous system. And this extends to all your senses too.' She pointed at his face. 'You may have noted a colour change in your eyes. That's because you're growing other receptors, on top of the usual rods and cones in your retina. We think you'll be able to see more, beyond the usual visible light spectrum.' She stared at him for a long moment. 'Neurochem is adjusting too – substances there we can map, whose function remains a mystery. Though we believe all these changes relate to your ability to perceive your surroundings, your ability to translocate, and to your perception of the process too.' She paused, taking a tablet out of her pocket and studying it.

He thought about that perception of his surroundings. His sense of the Complex around him hadn't diminished. He *knew* those two guards were still outside the door – it was almost as if he could see them there in some way. But he asked dumbly, 'My perception of the process?'

She nodded, lowering her tablet, and continued, 'The Fenris told you he wanted to create people who could "jaunt", but we're sure now that was a lie. It wanted people capable of that, but not without certain substances in those cybernetic flies. This wasn't some altruistic act to create powerful people, but to create people it could control. It didn't follow through, though – you must understand that you're turning into a, if you like, jaunting engine, but one without fuel. You cannot do it without those substances, which we're currently trying to synthesize.' She shrugged. 'Seems to me that creature was playing and just got bored with the game.'

Ottanger kept his expression blank. Her eyes turned kind of

glassy when she was lying. He could feel that the biotech of the flies was changing him into a creature able to jaunt without them, and without these supposed substances, but they clearly didn't want him to know that. Sure of this, even when he spoke to Axel, he'd left such details out of his fictional conversation with the Fenris.

'I'm turning into a meta-human,' he quipped.

'You are changing, certainly, but those changes bring with them a whole host of problems too,' she said. He didn't have to hear what she was going to say next to know that they were now off the science and onto the required script.

'With the previous subjects, we saw many medical problems developing. They started producing cancers we had to excise. One developed a heart condition, because his heart couldn't keep up with his other developments. Hallucinations were common, interventions frequent. All of them ended up on specially designed drug protocols, not only to keep them healthy but to keep them alive. I could go on . . . but this is why we're monitoring you so closely.' She pursed her lips in distaste, but whether this was a scripted reaction or her personal one to the series of lies she'd just told, he couldn't tell.

'Am I okay now?' he asked meekly.

'You have some nodes in your lungs we'll have to look at soon,' she replied. 'After your next jaunt would be best, since you'll need at least a few days to heal if we have to remove them.'

'Okay.' He nodded, looking worried as she headed to the door.

'Get yourself some rest now and eat healthy,' she told him on departing.

Retrospectively analysing the conversation, and her body language, he realized that she hadn't liked lying. Perhaps some integrity existed in the science world under the Committee after all.

★   ★   ★

Jillian visited him again, bringing a bottle of wine with her, and drank the first glass like she needed it. She then proceeded to start unbuttoning her blouse.

'I noticed someone out in the corridors I didn't expect to see,' he said conversationally.

She focused on him, her fingers freezing. Abruptly she took out a hand tablet and worked it for a moment, while glancing up at the cam. Finally, she replied, 'You're talking about Murcheson.' Then she hurriedly added, 'The cam is frozen – nothing is being recorded.'

'Yes, Murcheson. Is he in charge here now? With the Inspectorate?'

'The Inspectorate has oversight . . . and that concerns you?'

'He tried to have me killed.'

'Yes, I'd thought that too before. But the order for it actually came down from Committee bureaucrats, who are now dead. Like us all, he had no choice but to obey it. . . . You know about the terrorist attack?'

'Yes,' he said, expression bland, because of course she knew he knew.

'What happened to you before won't happen again. You're too valuable here. The Inspectorate had their own similar project and it's being amalgamated with our own, to the benefit of all. They've brought in some new and unexpected resources, which we're grateful for.'

'So Jones and Savarack are okay with this?'

'Just bruised egos. There's some infighting, but it's at the bureaucratic level and won't change how we've been conducting things.'

'That's good. I was worried,' he said, putting as much sincerity in as she'd put into her lies. She was a better liar that Dr Alison, but still seemed ludicrously transparent to him. He felt sure that even her work with the hand tablet had been a ruse, and the cam hadn't been turned off at all.

The sex was enjoyable but not so extended after that. Reading her intention, he tried to prolong it, but she told him that he should be rested for his next jaunt the following day. She promised that when he came back, they'd have an extra special time.

As she left, he stared at the door with a feeling of utter contempt arising, but then evaporating. They were making every effort to ensure his return, and smart enough to know that the carrot would work better than the stick, though Dr Alison's bullshit about cancer had some of the stick in it. He got up and raided his food supply, completely depleting it and going to bed with his stomach bulging.

In the morning the world felt even looser about him, more expansive, and transparent. He looked towards the door and *saw* the two guards out there. He then looked beyond them and saw Inspectorate and military personnel going about their various chores. He watched technicians at work and located Savarack, Jones and Murcheson sitting in an office talking. He couldn't hear what they were saying, and everything had the quality of illusion – had he imagined this vision of his surroundings into being?

When he got out of bed to go to the bathroom, the vision retracted to his immediate surroundings and a weird feeling washed through him – as though he had an alternative to walking into that room. It scared him and he locked down on it. If he was capable of jaunting now, he had no idea to what degree. He didn't want to try it and then find himself still stuck here, with the watchers knowing. Surely they'd try to find some further way to control him, if not decide he was too dangerous to keep around. He needed more fly pills, and then greater certainty in the extent of his growing ability.

They brought him a new undersuit to try on – altered to fit his larger frame. This confirmed the truth in his wide perception of his surroundings, because he'd already seen the technicians working on it, and bringing it. They then took it away again to alter, because even overnight he'd grown. No one had told him what time exactly the jaunt would be, so he headed to the shop again – the two guards falling in behind him. He bought enough food to last him many days, items of cookware and more clothing, as well as some luxury items and another bottle of wine. He put this on his table, with the two new glasses he'd bought standing next to it. Of course, the watchers would see all this. He ate hugely, but still had plenty of food left, for his *return*. Checking his account, he showed anger at how much he'd depleted his funds. Then he waited, and he thought, and for the cams, he apparently napped for a while.

Yorgos arrived with the techs who'd brought the undersuit previously. He was sort of glad to see Yorgos back and hoped any punishment hadn't been too severe. He stripped off his clothes and put on the undersuit, the techs checking and being satisfied with the fit. The jaunt was happening now, then. The techs disappeared and Yorgos stepped up close.

'We go,' he said tersely.

'Okay Yorgos,' Ottanger replied, his sympathy vanishing under the man's glare.

Yorgos led the way towards the lab, the two Inspectorate soldiers falling in behind once again. On the previous occasion, it'd been Yorgos alone who had led him there. The extra two confirmed Jillian's lie about changes only being at a bureaucratic level. Yet they were letting him jaunt, and quite possibly escape them? He felt certain that something new would await him and immediately started speculating what that might be, and how to prepare.

As he followed Yorgos through the doors into the lab, he thought about following through on a plan that had been taking shape in his mind. Inside, he once again had a large audience. The number of uniformed personnel had doubled up, with an even mix of military and Inspectorate, and the techs were moving to their positions. Over in front of the sphere, the two techs he'd seen before were waiting with the components of the outer suit. With them stood Dr Alison, Colonel Jones, Savarack and Murcheson. Something was up.

Yorgos led the way forwards, thankfully precisely where Ottanger wanted to go, right past the isolation booth where Savarack assembled the fly pills. As they drew closer to this, he reviewed his plan. The plastic booth should be easy enough to break open, then he'd be able to snatch up flies or pills, and just shove them into his mouth. He knew, in fact he could feel himself right on the edge of being able to jaunt without them. So perhaps just a little more of what they contained would be enough. He felt it worth the risk. But as they drew closer, he began to reassess.

Much was scripted here – Jillian, Dr Alison, his increase in comfort and 'wealth'. So what made him think that Savarack didn't follow a script too? He shouldn't fall into the misconception, with the increase in the Inspectorate here, that the military personnel were somehow good and the Inspectorate bad. They were all bad, all manipulative. They'd learned from the previous subjects and were applying that knowledge meticulously. There had been no particular reason for Savarack to allow him to see the pills being assembled, and where they were kept. As they approached the booth, he suddenly became utterly certain there would be no flies in the thing. Yorgos walked ahead, tension in his back, and then turned to him. Ottanger walked right by the booth, catching the expectancy in the soldier's expression. He'd read the trap correctly. Finally, they brought him to the others.

'I hope I get to see a little more this time,' he said.

'We hope so too,' said Savarack. 'For future jaunts, we're investigating a way for you to bring back samples. And, if we can figure it out, how to record other data.'

The man seemed distracted as he looked round at Colonel Jones, and then Murcheson. Jones glanced at him, face impassive, then shrugged.

'Dr Alison,' said Murcheson, beckoning to her. 'If you would.'

'But he didn't do it,' said Alison, somewhat shakily Ottanger thought.

Murcheson shook his head. 'It doesn't matter. We can't take the risk.' He looked to Savarack and Jones. 'We are in agreement?' he enquired tightly.

'Of course we are,' said Savarack hurriedly. 'We all have the one goal.'

Jones just pursed his lips and folded his arms.

Dr Alison shook her head in annoyance and turned to pick up something from the table, as techs became busy around Ottanger. They opened up the front of his undersuit, which they hadn't done before, and she stepped up close. He saw that she was holding a syringe and didn't like that at all. Nor when the two Inspectorate guards stepped in and took hold of his arms.

'What's this?' he asked her, as she swabbed his stomach and gave him a brief injection.

'Just to numb the pain,' she said.

The area she injected swiftly lost feeling, as she retrieved another device from the table on which the armour had been laid out. The chromed object had the appearance of a syringe, mainly because of the needle, which was large and wide bore. She stabbed it into the numb area, turned it up and activated it, the thing making a hollow click.

'What is it?' he asked.

She ignored him, dumped the device in a kidney dish with the anaesthetic syringe, then walked away with the dish, waving her hand towards Savarack, Jones and Murcheson. The three stepped in, and it didn't escape Ottanger's notice that the two soldiers still held onto him, while Yorgos stood close, his hand on a shock stick at his belt.

'It's an unfortunate, necessary precaution, dictated by others higher up,' said Savarack. 'We are now under pressure to do this sort of thing. I can only apologize.'

Ottanger gave him a puzzled look, but had a good idea what was coming. He also knew that Savarack's lines would have been different had he tried to break open the isolation booth to get to the flies it didn't actually contain. The man was lying – to script. Almost certainly a previous subject had felt the need inside too, and tried to grab the flies.

'But what is it?' he asked.

Savarack waved a hand towards Murcheson, his expression a well-rehearsed one of disgust.

Murcheson, it seemed, felt no need to follow any script. He looked at Ottanger with cold satisfaction. 'It's a timed-release capsule,' he said. 'In our own project we tried a poison, for which the antidote awaited back at our laboratory. But the subject came back barely coherent and unable to describe much of what he'd seen. In one hour, the capsule will release a nerve toxin into your body. Five minutes later you will be dead. However, upon your return prior to that, it can be deactivated by a simple coded transmission.'

'I see,' said Ottanger. He reached down and touched the injection site, and felt a hard lump, deep under his skin. A moment later, one of the techs slapped his hand away and closed up the undersuit.

He nodded at them, grimacing. 'This is the world we live in,' he said. 'I have no doubt that, whoever was putting on this suit, the same precautions would be taken. Even if it was one of you.' His words were to reassure them, though they did have veracity.

Savarack showed relief, while Jones's expression remained unreadable. Murcheson didn't believe it for a moment, and understood him to be saying reassuring things just because he was on to a good thing here and didn't want to spoil it. The man waved his hand and the Inspectorate guards released Ottanger's arms, then stepped back. He moved closer to the table and held his arms out to the side, in the position the techs had him assume when putting on the armour.

'Let's do this,' he said.

Chenghu

It was Chenghu's turn to gather information on the blast and its fallout politically. Rather than deposit himself in a sprawl and find screens there to view, as Chancel had before him, with all its inherent risks, he decided on somewhere else. While coming in, his holosense gave him a perception of chaos, a feeling of something badly wrong, but he couldn't clarify beyond that. His inability to do so annoyed him, for he felt he should.

The barrier walkway slid in below him, easily pinpointed by his instinctive homing sense, and he dropped down onto it lightly. Spread out ahead of him lay a patchwork of sea farms, secured against the stubs of turbine towers, with bulky robots running along rails beside these walkways to collect the harvest. Over to his right, he could see a collection barge into which the robots were spewing their loads of insipid modified herring. The next stop for these would be an onshore processing plant, where the fish were ground up and then pressed into protein bars, which were actually one rich part of the SA diet. They contained many of the amino acids and oils a human needed. Sadly they also contained the pollutants poured into nearby rivers from the numerous solar-panel reprocessing plants in this area.

Chenghu grimaced, took off his pack and removed a tablet, propping it up and sitting cross-legged in front of the thing. He then plugged in the special receiver Ektian had put together for him, and watched it search out then lock onto public service broadcasts. He sat there, absorbing the news as *homogenized* by the government.

Right from the start, they'd called it a terrorist act, and now various national governments seemed to have found people to blame. In fact, each country had uncovered its own particular candidates and was acting on that. European Bloc forces were annexing smaller states that had managed to resist being absorbed so far. Their police, with its large Inspectorate contingent, were arresting those members of internal groups who protested Committee diktats. Elsewhere arrests of a similar nature were being made, and already the USA was expanding its Inspectorate-run re-education camps. Meanwhile, Mexican forces were advancing into Texas. The UK, following a long historical precedent, had sent tanks through the Channel tunnels into France, and then rolled them south towards those obdurate people who ignored Committee diktats. These 'police actions' were occurring all over the world. At the same time the Committee – formed of subordinate bureaucrats and the swiftly replaced world leaders who were now drifting ash – was calling for calm and an organized response. One vocal member of the Committee, Alessandro Messina, with no particular political affiliations, spoke with gravitas about this, and it seemed he could be found on every channel. Chenghu felt a sinking sensation as he began to formulate an impression of what was going on.

The channels broadcast mostly propaganda, laced with real events to give it veracity, but peeling away that gloss, it was possible to see the underlying reality. The fact Messina was so prominent meant he was the leader being polished up for the position of chairman. Messina warned sombrely of how any remaining national divisions were a barrier to forming the Inspectorate into the truly multinational force needed to counter such terrorist acts. Quisling replacement leaders heartily agreed with him, and further police and military forces were coming under the aegis of the now 'worldwide' Inspectorate, under shared national command via the Committee. It also seemed, because sufficient uniforms weren't available, a lot of black armbands had appeared. Chenghu sat back. They'd not cut the head off a snake but from a hydra.

One of the sea-farm robots started heading towards him along the rails, down on the side of the barrier. Then he noticed things in the sky that looked like seagulls but certainly were not. Glancing inshore, he saw figures moving out onto the walkways there. He'd been spotted. If he stayed here, he'd be arrested, beaten, thrown into a cell, interrogated and tortured. And it seemed this was a state of affairs set to continue on this world. Could he learn any more here? Not really. What the jaunters should have done was set up some better way of gathering information before rushing into Irene's plan. This was something they needed to look into in the future, should they want to make further interventions. He shook his head. If there'd be any point in doing more – for it seemed a nuclear blast had made little change to the miserable course of history here. Had they even accelerated it?

He stood up, slipping the tablet back into his pack, and put that onto his back. It was time to go. But he felt reluctant to return to Caprock with a confirmation of what Chancel had already reported. He didn't want see Irene's obdurate expression, and then her long slow anger as she accepted the reality of the situation here. He wanted fresh air, not the polluted fish decay stuff here. And he needed peace, specifically without razorbirds lining up to cripple him, or Inspectorate officers coming to drag him off. He took a pace as if to step off the barrier, and the world slid under and through him. Utterly familiar with how he in a way sensed beyond vision, he observed the multiverse manifold tangled around him, including the sharp slope crashing down into the airless Earth. He could, if he wished, divert around it, but that would mean entering the parallels of his home world and he was sick enough of it. So he took the slope.

Coming out into the cold and dead air of this Earth, he stepped over a drift of gravel and kicked away one of the cactus-like plants that grew here, seemingly burned and shrivelled on the stone. Instead of immediately jaunting on to another place, he walked, knowing from Pranjab's studies and his own experiments that he could go without oxygen for a long time. The first few minutes were just like holding his breath, as his body used up every available molecule of the stuff. Next he'd feel a painful transition as it slipped into hypoxic function. He walked across the charred ground, noting burned lines of some growth, and then he looked up.

The moon hung high in the sky, bloated in comparison to the one above the Earth he'd just come from, and its surface was etched with human structures. So hive humans lived up there and possessed world-walking abilities similar to his own and the others. Though, judging by what Pranjab had told him, they required some kind of portal to cross the parallels. The Fenris had designated these people a danger – certainly, those who'd chased Pranjab, and that thing that hunted Irene, hadn't exactly been friendly. He wondered about them and their aims.

353

Had they destroyed their Earth, scouring it of life and oxygen, before shifting to the moon? These were aspects they were waiting on the Fenris to explain. But should they put all their reliance on that creature? He considered using his abilities to take him to that moon right now, to find out what he could, then rejected the idea. What the jaunters had designated a homing sense allowed them to hop from the surface of one parallel Earth to another. It corrected relative velocities and pushed them away from materializing inside objects. To make the leap to the moon, he'd necessarily have to fight all that, and he wasn't sure what the results would be. Perhaps another time, he decided, as his body made the harsh transition to hypoxic function. Then he looked down.

There'd been no corpses behind him in the place where, as far as he understood it, most unfortunate jaunters had arrived and died. Here he could see one or two, though, and the nearest was seared on one side. Something had happened here, perhaps related to the Fenris. Or perhaps some jaunter had managed to come through carrying an explosive. That would have been unusual, since it took a while to acquire the ability to extend the organic field of the body even to include clothing. There also seemed something odd about the dried-out remains of the human being before him. He stepped over it. The corpse looked somehow light and papery, and now he realized what his holosense was alerting him to. He focused on that. The thing was all but hollow, with just a few bones remaining inside. Further study revealed thin structural supports holding the dry skin in place. He then saw the threads eating their way along remaining bones and tracked those to a crack in the ground, where they disappeared deep down, beyond his perception. He recognized fenris biotech instantly and got some intimation of events here. Then he looked up again.

A ship had slid in above, without him noticing. It sat over a kilometre up, beyond where his holosense started to diminish, but he should have detected something so big moving in over him. Though this puzzled him, he felt no particular anxiety about the arrival, for he could step away to another world in a moment. He studied it.

The ship measured a kilometre across and looked like a chunk excised from some worm-eaten wood, with the burrows exposed in its fibrous structure. He supposed it a likely design for people who'd taken the route of social insects. It began to descend towards him, and as it did so, figures spilled from those burrows. Blinking and focusing in with his real sight, he observed numerous vaguely human forms, recognizing creatures like the one he'd killed when he intercepted Irene, those who had pursued Pranjab, and others besides. It was time to go. Chenghu stepped away, into the spaces between parallels, with a short map already laid out in his mind. But immediately he saw that something was wrong.

The manifold of the multiverse had blackened around him, with what looked like a cup rising up. From this multiple side tunnels fled down into darkness. He tried to push away from it in the direction he wanted to go, but felt a tug, similar to that of the slope from his nodal Earth into the airless Earth he'd just departed. The network inside him burned bright, drawing on his energy. He understood that if he didn't do something, he'd be pulled back into that world. He concentrated hard and he pushed, searching for a direction outside of the cup. With the feeling of something tearing inside, he threw himself aside. A surface came up below him, and he hit it fast, splashing water and then going under. Still hypoxic, he didn't panic, even as his weight and that of his equipment dragged him down and thousands of fish swirled around him. He fought this and swam upwards. As he surfaced, a metallic seagull skimmed above him and he knew where he was. Back on Committee Earth.

'You! Come to us here!' someone shouted.

He looked over at the police on the barrier. Their uniforms were dark blue and the armbands they wore were black. One was gesturing at him with a machine pistol. Chenghu snorted water and blood out of his nose. His ears were ringing, and he felt leaden and utterly exhausted. He swam slowly towards the barrier, but only to give himself time to breathe properly and take in some oxygen. A few metres out, he paused, treading water, and studied the two men. The black armbands were clearer now and the logo on them looked as if it'd been designed straight out of history, specifically the Second World War. It showed a stylized shepherd with cams on either side, almost like wings. He considered the machine pistol attached to the front of his riot gear, then rejected the idea. He lifted a fist out of the water and, when sure he had their absolute attention, raised his middle finger. They were aiming their weapons at him when he jaunted again.

14

The Fenris

The Fenris observed Chenghu's arrival on the airless Earth, and then his examination of a corpse, which the biotech was steadily ingesting from the inside. He contemplated making contact but decided not to. He just watched as the man finished his perambulation and jaunted away again. And that's when he realized the hive was becoming proactive once more.

He tracked Chenghu, and saw the strange manifold trying to route him to one location. Without a doubt, this lay right inside the hive moon. Destroying the corpses and being on watch to save any new jaunters who arrived there was no longer going to be enough. While researchers on Committee Earth continued to feed those fly pills to 'mutants', who would then inevitably jaunt here, the hive would almost certainly end up capturing a live one.

Chenghu broke away by dint of being a strong, experienced world walker. And the hive had yet to get its manifold working as it wanted. Evidently the thing had been initiated when Chenghu was spotted by a hive ship, so it hadn't manifested for long enough, nor with sufficient power, to generate a good grip on him. The hive's manifold seemed, at the moment, to be something that took time to power up and had little accuracy.

After Chenghu ended up back on Committee Earth, the Fenris kept tracking him, watching him jaunt away through the parallels, then drop hard on the mountainside of the world Ektian had previously resided on. The man was done – his biotech at war with his feeble human biology, blood running out of his ears and his body drained of reserves. He managed to retain consciousness long enough to stagger across the rocks to a nearby track, and there collapsed. The Fenris observed him, annoyed at this weakness, and knew it to be minimal in the man Ottanger and others, with their inherited fenris DNA substrate. He then made the necessary connection and looked upon one of the sea people there. He found the one whose shift it was to sit by the biotech 'brain' the Fenris had managed to penetrate and turn into a link to that world and its people.

'Hello,' he said.

The man jumped out of his seat and looked around. Then, realizing the voice had spoken from the melted-looking console in front of him, he started fast gill breathing as he sat down again. He shrugged himself, switched back to proper air breathing, then took a good long calming breath, before replying, 'Er, hello . . . is that the Fenris?'

'Yes, I am the Fenris. I need the help of your people as a matter of urgency.' As he said this, he also began putting together information about the hive world and its inhabitants. This was the sort of stuff the sea people liked, and it would set things up so they'd keep a look out for those hive human post-heads and warriors intruding on their world. But he also did this because the sea people were highly exchange oriented. It wasn't that they wouldn't do what he asked without some sort of gift of information, but the fact they were always aware of debt. As far as they were concerned, the Fenris was in their debt because they'd looked after Ektian.

'What can we do for you?' the man asked.

'One of my world walkers has arrived on your world in a bad condition. He is unconscious at this location.' Via the brain, the Fenris sent a map to a nearby gel screen, to highlight where Chenghu lay. 'He'll need rest, food and drink, then should recover quickly.'

By this time other sea people had entered the room. A big broad woman, whom the Fenris recognized as the head of the 'Fenris Project', began barking orders with ear-rattling subsonics. Chenghu would be in safe hands very quickly.

'We are glad to help,' said the man at the console, which was code for, *and what have you got for us?*

'I have sent a package to you, covering information on a culture of hive creatures. They can travel the parallels and may be a danger to us all,' the Fenris said.

'That is interesting,' said the woman, now coming up behind the man. 'Since we have had other visitors besides your walkers.'

'Perhaps you can send me information on that?' said the Fenris.

'Of course we can,' she said. 'And we would be glad to learn of any technologies we could use to defend ourselves against such dangers.'

They were fifty years out on the other side of a world war, with nation states treating each other with extreme suspicion, and they had their own biotech version of 'mutually assured destruction'. They'd never stated their interest in weapons outright, and this was the closest the woman had come to it.

The hive clearly wasn't unique in its assessment of, and preparation for, threats.

'I will send you something,' the Fenris said, then feeling a surge throughout his being. Those he was speaking to abruptly became so clear to his perception he could even see through them, into their organs and functions of their bodies, as well as into their surrounding technology. Suddenly excited, he pulled away, dropping the sea people down a perceptual well.

'What the fuck?' he said, speaking perfect English rather than the sea people's language designed for underwater. But it was a rhetorical question.

Another surge followed, and it felt as if the world was melting away all around, with him the only solid thing in existence. The multiverse opened out again, painfully bright to his perception. His sense of its detail expanded hugely, while his own world became a tissue-thin layer he could push apart with an act of will. Joy rose up, banishing long frustration and a great deal of anger. It was as if his biotech was running diagnostics on newly installed wetware. No, in fact that was precisely what it was doing.

The time had come. Adulthood had arrived, and at last he'd be able to jaunt.

Now he needed to venture out there and become active in dealing with the threat against him. He needed to guide his world walkers *firmly* along the correct course for dealing with their home world, and with the hive. And he needed them to be smarter than they had been. Their old biology predicated the requirement for leaders and the followers, for dominance and subservience. He could see that Irene, though diminished, would re-establish her dominance and might well lead them into disaster. She had to be replaced by someone powerful, with a more amenable and forward-thinking mindset, undistorted by bitterness and a need for vengeance. Someone who wasn't so limited by their old biology, and for whom the possibilities of development were endless.

The Fenris now turned his attention to the candidate he had in mind.

Ottanger

The techs moved in and began fixing the various plates to him in preparation for his jaunt. Jones moved away, waving Yorgos after him, as Savarack went to take a seat at one of the consoles. Murcheson went to join the audience, which now contained a few wearing Inspectorate uniforms. Ottanger read the dynamics of the room: the distrust between military and Inspectorate, how they watched each other. He then noticed Murcheson turn to speak to the woman beside him, who responded eagerly, flirtatiously, and it was of course Jillian.

With a large degree of cynicism, he continued studying the room. So no flies stored in the isolation booth – he was sure of that now. They'd dangled those as a trap for him, and it was to have been an excuse for the lethal capsule now sitting in his torso, spelling death should he not return. He'd not taken the bait but they'd installed the capsule anyway. It was clear the soft approach would swiftly disappear from this place as Murcheson established his position. Ottanger felt certain now that, upon his return, they'd also institute other methods of controlling him. How long before they considered the poison capsule in his torso not a sufficient safeguard against a determined person? How long before they tried something even stronger? Like the mental programming, brought about by drugs and torture, which put rebels on the screens sadly regretting their actions and apologizing for them. How long before they brought out Jane, or others he knew, and told him they'd torture and kill them if he didn't behave? He had to get out of this . . . now. But how?

The techs led him into the sphere and attached up the skeins of wiring. One of them inserted a fone in his ear, then the other opened the lid on the inhalator, as before, and inserted one of the fly pills. Over the fone, he heard the usual system check routine from Savarack.

'As before, Ottanger,' said the man at one point. 'Be ready for my signal to inhale. This time hold the breath for just ten seconds.'

Interesting, thought Ottanger. Savarack offered no explanation for this, but it was once again plain to him that the changes he'd undergone were making him less reliant on the pills. He peered down at the inhalator, and realized now what he had to do.

Finally Savarack said, 'Okay, Ottanger, use the inhalator.'

Had they covered this angle, Ottanger wondered, as he dipped his head to the device. Its actuator clicked, puncturing the pill. Ottanger closed his lips around it and drew in a long, deep breath. Even in the first seconds of holding it, he could feel his surroundings loosening and growing more insubstantial. But he steadied himself there and, still holding the breath in his lungs, closed his teeth on the inhalator, then bit down hard, breaking plastic, which sliced into his gums. He tore the lid away and spat it, still managing to hang on to that breath. The fly pill lay exposed. He bit on it and pulled it out, shifting it into his mouth, while fighting the urge to cough. A dry, bitter metallic taste sucked the moisture out of his tongue. And then, after more than twenty seconds, he let the breath out of his nostril as he struggled to summon the moisture to swallow the pill.

As he tried to get the thing down, he could see activity in the lab, but like ghosts closing in. The pill caught in his throat, as if it had produced hooks. Ahead of him, the surface of the sphere sprouted a rash of spots, with fracture lines around them. They were shooting at him. He felt impacts on his suit as he leaned away from the world. A vast pattern expanded before him, which he comprehended on a visceral level. Darkness gathered around a slope he somehow knew would take him straight to that airless place again. So he pushed aside from that, the urge to escape taking him further, perception opening out to show landscapes, seas, weird cities, strange plants and creatures. Momentarily he felt godlike, as if he could fling himself across eternity. But physical realities remained and, feeling the tether to his Earth still attached, he made a choice. He fell down upon a world that seemed bereft of human civilization, then found a specific surface and came out upon it, stumbling and going down on one knee.

Bright light flared around him. Choking and still trying to get that pill down, he turned his head to look up at a blue sky painted with cirrus, and framed by dark hooked shapes. He was uncomfortably warm straight away and felt humidity on his face and in his nostrils. The undersuit seemed to tighten around him; he sensed it trying to dislodge him from this world. They were trying to pull him back. He heaved to his feet and, as fast as he could, pulled off the garment and discarded it. The thing dropped to the ground, shimmering and writhing as if its mesh had transformed into a mass of golden worms. It faded for a second, then, with a thumping sound that lifted the soft, debris-covered ground around it, it solidified again, blackened and smoking.

Ottanger backed away from the thing, coming up against hard objects poking into his back. He could still feel a pull on him and began wrenching off those circular patches they'd attached all over his body. As each of these went, the pull diminished, but even with the last flung from him, it didn't go away fully.

Now he saw his surroundings impinging, through watering eyes. Leaf and wood debris covered the ground, and he'd arrived in a space between palm trees. He turned, realizing he'd backed into one of their scaled trunks. Beyond that a slope dropped away, draped with blue intestinal-looking vines, hanging between plants like mangroves, their wood a strange iridescent black. Returning his attention to the palm trees as he finally coughed up the pill, he realized they didn't look right either. The leaves above were bluish, and the scaled bark had more of a reptilian look than any image he'd seen on a screen. Weird fungus, like malformed white hands, clung here and there too. Another world, of course.

He took the fly pill out of his mouth and studied it. One end of the capsule was missing, exposing the fly inside, which looked mangled, revealing a glassy translucent interior. Finally generating enough moisture in his mouth, he tried swallowing it again and managed to this time. But his throat felt raw and dry afterwards. That done, he now accepted that he'd taken an irrevocable step, and he still didn't know if he had escaped. This world felt precarious around him, and the tug down an unseen slope towards Committee Earth remained. Not entirely sure how it all worked, he headed down the slope he could actually see, on the theory that if he relocated himself on this world, should he fall back to his origin, he would with any luck find himself outside the Complex. And he needed something else too. He had one hour before the hard lump in his torso broke open and killed him. He had to find something to cut with.

The vines hanging from their tangle in the black boughs above felt weirdly soft when he carefully tried to push one from his path, and he feared initially they might be some kind of animal. But they were otherwise unyielding. He pushed harder and the thing broke with a leaden sound, then collapsed, the smell of mushrooms rising to his nostrils. Some type of fungus.

He worked his way down the slope, feeling hard roots in the leaf matter under his bare feet. As he put one foot in front of the other, he kept looking out for sharp objects. Anything he might be able to use. The ground finally levelled off, and when he saw stones his hopes lifted. But the stone was soft limestone. He kept walking, still looking out, not knowing how much time had passed. He then heard water, as he found himself walking into the open again. Bluish moss, sprouting tubular red flowers, clad the stone slabs here, with dark red liverworts growing in between. This brought him to a stream, which flowed between the slabs, crowded with green at its edges, but was clear in the channel between, with stones on the bottom.

Ottanger waded in, stooped over, and stuck his face in the water, drinking until he thawed the horrible dry oily sensation in his throat. He then began to lift stones and toss them up onto the bank. Some looked viable for his purposes – he just wasn't sure. Returning to the bank, he scraped moss from one slab and used it as an anvil to break the stones he'd collected, smashing them against each other. He finally lucked out with one gnarled-looking lump that had a white exterior. Flint, he realized. Eventually, after further hammering, he managed to flake off a piece with a razor-sharp edge. He brought it to his torso, hovering over the lump.

Here Ottanger hesitated. The idea had been all very well in the planning, but now, having to slice into himself probably a centimetre or more deep, stayed his hand. He closed his eyes for a second, trying to summon the will. He visualized an inducer above his head as the alternative, because he had no idea what the neurotoxin might do to him. But his body's memory of pain just made the act of hurting himself even more inconceivable.

No. He opened his eyes and stared at where he'd positioned the chunk of razor stone. He shifted it just so, cleared his mind, then stabbed in and pulled across.

He yelled. The pain was terrible, and when he looked down, his torso and thigh were red with blood. The wound stretched a couple of inches across and had opened out, pouting like lips. Teeth gritted, he put the stone down on his thigh and probed the gash with his fingers. Again the pain speared through him, and reaching a layer inside the wound, he realized it was about to get worse. The lump was still there – underneath that layer. Picking up the stone once more, he inserted it in the wound, over the lump.

'Fuck you! Fuck you all!' he shouted at the sky, and cut again.

Ottanger came back to himself lying on the ground, his torso hurting badly. He'd never seen so much blood, and it was still oozing from the gash. He sat upright, then had to quickly slam a hand down because he felt dizzy and sick. But he couldn't allow his infirmity to stop him now. Swallowing drily, he reached down to the wound and probed it around the outside, wincing at the lightest touch. He then pushed his little finger inside it, crying with the pain, but he could feel no lump there any more. Was the poison capsule gone? He felt as if he was kidding himself with the question, and that he'd probably have to cut again. He searched around for the piece of flint and found it lying where blood had soaked into the moss. When he picked it up, out of the sticky mess, he saw something stuck to it: a capsule.

He cried and laughed now as he flicked the thing away, then lay back to rest, feeling dizzy and sick again. Briefly he fell into a doze, but the sound of movement brought him out of it quickly. He sat up and looked around. He could see nothing, but heard something moving up the way he'd come. It occurred to him now that he might be back on that world where he'd seen the mosasaurus, and other predators could be about. Predators smelled blood. He tried to push in that direction with the other strange sense he'd acquired, but got nothing. Perhaps he'd exhausted himself too much. Quickly now, he stumbled over to the stream, and scrubbed off the blood with handfuls of the greenery growing along its edges. He drank more water, because his throat felt dry again, and because of the blood loss. With a hand clamped against his wound, he climbed out the other side and headed away from that sound of movement.

Soon he made his way through those strange mangroves. It became muddy and slippery for a while and, seeing skittering movement, he turned. A large crab, its colour bright blue and red, backed away from him, claws held up. He eyed it for a moment, marking it, and the others he could now see moving through the mud, as a possible food source. But he didn't feel hungry yet. Moving on, the mud became gritty and steadily firmer. Stone began to displace it, then drifts of beige sand. The density of the mangroves dropped away until ahead he saw the glint of ocean. He finally walked out onto a beach.

Was this the same world as the first time? The beach didn't look the same. It was steeper and, though he had sand under his feet, further down it consisted of broken shells, then mounded whole ones. Moving forwards, he took his hand away from the wound – it didn't feel as painful now. On inspecting it, he saw it'd sealed closed already with black dry blood. The pull he felt – surely from Committee Earth – seemed less severe now too, but he dared not try any jaunts in case he ended up tumbling straight back there. Right now he was free, and had to decide what to do.

He moved close to the foaming waves, but only as far as his tender feet would take him over the shells, then sat down. He began sorting through shells and inspecting them. Of course he'd seen pictures of such, and recognized the shells of bivalves and other molluscs, but there seemed something off about them all. Their shapes and colours he didn't recognize from any images he'd seen. He finally discarded them as his stomach rumbled. Looking back the way he'd come, he thought about those crabs, and then other things he would need to do to survive. He stood up, naked on the shore, and headed into the mangroves.

He needed time for his body to complete its changes.

The changes were as fast as they were radical, and that, he guessed, might have been related to his blood turning black. His wound healed so fast he felt it might be part of a composite hallucination. After spending maybe an hour in the mangroves looking for crabs that stubbornly remained hidden, with his hunger becoming an intense animalistic thing within, he probed the wound with his finger, and found it painlessly healed shut. This was when he felt his perception opening out again. Estimating roughly, he supposed he could see everything around him in a sphere a kilometre across. He could see high in the sky, through enclosing jungle, and down into the ground too. That was when he finally spied the crab and dug it up, at the same time discovering those pincers of theirs were sharp and tough.

As the crab skittered away and dug itself down into free mud, he observed the dark, almost black blood oozing from the cut that had nearly taken off his little finger. He thought of the fenris DNA and biotech operating inside him, changing him, as he noticed his fingernails now partially folded into claws. He gazed at the seeping wound on his finger, and suddenly had a sense of it from the inside. His flesh shifted to his will, closing the thing up, and the finger pulsed as it healed. The sense of himself expanded too, and he realized he had control of his body from its autonomics and beyond – it was an extension of the control he'd already had over himself during interrogation. He sought out his hunger and shut it down, because he needed to think without it nagging at him. Walking carefully, he headed out of the mangroves, back up the slope. As he trudged upwards, he broke another of the fungus vines, and the smell nagged at the block he'd put on his hunger, so he took a piece off and put it in his mouth. Icons rose up and paired in his mind and, knowing at once what they meant, he chewed and swallowed. He stood there eating until his guts felt full, and the iconic language in his mind flagged up other things he required. He thought about that too, searching his mind, and his surroundings, and got to work.

Day progressed into night, which made no difference to the perception of his surroundings. He felt the need for sleep and found out how to banish that, then he worked unremittingly to ensure his survival. Days and nights ensued. He counted eight of them before he warmed his hands over a fire, while listening to the slosh of waves in the entrance of his new home. It amazed him just how much must have become imbedded in his mind during his time as a ZA on Committee Earth, though not through direct experience but from endless hours of screentime. He could now also surmise what information had been edited out of the government-approved programmes. The uses of flint had been part of that knowledge, giving him a way to start this blaze. The cave he was in had only been a recent find, after spending previous nights up in a palm tree, to avoid the giant pigs wandering the forest, until he decided they might be prey. He reached out and turned the spit – the fire had burned down enough now so the skin on the hunk of pork would turn crispy rather than burn, as he'd learned from the piece he'd cooked earlier. Other skin he'd dropped in a hollow in the rock, to tan it using urine. He sniffed at the smell of urine from the tanning skin and wrinkled his nose, wondering if he was getting that completely right.

Next his gaze wandered to his tool collection. Flint had provided him with a selection of blades and he felt quite adept with it. He'd killed this pig with a flint-bladed spear. He had tried knapping an arrowhead, though it didn't look quite as fine as those he'd seen in documentaries about the Stone Age. He planned to make a bow out of mangrove wood, with a string from cured and twisted pig gut. Shortly, he would also eat some gathered fruit and vegetables his biotech told him were edible. He felt happy here. Dangers were easily avoidable, and the weather always warm. He had plenty to eat, and no one to tell him what to do.

But was that reason enough to stay?

He looked at his hand. The fingers had grown even longer, tapering, and the nails finally folded into claws. He stood taller, and his body had drastically changed shape, while a glance in a reflective pool had shown him eyes of deep purple. But that wasn't the main thing. The pull of Committee Earth had lasted for the first four days, making the stability of this place seem precarious. This had now passed, and *he* could choose to make it less stable if he wanted to – in short, he could choose to go to another place safely now. The time was coming at last to explore his abilities.

And then? Committee Earth felt like a sore spot in his mind. During his time here, he'd replayed the things that had happened to him over and over again, and thought on what was happening to billions of others. If his new talents proved out, he could do something, start something, maybe help out. This was, after all, why he'd joined the resistance. His ideas were nebulous as he thought about what he might be able to do, but everything seemed to cycle back to what he'd experienced in the resistance.

Every fight, every attack, every effort to hold back the growing power of the government, and the increasing grip of the MDC over all governments, just resulted in civilian deaths. And thereafter, these all became excuses for the state to enforce more dictatorial measures. It seemed the ratchet went in only one direction. But surely, given time and experience, he could find a way. Certainly, he needed to get back there to find his sister Jane, before she ended up as a subject of Savarack's research.

The pig skin bubbled into crackling, and red vegetable roots finished roasting in the embers. He put these aside to cool. Overwhelming hunger and burned lips had taught him that lesson when he'd first cooked one of the crabs. He then looked at his meagre belongings on a dry shelf, as well as at the fire and pile of dry wood, and the stinking pig skin. He shrugged, before picking up his spear and heading to the mouth of the cave. The tide was on its way out now, and where the sea entered the mouth of the cave it was only inches deep. When it got deeper, he avoided it because of the sharks. Most of them weren't very big, but occasionally he'd seen fins the size of small sails passing further out in the ocean and, inspecting what lay underneath them with his wider vision, he certainly didn't want to get any closer to them. He waded through and round, back to the nearby beach. The sun was just coming up over the ocean and he smiled out at it, knowing the time had arrived.

Standing on the beach, holding his spear, Ottanger tried to change worlds. He pushed in one direction and the sun shot up into the sky, overhead and down. Nights and days juddered past with odd variations, like the sun leaping out of position or changing colour. He then halted, dropping a metre through air to hard-packed earth at the edge of a ploughed field. He puzzled over this, feeling that he'd made an error not coming in at ground level, and recognized a homing instinct operating within him, to bring him to ground level safely – some sense of the *right* place for him. This he now connected to the pull he'd felt back towards Committee Earth and the Complex. Perhaps it was a safety feature to put him back where he started, until he understood his powers. It felt right but he couldn't be sure. He looked up.

It was twilight on the world he'd transitioned to. Not far from him, he saw a large agricultural machine parked at the edge of the field, while in the distance he could see some industrial-looking structure, with lights glaring on it. His other perception confirmed massive machinery moving within it, and people walking gantries. He looked at his empty hand – his spear was back in the world he'd departed. No, this wasn't quite right. His perception had to be wider, more complete – he needed a holistic sense of it all, just as he now seemed to have with the function of his body and its wider perception. He stood up, blinked, and pushed again, while loosening his sense of material things.

Smooth as silk, the view of the multiverse as he'd seen it on his jaunt away from Committee Earth came back. He saw numberless world frames, caught in a great but fractured and disrupted web. Some of the worlds seemed more material than others, which multiplied out from them. He got a sense of whole-ness and shape. And, as with his wider internal sense, he could focus down on the detail of those worlds too. Scanning his immediate multiverse surroundings, he realized that the world he'd been on had been one of those less material, shadow worlds. A parallel of a core world, in fact the one he now stood on. He jaunted again, back along a course he now simply knew, and stepped out onto the beach to look down at his spear lying in the sand. He frowned.

Right now, he'd remain naked unless he cured that pig skin, which he now doubted he would. And unless he could find a way to carry things with him between worlds, naked he would always arrive everywhere. Stooping down, he hesitated for a second at the spear, then instead picked up a shell, closed it in his fist, and jaunted to the place with the factory and the fields again. There he opened his empty fist, for the shell had disappeared. He found a stone in the field and tried again on the way back, yet still came up empty. From the beach, he used a shell again, and this time felt the slightly perceptible tug of it leaving his hand. And it seemed this was enough, because a complex pattern lit up inside him, and out of this he deciphered a way to suppress the tug, and extend some perception of self to cover the shell. The next time the shell remained in his hand. He nodded to himself, satisfied. He'd known there had to be a way. He dropped the shell and jaunted back, then picked up his spear and tried with this, again arriving in that twilight place. There he paused, wondering just how far he could take this.

He walked over to the agricultural machine and studied it. The thing was many tonnes of metal and plastics, resting on caterpillar treads. Past ephemeral knowledge integrated in his mind, and he saw that it had an array of ploughs down from a large cylinder, and other tools were likely stored inside which could be deployed there. It had no seat for a driver, so was either a robot or remotely controlled. The thing had to be upward of ten tonnes. Could he?

Almost with a sense of abandonment, he encompassed the thing, including it in his sense of self, and jaunted. He felt the huge weight of it dragging on him, not with strain but with an almost joyful testing of strength. The beach came up at him hard, and he went down into a squat, while a huge crash and wave of seawater splashed in from the side, knocking him sprawling. He stood up, soaked, and observed the machine sitting in the sea. Lights now came on in various places, a motor whirred and other mechanisms clicked, as if the dunking had woken it up. Ottanger laughed, then cackled, and then found he couldn't stop. Until he thought about the disappearance of the machine from that other world. His laughter died as he considered the consequences. Maybe that world was like his own Earth, so the machine belonged to the state. Therefore, fuck the state. But it might not be like that, and perhaps he'd just stolen, or damaged, someone's livelihood. He was only half sure of what he was going to do when he did it. This time he arrived at his destination with more care, the twilight world etching in around him as he positioned himself, and the machine. He gently touched down. The machine did too, but then settled with a jolt on its suspension, spilling seawater. He hoped he hadn't damaged it, as he returned to his beach.

Ottanger went back to his cave to eat pork and vegetables, and tried to admire his collection of flints, but felt only disappointment. What was the point of flint blades when, through an act of will, he could grab some massive machine from another world? The multiverse felt loose around him, and huge horizons were opening out. This place had been a brief interlude while he grew into a power that provided limitless possibilities. He knew it was time to go from here, and to act. Filled with food, he found a comfortable spot on the earth floor and readied himself to lie down. Though he'd stopped his need for sleep over the last few days, it seemed the jaunting had actually raised some weariness. A pleasant dreamy space opened in his skull as a precursor to dreams, and he slid gently down into it.

The Fenris

The pleasure in taking that first step was incomparable. He was a seal discovering the sea for the first time, or a bird fledged from the nest. He was a world walker! It had its elements of danger, of course, and his first venture into a rocky desert had resulted in some fractures and a sore head, but the greatest wound was to his dignity. After that, he flew. The joy of stepping from world to world was undeniable, with different Earths below his feet, a whole spectrum of skies, strange versions of humanity, and other life. But the Fenris understood that his experience of it was at variance to those of his kind before him. They'd existed in a more homogenous multiverse, filled only with poor reflections of themselves. In this, he also understood that he'd been diverging from his kind since the moment of his birth. He was more human than he should be.

But wasn't this right? Though he'd wanted to make changes, wasn't he out of his time here, and so should adapt to this milieu? He wasn't dealing with rational fenris but primitive humans, with more power in their hands than their development warranted. That included not just the jaunters but the rulers of Committee Earth too. He also needed to deal with others who'd been human once but had now evolved into an obscenity. Could he seriously expect to still adhere to the dry fenris rules loaded into his mind concerning individual power, responsibility and free will? No, he could not, for he needed in some degree to become what he fought. At the moment he was constrained by the needs of manipulating the jaunters, *his* world walkers, but that would change, in time.

The Fenris stepped through from one parallel to another, until finally squatting down on some contorted stone on a mountaintop. Blue sky above and blue sea below were visible between the scattered islands here. He'd arrived in this place not far from where both Ektian and Chenghu had before too. Down below, he could see villages like white encrustations in the valleys, and over to his right lay the larger city of the sea people, where Chenghu was recovering from an excess of jaunting. Like the others, he had limitations, for all of them could only make a few

375

jaunts before the biotech's demands on their biology started causing damage. They couldn't move large amounts of material between worlds either. They'd required the use of a transport cage to move their nuclear device, whereas he knew in the core of his being that he could shift the mountaintop he stood upon if he so wished. As such, his group of jaunters were so far poor weapons to deploy against the hive, though they still formed the basis of what he now intended.

Ottanger had followed a developmental course similar to that of the others, but his progress had accelerated when he'd finally been fed fly biotech. Being part of the family he was, related to those who'd survived the viral implantation of fenris DNA, Ottanger was someone the Fenris had a special interest in, and hopes for his further development. But then he'd simply disappeared into the multiverse! Raiding databanks, the Fenris found out about the new Inspectorate methods of control, and hated to admit the possibility that a poison implant could very well have killed the man one hour after his jaunt. How had this happened? Were his plans to be cut down before he'd even got anywhere? He was then alerted to turn his attention to another of those pooled individuals brought in from the Inspectorate Complex. He would not let this woman perish.

The Fenris sighed in frustration at missed opportunities, and stepped from one world to another again, his foot eventually coming down on dry gravel and his breath huffing out in an atmosphere devoid of oxygen. It was an odd feeling to stand here, on this place he'd viewed and interacted with from afar for so long. He looked over at the hollowed corpses and felt the biotech in the ground below as a portion of himself. From it, and from the surface of this Earth, he gazed up at the moon and into the multiverse. The hive manifold still appeared as dysfunctional as before. However, more energy seemed to have become available. The thing could now power up more quickly, and zero in on a target more accurately. And it had done so.

Circumstances had changed since the researchers lost Ottanger, which was reflected in the way they'd taken care of their new subject. The mesh suit couldn't be so easily removed now, and the timed poison implant was made inaccessible. The Fenris had watched this new world walker jaunt, determined to help her survive. Instantly plotting her course to the place where he now stood, he'd aimed to contact her through the biotech here, then to shunt her on to somewhere safer, where she could breathe. But she simply hadn't arrived. In multiverse view, he'd watched the hive's manifold unreel a tube of its structure, then hoover her up. Quite likely she was dead up there now, on that moon – the poison implant in her rib would have activated.

Even so, her presence there dead or alive had suddenly become leverage, since she was Ottanger's sister. For, just as he'd been mourning the fact the man was a lost cause, automatic search had then detected something.

The flash of linkage had been almost invisible, only detected because the fenris biotech was established on a number of worlds. Ottanger had survived! The system had then enhanced it as the man jaunted, then jaunted again and again, between a nodal world and its parallel, his ability increasing hugely with every leap. Still, some function of Ottanger's biotech blocked the Fenris, but not enough to prevent him seeing that Ottanger wouldn't have needed a transport cage to move a nuclear device. And, because of the number of jaunts he'd made, the Fenris's probes into the multiverse were able to locate the man for him. But what now?

It was time for the Fenris to recruit the kind of leader he needed for his world walkers. Someone powerful enough to displace Irene from the top of the hierarchy she'd established:

Ottanger. He, and they, would then be a weapon to stand against the hive. It also suited the Fenris's purposes that Ottanger would be influenced by the fact that, in snatching his sister, the hive had killed her. But still, before deploying that weapon, there were questions that needed answering.

The hive manifold enabled its people to travel to many worlds. And the speed with which researchers on the nodal Earth had come to understand, and manipulate, jaunt technology seemed out of keeping with the technological decay of that place – the knowledge vacuum created under oppression. Could it be that the hive had been there too? Could it even be involved there? He saw extreme dangers, because Committee Earth was strewn with jaunt biotech, and knowledge in the form of all those who'd been infected, and all those who were being experimented on. Combining that with the way the hive had managed to grab Ottanger's sister, and tried to snatch Chenghu, signified its fast redevelopment of hive war technology. One thing was becoming clear: it was time to act. To deploy the soldiers, though not yet for all-out warfare. He needed, as the human colloquialism had it, to throw a spanner in the works.

He jaunted to the next world, and the next, honing his experience of it so that, with each step he took, another world came underneath his foot, and he truly walked each of the worlds. Finally arriving at his destination, he strolled slowly, analysing the likely responses to him, as he approached the promontory jutting to the edge of the sea, where the cave entrance lay concealed. By the lap of waves he halted, while looking in with his wider sense at the sleeping man. He had to remember Ottanger's powers and prepare for that, so he sliced claws across the back of one hand to bloody them. Next, wading through the sea, he analysed the required push, and saw that an aggressive approach would be required to initiate fight or flight, then briefly at least prevent the man using his ability. Water now came up to his knees, and he eyed a shark coming in towards him. He kicked it firmly on the nose to send it off. This seemed to set the stage as he ducked into the cave and, with the tone of his voice set to just the right amount of viciousness and arrogance, he spoke.

'I find you at last,' he said.

15

Ottanger

Ottanger jerked upright, instantly recognizing the voice and searching the halls of his mind for the place it'd spoken from before. Then he heard seawater splashing and saw the huge figure coming in through the cave entrance. He felt a surge of fear somehow related to the sharks out there and the tone of the words 'I find you'. Then his anger at this invasion of his space supplanted that. He rolled, grabbing his spear to rush forwards, not sure what he was going to do – attack or run past the figure and flee. An arm snaked out, and a clawed hand closed around his biceps. He swung his spear in, and its tip fractured on glassy armour. He next wielded it as a club and the shaft broke, even as the hand gripping his arm lifted him up and tossed him back into the cave. He tumbled, came up into a squat, then looked around for something else he could use.

'Well, that was irrational of you,' said the Fenris calmly.

The fight immediately started to drain out of him, and bafflement took the place of his anger. The creature was right. Why had he imagined its words to be threatening when it had never spoken to him like that before, and had actually helped him?

Why the hell had he behaved that way? He could leave here any time he liked, and he didn't need to use the entrance. He winced, looking down at his arm where it had grabbed him and saw black blood oozing. He put a hand over it, knowing the wound would close in just a minute.

The Fenris remained bent over until he was inside, then looked up at the low ceiling, snorted, and squatted down. He was too tall to stand upright in here. He focused once more on Ottanger.

In human terms, the Fenris was all wrong. The proportions of his arms and legs were at odds. His upper arms and legs longer than they should be, while the forearms and shins short, but hands and feet extended by an extra joint, while the fingers were long and tapered, more like claws – just as Ottanger's own fingers were becoming. The Fenris's body seemed too long as well, with the chest wide and inhumanly triangular. His face reminded Ottanger of Easter Island statues, which he'd once seen pictures of – those artefacts now packed into a museum space on Committee Earth, while their island had been adapted to multilevel agriculture. His ears were pointed, his brow jutting over narrow red-violet eyes. He wore spiky armour similar to what Ottanger had seen before, hung with numerous devices connected up in a web of pipes. However, it seemed bulkier now and was reddened, as if blood had been routed through inset capillaries, and some of those devices were definitely weapons. The Fenris grinned at him, exposing sharp teeth. Ottanger could plainly see where his additional DNA had come from.

'What do you want?' he asked, rebellious, but feeling as if his mind had been kicked, spiralling out of control. He knew that in jaunting he'd further driven something inside himself, and now this new input had accelerated that.

The Fenris made an odd gesture with one hand. 'I want many

things, and many of them I cannot have. Such as my entire race resurrected from the grave. I cannot easily fix your world either, without a long, slow intervention, while standing by to watch people suffer and die. And I cannot wish the hive out of existence.'

'Wanting things we cannot have is a driver of human existence,' said Ottanger, his own words surprising him.

'So you recognize me as human?' asked the Fenris.

'Something like that,' said Ottanger, not sure what he was thinking at all.

Now, having slowly recovered some balance, he assessed his perceptions. He had the sense of his surroundings in detail, within a sphere of about a kilometre across, but also in general lying beyond that. In addition he had the sense of the normal human functions in his own body, and how he could consciously control them – of the biotech laced through his flesh and networked over his bones, and its connections in his skull. And of the changes his body was undergoing, as his black blood ran as thick as jelly, and his muscles and bones grew increasingly dense. He also had the feed from his expanded senses, raising that iconic language in his skull, with which he could analyse and assess the world in ways that stretched beyond his human perspective. Moving out, he sensed the multiverse expanding from the central point that was him: vast, complex and potentially infinite. This perception was almost unbearable, so he pulled it in and focused solely on the creature before him. He saw the changes he was undergoing reflected there. Some were aesthetic, but most concerned function and capability and, as with him, built over a human core.

'Yes,' he continued. 'You're human, but highly advanced.' He puzzled over a thousand thought trains from that statement, then said, 'Advanced by biotech, your DNA changed by it, and in turn changing it over an evolutionary period. There are worlds far ahead of mine. Worlds in the multiverse are at different points of development.'

'Wrong,' said the Fenris. 'This multiverse is on a distinct timeline, and the versions of Earth are all nominally of the same age.'

'Developmental differences, then?' Ottanger asked. 'Difference Engines that were used?' He had no idea where he'd dragged that up from. An instant later, he remembered seeing a programme about the Babbage Difference Engine, glimpsed when he was first trying to walk. And then later, some fiction about an alternate Earth, where that mechanical computer had been developed rather than abandoned.

'There are developmental differences, yes, but they're not the reason for me, as I am.' The Fenris just watched him and he knew he was being tested. He also sensed probing at other levels, for that space where the creature had first communicated with him was open in his mind, and hinted at activity he couldn't quite parse.

'Time travel, then,' he said. 'You're from a future version of humanity.'

'Close enough,' said the Fenris. 'My world was flung back into your multiverse from a million years in your future, as the result of a project to partition *my* multiverse. Whether that project succeeded or failed is open to question. And my world being thrown back through time, to crash into an earlier multiverse, was not intended. But it does prove out theories of time travel burning vast amounts of energy and catastrophically reordering existence.'

There was so much to unpack from this, but Ottanger did understand the implication that time travel was an option never to be explored again. He thought about the multiverse as he'd seen it, and as he could see it now with just an effort of will. He considered in particular the sense of disrupted patterns out there and wondered if that might be the result of this project.

'So there are no more of you?' he asked.

'My people were all prey to entropy. I am the only survivor, born into this new world. And now I can see that your mind is no longer dull, and so this form of communication is too slow.' The creature tilted his head to one side, frowning at some thought. 'I need to take you somewhere to educate you properly.'

Ottanger blinked and focused on the interloper's activities in his mind. He understood, viscerally, that the Fenris was inspecting him from the inside. But he also sensed how he could close that space down and eject the creature if he wanted to. He thought then about the first comment it had made upon arriving here – how he must have been difficult to find. He contemplated his life until his existence here, being forever subject to the will of others.

'No thanks,' he said abruptly, and jaunted away.

The Fenris

Well, that had gone fast and not quite to his inchoate plan, but it had collapsed one probability and opened out another. The Fenris frowned at the space Ottanger had occupied in the cave, then tracked the man as he bounced out in the nodal world of which this one was a parallel. He startled an agricultural engineer who was puzzling over why a robot plough had ended up with a number of fish in its workings. Jaunting again and again, Ottanger began closing down access to his mind. He was very good, completely eradicating link after link, like the one that had squeezed his amygdalae when the Fenris arrived, and had driven him to action. And the one the Fenris had used to assess the growth of his biotech, and access the extent of his abilities. But the swiftly sealed cut on his arm had done its work – the few droplets of fenris blood deposited there had seized control of a small portion of his biotech. In his arm, Ottanger had what was essentially a tracker, which also gave the Fenris access to Ottanger's surroundings via his senses.

If he'd been one of the others, he would have been bleeding from various orifices and close to collapse by now, yet the man jaunted on. He truly was a world walker. The Fenris felt a frisson and excitement at this encounter, as he remained sitting on the cave floor and thinking. He hadn't had time to talk about the hive grabbing Ottanger's sister, and to use this as motivation for Ottanger to take action against the hive. But Ottanger was unusually powerful. And, being old-style human at the core, pretty much predictable. He would seek out power first, and then strive to protect those important to him, which the Fenris had to admit would have been his own instinct too. In all likelihood, this would lead him to Committee Earth in search of his sister. Ottanger would then inevitably need to use his strong jaunting capabilities in his search, which, considering what had happened to Chenghu, would draw attention and potentially lead him into serious trouble.

The Fenris coldly calculated that, through his link to this man, he'd learn a great deal. He could then use whatever situation might ensue as a way to leverage the other jaunters on a new course. That course would surely bring them into conflict with the hive and, he suspected, lead to necessary recruiting. He grimaced at his train of thought, again noting how reality was grinding down his fenris morality, and how human he was becoming.

NEAL ASHER

Ottanger

A man was working on the agricultural machine and daylight had arrived in this place. The man looked up, holding some sort of socket driver in one hand. He was big and thickset, wearing greasy overalls. Ottanger noted something odd about the shape of his face, his shoulders, and the length of his arms, and understood that here was a slight divergence in evolution. In a flash of insight, he speculated on, and extrapolated from, what the Fenris had told him, and came up with the idea of a time crash. He visualized the fenris world smashing into this multiverse, disrupting it not just in the present timeline but hurling debris into the past, and perhaps into the future. Maybe differences were scattered throughout multiple pasts: climate and other survival imperatives, perceptions of beauty, predators, asteroid impacts, diseases, food sources . . . the list went on and on. But something in this particular world's past had resulted in a form of humanity at variance with those on his home world. The man said something, and though it was a language utterly foreign to him, Ottanger automatically began translating. For it seemed his mind was continuing to explode into multiple patterns of thought. He needed to control this and focus on the immediate imperatives of survival.

Gazing into the multiverse, he jaunted again and found himself under a green sky, standing on hot sand. He jaunted quickly away from there, as his feet began to burn, and the harsh sunlight seared over his skin. Perception of destinations didn't necessarily result in good choices. A cooler place of thick grass seemed suitable, and there he focused internally to finish shutting down that fenris space in his mind. He felt numerous threads snap away. He then turned his thoughts to the necessities of his new existence. First on the list was clothing. But when his wide perception

386

picked up a huge monitor lizard stalking through the grasses towards him, these swiftly turned to protection and safety, and, inevitably, weapons.

Swinging around, he looked with human eyes at the mountains, which he'd already been aware of. Habitations filled the valleys and stretched up slopes and over peaks, as if poured there like molten metal, then solidifying as numerous bubbles burst all over its surface. He used his other sense at extreme range to peer in at humans dressed in skins and handwoven materials. They also carried tools and weapons, perhaps better than those he'd made, but certainly not what he wanted now. He jaunted again, just as the big lizard nosed into sight.

On another world, where giant gulls nested on a beach beside a pink ocean, he crept naked at dawn into a neat suburban estate. There the house roofs were tiled with green glass, and the grass grew blue on the lawns. Feeling both shamed and ineffectual, he stole clothing from a line, ending up with knee-length shorts decorated with teddy bears, and a sleeveless top that seemed to be made from fish skin, including the scales. These methods really weren't ideal, but what choices did he have? He needed to build up resources, to make a base. And he needed allies . . . Perhaps he shouldn't have fled the Fenris so quickly. But he hadn't liked the idea of faster education. On Committee Earth, that was something definitely to be avoided. His thoughts then strayed, as he jaunted yet again, to the resistance.

He had cut ties to his numerous contacts there, and had told them with certainty that he was done with fighting. They would be suspicious. In fact, he'd once feared they would come after him, to remove the threat he'd become, knowing their operations as he did. That too was part of the reason he'd left – the resistance didn't just regard totalitarian government as the enemy, but also anyone who wasn't a member of their own organization. As well as taking actions that resulted in clampdowns and casualties, they murdered innocent people who knew too much. But perhaps, with his new powers, he could go back to them and instigate a new approach. The thought strayed into a hundred speculations about what courses that would take. But they all just seemed to cycle round to an expansion of the things the resistance already did, and a consequent expansion of those clampdowns and casualties. So what *could* he do?

He looked around at his present environment, sitting on a slope looking down towards a rough track, along which a hover vehicle of some kind was travelling, kicking up a cloud of dust. What little he'd seen here revealed no shepherds, cams and readerguns, or Inspectorate. And, even if something similar existed here, there were other places where they didn't. Rather than fight something that seemed to have too much momentum to be stopped without disaster, he now saw the option of moving people out from its path: he could take people away from his hellish home. He next thought on who should be first and his thoughts immediately turned to his sister. His only close family left alive.

Jane had known that officialdom was looking for her, so consequently was keeping a low profile when Ottanger last saw her. She'd be able to stay out of the hands of those looking to snare up more people for Savarack's experiments, just so long as the search didn't become a serious one. Once AIs were deployed to that end, she would inevitably be captured. Ottanger had no doubt that Jane would eventually end up in the Complex, if she wasn't there already. He definitely needed to get her out, and others. He tracked the vehicle into the distance, thinking how it wasn't the size of that ploughing machine he'd moved. He could transport a great deal between worlds, and didn't yet know what his limits might be in that respect.

He needed to return to Committee Earth, despite his reluctance, and despite the thought that some trapping technology he didn't yet know about might be deployed. And if he was to go there, he'd have to be ready for all eventualities, which meant the weapons he'd thought about earlier. But on any world, weapons weren't something you could just pick up . . . Then again . . .

Ottanger riffled through worlds in his mind like cards, and gazed upon thousands of scenes in turn. The one that finally drew his attention was a world showing a scarred face, which at ground level rumbled with the thunder of guns. Mushroom clouds rose like a forest of fire trees on a horizon, in a landscape of broken buildings and the detritus of warfare spread wide. He chose his place and jaunted to where the chaos of battle seemed to be shifting like a receding tide, from burning machines and the abandoned dead.

The sky was yellow here, but whether that was its natural shade, or one imparted by warfare, he had no idea. He found a dead soldier down by a crumbled wall, flies buzzing up from him, and maggot riddled when turned over. He uncovered a handgun underneath the body and picked it up, then used a handful of wall insulation to clean off the stinking fluids. A shout to his right startled him, and he turned to see a figure standing up and aiming some rifle. Ottanger jaunted, but he didn't want to leave this place, so just tweaked the position of the world underneath him. He found himself standing a hundred metres from where he'd been, as gunfire clattered over there. The ease of it, and the smoothness of the transition, now opened up so many other possibilities. He simply hadn't realized he could jaunt not just from world to world, but to different positions on the same world. He could effectively teleport himself.

He jumped again, coming in behind the shooter, who now had his weapon held across his stomach as he looked in puzzlement to where Ottanger had been. Ottanger stooped and picked up another weapon leaning against a wall. It would be so easy for him to just kill now. Instead, he picked up a pack lying there too and jumped away again.

In a series of jumps, all around a battlefield that extended for thousands of kilometres, Ottanger gathered resources. He found resupply stations, and abandoned any rusted and damaged weapons in favour of those still under their filmy plastic, and wet with gun oil. Here and there he tested the weapons, gazed inside them and understood their workings. He settled on a stubby machine pistol, which took a hundred-round box of small, but ridiculously deadly, ammunition. He added grenades that popped out of a box like Tic Tacs and were the size of squash balls. Two of those boxes went on his belt – one next to a holstered twelve-shot revolver – along with further clips for the machine pistol. He filled a pack with more spares and other items. His previously stolen clothes he supplanted with a battle-dress in camouflage yellow and grey, with light expanded bulletproof armour sewn in. He found heavy boots that laced up to his knees, and a visored helmet that sealed up to the battledress in the event of chemical attack. In an abandoned warehouse, he put on what he could, then gazed at all the rest he'd stolen and stacked here. He could jaunt it all with him if he wanted to, but now it seemed so irrelevant. He'd be able to acquire what he needed at any time and easily, so why burden himself with all this? No, now he had to return to his home world, to pull Jane and others out of there.

Ottanger moved to the broken windows and looked out. He

had no idea what they were fighting about here, and he couldn't care less. A flash lit the horizon, and another mushroom pushed up towards the sky. Time to go.

It seemed to Ottanger he had a multidimensional model of the multiverse in his skull, and whenever he travelled anywhere in it, his route permanently etched itself out in that model. He didn't need to survey his surroundings much to know that his home Earth was over *there*, and he could look upon it. He wondered about jaunting all the way there in one go, since it lay a relatively long distance away, behind jumbled layers of other worlds. But he decided not to test himself too much in that respect. Though he'd felt no particular danger in jaunting, or in moving that massive ploughing machine, he did feel a sense of the *possibility* of weariness, and he didn't want to arrive tired in a place he knew to be highly dangerous.

He jaunted, closer to his home, impressions of the world shot through his mind in layers: enclosed fields patrolled by robots, seas networked with fish farms, or crossed by immense cargo ships, streets and tenements, and of course billions of people. But he also picked up on an emotional component, comprising fear and anger, arising around areas of disruption. Riots, always a part of his world, seemed to have spread around it like a rash, and in places they'd transitioned into a mix of warfare and plain extermination. He saw the scars of wrecked, collapsed and burning buildings through the sprawls, along with thousands upon thousands of dead. Armoured vehicles and soldiers moved in after high-atmosphere bombing of areas, and in some others the devastation of god-rod impacts. Why was this happening? He considered what he knew, and it came back to what he'd been told during his last days in the Complex. This was the result of the terrorist strike against the Committee, and yet another replay of the usual response to any resistance operation. The authorities were using it as an excuse to crack down, but now it seemed to be on a worldwide scale. He felt anger in his guts at that. This meant more restrictions, more shortages, and of course more mass death, in a population the ruling bureaucrats saw as excess and ultimately disposable.

He stepped out onto a road spearing through what looked like an endless banyan. The tree bore blue globes that might have been fruit, or its version of leaves. He further scanned his home, discovering that, just as with conventional vision, this other ability improved with proximity. He now understood that the unusual senses the biotech had gifted him were mostly to facilitate his ability to step between worlds. He also realized that taking shorter jaunts was good, because it enabled more precisely chosen arrival points. Like, for example, not landing barefoot on hot sand.

He soon found the site of the nuclear strike: charred and melted buildings in a sea of ash, with a collapsed and burned sprawl lying in a ring around that. Another ring grew further out, where massive machines were tearing down buildings and heaping up debris on the inner side, the clear areas swarming with shepherds. It was like a firebreak, though not for fire but for people. Fear would drive them away from the bombsite, but there'd be no room or resources for them elsewhere. Better to just fence them in and let them die. He turned his attention away bitterly from that and searched elsewhere.

Soon he was gazing into familiar streets. Pushing himself to remain focused on his purpose here, he wondered if he could simply track Jane down like this at a distance. As he tried that, however, he did find it straining something in his skull – like trying to focus through distorting glass. Next, recognizing general places and areas, he decided he'd held back long enough, and jaunted.

'What the fuck!' The woman staggered back into a man pushing a wheelbarrow, and he swore at her. Ottanger turned and moved quickly away, thinking about how it was almost impossible to come to his home without someone noting his arrival. Or, as had been the case with the woman, walking straight into him. He wrinkled his nostrils at the smell – a combination of sewage, body odour and putrefaction – then thought about how, all his life here, he'd hardly noticed it. Within a minute, he found his initial reaction dying as he fell back into an urban dweller's sense of his surroundings. He noticed change here. Urgency and fear were at higher levels, as if it was before, or just after, a riot. And he knew this was a reflection of what was going on in the wider world.

He pushed through the crowds with the air of self-importance that police usually had when moving amid the ZA population. This was something he'd learned while under an assumed identity and, with his present clothing, something he could carry off. People took one look at his battledress, which resembled that of soldiers all over the world, and moved out of his path. And if the uniform wasn't enough, the fact he carried a machine pistol was. He hurried, knowing his first destination and then wondering why he didn't just transport himself straight there. He rationalized that if he abruptly materialized in the tenement, that would be noticed, and would result in too many questions being asked, when he himself would want answers, and quickly. But the truth was he had grown suspicious of such easy powers, and the feeling had ramped up here where he had been accustomed to paranoia. ZA existence engrained such an attitude, accustomed as they were to having things they relied on snatched away, seemingly at a government whim.

Finally through to the edge of the main street crowd, he worked his way along a wall, past three or four doors. He then paused as his foot came down on a round iron cover. With his inner sense ranged out, he could see the shepherd folded up down there beneath it. No movement as yet, but he needed to stay alert. His strange clothing, and the fact he carried weapons, enabled him to travel quickly but would attract attention. At some point, a cam would read his chip and run a face comparison. Shortly after that, higher-level AI would be on his case and then the problems would start. He just needed answers before then.

Once in the tenement, he marched along corridors with people flinching out of his path, flattening to the walls. He hit the stairs, climbing past an old woman snailing her way up with a huge sack over one shoulder. He was busy and important, and he knew it was a mistake to step out of that role, but he took the sack from her.

'No! Noo!' she shouted, and gaped at him in fear.

'Which floor?' he asked.

She just continued gaping, and now he could see the signs of senility. However, something got through and she pointed upwards. He took a step up and gestured for her to come. She smiled in delight and began walking behind him.

Stupid, he told himself. It was precisely this kind of thing that always got him into trouble. And had led him into the resistance, then out of it again. One of his fellow fighters had said, 'You're too empathetic. Hard choices have to be made.' To an extent he agreed. He hated the suffering around him, and he hated being the cause of more of the same. And yet, the official who'd recognized him as having a false identity, when Ottanger had been working for the resistance, would perhaps have disagreed, had he been capable of doing so. The man hadn't suffered particularly, though, it had been quick.

He trudged up with her for three floors, painfully aware of the little white blisters of cams on the walls at each turning. Most had 'accidental' dirt on them, but the meta-material layer on the glass tended to shed that in time.

'This is as far as I go,' he said, when they reached the floor he wanted. He unshouldered the sack and handed it to her.

'Well, thanks for that,' she said sarcastically, taking the sack and trudging on. The original person had showed through the dementia and, like so many in the sprawls, wasn't exactly into niceties. He grimaced at her back, entered a short corridor, then pushed open a broken door to enter living accommodation.

Eight people, scattered about the room on ancient furniture, their kingdom and their belongings around them, looked up. Two of them had tablets, while the rest were watching some animal documentary on the wall screen. This had to be one of the rare occasions the power was on. The place smelled of bleach and, as ZA apartments went, was relatively well-to-do. He saw fear flash across every face, but then recognition in one.

'Ottanger!' said a heavily pregnant woman, pushing herself to her feet.

'Hi, Marianne. I'm looking for Jane.'

'She's not here.'

Marianne waved a bony hand towards the other doors through which some people were now peering. He wanted to tell her he knew that, but then of course couldn't explain just how much of the tenement he was able to see all around him.

'Why are you like that?' She indicated his clothing, frowned at the gun and then squinted at him. 'And your face. You look . . .' She trailed off.

'Long story and I don't have the time. Do you know where she is?'

The woman shrugged, but her expression had taken on a

shrewd look. He eased his pack off and put it down to his feet, then undid the flap.

'You're bigger too,' she said.

'I have food, and I want answers.' Besides the extra ammo and various other pieces of kit he'd thought he might need, he'd filled the pack with military concentrated rations. He began taking them out and dumping them on the floor. He didn't need them, and could always get more. The thought then occurred to him of transporting food into the sprawls. But, seeing the avid expressions all around him, he realized that again he'd probably create more problems doing this than he'd solve.

'They took her,' she said.

'Who took her?'

'Inspectorate.'

Ottanger's unpacking slowed as the horrible realities of what that might mean hit home. Not the officials, or whichever researchers had been looking for him and his sister, but the *Inspectorate*. He imagined Jane in one of those little cells in the internment camp, or perhaps undergoing interrogation even now. He had to get there.

'Any explanation as to why?' he asked, emptying out the last of the food.

'*Why?*' she repeated, raising her eyebrow.

It had of course been a stupid question. The Inspectorate didn't offer explanations. If they picked you up, you were automatically guilty, and of what they'd decide later. He stood up, shrugging the pack on again. Even as he did so, he felt the tone change in the building around him – in the sounds and constant undercurrent of people living out their lives, or perhaps just existing. Pushing downwards with his internal sense, he viewed the street and there saw a shepherd up out of its hole and unfolding. Meanwhile police in city uniforms, wearing black armbands, had entered the building.

'Hide this food,' he said. 'The Inspectorate are coming.' He'd hardly finished before she was scrabbling up the packets. He hadn't needed to tell her that – even though she didn't have his unhuman senses, she had as much instinct for that change of tone as he did.

He headed out of the door. A family was crowding along here – children snot-nosed and covered in the red blemishes of some sprawl malady. They watched him head for the stairs. Then, as he entered the stairwell, and was briefly out of sight of anyone, he jumped, relocating to another point on this world.

Nobody ran into him on this street. What crowds were here were sparse, and in a big hurry to be elsewhere. He faced the gates leading into the internment camp. The one he'd been taken into, and expected never to leave. He peered inside, riffling through thousands of cells in search of his sister – determined to focus on that one task and allow nothing else to distract him. However, when he found many cells where those imprisoned had simply died, and others were in the process of doing so, he felt a bitter anger growing once more. Watching those dying, he saw them all at the water spigots over the cell shit holes. Someone had turned off the water supply to the cells, for he saw it operating elsewhere in Inspectorate or bureaucrat quarters.

He then saw the corpses stacked like cord wood, in cells and rooms all around the constant grind of the macerators. Tired, ragged prisoners were steadily carrying them to the revolving mulching cylinders, while still other shabby individuals were bringing in more to stack. He peered into the mechanisms of the machines and saw that the composting tanks below were simply open into the sewerage system. Was this just the usual horror of this place? Though he couldn't know for sure, he felt that the killing had gone up a couple of notches, probably for the same reason as the tension on the streets, and the chaos around the world. He considered searching through the corpses and wondered if he'd be able to identify his sister's face there. For they all looked the same: skulls under translucent skin and flesh.

Then, as he was about to pull away, sure he'd set himself an impossible task, he saw the woman who'd interrogated him. She was standing up from behind a desk, in what might well have been the same interrogation room he'd once occupied. Two guards were in the process of removing a man from the chair below the inducer, while another was running a hose in to clean up the mess on the floor. The victim had obviously died under the inducer – just what would have been Ottanger's fate, had he not been grabbed by Savarack. His anger, a bitter twisting thing, flashed up and became something more. Before he even knew he'd made the decision, Ottanger jumped.

They were the product of an unjust society. It wasn't their fault they were born SAs, and then inducted into the Inspectorate or the Bureaucracy. They were people, probably with families, and maybe fathers and mothers. They could be changed, and they could be made into something better, for all humans were clay. All these thoughts went through Ottanger's mind as he drew his revolver, aimed it at the startled-looking woman rolling the hose out from the wall, and shot her through the face. As she dropped, he stepped into the cell and fired twice more, dropping the two guards there, then twice more through the backs of their heads. The bureaucrat woman had run to one corner of the room. As he watched her, she then sprinted across, behind the desk, to the other corner. It seemed almost like comedy.

'Sit down,' he said. 'I'm not going to kill you.'

The lie tasted sour in his mouth. And yet when he'd been in the resistance, lying to achieve his ends had never bothered him, until he realized where those ends led. He wondered about the changes he'd undergone.

The woman stayed in the corner and started making a strange whining sound. Ottanger turned to the door and closed it. There was a simple mechanical bolt on the inside, so he slid it across. The sound of gunshots here would be uncommon, because they tended not to waste bullets killing people when so many cheaper options were available.

'I said sit down!' he bellowed, and felt a guilty pleasure in his anger. He recognized that now, being fit and healthy, and armed and powerful, he could afford the burning emotion of *righteous* anger. Or was it his need for vengeance?

She was crying now, and he knew she couldn't believe he would let her live. He understood her reasoning came from an internal inspection of her guilt. However, she moved over, pulled out the chair and sat hunched over, arms crossed.

'Take out your tablet and make a search of those who've been killed here in the last two weeks, and those you still have here.'

'You're looking for someone,' she said, now taking her tablet out of a large inner pocket of her greywear. Reading her expression, he saw the same sort of shrewdness coming into it that he'd seen in Marianne. He wanted something, so now maybe she had a bargaining position.

'How smart of you to figure that out. Obviously you deserved the position you now hold in the Bureaucracy,' he said sarcastically. 'The name you must search for is Jane Reece Smith.'

She laid the tablet on the table before her. 'I can do this, but I need some guarantee.'

She rested her hands either side of the device, as though she wasn't going to use it until he gave that guarantee. He considered grabbing her left hand and smashing a finger or two with the revolver butt, then rejected that for another course. She hadn't seen how he'd arrived in the corridor outside.

'I need you alive to get me out of here,' he said. 'And anyway, my boss can handle the flak from some casualties, but not others.' He gestured to the guards spreading pools of blood on the floor, then to her.

She nodded. Inspectorate personnel at the sharp end were obviously not as valuable as those who sat behind the desks to guide and control. Ottanger recognized again, as when undercover, the almost delusional arrogance of the Bureaucracy. She propped up her tablet and quickly ran her searches.

'One of that name was arrested in our sector but didn't come here,' she said.

'Give me detail on that.'

'Apparently she was transferred to Special Operations Research, but where they have her I cannot say.'

'What can you say?'

'A lot gets delisted when it ends up in Murcheson's territory.'

'And that's all I need to know,' said Ottanger.

He studied her and she turned to look up at him. He'd engaged with her now, and saw her as a human being. He of course reasoned that all people were products of their circumstances and could be better. But now, with that sense of connection, it seemed to make what she was, and what she did, even worse. She saw it at the same time as him, and tried to leap out of her chair. He shot her through the side of the head.

By now there was activity in the corridor outside. No one was banging on the door to ask questions because they didn't need to. He glanced up at the cams in the corners of the room. Perhaps he should have destroyed them, but he knew they were only the visible ones, and there'd be others concealed in the walls too.

He looked straight through the door at the four guards outside, waiting with short machine pistols ready. Further out, he tracked the approach of another one carrying a shotgun. He recognized this as the kind used to blow out door locks and thought they might have some trouble with this particular armoured door. Then he jumped to another location.

'Open all the cells,' he said, pressing his weapon into the skull of the seated guard.

'I can't do that!'

'It's either that or I spread your brains all over your console.'

The man hurriedly pulled up a menu on a touch screen, then hit the general unlock tab for the two hundred cells in his block. Ottanger noticed other tabs there, like sleep dep., sanitize, gas (with numerous sub-tabs), a temperature scale that ranged from minus twenty to plus sixty, and a tab marked incinerate. And there were more besides. He heard the buzzing clonks of the cells opening. Without replaying his 'could have been better' refrain, he shot the guard and jumped on to the next cell block, knowing he could unlock the cells now without help.

Within the hour, those who could walk were pouring out of the open main gate. He detested that few tried to help their weaker fellows, and he detested himself as he stripped off items of bloody clothing, replacing them with Inspectorate gear. He felt sick to the core. But perhaps what caused him more concern was the rapid growth of callousness in that core. In his entire life prior to this day, he'd killed only one person, while today he'd killed thirty-seven of them. And to what purpose?

Those he'd freed would be snatched up again by the Inspectorate soon enough, or shredded by shepherds, or would simply starve out there. This internment camp was one of millions around the planet. And in doing what he'd done, he had guaranteed further suffering and deaths as the Inspectorate investigated.

However, having seen the full undeniable reality of the camp, he'd also needed to do something. He now no longer saw his walking away from the resistance as a correct moral choice. Yes, their actions were leading nowhere, but how did one square not acting with what he'd seen here? Still, in light of his new abilities, he needed to take a harder and colder look at the realities. He must take a more rational approach.

Finally, having replaced his fouled combat gear and transferred his belongings to a pack that wasn't so spattered, he considered the options. Jane was almost certainly at the Complex now, and less likely to end up dead there than elsewhere. Ottanger would go after her, of course, but it wasn't something he felt capable of doing right then since he felt too weary and sick to do more. He had to get out of here now, for he could hear the crowd roaring and screaming, which indicated shepherds were on the move out there. In fact, he could see them. He could also see fliers in the skies, and armoured cars coming through the streets. Meanwhile, surviving staff in the camp were still searching for him. Though, as ever, always in the wrong places. He needed to leave his home world again, recoup, and think things through before acting. But now he wondered where to go. Maybe that primitive place, with the big monitor lizards, or back to that war zone? He shrugged. It didn't really matter.

He concentrated on the multiverse, and now noted something odd. As if, at the centre of his internal vision of this immensity, a large black object had formed. He blinked at it, and found it shifting as he scanned around, seeming to stay at the centre of his vision wherever he turned. This, he assumed, must be the result of tiredness. Focusing required a strange mental effort in his internal vision, like using peripheral vision to get around this object, which appeared like a mass of pipes, a worm cast, or a *manifold*. Yes, that last word seemed somehow right. He focused on a world nowhere near as populous as this one, and there selected a wilderness running with deer. He needed to eat too. He then made the mental push and stepped over to that place, confident of soon feeling grass under his feet. But from the moment of transition, something was very wrong.

The manifold established itself in full like a shadowed flaw in sheets, with curves and shapes beyond three dimensions of its clear, glassy whole. It seemed to fall towards him, extending out tubes and funnels, and he had the distinct impression of some live thing attacking him. As if in the multiverse sea, a giant predatory squid had spotted him. He tried to fling himself aside, to go under or around and circumvent it, but it remained in his perception like the jags of migraine lights. He managed to evade it until it seemed to come up on one side of him, and he couldn't escape its tentacles. The thing coiled in towards him, funnel-mouthed and vast, and he finally slipped down what felt like the ice-slick throat of a well.

Even as he slid along a corkscrewing tube, he could still see the multiverse all around, and had a sense of where he was going. The manifold appeared to be some expansion of the slope that had taken him to that airless Earth on his first jaunt. Perhaps this was the result of him trying to jump over his home Earth's parallels and evade that world too? No, there was deliberation here, an entity behind it. Could this be a trap set for him by Savarack and his crew? Again no, because a trap of theirs would take him back to the Complex, when instead he seemed to be falling into the universe of the airless Earth, though this time apparently away from the planet itself. With an effort of will, he focused down the end of the long tunnel and saw his precise destination.

He'd seen this bloated moon, with signs of civilization on its face, once or twice before, and never really thought much about what it meant. But having recently come from the slaughter on his home Earth, callused up inside, and with a low opinion of humanity in general, he prepared himself.

With slow precision, he reached to his belt, unhooked his helmet and put it on, locking it down and closing the visor. He then raised his machine pistol on its strap, checked its load and held it in readiness. The moon came up at him fast – a curved surface seemingly writhing with structures – and then he was inside, snapping into reality.

16

Chancel

'Where's Chenghu?' asked Irene.

Chancel looked up from his tablet and replied, 'Still in his room. Perhaps he needed a break. The atmosphere here hasn't exactly been cheerful since his return.' He then cursed himself for replying at all. He'd sworn to keep his mouth shut and his eyes open here, just as he had when he was in the gangs. This technique had served him well back then, allowing him to move up in the hierarchy. Though he had to admit, his silence and introspective attitude made people believe he was smarter than he actually was. Anyway, better to let others damn themselves with loose mouths and open any opportunities he could use.

Irene glared at him, then turned to Ektian, who was at the computer yet again. The other woman looked up without Irene saying anything, shrugged and returned to what she was doing. And that was something else Chancel didn't like. He'd known what Irene was going to ask before she asked it, while Ektian had responded to her silent query. They had all felt this powerful sense of connection the moment they first met, but he hadn't realized just how far it went until Irene slapped him. He'd let her get away with that, when he never would have before. From then on, he understood their connection wasn't just a sense of each other, but something that bordered on telepathy, and it was hierarchical. The reason he hadn't hit her back was the same as why he'd just responded to her now, when normally he would've kept quiet: she was the *boss*.

After that slap, he analysed how she'd climbed up and asserted dominance over them all. With Chenghu it had been by the recourse of fucking the man's brains out – in fact an old tried and trusted technique. With Ektian it had been through agreement of aims. But he realized that her dominance over Chenghu had also enabled her to dominate Ektian. The thing was cumulative. And after the three of them arrived here, she'd quickly taken over, even though Chancel and Adriana had been at Caprock for months before her. This was why right now Adriana had taken a walk, along with Pranjab, down into the deserted city. It seemed that the only way to think clearly was to put physical distance between oneself and that hierarchical connection. Why Chancel hadn't gone was simple stubbornness, and the urge to resist Irene's power at its source.

'And the others?' Irene enquired.

Chancel fought not to answer, since the question had been directed solely at him, but then acknowledged that he couldn't refuse, and casually gestured outside. 'They went to the city. They're coming back up the path now.'

Chancel turned back to his tablet, teeth gritted. The question had been a dominance tactic too, because Irene surely felt Pranjab and Adriana approaching. She'd made him answer anyway. But annoyingly, he didn't know if she was conscious she was doing it.

Ektian abruptly looked up. 'Something's happening.'

Chancel glanced at her, feeling the shift too and something

untoward, with senses he had yet to become accustomed to. It was connected to the multiverse, about the parallels. The sensation initially resembled what he'd felt when others had first jaunted here. But it swiftly changed into a feeling of impending doom, as if something terrible had decided to wrench apart the substance of reality. He got the weird idea of Cthulhu horror rising from the depths of time – a creature he knew about after discovering that shepherds were made to resemble this classic image from ancient horror fiction, and then researching and reading the fiction concerned.

'What the fuck is that?' Adriana asked, as she entered their wide living room.

'You don't know?' asked Pranjab, coming in after her.

As Chancel leaned over the side of his seat, he glanced at the man. At least his eyes were no longer black, but he still seemed to have a spookily strong grasp of the biotech inside them. The machine pistol lay beside Chancel's chair. He snatched it up, along with two clips, slamming one of them into place. By the time he was on his feet, Irene was holding her machine pistol too, Ektian had stood up holding a nine-millimetre automatic, and Adriana had pulled a pump-action shotgun from beside her pack. Chancel winced, noting parallels here to the behaviour of those in the gangs: the moment anything untoward happened, everyone reached for a weapon. Except, in this case, Pranjab.

'What is it?' Irene demanded, gazing at their doctor suspiciously.

Pranjab looked back at her and smiled. 'Consequences.'

They all now felt the surge of a big jaunt. One side of the room, over by the windows that looked down the hillside towards the city, began shimmering and twisting. Chancel stepped back, remembering Pranjab's description of the portal those hive humans had gone through. Had the man left out something about his encounter with them? He glanced round, seeing Chenghu rush into the room, pulling on his bulletproof jacket while clutching the machine pistol he favoured.

A large object came into view, in a cyst in reality. It solidified with a thump, juddering through the floor, and came to rest partially in the house and out of it, scribing out a circle in the front window and part of the wall there. This material, unable to occupy the space it had arrived in, exploded in every direction. Octagonal fragments of armoured glass, rubble and dust filled the air. Chancel turned his back to the blast until it diminished, and then swung round, targeting a huge figure stepping into view.

'Sorry about that,' said the Fenris. 'I'm on the same learning curve as all of you.'

Irene's machine pistol crackled, and the shots made ringing sounds as they hit the creature's glassy armour. But already the Fenris was moving. He dodged once and leapt forwards, coming down beside her frighteningly fast. His hand swept across, grabbed her by the front of her suit, lifted her up and slammed her down on a sofa, at the same time plucking the weapon from her grip and tossing it aside.

'Don't you think you've done enough damage?' he enquired, a nasty edge to his voice Chancel had never heard before.

Ottanger

Ottanger had time to take in his surroundings – his sense of time extending, and the speed of his movements increasing to compensate. He'd appeared in a spherical chamber, between two structures like radar dishes. A flat floor, supported on a metal framework, came up at him, but slowly in this low gravity. All around, the walls were wormed with covered burrows and scattered with the mouths of further burrows spearing away. He tracked them with that other sense and found nothing but more burrows and smaller chambers for as far as he could perceive. Glancing down, he saw people swarming out onto that floor as he approached it. He then did a double take, taking in their strangely shaped heads, body shapes and limbs, recognizing those creatures his interrogators had shown him on a screen. The ones directly below, with binocular heads and large muscular bodies, were from the second picture. Back from these, around the circumference of the floor, clustered groups of the other kind, with narrow heads that seemed to be just extensions of their necks. These figures held up arrays of organic-looking instruments, whose wires, controls and supports threaded into their bodies like subsidiary antennae, ears, dishes and probes. The muscular, armoured, *fighting* kind, the *warriors*, he noticed were dragging out a flat slab, inlaid with the shape of a human being. This had numerous straps and clamps hanging loose around it. As they swirled around a central point where he was due to fall, it didn't take much thought to realize the slab was intended for him. Whatever these things were, they'd aimed to capture him, and he needed to change that.

How should he respond? He hadn't chosen to end up in this place. They had blocked then snatched him with evident bad intentions during his jaunt. He had some misgivings, but his inner, callused self overrode them. He never wanted to be a captive again. And, as with the Fenris, he never wanted to be subject to the will of others. The grenades snapped easily out of the box on his belt. He tossed a number of the fragmentation kind away from him, on their set detonation time, but retained a stun grenade. On this he clicked down its detonation time, then tossed it away from him while coiling himself into a ball. The blast slapped him tumbling through the air. Even as he unfolded, feeling the bruises and seeing his clothing smouldering, he crashed down amid the crowd, to one side of where he'd been expected. He slammed two of them to the floor, as the other grenades detonated all around, throwing up body fragments and trailers of intestine. Coming up out of a squat, he lashed out with the edge of his hand at the nearest figure, chopping into its neck and dropping it. Spinning that into an elbow strike, he crushed the binocular vision of another, and opened fire one-handed with his machine pistol. The creatures dropped before him, and he rushed for the gap. But this was the moon, with its weaker gravity, and he found himself flailing through the air, the strides he made propelling him up rather than forwards.

Something snapped out at him, and coiled like a jointed snake around one arm, then tightened. He looked around to see it came from the gunlike device one of the warriors held. Hitting the ground, he tore the thing free from his arm, and opened up on others bringing these devices to bear. Still more crowded in behind him, trying to grab his arms and legs. He flailed and kicked, surprised at how easily he broke their grip, and them. But then he saw the logic: they were dwellers of the moon, so didn't have the strength of bone and muscle as someone Earthbound. He nearly reached the edge of the floor, and was eying up the mouth of a tunnel, when further snakes wrapped around his legs, and then, in quick succession, around his torso. He turned again and fired, until the clip emptied, then grabbed for another and found they'd been pulled from his belt. He used the gun as a club instead as he groped for his revolver, but found that gone too, as the whole host came down on him in a wave.

Ottanger lashed out, feeling bones breaking under his blows. A space briefly opened, and he thought to throw himself towards it. But the flash of weapons threw the other narrow-headed kind in silhouette, and stun charges slapped into him, deadening his limbs and bringing on a horrible weariness. At the last, he reached out with his ability into the multiverse parallels and threw himself in that direction. The black funnel of the manifold rose up and recaptured him, though, and he fell down the frozen well. He came out in the same chamber again, between those two radar dishes, as stun shots below converged on him. An electric mist swathed him, even shorting with a brief spurt of discharge into one of those dishes. He could hardly move as he hit the floor the second time, and they swarmed in over him again.

Consciousness came back with a hard flash of anxiety. Ottanger immediately went into a fighting mindset, but found he couldn't move. He felt terrible – beaten from head to foot and unutterably weary, though that wasn't the reason he was immobile. He was lying naked in the slab's indent, metal bands and straps securing his limbs, torso, head and even the individual fingers of his hands. He then suddenly thought how this was perhaps for the best as, reviewing his recent actions, shame washed through him. Why, when he'd arrived in that chamber with the creatures waiting below to trap him, hadn't his first thought been to try jaunting away again? Why had his immediate choice been violence? Sure, he'd attempted a jaunt later, when his capture seemed certain, and only then realized there was no escape. But using that as an excuse was a rationalization after the fact. He felt there were two facets at war inside him: the moral Ottanger and the one looking for excuses to do murder.

The slab was on the move and, out of peripheral vision, he could see the creatures on either side carrying him. His other sense showed a crowd of them extending along the burrow ahead and behind, and further creatures moving along in consonance in surrounding burrows. Was he being taken to see their king, or rather their queen? He remembered the Fenris mentioning a hive, and his surroundings did remind him of such a place. Just as those around him seemed to be the kind of creatures that would occupy one. An affirmation of this then arose within him, the source of which he couldn't trace: these were hive humans.

As the procession followed a spiralling course down and down, he started to feel a little better. And, since he wasn't going anywhere, he concentrated on his internal state. As with his perception of taste and smell, this began to raise molecular shapes and weird icons in his mind, connections and interrelationships. Just for a second, these baffled him. Then, in a flash, he knew them to be internal diagnostics, and a moment later understood them perfectly. He had broken bones, but the biotech had worked to secure them, just as it was working to clear the detritus of heavy bruising, and a chemical malaise brought on by those stunners. Their effect had been to turn over molecules in a large portion of his ATP, and render it ineffective. He blinked on that. Remembering the term ATP being mentioned in a resistance briefing, in connection with the function of inducers. He then discovered a thousand other smaller connections that gave him the sense of what it was. His body was working hard to recycle the damage. It had already burned off what little fat he'd accrued in the Complex to this end. And, he surmised from those weirdly twisted shapes, he was now sucking on empty.

Next he eased into jaunt mode to view the local multiverse, and yet again found the black funnel of the manifold awaiting him. If it always routed back to that previous chamber, then that was one option. But in his present state, he didn't think he'd get far from there. Another option, viewing the endless burrows around him, would be to jump to other locations. Surely he would be able to find food and drink to top up his resources, and evade capture? But then what? If he couldn't make it out of their trap, he'd be forever stuck here, merely surviving. He needed to be rational. Other than the beating he'd received, and the stun shots, he wasn't in too bad a condition, and he wasn't dead yet. In fact, from their methods, it seemed they wanted to keep him alive. He decided to be patient and see what he could learn, what resources he could garner, and whether there might be better options for escape.

Down and down they went, finally bringing him out in another chamber. This one was oblate, having a low ceiling hung with odd chandelier-like instruments, and walls tangled with either technology or something growing, he couldn't quite tell. Certainly there seemed to be hive humans in there doing something. In the centre of the chamber, they tilted up the slab he was on and dropped its bottom end into a slot in the floor. The creatures swarmed around him, as if unsure what to do now, occasionally reaching out to prod or caress him. He noticed some of them moving erratically, and these showed signs of illness, with their eyes watery, blotches on their skin and snot running from their noses. Whether that might be relevant to his circumstances he didn't know, but he just watched and waited.

Groups of the creatures began to drift off, while others lingered, sometimes sitting on the floor. He guessed some had been reassigned and others were waiting on that. While this was occurring, he became aware of a weird pull at the core of his being from his surroundings. More closely studying them, he grimaced. The stuff around the walls did seem like hard technology, overgrown with something fleshy, but now he could see other things in there too. Hive humans were as much a part of this machinery as in other cases machinery was part of

413

them. Some of them blended into the frameworks, and extended arms of complex instrumentation. Others were stooped over nuggets of flesh, devoid of limbs, and their heads transitioned into things like large microscopes. He realized that the biotech he was seeing, binding all together, was an extension of them. He then focused on what they were studying, and began to distinguish it from their own flesh: human corpses. The pull he'd felt came in a diffuse manner from all around, but most of it seemed to come from these corpses, or their parts, and this baffled him.

Finally, managing to distinguish the bodies more clearly from the mutilated hive humans, he counted five or more in various states of decomposition and dismemberment. Some were wrapped in plastic films, one floated in a tank of cloudy fluid. Others were in what appeared to be different stages of autopsy, penetrated by the hive growths, the hard tech and various slowly bubbling tubes. Yet even though they were in such a state, he recognized them as the corpses of humans. They had standard proportions and positioning of facial features, though perhaps a little bit longer in limb than usual. Remembering those he'd seen on his first venture to the airless Earth below, he assumed they must have come from there. Concentrating intently, he watched the dissectors' slow movement – peeling back some dry skin here, the steady ablation of a length of bone there – and understood their meticulous examination likely went down to the molecular level. Then he realized it was the corpses' biotechnology under examination, and the pull he'd felt was from that – some sort of connection to it. However, that didn't explain the more diffuse pull beyond it.

Ottanger considered how he might end up joining those corpses being examined, though he guessed they had something else in mind for him first, since they'd gone to such great lengths to capture him alive. He got some intimation of what that might be when they brought in another live captive.

There was something about the woman who, even in the moon's low gravity, seemed to be labouring under a heavy load. She was surrounded by post-headed hive humans and had a ring around her neck, with numerous loops about it. The creatures led her forwards using long poles with hooks at the ends, which engaged in those loops. She was also wearing some sort of technological backpack, with various tubes and wires leading up to hardware that was actually penetrating her skull. From this, various tubes and wires then ran down her guards' poles, which in some cases were just the post-heads' arm extensions, and penetrated some of them. She also had on a suit that looked vaguely like golden chainmail. Ottanger stared at that, because it closely resembled the one they'd put on him in the Complex. Then slowly it began to dawn on him what he'd been denying, and he studied her face more closely.

Recognition crashed down on him, along with a feeling of unreality. How could such a coincidence be so? It was as if something was testing the limits of his sanity with all this horror and madness. His thoughts exploded into crazy extrapolation about the holistic universe or multiverse, supernatural influences, then honed down to manipulation and connections he couldn't yet see. He had to push this aside, though, because no matter what had led to this point, this juncture, he simply had to deal with the reality of it now.

'Jane,' he said hoarsely.

His sister showed no reaction. He realized that he hadn't recognized her at first because of the mutilation of her skull and body, as well as her lax expression and the fact that she didn't even move the same way as before. He made the chilling connection then to the homogenization of appearance in the corpses he had seen in the internment camp, and saw this to be akin.

Deal with it!

He hardened himself and peered inside her, at the numerous technological intrusions into her body – the inside of her skull was a mess he couldn't fathom. The suit connected to her skin he saw, while bars inserted through this ran to rings around her bones.

'I am here to speak with you,' she said haltingly, in a voice he little recognized.

Thinking about what the Fenris had told him, the stuff he'd already extrapolated, and utilizing the accelerated facilities of his mind, he put everything together. He reckoned she must have been snatched up by the Inspectorate jaunt research project at about the same time as Savarack took him. They'd turned her into a jaunter, and she'd ended up in the same place as he had, on the airless Earth below. Obviously, the hive humans had captured her down on the surface and had wanted to stop her jaunting away again. Judging by their examination of the corpses, and studying her biotech, he guessed they'd now found a further use for her. It seemed odd that she still wore the suit. Surely its function was to drag her back out of this place, to Committee Earth? Or had these hive humans altered it, now to keep her here?

Whatever the answer to that, it seemed evident the material intrusions into her body were not just about examination, but about keeping her a captive. As a new jaunter, he'd struggled to carry anything beyond himself on his journeys. Loading her with materials like this, actually connected inside her, would act as an anchor. But it went beyond that too. From her, he also felt that pull. And, since she was actually alive, he tried to track back along it to her. This worked until he hit some barrier, and realized the technology enclosing her blocked him as much as it did her.

'When you give me food and drink, I'll talk,' he replied, and said no more, utterly aware that he wasn't addressing his sister.

'I am to ask you questions,' she said, following her script.

Ottanger simply didn't reply. He concentrated on his surroundings, continuing to absorb detail. In the post-heads – yes, that was definitely the right name for them – he could see certain semi-biotech structures around their diminished brains. Other hive humans of different designs were similarly lacking in skull capacity and had those same structures. He supposed this a requirement, in fact a necessity, for creating a hive out of humans: individuals diminished of intelligence and will would be good components in the overall machine. This reflected human societies on his home world too. The greater the authority of the collective, the smaller the requirement for independence in its members. Admittedly in the case of his Earth, the authority of the herd was concentrated in the Committee. Yet he could see how even that would seep away as the strictures they placed on others would eventually apply to themselves, though later.

He could see a similar semi-biotech structure to theirs had also been implanted in Jane. He surmised that, with this, they'd made her a translator – a conduit to the *hive intelligence* here. This brought home just how much its methods of communication and thinking must be hugely at variance from his own, for a conduit to be necessary.

'I am to ask you questions,' Jane said again.

Ottanger ignored her and continued his examination of his surroundings. The corpses were interesting, because when he'd tried to reach out to Jane, he'd felt something more from them. He pushed into that further and firmed the connection, receiving a weird mental boost, and a sense of greater strength and available resources. He then strayed beyond this chamber, to the movements of the hive humans in the tunnels beyond. There he saw a group of a different type he hadn't noticed before. They had the binocular heads of the warrior kind, but were lightly built, with thin arms, long fingers and exterior hardware running down those fingers. There were four of them heading in this direction, with two wheeled pallets. Two were pushing, while two more of them sat at the end of each pallet, cut off at the waist and positioned in thick discs of hard tech. Numerous mechanical surgical extensions went into their hands and fingers, as well as optical extensions to their eyes. Ahead of these on the pallets lay other neatly arrayed components, the same as those they'd put into Jane. He designated this group as surgeons. Why had they not, right from the start, done to him what they'd done to her? He studied his sister as her face went slack after speaking, and blood trickled out of one of her eyes. It tore at him, and he really wanted to let go, as he had in the internment camp, but he needed to stay as calm as possible. Evidently their operations severely damaged the recipient, and the hive mind wanted as much information from him as possible before locking him down in a similar way.

'I am here to ask you questions,' she said yet again.

'Food. Drink,' he stated, and left it at that.

A long pause ensued with nothing much happening. Then one of the post-heads scuttled off on all fours, to enter an alcove running into the surrounding tech. Ottanger tracked it to a limpet-like device attached to one wall and saw pipework from there running off into the hive, also supplying other such devices at other locations. The thing squirted out a turd of white matter, which the post-head took. It then squeezed out a bulb of water, which detached, revealing a teat. The post-head rushed back with these and scrambled up him, until right in front of his face –

obviously personal space wasn't a thing here – then thrust the turd towards his mouth. Ottanger hesitated. The post-head's breathing was laboured, liquid rattling in its lungs, and snot was bubbling from one nostril. He certainly didn't want to catch what it had, but they might also be trying to insert some of their tech inside him through this food. He scanned the white thing, but could detect nothing untoward, while his sense of smell raised approval icons in his mind. He opened his mouth and the creature thrust the food in, near choking him, but he managed to keep the stuff down. His sense of taste now offered further icons and he understood, on a visceral level, that he was being given what he needed. When it also thrust the teat of the water bubble at him, he kept his mouth closed until he'd swallowed all the food. Then he allowed it, drinking until the post-head threw away the shrivelled bag and finally scrambled off him. He watched it scuttle away to the wall, and there crouch down, with its arms wrapped around its legs. It looked very ill.

His insides bubbled and he felt the nutrients entering his system fast, as he had on other occasions. His exacting mind now told him of fats, sugars and proteins, and his body sucked them up hungrily. As a result of this his level of consciousness stepped up too, and it seemed to allow further emotion to seep through, feelings he hadn't had the energy for before. *Jane.* He now truly felt the horror of what they'd done to his sister, mixed in with fear of what would almost certainly happen to him if he didn't escape here. A wave of shame then swamped that, as he felt that perhaps he deserved this, after how many he'd so recently killed. The nutrients initiated a rising surge through his biotech too, with that network lighting up inside him. It increased his connection to the corpses, as well as the general all-round feel of *something,* and to Jane too, despite the blocking tech.

The hive creatures stirred and shifted about in agitation. From this he assumed they'd also detected the change. He concentrated, and it was as if different filters clicked into place, one after another, in his internal sense. And then he saw the glimmer of terahertz radiation, the wave patterns cutting through the air, and the precise beams scanning him up and down. He felt their warm prickly intrusion as they dug data out of him. As a footnote, he saw the surgeons, who until then had paused their approach, start back into motion.

'So what do you want to know?' he asked, more to keep up the delays than because he wanted to give the hive mind any information at all.

Chancel

The Fenris stepped back from Irene and stood upright, looking around at them all. Chancel had seen the creature previously in his mind as a kind of projection, as they all had, but the reality was somewhat stronger. He stood well over two metres tall, had a solidity that'd been lacking in those previous communications, and he seemed to extend beyond the here and now. As if his form slewed into the other dimensions of the parallels. He seemed more aggressive and dangerous too.

'I thought we were under attack,' said Irene, sitting upright.

The Fenris peered down at her. Though his face hardly seemed human, Chancel could read a hint of contempt there.

'My arrival was somewhat tumultuous,' the creature conceded.

He waved a hand, and the ribs of a transport cage detached from the object he'd brought with him, then rose up into the air to swirl around each other, finally snapping together in a seed form. This then blinked out of existence, or at least *this* existence. Irene moved to stand up, then thought better of it, sitting back casually. Dominance games, Chancel thought. Standing she would suffer in comparison to the sheer size of the Fenris, but sitting casually she could still play the part of the lord of the manor receiving a visitor. Chancel realized something else he'd felt during that arrival. He'd seen the ribs of the transport cage and instantly recognized the Fenris, so it seemed likely Irene and the others had too. But he'd felt her spurt of fear and accompanying anger before she fired. Did she see the Fenris as a threat to her power? She obviously wasn't as in control of herself as she would have liked them all to believe.

'And why are you here?' Irene asked.

'To advise and help,' the Fenris replied. 'By now you have some awareness of what your recent action on Committee Earth resulted in, but your access there is only limited to what you can glean from the propaganda.'

Irene looked away, unable to meet the creature's gaze.

'It wasn't good the last time I looked,' said Chancel, feeling a slight frisson that he was going against Irene by saying this. 'And what Chenghu found out wasn't much better.' He glanced at the man. Chenghu seemed pained as he looked from the Fenris to Irene. Chancel could sense the battle inside the man. He wanted to support her, but he was rational enough to know that she'd been causing more problems than she'd solved.

'The Committee is using the "terrorist threat" as a means to establish further power over the nation states,' said the Fenris. He turned and walked back to stand beside the huge grublike thing he'd brought. Waving a hand, he opened out a filmy surface that seemed to extend from him, and his suit, like a butterfly wing. This surface then coloured in, blocking out everything behind it, and divided into triangular segments, each displaying scenes from Committee Earth. 'What he didn't find out much about, is this.'

The scenes showed riots, wars, massed Inspectorate forces, shepherds ripping through crowds, fires and explosions, jets in the skies and a space plane crashing into a sprawl.

'And what is this?' Irene asked leadenly.

'You cut the head off the snake, as you said, but in doing so you also upset a delicate balance. The Committee doesn't consist of those leaders and other members who take the title. It's rather a culture of control, established over a century in the bureaucracies of the world. Those leaders, though only in agreement to maintain more power in their hands, also acted as a buffer between the Committee and the people they effectively ruled. Many Committee diktats were toned down, or slowed in their delivery. In killing these people, you've allowed the bureaucrats to occupy Committee seats, within just hours. And now, given the justification of the "terrorist threat", they are acting.'

Irene said nothing, but Adriana asked, 'And how are they acting?'

'Their new chairman, Alessandro Messina, just put in position four hours ago, has said that it's national divisions that have allowed this atrocity to happen, and that with nuclear weapons in play, these can no longer be permitted. They're applying a plan, long drawn up, to divide the world into sectors, under governors appointed by the Committee as ultimate authority. Some countries disagree, of course, but others whose leaders you killed have mobilized armed forces against them.'

The various images flashed brightly, and familiar mushroom clouds arose.

'As you can see, nothing must stand in the way of this plan, and any means will be used to bring it to fruition.' The Fenris focused down on Irene. 'In trying to stop the world becoming a totalitarian state, you actually accelerated the process.'

'They can't do this,' said Adriana doubtfully.

'They can and they are. But that's not all of it. Due to the disruption caused by, at present count, five separate wars, the whole system is in a state of collapse. Infrastructure is failing – power generation, water and gas supplies, and food shipments. This is generating riots and Inspectorate clampdowns without restraint.'

Irene looked up sharply. 'Then the Committee won't be able to push their plan through. If the whole system collapses, they'll lose their grip and separate polities will establish.'

The Fenris shook his head. 'No. It will succeed, because it's too deeply imbedded in every country. The only thing in question will be the level of death toll before its grip is firmly established. At present it's at a hundred and fifty million. By the time this is all done, it will be over a billion.'

'That can't be true,' said Irene, fists clenched.

Chancel noted a whine in her voice he'd never heard before. And with that, he felt something snap in the room, in the connection between them all. Suddenly, there on the sofa, she looked exceedingly small, and in consonance with this, the others came into stronger focus. Chenghu shrugged and seemed to stand more upright, the confusion in his expression winking out. Chancel realized that despite her protest, she'd accepted what the Fenris was saying. And in her doing so, her dominance had diminished.

'You know it's true,' said the Fenris. The creature now looked bitter and, he felt, just a little bit jaded. 'Committee Earth is not something that can be fixed by the simplistic approach you used. Every leader you kill leads to thousands if not hundreds of thousands of deaths amid the ZAs you once were. Every system of oppression you try to blunt results in a harsher one taking its place. And, in the end, there is a multiplicity of worlds out there, so why are you trying to fix just that one?'

'That sounds suspiciously like projection to me,' said Irene resentfully.

The words had come across as projection to Chancel as well, though to his mind they felt more like a lie. He kept this observation to himself for later analysis. In fact, he realized he could keep it to himself completely, and felt no need to blurt it out to Irene.

'You cannot fix what is so badly broken,' said the Fenris. 'But meanwhile you can look to yourselves, and a very real problem that's within your power to deal with.'

He raised a hand and closed it, snapping shut the butterfly wing and the images it showed. Another cutting gesture with the flat of his hand triggered the grublike thing to coil up and open out gaps between its segments. Recognizable items were then revealed inside: weapons, suits and other hardware.

'State-of-the-art combat suits and weaponry I'm certain you'll have the intelligence to understand swiftly,' said the Fenris flatly.

'What use is this to us if we have to stop trying to fix things?' said Irene, and now she did stand up.

Chancel felt her dominance trying to re-establish via their connection, but it was still a lot weaker now. He knew she needed time to recover from the blow to her certainty, which, he now realized, had started fracturing when they'd all stood on that rooftop and watched the nuclear blast eating up the sprawl. The Fenris just stared at her for a long while, and she appeared to wither under his gaze. Then he spoke.

'Actions on Committee Earth are not to be discounted, and perhaps some good can be achieved there. But you are world walkers and must think on a larger scale, and consider that you face a greater threat now: the hive.'

'Just another world,' said Irene. 'Maybe a few of them can travel, but what does that matter to us? If our own world isn't something to fix, then, as you say, there are other places for us.'

She was pushing it – again searching out the words and attitude to re-establish control. Chancel grimaced and fought against it, not liking how he was feeling the urge to agree with her again.

'Chenghu has told you what happened to him when he tried to leave the airless Earth,' said the Fenris. 'But now you need to understand that the hive engineered those spaces between to make that place a trap. All the jaunters who died there are because of this.'

'Why would they do that?' Irene asked.

'Because the hive assesses potential threats and seeks to negate them. It evidently uses high-energy machines to open tunnels between parallels. But now, having discovered it's possible for individuals to jaunt between worlds, it wants that technology too. I have managed to destroy my biotech in the corpses on the airless Earth, as Chenghu saw, but have since learned that the hive grabbed some other jaunter corpses before this, to examine them.'

'So you want us to raid this hive and steal back, or destroy, the corpses?' Irene looked round at them all, expression and attitude derisive. This also reflected in them, as her dominance grew.

'No,' said the Fenris. 'The fact the hive has obtained some of this technology cannot be undone. Though I suspect it will take it many decades to come close to unravelling the biotech from corpses.'

'Then what?'

'The hive has two live jaunters, two of your own kind, held captive.' The Fenris scanned them all. 'From these two, it can more swiftly understand the technology. I suggest it might be a good idea to rescue them and then –' the Fenris turned his gaze on Irene again – 'focus on the research into jaunters being conducted on Committee Earth.'

Ottanger

'How did you acquire the biotechnology in your body?' asked the spokeswoman for the hive, who might or might not still be his sister Jane.

'Biotechnology?' Ottanger asked. 'What biotechnology is that?'

This seemed to cause a stir, with all the hive humans in the chamber shifting, turning to each other, making odd hand gestures and generally looking agitated. Jane was jerked to one side by her neck ring, but it didn't seem to bother her. Her expression turned blank and moronic again. He meanwhile noted that the surgeons had paused again, and looked similarly agitated. This went on for some minutes, while he continued to explore the reach of his abilities, and think on some other interesting factors.

Why was the hive so interested in the Fenris's biotechnology if it could already manipulate the multiverse, to the extent of putting a trap in the places between? Surely it must have the same abilities that the biotech imparted? But no, that wasn't necessarily the case. The mere fact that it was so interested meant it surely didn't have the technology. And now, understanding this, it was his instinct to try in every way to deny it to them. He explored his links to the fenris biotech around him further, and closely examined the sense he'd had of an increase in power. Those with the biotech inside them could jaunt. But now, seeing there was some kind of connection, he studied feedback loops. Gazing into the multiverse while focused on this connection gave him a surge – a greater clarity in his perception of that whole, and a feeling that he could spill into it almost inadvertently. He realized the process was synergistic. And, with one lead in control over the connected biotech, the accuracy and other subtle nuances of the power expanded.

'You are lying,' Jane said abruptly.

Ottanger looked at her in surprise. Her face gained some humanity as she pulled upright against her restraints. He was reminded of her response to him once when he'd been going about resistance business, and he'd lied to her. But it could all be just facial muscles falling back into familiar places, and perhaps fragments of a mind doing the same.

'No I'm not,' he replied, turning away to explore further.

His links to the corpses, and even to Jane, had expanded his ability to see across the parallels, to perceive the multiverse all around him, as well as in him. He inspected the hive's manifold, with its black funnel and collection of tunnels leading away, and then looping back. A memory of screentime nagged at him, and he recognized something like the structure of a Klein bottle. Whatever. The thing had to be an artificial construct, somehow maintained by machines in, or on, this moon. He began tracking the relationship between the multiverse, the manifold and the reality around him, then pushing and testing.

'You are lying,' Jane said again. 'We gave you food.'

'You would be poor hosts if you hadn't,' said Ottanger. He could play these word games for as long as the hive liked, but he doubted it would like them for much longer.

'You must answer our questions, or we will cause you pain and physical damage,' Jane told him.

Not long at all, it appeared. And now he noted how she'd slipped into using 'we' rather than 'I'.

'Okay, I have biotechnology in my body, but you knew that anyway,' he said.

The hive mind response was quicker this time. 'That does not answer our question.'

'I was born with it,' he replied, which was a half-truth, and not at all helpful.

'That is not the entire truth,' Jane responded quickly.

427

He peered at her, acknowledging the hive must have gleaned knowledge from the corpses, and from her, and was applying it at the level of the connections he felt here – the veracity of his words was being checked via this route. He pushed into the multiverse that much harder, mapping the black funnel to the reality of his surroundings, and pushing to extend the range of his perception. The hive opened out further to his internal sense, multiplied by the synergistic effect of the fenris biotech around him. It all turned a bit misty, but now he detected some kind of fault, or flaw, lying higher up, and just below what he surmised was the surface of the moon.

'I don't know the entire truth,' he said. 'I found myself able to travel between the parallels, and have been learning ever since.'

'These are obfuscations,' said Jane. 'There is something you are avoiding telling us.'

He stared at her, noting the increase in hive vocabulary, and its sense of what he was thinking. Those connections he felt to her were definitely creating some kind of feedback loop, providing the hive with more insight into his responses than from the mere verbal. Was it just gathering this from his sister, or from else-where?

'Perhaps you could make your questions more specific?' he suggested. He then wondered about his instinct to impart as little information as possible, and why he resisted telling this entity, of which Jane was just the mouthpiece, about the Fenris.

No matter. His situation in essence remained the same. If he tried to jaunt away now, the funnel would catch him and turn him round, delivering him back into the chamber in which he'd first arrived. If he jumped locally, that would lead to him endlessly evading capture. And, it suddenly occurred to him, they might learn enough to alter their trap to catch local jumps too. But having eaten and drunk, and with his local connections expanding his perception, he saw there might be another way out.

'You must tell us how you acquired your biotech,' said Jane. 'We are aware that you are prevaricating. Tell us everything and in detail. If you do not, we will cause you pain and damage.'

'Okay, I'll start from the beginning. In my early teens I became aware that my mother was regarded as an outlier to what was acceptable in our society. She had visible mutations. However, despite being shunned for these, she was also seen as exotically beautiful. I guess that's why she ended up as a whore.' Yes, he could keep this going for a good time. Meanwhile, it seemed the surgeons were still on pause. But at some point, the hive would realize he was just drawing things out, and those surgeons would come in anyway, no matter how much he told them. He was an object of study, and this interview was just the first stage of his dissection. He'd end up like those in the walls, or like his sister – he wasn't sure which would be the worse.

He continued, 'I then realized, by the attitude of those around me, that I too had these visible mutations. . .'

By compartmentalizing the story he was telling, switching it over to a conversational low-function part of his brain, he managed to keep his main concentration on planning a way out of this situation. Did the hive understand he could jump in three spatial dimensions here? Almost certainly not, otherwise it wouldn't have used this approach. It must think it had plenty of time available and could just keep grabbing him whenever the funnel routed him back. He knew he was dealing here with reasoning and views at variance from the conventionally human.

'In puberty, my mutations became more pronounced, and therefore more noticeable to others. I wasn't considered beautiful like my mother, but a big ugly fucker.' He paused and studied Jane. 'Unlike my sister, who many *did* think beautiful.' Utterly no reaction. Feeling a sinking sensation in his gut, he continued, 'The first time I was attacked and beaten, I took my knocks. I recovered very quickly, though, and this highlighted the internal non-visible aspects of my mutation. The next time it happened, I defended myself, and badly beat two of the gangbangers who'd attacked me. This brought me to the notice of the resistance, because I'd shown myself to be a suitable recruit.' Was he revealing too much with this? The hive might be able to extrapolate some of his capabilities from it. No, because it had already seen him fighting, when he arrived.

So, jumping locally with no goal, he'd eventually be captured again. Almost certainly he'd then receive the attention of the surgeons. But with food and drink supplied by those machines all over the hive burrows, he'd be able to cover quite some distance. He now focused up on the distant flaw in space–time. He needed to remove what was holding him here, and it lay there.

'I enjoyed the training, and grew stronger and more competent – carrying out steadily more and more important missions as I grew up. However, my physical size, plus my mutations, made me a target. And my presence tended to create more problems than it solved. Then I started to realize that all resistance actions were similar, for they seemed to create more problems than they solved too.'

'The detail you are giving us is not pertinent to our initial question,' Jane dropped into the pause. 'It is evident this obfuscation and extraneous padding will continue. You require instruction.'

Ottanger allowed himself a mild grin, noting that the surgeons were coming. Why wait any longer now he knew what he had to do? He garnered his resources and focused on a location in a cyst chamber over to his right. He then began pushing, thinning out the world and bending reality. The funnel slid down on him, slewing his aim to that location, and he pushed back.

'What are you doing?' Jane asked quickly. 'You cannot escape.'

There were post-heads over there, but fortunately none of the warrior kind nearby. He focused on her. 'Perhaps we'll have a chat about that, but not here.' He stretched out, his power echoing into the network formed by her and the corpses, and he jumped.

17

The Fenris

They were on their way. They might succeed in rescuing Ottanger and his sister, whom he now saw the hive had used as a conduit, or they might not. Extrapolating, he saw that Ottanger, now on the move, would likely cause enough disruption to make an opening for rescue. And at least being aware of it, and with the strength of their synergy, they should be able to get through the hive manifold.

Initially, the Fenris had considered going with them, sure that his presence would have guaranteed the rescue, but had then changed his mind. He needed soldiers who could operate independently. Anyway, he had to stand back and once more take the long view. The future of Committee Earth, and likely a large portion of the multiverse, couldn't just depend on the actions of a handful of world walkers. More important now was to analyse the data coming through the same link he'd established to enable his walkers to track Ottanger. And that data appalled him.

Two things became apparent at first. When he saw the mesh suit that Jane wore, he finally made a connection he should have noticed long ago. It was hive technology adapted by the

Inspectorate research complex. And, when he searched their systems, he discovered the hive had visited that Earth in the past, with those visitors brought down by readerguns. The second thing was the number in the hive showing symptoms of viral infection, which he was certain they'd picked up from the jaunter corpses. This terrifying reality meant the hive was already partway to obtaining his biotech, and he had to stop it going any further. Everything else he saw in that place confirmed this for him too.

What he could see of the hive extended as far as Ottanger's senses did, so was accurate within a sphere a kilometre across, and with diminishing returns outside that limit. But this was enough to glean an overview, and to then be able to extrapolate what the moon contained. Ottanger had gone down deeper than the Fenris had first been able to see in. And it seemed the burrows might go deeper still – in fact right to the moon's core. Calculating from the observed population density, this put their number maybe even as high as a trillion. The hive had massive material, agricultural and manufacturing resources to support this population, but also had huge reserves. As he'd earlier surmised, the hive had been locked into an enclosed circuit of birth from vast chambers filled with artificial wombs, through to death when its old and worn-out citizens simply walked into the recycling plants – whether willingly or otherwise, he couldn't tell. The only slight bleed away from this circuit had been gathering rare materials, through that organic mining machine, and threat assessment. But now, a threat having been identified, everything had changed.

Artificial wombs were filled with warriors, and other human iterations that didn't match the general demographic of the hive. Huge factories had switched over from manufacturing the necessities of lunar life, to weapons and other machines of war. Meanwhile, glimpsed here and there, and distantly sensed at the surface, machines that resembled many from the Fenris's own engines were activating. Judging from hive history, he guessed that these were weapons and devices used in high-tech, inter-hive warfare. This enormous civilization – if that's what it could be called – was moving steadily onto a war footing.

With a claw closing in his guts, the Fenris wondered when this activity had all started. Having narrowly escaped from its past inter-hive warfare, this hive had been propelled here, into this multiverse, damaged but war ready. In the ensuing years, with there being no threats around it, it had then dropped back to conventional function. The hive was like a dumb beast, perhaps an insect, which, having survived a predator taking a chunk out of its body, just returns to feeding, and to its routines. It had its systems in place, ready to activate and deal with threats, but on the whole its purpose was simply to exist. But then this wasn't so completely different from the usual run of humanity. He saw that the memory of threat, in a mind that overall was immortal, was the same as it was with general humankind: spanning maybe only a couple of generations.

The hive had responded when he'd first penetrated the multiverse. The state of the ship it sent the second time confirmed his assessment that it had been somnolent, unready. Further penetrations by the jaunters had elicited a larger response, with it setting its trap. Judging by the corpses it had been examining, this was also to do with threat assessment. Now it was trying to acquire jaunt biotech, because it didn't have something similar. The difference between the hive method of travel and that of the jaunters was the equivalent of someone being confined to a transport system, while others could wander at will. He saw that the hive method of crossing the parallels reflected its composite mentality, for it was the *hive* that travelled, not individuals. So how could he stop it acquiring jaunter technology, and how could he halt its development into this warfare mode?

The Fenris feared there might be no easy way to shut it down. It'd be impossible for him to transport enough bombs or viruses directly inside the moon to destroy a civilization so huge. Viruses would certainly result in sterilizing exterminations in the hive, only to be followed by rapid replacement of those excised. But he was at war with himself, old morality battling present exigency. Though he accepted the concept of command structures, and some suppression of free will, he simply couldn't make a first strike like that. He wouldn't accept the idea that a full extermination of a potential enemy was the answer and rejected it unequivocally.

The Fenris then returned to what he saw as the only course, and ran through a thousand models of warfare. He struggled with the appalling reality of a numbers game, with the hive having those numbers. The thing was a behemoth set into motion, and bringing it to a stop required the long view once again. Gazing down upon his own world, he saw all its resources and lack of people. The solution it seemed, when he turned his attention to Committee Earth and other worlds, lay there. War was coming and he needed more soldiers – probably millions of them. On its surface the idea sickened him, but deep down he felt a sense of power and purpose.

This was only the beginning.

Ottanger

The chaotic transition felt like running across an icy slope, only just maintaining balance, and he understood that the manifold trap was affecting his ability to jump. Points swirled around him, the network flashing in and out, then he briefly hit the synergy required and made it through. He flew out of the air in the cyst, a metre above the floor and travelling fast. Hitting the floor at an angle, he took the momentum into a roll, crashing one post-head aside and slamming another into the edge of an examination slab. Other objects that he'd brought appeared with him, crunching down and flaking their dried skin and flesh, some hitting wetly and smearing fluids across the floor. The stink of rotting corpses arose. He bounced to his feet. The post-head he'd crushed against the table simply dropped, as the one behind staggered to its feet. He lashed out with a side kick, folding that one over, and turned to the table.

Laid out across the surface were his belongings – neatly positioned like some disassembled machine for renovation. He eyed the two post-heads on the other side of it, long instruments attached to their fingers, and single-lens scopes sunk into their eye sockets. He reached up to his ear, then studied his fingers, wet with blood. The jump had damaged him in some way, and he felt tired. This was something he'd sensed as possible but never encountered until now. No matter. He was here. He reached out and picked up the parts of the machine pistol and, with calm ease, reassembled the thing. The post-heads seemed baffled, and he guessed this to be an advantage he had – they needed instruction from the overall mind before acting.

Beyond the chamber, through his inner sense, he saw warriors on the move in his direction. He checked the action of the weapon, loaded a clip, knocked it down to single shots, and fired twice. The two dropped, with their lenses smashed, flesh and bone flowering out of the backs of their narrow skulls. He turned and fired once more to kill the one he'd kicked too, then again felt a moment of shame. How innocent or guilty they were of what the overall hive wanted to do to him he couldn't fathom, since they were mere components, but still they'd been living humans.

Next he focused on those who'd arrived with him. Whole corpses and various body parts were strewn across the floor. He still felt a connection with most of them, but in some this link had died now – specifically in the wet mass of internal organs smeared in a line over to his left. Over to his right, against the far wall, there was one still in motion.

He resisted the impulse to go over there, as Jane made horrible grunting sounds. Instead he quickly pulled on his clothing and boots, without doing anything up, while keeping a careful inner eye on those approaching warriors. She heaved upright, and he saw that the backpack was gone, and the ring was missing from her neck, as well as some of the hardware from around her skull. Her head was bleeding, pulses coming out of a deep hole. She looked at him with bloodshot eyes, then reached up and pushed a finger into the hole.

'Kill me,' she said.

It had already crossed his mind, because he'd thought nothing remained of his sister in that body, and since the biotech still generated that synergistic effect even in corpses. But now she herself had spoken, he realized some of the rational human being did remain. He wanted to go over to her, check on her and do the things a brother should to, but there was no time. He had to remain focused, for her sake as much as for his own.

With everything now on, if only loosely, and his helmet hanging at his hip, he peered up through the hive, in the direction he wanted to go. Pushing this time was much harder, while his body screamed protest at a lack of resources, a lack of energy. Icons and molecular models swirled in his mind – some he could understand, and some completely escaped him. He garnered what he could, and tweaked where he could, as he pushed closed Velcro seams, did up buckles, buttoned and zipped. Then, at the last moment, just as one of the warriors

437

came through the door wielding a lariat gun, he jumped again, his companions in tow.

The arrival was just a drop to a floor, his body hot as it burned up meagre resources. Post-heads swirled around him and he immediately jumped again, falling from a ceiling and jarring his legs, then once more because hive humans were still close by. The arrival this time was harder, as he went sprawling and skidding into a hive tunnel, or burrow, and bashed his head against a wall. Staggering to his feet, seeing stars, he damned himself for not putting on the helmet. Locally, the area within this compass seemed all but deserted, but he knew it wouldn't remain so for long. He winced as Jane rolled over, vomited and tried to pull herself up. Now all the exterior hardware was missing from her skull, but at least the bleeding had stopped from that large hole. However, blood had run from both her ears, as well as gathered in one eye as she turned to look at him. He touched below his own eye, fingers coming away bloody too, and realized it had compromised his human vision. He was mostly using his inner sight now.

'I know you?' she asked, her voice hoarse.

'Yes, you know me,' he replied, looking within.

His body was screaming for resources, and warning him it had begun to burn muscle, while also struggling with toxins. Though he could move beneath their trap in local space, the strain on him was horrific. He also realized that, although the synergistic effect from the biotech in Jane, and the corpses, helped the process, their dead mass seemed to hinder it in other ways too. However, he was damned if he was going to leave anything behind for the hive to examine or experiment on. And that very much included his sister. He pulled out of internal inspection and scanned around for one of their food machines. The nearest was a hundred metres down the tube. Seeing movement coming in his direction all around, he knew he wouldn't have time to reach it and grab something. But he needed calories if he was to survive this and, almost as if directed from within, his gaze fell on the battered jaunter detritus littering the burrow. Hunger rumbled his stomach and brought saliva to his mouth. Coldly sure of what he was doing and why, he stooped, picked up a ripped-off arm, then bit into the biceps.

'The fuck are you doing?' said Jane. But her attention was wandering to the remains too, and he could feel her hunger.

His teeth sheared through flesh, because of course they were sharper and more pointy now. And he gulped down lumps of it, with little in the way of chewing. As it reached his stomach, he could feel it dissolving and disseminating, and felt a stab of curiosity about his internal biology, now acting so fast. By the time he'd gnawed the upper part of the arm down to the bone, Jane had dragged herself to a lump of human liver and was cramming it into her mouth.

'Again,' he said, as warriors now came into sight at the end of the burrow.

This time he seemed to skim along below a sky made of contorted black glass. It stabbed down glassy tornados to try to spear him, but they were random and far off target. Their disruption strained and tore at him, however, until he and the others tumbled out in yet another burrow. There, still clutching the arm and chewing, he understood how his perception of the multiverse was all a matter of interpretation. His finite, linear mind was imposing images over something it had just not evolved to perceive. And yet, growing from some inner core, was a perception that did extend there. The biotech, of course.

'Now it gets shitty,' he said, trying and failing to give his sister a reassuring smile.

She'd lost even more of the extraneous hardware, but still

retained the mesh suit. Peering within her, he could see the rings around her bones, and other probes and monitors. He could also see internal bleeding and fractures. Nevertheless, this time she grabbed at protrusions from the wall, and pulled herself upright.

'I don't understand this,' she said.

'Time for understanding will come later, sister,' he said.

'Sister?'

'You are my sister, and your name is Jane.'

'Jane,' she repeated, tasting the word.

He checked through his pack, hooked remaining clips on his belt, topped up the grenade boxes and dropped the remainder in his pocket. He checked the action of his revolver and considered giving it to her. But there was no guarantee she wouldn't decide to shoot him, and quite possibly herself. He then looked up.

The moon's surface sat a kilometre above them. Meanwhile, the flaw in reality that had made this last jump strangely easy, as he seemed to be sliding down towards it, centred on a chamber just below the surface. The device from which this flaw seemed to initiate hung in the centre of the chamber like a neuron. It was a sphere of hard and organic technology, braced at the centre by frameworks running in energy and nutrient feeds. His internal sense alerted him to the massive concentration of energy there, punching through the parallels. It was also logical to assume that, once it lost that capability, the energy would have to go somewhere here. Earlier, when he'd first got a look at it, the thing would have been an easy target. Now, however, warriors and post-heads were swarming in. For it seemed the hive mind had ascertained his target.

'Just keep your head down and try to stay alive, Jane,' he said. 'I'll come back for you.' Hardening his resolve, he made the requisite disconnection and jumped once more, towards the device, leaving her behind.

This time it was all so much easier, as if he'd come into the calm at the centre of a hurricane. He could tweak things, choose relative velocities and position himself to best effect. Ottanger chose to appear in the open space of the chamber, between the support frameworks of the device, rather than down on the floor, or around the edges where hive humans were crowding. He tweaked relative motions, so he fell in towards the device, with his accompaniment of bodies and body parts swirling around him. At once he flung handfuls of grenades towards the thing, just as stun charges and lariats whipped towards him. Then, because he could, he jumped again. In another position, he detached a box of grenades from his belt, took out one, flicked its cap and dropped it back in the box, then threw the box towards the device.

He jumped again, coming down on a framework, and flung the other box as the first grenades detonated in a staccato rattle of explosions. A massive discharge flashed out from the device to the chamber wall, while a support frame not far from him glared red, and then simply melted. As he'd ascertained, the energy had to go somewhere. In that moment, he felt some of the other biotech going out, as the discharges cremated those erstwhile jaunters. He forced his disconnection from them, feeling sure that very soon nothing much would remain of them. Then, from the surface of the device, a blinding light started to expand. Time to be gone.

Ottanger thumped down into a crouch in the burrow. Jane was up against the wall, arms wrapped round her knees and eyes tightly closed. A warrior was reaching down to her, while a gaggle of post-heads shifted about in agitation behind him. A short burst from Ottanger's machine pistol spun the warrior against the wall, and another burst scattered the post-heads. He stepped over, reached down and grabbed her hand. The warrior now

441

lurched up and he saw that, though some of his shots had penetrated, many had made craters in its subdermal armour. He fired again, concentrating on its head, until that was all but gone. It staggered on past him, groping at those shredded remains.

'Now?' Jane asked.

He pulled her to her feet as the burrow shook. Above, he could see only a growing sphere of fire.

'We're out of here,' he said.

The realization of his limitations put Ottanger on the verge of panic, as the manifold's funnel scooped him up yet again. It dropped him between the two dishes of the first chamber, falling towards that same floor again. The moon was shuddering all around him, and the hive humans below were running around in seemingly aimless confusion. He'd certainly caused some problems here, but had he destroyed the wrong machine? No, the manifold – that structure that had routed him back into the moon three times now – was definitely fracturing and twisting. Perhaps the machine had been one of many now put out of balance. Or perhaps its destruction didn't immediately dispel its effect.

'Please . . . no,' said Jane as they fell.

He looked at her, inside and out. The rings around her bones had shifted, and further fractures had appeared. She was bleeding internally, in reflection of her exterior, where various wounds had opened all over her body. Her chain mesh suit was steaming. Still holding tightly to her hand, he realized that if he kept trying to push through as he had been, he'd soon be towing a corpse along with him. He scanned his surroundings, as the creatures below received direction and crowded in towards the centre of the platform, wielding their various tools of capture. Then he jumped yet again.

Jane groaned as they landed in another chamber, and rolled on into the far wall. Releasing her hand, Ottanger stood up quickly, drawing his revolver and snorting a spray of blood from his nostrils. He rushed over to the entrance and swung shut a heavy door, made of some composite material, then turned the wheel on its inner surface to lock it. He'd chosen this place because it was one of the few enclosed rooms that actually had a door. But now he saw it could be opened by a wheel on the outside too.

Think!

He stared at the mechanism inside the door, placed his revolver barrel against it just so, fired one shot, then, after a moment, fired another. The cogwheel running on the rack of the locking bar shattered. He stepped back, even as hive creatures swarmed in towards the door. It wouldn't hold them for long, but perhaps long enough.

'How do you feel?' he asked, walking back to Jane. Then internally he berated himself for asking such a stupid question.

'I'm dying,' she replied. 'Just leave me here.'

He gestured to the door as the wheel spun back and forth – post-heads on the other side were seemingly unable to grasp that the thing wasn't working. He noted warriors coming too, carrying tools like pickaxes, and knew the hive had issued new instructions.

'If I leave you here, they won't let you die.'

She closed her eyes, expression pained, focusing inside as it seemed she tried to direct some repairs. Seeing this, Ottanger turned his own attention inwards. Once again, he'd seared through conventional resources, and now his body was trying to raise chemical energy by burning up its very structure once more. He scanned around, hoping to see one of those food machines. But all that occupied this place was the two of them, and a sphere two metres across, set down in the floor. He studied the thing, seeing power lines blossoming from its lower hemisphere into a chamber below. Peering inside, he mapped out its complexity, and found that beyond a certain point, he could look no further – the sun burning at its centre glared too brightly even for his odd internal sense.

He was wasting time.

Ottanger focused again on the structure of the surrounding multiverse and tried to parse what he could do. The manifold was continuing to slew and twist out of existence, like a rickety raft caught in a sea storm. But still it blocked him, and would keep turning him in, back towards the moon – probably hand in hand with a corpse. However, that portion of it that kept routing him back here was a local phenomenon, connected and integral to the trap on the airless Earth below. The thing was directional, almost like a Chinese finger trap, in that the deeper one went, the harder it was to get out. If he could put some physical distance between the core of that trap and himself, perhaps without killing his companion, he might be able to push upslope, at least to jump to Committee Earth. But first he needed to make it to the airless one, and didn't know if a jump that far was even possible. He shrugged, turned back to Jane, crouched beside her, and took up her hand.

'Hyperventilate,' he said.

She looked at him in panic, and then obeyed. He noted that this close, and actually touching her, he could see much more of what was going on inside her – the iconic language in his skull detailing it for him. He saw her oxygen levels climbing, as pick-axes smashed into the door. He gave her all the time he could, until the door finally ripped open and warriors burst in to aim their lariat guns. He even allowed them to fire, before he gasped in a breath, held it, and flung them both into the void.

An eternity passed, with Ottanger and his sister seemingly

hanging in the flaw, in a dark crystal amid masses of clear ones. Then they came down, crashing and rolling on hard rock. He bashed his shoulder and came up into a crouch, dreading what the impact might have done to Jane. She began breathing fast in the oxygen-free atmosphere, eyes wide and panicked. He recognized the Cheyne–Stokes breathing of a body struggling to stay alive. But no time to check anything, or stop, as he focused blurrily on his home Earth and forced them back into the between place. His shoulder screamed, as if he was using it to push against a locked door, then the rest of his body screamed a moment later.

They came out in bright sky, with clouds around and the wind hitting them like a hammer. Travelling too fast and too high. He corrected with another jump, grabbing for a place that looked marginally safe. And this time, with just a stagger and collapse, they were finally out.

'Jane?'

She gave no response externally or internally, or in any way to his sense of her presence. But at least she wasn't dead – just in a deep coma. He staggered upright and looked at the green-houses looming all around, packed with plant life. The path they were on was a narrow one, running between these. With his other sense, he could see they were on a tenement rooftop. This was gang territory, with the protection in the floor below looking to fend off any interlopers from the streets. So what now?

He was beaten. The mere thought of either jumping or jaunting anywhere raised a psychosomatic pain that seemed worse than the ones he was already suffering. But eyeing tomatoes in one of the greenhouses, he saw that here he could recoup at least some of his resources, and then perhaps jump to the nearest SA area to steal medical supplies. He stooped down and took hold of his sister's hand. Again he found he could look deeper inside

445

her this way. Her injuries were severe, with bleeds and broken bones everywhere. As he watched and assessed, he finally understood that her biotech had put her into this coma state to slow things down, and keep her alive for as long as possible. Yes, first he would eat, and then he'd look for what she needed . . .

The feeling of the world wrenching apart preceded a crash and flying glass. A hollow roaring ensued, which sucked away an entire greenhouse, even as he clamped down on Jane and grabbed at welded-down floor gratings. Imbalances corrected and air pressure equalized. Another greenhouse went down, and now he could see across an open stretch of rooftop to the edge. A black mouth had opened there, very like the funnel that had scooped him up numberless times. He could see it in the real world, as well as the structures that pushed it out of the places between worlds. At the centre appeared a pale area, so for a second it took on the appearance of an immense eye, until the figures came into view, moving like deep-sea divers. The thing seemed unstable and kept shifting, while the figures rushing towards the mouth kept compacting together, and then abruptly stringing out, as if seen through a distorting lens. Finally they started to come through.

The first three, one brandishing a lariat gun and two others carrying things that looked decidedly lethal, stepped out with binocular heads zeroed on him. Then they just dropped. They didn't even scream. One managed to scrabble at the edge of the building, before losing his grip and falling after his fellows. And that was it, gone. The eye adjusted and shifted, carving up debris like a cutting wheel to spin about its circumference. The next warriors to spill out arrived actually on the roof. Ottanger stared at them, feeling beaten, no fight left in him. He could jump away, but that would probably kill his sister. Then, with his energy further diminished, these creatures would be on him again anyway. Yet as he gazed at them, he felt a sudden surge of hope. For biotech connections blossomed all around him, and in their synergy raised his strength. He didn't understand it, but still he stood up, raising his machine pistol.

The fast burr of machine pistols ensued, but not from his weapon. Approaching creatures staggered back as armour-piercing bullets smacked through them, raising chunks of their subdermal armour and blowing out fogs of blood behind. A figure stepped into view to his left, and just for a second he thought Inspectorate soldiers had arrived, but the suit looked far too sleek and modern. The woman raised a hand and gestured, and he felt some sense of an order given. A big man stepped into view with an RPG over one shoulder. He knelt and fired, the missile streaking straight into the swirling eye. Then he took the weapon from his shoulder and loaded it again.

'So you're Ottanger,' said the woman, peering down at him through the near-invisible bubble visor over her face.

'I don't believe we've met,' said Ottanger, trying to keep calm as an explosion bloomed deep in the eye, and another missile shot in. He could also feel an odd pressure around him, as he spied the other figures on the roof – they were in some network, and seeking to incorporate him. He instinctively resisted the feeling of subjugation from the core of that network, keeping to his vow of never allowing another to have power over him.

The woman frowned, for on some level she knew he was fighting her. 'If you were to know me at all,' she said, 'it would be as Subject Alpha, but my name is Irene.'

Missiles continued to explode deep down in that glassy black funnel. Hive human debris swirled out, dropping on the roof, and then down towards the street, as the funnel slewed back from the edge. Then, with a crash, the funnel finally closed. The man with the launcher wandered over, while four others closed in.

'Best get out of here now,' he said. 'They obviously have more than one or two of those machines.'

Ottanger couldn't argue with that.

The jaunts were strange. Ottanger could feel Irene directing it, while the others orbited in a subservience he'd already sensed. He clung on, holding Jane, and borrowing their power as they swept around the disrupted manifolds of the hive and onwards. They stopped maybe two times. His memory of that was blurred as he concentrated on Jane, though he did remember some potent energy drink being handed out. At their final arrival point, he could see the residence on the hill and presumed it to be theirs, as Irene brought them out on the flat stretch of a flier landing pad beside the place. Why? Because her degree of jaunt control was imperfect, and she didn't want to bring through a bunch of people somewhere cluttered. The moment they arrived, he stooped down to Jane, still gripping her hand, and peered inside. He noted further bleeds her biotech was shutting down, as it fought to stabilize her.

'I'll take her.'

The man had removed his helmet to expose an Indian face altered by the mutation Ottanger knew well. His accent was thick, so Ottanger guessed he must come from that continent. He focused in on the blood leaking from one nostril and pushed into the man. There he saw similar damage to that in Jane, but he immediately felt the man's affront, that he'd stepped beyond some newly establishing social more, and he withdrew swiftly. Others were opening their visors too, and some taking off their helmets to hang them on hooks on their belts. They were a wide variety of people, but all with the same bonding mutation. And all, he noted, looking weary and leaking blood. The big man with the launcher even had it running from the corner of his eye. They must have been doing a lot of jaunting to have taken such damage . . .

Pranjab

The moment they'd used the connection the Fenris had given them to track the man, Pranjab had felt it. He wondered if Irene could yet too. Or perhaps sense it on her instinctive level. It had been difficult at first, and had taken all of them working in synergy to punch through the manifold generated from the hive moon. And even then, they'd needed to jump to separately distant locations for triangulation. They'd traced a series of the man's jumps – one of them apparently from the moon to the airless Earth – and finally the jaunt to Committee Earth. Then they'd seen the protrusion snapping out from the manifold towards that world, perfectly locating this Ottanger for them. The man had managed a great number of jumps and jaunts, which would have left most of them semi-comatose and bleeding badly. He loomed huge in their network, yet stubbornly failed to connect.

'I'm Pranjab,' he said, squatting down to put his arms underneath the woman who was apparently Ottanger's sister. She felt light as balsa to him – everything did now.

The others moved in around them, intent, saying nothing, and sensing all. Pranjab stood up and studied Ottanger. If anything he was bigger than Chenghu. He seemed to be one of those tall and blond-haired people of Scandinavian descent, for whose kind Darwinian selection had involved battleaxes. His hair and beard were cropped to a single depth, probably by some military cutter he'd obtained along with his other gear, which underneath the Inspectorate jacket only looked familiar in it being military. He appeared more advanced in his mutation than all of them – his pale skin showing the purple-grey colour change, teeth decidedly predatory, claws well developed, and his eyes like amethysts. It was altogether an outward expression of what Pranjab could sense within too, and one word covered it: powerful.

'You all speak English?' Ottanger asked, gaze switching from face to face.

'We do now,' Pranjab replied, 'but it's my second language.' He turned to head for the house, but slowly, with his holosense remaining focused on the man.

'The Committee once wanted everyone to speak the same language,' said Chenghu, moving in on one side of Ottanger. 'They then changed their minds about that concerning ZAs, since a common language can be a unifying force.' Typical of Chenghu, since the man's guilt at being part of the 'system of oppression' inclined him to highlight the things that system had tried to impose.

'Your second language too?' Ottanger asked.

'We learn very fast,' Chenghu replied, perhaps disappointed by the lack of response to his observation.

'And now we need to learn what you know very fast,' said Irene from his other side. 'But we also need to eat and rest. That number of jaunts in quick succession, carrying all our stuff, was hard enough, even with the synergy. And then there was that manifold the hive created . . .' She looked at Ottanger questioningly.

Pranjab smiled at that, feeling her will pushing at the man. He couldn't read Irene's mind, but knew she was probing for information. He understood her need to find out more. Together, dodging around that manifold and tracing Ottanger, they'd struggled with the jaunts. Yet this Ottanger had made at least that many by the time they got to him, and quite likely he'd made many before that without rest and sustenance. Pranjab itched to get a look at his biotech. But for the present he would have to be satisfied with what his iconic inner readout was giving him on the man's sister. And that was enough to keep him occupied for a while.

'I have no more idea about it than you,' Ottanger said,

450

sidestepping what Irene was really after. 'I've jaunted, survived and learned. I headed back home to try to find my sister, then fell into a hive trap made with that thing, and found her there.'

He gestured towards Pranjab with Jane in his arms. Pranjab shivered, feeling a brush of connection with him in the network.

'How did you find her there?' Irene asked sharply.

'Pure lucky coincidence that the hive was using her as a conduit, an interpreter, or perhaps something else I simply don't know . . . some manipulation.' He shrugged.

'And your escape?' Irene asked.

'I destroyed one, or part of, the machine, or machines, that generate that manifold, and then you came. That's all I know.'

'Detail can come later,' she said, her gaze straying away.

Pranjab caught her look of peevish annoyance and felt it in the network. She understood Ottanger was being deliberately obtuse, but that wasn't what was annoying her. She'd put the kind of pressure on him they all felt through the network – that sense of connection – and he'd not responded as expected. As they moved on towards the house, Pranjab tried not to get too far ahead, because he didn't want to miss any interactions. But the doctor in him also couldn't deny that Ottanger's sister needed help, and that he must provide it quickly.

'What happened there?' Ottanger asked, pointing.

He'd noticed where the Fenris's arrival had scooped a chunk out of the side of Caprock, shattering a panoramic window and removing part of a wall and floor. Rubble and broken glass lay on the ground all around it. Pranjab reached a door and turned to see with human eyes Ottanger focused on Irene. But his sense of the network showed him more, as within it the man was *pushing* her.

She snapped her head towards him, startled, and answered quickly. 'The Fenris came. He brought these but didn't have full control of the transport cage.' She gestured to her suit and weapon. 'He told us about you and your companion being captives of the hive. You know about the Fenris?' She was almost babbling and Pranjab noted all the others, but for Chancel, looking at her in puzzlement. He and Chancel locked eyes for a moment. They both knew what was going on.

'The Fenris contacted me and told me what I am,' Ottanger replied smoothly, then obviously decided not to elaborate. There must have been more between this man and the Fenris, and he was keeping his cards close to his chest. He'd sensed the dynamic here, and perhaps understood that if he was too amenable, he might be subsumed under Irene's rule as well. Pranjab reckoned this man would not be ruled.

When Adriana held the door open for him, Pranjab entered. But he still kept the bulk of his attention focused back on the group, through his holosense. A narrow corridor took him to a short staircase, leading down into the main area.

'So much wealth,' said Ottanger, gesturing around once inside. 'What is this place?'

'Once home of a Committee bureaucrat,' said Chenghu.

Pranjab paused and looked at their home with renewed eyes. From a ZA perspective, the interior of the house had a luxury never seen anywhere except on a screen. The window that had curved around one side of the oblate room was gone now, along with part of the floor, and the wall to one side had been ripped away. Stacked beside this were the numerous containers the Fenris had brought, with the look of seed pods or eggs. Many of them stood open, revealing a supply of the hardware they'd raided before heading out. The central pit, containing comfortable chairs, sofas and tables, was bigger than a three-family ZA apartment. The kitchen, dining area and computer stacks occupied a surrounding raised section that could have homed another six families. Pranjab snorted annoyance at having become so quickly accustomed to all this.

Irene moved away from Ottanger, after Pranjab headed for the door down to Medical. Obviously Ottanger's lack of subservience made her uncomfortable, but as ever Pranjab wondered if her knowledge of that was conscious. While Ottanger followed her, Pranjab sensed him *pushing* Chenghu. Momentary resistance gave way to what felt like willing acquiescence. The man had been slowly breaking away from Irene anyway.

'This is a parallel of Committee Earth, split away in some fashion by that airless Earth, by the hive. I don't know what that means, but . . .' Chenghu went on to talk about the plague here, and Pranjab felt shock in Ottanger, and some shift in his pattern of being. The man then continued with the verbal prodding, and Chenghu talked about his own past, and how they'd all come together. The questions Ottanger asked indicated he was sucking up knowledge like a sponge. As Pranjab reached Medical, he couldn't help but grin again. They hadn't rescued a wounded dog, but a tiger.

'So Irene killed the bureaucrat responsible for interrogating her, this Garrick?' Ottanger enquired.

As Adriana opened the doors through the biohazard lock, to let Pranjab into *his* medical area, he paused. This question had been loaded, and he was anxious to find out why. He went inside, depositing Jane on one of the slabs, and quickly turned on the intercom so he could hear the rest of the exchange.

'He deserved to die,' said Irene, as they grouped outside a window looking into the medical area. 'Just like the leaders of the Committee did.'

The additional phrase dropped like a bomb, and Pranjab read numerous changes of expression, just as he noted the doubt behind the supposed firmness of her words. As had been evident when the Fenris visited, she was a few notches out of synchrony with the others – her own doubts undermined her dominance. Her sense of the network had so diminished, she hadn't realized she held no control over Pranjab himself. Because thus far, she'd felt no need to push him, though she did instinctively know she was losing her grip on Chenghu and Chancel.

There was a silent pause, into which Ottanger spoke.

'So it was you who nuked that place.' He looked around at them all, and it was notable how few would meet his eyes. 'Quite a strike against the Committee.'

'It was necessary,' Irene affirmed.

'Indeed,' said Ottanger.

Pranjab had no need to track further reaction to that. Anyway, he had a patient before him to attend to, and in the process learn from. With fast efficiency, he attached up drips and wheeled over the medical devices he'd need to use first. He could get into the other stuff after he'd stabilized her.

'He knows what he's doing?' he heard Ottanger ask, segueing away from the previous subject.

'He was a doctor and, like us all, has only become better at what he did before,' Adriana replied. 'He seems to have an instinct for it.'

'And you are?'

'Adriana.'

It then came time for introductions and, as he worked, Pranjab felt Ottanger subtly pushing, getting potted biographies and perhaps some sense of the others. Even Irene acquiesced, and then looked puzzled when she finished telling her story. Perhaps her instinctive understanding of her dominance had begun to slide into an intellectual one.

'And your story could do with some elaboration,' she then said, this coming out as an angry barb.

Ottanger was handling himself well, but now Pranjab felt a wave of utter weariness from the man. Pranjab had no need to read the icons and molecular models from him, as he was doing from his sister, to know the adrenalin was now running out. And though via his biotech he'd clamped down on his injuries, Ottanger needed food and rest. He chose this moment to play one of his cards.

'My story starts with you,' he said to Irene, 'since in killing Garrick, you're the cause of the riots in which I was arrested. And, as ever with such actions, the reason many thousands ended up dead.' He paused, pushing out to them all. 'I'll tell you the rest later on, but right now we all need food and rest.'

Pranjab felt their confusion as Ottanger turned away. Surely it wasn't for him to deliver such instructions? As he disappeared up the stairs, a brief pause ensued and then they flocked after him. Pranjab smiled yet again, and then dismissed them from his focus. He placed a hand on Jane's forehead and the iconic language rising from her clarified. He grimaced. He had his work cut out, literally.

Ottanger

He kept his feelings to himself, verbally and in the network between them. He'd figured that they must have been intervening on Committee Earth, but still the news about what they'd done had come as a shock. They'd caused the riots leading to his capture, and exploded the nuke that had led to the mess his world was in. He understood their need to do something, and just a few weeks ago he would have considered their actions as rash and destructive as the rebels he'd left. However, the reality of what had happened to *this* world they were on now had him questioning his past decisions further.

The fridge Adriana showed him was full of preserved meats, cheeses, fruit and other concoctions he simply didn't recognize. He knew that in the condition he'd been in before Savarack grabbed him, he would have struggled with such rich food. As it was, he helped himself to an armload of the stuff, then went over to the dining table as others grabbed food too. He gave terse replies when questioned, and asked his own questions, trying to garner as much information as possible. But he was still just mostly unutterably weary. The group swirled around: Chancel and Adriana moving off, Irene distancing herself down on one of the sofas, and Ektian joining her there. Only Chenghu seemed to stay nearby, as if he had some hope of Ottanger. The dynamics were logical in one sense, but odd in another. He felt himself amid solid individualists, whose every instinct was individual, for they were too intelligent to be otherwise, but who were unnaturally welded together. Like the rebels? No, not really.

He ate steadily and methodically, having occasional brief spats of conversation with Chenghu, but his own terseness tended to shut them down. The initial food – some kind of meatloaf – he could feel leaching out into his muscles and bones, as if his guts were dissolving each mouthful before the next. Cheese and dried fruit followed, then preserved sausage and nuts, then a second round from the fridge. He washed this down with a large beaker he filled twice with water.

'There's piles of stuff in the freezers too,' Chenghu told him. 'But no one has been inclined to defrost and cook it yet.'

Ottanger nodded. Apart from Chenghu, they were all ZAs and tended to eat whatever was easily and immediately available, and more likely to spoil. Food had never been a gastronomic experience for them but the fuel of survival.

At one point, with icons and molecular messaging rising to

his skull-aching jumble, he concentrated internally on trying to cut down the noise of it, but then found himself falling into mentally tracking the nutrient flow and demands of his body. He managed to get a grip on it and understood some curious demands, which he then saw would process more speedily with sleep. Eating the foil wrapping on a piece of cheese supplied one of them. Searching through kitchen drawers rendered the answer to another. Using his unnaturally strong fingers, he bent the iron nail he found into a ring, around the handle of a knife, then wrapped the nail in some cheese and swallowed it. Chenghu then told him about when he'd eaten rust off an old car. Finally, icons still surfacing like bubbles in a pool, he knew he'd had enough, so stood up and headed away. He'd already mentally explored the house, found everything he would require, and selected a room it seemed no one else was using. He needed rest, so he could be much more mentally prepared to deal with Irene and the power plays that would undoubtedly ensue. Jane came to his mind too – had she suffered too much damage? He hoped Pranjab really did know what he was doing, but found he trusted the man already. In the room he'd selected, he paused to close and lock the door, before falling headfirst onto a dusty bed and immediately into sleep.

Time passed.

One sharp rap against the door, and the rattle of its handle pulled him straight into consciousness, sitting upright. His eyes were dry but his other sense, what he'd heard the jaunters here name a holosense, immediately expanded. He saw Irene standing out there just as clearly as he knew she could see him.

'We have things to discuss,' she said from the other side of the door.

Reviewing his biotech gave him a sense of time having passed, and checking the watch he'd taken from a dead soldier gave him a comparison to that. He had slept for seven hours. With his internal time sense now firming, he knew he'd never need the watch again. Now studying Irene he saw she had piled her hair up on top of her head in a way that looked messy but had probably taken time to arrange. Her face was made up. She wore skintight leggings and high heels, a low thin top without the benefit of a bra underneath. Having understood her interaction with Chenghu, he was reminded of Jillian and felt a surge of cynicism as he swung his legs off the bed. She had tried to incorporate and dominate him in her network and, that not having worked, she had decided to fall back on a tried-and-tested method. He did not know whether to be angry about that, since he didn't think her conscious of what she was doing and just following through on her biological programming. He mentally stacked and sorted through various ways of dealing with this, and decided he didn't want to deal with it right then.

'I'll join you all out there in a little while,' he replied, and watched.

She stood at the door, features twisting with flashes of anger, disappointment and then finally and contrarily, some hint of satisfaction.

'Okay,' she replied.

Ottanger watched her go and then scanned out into the rest of the house. In their room, Adriana and Chancel were fucking vigorously and he snapped away from that quickly, feeling like a voyeur. Ektian was in the main room at one of the computers, while Chenghu was on a sofa studying a tablet. But they weren't what he was looking for. Pranjab was still down in the medical centre overseeing Jane. He looked tired as he connected up a drip full of milky fluid, and it seemed he'd been working all this time. A nearby stainless steel trolley was loaded with hardware he'd stripped off, and apparently out of, her body. From this distance, Ottanger couldn't look so deeply inside her, but he could perceive the numerous stitches, staples and glued wounds under the dressings, and he did get some sense of how deeply Pranjab had delved. Returning his attention to the trolley, he saw some of the rings that had been wrapped around her bones, and other penetrating hardware, along with the mesh suit. He accepted she was in the best care she could be now. At that moment, Pranjab looked up and turned his gaze directly towards Ottanger. His eyes appeared completely black, but then this faded as he gave an amused smile and turned away again.

While stripping off his clothing and heading into a shower room, Ottanger continued to watch the man work. What was it about Pranjab? Ottanger judged that Irene's perception of the network, and that of most of the others, was on an instinctive level. Yet with Pranjab he felt it to be on an intellectual one. He focused his attention on that network, and perceived it as a microcosm of the overall multiverse. He saw them all as small worlds in orbit of Irene. And yet the greater the substance of each, the less her influence. Pranjab bulked there, with Irene's influence on him being minimal. This model brought understanding and, with a small leap, Ottanger saw it as a reflection of the man's intelligence. So why hadn't Pranjab come to dominance, since he appeared so much larger than Irene?

Once showered, Ottanger found a clean tracksuit in one of the cupboards, but finding no footwear that fitted, he put his boots back on. He next opened some glass doors and walked out onto the room's balcony, then gazed down at the sprawl. He needed a little more time before he could decide on what to do next. His mind blazed with extrapolation, and momentarily he found it difficult to track how his speculations had taken him to where he was. But even then, another thought thread gave him the obviousness of the answer: expanded inner and outer senses had raised his mental activity, from areas of perception that simply weren't human. It wasn't as if he had to accept them as something separate and alien either, for they felt as comfortably part of him as eyes that could see and ears that could hear. He adjusted the microcosm of the group's network in his mind and saw that he bulked largest of them all. This just seemed an inevitable by-product of his greater facility for jaunting. From that, he then followed a thought thread that gave him the answer as to why Pranjab had not asserted dominance here: he didn't need to. The man's greater intelligence had amplified his self-assurance. He was a jaunter who could go anywhere, and he had attained powers that went beyond the human. He didn't want or need power over others too.

Intelligence was the key here. Ottanger saw it reflected in the hive, in Committee Earth, and in thousands of other hierarchies clamouring for his attention. Irene's dominance and the acquiescence of the others was a product of fear, and lower relative confidence and intelligence. Because of these, she wanted control, and they wanted to be controlled. It was rooted in old biological drives. But now he realized it was a hierarchy that couldn't last, with their intelligence, their abilities and their confidence in these growing, as a result of their new enhanced biology. In fact, he could already see the dynamics breaking down. It would be slower with Irene, because of course those who grasped power were usually the most fearful of losing it.

Ottanger turned back inside from the balcony. Everyone but Pranjab was in the main room now, and he was on his way up from the medical centre too. Ottanger still had no idea about his future course, for his ever-busy mind seemed ready to explode as it mapped out far too many options. He headed for the door, knowing events would resolve that course. He then wondered if being able to perceive too many possibilities was why those with intelligence beyond a certain level didn't seek power. He would have to watch that, since thinking and never acting could also be a route to disaster. On that thought he paused, and cycled back to something he'd been avoiding: the reality of this world. He now understood that in leaving the resistance he'd escaped into rationalizing and not acting. The billions dead here, slaughtered by a Committee plague, put the lie to that. The problems and the deaths the resistance had caused could never outweigh what had happened here, and could happen on his Earth. Not acting was unconscionable.

Irene had slung on a military-looking jacket and abandoned the heels for a pair of flashy trainers. He could feel her probing for him through the network, and again recognized it as an instinctive thing as she swung towards him. He also acknowledged that the clothing change reflected her intent towards him: she had only partially concealed it, but it was still there. Abruptly she got into motion and headed over to him.

She gestured to the table he'd first eaten off. 'Get yourself a drink and something to eat, and then join us. There is, as I said, much to discuss.'

She was taking the lead again and trying to re-establish herself. He felt vaguely amused seeing it in the microcosm of the network. Changing the visualization in his mind, he saw her as an amoeba, stabbing out pseudopods to snare others around her. As before, he saw Ektian was the one she had the firmest grip on, Adriana next, while she was losing Chancel and Chenghu. Meanwhile he, and Pranjab who'd just entered, were slick as glass.

At the table, he gazed at the food and drink and again felt a little shocked at such profligacy. Various bottles and glasses were out, a coffee pot bubbled on a nearby counter, while the quantity of food seemed obscene. Nevertheless, he picked at things

461

while filling a plate, then poured what looked like expensive whisky over ice in a glass. He then took this and his plate over to a comfortable chair on the periphery of the others, placing both on a table beside him. As soon as he started eating, he knew that the one plate wouldn't be enough – his hunger doubtless exacerbated by repairs made during sleep, as well as the furious activity of his mind now.

'How is she?' he asked, as Pranjab moved past him holding a plate heaped with food and a beaker of something in the other hand.

'She'll live and she'll heal up,' said the doctor. 'The deeper I delve into the changes the Fenris wrought on us, the more amazed I am. But then I shouldn't need to tell you that.'

'I suspect I know rather less than you.'

'I suspect you know rather more than you admit.' Pranjab gave him a hard, assessing look and stepped over to a chair nearby.

'Perhaps we'd all like to hear about the condition of our other guest,' said Irene, sitting on the arm of a sofa and therefore elevating herself above the rest of them.

Pranjab chewed calmly for a moment, then replied unhurriedly.

'She's recovering. Even as I removed some of those additions from inside her, her biotech sealed bleeds, closed up wounds and routed blood supply to where it was needed. This brought in nutrients, amped up her immune system, and what I'm certain now are nanomachines. It was almost like having an assistant.' He paused, looking thoughtful. 'On more levels than the physical one too, considering the information I was getting.' He tapped a finger against his head. 'Remaining damage will only be memories lost from the procedures on her brain, and perhaps memories she'd rather not have anyway.'

'And what have you learned about those additions?' Adriana asked.

'There are anomalous consistencies, and wide differences between the two technologies.' Pranjab waved a large chunk of cheese as if it might contain them. 'The Committee Earth stuff I could wean out, like the microwave-controlled neurotoxin rod in one rib.'

As the man paused to eat, Ottanger decided it was time for him to interject.

'They started that with me,' he said.

Seven faces turned towards him, and he felt the odd shifting of dynamics. He knew that if he played this in a particular way, he could take control now. He didn't want or need to right then, though, and much preferred that the right answers should arise through this interplay, not by him dominating the conversation. He glanced at Irene, almost giving her permission.

'Explain,' she said.

He pointed to his waist. 'They put a neurotoxin capsule here, with a timed release set to one hour – that release could be stopped by a coded transmission upon my return.'

'How did you deal with it?' Pranjab asked, eyes narrowed.

'I cut it out with a piece of flint.'

Pranjab turned to the others. 'I think I like this guy.'

From this Ottanger felt a subtle encouragement from him: *Take it if you want.*

He continued, 'That was after I took off a mesh undersuit, just like the one Jane was wearing, because it was designed to drag me back to the Complex.' He paused as tension increased, and curiosity. 'Even though Irene here was designated Subject Alpha, I can see you know little about the Complex, the fly pills and their experiments there later on.' He turned to Pranjab again. 'The undersuit you took off Jane was different – more of a permanent solution, just like the neurotoxin rod in her rib. Which incidentally should have killed her when she didn't return.'

Pranjab nodded, then said to them all: 'The neurotoxin rod was effectively sealed off in a fast, violent procedure. Looks like the hive humans simply drilled in and injected a resin to encapsulate it, because it was primed to activate if interfered with. In fact, it *was* activated, but the resin stopped the toxin spreading. To remove it, I'll probably have to take out a chunk of her rib. But this will grow back, as is the case with all of us.'

He let that comment rest for a while as they absorbed the implications. How much damage could they survive and regenerate from, Ottanger wondered. How long could they live?

Pranjab continued, 'It took me some time to get to that, along with the other internal tech, because of the procedure to remove the suit. It was effectively bonded to her skin with meta-material hooks and glue.'

'We need to hear more about this Complex,' said Irene, now pushing. 'Especially taking into account what the Fenris said . . .'

Ottanger ignored her, keeping his focus on Pranjab, and asked, 'And those anomalous consistencies you mentioned?'

Pranjab acknowledged this with a nod and reluctantly put down his cheese. 'I can distinguish the technology of this Complex from that of the hive, but there are similarities between the two technologies that, to my mind, go beyond parallel development. The mesh suit, for example, is definitely of Committee Earth, but it uses alloys and meta-materials that ape those of the hive tech wrapped around her bones.' He paused for effect. 'As if those on our Earth had seen hive tech and sought to copy it.'

'That's because,' said Ottanger, 'hive humans have been to our Earth before, and some were captured or killed. They showed me autopsy pictures of them during an interrogation, after my first jaunt.' He noted those around him wince, because they all knew what interrogation meant.

Irene pushed harder and, because he saw no reason to block her right then, he allowed it. He next felt the urge to elaborate on everything he'd said, and to share information with her, which amused him.

'On our Earth, I was part of the resistance,' he told them, and felt something in the network like a sharply indrawn breath. It was another thing he could use as a dominance play, but he didn't, and went on to tell them his story. Now he felt no urge to edit but, recognizing this came from Irene, he still did. He glossed over the extent of his abilities to jaunt and jump, and how little it affected him, until he was fighting the hive manifold. Nevertheless, he couldn't hide it all from such intelligent people by any other means than lying, for they'd extrapolate the gaps in his story.

'After escaping, I made it to the surface where I'd detected their machine, and then blew it up with grenades. That disrupted things enough for me to jump with Jane to the airless Earth and then jaunt to our Earth, where you found us,' he finished, wincing at the large omissions there. He now expected detailed questions to clarify his escape from the hive moon. Thankfully Irene quashed them before they started, since she'd been getting edgy and uncomfortable about him being the focus of attention for too long.

'The Fenris has told us the hive is a danger,' she said abruptly. 'We've seen for ourselves that it is, and that its aim is to obtain the biotechnology inside us. At the very least, we need to stop that.' She focused on Ottanger. 'The research on Committee Earth seems to be established in one place, where they have all these inocular flies, their researchers and their data.'

'Indeed.' He nodded, knowing precisely where she was going with all this.

'Seems to me,' she addressed them all, 'that the hive wasn't

465

yet organized before, making mistakes when its warriors came after me, and later sending the post-heads for Pranjab. But judging by what happened to Ottanger, it's getting more efficient now. And since it has been to Earth before, it likely knows about the inocular flies there being a source of the fenris biotech. So it'll almost certainly focus its attention back on our Earth. That Complex would be a jackpot of resources for it. As I said, they have the flies, the data, the researchers and no doubt more jaunters. And now, under Inspectorate control, the operation will be expanding.'

'So what do you suggest?' asked Chenghu, in response to her mental prod.

'I suggest that we burn it all down,' Irene replied.

18

The Fenris

Ottanger's escape from the hive had been illuminating, not least because it showed the amazing strength and capability of the man. But now the mass of data the Fenris had gathered through Ottanger's senses shone a light on so much more. The fusion flash of the explosion from the device had lit up the moon for a fraction of a second, and what it revealed had probably not been visible to Ottanger. It took the Fenris some time to wean it out of the data too. But now he knew that the hive did indeed go right the way to the core of the moon and, as he'd estimated, was over a trillion strong. The engines that generated the manifold were spaced equidistantly all around, just below the moon's crust. But it was the one Ottanger had jumped to that the Fenris focused his attention on.

Ottanger had been intent on destroying the thing, subtly shifting his jumps there to take in the disposition of the hive humans arrayed against him. He chose to see what he saw – his mind honing down what it obtained from his holosense. However, that sense covered everything, and using what he'd taken from it, the Fenris could now examine the machine in detail. The

467

technology used a different route to its goal, but in effect was much the same as mothballed portions of the fenris engines. These penetrated the multiverse to transport material objects through it. The fenris had transported themselves and their technology this way when first exploring that continuum. But later, via their biotech, the fenris had shifted that function over to individuals of their kind, using synergetic mass transports and transport cages instead.

The hive had obviously not taken that route. It simply hadn't been an option for a culture like this to devolve such power, responsibility and necessary intelligence to its specific members. For the hive stayed together in precisely the opposite fashion. As he'd seen by what lay in the hive humans' skulls, individual intelligence was not a priority, while responsibility and power resided in the overall consensus intelligence. So what would it do? Sure, right now it was after fenris biotech, but supposing it obtained it, what then? Having seen others develop the means of travelling between multiverse worlds, it would stay in a counter-threat mode. He had no doubt that, now stirred into action, it would spread. And like the massed hives in their war, it would seek to incorporate or exterminate others. The Fenris still needed soldiers to stand against this threat, but then realized his thoughts had been straying away from present responses and he pulled them back.

Judging by the increasing strength and penetration of the manifold, not all of those machines on the moon had been up to speed. But they were swiftly getting there. Already his biotech underneath that frigid ground of the airless Earth was becoming increasingly difficult to access because of this. It would result in the hive having greater control around itself and, by extension, of Committee Earth and its near parallels. He needed to do something about that, not least because of the dangers it would represent to the jaunters' mission to 'burn everything down' at the Complex – a move he thoroughly approved of. He made his mental demands and began pulling up data that, from his perspective, was for technology millennia old.

It was like moving from the examination of an artificial cell and its workings to that of a steam engine. So much of the hive's technology was about brute energy – punching between worlds rather than sliding between them like jaunters. He modelled the hive machines and their effect, and saw its chaos lay in an incomplete array of them. And, in being insufficiently networked, they were prone to feedbacks. Meanwhile, he transmitted orders to bring the same old technology in his engines back up to speed. An hour later, he had what he needed: a hole hovering out from the orbit of the fenris world, programs queued up, and reconstruction in the engines underway. At present all he could do was open a tunnel through to one location, but that was all he needed. For the response would be predictable. So now, with everything prepared, and seeing the jaunters getting ready to set out too, he thought about a confirmation he'd been avoiding.

It was time to ask some questions.

Ottanger

Back in his room, Ottanger pulled up his sleeve and inspected his arm. The wound was now almost invisible. The device Pranjab had used had just been a squat cylinder externally, with a button on top. He'd passed it over Ottanger's arm until it beeped, then pressed it down. After a brief spike of pain and a trickle of black blood, Ottanger had felt the ID chip dropped into his palm. He'd stared at the glassy little capsule then let it fall and crushed it under the heel of his boot, aware of all the others watching him, aware that he had become completely one of them. Now it was time to put on their uniform. He stripped off his old clothes, then pulled on the padded undersuit, before moving on to the armour. This reminded him of the tech assistants cladding him ready for a jaunt from the Complex, but now his purpose was very different indeed.

Arguments had ensued from Irene's suggestion to target that place, even as she'd pushed to make it much more than that. Hadn't the Fenris shown them how their previous intervention only made things worse? But their intervention before hadn't been with a specific outcome in mind, beyond the deaths of world leaders. Still, it could cause chaos! Could things on Committee Earth get any worse, really? Anyway, now they'd been made aware of a greater danger in the multiverse that needed to be countered: they had to shut down or destroy everything concerning fenris biotech on their home world, to keep it from the hive. And so it had gone on.

He pulled on the armoured oversuit, closing the front seam up to his neck. The boots went on next, loosely at first, but when he attached them to the leg armour they shifted, changed shape and closed up to fit his feet snugly. He stood up, shrugging, then as Chenghu – the military man – had instructed, he pressed a control over his breast. The suit closed up like the boots, fitting perfectly, but when he moved, he felt tight restriction.

Ottanger had listened to their discussions, made a few non-committal interjections and closely observed the dynamics. Ektian of course agreed with Irene, and that complemented her weight in the network, as she first incorporated Adriana, then steadily convinced Chenghu and Chancel. Pranjab stayed out of it, as non-committal as Ottanger, and seemed to be waiting for something from him. Ottanger did know what he wanted to do, but wasn't prepared to offer it just yet, and was in fact too interested in all this interplay to intervene. Finally, when Irene showed a flash of anger and he saw this germinating in the others, he'd understood. Their connection wasn't telepathy but a more elaborate form of empathy, which had then become a hierarchy. Also, as he'd noted before, with stronger individuals the hierarchy dissolved. Thereafter only empathy would remain. As the anger increased, cycling between them, he'd decided it was time to speak up.

'She's right,' he said, pushing himself into Irene's orbit. 'The Fenris implied that you shouldn't concern yourselves just with one world, when intervention there leads to more chaos and death anyway.' Ottanger paused, thinking about the mounded dead rotting all over this Earth beyond Caprock, then continued, 'But with the hive able to access as many worlds as us, this isn't only about the one world.'

'You see,' said Irene, gesturing to him and resenting it at the same time.

'But I should also say that's all a bit high flown, and I'm going no matter what you decide,' Ottanger added. 'That fucking research needs to stop, and there'll be people there to release.'

'Are we agreed, then?' Irene asked, pushing again, with Ottanger's weight behind her now. Anger and argument died. Pranjab had just looked at him briefly, black eyed, then headed back down to Medical.

'So we must make our plans,' Ottanger had said into the silence.

Ottanger picked up the pack next. It contained the power supply and other key things – a medical kit and some subsidiary items for the other equipment they'd be taking. The bag was a rectangular block, with just two tab straps he used to sling it on his back, then holding the straps in position at his shoulders. Once in the right position, it bonded and, pushing the tabs down

471

against his shoulders, they stuck in place too. Its power supply also connected, and now he could move with ease. The suit, powered up, could 'assist' his movements as well. Chenghu had demonstrated this by picking up a heavy table and holding it straight-armed in front of him. Ottanger wondered if the man could do that without suit assist, since they were all so much stronger.

He tucked the suit gauntlets in his belt and turned his attention to the helmet. It fitted his head snugly, while the neck covering, which could be pulled down from it, then bonded to the neck of the suit automatically. The visor folded down from the crown, and was designed to bond too. The suit was airtight, and connected to a highly compressed air supply in the pack. He was ready and he'd had some time to think things through, without the distraction of the others around him. He'd decided he would just play along for now, demonstrate no superiority, and allow Irene to run it. He headed out.

First off, he avoided the others and went down to Medical. Pranjab was in there with arms folded, while he studied Jane pensively. Ottanger went through the clean lock, then over to her slab, and gazed down at her. She was still out of it but looked a great deal better now. In fact, she looked like his sister again. He noted Pranjab had stripped away a good amount of the support gear, and all that remained was a nose plug feeding oxygen and some anaesthetic, as well as two drip feeds into her arm, one for saline and another for some liquefied food, and finally a catheter arrangement below. Peering inside her, he saw that the technology remained and noted the changes there.

'Your assessment?' he enquired.

'Do you need it?' Pranjab asked.

'Yes, since this work has been your focus and not mine.'

'As I said, she'll recover. I stopped removing the hive tech in her because it seems her biotech is dissolving it, or incorporating it, and with a lot less damage than surgical removal would cause.' He studied Ottanger carefully. 'One must know when to intervene and when to leave things to run their course.'

'Yes, that's very true,' said Ottanger, knowing his amusement showed.

'But interventions may be required,' said Pranjab, obviously not talking about Jane any more.

Ottanger nodded. 'The base facts are unchanged: Committee Earth and what it ultimately becomes – the hive – are abominations we need to do something about. Irene's hard approach has its merits and its large drawbacks. We must also consider that the Fenris is not all knowing . . .'

'Born from an artificial womb. And now, as far as we can gather, as much as a hundred and fifty years old,' said Pranjab blandly. 'Yet, only recently acquiring the jaunting abilities we possess. What does that tell you?'

Ottanger rolled this information through his mind. He'd already learned that Ektian's changes had accelerated with puberty, and it was notable that none of the jaunters he'd seen, alive or dead, were children. He speculated on how long childhood lasted for a species a million years in the future. He then considered the mistakes the Fenris had made, and the actions he'd taken.

'It tells me precisely what you expected it to,' he replied. 'That the Fenris may . . . be in error.'

'And I sense that error may be war,' said Pranjab flatly.

'A doctor's analysis,' Ottanger noted. 'But I agree. We mustn't allow authority to take us along the wrong course. Fierce intelligence doesn't imply wisdom.'

'Good talk,' said Pranjab. 'Shall we join the others?'

Only Irene and Chenghu were there when they arrived. Chenghu had brought out further toys, and they were scattered on the tables and furniture at the centre of the room. As Ottanger walked over, the man turned to him.

'You've used weapons before,' he said. 'These are somewhat different, though.'

'I'm sure I'll get the hang of them,' Ottanger replied drily. Then, catching a whiff of disappointment from the man, he added, 'But show me anyway.'

'Okay, close up your helmet.'

The short assault weapon looked half-melted – all smooth curving lines. A bead ammunition clip attached on one side of it, and the energy package on the other. He had spares in his pack, but Chenghu doubted he'd need them, or that any of them would need them, because the clip contained a thousand shots. To ensure they didn't kill the wrong people, Chenghu had asserted master control over the weapons, so they'd shut down if pointed at any of them in the group. A targeting frame came up in Ottanger's visor – all very simple. The same frame appeared for the sidearm, but it fired single shots and had a mere one hundred in its clip. Low impact, apparently, so probably wouldn't penetrate the bulletproof gear the soldiers wore. The grenades put up a timer in the visor. He could alter the timing using a wheel on the side of each cherry-sized device. A click down on the wheel set the timer running.

'I'm giving these to you because, well, we might encounter more than expected,' said Chenghu. 'But otherwise don't use them. They won't shut down if close to one of us.'

By now the others had arrived, and Chenghu turned to them. 'I have master control and have set the weapons so we can't fire on each other. Everyone else is viable.' Frowning, he gestured to two flask-sized cylinders on the table. 'It doesn't really matter.' There was no need for a transport cage, for the devices were light. None of them had been sure about the tech inside these cylinders, though they had speculated on antimatter. Chenghu, checking the screen instructions on one of them, had found out their yield, and commented that he hoped this fenris tech would be more accurate than the tactical nuke they'd used before.

'And those we apparently don't want to kill?' asked Irene, a slight sneer in her voice.

'Be careful where you shoot.'

'We may not need those devices anyway,' said Ektian. 'Once I gain access to their system, I'll find all we need to know.'

'Secondary, off-location backup,' said Adriana.

'It's a standard protocol to have one. I should be able to find it.' Ektian shook her head. 'A map location will be enough to get a contingent of us there.'

'Irene, myself and Ottanger,' said Chenghu. 'We don't want you taking down the system and initiating some kind of safety data distribution, so you stay in the Complex.'

Ektian nodded curtly.

They all collected their weapons, and Ottanger felt they looked more efficient and professional than the soldiers they'd soon face. They were also superhuman and intelligent, for the biotech was continuing to change them in the same way as it was changing him. He studied them all – their tall frames and narrow faces, those violet or red eyes. They didn't really look human any more.

'So I guess we're ready,' said Chenghu. 'We're all clear on what we need to do, and why?' He looked in particular at Ottanger when he said this, as if for permission rather than out of doubt. Ottanger nodded. Oh he was very clear.

'On my lead, then,' said Irene, and it sounded like a challenge.

Ottanger shrugged agreement. He looked over at Pranjab, slightly surprised the man had decided to come too. Pranjab nodded to him, watching on so many levels, and waiting.

He'd been dragged along with them before with Irene leading, but the sensation was different this time. He could feel her pushing in one direction and he went with it, fighting the urge to insert himself into the jaunt more firmly, knowing he could seize full control, but still reluctant to reveal the extent of his power. He didn't want control anyway, at least not yet. And he knew that once they understood his real capabilities, they'd end up falling in around him. That hierarchy wasn't so much about dominance, but submission.

One moment they were in Caprock, then it quickly grew insubstantial and they were falling down to the sprawl. This seemed to change as they fell, sprouting and dropping towers, rashes of low buildings spreading in some places and dying in others. Then they were on the ground in what looked vaguely like a street. The buildings here were carbon trees, tangled with chrome strangler figs, and the street had many levels, formed in boxes of some gridlike structure. A multi-limbed robot, like the by-blow of a giant spider and industrial machinery, was heading towards them. Irene took them off again and the buildings twisted into glassy spirals. Then night fell, sweeping all away into infinite black. Not having seen so much variety in the transitions before in his jumps, Ottanger analysed and understood. They weren't just seeing whole worlds but reflections, shadows and parallels amplified through the lens of their synergy as a group.

When the lights came on again, they landed, staggering in a bright desert. Ottanger watched a raptor dinosaur raise its head from a mess of blood and bone, hiss at them, then begin backing off. Chancel fired into the sand in front of it and it ran away.

Ottanger thought about the mosasaurus he'd seen, and realized the diversion in the course of multiple Earths had in some cases been tens of millions of years back and resulted in the circumvention of the asteroid extinction event for some.

'We all good?' asked Pranjab, touching below his nose and at his ear, his fingers coming away dry.

'I need a moment,' said Adriana.

Agreement on an emotional level came from the others. She used a tissue to wipe blood out of her ear. Chancel wiped blood from his nose and turned away in annoyance. Surveying them on multiple levels, Ottanger saw the ruptured blood vessels, and biotech squirming to cut the bleeding and make repairs. He also noted that the internal damage was in inverse proportion to their weight in the network, and from this realized that it wasn't an energy thing but a mental one. Their expanding intelligences gave them more control, and it was the lack of control that damaged them during jumps. Pranjab had sustained very little, Chenghu and Irene too. Ottanger, inspecting himself inside, saw no ill effects at all.

They sat or squatted on the sand, pulling out drinks bottles and nutrient bars. Adriana, after wolfing down two bars and draining a bottle, sat in a meditative pose with her eyes closed. She'd gone into a brief doze, closing down her energy-hungry brain so her biotech could get on with the job. The respite lasted half an hour, before Irene's impatience began to infect them all. She stood up and began pacing.

'Are we ready?' she asked tightly.

A further long jaunt ensued to a jungle, and then to mountains where they rested again. All the others had their damage this time, and Ottanger noted the speculative looks cast in his direction. He could feel their puzzlement and query in the network, except of course from Pranjab. Catching this, he

477

sought ways to block it, as he dropped leadenly to the damp ground, pretending weariness. He doubted anyone was fooled. They ate from their supplies while commenting on the fairy city lying in the distance, jutting up through a layer of cloud. Everyone then slept for a while, and ate and drank again, until the time finally arrived.

'This will be nasty,' said Irene.

She was talking about the hive manifold lying ahead, but to Ottanger the nastiness really lay beyond that. He looked down at the weapon attached to the front of his suit and knew there would be no choice but to use it – Inspectorate and military guards would ensure that. He and the others would have to kill to ensure their own safety, while grabbing the people they needed to. And he knew that for those cases, more than defensive violence would be required, because those people wouldn't want to answer questions. He didn't like it, but precisely what he didn't like was debatable. Was it the killing? No, he didn't like the fact that on a base emotional level he *did* like the idea of *justly* punishing the people in that place.

They launched from the mountaintop into the places between worlds, and soon began passing through the manifold. It seemed as if trains or giant worms rushed past them. Maelstroms rose all around from every angle, and even those beyond four dimensions. They passed between the surfaces of turning spheres, or worlds, and the whole buffeted them, throwing them outside of a set course – trying to push them down to the moon. The network linking them, and creating their synergy, strained and twisted. He could feel this feeding back into Irene, and her growing pain, as well as that of the others, as she struggled to hold them all together. He maintained his place, and held off doing more. And then, as it seemed they were about to break apart, Pranjab intervened to take the strain, shunting Irene aside. Ottanger still held back, until he could feel even the doctor suffering and beginning to lose his grip.

It was time.

Ottanger slammed Pranjab aside, grabbing up the cords of the network and pulling them all in close. He could feel the manifold snatching at him, but he tightened up their connection, fully utilizing their synergy, with him as prime. The manifold effect became like a storm wind – he could feel it, but it had no strength to stop him. He arrowed down through it and out, no longer following Irene's map but his own. For even those early jaunts from here remained etched in his mind, and he zeroed in easily, hurtling them in over the Atlantic into continental America, down towards New York, then sliding aside from there.

The Complex came up at him – his perception of it was a firm shape, a core within a mass of growth. Coming partially out into real-world perception, he then saw the changes. The Complex was still there but the grounds around it had been levelled. New foundations had been put down in some places, and in others large emergency-use buildings had been erected. He saw too that a road had been opened through the sprawl beyond, without any thought about urban planning. Buildings had been dropped and dozered aside. He wondered if they'd bothered clearing the resident population before doing this, and with his mind reaching out at the thought, he saw that they hadn't. The road had obviously been made to provide access for massive cargo transporter trucks, which even now were being unloaded.

'What is this?' Pranjab asked through the ether.

'The original Complex was military and now the Inspectorate project has been moved in,' Ottanger replied, gritting his teeth against the anger – against the disregard for human life he knew he was shortly going to have to adopt.

'I see,' Irene ghosted in, for they could all see the uniforms. 'Be ready, people.'

Ottanger noted her attempt to take back power, after being pushed aside first by Pranjab and then himself. He felt the need to push back again, but resisted it, slowly easing away and handing the reins to her once more. She took them eagerly and they fell down on the Complex. Perception filled with dull colours and shapes, steadily gaining substance. They arrived in the laboratory with a snap, and immediately focused away from the multiverse and onto the locally real. Three of them came down on tables, the rest scattered about the room. As Ottanger took it all in, one of their weapons thrummed and crackled. A soldier spun and crashed into a wall, leaving sprays of blood, before sliding down. He felt something hit him, turned and targeted, but the soldier there shuddered, his combat gear flinging out wisps of bloody shock fibres, and he dropped.

'Stay sharp!' Chenghu bellowed.

Two techs stood up from their workstations. Ottanger had them in his sights, but hesitated long enough for Pranjab to send them staggering and bloody.

'We do or we don't,' Pranjab said.

Ottanger spun, targeted and fired a short burst, throwing an Inspectorate guard back through a door. He'd hesitated because the first two had been military and the researchers were civilians, but in the end it didn't matter – none of them were getting out of this place alive.

'Ektian,' said Irene, as Adriana and Chancel moved towards one of the two room entrances. Ektian was already over by Savarack's consoles, pulling out a chair and undoing her pack. She connected up a DNA drive to record the entire system, then set to work.

'Chenghu,' Irene pointed to the doorway, even as the man

was already heading over. When Chenghu glanced at him, Ottanger nodded and set out after him. Irene and Pranjab had their section to cover, while he and Chenghu another. Chancel and Adriana would stay to keep watch over Ektian as the woman hunted through the computer systems. They needed to move fast, before too much resistance had a chance to build up.

Everything here seemed hauntingly familiar, yet slightly dislocated from his mind. Like returning to a childhood home in late adulthood. Two soldiers appeared at the end of the corridor. Without hesitation, he targeted and shot the one on his side, while Chenghu took down the other. As they moved on, he thought about just how many people he'd now killed and didn't feel great about it. All were victims here. But, staying coldly rational, he knew the two hadn't come to check on their well-being. They approached a corner and here their advantages played out, as Chenghu glanced at him and shrugged.

'Well, that was quick,' he said.

They halted at the corner, knowing that just around it and down the corridor, four soldiers had put a tripod-mounted machine gun in place. Chenghu pulled two grenades from his belt and flung them down there. Two bright blasts ensued, then he rounded the corner, Ottanger right behind him. A fire burned, and insulation snowed through the smoke. They ran on, stepping over dismembered bodies. Ottanger paused to look at two of them. They wore military uniforms but with black Inspectorate armbands.

They worked from room to room, kicking open doors. Chenghu went first, and usually by the time Ottanger came in there was no one left to kill. Kick. Another door. Chenghu yelled as Ottanger stepped in after him, and he felt a wash of agony down one side of his body, then a moment of recognition. His second interrogator, the man Axel, was drawing an automatic from a shoulder holster. Two other 'crats attempted to hide behind the desk. Ottanger put five shots in Axel's chest, blowing his ribs out of his back and tumbling him over the desk. He then turned and put his next burst into the inducer above him, which had disabled Chenghu. The man responded at once, firing low, splintering the desk in two bursts and shredding the two grey suits there.

'Fucking things,' said Chenghu, looking up at the shattered inducer.

Indeed, Ottanger thought. The device had come as a timely reminder of what this place meant, and a warning too that even though they could see through walls, they still weren't invulnerable. They moved on again, with techs and 'crats running away, and only opening fire when necessary. But any reservations Ottanger had brought here were gone now. He felt the callousness thickening on his mind, almost like biotech growing on his bones. Scanning ahead, they could easily see where they needed to go, but of course they had to go carefully. Coming to the refectory, they brought down four soldiers trying to set up another tripod-mounted machine gun outside.

'Targets located,' said Chenghu, shooting out the glass of an internal window. That wasn't for Ottanger's benefit but for Irene's. Ottanger threw himself at the shattered glass, aware of Chenghu directly behind him. He shouldered a table and rolled free. Two bursts brought down two more soldiers, and then she was before him, weaver stance, pumping shots at his chest that only staggered him a little as he closed, then slapped the weapon from her hand and slammed her face-down on the floor. Jillian.

A tech flew past him – one he recognized as the guy who'd clad him by the sphere. Spine broken. He put a foot down on Jillian's back and, as shots hit his armour and didn't penetrate, he turned, bringing down another soldier. He turned again, feeling a wash of pain, but Chenghu shot down the 'crat wielding a handheld inducer. Movement. Swinging back, he saw a figure scrabbling for the weapon of the soldier he'd brought down just before. He released a burst into their white-coated back. As his finger came off the trigger, he recognized that figure, the weapon falling from her hands. He'd seen it many times when she left his room after examining him.

'We got them,' said Chenghu, hauling Colonel Jones to his feet and shoving him ahead. Ottanger stooped and, grabbing Jillian by the back of her jacket, hauled her up too and pushed her ahead. He felt angry now – not because he'd killed Dr Alison, but because he existed in a world of such cruel necessities.

'Is that you, Ottanger?' Jillian managed.

It surprised him that she recognized him, but he didn't answer.

As he and Chenghu brought their prisoners back to the laboratory, Irene and Pranjab arrived with Savarack and Murcheson. They all looked scared, and Murcheson appeared particularly pale and frightened – his bald head sheened with sweat. Ottanger pushed Jillian down in one of four chairs placed in a row, while the others were also seated. Pranjab, his expression cold, took out a bunch of plastic ties he'd found and efficiently set to work. Murcheson fought it, until in a fast move Irene stepped over and shoved a gun barrel in his eye.

'Ektian?' she enquired, retracting the barrel once Pranjab was done.

'I have the Complex system isolated, so nothing is going out. Following some leads on the backup location, but it's taking some time.' Ektian grimaced and looked over to the prisoners, before returning to her chore.

'We need the information quickly,' said Irene. 'How long?'

Ektian flung her hands up. 'I don't fucking know.'

'Then we must go to our other source.'

Chenghu glanced at Ottanger, concern writ there on his face. Ottanger could feel the eyes of the others on him too, and particularly those of Pranjab. In the network – vaguer now after the jaunts – he could feel the shifting and jockeying. They now considered him to be the most capable of them, and he could feel something horribly like obeisance filtering through. They wanted him to take command and instruct them, and this angered him. He recused himself – pulling away – and snapped the threads of need. The triumph in Irene's expression lasted just a fraction of a second, then seemed to wind down through sadness and disappointment, before flaring to cold rage. She turned to the prisoners and stepped forwards, removing her helmet and hooking it on her belt.

'I am Subject Alpha – you may still recognize me,' she said. 'I have questions to ask you. Answer them and you live. Refuse to answer, and I will hurt you until you either answer them or die.'

They stared at her. Ottanger had to admit she was a formidable sight. He also noted how her approach resembled that of the hive, and felt some misgivings return.

'You will kill us anyway,' said Jones.

Irene drew her sidearm and shot his kneecap off. Ottanger jerked. Did it have to be this way? Jones shrieked and then just sat there groaning. The others transitioned to terror, with their fears confirmed.

'Where are the inocular flies and other materials of that nature kept, and where is your backup data store for this project?' Irene asked calmly. 'Answer now or else another of you loses a kneecap.'

They looked around at each other, panicked. Irene gave them just a moment, then moved forwards again. Making precisely the choice Ottanger would have made, she put the barrel of her gun against Savarack's knee.

'No! Wait!' Savarack shouted. 'I'll tell you!'

'Talk fast,' she instructed.

'The flies are here in this Complex. Coded storage.' He nodded to one of the doors. 'They're down at the end, before the medical area. You need my handprint and retinal scan to get in.' When he finished saying this, he suddenly looked even more scared. Because, as he'd no doubt surmised, his hand and his eyes didn't need to be attached to his body to be used for that.

'Should we take them?' Irene shot at Chenghu. 'As they're easily accessible?'

Chenghu nodded. 'The blast will fry this place, but some kind of safe might survive.'

She turned back to Savarack. 'Do you know the location of the backup storage?'

He shook his head, dumb for a moment, then began babbling, 'They didn't want me to know, said I was a risk. It's military and some in the Bureaucracy know.'

'Right about the risk,' said Murcheson.

Irene turned calmly and shot him through the head, spraying his brains over Jillian, who let out a scream, then quickly choked it back. Ottanger stared at the slumped man, someone he held responsible for so much, with an odd mix of emotions arising. He also noted that Irene had made a stupid mistake. She'd killed Murcheson to scare the others into talking. But as head of the Inspectorate here, he would have been the one most likely to know the location of any backups.

'Pranjab,' said Irene, pointing to Savarack.

Pranjab flicked a glance at Ottanger, shrugged, and came over to cut Savarack loose, then haul him off to collect those flies. As he watched them go, Ottanger knew that would be the last time he saw Savarack alive. Pranjab might be a doctor but had already demonstrated his commitment to their course. This was all so utterly savage, and necessary? Ottanger tried, but he couldn't make the emotional connection to the danger the hive represented. Perhaps it was a facility he had yet to own.

Irene next stepped over to Jones, who was sitting with his head down on his chest. She slapped the barrel of her gun against his ruined knee. He yelled, his face clenched up with pain and tears running out of his eyes.

'Where is the backup data stored?' she asked.

He looked up at her and said succinctly, 'Fuck. Off.'

Irene shot off his other kneecap and waited for him to finish yelling before saying, 'Why so intransigent? Do you admire what you serve?'

'I have family,' he managed.

'No one will know you resisted.'

He looked up at the ceiling. Irene smiled coldly. 'Ektian has isolated the system so nothing recorded by the cams here will be seen.' She pointed to the two cylindrical objects Chenghu had brought along. 'Only one of those is needed. The yield of each is five kilotonnes.' She brought the gun barrel down against his elbow. 'Now talk.'

Closing his eyes, he just started repeating, 'Fuck you! Fuck you!'

Irene transferred the barrel to his skull and blew his brains out.

'And that leaves you.' She turned to Jillian.

'I can tell you where it's kept,' Jillian said quickly. She looked to Ottanger as she spoke, her expression pleading. He glanced to Irene, who'd just killed the last of those who might have been able to tell them about the backup, and wondered if she knew Jillian was lying.

'It's okay, guys,' said Ektian. 'I've found it – we don't need them.'

Irene shrugged and raised her gun. Ottanger decided he'd procrastinated for long enough. Irene had made too many errors.

'Prisoners, the other jaunters here,' Ottanger said succinctly, meanwhile pushing back into their network.

'Yes!' Jillian shrieked, while staring at Irene in terror. 'There're things you don't know!' When Irene hesitated, Jillian turned to Ottanger. 'Your sister is here!'

Irene jolted, but it wasn't because of Jillian's obvious lie. She looked around, almost in panic, again reminding Ottanger of her merely instinctive grasp of her dominance. He felt her confusion at his incursion in the network, and the consequent anger rising from it as she swung her gun back towards Jillian. By then he'd moved up beside her. He closed a hand on top of the gun and pushed it aside.

'The prisoners,' he stated.

Still Irene seemed confused and just a little lost, but then managed to salvage something from her fractured ego. She pushed his hand away and rested the weapon back on one shoulder.

'Keep talking,' she said to Jillian. He took a pace back, confident she'd dropped down in the hierarchy below him, because she dared not point the weapon at Jillian now.

'They're in the cells,' Jillian said quickly. 'The doors are—' A shot rang out and she looked to where Pranjab had taken Savarack. Jillian closed her eyes for a second, and Ottanger knew what was going through her mind. They were going to kill her, definitely when they discovered her lie about Jane. She opened her eyes. 'The doors are coded but I can open them.'

Quite, thought Ottanger. Even though Jillian fully understood they were going to kill her, right now she was alive, and wanted to stay that way for as long as possible.

Irene holstered her weapon, picked up a box-cutter from a nearby desk, and went over to cut Jillian loose. She then pulled her to standing. Ottanger could feel Irene at war with herself. She wasn't sure if she was doing this on her own authority, or at his behest. Meanwhile, Pranjab returned carrying a large sample box under his arm – the inocular flies. His expression was grim as he took in the scene, nodded once, and went over to lean against a desk.

A brief silence ensued as they all felt the change in dynamic. Ottanger caught Chenghu staring at him, and when he returned the look, the man pointed towards one wall. Focusing out, Ottanger saw the activity beyond the Complex. Many who'd been inside had fled out that way, but now others were coming in. They must have been barracked out there in those new buildings, as they hurried in slinging on bulletproof gear and checking weapons.

'We've got maybe ten minutes,' said Chenghu. He stepped over to the two cylinders, stabbed at the console of one, then picked it up and stuffed it into a cupboard.

Another hiatus ensued, and Ottanger knew it was time to step fully into command. 'Irene and I are going for the prisoners. The rest of you deal with the backup.'

Chenghu just nodded and picked up the other cylinder. Ottanger turned back to Irene. 'Bring her.' He gestured at Jillian. Irene looked bewildered again, but still shoved Jillian ahead of her to the exit. Pranjab stepped over to Ottanger, holding up the case of flies.

'Turn round.' It was more of a request than an instruction.

Ottanger turned and felt the man putting the box of flies into his pack. He understood the reasoning of this perfectly. Those who went after the backup had a marginally lower chance of getting out, but it was also an acknowledgement of his authority.

Pranjab slapped him once on the shoulder and muttered, 'About time,' and turned away.

Ottanger quickly headed after Irene. Jillian, walking ahead, tried to go as slowly as possible, until Irene grabbed her shoulder and hauled her forwards faster. Glancing back, he saw the others moving closer together, and felt the tug of the jump as they winked out of existence – a sucking thump of air rushed into the place they'd occupied. The network tether to them snapped taut and thin, and as a consequence, this highlighted the dynamic between him and Irene. She looked back at him, wary and still puzzled.

As they moved through corridors riddled with gunfire, and scattered with corpses, he thought about that network connection. It was implicit in their biotech, but how far did it reach? He'd already known things in the hive that were affirmed by the jaunters, like the descriptions 'post-heads' and 'warriors', and he felt sure those had filtered through from them. He understood that this had been the binding force of the fenris civilization. But there was no civilization now, just the Fenris, alone and distant, and making decisions with fierce intelligence and knowledge, but perhaps little wisdom. He then surveyed further corpses and thought about the meaning of the word 'civilization'.

He'd not been keeping count, but in retrospect realized they must have near depopulated the core of the Complex, except for those who'd managed to flee or hide. Outside he could see that those who'd escaped were being detained by part of the force there, while the rest of the Inspectorate soldiers were coming in.

'Down here,' said Jillian, finally indicating a door. She pressed a hand against a reader and lowered her head for the device to scan her iris in a flash of red. Nothing happened. She tried again and still no response. She looked round in panic.

'Your attack . . . it must have locked down!'

Ottanger could see what lay beyond the door and considered just jumping them through. But he didn't know what automatics might be in there. Before he did, almost as if keying off his thoughts, Irene stepped forwards, taking a flat round case off her belt. Chenghu had covered this in his weapons briefing. Ottanger stepped back and let her get on with opening the case, and unreeling explosives like chewing gum sticks. She detached a number of these and stuck them around the door, then ran a finger over each to push up a touch slider control. She finally grabbed Jillian and pulled her off to one side. Ottanger stepped to the other side as she pressed the button at the centre of the reel.

The explosives crackled, flaring with arc-bright light. As he swung round to look, the door toppled down a stair within. Irene shoved Jillian ahead, over the door, then stooped down behind her to use her as a shield, with her weapon pointing over her shoulder. The stair led down to a corridor, with cell doors running along one side of it.

'Maybe I can open them from here,' Jillian said, indicating the same retinal and palm lock as above. She looked desperate now.

'Try to open them all,' said Irene.

Obviously delaying and drawing out every moment of her existence, Jillian placed her palm carefully on it, then stooped to have her eye scanned. Next she worked a touch screen. As a clonking sound echoed all along the corridor – with the lockdown clearly not extending to down here – Jillian quickly turned to them. 'You don't have to kill me,' she said. 'You're obviously here to shut this down. I don't know much, but I could find out if anything of value is kept anywhere else.'

'Could you indeed?' said Irene.

Ottanger meanwhile moved to the first cell door.

'Ottanger,' said Jillian. 'Surely what we had means something?'

She was trying to keep her voice level, but couldn't disguise the pleading. Ottanger looked around to see Irene giving him a questioning look. The impression now from her was that of a subordinate, though a professional one.

'What we had,' he said, 'was you thrown in as part of a concerted attempt to buy my loyalty, and keep me onside.' He glanced into the cell. 'But I have little doubt that, even had I been a good obedient subject, I would still have ended up like that.' He stabbed a finger into the cell.

Irene grabbed Jillian's jacket and dragged her forwards. The interior of the cell was larger than his one had been at the internment camp. The subject lay on a slab, clad in a mesh undersuit, which had wires leading to it from various devices in the room. More wires and an assortment of tubes entered her skull, which had been shaved, and had chunks excised from it. Moving closer, Ottanger peered at the holes, seeing them filled with clear gel, through which he could see the surface of the brain. It was webbed with organic-looking electronics.

'We have no time for this,' said Irene.

He nodded. They had no time for medical interventions, no time to rescue these people with care. But maybe the biotech of the Fenris could help here? He put his weapon down on a pedestal device from which most of the tubes ran. Then, as rapidly as he could, he began unplugging everything from the woman's body. Her eyes flashed open as he did this, and she began moving, her hands up as she swiped at things he couldn't see. Suddenly she sat up, stared at him with a kind of dead-eyed assurance, then abruptly started convulsing and rolled off the slab. The violent movements lasted only a few seconds, until she lay there shivering, eyes open. Ottanger picked up his weapon.

491

'The others.'

They went from cell to cell unplugging the five of them who were also there.

'Where's my sister?' Ottanger asked casually, but then felt disgusted at his cruelty. 'She's not here.'

'I'm not part of this,' said Jillian hurriedly. 'This is Inspectorate.'

Ottanger studied her. Maybe she was telling the truth. And of course, everyone here, whether ZA or SA, had to obey their orders or face the consequences. But he'd seen her sliming up to Murcheson, and doubted she raised objections during any discussions of their procedures here. She was just like all of them who'd been in the audience watching his jaunts – power-hungry climbers. Also, if she wasn't part of this, why did the locks here respond to her?

The two in the last cells had obviously been further along in the process, or at some critical stage. When their convulsions ended, they sighed away their last breaths. Ottanger checked the pulse of the first one and tried some CPR, but the man didn't respond at all, and blood started running out of the holes in his skull.

'The Inspectorate wanted control – utter control,' said Jillian.

'And these are all you have here?' Ottanger asked.

'Yes, though thousands are lined up in camps ready for when . . . they have the equipment ready.'

When the second one died, Ottanger didn't try to revive her.

'We take them with us.' Ottanger nodded back towards the other cells as he spoke, looking across at Jillian, who was back against the wall with her head bowed. She looked up abruptly, hopefully, took in his expression and bowed her head again.

'We can try,' Irene replied. 'Just so long as their own abilities don't interfere.'

They turned to head out, but paused because he and Irene could both see what lay in the corridor without. Ottanger glanced across at Irene as Jillian continued to the cell door. Something of his thoughts and anger cycled between them, and neither of them stopped Jillian as she stepped out. Shots crackled in the corridor, and Jillian pirouetted in a spray of blood, going down. A second later, almost like a conjoined weapon, Ottanger reached low round the door jamb, with Irene high, and they fired simultaneously, without having to use their eyes to find the target. The soldier there staggered backwards as they stepped out, and went down on his backside. He sat there, stomach a bloody mess, trying to reach for his weapon that'd fallen out of his reach. Ottanger walked along the corridor, seeing one of those he'd freed coming to the cell door, already looking better, apart from those holes in his skull. Reaching the soldier, Ottanger kicked the weapon further away, then said, 'Hello, Yorgos.'

The man looked up, face white, panting as a pool of blood spread out around him. Ottanger turned away and walked back. The others were all out of their cells, not moving too well, but at least moving. He looked beyond them to where Jillian lay. She'd left a trail of blood in her slow crawl to the blank end of the corridor. Irene looked round too, then shrugged and turned back.

'Time to go,' Ottanger said.

19

The Fenris

Worlds passed under his feet, and scenes from them passed through his perception in detail now, as far out as two clear kilometres, and distinct enough beyond that for thousands more. Finally he slowed and stepped through into the place where he'd arrived so impactfully the first time at Caprock. He eyed the open grub form in which he'd brought the weapons and armour here, and walked on. He had to duck through the side door and stoop all the way along the corridor, but was at last able to stand upright again upon reaching the medical centre. He gazed through the viewing window at the figure lying on the bed, equipment arrayed all around it. Glancing at the side access door into there, he winced with annoyance at its small size, and so jumped instead again just a few metres, coming in to loom over the bed.

Pranjab had done all he could with the medical technology available and the Fenris was impressed with how much. According to the recorded data, Ottanger's sister had been snared in trawls the Inspectorate carried out through ZA sectors, checks they'd instituted even before the two jaunt research complexes were combined. It hadn't been her identity that

494

alerted them, but that she possessed the visible 'mutations', though that wasn't the correct word. They'd only discovered her relation to Ottanger after that. Even now, thousands like her were being moved to relocation camps and queued up for transferral to the place Ottanger and his crew were currently storming. Unusually, they were receiving better food and treatment in the relocation camps than they were accustomed to. But of course, they'd now become useful.

Jane had then become part of the Inspectorate jaunting project. And she'd been one of the first to be given the meta-material mesh suit – the technology for which the Inspectorate had evidently got their hands on following a hive visit to their Earth. Shortly after that, the Inspectorate had shared this suit tech with Savarack too, because he'd been the best mind for the job, and they'd been certain they'd be taking control of the military complex soon anyway.

He walked over to a table, hooked a claw into the mesh suit Pranjab had removed from her, and raised it. Studying it with his holosense, he quickly understood its workings. Yes, it was hive technology that acted on whoever was wearing it to amplify their homing instinct. For the hive, that meant drawing its members back to whichever incursion they'd passed through, and thence to the hive. For jaunters, the effect was more subtle, acting on their inner biotech homing instinct, which enabled them to return safely to an original location when first getting to grip with their powers. He dropped the thing. All of that was immaterial to his purposes now. He leaned forwards, grasped Jane's arms, and drove in his claws.

This time there was no necessity to cut himself in order to deposit blood on those sharp points. The claws, just like the entirety of his body, could be adapted to purpose and now, through what might also serve as poison glands, he injected his blood into her. It quickly began to spread through her system, lodging itself in the required places in her biotech. The feed then came back swiftly, its iconic language relaying to him her condition. She was recovering fast, as they all would now from the most extreme injuries. She'd only remained unconscious because Pranjab had rigged up a steady anaesthetic gas feed. The Fenris pulled out the tube running into her nose and stepped back.

'Wake up, Jane,' he said.

Her eyes snapped open, but it took her a moment to focus on him. She startled, her yell truncated into a simple grunt, then the accelerated thought and calculation edged in. He smiled, because it was always good to see an intelligence firing up like this. Then he regretted what he must now do.

'Who are you?' she asked. 'What are you?'

He gave her the pat explanation he'd given to all the others, and then segued into recent events and how she'd ended up where she was. It was enough, because he only needed to give key points and then watch her extrapolate from each. He reckoned by the time her body and biotech had fully recovered, she'd be a strong match for the others.

'But you missed me,' she said accusingly, when she'd heard him out and ceased to ask questions.

He shrugged, holding his hands out to the side. 'I did what I could.'

'Not enough.'

'I will do more for you all, but now I need you to do something for me.' He felt ashamed about that, because it appeared he was offering her a choice in the matter, when he wasn't.

'What?'

'You were a conduit for the hive,' he explained, meanwhile linking back through his massive biotech in the ocean here to the engines of his world. Back there, they began their first operation of drilling a hole between worlds, but not breaking through as yet. The tunnel, narrow as a finger, was already stirring up activity in the manifold but hadn't yet approached anywhere critical that required an energetic response from the hive.

'Yes.' She nodded tightly and then flinched, though whether because her head hurt or at the painful memory he couldn't know.

'And I want you to be a conduit again.'

Her response was immediate and succinct, 'Fuck off!'

The Fenris sent an instruction to his blood inside her and it dropped her into unconsciousness once more. Why had he woken her to try to talk her into volunteering for this? His self-contempt offered the answer: if she'd volunteered, he wouldn't have felt like such a shit doing what he was about to.

His blood, swimming through hers, reached into her skull and there he took control of her biotech. Pranjab had been skilful with his surgeries, but hadn't taken the risk of opening up her skull to remove the bioradio, so in the end it was a simple task to reactivate it and set it broadcasting its carrier signal. The problem was getting that to where it needed to be.

He received the signal in his own body, then rebroadcast it to his ocean biotech and thence back to the engines around his world. Upon receiving this, and his next instruction, the engines pushed the narrow tunnel on. Via the feedback, he saw it snap through, beyond the hive moon's orbit, but not so far as to produce more than a fractional delay. The manifold, surprisingly, didn't respond further, nor was there any response from the hive on the moon for long minutes. When it came, he ensured it was free of malware in his engines, then allowed it through. Jane's eyes snapped open again and she abruptly sat upright.

'What are you?' she said, and he knew it was no longer her looking out of those eyes.

'That is not necessary for you to know, but I'm sure you'll work it out in time.' As Ottanger had noticed and the Fenris had noticed through him, the hive's vocabulary and understanding had increased swiftly, and he didn't suppose it had lost that yet.

'You are the originator,' said the hive.

'Yes, I am the originator,' he replied.

'What do you want?'

'I want peace and tranquillity, but it seems I cannot have these because of your aggression.'

Jane just stared and blinked as the hive mind processed this. He wondered what it was having difficulty with – perhaps the terms 'peace' and 'tranquillity'.

'We are eternal,' said the hive. 'All threats to that course must be countered.'

'I am not a threat to you, and nor are the jaunters you've been killing on your Earth.'

'You are a threat that must be countered.'

The Fenris felt a flash of irritation and continued tightly, 'In what way are we a threat to you?'

'You have technological advantage.'

'That does not make us a threat.'

'Threats must be countered.'

'How can I convince you that we are not a threat?' he asked.

Again the long delay and the blinking, then the hive replied, 'Give us your technological advantage.'

Now it was the Fenris's turn to mull things over. The hive's view of reality was a simplistic thing but, for all that, not necessarily wrong. Those who had an advantage could be dangerous and were therefore a threat. The intentions of those others had no bearing on the matter. He considered his options – making promises, making threats – and dismissed them. The hive would see others with any 'technological advantage' as a hazard, no matter what. But if he handed over jaunt biotech to it, it'd become even more dangerous than it was at present, with no guarantee that it'd cease to consider him and the jaunters as a threat after that. And anyway, he had no intention of giving it *that* advantage.

'I can't do that. I cannot trust you,' he replied.

Just one blink then, 'Give us your technological advantage or we will cause you pain and damage.'

The words aped those it'd spoken to Ottanger. Analysing the exchange thus far, he could see no room to manoeuvre, no ploys or plays, and no chance of negotiation. He grimaced, for he'd expected this, but it had been worth a try anyway. Finding alternatives to the use of force required imagination, and that was something the hive as a culture had sacrificed long ago. With a thought, he shut down the contact, even as the malware and viruses began to arrive. Jane slumped back onto the bed and, after checking on her, the Fenris turned away, depressed by the certainty of what was to come.

He jumped to another location outside the residence, the world whipping past and through him, until his tread came down on spiky brittle grass along a sea wall, beside a massive container-storage facility. Inland he could see a couple of large containers seemingly dissolving into the ground, wrapped in the white snakes of biotech. His arrival, immediately having been sensed, boiled the sea. He turned towards it as, near the shore, an underwater slab of flesh rose up and protruded two jointed tentacles ending in hands, much like his own, with eyes in the palms. He wondered then at the design of this, for it'd not been his own – some conceit of one of his ancestors.

Immediately moving his perspective to inside the biotech, he sensed its great mass and all the things it could do, as well as produce, and he felt tight regret. But he then shoved this aside. Though resources such as this would be needed as conflict grew, the jaunters' base was here and would surely be lined up as a target by the hive. He sent instructions and the biotech began its process of self-destruction, starting out in the sea. As with his biotech on the airless Earth, he simply couldn't allow the hive to grab hold of this and reverse engineer it. However, as it destroyed itself, he directed it to gather fissile materials from its massive spread, and route them to the inshore biotech. The stuff on land he then gave different instructions. There it began retreating from the surface of the Earth, and retracting its spread. It would maintain a foothold on this world, a link he could utilize. But he also set it up to trigger atomic obliteration the moment anything interfered with it, even if he went out of contact. As he turned away, the sea boiled behind him and lianas of biotech collapsed into dust ahead. Meanwhile the biotech underground started forming an egg-like shell of metal, and filling it with a deadly explosive load.

The Fenris returned home to find his defence system already in operation, for it seemed the hive had worked out who he was. Four holes had opened in the firmament even closer to his world than before, and they seemed a great deal more stable than the last ones – further confirmation of the hive getting its machinery up to speed. The first fusillade of missiles showed up as a glowing cloud of vapour across vacuum, having been destroyed some minutes before he returned. The second came through even as he arrived. With a hollow feeling inside, he walked across the control deck of his engine and sat down in a sensory throne, making his connections.

The next missiles came in with the explosive acceleration of the first lot, burning solid fuel boosters. The defences responded, webbing vacuum with bright yellow beams and explosions. This attack puzzled him, because the hive had to know it couldn't succeed. He then understood the reason, as other holes opened a moment later.

The biotech brain of the sun tap informed him of them, as it diverted just a small percentage of the energy it routed to him into its own defences. The cloud of missiles hardly had time to leave the hive's manifold before focused solar radiation turned them to glowing fog. Bright white lasers then flared from the sun tap, to disappear into those holes and blow up something far back inside them, and they winked out of existence. The Fenris stared. This had been an intelligence-gathering exercise. Then he felt a stab of fear, because he had no idea what intelligence had been gathered. He'd need to study this more closely to divine the hive's next likely moves. However, before that, he had to make pre-planned moves of his own.

First he turned his attention to the biotech growing underground on the airless Earth. He'd wanted to retain it to shunt on any entrapped jaunters, but that was rapidly ceasing to be a useful option. There had been no one since Pranjab and, with research about to be shut down on Committee Earth now, there'd be no more. He hoped that no inocular flies survived there either to push the 'mutated' through the final step in their evolution. He'd also wanted to retain the biotech there as a spy on the hive, but with its abilities and technology steadily increasing, that was becoming too dangerous. It might detect the biotech and seize it before the Fenris could do something about it. Also, because of the dearth of energy and materials there, it wasn't something he could usefully weaponize against the hive. It was time for it to go away.

Linking into the tech fully, so he occupied that subsurface realm while peering out omnisciently from there, he checked out the situation. Activity on the hive moon was evident, even without magnification, for the temperature had ramped up there, and it was putting out a lot more infrared. Magnification showed movement on the surface: old damage being excised and new structures going into place. The flow of hive humans at work resembled rivers moving along deep channels. Withdrawing from that, he concentrated on the biotech itself. It had retreated to just below ground, ready to react to new jaunters, and on the surface it had completed its previous chore. The corpses there were now all hollow shells, only retaining their shape because of the injection of aerogels and carefully placed carbonate structures. He sighed, once more regretting his task, then gave the biotech an instruction he'd given to it before.

The thing had no consciousness and was in fact just an extension of his own mind and body, but his regret seemed to be reflected in it, as though it were a separate personality, and a faithful servant dispensed with. Faithful it remained, however, and his instructions were processed. Out at its furthest reaches, chemical energy stores began to combine and react destructively. Filaments of biotech simply collapsed into dust, from their terminal point to their source. Ribbons and sheets of the stuff smouldered out of existence like fuse paper. Larger tentacles and trunks collapsed in on themselves, like corpses in accelerated decay. The sensation was horrible for the Fenris, for it wasn't only like part of him dying, it actually *was* a part of him dying. With sensors near the surface the first to go, he soon lost sight of the moon. And from then on, his perception of the biotech's surroundings diminished to the point almost of introspection. Last to go were the neural nodes and larger neural structures. As each went out, it felt like explosions of shadow in his mind. At the last, he disconnected and came back to his view of the multiverse through himself and his engines, and this had become like a painting scrubbed of colour. No matter.

With the last of that biotech turning to ash, his next instructions were to the engines around his world and had them generating their long tunnel towards the hive moon. With luck, the hive would think this another attempt to communicate, when in fact he'd summoned some cylinders from storage, similar to but larger than those ones the jaunters had planted, ready to explode, on Committee Earth. Now, loosely linked via his implanted tracker within Ottanger, he saw it was time. With a nod, just for himself, he made the final instruction. It was a tacit acknowledgement that war had really begun.

The tube abruptly extended and widened out, while the systems within one engine propelled the cylinders through it. Transit time was fractions of a second, and it took the manifold just about the same time to respond. Almost like a tentacle lashing out, the thing knocked his tube aside, its exit point folding out into reality far away from the moon. However, he saw he'd still managed to get one of the cylinders through as a bright detonation gnawed a chunk out of the moon's curve. Further detonations then occurred out in space, in a line thousands of kilometres long, before the tube collapsed and went out. Feedback flared in one engine and, with his wider vision, he saw an explosion there too, lifting up a scale of its hull and spewing debris into space around his world.

This attack had the predicted and necessary effect. The manifold retracted around the moon protectively, wrapping it in a shield impenetrable to jaunts, and only permeable using the tube method, which would now require the application of ruinous amounts of energy. This meant the hive would be unable, for a while at least, to grab the world walkers.

The Fenris sighed and rested back in his throne. He'd expected to feel glad at having finally taken this step, but he didn't – he felt nauseated. With a cloud of horror growing inside, he estimated the damage he'd caused to the hive. The fact he'd taken out far below one per cent of the population, and even less of its resources and abilities, didn't negate the reality of him just having snuffed out hundreds of thousands of lives. He then shuddered and forced himself out of the introspection into which he'd been sliding. It wasn't as if they were truly *human* lives.

The first real blows of the war had been struck.

'Your move,' he said tightly, trying to acquire a cold, pragmatic martial sensibility with the words, but failing.

Ottanger

They linked hands in the corridor, while above them the sounds of movement and shouts of, 'Clear!' filtered down to them. Ottanger of course took the lead for their jaunt, reaching out to encompass them all. Irene complemented him, strengthening the field, while he also felt the mismatched instinctive attempts of the three erstwhile prisoners to do the same. Ottanger included their efforts, enhanced and guided them, and Irene fell in with him. It was a form of communication, but without words – only a perception of the flows of energy.

The world grew thin around them, then seemed to flood in, surrounding them like a thick fog. In a between place they'd slid underground, and if they were to rematerialize here, it would have killed them at once. His alien senses rebelled, even as he thought about this. It would be akin to stepping off a cliff, or walking into fire, which wasn't to say it couldn't be done. He hauled them up into the Complex's building site, passing through a fast-moving armoured car like mist, and then higher and higher relative to their departure point. There he held it, expanding his view of the Earth below, because he needed this completion.

Time ticked in his skull down to zero. White brightness opened in the centre of the Complex and expanded to encompass that core. The blast wave whipped out, flinging temporary buildings ahead of it, and rolling the heavier cargo transporters. It hit some surrounding sprawl too, peeling off composite slabs and windows from the nearest buildings, and dropping two more, before dying in dust and smoke as the central boiling explosion rose on its hot stalk. The blast had been a lot more surgical than the previous bomb that'd hit the heads of governments. But, like most surgery, it took out more than just the cancer. Ottanger allowed his guilt to rise at the pain they'd caused to the innocent. Next, he brutally suppressed this as an emotion he couldn't afford, and wondered what he was becoming.

The second explosion opened its distant eye, highlighted by the jaunt he felt there just a moment before. But this also brought to his attention other blasts opening here and there, all around the planet. The Committee takeover was still continuing. He grimaced at that, and took them away, their surroundings fractionally darkening into nothingness before, from a zero point, the multiverse exploded into view. As he'd surmised before, his perception of all this had previously been an interpretation through a linear mind, but now he was seeing and encompassing more elements that defied description in human language.

He felt the three ex-prisoners expressing confusion and their connection threatening to break. But he clung onto them as he mapped ahead, even while one of them seemed to have slid into a cycle of repeated attempts to materialize. Weighed down by this load, he dreaded the manifold, yet the thing seemed to have collapsed to a point that lay out of his path. He puzzled on this, and saw that it'd retracted in multiverse terms to the region

505

directly around the hive moon. It had become defensive, and it didn't take much deliberation to realize the Fenris probably had something to do with that.

He followed the course they'd taken on the way out. The stopping place they'd used slid into range, and he felt Irene's slight tug towards it. He swiftly tugged her back and took them on, now no longer feeling any need to conceal his ability. Far clear of the manifold, the woman who kept trying to materialize began disrupting the network. He could have continued to drag her on with no problem, but knew that her efforts would likely kill her. So he chose a location and brought them out.

A rocky slope came up at them, a glaring line cutting ahead and smoke boiling above. The woman, making another attempt at just the wrong point, screwed the transition and they came in a few metres above the slope and at an angle, landing and tumbling.

'Fuck,' said Irene, pulling herself upright. 'You could have chosen somewhere softer.'

Ottanger spat grit from his mouth – it tasted salty. The air was sulphurous, and up above smoke boiled into the sky from the low rumble of a volcano. He turned to the glare, feeling its heat on his face like desert sun. A river of lava was running down over there, and that was why he'd chosen this place.

As he stood up, he returned his attention to his companions. The man they'd rescued got up onto his hands and knees, then rose fully. One of the two women was standing too, but the one who'd caused the disruption lay on the ground thrashing, expression terrified. He went over to her and rested a hand on her torso to explore within, and this seemed to calm her. The iconic language he saw expressed in great detail just how much of a mess she was in. The mesh suit connected to her skin had partially activated to force her out onto a world. He examined it deeper and found himself extrapolating its function, realizing that the explanation given to him when he'd first seen this thing had been complete bullshit. The biotech within them keyed off their own minds, looking for the familiar, as a safety function. This was all part of its initiation to prevent new jaunters killing themselves – it was an instinctive push to arrive back into the real at ground level, and in parity with the motion of a world. The mesh amplified that effect. And the partial activation of it had kept pushing her to return to the familiarity of a world. If she was to survive their journey, this couldn't continue. So what to do?

He felt Irene stepping forwards before he saw her squatting beside him. The sequence between them operated in the same way as it had when they'd both allowed Jillian to step out into that corridor – no words and no coherent communication was necessary. On the empathic level, she knew what he wanted and sought to provide it. She uncapped a short cylinder and pressed it against the side of the woman's neck, who a second later sighed into unconsciousness.

'We'll take her as cargo,' said Irene. 'No problem.'

He nodded, reading her expression and more besides. It surprised him to find no resentment there, and instead relief. This then connected to earlier reactions when he'd seen sadness and disappointment. She was actually glad to have had the responsibility taken away from her, despite her initial struggles for dominance. The interactions between the jaunters were so obviously rooted in evolutionary psychology, biology and the natural hierarchies they engendered. She'd needed to take control because of her history and desire for safety, but mostly because she was the strongest of them all. The necessity had also raised resentment and bitterness, however, because old biology had made her feel she shouldn't be the strongest. He noted with a degree of cynical amusement that she now seemed a lot more feminine to him. His thoughts segued into how this related to the Fenris. Its driving psychology and biology were a million years further on, yet it still connected to them via the empathy – not least because some, like him and his sister, contained its DNA. How was the Fenris affected by old hierarchies that his kind had supposedly outgrown?

'They gave us numbers,' said the man abruptly from behind, snapping his thought train. 'After you, they added numbers to the Greek letters.'

Ottanger stood up and turned, Irene rising and turning just a fraction of a second later, as if drawn by parallel strings.

The man pointed at the woman on the ground. 'They labelled her Theta Six.'

'How're you doing now?' Ottanger asked. It was a throwaway question, as he peered inside the man and the other woman to see for himself. In both of them, he could see biotech veins and coils shifting around their wounds, and even observed new bone forming in the holes through their skulls. He was glad of that but predicted problems. As they regained their function, so too would their mesh suits. And just as with Jane, the things could only be removed with surgery.

'Learning fast,' said the man, with a hint of a confident smile.

Ottanger nodded, then looked at Irene.

'Just one thing to do,' he said, noting she'd taken two more of those cylinders out of a pocket in response to his fears.

He headed over towards the lava flow, where he unhooked his pack and removed the box Pranjab had shoved into it. Popping it open, he peered at one side neatly filled with all the black and white capsules, while the other side had clear containers packed with dead flies. Moving closer to the lava, with heat trying to blister his face, he turned the box over, tipping out its contents. These flared and burned, raising a stink and more heat to drive him back with watering eyes. He tossed the box after them, wishing that would mark the end of people becoming numbered experimental subjects, but knowing that not to be the case. As the box began spewing flame, then melted, he turned and headed back to stand over the prostrate woman.

'We need to get out of here,' he said, gesturing the others over. The man and the other woman linked hands, then he carried them all away.

Jane was sitting on the edge of her bed as Ottanger walked into Caprock's medical centre, carrying the unconscious woman, with the rest following behind him – Irene supporting the other woman. She'd found herself a set of paper overalls and watched them expressionlessly, then abruptly got off the bed. Ottanger nodded an acknowledgement and laid the unconscious woman down on it. Irene left the other woman leaning against a pedestal-mounted scanner, while pulling other beds out of storage in the walls. The man stumbled over to one and sat on it.

'I can feel it pulling me,' he said. 'The world seems like tissue.'

Ottanger could sense it too, with the effect on them also transmitted through to him, making him feel forever on the edge of a jaunt. It was a constant effort for him to maintain the network and stop the three of them slipping away.

'We need Pranjab,' said Irene.

'Cut them,' said Jane.

Ottanger glanced at her. From the moment of their arrival, she'd appeared to attach herself to the network as an adjunct, while her status varied. She wavered between being as high up as Pranjab, then down below the weakest of them. Her highly active biotech and biology was still repairing damage, but mostly centred on the bioradio in her skull. He'd assumed the biotech was trying to get rid of the thing, but closer inspection revealed otherwise. It was attempting to incorporate it, and bring it under her control.

'What do you mean?' he asked.

His question panicked her, but then her expression changed to frustrated anger. She turned and headed over to a sterilizer on a side counter, opened the door, and pulled out a tray. From this she picked up a probe and a pair of snips.

'The hive . . . me do it,' she said.

Ottanger simply nodded and gestured her over to the man. He now understood her frustration. The bioradio was attached to the language centres of her brain, and all the activity around and in it was messing with her ability to talk. She reached up beside the man's head and, using the probe, levered up something in the hood. Inspecting with his internal vision, Ottanger saw her reaching for a wire that ran to one of the circular patches he'd thought were for monitoring. Hooking a loop of it through the mesh, she snipped it. The thing sizzled and the man swore, jerking his head away, but Ottanger immediately felt a reduction in the pull. The man showed puzzlement for a moment, then turned and presented the other side of his head. Ottanger exchanged a look with Irene and the both of them quickly went over to the drawers containing more surgical tools, then got to work. With each cut and sizzle, the world solidified around them. And then something penetrated that world.

Feeling the arrival, Ottanger peered up through the house at the other jaunters who were appearing in the main room. His network immediately snapped out to include them. Their return journey had been quicker, likely because Pranjab had led it. A second later, the doctor blinked out again, then reappeared with a thump and waft of burning in Medical.

'I'll take it from here.' He put aside his weapon and eyed Jane. 'And you can assist me.'

Ottanger nodded, walked over to drop implements in the sterilizer, then headed to Jane and put a hand on her shoulder.

'We'll talk later,' he said.

Jane shook her head, reached up and grabbed hold of his hand. 'Wait.' She reached up to tap a finger against her skull. 'Bioradio.' She took a breath, and he could feel her drawing together resources, concentrating intensely before continuing, 'The Fenris came. He used me . . . to speak to the hive.'

'To say what?'

'Assessment . . . an attempt to negotiate. The hive is . . . intractable. It wants our biotech and will not stop.' The words were flowing faster now. 'I think it just confirmed what he already knew. There will be war.'

Ottanger suppressed the urge to question her conclusion, because he had no doubt her assessments now had a clarity beyond the conventionally human, and he felt the same. He glanced over at Irene, who was watching with a grim expression, some hint of her assertion and urge towards violence impinging on the network. He transferred his gaze to Pranjab, who looked up from attaching a drip to the unconscious woman. Pranjab nodded agreement with Jane's statement, but also with something else beyond that. The last time he and Ottanger had spoken down here a subliminal *consensus* had come into being.

'Help Pranjab now,' Ottanger said to Jane. 'You can give me detail when you're better.' He withdrew his hand from hers and turned away to head up to the main room.

The others were feeding themselves – sprawled on the furniture with a selection of food and drink, whose only similarity was quantity. He headed over to the kitchen area, gulped down a carton of some unidentifiable fruit juice, then picked up any available food and began eating, refuelling, hardly noticing the taste. The jaunters all looked physically and mentally tired, but

Ottanger saw that they'd all toughened up. None of them had bleeds this time and, reaching out mentally, he could now raise iconic analysis of their condition in his mind. Their epigenetic adaptation to their biotech was in turn making fundamental changes to their DNA. This cyclic process would result in them becoming more like him; in fact closer to becoming fenris. He also noticed little offence was triggered at his inspections of them, because the social more that'd been formed in that respect was hierarchical too. The only one who might have looked askance at him was Pranjab, who by dint of having stepped somewhat beyond his old biology, made his position in the hierarchy a matter of choice.

'So we've destroyed jaunter research there. What now?' Irene had loaded a tray with food and followed Ottanger down into the main area.

The question opened out numerous courses of action in his mind. For they were powerful, and there were hundreds of ways they could frustrate the hive, or attack the Committee further. Yet as he sat down and reviewed them, his mind flashing through perfect logical constructs, running them through to their completion, he discarded each in turn. He continued to eat his food, feeling their expectation.

'First you need to know what Jane just told me.' He looked around at them, assessing. 'The Fenris came here while we were gone, and made contact with the hive through her. She says the hive is intractable and won't stop until it has jaunter biotech. There will be no negotiation.'

'Fight or flight,' said Chancel, surprising them all by speaking out.

Ottanger studied him while continuing, 'We had a hard time getting to Committee Earth because of the hive manifold, yet when we left it was retracted defensively. The Fenris did

512

something and I surmise that, from his side, the fight has already begun.'

'That doesn't necessarily clarify our position,' said Chenghu, looking up.

'There are many things we can do,' Ottanger replied. 'Presupposing our understanding of the situation is correct. Presupposing basic premises are correct.'

'You have doubts?' Chenghu asked.

'I told you I was in the resistance,' Ottanger replied. 'What I didn't tell you was why I left the resistance. I quit because the actions we took didn't lead to a better world, but in fact worsened the situation for many, and resulted in the deaths of many others.' He focused on Irene. 'Actions have consequences, as you know. What I saw in microcosm in the resistance, you saw on a larger scale when you killed Garrick, and then when you assassinated world leaders.'

Irene winced then said, 'But that's Committee Earth – the same paradigm does not necessarily apply to the hive.'

'Is that because they're not human?' he asked.

This instantly troubled her and she lowered her eyes.

'Inaction has consequences too,' said Chancel.

Ottanger looked with amusement at the man – in his terms, he'd become almost chatty. 'Yes, I am painfully aware of that too.' He gestured at their surroundings, taking in the world they occupied. 'My reasons for leaving the resistance are no longer valid in light of what happened here, and could happen on our own Earth. Inaction is unconscionable. If we'd not acted today, thousands would have suffered in the name of jaunter research. And we have, I hope, eliminated at least one imponderable from our calculations. However—'

There he stopped. They all stopped, because they could all feel it. Ottanger stood up and focused out on the multiverse as it seemed to crash in around them. It grew dim to him, as his holosense truncated, and as their actual surroundings darkened. The world became stifling. To test this he threw himself into a short jump, but it felt like swimming through treacle – much more difficult even than when he'd been jumping in the hive moon. He came out of it standing at the gap where the Fenris had smashed the window, and looked up as the others rushed up behind him by more conventional methods.

'That does not look good,' Chenghu observed.

The Fenris

The hive had made its next move, and the alert, coming in through his biotech, almost came as a relief to the Fenris, after the tension of waiting. Within the blister he'd just brought back from the Geostation, he turned and looked up, but could see nothing with his normal vision, while his holosense gave him a series of dark blots across vacuum. The sensors in the engines all around his world filled in detail, as he hurried to the control deck. By the time he'd sat down in his sensory throne, and made hard connections, he'd received information on the strength of five incursions three million kilometres out, beyond the moon's orbit, and then saw something coming through them.

The missiles dropped through and immediately took off under heavy acceleration, on wildly varying courses. They were big – as large as Committee Earth skyscrapers – and if their atomic load reflected their size, he couldn't afford to let any through. They were too far out for the defences to react yet, so he commanded a reaction. He had no doubt the hive wouldn't repeat its previous clumsy methods of attack. Honing down its multi-spectrum beam width, the engines began firing, and selected those missiles heading in his direction. The objects quickly disintegrated into long boiling clouds across vacuum. Spectral analysis showed little in the way of radioactivity, while the clouds they produced had a very high albedo. They must have been composed of something hugely dense. When he went into deeper analysis, he saw that shortly after being hit, the smoke they effectively became began to crystallize into flakes of a wide, molecular dispersion form of iron and carbon. And the things just kept on coming.

The Fenris sat back and speculated. Judging by their mass, he could see that the missiles probably didn't need nuclear warheads. If they came down on the planet, they'd have more than enough destructive impact. Yet, being so large, it took them time to generate speed or change direction, which made them easier targets. Perhaps the hive was running out of fissile materials? The idea gave him hopes for a swift resolution to the war, yet he still couldn't decipher its aim here. He watched, studied and speculated as the attack continued for a further hour, then, at length, he began to see a pattern. Missiles his defence system had avoided, because they weren't heading his way, were adjusting course, while the ones his weapons were hitting were getting further and further from the incursions. Meanwhile, those missed missiles were set to swing around the sun, then head on towards the sun tap. He realized brute material force was being employed here. If the hive could keep up this rate of firing, the missiles would get closer and closer to both targets and inevitably hit. Yet that seemed ludicrous, and when he made the calculations he saw that it was.

It would take upwards of a hundred million missiles being destroyed before any of them impacted, and that would be fifty years hence. The hive would certainly have to venture out from its moon to supply the materials, and a huge portion of its manufacturing resources would surely be taken up making the missiles. Numerous responses now occurred to him. He could just let this run and allow the enemy to exhaust itself to the point when it was forced to venture out for resources, and at that point attack. But the moment he considered this course, he felt he might be deluding himself and not seeing some ploy here. He needed to shut this down. Even as he came to that decision, the incursions began to narrow as they turned to face away from his defences. In multiverse view, he could still see them, of course, like worm burrows stretching away to infinity, but they were closing themselves off against the beam attack from his engines.

'That's enough of that,' he said, trying to feel potent, and gave his engines a mental nod.

Across ten of them, large crusty sphincters opened and spat out their loads – two from each. Coil-driven at first, these shot out, looking like barracuda aiming to scour out a bait ball. A couple of hundred kilometres out, half of them then opened up fusers and headed towards the fenris moon. One slingshot around there would take them out, but their grav-engines would swing their course into a parabola and bring them in to hit those incursions in their present positions. The other half were on a direct course and much slower. It didn't matter which way the incursions turned, the missiles were capable of adjusting their courses from either direction to hit them.

Next, the Fenris raised massive turrets from other engines, ready to fire up even heavier phase-shifted plasma beam weapons. He put them under programming. They would now target any new incursions that opened and would deliver a nasty pulse of ionized matter into the hive moon. He considered other options. Thus far the hive had struggled in the positioning and repositioning of its incursions, and that couldn't last. It wasn't able to place incursions in close proximity to anywhere critical, since everywhere was protected by an equivalent to the hive manifold, including the sun tap. But it might find a way to zip incursions all over the place, taking pot shots at him. He gave another mental instruction to the engines, and they began to launch further missiles, strewing them out from his world. Out there, they would patrol and await opportunities as they arose – the hive opening incursions to attack meant it was also opening windows through which he could attack it too. As a subtext, he increased manufacturing, selecting out whole arrays of weapons from fenris history. The small alert concerning available energy slid under his perception for a while as he concentrated on these chores. But when it increasingly came to his attention, he couldn't ignore it any longer. The energy from the sun tap had diminished.

The Fenris obtained a diagnostic from his biotech in the sun tap, hopping over the light delay via multiverse communication. As with all biotech physically distant from him, it did have some independence, and he expected it to inform him of how it was garnering reserves against those approaching missiles. But the report surprised him because no, it wasn't doing this, since a brief diversion of energy a few months hence would turn them into spreading clouds of hot gas. And there, in that instant, he knew the hive's strategy. The high albedo clouds of matter were obstructing the microwave beam transmitting energy from the sun tap to the moon here, and thence to his technology around the world. At present it was minimal, but in time it would have an effect. Even upon his realization of this, another alert came through: the hive manifold was changing.

The Fenris flung up various views onto the surfaces around him. He saw the hive moon in one surface, and reflected in another as a multiverse representation, with the manifold wrapped around it like a vast spherical worm cast. The thing was shifting, seemingly boiling, and then it threw out a great braided rope of incursion tunnels. The braid hit a representation of a world in the multiverse format. From the apparent point of contact, the thing then spread out around that world, effectively smothering it in a manifold. This immediately blocked travel across the parallels to that place. He'd expected an attack there, upon the split-away parallel, but not so soon, and nothing like this. He felt a claw of fear in his guts. This leap in competence simply didn't track with what had passed before.

He sat watching, frozen into inaction by the abruptness of it all, but the claw of fear twisted a little and he knew he had to act. He simply couldn't allow the hive to grab the jaunters. If it did so, he saw a future of being confined to his world, defending himself, because venturing beyond it would mean forever being hunted by those creatures, who'd be free to move anywhere in the multiverse. Issuing instructions to that older technology in his engines, he began to extend his own tunnel again, like the one he'd extended to the hive moon, while within one engine he initiated a transceiver satellite. When his calculations apprised him of the ruinous amounts of energy he needed, he shut down the beam weapons. Seemingly in response to this, the five hive incursions abruptly closed too. This gave him hope. The hive couldn't fully maintain such attacks on two fronts and that likely meant weaknesses in the new world-wrapping manifold it had just generated around the shadow Earth and Caprock. He determined to penetrate that.

Ottanger

The sky had darkened to deep grey, mottled with darker structures that were sliding through it like endlessly tangled and knotted worms. Ottanger pushed at the multiverse again, recognizing the effect of seeing it as though through dirty, distorting glass. Somehow the hive manifold, previously confined to another region of the multiverse, had arrived here. Worse than that, the hive seemed to have managed to refine it, so it now interfered with holosense and the ability to jump locally too. He inspected it closely, his head aching, but his understanding of the thing had expanded. They were all now in the trap he'd been caught in before, and this time it was a lot tighter. Then, within this multidimensional view, he saw a pipe arcing down. He lowered his gaze to its exit point and saw the black mouth ploughing through the sprawl, eating up buildings and hurling wreckage behind, almost as if a giant spinning cutter had come down there. It finally settled at a point two kilometres away and began spewing out an endless stream of warriors, post-heads and hive humans of other designs.

'Can you take us away?' asked Irene. 'I can't . . . move.'

He looked over as Chancel stepped up to the stacked crates, pulled up a lid and started taking out ammo clips. The man had the right idea.

'It's something I don't want to try more than once.' Ottanger decided not to mention that he simply didn't know. He could feel strong resistance and it seemed likely that a substantial jump, taking them all with him, would rip the biotech out of his flesh. 'Ektian –' he turned to the woman – 'see to the house defences.' She nodded and ran for the main computer console, rubbed her hands together as she sat down, and then set to work.

Pushing his holosense and feeling a warning ache in his skull, he next surveyed the entire house, even as roller shutters came down over the windows, and the thumping of locks on the lower doors resounded, all on Ektian's instructions. To one side of the main, missing window, a motor whined and a shutter protruded a couple of inches then jammed. Before he'd thought to give an instruction, Chancel and Adriana picked up a weapons crate and repositioned it. Yes, they had defences and could build a barrier here, but what then? He turned on suit com and, while giving the man a jab through their network, said, 'Pranjab?'

'Yes, I know,' Pranjab replied.

Ottanger peered down into Medical as if through coagulating shadow, the ache in his skull settling permanently. He saw that Jane had worked quickly getting the three they'd rescued tubed up, and Pranjab was already halfway through removing the mesh from the man there. The hood was gone, and Jane was filling the holes in his skull with a collagen foam, then applying dressings. The doctor was also removing the sections of mesh by some new, swifter method. Ottanger snapped his holosense away, not wanting to push it too hard.

'How long?' he asked

'Not long for the mesh. As long as a piece of string for anything else.'

'Chenghu.' The man looked up from the crate he'd opened. Ottanger held up three fingers. 'Three suits and sets of weapons down to Medical.' Chenghu seemed glad to have been given a chore.

'We have access here to more than just house defences,' Irene noted.

Ottanger just looked at her.

'I'll help Ektian.' She turned and headed off.

Ottanger returned his attention to the hive humans, focusing in with both perfect sight and denuded holosense. The warriors carried lariat guns and the post-heads their stun pistols. He could see other weaponry but had no doubt it was of the non-lethal variety. The hive wanted them captured unharmed, to be taken back for examination. And doubtless the harm would begin then. He inspected the other hive humans, of designs he hadn't seen before. Some were big bulky creatures, heavily armoured, with large grasping hands – all the better for catching one with. Others were painfully thin but fast. He could see little in the way of facial features. Running on stick legs, they streaked out ahead of the rest, pouring through the streets. At a glance, he might have supposed them unarmed, but on deeper inspection the trumpet mouths of stunners became clear, where hands should have been. Technology was laced up through their arms, and wired to stuff in body cavities that should have contained a digestive system. They were short-lived, disposable human beings, he realized.

'Not much defence against those stunners,' said Chancel. He then gestured to the house all around. 'Electrics will be vulnerable.'

Ottanger nodded and spun towards Irene and Ektian. 'Computers will go down,' he said. 'Make sure you're prepared for that.'

'Initiating set programs,' said Ektian. 'The readerguns will keep firing,' She shrugged. 'Until they're shorted out, or run out of ammunition. . . . Razorbirds are going.'

A flock of them streaked above, from behind the house, and he saw them launching down at the edge of the sprawl too. The ones below were flapping their wings to gain height, while those above simply fell like missiles. He shuddered, always having been at the bad end of such things. The diving ones appeared black against the sky, then gleamed when they fell lower and abruptly opened out molecularly sharp wings. He heard and felt the impact as they scythed into the hive runners. The white creatures seemed to break like porcelain and strew themselves along the street, until a moment later when the blood came spraying out. Runners behind still came on, trampling over their fellows even as the razorbirds launched back into the air amid them.

Ottanger swallowed drily, then stepped over to one of the

crates, as Adriana came up from the central pit of the main room carrying an armchair to dump into the barricade. Chancel was also down there, picking up the sofa she and he had sprawled on earlier. Ottanger put a finger down one edge of a container in the crate, which caused it to split open and reveal rolls of assault rifles. Another touch had one roll opening, and he picked out the weapon for inspection. The thing looked vaguely like an AK-47. However, it had a fancy screen sight, and a back-curved magazine full of bullets the size of rice grains. The barrel bore was exceedingly narrow and punctuated with coil sections. Hydraulic recoil absorbers ran down the sides, while the forward grip seemed to consist of some laminated and coiled material. Wincing at the effort, he scanned through the thing, guessing at function, and guesses turned into certainty. This was a coil gun, powered by some form of capacitor in the grip. The kinetic impact of the bullets, small as they were, was evidenced by the heavy recoil system. He noted that the magazine was integral. Maybe as many as five hundred shots, but then the weapon was throwaway – the whole thing including the barrel probably worn out.

'Chancel!' Ottanger tossed the first weapon to him as he dropped the sofa in place. The man caught it without looking round.

Ottanger took out the rest to distribute along the barricade and handed one to Adriana as she returned to dump their erst-while food table as another part of it. She frowned at the thing, then stepped over to join Chancel. Chenghu returned, carrying the missile launcher he'd used during their rescue of Ottanger. He also dragged out another odd-shaped container and opened it to reveal a selection of RPGs. He chose one and loaded it, then looked to Ottanger.

Nobody had opened fire yet, though easy targets aplenty lay below. Ottanger supposed they felt the same about this as him.

It just seemed wrong to wait here, blasting away at what were in essence, barely sentient versions of humanity, driven towards them by a controlling mind they couldn't kill. But the reality of the hive's intent remained, and the humans below were portions of that same mind. If he and the jaunters were captured, they would end up, eventually, on a dissection slab. He knew he would have to take the lead in this and, raising one of the weapons, looked at the sight screen. The hive humans leapt closer. He hesitated, looking for reasons not to fire, almost as a matter of form. Then he finally did.

The weapon thumped against his shoulder and put out a jet of vapour to one side as the barrel and breech jerked back against the shock absorbers. The shot hit one of the big armoured things squarely in the chest, and it seemed to show no sign of penetration there. But a cone of vapour, licked through with flame, exploded from the creature's back. A warrior directly behind it fragmented, another lost his right arm and most of the right side of his body. Beyond these, others went crashing down. Some struggled back upright again, while many just disappeared under the horde advancing from behind.

'The hive cares little for its members,' Chenghu observed as he fired, and then swiftly reloaded. The RPG landed just inside the hive's incursion tube, its blast raising a fountain of body parts. He fired again, quickly, and the next missile streaked in through the thing and out of sight. Deep inside it, a hot eye opened and then closed. Now Chancel and Adriana opened fire – their shots had the same effect in the mass as Ottanger's did. On Chenghu's third shot into the incursion, he thought it was closing up, as it seemed to grow steadily narrower. Yet the same mass of hive humans came streaming out of it. Focusing on it more carefully, he then saw it turning, grinding up composite and shuddering. It apparently thinned to a line and then winked out. But now he received the weird perspective from behind of the horde just appearing, swirling out and round, then joining up with the rest. The mouth of the thing had turned to face away from them, out of range.

Irene came up beside him.

'Other defences?' he asked.

She pointed upwards. 'The program is set and should kick in shortly. It'll last as long as the super-capacitor up on the satellite.'

'Firing now!' Ektian called.

It started with wisps of smoke, or steam, cutting lines through the horde. Only as the line traversed back did they see the hive humans dropping, to disappear in the crowd. And then, only as the air clouded with steam and smoke, did that pick out the red needle flickering of the lasers from orbit. Meanwhile, runners had now reached the lower fence around the hill on which Caprock stood. There was no subtlety. They crammed up against the chain mesh and began scrambling up it en masse, until the whole thing collapsed. A second later came the triple-tone thumping of readerguns. But corpses where they fell just kept disappearing underneath the surges of more and more hive humans. As he crouched down and rested his weapon across a crate to fire shot after shot, and as the smell of cooked flesh finally reached him, Ottanger thought of the thousands upon thousands of them he'd seen in the hive. Calculating on the assumption of similar population density throughout the moon, he came to a simple conclusion. Chenghu was right: the hive mind cared little for its individual members. Seeing the jaunters as an existential threat, it would keep sending its members, because it could. Eventually capacitors, readerguns and their own ammo would run out and they'd be swamped.

He needed another option.

The hive humans came on, up the hill, in a wave, sweeping their dead in underneath as they rolled on. The runners were in the lead and so died in their thousands first. As he fired methodically, he understood they were an advance whose purpose was just to soak up shots. The landscape visibly changed shape down there, growing a mound of corpses, which the others scrambled over. He glanced aside as a figure newly suited came to the barricade and stared out at the approaching horde.

'Your name?' Ottanger asked.

The rescued man turned to him. 'Jordan.'

Ottanger just pointed to the weapon leaning against the barricade nearby. Jordan looked down at it, abruptly picked it up and inspected it. He seemed about to say something more, then just shook his head and started firing. A short while later, Jane and Pranjab arrived. This seemed to harden the network, and he felt the query in it. They all knew this to be a fight they couldn't win. But what could he do? They were deferring to him, and he could see no way out of this. Perhaps attack the incursion and fight through there, to jaunt out the way he'd escaped before? No – the fact the hive could reach out to this world meant it would have even tighter control around the moon. His only option, it seemed, when the ammo ran down, was to try to jump them to another location on this world. Almost certainly the hive would then come after them in a less defensible position, and with them having fewer resources to defend themselves.

The two rescued women showed up next from Medical, as the hive attackers reached halfway up the hill. The two held back, low in the network, confused and not knowing what to do until Chenghu called them over. Ottanger pulled back from the barricade and, straining with holosense, viewed the overall situation. The fences were down all around and hive humans coming in on all sides. He now saw some readerguns tracking and no longer firing, while one or two were locked and smoking. And now the hive began to fire back. The shots came up like fireworks in slow arcs – sizzling balls of electrostatic energy. They hit the walls and the barricade, spreading crackling energy and raising smoke. Chancel yelled and staggered back, dropping his weapon. Down below, the readerguns died and the horde surged forwards, warriors shoving away remaining runners and pelting up the hill. Weapons went over to full automatic, ripping into them, but those behind continued to run over their dead.

Then it was suddenly as if a spike had punctured through the stifling blanket of the manifold. Something hit the thing and, in the visible world, sent ripples across the sky. In the multiverse vision, Ottanger saw another tunnel winding down to the planet, shuddering as it came. Was this something more from the hive?

A warrior reached the barricade, leaping over even as it fired its lariat gun. The snakelike projectile whipped around one of the new women and dropped her to the floor. Chenghu shot the warrior through the waist and it folded over, falling in two halves, with the back blast of the shot rolling one of the armchairs, on fire, over the edge. Ottanger reached out to them all and tightened a grip on them. He could see no entry point to this new tunnel, just an awareness of the thing cupping over them. If they stayed here, they'd definitely be captured. He yelled and, with one great expulsion of energy, threw them into a jaunt.

It was different this time. The world faded even as a ball lightning passed through his body, leaving an odd sick burning behind it. This spread up through his chest and through one arm, deadening his grip so he dropped his weapon. He saw warriors now clambering over the barricade, firing their guns, but the lariats passed through the others into the room beyond. His weapon fell, gaining solidity to bounce on the floor. He had little sense of the multiverse as a whole, but a strong sense of coming to a huge slope, like the one down to the hive's version of Earth. They were locked by this new intrusion, and there was only the one place to go. He fought against it but it began pulling them in.

They fell into darkness, spinning around each other like leaves sucked up a vacuum pipe. They gazed at each other across the no-space between worlds, as the tunnel revealed itself around them. He sensed the manifold falling behind, felt grateful for that, but didn't have the energy to think beyond. Then something appeared, far down this virtual tube, and sped up towards them, or they down to it. Out of the dark, it revealed itself as curved ribs of translucent glassy yellow, like a claw, and it was coming straight at him.

20

Ottanger

Ottanger groped for the short machine gun attached to the front of his suit, and in consonance with him, the others reached for their own weapons too. Abruptly a new force impinged on them. He felt the network stretching and the others growing distant, as if physically moving tens and then hundreds of kilometres away. The claw singled him out and began to close up around him. His connections finally broke and the others fell away into black, with Irene desperately grabbing them up. Distantly now, he sensed Irene's chagrin as she had to take control, and their network reordered with him excised. He dropped away in what he now recognized as a cage sphere. It locked together, and the black between its bars turned to grey. A sense of massive acceleration ensued, though it had no physical effect on him. But the actual deceleration soon after slammed him into the side of the cage, signifying arrival.

He dropped to a metal floor that looked like brushed aluminium, with the cage around him half-buried in it. Beyond it other structures had appeared: cylinders, networks of pipes and ducts all wound through with woody biotech. Within this knobbly arms, terminating in hands with multiple fingers, shifted here and there to operate odd-shaped imbedded controls. The whole had the look of the interior of some industrial structure, but with lines and curves smoothing into each other, and objects appearing half-melted or organic. He observed a wall to his right, and then another to his left. Ahead and behind, the floor cut between these, but not in a straight line, rather winding like a river, as if it had been poured in the gaps. The walls rose to a ceiling far above, marked with lines and swirls like the patterns on Celtic stones. Yet he felt blind, because though he could see these things with his eyes, he had no sense of his surroundings with his holosense. It seemed suppressed, stifled.

He only had time to realize this before a figure loomed between the two walls and strode towards him. Though he recognized the Fenris at once, the violence of expectations still fizzed through him. He came up into a squat, weapon pointed and other hand groping for grenades, before conscious thought re-engaged.

'You,' he said.

Drawing closer, the Fenris waved a dismissive hand. Around Ottanger the cage sphere crackled and began splintering. The thick vapour that rose from it smelled strongly of sulphur, and this seemed apposite. It steadily decayed, the vapour flowing away across the floor, and by the time the Fenris loomed over him, it was all but gone. Ottanger stared up at the creature, glad of the rescue but with a degree of healthy paranoia at the forefront of his mind. He didn't like that the Fenris had used technology similar to that of the hive, or the sense of anger that seemed to be emanating from the figure before him. And he certainly didn't like how he'd been snatched away from the others, their connection broken. He wondered where they were now.

'War is here,' said the Fenris. 'Come with me.'

The Fenris strode off the way he'd come. Ottanger took a breath, suppressing his adrenal response, shrugged, then stuck his weapon to the front of his suit and followed.

The path took them to where it abutted a long tube. Set in the opposite side of this were glassy spheres, each five metres across and giving a view out into starlit space. The Fenris walked up to one lying directly ahead, whose rear hemisphere was apparently missing. Ottanger followed, stepping out onto a rough flat floor in the hemisphere. Now with the view much less distorted, he could see that more than starlit space lay out there. A world hung down to his left, while far ahead was a massive machine hanging in orbit. He could also make out other satellites and structures distantly, and chafed at his simple vision, as excellent as his had now become.

'Look,' said the Fenris, tapping him on the shoulder and pointing.

Far out from the world, up to his right, he saw a rash of flashes sparkling across vacuum, lighting up what appeared to be streamers of smoke. He stared at these, puzzled, realizing his senses might be blunted but he was just getting too much input.

'Where the fucking hell am I?' he asked.

'You cannot see,' said the Fenris, then reached down to grab his arm. Claws went straight through the armour of his suit and into his arm. He tried to pull away and again adrenalin surged through him. He began to reach for his weapon but his holosense exploded out around him, instantly stilling him in wonder.

'The technology I use to prevent hive incursions here, on my world, blocks what you jaunters call your holosense. You are now seeing everything through the biotech in this engine.'

Ottanger located himself in this vast device, in orbit around a world scaled with slabs of biotech. Other such 'engines' hung in orbit all around it too, while what looked like a space elevator speared down to the surface from a large space station. However, as he took all this in, he could feel a pull from the Fenris, directing his attention outwards. His perspective rushed towards those flashing lights, surely taking him beyond the range of usual holosense. And now he saw energy beams high-lighted in a fog around the swarm of missiles that was their target. Huge explosions opened bright in vacuum and died to fading embers.

'I am blocking my world from attack in the same way the hive blocks its moon – my manifold prevents penetration of the parallels here, both for the hive and for us. But I cannot stop its incursions out there.' The Fenris paused, seemingly lost in thought, then added, 'It opened five incursions to put those missiles through, but couldn't maintain them when it went after you and the others.'

'It's trying to bombard you?' He tested things then, edging his biotech towards a jaunt, and found precisely the same as he had in the hive moon. He couldn't jaunt away from here. But with effort, he'd be able to jump locally.

'Yes and no. If I don't destroy those missiles, they will drop on my world. But in destroying them, I am creating a high albedo cloud that's blocking transmission of microwave energy from my sun tap.' Again the pause and then, 'I expect this attack to recommence, once the hive has the resources it needs.'

Ottanger had seen where he was and bewilderment passed quickly. He understood 'sun tap' by context, and what was going on with the attack here. But even though he was hungry for more information, there were other priorities.

'Where are the others?' he asked.

The Fenris turned and looked down at him. Now, beside the creature's seemingly angry demeanour, he noticed something else. The Fenris had looked at him with disappointment, but also seemed haunted, and it worried him that such an apparently powerful being could show such weakness.

'You will be able to see and to understand better from the control deck,' said the Fenris, then just turned and walked out of the blister.

Feeling rebellious, Ottanger stared at his retreating back. Finally, accepting he could do nothing here but tag along, he followed. More routes through the engine brought them to a huge chamber. He and the others had glimpsed the background of this before, during communications with the Fenris – this space with its translucent surfaces seemingly sprung like leaves from a tangle of organic technology. A chair stood in the middle up on a stalk, and the Fenris sat down in it. Transparent tendrils like living optics oozed out of the chair and mated with the spines on his glassy armour. The Fenris's eyes turned black just as Pranjab's sometimes did. The doctor had explained this to him as being a sudden routing of his blood to the biotech in his visual cortex, allowing for a massive expansion of holosense and visual processing. The explanation didn't make it seem any less sinister.

The chair tilted and turned on its stalk, while translucent surfaces became windows into other worlds, and into the structure of the multiverse. Ottanger scanned them all, his brain activity ramping up so much it seemed it would boil in his skull. Then, hardly giving it a thought, he walked up to the display and rested his hand on it. The iconic language spoke to him, offering alternatives. He made selections then paused, rubbing at where the Fenris had punctured his arm, and suddenly remembered when that had happened before, in the cave.

He gazed inside himself with that inner sense, and in great detail. He saw alien blood swirling immiscible with his own, attaching to the biotech etched into his bones and woven through soft tissues. Fenris blood. Also, his own blood supply had increased to his skull and he guessed his eyes had turned black too. It almost felt as if his blood was sweeping up information generated by the static biotech throughout his body and depositing it there. He had no sense of panic about this, just an amazing precision of thought. The Fenris had done something – boosted him somehow.

Next, withdrawing from internal perception brought something else into view. In his mind the image bloomed of the split-away parallel Earth they'd been on, and from a hundred perspectives he saw the sky mottling. He took his hand away and watched as, in the first image, one hive incursion tube stabbed down to the ground. A new image offered up made him grimace when he recognized Caprock, with the hive incursion opening in the sprawl below, and the warriors and post-heads pouring out.

'The hive blocked the world first so we couldn't escape, and then sent in its forces to grab us,' he stated, turning to the Fenris and seeing him watching intently. 'I fail to see why you're showing me the obvious.'

'The hive is operating in a much less chaotic manner than before,' said the Fenris. 'In its determination to capture jaunt tech, it has put itself on a war footing.'

Ottanger just took that in. It seemed that the Fenris was forcing himself to use the word 'war'. It reminded him of a person belligerently stating 'facts' to broadcast their acceptance of some distasteful reality. Returning his attention to the recording, he watched hive humans flooding around Caprock and up the hill, dying in their thousands. He then pushed the recording and ran the progression forwards, until it blinked out.

'Your arrival was timely,' he noted. The last images had shown hive humans clambering up over the roof of Caprock and affirmed that, had they not left at that moment, they would have been buried underneath the things. 'After you and I took the jaunter bodies away from it, of course it was going to go after the live ones next, in its mission to obtain jaunt biotech.' He paused to inspect the statements he'd just made. How did he know the Fenris had destroyed bodies on the airless Earth? The information was simply there in his mind, washed up from his biotech.

The Fenris gave a nod then said, 'I presumed that to be its aim, but didn't expect it to be able to reach so far, with such power and accuracy. The fact I got you out when I did is just a matter of pure luck.'

'And luck should never be discounted in tactical and logistical calculations,' said Ottanger flatly. 'What will the hive do now?'

'This will initially be a war of resources. Proof will come with whatever happens next on the Earth you just came from.'

'What proof? Its manifold cut your feed to there.'

'Manifolds are local phenomena, just as jaunter travel is that way – we can travel across parallels from one Earth to another, but the energy needed increases exponentially if you want to jaunt, or extend a manifold, beyond a nodal Earth.'

'And?' Ottanger absorbed the idea of these only being a local effect. It seemed that, even with his power to jaunt across multiple Earths, he couldn't escape any real distance away from those Earths. His thoughts strayed to speculating on how it *would* be possible to get to a world enclosed by a manifold, but you'd need a spaceship to do so. He filed the thought away for future inspection.

'I've sent a satellite outside the manifold there,' the Fenris continued, confirming his speculation. 'And it's communicating via radio with my remaining biotech on the surface. The feed is only now arriving because of the transmission delay.'

At another wave of his hand, new images began appearing on the screens, and in Ottanger's mind. He saw a multiverse view of the world, with numerous tunnels stabbing down from the conglomeration of the hive's manifold around it. Views down on the surface showed incursions landing in sprawls, in croplands, in sea farms and even out on the oceans. These hung in place for a brief period, before the detonations. Flat blast waves spread out from the sprawl incursions, dropping buildings and opening out wide areas of fallen rubble.

'They're doing it to take out the readerguns, I assume,' said Ottanger.

'Establishing a foothold, yes – to remove immediate threats,' the Fenris replied.

Next, thousands of hive humans began pouring out and spreading. He watched as flow patterns established, and closer imagery showed the creatures gathering up materials and heading back to the incursions laden down with loot. He saw one of the larger hive humans carrying a couple of steel poles with cams and readerguns still attached, and was reminded of lines of leaf-cutter ants hauling their prizes back to the nest. But obviously this wasn't enough, nor fast enough.

Imagery juddered and next came the machines. These were iterations of bulldozers and earth movers, driven by hive humans who were melded into the mixture of organic and hard technology of them. Other things came out looking like mechanical versions of amoebas, throwing out long tentacles to gather up materials. Then came huge machines with vast digging wheels chewing into the wreckage and the ground before them, leaving trenches wherever they went. They poured out their haul into great loaders that were perpetually connecting up behind. These loader machines obviously had sorting hardware inside them, because they issued a spill of broken concrete to the sides, while behind they collected up metals and, it seemed, anything organic such as plastic, occasional plant life, and even old road macadam. The scenes held him riveted as he speculated on how all this would feed industry within the hive moon. In overview, he saw the world dotted with spots kilometres across as the hive chewed into it. Checking the time since he'd started watching, it startled him to see that hours had passed.

'This is coming to an end now,' the Fenris told him.

'What do you mean?'

'I couldn't allow the hive to seize my biotech there.' He paused, then affirmed, 'These creatures must never obtain my technology.'

A new view appeared at ground level, through what looked to be the container-storage area of a port. Beyond this, two huge digging machines were stationary, while hive humans had swarmed in around the containers and were breaking them open. Ottanger guessed that everything that supplied a sprawl could be equally useful in the hive. The flow patterns of workers established here again, as the creatures emptied the containers and flooded back to the nearest incursion with what they'd found. It was all very fast and efficient, but then they weren't individuals but one organic machine. At a certain point, the routing changed, with the hive humans heading off to the sides as they drew closer to his viewpoint. In the background, the digging machines started up and began advancing, slicing down into the ground thirty metres, also scooping up empty containers and the big trucks the hive seemed to have no use for, beyond their materials.

'And that is it,' said the Fenris.

With a blinding flash, all the close surface views of the world winked out. All that remained was the multiverse views, which showed little of what was effectively a massive strip-mining operation. However, the flash did penetrate from down on the coast of India.

'What did you do?'

'I set the biotech there to self-destruct the moment the hive came too close. Thermo-nuclear explosion of five megatonnes. There will be nothing of it left, and no chance of any reverse engineering.'

The explosion seemed like a final confirmation to Ottanger and he just nodded, now fully recognizing the Fenris's fear of the hive rising to a technological par, and his utter commitment to preventing it. And yet, this also looked like a retreat – the Fenris pulling in and closing down resources in the greater multiverse – and he found himself searching for other options. He really needed to think hard about this.

He pointed to the scene showing the explosions out in vacuum, around the Fenris world.

'So they need resources,' he stated simply.

The Fenris gave a slow nod. 'Materials for missile manufacture, to send more through which will feed that growing cloud.'

'I see.' Ottanger began extrapolating what that meant. The hive moon and the fenris world were locked down. The hive had grabbed another world for resources and was taking it apart. So would the Fenris do the same thing?

'I asked you where the others are,' he said abruptly, returning to what was most important to him, making an effort to at least push away from a projection of the future he felt was locked in the creature's mind.

After a long pause the Fenris replied, 'Down on the surface.'

Ottanger reached out and touched the nearby screen again, summoning images. These then fell into his mind, opening out as wide holosense perception. He found himself spiralling down to the world below and tracking information autonomously. Down there, he gazed into a spherical garden with a sun floating at its centre and alien growth sprouting from the walls. Irene and Chenghu stood on the inner face of the sphere, looking around. Tracking back down a short tunnel, Ottanger found the

537

others in a wide room, with human furnishing amid fenris biotech. The man Jordan and one of the new women sat talking to Ektian. The other woman lay on a flat couch with her eyes closed, while Jane sat at a table eating odd-looking red fruits from the garden. Apart from her, the new jaunters all had tubes running back to a biotech robot, crouched down on four spidery legs and overseen by Pranjab. With access to more than visual information, Ottanger realized Pranjab was using the robot to feed programming and materials into their biotech to heal them. He was taking a download similar to the one running into Ottanger's mind too.

Seeing this, Ottanger now tracked and analysed his own sources and realized his biotech was hoovering up information being broadcast by the biotech of the engine. He examined data coagulating in his mind. The history of the Fenris was just there, and he hadn't even noticed its arrival. Technical knowledge layered up like silt, with data about the hive dropped in its bombshells.

'Updates,' he said looking at the Fenris.

'It's similar to the educational download I received when I was born,' said the Fenris. 'It enhances curiosity and need – the demand of your mind. Though it's necessarily limited, otherwise it would overwhelm you.'

That was true, for he could see the history of the fenris race only as a vague shape in the background. More recent events were there for him in greater detail, and he scanned the Fenris's youthful altruism and failure, encounters with the hive, and the long periods of him leading an isolated existence here, wrapped up in the technicalities of this world. Whenever he focused on some technology or event, more detailed knowledge expanded out. It was just like remembering things he knew as an unbiased observer – the information always being collected by the biotech.

'And thus we all end up thinking the same,' he stated. This was certainly a danger but, in recognizing it as such, he realized he'd already begun to resist it. The information seemed like rain on the landscape of him, little changing it. He considered it pouring into his skull and complementing his adult mind, then thought about similar information landing in a juvenile mind. He remembered his terse conversation with Pranjab regarding the Fenris in light of what he was seeing, or rather *remembering*, now. Again he observed that knowledge did not imply wisdom.

'No fenris thought the same as any other,' the Fenris said, a little defensively, Ottanger thought. 'Variety of thought was the driver of our civilization.'

'And yet, how different is this method of education from the hive feeding information to the bioradios in the skulls of its members?'

'It's utterly different from that!' the Fenris replied vehemently.

Ottanger pretended distraction as he mentally scanned out from where the jaunters waited to a small spread of accommodation, expanding in surrounding fenris tech. He then shunted aside the mental images and focused back on the creature before him. There he sat in his throne, a hugely intelligent being, linked to a world of super-advanced technology that was powered by a tap on the energy of the sun itself. And yet the Fenris was scared and had been utterly alone. Like anyone in such a position, he wanted those he did encounter to fall in with his paradigm, and Ottanger could see how the information he was receiving was shaped to that end. The process might not even be a conscious effort on the part of the Fenris – just an effort to provide 'what they needed to know'.

'How many years have passed since your educational download?' Ottanger asked.

'In your terms, over a hundred and fifty, and I have learned a great deal more in that time.'

This seemed defensive too and further illuminated his doubts.

539

The Fenris had been unable to travel until only recently, so in that time he'd been isolated here on this world. Sure, he had massive resources and access to huge knowledge, but no experience with other people, and its more complex iteration in the form of fenris empathy. What stood before Ottanger, no matter how the Fenris looked, was a hundred-and-fifty-year-old teenager. This creature had made mistakes that cost lives, and thereby learned from them, but could he learn from others? Ottanger had already seen the Fenris's reaction to his observation about the similarities to the hive bioradios.

'Your conviction, which arises out of the history of your kind, is that a sense of personal power, durability, safety and the control or suppression of old biological drives are what enabled the fenris civilization to prosper.'

'That is so,' the Fenris replied, looking slightly puzzled.

Ottanger nodded. 'It was your aim to provide those to us on Committee Earth, to push us out of our dark age into a utopia.'

'That's not a word I like,' said the Fenris, 'but that was the essence of it, yes.'

'But then a greater danger, not just to our world but all, revealed itself.'

'Yes, the hive.'

'Ultimately what Committee Earth would become without changing course?'

And you hate it, don't you, Ottanger thought.

'Yes, and it must be fought in every manner possible. It's bad enough that it can cross the parallels, in its own way. We cannot allow such a . . . culture to obtain my jaunt tech and do so freely.'

The reaction fizzed up through Ottanger's body, and he fought to suppress it as he began to see clearly what was happening here. He realized he wouldn't have perceived what he did now without the experience of a long hard life on Committee Earth, and without his experience of the resistance, illustrating how the best of motives can in the end be turned to evil. He also wouldn't have perceived it without the expansion of his knowledge and intelligence upon that foundation, and the much larger expansion of all that even now.

In failing miserably in his initial altruistic intervention, the Fenris had retreated to non-intervention, merely rescuing whoever he could of the survivors. He'd then discovered the hive, and his detestation of that culture, so antithetical to his own, had increased upon discovering it was the cause of many of those jaunters' deaths. The hive attacks here had finally snapped him out of a malaise and straight into preparation for war. It was the pacifist apparently driven to self-defence, and feeling obliged to use the gun pressed into his hand – the act done not because it was the best option, but because he was afraid. This big, powerful but inexperienced creature, surrounded by wonderfully potent technology, was still deeply fearful. And he'd done what fearful people did with their enemies: he'd dehumanized them.

This was the conceptual barrier Ottanger crossed in his under-standing of the Fenris. He shrugged and searched round for something to say as a cover for the furious activity in his mind. 'So is this hive with or without a ruling class, or queen?'

The Fenris's eyes were wide, and he spoke flat facts without justification. 'Without, I have learned. Those who rule and drive humanity towards such a milieu fail to realize that they're not above the systems they put in place, and so they die out. All that remains is the system; the hive.'

'Mob rule,' Ottanger quipped, seeing how the Fenris's thoughts tracked his own on that matter. And he felt he'd managed to take the conversation away from dangerous territory. But he needed to take it further, into his apparent agreement. 'So the hive mustn't obtain any more power than it has, and definitely no jaunt biotech, as you say. That leaves us with a big problem.'

'Go on,' said the Fenris.

'There are tens of thousands of people in internment camps on Committee Earth with your precursor biotech inside them.' He glanced at the screen image of the split-away parallel, hive humans swarming it, and continued, 'The hive is being wary, and you have made it so. It doesn't want to allow easy direct links back to itself. So what it's doing there,' he pointed at the screen, 'I would guess is more than just a resource-gathering exercise. It's also a staging area for the invasion of the next world.'

'Yes,' said the Fenris, eyes black and looking elsewhere, 'to Committee Earth, to grab the mutated jaunters there. And of course gather more resources.'

'So you're placing your own manifold there, before the hive can,' Ottanger stated, feeling the change in the engine around him and beyond. He reached out and touched the screen, not needing that contact to bring the images into his mind, but feeling almost obliged to take physical action. He saw the fenris manifold shifting and then throwing out a braid of tunnels, perfectly aping the one the hive had sent to the split-away parallel. He watched it splash on Committee Earth and engulf it, while here a further tunnel opened from the manifold, connecting down to the surface of the fenris world.

'Yes, I am enclosing Committee Earth to prevent access. How long I can maintain it is a matter for conjecture.' The Fenris pointed again at that rash of lights out there. 'Energy.'

'And then what?' Ottanger also perceived a reluctance to act in the Fenris. Preparations for war were a similar thing: all the readiness to fight without actually getting on with the fighting.

'You and your jaunters will pull out all the mutated people you can.'

'Of course,' said Ottanger flatly, seeing the path the Fenris was laying out, and understanding he'd been given an order.

He now realized that the resources for this war weren't just the materials and energy the hive required, but the people the Fenris required. He saw that, with this world and the hive moon locked behind defences, the war would inevitably expand, with other worlds eaten up in the search for, and depletion of, these resources. The whole scenario reflected the power blocs of Earth before the Committee – and whose paradigm it was supposedly now negating. And there would be no direct head-to-head conflict, but endless proxy wars. He also saw that, with his fear and detestation of the hive, the Fenris could see no way from this path unless instituted by himself. He'd invested too much. His fears of the hive and its goal to obtain jaunt tech were self-reinforcing, and he wasn't persuadable otherwise. Certainly, he wouldn't be swayed by primitive humans burdened with old biology and hierarchies.

But there had to be another way.

The Fenris

As he watched Ottanger descend in the space elevator to the surface, the Fenris felt discomfited. Here on his world, he'd been an omniscient observer and then tinkerer in the worlds of others. He had been distant and godlike, and only became part of everything he observed and influenced when the hive incursions truly turned into a threat, forcing him to act. But even when he'd ventured out, he had still felt as if he was just passing through to drive events along a course he'd deemed appropriate.

During his brief physical encounters with the jaunters, he'd felt their influence pushing and pulling at him; he had pulled firmly away from it, since their network was trying to place him at the top of their old biology hierarchy. Now they were actually here on his world, he could feel it there again, niggling at him constantly – the jaunters' consensus influencing him. As a result, he had reluctantly to concede that they felt like an invasion of his world. They weren't in consonance with him. The things they saw as important were not aligned with what he did, and now he was beginning to question bringing them here.

This was obviously the result of his long life thus far being that of a hermit, and now having to deal with actual people. Though he really wanted to resolve it somehow, he instead decided just to force himself to become accustomed to it, since everything else was progressing as he desired. His idea that they must gather up forces to stand against the hive would go ahead, despite Ottanger seeming lukewarm about it, rather than giving his wholehearted agreement. And, despite Pranjab being lugubrious about the prospect of warfare, he'd raised no objections either. Being the strongest amid the jaunters, those two would lead the others, at least until their old biology hierarchy broke apart. His niggling sense of something wrong, something not aligned, was simply the reaction of a long-time loner having to deal with others who weren't perfect mirrors of him. Perhaps it would have been different if they were really fenris, and perhaps it would be different in the future.

The Fenris snorted and returned his attention to Ottanger, now down there on the surface. The jaunters were quickly becoming accustomed to their new home and, via the biotech around them, which was feeding them updates, he listened in to Ottanger detailing what he'd been told, and what they'd been ordered to do next.

Over the next few days, he watched as they explored their surroundings further, venturing into the accommodation that expanded out from the location they'd established as their base. And they made their plans. With access to a massive body of information, and growing understanding of the manifold, they went out onto the surface of their city slab to the designated place. From there, their holosense opened out in the throat of a tunnel stretching all the way over to Committee Earth. Chenghu volunteered to be the first, and took with him a transport cage he'd grown for himself. He returned with his armour cratered with readergun shots and five other people. One of them was shot too and taken quickly down to the medical area Pranjab had created. The next to go was Irene, as they steadily refined the process. Only observing for now, the Fenris felt no need to intervene. That is, until the incursions came back.

The things flicked into being facing in towards his world. As he'd prepared, phase-shifted plasma weapons turned on their turrets, targeted them and fired. Explosions inside two of the hive incursions put them out, but within minutes two more opened, facing away from his world this time. His barracuda missiles out there homed in, yet in the hours before reaching their targets, more of the big hive missiles had swarmed out. He closed more incursions down with his missiles, but more opened, and it seemed the inevitable course had been laid, as the cloud continued to grow and power from the sun tap slowly diminished. He finally left this defence on automatic as he turned his attention back to the world.

The potential jaunters were growing in number, but they weren't yet what he needed them to be, so he planned. If he released inocular flies down to them all, the transformations would be fast, but he didn't want a repeat of the disaster on Committee Earth. These people here wouldn't be able to jaunt away from his world because of the manifold, but they would certainly be able to jump. And if they didn't end up scattered, they might well kill themselves with sloppy transitions. However, the hive had supplied him with the solution. The backwash from its manifold suppressed even that ability, and he could create, and refine, a similar effect – essentially harnessing prospective jaunters until their ability had fully developed. In fact, he now saw that in suppressing them, and preventing dangerous jumps, he would have the option to make some other changes. He worked on updates to the schematic of the inocular flies, adding in a higher component of his DNA substrate, so they'd become more like Ottanger and stronger. Further updates and changes could operate through his biotech, to prevent it from killing them, as well as allowing them to develop in a safe way.

The killing would come later.

So the hive had isolated the split-away parallel Earth for the resources it was now using, while he'd managed to isolate Committee Earth for the jaunters to gather up the 'mutated' from there. The hive was doubtless harvesting its captured world for all forms of energy available: fissile materials, hydrocarbons, deuterium and tritium for its fusion reactors. It was also harvesting the material needed to make the missiles now steadily blocking his source of energy. He ran calculations again and saw the hive had set itself in for the long game. It didn't matter if it couldn't keep up the present rate of firing because the cloud, slowly spreading and thickening out there, wouldn't be going away any time soon. In fact, it was on course to fall in towards the fenris world and become even denser as it did so. This would take decades and was just the beginning of the resource war. How far it would then extend, he couldn't know. It'd end when the balance tilted one way or the other.

And that's when a hot war would ensue.

Chancel

They were supposedly safe here, and did have access to huge resources, but comfortable wasn't the way Chancel would describe this place. Nor, by what he sensed through the network, would any of the others. In one way he rather liked it, since at Caprock he'd felt a complacency setting in, whose disruption had been long overdue. That disruption had begun with Irene and then continued with Ottanger. But he didn't like it here in other ways.

'It's hard,' said Adriana. She took her hand away from her stomach area to wave it in the air for a moment, then returned it. It seemed she kept it there all the time now, as if offering another layer of protection for the child growing within her. Their child.

'All the information,' Chancel agreed, as they walked along a tunnel resembling the internal view of a large intestine, braced with metal straps.

Over their time at Caprock, it had been disconcerting actually to feel his own intelligence expanding brutally in his mind and biotech developing. He'd come to understand that, as a captain in a street gang, he'd always felt a bit of a fraud in that respect. But at Caprock, he'd grown both physically and mentally. Languages became easy, whether from the human tongue or in computers. Information in any form landed in his skull indelibly, from whatever source. Memories he never knew he'd retained came back to him with new context and connections. He'd felt dominion over what he now saw as the simplicities of the world he'd known, and recognized this to be a side-effect of his perception opened out to the multiverse in all its vastness.

This had changed with the arrival of Irene and what he felt to be the establishment of an atavistic hierarchy. He'd found his place in it, as did they all, but the thinking didn't stop. Again, he'd resented her dominance, questioned her leadership, and found himself growing in rebellion against it. His increasing knowledge was obviously a big reason for that, but the expansion of memory, and putting that knowledge in the context of experience, was a bigger one. Ottanger's arrival had then come as a bombshell dropped on Irene's dominance. The presence of the man had been huge, breaking the previous hierarchy. It had subsequently fallen into a different shape, which wasn't about forced obedience to a stronger personality, driven by anger and hate, but acquiescence to respected leadership. And it seemed Ottanger had now led them here.

He'd felt all the information washing into his mind the moment they arrived, as the biotech updated them as if they were computer adjuncts to itself. Though it instantly opened out his thinking, and provided intricate data on whatever might concern him at any time, he hadn't liked it. It felt as if it was pumping him with information in order to set him on a predictable course – one they'd followed by adhering to the wishes of the Fenris and starting to rescue the mutated from Earth. Later, they'd managed to exert more control over the data flood. Pranjab, on returning to their base from one rescue, showed them how to. He'd just looked around, with his eyes having gone black, and walked up to a wall and pressed his hand into a soft pad. He then stood there, seemingly unconcerned, as the thing folded out pincers to take his blood. His knowledge suffused their network. Irene had been next, and Chancel also allowed the surrounding biotech – still nominally controlled by the Fenris – to take his blood, for recognition and information feeds. This gave him more control over the thing feeding him, both mental and physical, but still they'd stepped into a new paradigm.

'Do you see it?' Adriana asked, pausing to rest a hand against one wall. 'Down below.'

Even though the realm of information had expanded, their ability to jaunt or jump had been suppressed. And that meant they'd lost much of their holosense too. However, they'd soon found that making a physical link to the system returned a facsimile of it. He stepped over and touched the wall, skin cells in his hand bonding with biotech keyed to his blood, and the connection quickly established. He gazed down into the constantly moving bio and hard technology of this place. Amid the masses of it, going down as far as this perception allowed, he saw the chambers still opening out – cell-like rooms expanding, passages routing between them like blood vessels. More information was offered in the form of familiar infrastructure, like water supply, the strange food plants growing in mini-gardens, and cyst factories producing both the necessities and luxuries of human existence, but also the paraphernalia of an army.

'It's preparing for larger hauls,' he noted, taking his hand away and abruptly flicking it up to snatch something out of the air. He crushed the thing, then held out his hand to show her. 'The next stage.'

She peered down at the squashed inocular fly and nodded. He inspected the thing, seeing its metallic ichor spilling from glassy insides, with his vision somewhat more than twenty-twenty, and then discarded it. The things had appeared in the last few days and were already wreaking their changes on those occupying the accommodations below.

'I think we're far enough away now,' said Adriana.

'Okay.'

They moved further along the tube to a soft section, where he formatted an instruction and delivered it with a touch of his finger. The wall, like psoriatic skin, opened up with an unzipping-type sound, and they stepped through a short passage into an expanding cyst. It rose like a bubble, stretching the passage behind and below, then the section ahead cleared to almost complete transparency, revealing the fenris world to them.

'We can't walk out, there's no oxygen,' he said. 'Unless you want to go hypoxic.'

She rested her hand on her stomach again and shook her head. Despite all the knowledge and downright power to hand, some instincts were hard to defeat. It was one he knew the fenris, as they had been, had dispensed with completely, as they'd transitioned to birthing halls and artificial wombs.

'So why the necessity for distance?' she asked.

'Clarity,' he said.

'I'm not so sure it works the same way here.'

They'd done it many times from Caprock, after Irene had taken over. Creating physical distance by heading down into the sprawl below had enabled them to escape her dominance and think for themselves. Now, he understood Adriana meant this wouldn't get them away from their biotech feeds, but still felt it separated them from the reinforcing effects of their jaunter network.

He pointed towards a wide, fenced-off area in the distance, on the top of the city slab.

'He's on his way back,' he said. 'It feels like an age has passed here, yet it's only been a few weeks. We're doing the will of a creature who apparently believes utterly in the idea of free will. Ottanger is our leader and the mouthpiece of that creature, but I'm not sure he believes what he tells us. We're handling massive amounts of information and, in all honesty, I feel as if I'm drowning.'

'But we're not. We're swimming in it.'

'The wave carries us along with it, and that wave is at the will of the Fenris and Ottanger,' he said. 'We're in their paradigm as much as we were in Irene's, and we need some space, to step away from it and to question it.'

'He doesn't dominate us, though,' she replied.

'Who?'

'The Fenris doesn't, and neither does he.' She pointed at the distant platform. 'Right from the start, Ottanger only took control when necessary. Since then, he's just presented us with information and allowed us to decide. In no other way has he made me do anything I've had second thoughts about. Have you felt differently?'

'No. But his influence on the others, and through them, has its influence on us, hence me wanting to put this distance between.'

'So, with the distance, do you feel differently now?'

'No,' he admitted. He was finding it hard to express the misgivings he'd had earlier, in the seeming rush into this new world.

'He went along with Irene's idea for the destruction of jaunt research on our Earth, and I saw no fault in that. Just as I saw no fault in him displacing her leadership when necessary. I also see nothing but logical extrapolation in everything the Fenris has done, and all he's preparing for. We know the hive is anathema, and it's what the eventual future will be of the Committee-controlled Earth, on its current trajectory. It must be fought,' Adriana said, her expression firm.

Chancel studied her. As they'd become lovers, he'd admired her strength of mind and her certainty. Everything that'd later occurred had seemed the ultimate upshot of this, however strange their lives became. But now, with his mind operating as it did, he knew it to be an illusion. He understood her certainty had focused on what she wanted, which had been him. Now it had shifted onto what she wanted next, which lay under that hand on her torso. He recognized old biology at work here, for the perception of safety arose from being sure about something. She couldn't allow herself to entertain doubts about their course now.

'It concerns me that we act on the information available, and its format,' he said. 'There's much of it, and it gives us the illusion of certainty. Yet that information is inherently of the Fenris, and his perception of reality.'

'You doubt your ability to decipher the truth?'

'Truth is mutable.'

'Yes,' she said, and they were no longer talking about the actions of the Fenris, or Ottanger or Irene, but what lay between them.

Old biology had pulled them together in terrible circumstances. They'd escaped those circumstances by fantastical means, and that'd seemed to affirm their love. But now they were changing fast, as logic, reason and the tech growing inside them dissolved the roots of that old biology. It would disappear more slowly with her because of the child, of course, but it would still go.

'It's okay,' she said, sensing him on so many levels.

He shrugged. 'Yes, oddly it is.'

What was happening to them reflected the standard way of things between standard humans. The rose-tinted passion was fading, but it wasn't sliding into the usual dominance games, because their new biology was taking them away from that. He reached out and rested a hand on her shoulder as they gazed out at the new world. He still loved her and she him, in varying definitions of the term. That would change over time too and, yes, it was okay.

'Something is happening,' Adriana said.

He thought she was referring to what lay between them, but in a glance saw she was looking up. He did too and saw a rash of lights flaring in the twilight sky. He didn't need to wonder about them, since downloads told him. It seemed the hive, having stalled its attack here while consolidating its seizure of Caprock and that Earth, had restarted its assault.

Irene

The landing pad sat up on the surface – a circle of composite on top of this city slab. The slab went down two kilometres, with human accommodation areas expanding in it like cysts, as hardtech and biotech constructed them to fulfil demand. The pad was one of twenty such places, on top of twenty such slabs. Irene, coming up the stairs from below, gazed across at it. She huffed in the thin air – now only breathable as the biotech continued to rebuild the atmosphere – and looked up.

The sun was above the horizon, with a cloud bank lying below it like a wave foaming over. Weather was becoming an interesting phenomenon here, what with the atmosphere changing, the constant orbital drops and launches, the shunting of materials and components up and down the space elevator, and the technology of this world heating up. Turning the people they'd rescued from Earth into jaunters wasn't the only preparation being made for war.

She focused on the sun, intently, able to because her eyes were no longer strictly human. Comparing it precisely to how it'd appeared when she'd first seen it, she noted how it had taken on a greenish hue now. Next, carefully filtering, she began picking up on the dark spots of explosions in silhouette, and the glints of them elsewhere. The cloud out there was continuing to grow, slowly but surely cutting energy. In fact, a lot of the activity down here was the manufacture of fusion plants and zero-point collectors. She grimaced at that, lowered her gaze and headed along the caged walkway to the landing pad.

A fence consisting of interlinked rings encircled the pad, with other caged walkways running out to other stairwells. They'd all hated this, because it resembled the fences of the internment camps too closely, but it was necessary until the people who arrived here were able to understand their situation properly. Only as she stepped onto the platform, which was the target for one of the Fenris's tunnels through to Committee Earth, did the multiverse start opening out to her perception again.

The tunnel seemed to extend above her head, through the world's defences, but that was of course just her linear mind's interpretation of it. Here she paused, because her holosense, which previously she'd thought relied on conventional radiations, was also a function of her multiverse perception, and it too had come back. She gazed down through the massive structure below. Chenghu and Pranjab had returned, via the surface transport system, from their heavy jaunts and were now in their quarters below. Jane was there too, recovering from her very first transport job. It seemed the bioradio in her skull, and other tech still dissolving in her body, interfered with the process. Chancel, Adriana, Ektian and the others of their limited group were returning from other city slabs and were due back here, where they'd made their base, sometime soon.

Irene was still sore in body and mind from the biotech updates and educational downloads she'd experienced on arrival here, as well as exhausted from her last jaunt to Committee Earth. It would take her a little while longer before she could go again. She wasn't related to Ottanger, his sister Jane or the woman Callis, who was apparently a distant relative of theirs too, so didn't have actual fenris DNA melded into her own. She still had to use a transport cage too, to enhance the process, and it left her feeling on the edge of death. She fought down the annoyance she felt about this, suspecting it arose out of her initial anger and bafflement at losing control of the others to Ottanger. Frankly, she didn't want control now, because things had got very complicated very fast, and she didn't need that responsibility. She closed her eyes and remembered her first jaunt from this place.

With all the new information boiling in her mind, it had been a vertiginous experience, and she'd arrived at her destination baffled and out of sorts. Had she not been wearing her suit, she would have instantly fallen prey to the readerguns in the guard tower. But she'd managed to jump to a new location after the first triple impact of slugs on her back.

Inside one of the long barracks buildings, she'd eyed the people crammed in there. All her mental facilities came back at that point, and she'd gazed into two similar buildings. Following through on the plan, and the mental program Ottanger had designed, she'd tugged her transport cage out into visibility but not full materialization – the thing hovered in the middle of the barracks, as people shouted and tried to get as far away from her as they could. She'd opened it out, into cage form, then separated this into its different components to disperse around the three buildings, before bringing them fully into this world. Next, running the mental program, she'd found the biotech in those all around her and tugged them into a steadily expanding mental network. The people had grown quiet and attentive after this, and those nearby began to move back towards her. At a certain point, the collection process had gone into cascade, spreading to everyone in the barracks, and even spilling out of the internment camp and finding others. With an effort of will, she'd halted it there, and pulled it back within the compass of the cage components. Ottanger had surmised that any outside the cage would fall out of her control and end up like so many dead jaunters before. Then finally, she'd jaunted with her massive load, just as the Inspectorate guards crashed through the doors.

The long scream of transition haunted her even now, and it had screwed with her on every subsequent jaunt. But at least now she didn't collapse into a coma afterwards, with blood running out of her every orifice. The continuing mental exercises and biotech updates had helped with that, and the fly bites too, which were apparently implanting some of the Fenris inside them all.

Irene felt it happening then, perfectly on time with her internal clock, so turned and walked off the platform, back into the caged walkway. The mass transports had their inaccuracies, what with having to correct for relative velocities, and such a narrow window of access, and Ottanger really didn't need someone standing right where he was about to materialize others. It began as that concerted screaming in her mind, and she flinched. It seemed louder and more intense this time, as if someone had opened a doorway into the suffering of hell. No longer able to gaze into the multiverse, she just concentrated ahead for visible signs. First came a flickering, like gas flames burning to their source and snuffing out. Then came the ghosts of thousands crammed together. And finally the actual people arrived.

A blast of displaced air shoved Irene back a step. Within the perimeter of the fence, the people dropped and tumbled, until pushing up against it. They began spilling into the walkway too, so she moved up against the cage. She gazed upon those she and the others had once been. They were dressed in a variety of clothing, some of it the rugged kind passed from generation to generation, some of cheap manufacture being worn to destruction. The men, women and children were mostly Indian, since these came from Pranjab's home territory, but they all bore the same recognizable features as everyone else they'd taken: the purple-blue tint to the skin, ears with slight points, and eyes at the red-violet end of the spectrum. Irene winced as the smells of urine, shit and body odour washed over her. Surprisingly, there wasn't much panic or shouting, and the scream was apparently a subconscious thing. It arose in people who weren't fully jaunters panicking at the sense of the multiverse, without the mental capability to interpret it.

'Down there.' She directed those looking at her in bewilderment to the stairs. Shortly after she spoke, another voice issued seemingly from the air all around. Speaking in Hindi, it said, 'Take the stairs down into the city. You will receive further directions down there about food, drink and accommodation.' Irene frowned. They'd considered adding to the message something about them now being free of the Committee. But Ottanger had scotched that, saying, 'They're scared and internment camp compliant. Let them stay that way until we've got them where we want them. Time enough for them to learn the realities of their new world later on.' It had been quite cold and heartless, yet utterly pragmatic and correct.

The people flowed steadily past her, while over to the left and the right, she could see them going along the other walkways. Only then, because she hadn't been able to use her internal sense, did it occur to her that there seemed a hell of a lot of them. Abruptly she moved back along the walkway, people hurriedly stepping out of her way as she did so. The moment she moved back onto the landing pad, her sense of the multiverse returned, as did her greater holosense of her surroundings. The whole pad was utterly packed with people from fence to fence, and the pressure only eased as they surged along the walkways. There were thousands of them. She began pushing through, with her holosense ranged ahead, to a small open spot right at the centre in which Ottanger crouched. It was a long battle, since even though people wanted to get out of her way, with her advanced changes marking her out as intimidatingly alien, they were caught in too much of a crush.

Finally, with the crowd density thinning out, and the sound of announcements in Hindi drifting up from below, she made it through to him. He remained crouched, the fingertips of his right hand against the ground, forefinger of his left rubbing his nose. He looked thoughtful, and relief flooded through her on realizing he was unhurt. Rationality then prompted her to note that he'd done this over twenty times before and not caused himself any particular damage.

'Showing off again?' she asked.

He looked up at her and smiled. 'That was about my limit.' He stood up and looked around at the departing people, then focused on her again. 'Now we've figured out how to work things at this end, we need to get on with taking bigger hauls. The Inspectorate has been slow to react so far, and I'm guessing they're just not sure how to. But they will do.'

'And of course, there's that,' she added, pointing up towards the disappearing sun.

'Yes – energy may become a problem.'

They started following the crowds towards the nearest stair.

'How do you think the Inspectorate will react?'

'At the least, dispersal,' said Ottanger. 'At the worst, they'll see the "mutants" as a threat and begin exterminations.' He paused. 'Any more strays?'

'None. Destroying the Complex ended that. The five we rescued all came into contact with dead inocular flies by chance, as far as we can gather. Strange that the Fenris hasn't sent more flies there – the jaunters would all end up here.'

'It's too disorganized,' said Ottanger. 'Many would die in Earthbound transitions, and when arriving here. And, of course, he's reluctant to release any more jaunt tech out there, which the hive might get its hands on.' He paused, and then added with an edge to his voice, 'And we wouldn't want that happening now, would we?'

She absorbed this but felt there was more to it that he wasn't telling her. And this was connected somehow to another thing he wasn't telling all of them. The silence grew uncomfortable.

'So group lifts,' she said abruptly. 'That's why you wanted us back here?'

He glanced at her, expression unreadable and, she felt through their connection, deliberately so. Right from their arrival here, when he'd come down from orbit after his meeting with the Fenris, she and the others had sensed him to be hiding something. It wasn't the fact that the people they brought here were almost immediately bitten by inocular flies, to transform them into jaunter status. Nor was it that they were intended to serve as soldiers in a war dragging itself into life – that had all been obvious by the provision of further armoured suits, weapons, weapons training, and the martial nature of the uploads they received. It was something else they all recognized he didn't want to discuss out loud, and so they kept their mouths closed on the matter.

'Yes, group lifts,' he said as they reached the stairs. 'The others?'

'On their way.' She didn't bother mentioning those below, since he should have seen them clearly enough via holosense when he arrived. 'I'm not sure if I, or some of them, will be ready for anything soon, though.'

'I'll take the load on the way out,' he replied. 'We'll divide into threes to hit the selected camps.' He gestured behind. 'We'll need to take down the fences too, since there'll be floods of people.'

'Okay,' she said, wanting to ask him what this was really about.

'Y'know how, in the beginning, we could only carry stuff inside our biological field?' She waited, knowing this was something to do with that other matter, and he continued, 'I've found out how to actually remove things from inside ourselves by the same method.'

The comment hit home, because she could guess what that was about. He'd discovered that the Fenris had used its own blood to grow a tracker in the biotech of his arm. She said nothing about this and instead quipped, 'So we can jump and leave our tumours behind.'

He nodded once. 'Precisely so.'

Down below, they entered corridors running off into the massive accommodation spread throughout the city slab. The Hindi instructions and various arrows were directing the new arrivals there. Now familiar with their surroundings here, Irene and Ottanger ignored them.

'They're always remarkably calm,' she said, pointing to a man and a woman with two children ahead, taking a turning and heading off.

'Yes – it's more than the fact they've been conditioned to obedience by readerguns and Inspectorate shock sticks. It's the empathic connection, and the hierarchy establishing here. With the first, they realize they're being rescued, and with the second they become obedient to the primary in charge.'

'Like me,' she said tightly.

'Less so as time goes on,' he replied.

'And we'll all be free when we rise above our biology,' she stated

He shrugged.

The door into the section the jaunters had occupied opened at his touch, which it wouldn't do for any of the new arrivals. They went through a short pipe into a living area, which closely resembled their main room at Caprock. As they entered, Chenghu came sauntering back through the tunnel leading to the spherical garden, popping open some pods and slinging the brassy-coloured beans they contained into his mouth. He simply nodded at them and went to take a seat. Ottanger turned to her.

'I need to talk to Pranjab,' he said, and she tried not to resent that he meant 'alone'. She waved a hand towards the door leading into the steadily expanding section where Pranjab spent most of his time.

Ottanger

The strain of saying nothing was becoming telling on Ottanger. His brief slip into sarcasm back there had been a sign of that. But he couldn't tell them his plans because the Fenris could listen at any time and, in fact, probably did listen all the time.

He knew the others realized he was holding something back and, via their connection, were constantly pushing him to speak up, though they weren't consciously aware of that. He touched the door, sensing Pranjab ahead rather than seeing him with his holosense. The door didn't open until Pranjab shot over his mental permission, and Ottanger then walked through. The laboratory was as wide as the main room and had another section expanding beyond. Within it was a weird combination of recognizable human-level instrumentation and fenris biotech. Pranjab, wearing a lab coat that reminded him uncomfortably of Savarack, turned from a wide slab against one wall. On this lay a corpse mid-autopsy, pinned open and carefully eviscerated, various

561

organs scattered around it on higher platforms, or in globular transparent cysts. Biotech laced the air between them, like purple and black branches and twigs, while two of those jointed tentacle arms worked at some chore in the open torso. The hands they terminated in had long delicate fingers and Pranjab's eyes in their palms.

'It's working for you now?' Ottanger enquired.

It was even more difficult here with Pranjab, because he didn't simply have to lock down on speaking about his plans, but had to communicate them in a grey area of word games, hints of emotion through the network, gestures and other subtle methods. But from this Pranjab knew his plans and was assisting him in them, even though it wasn't something they'd discussed outright.

'The Fenris withdrew his control, and that of the others, from the biotech here, so I inoculated it with my blood again,' Pranjab replied. 'It now functions as a much clearer extension of my mind.'

'And him?' Ottanger gestured to the corpse.

'One of a hundred and forty-two, out of forty-three thousand arrivals so far,' Pranjab replied. 'The accelerated transformation isn't working out so well for some.'

Ottanger nodded. This was old news. The inocular flies down here were a different iteration from those sent to Earth. The Fenris wanted jaunters as capable as Ottanger, Callis and Jane, when she finally had herself in order, which meant the installation of fenris DNA. Because that DNA in pure form killed most of its recipients, he'd initiated a new form to lay the foundation for a long series of updates in its recipients. It still killed some people, however.

'Any luck with the flies?'

'The Fenris gave me their schematics and I'm learning a great deal from them,' said Pranjab bluntly, for they were now venturing into dangerous territory.

'I'm surprised.'

'He seems quite pleased I'm showing an interest and, with my different perspective, says I might even come up with a better method.'

'Yes, perspective is a thing,' Ottanger said drily.

Pranjab gave him a warning look, then gestured to the other side of the room. They walked over to another slab, with a series of wide cylinders arrayed underneath. Above it, a section of the wall – wetly translucent – faded into life as a screen. It displayed an inocular fly that'd been opened up, like the unfortunate on the slab behind. Inside were the standard organs of such a creature, but seemingly made out of bright metal and glass. Magnification brought it forward to fill the entire screen. Subsequent magnifications showed micro-structures, then smaller structures still, down and down. Ottanger viewed the components of fenris biotech with apparent interest, while he thought how to lead on to what he really wanted to know.

They still didn't know how closely the Fenris watched them. Having set things in motion down here, he seemed content to leave the rescues, and the building of *his* army, to Ottanger. He occasionally raised his own incursion tubes and went away to other worlds, then on his return fed them data from his travels, looking for hive activities elsewhere. He'd found no such activities, and even reports of them on the world of the sea people had turned out to be their version of alien greys. That is, they didn't exist.

'So you have enough to work with?' Ottanger asked, taking a risk to get to his real point of interest. Their conversations had become increasingly opaque ever since the one they'd had when the inocular flies first appeared down here. Their words and phrases had been a convoluted ramble about the effect the flies had had on Committee Earth, and apparent concerns about the effects on the people they'd brought here. But raised in the nuances of their connection, they'd been having an entirely different conversation, and had come to an agreement. He understood that their ability to communicate in such a manner arose out of their having been ZAs on Committee Earth – there was so much there that couldn't be said directly while observed by the cams and AIs. The same went for the SAs too.

'Plenty,' Pranjab pointed to the cylinders. Then, after a pause and a shrug, he stepped over and pulled one out from under the slab, sliding it easily on fibre pads. A series of tubes extended out with it, plugged into the centre at the top. The thing measured over a metre in diameter and, when he tapped a finger against the top, the milky polymer cleared. The inside was segmented around a central core, of which Ottanger could just see the top. And, straining his holosense, he managed to perceive it went right down to the bottom. The mixture of biotech and hard tech looked like the electronics of Earth a hundred years before, but only had such scale because of millions of miniature moving parts. From previous visits here, Ottanger recognized a series of bioprinters and they were at work too. The segments were nearly full to the brim with dark red chrysalises, and more were feeding out from the printers.

'With the schematics I have,' Pranjab continued, 'I can print them out in this chrysalis form, and in that way they're somnolent, until a little application of heat. They hatch out very quickly then.' He paused again and Ottanger realized it was his turn to take a risk. 'I'm investigating the possibility of difficulties across multiple printings, though the Fenris says problems there are unlikely. I disagree, since this is nanoscale stuff, so not every fly is exactly the same. I've tracked iterations across a thousand generations.' He pointed at the cylinder. 'There's a hundred thousand of the little horrors in there.'

And that was all Ottanger needed to know.

'Let me know if you find something.' Ottanger gestured to the corpse. 'We don't want to lose any more *soldiers*.'

'Of course not.'

They chatted more, just to bury the important exchange in verbiage, then Ottanger headed for the door. As he stepped out into the main room, he focused on Jordan and Callis, who'd just arrived. Even though he couldn't actually see them, he could also feel the others approaching.

'All good?' he called.

Jordan held up a thumb and Callis just looked askance at him. Conversation had been limited to necessities between Ottanger and the rest ever since they'd realized he was holding back on something, and understood they must remain close-mouthed on the matter. The strain was telling on them as much as him.

He headed across the room, and then out through the tunnel leading into the garden. Stopping by what they'd dubbed the steak tree, he plucked fruits and ate leisurely, while sensing in the network that the other jaunters had finally arrived. He walked over to one of the eating areas, or rest spots, or whatever they were, grabbing up a selection of strange fruits on the way, then sat down and continued feeding himself. The thought went through his mind that this might be the last time he ever did so. Then he pulled on the jaunters, gently and persistently, through the network, drawing them in.

Jordan came first, shortly followed by Irene, and then the rest filtered through to pick food and finally join him. He looked at the other woman of the newer jaunters and remembered her name to be Agaia. She'd caught up quickly with them, and her weight in the network was as much as that of Adriana. Jane was weightier still, but damaged. Pranjab, recognizing the pull and having discarded his lab coat to come out of choice, was the strongest of them all.

'You brought the flier,' Ottanger said to Chancel.

Chancel just shrugged.

'I'm not sure I see the necessity,' said Agaia, then closed her eyes and wished she hadn't spoken when the network reaction came through to her. The need for a flier had been part of the *something* Ottanger didn't want to speak about. But since a question had been posed, he felt the need to answer it, to maintain the facade

'The Inspectorate will soon start reacting, and energy might eventually run too low for the Fenris to maintain his manifold at Committee Earth. We need to move more people more quickly. The first big jaunt, run by myself, Irene, Chenghu and Jane, will take some time to set up. I don't want to be on the ground while doing that . . . well, you know.'

'Birds and readerguns,' Agaia supplied, looking relieved.

'Chancel, Adriana and Ektian will jaunt the Carvort Camp, while I want you, Jordan and Callis to go for the site in East London. They're about the same size, and your abilities balance out about right.' He looked around at them all. 'We go in four hours.'

'You failed to mention me,' said Pranjab.

'You'll be at the controls and defences of the craft,' said Ottanger.

Pranjab showed puzzlement, but of course it wasn't real. 'I would have thought Chenghu a better choice for that . . .'

'The present stalemate in this war cannot continue,' said Ottanger, again scanning expressions but also delving into them at a deeper level, to see their response to this statement. He was satisfied with what he found. 'You, Pranjab, have spent far too much time in that laboratory, and though that's useful, I need soldiers. I've yet to ascertain that's what you are.'

He felt the wince from the rest of them, then a buzz of confusion as they detected an undercurrent in the exchange. Pranjab apparently issued chagrin, but he was good at hiding his responses.

'The craft?' Pranjab enquired of Chancel.

'Mixture of hard tech and biotech, as them all,' Chancel replied. 'General-purpose for any environment, atmosphere sealed, grav-tech, thrusters and a main fuser drive. The weapons were an add-on: anti-munitions bead coil guns, two heavy lasers and a missile launcher. The bio is neutral and ready for any of us to take control of it.'

Ottanger shot him a glance, wondering from that description if Chancel had some idea of what he really intended. It'd been highly convenient for him that fenris technology was now so advanced that any vehicle capable of independent flight was 'general-purpose'. The Fenris would've had suspicions if he'd wanted something only capable of space flight for an Earthbound mission.

Pranjab stood up. 'I'll take a look at it.' He turned to Chenghu. 'I've got some research gear I want to bring, and since we can't use transport cages down here . . .'

'I'll help you,' said Chenghu, standing up also.

Ottanger watched the two of them go, then turned back to the others.

'Get some rest and prepare yourselves. This is going to be the first of many bigger groups we grab.' He wanted to say more, to offer hints of an explanation to come, but once more it was simply too dangerous to do so.

21

Ottanger

The intrusion, the *arrival*, snapped Ottanger out of sleep. Though the engines up in orbit generated distortions in the local multiverse that prevented jaunting and, more important, kept the hive manifold from penetrating here, as well as severely limiting senses reliant on the multiverse, all the jaunters could still feel arrivals and departures via the Fenris's tunnels. He sat upright, immediately aware he'd slept for two hours, and that'd been more than enough to bring him up to optimum. The knowledge surfacing from a level below conscious thought also told him who'd arrived, and he felt a surge of anxiety. He climbed out of bed and, rather than rushing out, enforced calm. He sauntered to his shower and, while he washed, ensured he had his mind in order. Then he took his time dressing in the padded undersuit and combat armour.

He was ready. As he headed for the door, he was reminded of his preparations for the interrogation with Axel, what felt like an age ago. There'd be no lie detectors running this time, and no AI to analyse his reactions, but something that combined both in one mind.

The Fenris was waiting for him, out in one of the main corridors coming from the stairways to the caged walkways above, gazing pensively into the nearest large accommodation section. The ceiling was of course high enough for the creature here, since he'd designed this place. Ottanger eyed him. The Fenris still wore his reddened armour, yet it seemed to have taken on bulk – whether the armour or the being underneath it, he couldn't tell. Still, there was a sense of the martial about him. Ottanger's mind, having strayed back to his time in the Complex, drew comparison between the Fenris and Colonel Jones. Jones had obviously been a tough soldier in earlier life, but had later taken on the gravitas of rank, while his bulk expanded with that. The Fenris had that sort of air, though without the underlying experience that created it.

'Nice of you to visit us,' Ottanger said, not hiding the sarcasm.

The Fenris turned to inspect him, head tilted to one side. Ottanger could read much of his expression, since he did have features placed in a near enough conventionally human fashion, but still the face wasn't as easy to read as those of his fellows. On another level, he sensed the creature's weight in the shifting networks down here. The Fenris was larger than all of them, and in fact wasn't distinct, seeming to dissolve into infinity all around. He had the state of independence, probably from birth, which they'd all eventually achieve, so didn't seek hierarchical dominance. However, that didn't mean he didn't dominate, because the hierarchies weren't just about top-down pressure but also submission from below. Ottanger could feel that pressure, as could the others. This was why there'd been so little questioning of the directives . . . they were the orders the creature had given.

The Fenris pointed into the accommodation section.

'Walk with me.'

They moved on through, passing the various styles of rooms where the refugees had secreted themselves. Ottanger had wandered through this place before it'd been occupied and knew the people here had much more space than they were accustomed to. A few doors stood open, and some people were moving along the corridors, so he and the Fenris were soon noticed. The effect spread in inchoate networks, like ripples from a stone cast in a pool. He could feel the excitement, awe and in some cases fear, spreading out around him. He was of course larger than them all, and could pull all the threads together in one massive network to dominate it, as all the original jaunters did in microcosm when transporting them. This was perhaps what the Fenris wanted him to do, but he'd resisted so far. He also noted with interest his own reaction, for the temptation of so much power seemed balanced out by a fearful responsibility. Perhaps this was why the Fenris didn't grab up those threads too – it was easier not to take responsibility for what people did with *advice*.

Further along, they halted and turned into a long training hall. Here people were running gym assault courses, which some among them had set up. All were clad in uniform pale blue sweatsuits printed up by fenris tech. Ottanger recognized army formation as a kind of grassroots impetus. None here had been told they were going to fight, but they'd been provided with information about the hive, with activities such as this, with armoured suits to try out and become accustomed to, as well as with weapons that only activated in various shooting ranges.

'They are cohering, and they need a firm lead established over them,' said the Fenris. It felt uncomfortably as if he'd been reading Ottanger's mind.

Some of those working out here now turned away from their activities to gape at the two of them. Others on a nearby circuit, hurling themselves over a vaulting horse and then scrambling up a rope net, were pushing themselves harder, doubtless in a bid for praise, or at least notice. It was as if a king had come to walk among them, accompanied by a god.

'Remarkably fast, it would seem,' Ottanger replied.

'That's not something I need to explain to you.'

'No, it's not. You established an ethos right from the start. This place resembles a military camp base, even down to the colour scheme. You've shaped their access to information, their communication and media, in fact everything to the smallest detail, to one end. If you were to tell them they're *not* going to go fight, either the Committee or the hive, most here would be angry with you.'

'And that is a bad thing?' the Fenris enquired.

Ottanger closed his mouth, not because he was drifting into dangerous territory, but because he sensed doubt from the Fenris he'd never felt before. It shocked him down to a very deep level. His whole aim was predicated on this creature's utter certainty that protracted war with the hive was a foregone conclusion. He almost felt like pressing into that doubt, but stopped himself. It was the empathy, he realized. The hierarchical nature of the human networks was just an upshot of their ancient biology. A fenris network was empathic alone, and this was why the creature hadn't even tried to assert dominance via that route. However, the Fenris wasn't immune from the empathic connection either. He had doubts now because he was picking up on subconscious cues from Ottanger, but that would likely change as soon as Ottanger wasn't present. Anyway, it was an emotional thing, and the Fenris had convinced himself he operated on logic and dry, hard facts. He little understood the complicated circuit of them being a veneer over emotional responses, and a driver of the same.

The Fenris saw the hive as the antithesis of everything his race

571

had been and achieved, and had been repulsed. Repulsion had swiftly acquired a sense of threat, which by its actions the hive had exacerbated, and he'd leapt straight over other alternatives into a justification for war. False altruism keyed in, because wasn't the Fenris aiming to prevent the hive from taking over other worlds? Ottanger had no disagreement with the Fenris's prediction of what the hive would do, and he found the thing as antithetical to his own perception of the best course for humanity too. His disagreement lay elsewhere.

He shrugged. 'It's neither a good nor a bad thing – just a practical one.'

'So now we must turn back to that firm lead . . .'

'You could take control in an instant. You have to be aware of your weight in the mental network.'

'Hierarchical domination is not the fenris way,' the Fenris replied.

Ottanger acknowledged this with a wince but then hurriedly buried his cynicism. 'I tend to disagree. It might not be the way in times of peace and plenty, but when the pressure is on, the fenris revert to the original blueprint. Don't forget you loaded us with a version of your educational upload, your potted history, and gave us access to your data banks. I know what happened directly after the Great Project, and I saw those dried-out corpses you disposed of.'

'A rare occurrence.'

'Really? Did you not delve into the history of your race?'

'Yes – tens of thousands of years of peace.'

'Because you were comfortable and life was easy. Yet every time things got a bit gnarly, you all started fucking each other up.' Ottanger reached out with one hand and rapped a knuckle against the Fenris's armour. 'Standard dress for a fenris throughout many ages.'

'Are you being deliberately provocative?' the Fenris asked calmly, but with an edge in his voice.

'Perhaps I am.' There was no perhaps about it. He wanted to throw in a disruption like this to prevent the creature discovering his real intentions. 'That being said, yes, I'll establish a command structure here, with me at the top, and I'll get our army ready.' He paused, as if a thought had only just occurred to him. 'Thousands here are jaunt ready now and frustrated by their inability to do so.' He pointed to the gym equipment all around. 'That is training we won't be able to do here.'

'The hive has made no attempt on other worlds yet, and I doubt it has the resources ready to do so. Its main focus is here on us,' the Fenris observed. 'But its focus will turn to other worlds if jaunters go there. Its drive to grab the biotech overrides all other concerns.'

'A necessary risk,' said Ottanger, feeling the Fenris's stab of fear.

'One that you as a commander will have to weigh up.'

Ottanger nodded smartly, ready to break this off and be about his business recruiting for, and fashioning, this army – the very image of the efficient lieutenant. But now as the time drew nigh for him to take an irrevocable step, he felt beholden to ask some questions. In a sense, this was much like the Fenris questioning the hive through Jane: a meagre hope of a positive outcome, but in reality a confirmation of intent.

'You never thought to rescue them,' he said.

'What do you mean?' the Fenris peered at him suspiciously.

'You saw Committee Earth and your instinct was to wreak changes there at once – to divert the course of humanity away from a nightmare regime. But you had no instinct to save the hive from that . . .'

'Definitions of humanity,' said the Fenris, anger flashing across his features. 'The hive is a trillion strong but just one individual. It is a consensus intelligence that lacks any of the qualities of humanity, and as such has become an infestation. There is no saving it, there is only resistance.'

'That sounds like an emotional judgement.'

'You can be damned sure of that. The hive is the end result of the imposition of inhumane rule over centuries. I wish I could say there is something there to save, but there is not.'

'Then resistance is a passive response,' said Ottanger, studying the Fenris closely. 'We need to stop thinking about standing against the hive, and the inevitability of having to fight its spread. We must think in terms of extermination.'

'Perhaps that is so . . .'

Ottanger continued relentlessly, 'If we are to suppose the hive lacks any redeemable qualities, we must look upon it as the infestation you named it. We must destroy it by any means at our disposal.'

'With its manifold in place, that's no easy option,' said the Fenris, expression bland. 'But these are things that you, as the commander here, must consider.'

Ottanger gave a cold smile, everything locked down inside himself. 'Okay, but right now, as a commander, I have more immediate concerns. We still need to get as many away from Committee Earth as we can first. So if you don't mind, I'll attend to that now.'

The Fenris waved a dismissive hand. Ottanger turned and headed away, everything now confirmed for him. He'd felt the Fenris's fear when it came to risking the hive grabbing jaunt tech, the flash of panic when he'd mentioned extermination, and he'd then felt the relief when he accepted the role of commander. Fenris morality held the creature back from making the harsh decisions, and 'preparations for war' were a half-measure –

procrastination, in fact. That morality, and the Fenris's belief that he only turned away from it out of necessity, had also blinded him to his own bigotry in being certain the hive was irredeemable. Ottanger picked up his pace, telling himself it was just paranoia that he could feel the gaze of those violet eyes boring into his back.

The fenris craft wasn't spectacular, and could easily have been mistaken for something manufactured on Committee Earth. Nominally ten metres long, half that wide, and a quarter deep, it had the appearance of a metallic mango pit that creatures and infestations of hard tech had come to occupy. The nose was rounded. A rear section, containing a main drive, could hinge up and down, and side to side. Stubby wings protruded, with steering thrusters clinging to them like aquatic lice. The squatting crab of a missile launcher sat on top of it, while the other weapons deployed from similar structures attached underneath. Pipes and ducts ran over its surface as randomly as thread veins. It sat on its belly on one of the arrivals platforms, with a sphincter open in its side. Ottanger strolled across to the thing, while observing the fences and cages around the platform unravelling and disappearing into holes, as if being wound onto hidden reels.

'There's going to be quite a crowd here to deal with when we're done,' said Ottanger cheerfully. The presence of the Fenris down here had been concerning. Ottanger had felt sure he either knew or suspected something. But after taking a lone tour of the human accommodation, or *barracks*, he'd then returned to his engines in the sky.

'It's going to double the number we have here,' said Irene.

'Indeed.'

'My head aches just thinking about it,' Chenghu interjected.

Ottanger glanced at him, smile fixed. As during Axel's inter-rogation of him, he was keeping himself rigidly under control. He allowed enough anxiety and excitement through that he deemed suitable for what they were apparently about to do, while deeper inside he locked down wilder and more explosive emotions. Reaching the end of the walkway, his holosense expanded again, the tunnel apparently extending above to infinity, and down to pierce through the world. He could see below where thousands of soon-to-be soldiers lived, exercised and trained, and felt a tug almost of disconnection. Peering into the craft, he saw Pranjab in place in a front bubble, like one of those viewing blisters on the engines in the sky. Jane, Jordan, Callis and Agaia were in misshapen and soft inward-facing seats in the rear section, while behind him he could see the rest stepping out of the stairwell. His tension still contained, he stepped up and entered. He nodded to the others and moved on past them to the bubble. This had a sphincter door to its rear, presently open. The whole bubble was apparently clear, with the front section giving a view out across the top of the city slab. A melted-looking console ringed it inside, and in that ring two seats stood on stalks. He ducked in and dropped into the empty one.

'Did you get your research equipment aboard?' he asked.

Pranjab gave him an amused look. 'Of course.' He stabbed a thumb behind.

Ottanger didn't need to look round because he could see packages attached to the inside of the hull at the back.

'Control of the vessel?' he enquired.

Pranjab simply pointed to a pad on the console ahead of them. The thing looked like a low flat mushroom. They both knew what it was, but neither of them wanted to talk about it right then. Other controls consisted of hand units that pulled out on translucent cables, in which some fluid ran. Ottanger had a good idea from his mental downloads how this all worked, but he would get a better idea soon enough.

The others entered, dumping equipment in a centre aisle, where mechanisms like squid tentacles folded out of the floor and secured them. They then sat in the remaining inward-facing seats. There were no visible safety straps – all that would kick in on the basis of need. They exchanged few words, and that had become pretty much standard, with little need for chatter on top of their empathic connection. This was excepting the one question they all wanted to ask: *What are you hiding, Ottanger?*

Pranjab pulled one of the hand units and brushed a finger over one surface. The hull sphincter closed up with the sound of a vacuum pipe hitting a plastic bag.

'It's quite warm in here,' said Ottanger.

'I'll make it cooler, just a little,' said Pranjab, thumbing another control. The two of them exchanged meaningful looks.

'Take us up off the ground,' Ottanger instructed.

Pranjab grimaced and grabbed another control. He worked this for a second, put it back to take another, and tried that next one. Ottanger felt grav come on, and with holosense observed the craft rising. Of course it had taken Pranjab a second to find the correct control because he needed to download knowledge of how this thing operated.

'Are we ready?' Ottanger asked loudly, while casually leaning forwards and pressing his hand down on that mushroom object.

'Yes, we're ready,' said Jane – the only one who answered verbally.

The thing sank under his palm. Then pincers, like those of some mud-dwelling worm, punched out either side of his hand and into the back of it. It hurt, and through his holosense he could see the thing sucking his blood. This was yet another danger point, where the Fenris might grow suspicious, if watching, and shut down the tunnel. He sighed out a careful breath, sensing the curiosity rising in those behind, and then, as the pincers retracted, felt his sense of self expanding through the veins and capillaries all around him in the vessel. The iconic language played in his mind, and now he could read it even more easily than written English. He felt his blood hitting home in neural junctions, and his downloaded understanding of the vessel expanding. It was perhaps like the difference between having a technical understanding of running, and actually doing so. His grip on the vessel continued to grow, but now he had enough, and even with the thing slippery in his grasp, he finally threw it, and its contents, into a jaunt.

It felt easier to shift such a load now than it had been to move that agricultural machine. The multiverse opened out, distorted through the walls of the tunnel, and since there was only one way to go, that's where he took them. The biotech network inside him seemed bright, and it webbed out to the others, as well as the ship. He took nothing from them to assist the jaunt, since they'd need all their energy for the rescues they were about to carry out. They shot down the tunnel, and all seemed well until they approached their destination. Here the tunnel punched through the regularly knotted hive manifold, where incursions groped down the tunnel wall like lampreys against glass. When they passed beyond that, Committee Earth loomed ahead, with the tunnel running right to the Fenris's manifold there and to the surface. Ottanger pushed before they reached this destination and reality fell back in around them. He sighed out his relief.

The vessel exited as planned in high atmosphere. He held out a hand and Pranjab handed over the control he'd been clutching. Ottanger slid his fingers over its surfaces to engage grav and stabilize the vessel. He could have done this mentally, but didn't want to focus more attention on the thing's biotech than necessary. Internal vision showed him nothing nearby, while longer-range sensors of the vessel gave him distances to the nearest objects – there was a satellite passing above, and a space plane heading up to a space station wrapped around a captured asteroid, both hundreds of kilometres away.

'Well, we're away now,' said Jordan meaningfully.

Ottanger turned, finding the seat turning with him on its stalk, and just went with that. He studied them all with more than human eyes. Could he trust them once they'd done their job here and gone back to the fenris world, out of his influence?

'Get your gear together and prepare to jump to your locations,' he said.

'No explanations?' asked Agaia.

He decided it just wasn't worth the risk, at least with some of them.

'Explanations will come later, I promise you that.' Annoyed expressions met his gaze, but he did feel some relief in the network now they knew there *would* be an explanation. Except for Chenghu, Irene, Jane, Pranjab and himself, the others collected up their gear. They shrugged on packs and readied weapons. Chancel, Adriana and Ektian moved to the centre of the vessel and loosely linked hands. All three of them showed their annoyance by not waiting for his go-ahead. With a clapping sound, they disappeared. Next Agaia, Jordan and Callis gathered together.

'No reneging on explanations,' said Jordan.

'You'll get them.' He tipped them a nod and, with the same clapping sound, they disappeared too.

'So the inner council remains,' said Irene, moving up. 'Bar one.' She looked around at Jane.

'Jane is essential to what I do next,' Ottanger replied.

'And what is that?' Chenghu asked.

Ottanger scanned them on all levels available to his senses and found them sufficiently trustworthy. Anyway, Chenghu and Irene would need something from him, when they discovered that Pranjab was set to join them in handling the refugee jaunt, while he and Jane wouldn't be going.

'I told you some of my history in the resistance. How every violent action we took led to a worsening situation, and you've experienced the same with your interventions here.' He pointed a finger down at the planet below and gave Irene a meaningful look. She winced, then shook her head as if to dispel past pain.

He continued, 'The Fenris is right to say the hive is a danger to us all. But what do you think the result of the present course will be? The Fenris wants to shut the hive down, while it wants jaunt biotech. Neither, in my estimation, is likely to back down.'

'Actual fighting in this so-called war. It's what we've been preparing for, after all,' said Irene, and he was glad to see the words were bitter on her tongue.

'Correct, but meanwhile we have the hive moon and the fenris world virtually untouchable. What is the endgame here?'

After a long silence, Chenghu said, 'I don't see one.'

Ottanger nodded. 'It'll be a perpetual garnering of resources and power, with which the two sides will strike at each other. Meanwhile, they'll attack each other on worlds other than their own. This will result in proxy wars with no end in sight – a steady expansion of the battlefield. Committee Earth will be first to go under, then others will follow.'

'Seems likely,' said Chenghu, sounding unsure.

'It's like old bloc powers fighting through others, because they're terrified of the real fight between them and what it really means,' Ottanger grimaced. 'Or at least one side is.'

'So what do you propose?' Irene asked.

'I propose to end this right now. I propose to give the hive what it wants.'

The argument lasted for some time, but in the end he'd convinced them. When they found out Pranjab had known from before the first rescue jaunt, and was in complete agreement, that tilted the balance. Ottanger could have pushed them, and demanded submission through their network. But he wanted their agreement without that. It was risky telling them, because they'd carry out their rescue and be back at the fenris world long before he was done – then one of them might just have a change of heart and tell the Fenris – giving the creature time still to stop him.

After Pranjab, Irene and Chenghu finally clapped out of existence, Ottanger turned the vessel nose up and accelerated steadily out of atmosphere. Internal grav and inertial damping came on. Jane took the opportunity to move into the cockpit bubble and drop into the chair Pranjab had occupied.

'So that leaves me,' she said.

'I don't feel good about what I need to ask of you,' said Ottanger, 'but it's essential. Otherwise we'll end up on the bad end of a hive missile. I want you to—'

'I hear it sometimes,' she interrupted, 'even back on the fenris world. I know. You want me to open up to the hive and become a link again, just like I did with the Fenris.'

'Yes, I do.'

'Isn't there some danger, in that I know what you intend to do?'

He shook his head. 'I've inspected that bioradio in your head for some time. The hive cannot read your thoughts. It just has some control over your language centres and visual cortex.' He turned to look at her. 'Think about it. If it could read minds

581

with such an implant, why didn't it just do that with me, rather than question me?'

'Yes, I see. Makes sense.'

'You'll just talk to the hive for a while, and be its eyes, then either you or I can turn the thing off again.'

'It still isn't pleasant.'

'I'm sorry.'

She shrugged. 'It seems to me the only way, and it will save billions of lives. But I want one promise from you.'

'What's that?' Ottanger flinched internally, because though he wanted to stop a war that could eat up whole worlds, and those billions of lives, there was still a cost in lives.

'If it doesn't work out as you expect, I want you to kill me.'

Ottanger didn't know what to say. It seemed highly likely they'd be captured. He had various plans and he knew he was strong enough to push against the hive manifold, but the hive would be a lot more organized this time, and unlikely to be caught out as before. His hope was that once it had what it wanted, though perhaps not in the way it wanted, it would either let them go or be so busy they could slip away.

'I promise,' he finally conceded.

The vessel kept on rising and he noted vapour trails heading towards his location, but much lower down. They were jets, and not vacuum capable, so would be no problem. Higher up, he observed the space station in all its glory, noting just how much wealth was being thrown into that. Perhaps they wanted to take humans properly interplanetary, and make a larger base than they presently had on Mars. It would perhaps help, though he doubted the capability, or inclination, of the Committee to transport people off planet at a rate even approaching the birth rate. More likely this was about opening up space to only the upper echelons. Finally, the biotech in the ship, that extension of himself, told him they were in vacuum, at which point he hit the main drive. Inertial damping compensated but he still felt some of the acceleration and his chair tentatively began to close about him.

'Pulling clear,' he said.

His mind, struggling to find interpretations, showed him the fenris braid of tunnels, splayed at its end and gripping the Earth. In proximity to this, the multiverse was a distorted thing, but as they drew further out, it began to clarify in his holosense. He felt some inner tightness coming off at this expansive vision, and overlaid on it the maps in his mind. There, distantly, he could see the airless version of Earth and its hive moon. The hive manifold was wrapped around them both, making it impossible to jaunt directly to either.

Spearing out from that dark multidimensional blob in existence, the manifold's arcing braid of tunnels stretched across to the sheared-away parallel of Earth, which it also encapsulated. He saw how it would go. If the Fenris couldn't keep up the power supply, his manifold would collapse here, on Committee Earth. The hive would then throw another series of tunnels over to encapsulate this world too. He imagined the nightmare ensuing, as the hive flooded through to seek out anyone with precursor jaunter tech in them. The Committee would fight, of course, and with no concern about casualties. The death toll would be in the billions. And that was only on the first of a series of worlds.

'You know I figured it out a while ago,' said Jane.

He ran the drive for longer, until he couldn't feel the pull of the fenris tunnel any more, and all became clearer too.

'The others didn't,' Ottanger observed.

'I'm your sister so have a little more understanding of how your mind works. I didn't figure out exactly what you intended, but I knew you'd be going there.' She pointed vaguely, but he knew she was indicating the hive moon, even though in multiverse terms it wasn't something she could point to.

'How?' he asked, as he observed a launch of something from the space station.

'Your explanation of using this ship as a platform while you finalized the rescue jaunts just didn't gel. So I knew you wanted to go somewhere you couldn't jaunt to, because it'd be vacuum. The hive seemed the only logical place. I thought you were going to load up with warheads.' She gestured to the back of the vessel. 'I didn't expect that.'

With the fenris manifold in place, jaunters from Committee Earth ended up only on the fenris world, and vice versa. The hive moon was defended from jaunt attack and presently only connected to the split-away parallel, so to go there, or to a point in space directly adjacent to the hive moon, required him to distance himself physically from both manifolds.

'Strange the others didn't figure that out,' he observed. Two missiles, which could be either sensory probes or weapons from the space station, were drawing closer. They didn't matter – they couldn't reach them.

'I think they got as far as me,' she said, 'but we didn't talk about it because of the pressure you put us under to keep silent. It hurt my head sometimes.'

'Again, I'm sorry,' Ottanger said.

The main engine continued to roar and internal perception, magnified through the ship biotech, showed him the Earth receding behind. They streaked out and out, and he noted the two missiles ceasing their burn and dropping behind. Time passed. Jane dipped her head and from her he received a sense of inward-looking calm. She was preparing herself, and so should he. Using a control Pranjab had shown him, which he knew well now anyway, he turned the internal temperature up a little. He sensed it exactly and knew the requirements: a much higher temperature later on.

The standard moon of Committee Earth lay visible ahead to the left, slowly drawing closer and then past. He gazed at the bases scattered about its surface and wondered if any of them were still active. According to broadcasts, mining and manufacturing were very busy there and constantly supplying products to Earth. That was probably a lie. As the moon dropped behind, he felt tethers of existence sufficiently stretched. This baffled his inner facility that zeroed him to survivable regions from world to world and, groping for something recognizable, it fell into a new format, coming more under his conscious control.

He scanned the multiverse, ascertaining they'd now achieved sufficient physical distance from Committee Earth not to be dragged into the fenris manifold. Twisting his perception, he saw this expand and in some sense wrap his Earth and its moon, but also the split-away parallel, and the hive moon with the airless Earth it orbited. Contending manifolds were concentrated around their own seized worlds, and then shadowed across those of the opposition. This continued shadowlike across multiple Earths, arcing to infinity. Trying to elucidate it was like trying to describe a three-dimensional object to a two-dimensional flatlander. He could see it, but his old biology human mind struggled to make interpretations.

'Far enough?' said Jane quietly, raising her head.

'Far enough,' he agreed.

He reached out again to grasp the vessel's biotech and everything within it, then tracked close to an old mental map. He turned the ship to face back towards the Earth and the bright crescent of the moon. Then, with the network inside him glaring, he threw everything into a jaunt. The universe seemed to take a breath. Star fields loosened, and the entire Earth shifted and became denuded of colour. The moon zipped over to one side, expanding as it did so. They came out of the jaunt with a crash – things out of alignment and the stab of a harsh headache immediately hit him. The expanded moon now had hive structures etched all over its surface and glared in the full light of the sun. He took a breath and then set the vessel on a course towards it.

'Now would be good,' he said, turning to inspect Jane.

She nodded and, looking pale and ill, dipped her head. He looked within her and saw, as he had done before, the bioradio in her skull. She'd routed her black blood to the capillaries supporting it, through a more permeable blood–brain barrier. The thing shifted slightly, like a parasite getting more comfortable in her skull, and she winced. Adjusting his perception across the EM spectrum, he saw it powering up and its signal transmitting, the waves rippling out. Deep-linked into the ship's biotech, he picked up that carrier and retransmitted it. The reply signal came back almost instantaneously, but it was a short while before Jane responded. Her head came up and she looked at him.

'You are a threat,' she said. 'You will be destroyed.'

'I have brought you the jaunt biotech you've been seeking. We do not want war,' Ottanger replied.

A long pause ensued. Jane raised a hand and revolved a finger at her skull. She still had control of her body, just not the voice centre of her mind. Which made sense. When he'd first seen her, the hive humans had been towing her along with rods attached to a ring around her neck.

'You are a danger,' she abruptly said.

'I have no way to attack you,' Ottanger replied.

'You have weapons.'

Ottanger grimaced, now seeing a number of launches from the moon. He hadn't wanted to throw away advantages he might need later, but it seemed he had little choice in the matter. The weapons for this craft were all add-on and, through the biotech, he gave a series of instructions. Clunks and whines, and liquid sliding noises resounded through the vessel, then in his larger view he saw the launchers and guns detaching and drifting. A tweak of the drive pushed the vessel sideways, making those weapons drop away. In response the missiles – and they were definitely that – changed course and fell into orbit around the moon.

'We are observing,' said the hive.

And the hive certainly was. Linked into the biotech, he could feel the intrusive scanning passing through the vessel, or him, and the waves of radiation lapping against the hull. This just went on and on, and he began to warm up, seeing beads of sweat on Jane's face too. The hive was making sure he had nothing nasty aboard, like a fusion nuke. It would recognize their laminar power storage as something of little danger. From what he knew of the hive thus far, it probably didn't recognize the zero-point collector in the hull as anything more than protective layers either. Still, this scanning was going on too long, and he cast a concerned glance to the packages at the back. Things there were okay thus far, but they wouldn't be for much longer.

Finally the hive spoke. 'The jaunter biotech is in you.' At that moment the scanning stopped, and Ottanger wiped sweat off his brow.

'Yes, but I have no intention of letting you take me apart to get to it.' He grimaced. 'Anyway, it seems to me that you had some problems figuring it out from those jaunters you . . . examined before.'

'We learned much.'

'But not enough.'

'What do you bring?'

'First some detail. Do you understand that the initial biotech, as it is on Committee Earth, was put in place by a series of viruses?'

'We understand this.'

'Then do you know the rest of it was installed by a larger organism the Fenris sent?'

'We understand this was done by the creature that fights us. We understand this from information gathered.'

'Okay.'

Ottanger stood up and beckoned to Jane. She carefully got out of her chair, and he realized her human eyes were blind – she was operating wholly on holosense. He led the way back through the vessel to the packages attached to the back wall. These were long bags of a material much like canvas. He pulled up the flap on one, pulled a long cylinder segment halfway out, then tapped the top. The plasmel cleared to show some of the hundreds of thousands of neatly packed chrysalises inside.

'The Fenris sent viruses because in the beginning he didn't have the power to send anything larger. Later, as his power grew, he sent bigger organisms whose bite imparts the remainder of the biotech.'

'The inocular flies,' said the hive.

It obviously *had* been information gathering, probably right back from when it sent those hive scouts whose corpses he'd been shown during his interrogation. This made things a little easier.

He gestured to the exposed segment. 'These are the chrysalises of those flies. They can be hatched out and studied.'

'Bring them to us,' said the hive.

Exterior view showed one of the missiles break from orbit and head out towards them. As it approached, it shed its warhead and then adjusted course away from it. Doubtless the device would lead them to where the hive wanted them to go. But this had to be convincing, so resistance was required.

'Sorry, I can't do that. I am here to deliver this technology to end a war, but I'm not suicidal. You can send a ship out to collect them or, alternatively, I can dump them in vacuum for you to collect.'

Now the other missiles started heading out from the moon again, while the ship's sensors highlighted energy surges down on the surface. Jane grimaced and closed her eyes, holding her palms against her temples. She went down on her knees. Ottanger felt the shift a moment later and, in the multiverse, it was as if a black wave had come down. The hive had expanded the effect of the manifold out to encompass them, so there was no way he was jaunting this ship away now. Just as at Caprock, his holosense collapsed too, and he knew that within this manifold the chances of jumping locally were highly suppressed. Other activations came to his attention, and in a long view, via his vessel's instruments, he saw hive ships out at a Lagrange point, firing up their engines. He'd expected something like this. The hive wanted to grab the opportunity presented here, which meant not just the inocular fly chrysalises but him and Jane as well. And he had no doubt that if it didn't understand the tech from these, it would still go on to Committee Earth to grab the 'mutated' there. This would give it pre-jaunt humans, the flies and two jaunters to experiment with endlessly.

The missile that'd shed its warhead turned and decelerated towards his vessel. Then a few kilometres out, deceleration transitioned into acceleration back towards the moon. Those ships out there were getting up speed too. He wondered if frozen hive human crews had been thawed out. He shoved the cylinder containing the chrysalises back into the bag and closed the flap, having noticed one chrysalis starting to hatch out.

Jane dropped her hands and looked up, dead faced again. 'You will follow the unit ahead of your ship to internal bay.'

'Or what? You'll blow up my ship?' Ottanger exclaimed. 'Seems like a really stupid thing to do. Here I am, offering you what you have mobilized your civilization to obtain!'

'Our weapons can disable by electromagnetic means,' the hive stated.

'Why the hell do you want us to land?'

'We want all information you have on the technology.'

That was a half-truth, of course – the information the hive wanted would be peeled off their bones.

'I can tell you what I know from here,' Ottanger protested.

'You will come to us.'

Gazing down at Jane, he found his sense of her blurred by her connection to the hive. But there was still enough of a link for him to give a little push, while bringing a finger up and drawing it across his throat. Her expression turned agonized, and inside her he could see the blood routing away from her skull, with the bioradio shutting down. He instructed the ship to stop retransmitting from her, and to cut the signal coming in from the hive too. She slumped and looked as though she was about to go down on her face, before he caught her and lifted her up. He took her forward, into the cockpit bubble, and down into a chair. Further mental instructions had the chair closing round her, supporting her.

'That was . . . horrible,' she said.

'Yes, I understand,' he said, now taking up the flight control and directing his ship to follow that beheaded missile. He then picked up another control Pranjab had used earlier. It was for the ship's internal environment and covered a huge range of pressures, gas mixes and temperatures. He put the temperature up twenty degrees. Jane finally opened her clenched eyes. She looked tired and somehow a lot older than before.

'I really hope you're right,' she said. 'I could sense a lot more of it than before. It wasn't just in my language centres and visual cortex but in other places.' She shuddered. 'Empathy is a little thing compared to that – it was invasion.'

'It cannot read your thoughts, no matter how much of your brain activity it monitors, because it has no template to work from.'

'You sure about that?'

He thought about those corpses he'd destroyed on the hive moon, and the way Jane had been inspected. No, he wasn't entirely sure, just like he hadn't been sure earlier that he could fully trust those he'd revealed his plan to.

'I guess we're about to find out.' He shrugged. 'Because all it will change, in the end, is the method of delivery.'

22

Ottanger

As they drew closer and closer to the moon, Ottanger could clearly see the structures all over its surface. It was as if someone had constructed a vast city out of a rubbery material then squeezed it into a ball. There seemed to be no natural surface of the moon left. Despite the manifold crippling his holosense, he amplified it through the ship's sensors to view the shape of the multiverse locally, or parts of it at least. Things like vast tornados rose up evenly spaced around the moon's crust, then opened into the infinite surface of the manifold, slewing around, out from the moon's orbit, to enclose it and its Earth. Now inside the thing, he could also see the Earth enveloped, as well as the split-away parallel, which in exterior view looked like long tunnels through the multiverse. With his head starting to throb, he closed down his struggling holosense and focused on real-world stuff from the sensors.

The 'tornados' were rising from structures on the moon's surface, which looked like flattened-down roses, constructed of blue-green metal. Some kind of meta-material reflector or ampli-fier, he assumed. The manifold driving machines, like the one he'd destroyed, doubtless lay below the centre of each. Around these, the rest of the crust mostly consisted of distorted blockish structures with deep valleys running between, filled with pipes at their bottom. Towers and spines also protruded; he didn't think them likely to be dwellings, but sensors.

Their guide slowed a quarter of an orbit in, above all this. Ottanger reduced their speed as well, to maintain a kilometre's distance behind it. The thing then began to descend, and he followed it down. He glanced at Jane's worried expression as she closed up the visor on her suit. He did the same – it was now getting very hot inside the vessel and the suits had a cooling function.

The headless missile dropped into one of the valleys, between two vast buildings resembling partially collapsed cylinders. Down at the bottom, he could make out figures moving over the long clumps of pipes. Focusing in, he saw suited post-heads and larger creatures, like human earth-moving equipment, busily at work replacing a section of pipe. Meanwhile, the missile slowed to a stop and, on stabs of steam thrusters, drifted in towards the wall of one of the buildings. As it approached, ribbed sections of the wall slid aside to reveal a brightly lit interior, in which frameworks held octagonal landing pads, mostly occupied by the hive's odd-looking laminar ships. The missile slid on inside and he followed it. The thing descended to the side of an empty pad – he brought his ship in over it and landed.

'Well, this is it,' he said, still observing through the ship's sensors.

Jane was staring out of the front screen at the view. She just nodded mutely.

A dome of some green glassy material began to slide up and over from one side of the pad. Ottanger watched it, feeling a trap closing. The lack of ship's weapons had crippled his options for getting it out of here, and he now felt deeper reservations about what he'd committed himself to. It was all very well believing your actions could end a war before it got going, saving billions of lives, but the personal need to survive didn't just go away. He shot another glance at Jane and his guilt hurt him almost physically. He'd given her no choice in the matter. And frankly, if she hadn't been amenable, he would have forced her compliance. He felt the irony of the lengths he'd gone to rescue her from this place, only now to bring her back again.

The dome closed with a shudder he felt through the deck, and the ship's sensors indicated rising air pressure outside. As it reached optimum, an iris opened in the platform fifty metres from the ship. Even while the thing was still opening, post-heads and warriors swarmed out towards his vessel. They carried weapons, large packs and a variety of tools. He knew that if he and Jane didn't step outside, they'd take the vessel apart around them. He stood up.

'Remember your promise,' said Jane, standing also.

He nodded curtly and moved back into the main body of the ship. Here he stopped to pick up a large backpack from the central luggage area and opened it. He took out two machine pistols and handed one up to Jane, then clips, a sidearm, and a strip pack of grenades. For himself, he stuck a machine pistol to the front of his suit, then the revolver he'd first acquired on the warlike world he visited, which he concealed inside his suit. Meanwhile Jane hid grenades all about her person. This done, he headed back to the canvas bags containing his special delivery for the hive.

'They won't disarm us,' Jane called after him. He just turned to look at her, until she continued, 'Having a few hundred, or thousands, of its members killed is about as relevant to it as us losing a few drops of blood.'

He nodded. 'It made me disarm the ship because . . . economies of scale.' Wondering if this conversation was a rationalization for killing, he turned to the canvas bags.

There were four of them, each containing three of the long cylinder segments, and he brought them back in four trips. The things felt hot under his hands, and were vibrating like faulty transformers. He took them out of their bags and laid them in a long row, then next took the last item from the backpack: a reel of explosives. Just like the ones Irene had used to blow the door to the cells in the jaunt research Complex. Unwinding these, he stuck them all over the segments. He then used the touch slide on each to wind the explosive yield right down to the minimum. With that ready, he set the detonator that would send the signal to blow them all. Finally, he shoved the segments down into just one big pack. They protruded out about halfway, but he could carry them like that. Lifting the pack was an effort, though, even for him, until he realized his stupidity and instructed the biotech in the vessel. Internal gravity gradually died, leaving them subject to that of the moon.

'Are you ready?' he asked.

'I'll never be that,' Jane replied. She looked towards the screen where the hive humans were now visible flooding around outside, ringing them completely. 'When we go out, they'll simply grab us and take what they want.' She shook her head and looked lost and frightened. 'I was stupid to make you promise to kill me, since you won't even have the chance. And you were lying when you made that promise.'

'I don't think they'll grab us straight away.' Ottanger felt like a shit as he said this. She was right at least about the killing.

'Your reasoning?'

He slung on the huge pack and stabbed a thumb towards it. 'The hive wants these but doesn't know whether I can destroy

595

them, or if they might be damaged in some violent action. It'll go carefully and patiently while we're bringing them in.'

'You're presuming rationality.'

'I've seen no reason to presume otherwise. The hive might be a vast human civilization, but it's also a rational individual with quite a simplistic, almost childlike approach.'

'And then, once it's sure it has what it wants?'

'It'll likely have what it wants sooner than expected,' said Ottanger, 'then we'll see what we see.'

She turned away to look out the screen again and said, 'Fait accompli, anyway.'

Ottanger had no reply for her, so gave the vessel the instruction to open its door.

The hull sphincter opened. The noise of movement, of mechanisms, a concerted sighing and the shifting of a large crowd, permeated from outside. Oddly, there was no shouting or calling at all. But he already knew hive humans didn't have vocal cords. With no sudden onrush of creatures into the craft, they were able to move over to the opening and peer out.

The sighing sound went up in volume, and he ascertained this to be their only form of vocal expression. Post-heads crowded the whole area from the iris opening right up to the ship, with warriors scattered throughout them at a ratio of about one to twenty. But none seemed inclined to enter. He glanced at Jane as she came up beside him and, switching over to suit radio, said, 'Do you see?'

'I see nothing but nightmares,' she replied.

Again Ottanger had no answer for her. Now they were down on the moon and about to enter it, he pushed out with his wider senses of the multiverse. Unsurprisingly, the ability to jaunt was utterly clamped down. Jumping in-world and holosense were also even more severely limited than they'd been his last time here. He saw jumping as only a final option. Without being able to see clearly, he'd likely end up putting the both of them inside moon rock.

Shrugging the pack to a more comfortable position, he took the first step and noted the change of tone in the sighing. The crowd shifted and jostled and, thankfully, he could see none of them bringing weapons to bear. He noted vapour forming ahead, as the hot air from the ship hit the cool air out here. Just because he could, he hit the control that drew his visor up into the top of his helmet. Now the smell hit him. It brought back memories of the sprawl, with that combination of body odour and sewage, but it also had an acrid taint, accompanied by a strange sweetness. It was just far enough from the smell of the sprawls for him to classify it as not quite human.

'Come on,' he said.

Jane opened her visor too and they stepped down to the front of the crowd. As he'd expected, the hive humans jostled hard against each other to open a path towards the iris. This path lay just wide enough to keep the two of them out of reach, though it seemed from those nearest stretching out their hands that the creatures wanted to touch them. In the moon's gravity, they moved in long loping steps, covering the distance quickly, which worked for his plan because he didn't want to give the hive too long to think.

Scanning these creatures, he again saw what he'd noticed while a captive here: many of them showed the customary signs of viral infection. Snotty noses and watery eyes abounded, accompanied by dark blotches on the skin of those infected. It had surprised him when he'd realized what this meant – that they'd picked up the biotech virus from the jaunter body parts they were examining. And the fact it was establishing in them had been the reason for the diffuse pull he'd felt when he was here last. But surely a monoculture as vulnerable as the hive would have severe forms of biosecurity? Then, comparing the hive to the fenris – both from distant futures – he realized that, although in those far-off ages all biology had been turned to human purpose, the rogue kinds arising from mutation, or perhaps an attack, weren't unheard of. And they both had their different methods of dealing with these, which reflected their cultures. In the fenris, their biotech and amped-up immune systems protected them. With the hive, the method was simpler: easily disposable and renewable humans.

'It's trying to talk through me,' said Jane tightly.

'Allow it to do so,' said Ottanger coldly.

'What's the point of that right now?'

'Just do it.'

It seemed Jane was now baulking at just the wrong moment so, disliking himself intensely, he pushed her through their singular network. She made a nasal whining sound and stumbled a little, then straightened up.

'You bring the biotech,' she said, voice leaden.

Ottanger held up the little detonator high, knowing the hive would be looking at it through the eyes all around him. 'I've also brought a way to destroy it, attaching explosives all over it. I am bringing it to you now, and I will answer your questions, but I fully intend to leave afterwards.'

'This is danger to our purpose,' said the hive.

Ottanger noted the double meaning of that and ignored it, continuing, 'I will bring this biotech to where you require it to be, and then I will return to my ship. From my ship, I'll answer your questions, and then you will allow me to leave. Once I am clear of the moon, I will deactivate the explosives and depart.'

It was all utterly specious stuff, and he knew that if he'd been saying this to someone with a good grasp of human language and interactions, it would've been shot full of holes. Why couldn't he hand the things over to the post-heads here? How could he believe the hive would let him go when he departed the moon? Perhaps the hive was debating these matters with itself, or perhaps everything had flown straight over its naive head. It wanted what he carried, it wanted him and Jane, and all it knew was that these were heading in the right direction – which was through the iris opening they'd just reached and down some long stairs, with human steps made for moon gravity.

'You must remove the explosives,' said the hive, in what seemed almost a sullen tone. 'You must answer the questions.'

It was funny really. The hive had its limited facility with language, and could distort things a little, but he realized that the concept of saying anything but the truth seemed to evade it, just as much as the perception of anyone else not telling the truth did too. But then perhaps this was like the technological development here – later the hive would grow sophisticated enough to detect, and tell, elaborate lies. That's where societal sophistication led.

'You will have everything you want,' said Ottanger, telling a half-truth in precisely the same manner as the hive did.

He and Jane descended the steps two at a time, rapidly plunging underground. Post-heads and warriors lined the way down on either side, while the crowd above closed in behind. This felt even more like a trap closing. Beside him Jane shuddered and looked at him with bloodshot eyes.

'You forced me,' she said.

'It's a function of the empathic network subsumed by old hierarchical biology,' he explained. 'Irene could do it to a certain extent with the others, but I'm stronger than her.'

He saw Jane's flash of annoyance and knew he'd been throwing out fancy words to cover the guilt he felt.

'I'm sorry,' he said.

'It doesn't matter how much you apologize if you keep doing the same things.' She faced forwards again.

'Indeed, but another aspect of human hierarchies is apparent altruism, with a basis in selfish genetics. We are both smart enough to know that billions will die if the hive and the Fenris go to war. And, having accepted my thesis as correct, we both see the value to humanity overall of the sacrifice we may have to make. You came willingly, remember.'

She glanced at him again now with amusement. 'I don't think any number of apologies will be sufficient for that pompous speech.' She stopped and scanned around, for they'd reached the bottom of the stairs, where tunnels speared off in three directions. Hive humans were packed in down here, blocking off all but one of the burrows, which they lined on either side, offering a path further down. 'Where will you do it?'

Ottanger turned into the path, again keeping to a fast pace.

'Your memories of me getting you out of here are probably unclear,' he said. 'I tried to jump out a number of times and it was killing you, so I took us into a generator room. It was unusual in that it was the only enclosed place I could find that had a door.' He pointed upwards. 'There are pressure doors on the surface, and occasional bulkhead doors down here, but everything else is almost like open cell foam. Hive society has no requirement for privacy, and doors are a waste of resources as well as a hindrance to its activities.'

'So anywhere apart from those rooms,' she said.

'We're here now, so let's go as deep as we can – that will give us a better spread.'

'Let's just hope it works quickly.'

He nodded. 'In the Complex, you and I were only dosed with small amounts of the biotech, to drive jaunts while also keeping us under some degree of control. With the others who were actually bitten, it worked much more quickly – in many cases they started jaunting almost immediately afterwards.'

The tunnel continued to slope down and, though he could hardly perceive beyond what his eyes could see, he estimated they were half a mile down when they hit a steeper curving slope. They kept on going, quickly but not hurriedly, and he realized they were loping down a spiral that drilled down into the moon. He was in two minds about this, and he guessed the hive might be too. The hive was determined to ensure it had them in its grasp, while at the same time, it would surely be conflicted with regards to the explosives he was carrying down here. For his purposes, he too needed to be deep inside, but once he'd achieved that goal, he also wanted both of them to be able to escape.

'Tell me what happened to you on Committee Earth, since I last saw you back home,' he said. 'We haven't really had the time for normal conversation.'

Jane gave him a puzzled look. 'There's not much to tell.'

'Tell me it anyway.'

She shrugged and launched into it, detailing how she'd followed her roaming lifestyle within her sector, knowing the authorities wanted to talk to her. Then about how she'd evaded street political officers, only to be caught up in an Inspectorate sweep. They hadn't been grabbing specific people, just those with any signs of 'mutations'. He kept throwing questions at her whenever she faded off. Her puzzlement turned to realization, and she started throwing questions back at him too. It was a way of keeping the hive mind distracted. For while it listened to their chatter, trying to glean information and a way to separate them from the inocular flies, as well as from the explosives, it perhaps wouldn't think so much about other matters. And it also passed the time.

The tunnel wound on, down and down. And then, having been in motion for the best part of an hour, they came to a point where the route straightened out. When he vaguely sensed a sizeable space lying ahead, Ottanger estimated they must be kilometres below the surface now. A short while later, they stepped inside that space, a large chamber packed with hive humans and equipment. To the right and left, loose conglomerations of hard tech and biotech occupied the volume up to the walls. It was an open organic scaffold, almost like the skeletal remains of wood's cellular structure writ large. Devices, or perhaps living things, clung to this like aphids. Tubes ran through it all, like roots connected to globular glass vessels. Post-heads, and the creatures he'd once designated as surgeons, worked amid it, moving like apes in trees. The similarity here to fenris technology didn't escape him, or the slew of implications from that. What were the real differences between the two cultures? He paused to gaze at recognizable human remains hanging on wires. But, taking a step further, he saw the corpse had been split and folded open to reveal a hollow interior. And its shape was maintained by denuded bones and some aerogel material. Obviously the hive had snatched up the remaining jaunter corpses and found them empty of the biotech it sought.

'Tunnels everywhere,' said Jane, gesturing to the solid walls behind these structures.

She was right. This seemed like a junction of sorts. And, judging by the hive humans blocking the path ahead and edging in behind, he gathered this must be their intended destination. He also understood he'd been procrastinating. While they were walking and talking, they'd remained unharmed, and he'd not had to take the final step. But now was the time.

'I guess this is where it wants the biotech,' he said.

'It certainly wants to talk again,' said Jane, her voice strained.

He turned to her and touched his visor control once more, closing it up. Her expression edged on panic as she did the same, for she knew what this now signified. With slow deliberation, he shrugged off the pack and put it down on the floor, leaning it against his legs. Meanwhile he noticed the hive humans edging in ever closer. He had to remember they weren't individuals but components of the thing now straining to speak through Jane. Opening the backpack, he slid out two of the long segments and weighed them in his hands like spears. They felt heavy to him, even in this gravity.

Now.

Abruptly he threw one ahead, straight over the crowd there, then turned and threw the other one behind, towards the tunnel they'd entered through. He heard them thud and drop to the floor with a glassy ringing. They'd certainly hit hive humans before falling – with all of them clustered so close it would have been difficult not to. Without pause, he stooped to the pack and took out two more, then threw these to the sides – one thudding into the hollow human corpse. Around him the sighing, which had been a constant susurration, increased almost to a roar. The post-heads, warriors and surgeons surged back and forth, pushing into each other, and even scrambling up the walls. Yet still they kept themselves at a distance from him and Jane. Ottanger stooped again, and threw again. It was at that moment he knew something had changed, and he grabbed up the detonator remote.

The crowd seemed to pause, every member of it shivering. Ottanger raised the remote while kicking the pack away from him, and triggered it. Since he'd dialled down the explosives to a minimum, the sound was simply of firecrackers going off. The backpack jounced along the floor, splitting open to spill any remaining segments. With the integrity of their glassy ceramic sufficiently damaged, they broke into pieces. And they seemed to boil with smoke – those before him, and the others he'd thrown too. A deep buzzing then impinged as thousands upon thousands of newly hatched inocular flies rose up and scattered. Hive humans nearby twitched and jerked, bitten at once. Every space seemed to fill up with the buzzing things. Then, as they began to spread into the surrounding tunnels, and the dark speckled fog dispersed, the hive humans finally surged forwards.

Jane's machine pistol thrummed and collapsed the wavefront of hive humans, and they started to trip over their own dying. Ottanger turned and fired behind, stopping them there, then grabbed her shoulder and dragged her towards the nearest scaffold. Lariats smacked through the air, and one hit his waist then wrapped around it, its end groping out to snare his arm. But such was the crush no warrior could get a clear shot at them. They dived into the structure, with numerous hands groping after them, methodically firing short bursts about themselves. Dying hive humans fell all around, continuing to block the ones trying to push in from behind. A grenade blew out in the main mass, flinging body parts, and then Jane tossed another through a gap in the scaffold, to where a cluster of surgeons were worming their way through. Given a brief breathing space, Ottanger switched his suit to assist and tore away the lariat from his waist. They moved, pushed by the pressure of the crowd, and only able to go where the space allowed. Then something else changed.

The nearest post-heads seemed to lose track of what they were doing and began groping about themselves aimlessly. One nearby had drawn a stun pistol, but then dropped it as if not knowing what it was. The multiverse stuttered. Ottanger felt an immediate sense of relief, as if walking all day under a cloudy sky and then seeing the sun breaking golden through it. He grabbed Jane's arm and incorporated her as, in a flash, he clearly saw their environment with his holosense. Hive humans crammed the surrounding tunnels, like lymphocytes attacking a bacterium. It was a window and probably a brief one, but he had to use it, and so he jumped them.

The multiverse stormed around them – it was just another snapshot, but in it he saw the manifold disrupted. It seemed they slid along a plain of black ice, until it fractured ahead, dropping them back through into reality. Ottanger immediately slammed into a wall, the bones in his left forearm breaking, and everything below that utterly numb. Jane hit beside him and bounced away, going down on her back. Why the same hadn't happened to him soon became evident when he looked down. His hand and lower forearm were imbedded in the wall. He stared at it in horror, knowing that part of his arm now consisted of a mixture of this wall and his flesh and bone. His biotech reacted quickly to the break, driven by adrenal surge, but it could do little beyond that point. He brought the machine pistol in and fired into the wall around where his hand entered it, shattering away a foamy stone. Clamping down on the pain, he then stuck the machine pistol to the front of his suit, pressed his right hand against the wall, and heaved. His left hand finally came free, caked in stone and utterly dead.

'Fuck fuck fuck!' said Jane, standing up. She then got a look at his hand and her eyes grew wide. He pointed along the tunnel they'd arrived in, where it sloped upwards, and they set out at a long, steady-paced jog. He'd no real idea where they were in relation to anything, but to get back to the ship, they needed to head towards the surface. Pushing with his internal sense, he could only perceive very little once more, though he could feel the disruption. It seemed the manifold was back in place. Movement behind alerted him to post-heads filling up the tunnel

NEAL ASHER

a hundred metres back. Their jog turned into a nightmare run, tracking round the steady curve of the tunnel. Then ahead, warriors came into sight.

Four of them were in the tunnel. Another wave of disruption came through the manifold, opening a gap, too brief for him to take advantage of it. He pulled out his machine pistol, but didn't fire. And, keyed to him, Jane didn't either. There was something wrong with these hive humans. Two of them were down on their knees, heads tilted up and hands against the floor, as if they wanted to hold the world steady. The other two were back against the walls of the tunnel, arms spread in a similar effort. Drawing closer, Ottanger saw the flies launching from their skin and coming to buzz around him and Jane. They landed briefly to test mouthparts against their suits, then flew on. As they came right up to the warriors, he saw further flies still biting them, and the numerous welts on their tough skin. Around those welts the hide had taken on a mauve hue, which could have been bruising but looked much like the colour of fenris skin.

They stepped past the warriors and then on, breaking into a run again. Another manifold gap passed, and this time Ottanger managed to locate a route up to the surface. Though what they'd do upon reaching it he wasn't sure. In all honesty, he'd expected to be a prisoner by now, finding ways for them to survive until the effect he expected here took hold.

'Look!' Jane exclaimed, elbowing the wall to turn, and coming down in a skidding halt. He did the same and peered back towards the warriors, as the post-heads flooded towards them. Only three of the warriors now occupied the tunnel, and no way in the physical world could one of them have gone elsewhere.

'Hundreds of bites,' said Ottanger. 'Obviously speeds up the process. Come on, keep moving.'

Another opening passed over them – another apparent break

606

in the manifold cloud. Ottanger felt the temptation to jump closer to the ship, but with the disruption he feared a repeat of his arm in the wall, and worse. Back the way they'd come, post-heads flooded past the warriors, but the scene took on a weird twist as some of them simply blurred out of existence, while others stretched out, seemingly into long lines, punching through the walls. He and Jane swung away and kept running.

The tunnel transitioned into a spiral going up. It might have been the one they'd come down, he didn't know. More waves of disruption passed through the manifold. He'd hoped for this, but not expected it, since he hadn't known precisely how much control the hive had over the thing, and how much was automatic function. He now guessed, by the way the hive incorporated its members into its technology, that the former was the case. A few turns up the spiral, they felt the manifold come back hard. Seemingly in response to this, part of a nearby wall exploded, slinging out a cloud of dust lit by a bright internal fire. They stopped to gaze at a post-head, half sunk into the wall. Its upper chest, shoulders and head protruded, as did its right leg. An electrical fire burned in a dark crater, down where he assumed its right hand had been captured. Obviously those stun weapons didn't react well to being rematerialized in foamed stone. It blinked at them, sighed, then its head dipped.

'They're already moving things with them when they jump,' said Jane.

'Damn, yes,' said Ottanger.

New jaunters usually struggled with that, as he had at first. But it seemed the hive humans, infected with the virus and now bitten by numerous flies, were changing very quickly indeed. He speculated that this could be because they didn't possess too much intelligence, or a firm perception of the world, to get in the way of what the biotech had honed down to an almost autonomous process. He tilted his head to listen. The sounds of chaos reached him: a constant crowd roar, as if the people here had discovered vocal cords, and a rumbling interspersed with explosions. They kept moving, and with each wave of disruption through the manifold, and each opening, further explosions occurred. A group of twenty post-heads blocked their path at one point, and they both opened fire simultaneously, then charged through. A feeling of shame bounced between them after that, and they didn't fire when encountering the next such group. The creatures were simply no longer reacting to them.

'It's trying to get it under control,' said Ottanger.

'Yes,' Jane replied bluntly.

The hive had its jaunt technology now.

And then, almost unbelievably, they were at the stairs they'd first come down. They bounded up past post-heads crouching against the walls, and around a warrior sunk to its waist in one step. When they came out of the iris, more hive humans milled about above, and they loped through them easily to the ship. Three post-heads were inside it, with a variety of tools laid out on the floor. They were crouching, like those on the stairs. Even as Ottanger decided what to do with them, another wave passed through and, with a whistling crack, one of them simply disappeared. He shook his head, stooped to grab one by the arm, heaved it up, and then pushed it out, tumbling down the steps. Jane brought the other, guiding and supporting it like an invalid to the steps. Once released, it walked obediently down.

'Now we have to figure out how to get out of here,' she said.

Once again connected to his surrounding biotech, Ottanger ordered the hull sphincter to close. He then moved forwards and took a seat, Jane dropping down in the one beside him. Picking up one of the control devices, he affirmed his connection.

'This is tough technology,' he said. 'And since we have suits, the ship doesn't have to be airtight.'

Realizing what he intended, Jane grabbed the sides of her chair.

He fired up the grav-engine and thrusters, lifting the vessel's nose, and then simply hit the fuser drive. The thing roared forwards and up, the drive flame searing the landing pad behind. Anticipating him, the system activated the chairs and the material snapped around the two of them. The hard impact tried to fling them through the front of the bubble, beyond which the dome shattered into hexagonal chunks. Cracks ripped around the cockpit bubble, and sections to the fore turned black. He saw dome material now blasting out ahead, and a second later hive humans tumbled through too, as air from the dome poured out into vacuum. Orienting the ship, he sped towards where they'd come in. The dome had been easy, but what lay ahead was a completely different matter. Calculating quickly, he ramped up their speed to the wall. Then, at the last moment, he spun the ship on thrusters, directing the fuser flame towards it. They decelerated fast, with the hot flame searing into the material, and then the rear end crashed into it. This time the impact tried to throw them back into the ship, and the chairs bent back on their stalks.

Air now roared out through a split opened down the side of their ship, while the biotech sent him an avalanche of errors. The vessel wasn't moving. Swiping aside the overload in his skull, and getting to the remaining sensor data, he saw it had punched partway through the wall, while the drive flame had gone out. He searched out and found the ignition sequence, then tried it. Something clattered, like an ancient engine starting up to the rear, but the flame re-ignited, burning dirty orange out into vacuum. With a horrible ripping sound, the ship surged back into the huge building, debris from it and the wall spreading out all around. Using just the few thrusters remaining, he flipped it over. He saw, through the cracked screen, the hole they'd made and accelerated towards it once more. Another crash, but then a moment later they were out into the trench. With the chairs sinking down into the floor, Ottanger angled them up hard, but they still bounced off the curve of the adjacent building. Finally, within a few seconds, they were speeding away from the moon.

'I didn't expect to get this far,' said Jane over suit radio.

Ottanger wanted to agree with her, but decided to keep his mouth shut. He scanned, seeing the other ships out there coming in, and wondered how much of a grip on them the hive mind had. He checked for incoming missiles and saw none, though he did see sprays of debris leaving the moon's surface. Then, pushing with his ability, he saw the manifold from the inside, roiling like a stormy sky, with moments of brightness lancing through. As one passed over them, he received an expanded view and saw a rash of disruptions within the moon, spreading out like a metastasizing cancer, and deep down where they'd come from.

'I'll push to jaunt if those ships come too close,' he said. 'Otherwise, we'll try to get clear of the manifold.'

'You didn't expect this either, did you?'

He turned and looked at her, wincing at her betrayed expression. 'The Fenris often talks of taking the long view – of working over stretches of time to achieve a goal. You're right. I didn't expect this, though it was in my calculations as an outlier. I hoped for sufficient disruption to allow us to escape, but I expected us to be taken prisoner. I hoped that with its hands on jaunt tech, the hive would no longer see us as relevant, and we'd be able to get away. My actual expectations were grimmer.'

'You expected us to die.'

'There was also the option to jump within the moon, evading capture. Despite the hive managing to clamp down on that too, it was still possible, but . . .' He held up his petrified hand.

Jane said nothing, just stared at him.

Ottanger faced forwards. He thought about it all for a while and felt the need to explain himself further. 'The hive is the ultimate outcome of what's happening on Committee Earth. How the Fenris—'

It came through one of those openings in the disrupted manifold: the incursion of a tube from beyond, stabbing in like a spear through a gap in armour, and over their ship. Ottanger gathered everything within his power and hurled them into a jaunt. They fell fast into the pipe, ships and the reality of this universe sliding past. With his internal vision opening out, he got a proper look at the twisted wreck their vessel had become, and was amazed it'd been able to fly at all. He then saw the cage sphere coming up, and opening out into a claw. He had time yet to fling them out again, for now they were beyond the hive manifold, and thereafter he could take them wherever he wished. He didn't, though, because he owed too many too much. The claw split into its separate components and closed in around the vessel, juddering it in no-space. He felt the hard pull almost as an expression of the anger of the one directing it, and whom he would soon have to face.

As the vessel settled towards the landing pad, Ottanger could see human figures near the edge. And as their connection firmed, he knew everyone was there. No sign, however, of a larger figure amid them. A whining sound then kicked up, and he could feel something pushing at reality, for they had yet to materialize fully. A flash came behind and he turned to see one cage sphere component sliding towards him through the passenger compartment, while holosense showed them closing in all around. They snapped in to envelop him in a globular form. He glanced at Jane, seeing her shock, then her vision sliding past him as the cage tugged him away.

In internal vision, he saw the tube now curved above. Contained in the cage, he slid out of the ship and into this tube. Acceleration dropped him to the bottom of the thing, with its ribs pressing into his back. Managing to turn his head, he glimpsed the ship landing. As the cage surged upwards, it gladdened him the jaunters were all down there, and that only he had to answer for his actions. The tube curved in, narrowing now as it funnelled towards one of the great engines. In an eye-blink, he punched through the hull, and he and the cage rematerialized, bouncing along a metal floor and then crashing into a wall of fenris machinery. No gentleness or care for him, and had he not been wearing his suit he would have been a mess. As it was, the partially healed break in his forearm sprang open again. The cage dropped and rolled, then shuddered as the jointed tentacles snaked out and grabbed it with fenris hands. One of them spread between two of its ribs and gazed at him with a livid violet eye.

'Surely you understand what I've done,' he called.

'Surely you do not,' replied the Fenris, voice booming and echoing.

The tentacles rolled him along a metal path between walls of machinery. Meanwhile the cage began vaporizing into sulphurous smoke. He coughed on that and managed to get his visor closed as he clung to the ribs. The tentacles knocked the cage through a wide hole in the surrounding machinery and it dropped into an oblate chamber. As it hit the floor, the remainder of the cage shattered and spilled him out.

It took him a short while to recover, focusing internally on the newly opened break, killing the pain and ensuring his body and biotech worked to put it right. Beyond the break, where his hand had gone into the wall, he had some sense of it via the biotech, but little more. He tried removing the gauntlet, but the wrist mechanism was gummed – that whole section was a mixture of arm and hand, suit and foamed stone. He sighed, not really knowing what to do. Next he scanned his surroundings and found that his holosense reached only as far as the walls. He tried pushing for a jaunt or a jump, but there was just nothing – as if he was a normal human being. It seemed the Fenris had perfected his methods of suppression here. A blister pushed out of the wall, steadily expanding and growing translucent, and in it he could see a large familiar figure drawing near. He stood up.

The Fenris pushed with his claw tips, then stepped through it. Light patches ignited in the walls, dispelling the gloom. The creature glared down at him, leaving him in no doubt of its anger.

'Explain yourself.'

'You haven't figured it out yet?' he asked.

'Yes, you treacherously handed over jaunt technology to the hive, and in seeking to eliminate threats to itself, it will use that tech to spread itself through the multiverse endlessly. The result of your single act will be the suffering and final inhuman subjugation of billions.'

'Wrong,' Ottanger replied.

The Fenris stepped forwards to loom over him, clawed hands clenching and unclenching. And then it seemed he could contain himself no longer. One hand came up, then snapped down and around. Even with his suit on, the blow cracked Ottanger's ribs and launched him into the wall. He hit hard, feeling material bow behind him, and slid down to sitting, with his feet out ahead, fighting for breath.

'Do enlighten me as to why I'm wrong,' said the Fenris viciously.

'You're wrong . . . because hate and fear blind you,' Ottanger managed.

'The fenris do not allow such emotions to blind them.'

'And there you have it: the fenris race, not the Fenris the individual.' Pushing his back against the wall, Ottanger levered himself to standing again. 'We've been here before, when I questioned your belief in why fenris society didn't descend into totalitarianism. You contend that dispelling the need for individual safety in the acquisition of power, and its basis in the passing on of genes, your people avoided the road to becoming the hive.'

'Not contentions but facts.' The glare had eased a little now, so Ottanger reckoned he had a good chance of not being torn apart right then.

'It took a long time for fenris society to evolve, and through many conflicts. Personal freedom and power were part of it, but those alone would have led to fragmentation and not a society. In the end, what stabilized things was the connection through your biotech: empathy.'

The Fenris just stared at him, waiting.

'Interestingly, in the end what saved you,' Ottanger continued, 'is in part an aspect of communal societies like the hive.'

'Oh, so you admire the hive, do you?'

'I hate what it is just as much as you, only I didn't allow my hate to blind me to what it is. I, mere human, could see other roads to take, rather than heading directly into a massive escalating war that would kill billions, and was, in essence, an evasion of responsibility.'

He saw a flash of puzzlement in the Fenris's expression. Perhaps now was the time to shove his point home. The creature was, after all, highly intelligent. He just wondered if he'd survive doing so.

'When you arrived here you looked upon Committee Earth and hated it. You saw that the way to change the tens of thousands of years of suffering was through your biotech. You then looked upon the hive and were repulsed. You didn't even think to try changing it – all you did was retreat and make preparations for your war. Don't you see the contradiction there?'

The Fenris folded his arms. 'Go on.'

'You felt sympathy for the humans on Committee Earth – empathy, in fact. But when you looked upon the hive, you didn't see humans at all, though you may have labelled them as such. That, along with the hive's aim to obtain jaunt biotech, made you afraid. So you backed away, fortified, and prepared for a future war instead of doing the right thing.'

'The right thing is to destroy the hive, not provide it with the tools to spread and take over the multiverse.'

'I have done both,' Ottanger replied, 'while you avoided its actual destruction because even with your hatred of the hive you could not bring yourself to make that harsh choice, because of your *morality*.'

The Fenris just stared at him for a long moment then finally said, 'Explain.'

'What happens to human intelligence as it transitions into something like the hive?'

'It decreases on the individual level.'

'Yes. It begins with an elite class accruing power and suppressing the masses. They're programmed through crude methods at first, and then more sophisticated ones as time passes and technology permits. However, the ruling class is eventually subsumed too, because it cannot avoid becoming subject to the systems it puts in place. Individual intelligence ceases to be a survival characteristic and is evolved out, or simply removed. Communal intelligence takes over, and by and by the hive comes into being.'

The Fenris shrugged. 'It's a successful strategy, as the social insects demonstrate.'

'Intelligence resides in the hive overall, while individual members are just like cells in a brain. They're mindless drones, running the programs of the overall mind.'

'You are not telling me anything I don't know.'

'The hive travels en masse, while jaunters travel mostly as individuals. Your biotech, in us, leads to a boost in intelligence – usually increasing after our ability to jaunt has kicked in, since it's a function of multiverse perception.'

'Yes, that's true.'

'So what happens to brainless hive humans – the cells in a brain – when they abruptly start jaunting? How much control will they have? How long will it take creatures that've been deliberately denuded of brain to start developing the intelligence to control it?'

The Fenris just stared.

Ottanger continued, 'You saw your biotech as a solution to Committee Earth, but it pained you to see so many dying before they could control their ability. How is it that you failed to see it as the solution to the hive?'

The stare was now becoming seriously unnerving. The Fenris then unfolded his arms and held up one hand, studying it. 'I sacrificed this hand so I could have the power to bring about an altruistic act, or so I thought.' He returned his gaze to Ottanger. 'You need to remove your lower arm above the dead area and regrow it.' He turned away and started heading back the way he'd come in.

'That's it? That's all you have to say?'

The Fenris looked back. 'Building defences and preparations

for war are not the same as the act itself, or its ultimate objective. If you're wrong, you have destroyed our chance to fight the spread of the hive, for it will be able to step from world to world with ease. If you are right . . . then you have perhaps been more ruthless than I could ever be.'

He stepped through the blister and it turned dark, sinking back into the wall.

23

Ottanger

How long had it been? Checking inside, Ottanger counted ten days, fifteen hours and sixteen minutes, and didn't bother with the seconds. On the first day a tube opened into his prison bringing a selection of fruit from one of the gardens, wrapped in gel that provided the fluid he needed. Doubtless one of the Fenris's hand tentacles had picked it. After filling himself up, he slept on the hard floor, and woke up to find a hole in that floor, with a water spigot above it. The thing reminded him of the toilet arrangement in the Inspectorate cell he'd once been thrown into.

On the second day, after shouting at the walls for a time, he concentrated on his injuries. The Fenris had told him he must cut off his hand . . . no, that wasn't right, he'd said *remove* it. Concentrating on the point where feeling ended, he raised icons and with them came understanding. He set the process in motion, while steadily removing his suit. A little work with some of its tools freed the gauntlet fixing, and he was able to peel its material steadily from his stone hand. He sat down and focused fully on it. At the division point, arteries and veins closed and retracted, spilling just capillaries behind to feed the change. Muscle cells transitioned to skin, but tough bone still remained. He denuded it a bit, and knew he could bring about the separation with patience. He lost patience on the third day, however, drew a combat knife from his boot, and cut down through the dead muscle. With the internal skin nub on one side, he then hacked. At this point, he was sharply reminded of afferent nerves.

Days thereafter passed with him watching the hand forming in the end of his stump. He stopped shouting at the walls, because he felt it was just too undignified, and he suffered enough indignity shitting into that hole in the floor. Instead he meditated, explored his abilities, and the library cache of iconic language in his biotech, absorbing the knowledge it could impart. He also analysed all his actions, those of the others, and of the Fenris. And he found his certainty about how things had played out diminishing. Sometimes he even thought he'd got things totally wrong, because wasn't he utterly arrogant to believe he possessed more insight and understanding than a creature like the Fenris? On other occasions his certainty that he'd been right was a painful thing. It raised him into an anger that would have pushed him into shouting at the walls again, if he hadn't had the control he did.

Then, a more insidious and frightening thought occurred: he had been utterly right and correct, and the Fenris was punishing him for that. He wondered about the others in this respect. Did the Fenris so detest being wrong that he'd imprisoned them too? Or even worse, simply killed them? And what of the thousands who were set to be the Fenris's army – what had happened to them? Ottanger only contemplated these things once, realizing he was straying into paranoia, and dismissed them. The Fenris was rational, and he must remain so too. So he waited.

★   ★   ★

The cell wall split, and its edges rolled back to open out an exit.

Ottanger gazed at the opening through the mixture of hard machinery and biotech, and wanted to go through at once. But he turned away and, since the Fenris had made no announcement, he said nothing. While in the cell, he'd stripped down to his undersuit and now set to putting the combat suit back on over that. Meticulously insuring everything was in place, including the patch over his arm stump, he didn't hurry, because fuck the Fenris. One of the jointed tentacles came in through the gap to inspect him with a fenris eye, its surrounding fingers flexing impatiently, then withdrew.

When he finally stepped out, his holosense expanded shockingly bright and clear beyond the cell. He could see the massive machines all around him bound together by organics, almost like old electronics writ large, and through which a fungus had grown. Though the extent of his detailed perception now ended at over a kilometre from him, he could still see beyond that, just with diminishing detail. He saw the other engines and satellites, the Geostation and elevator. He saw the fenris world and its sun glaring over the horizon. Yet down on that world, things were hazy. It looked as if the Fenris had shut down the defences against hive incursion, and by default against jaunting up here. But some interference continued below. He felt true freedom when he looked out into the multiverse, since there was nothing to stop him leaping away to anywhere he wanted right now. But what he also sensed, just half a kilometre away, stopped him doing that.

A series of hands protruding from the surrounding structure watched him for a moment, then all pointed in one direction. Further hands needlessly signposted his path through the corridors of the great engine. He walked strange halls, whose floors seemed to be made of poured metal between tangled jungles of metal and flesh. He crossed a bridge over a space in which large golden cylinders hung, twisting the multiverse around them. And he traversed a tube free of gravity to a huge bulkhead door. Here he paused, viewing what lay ahead.

It seemed almost like a chunk bitten from an apple – part of the engine had been excised and returned to position, slightly out of place. Studying this thing further, he realized a vessel had been formed there – a thing shaped like the flakes of flint he'd once made. He stepped up to the door and eyed the mushroom control, then with a shrug pressed his hand against it. As expected, the thing extruded pincers to extract his blood. And as the door wafted open, he began to get a stronger sense of the ship around him, and some degree of control commingled with that of others. He walked passages, towed himself through zero-grav tubes, and at length came to another door. There he raised a mere mental indication and it opened ahead of him. He stepped in.

'You weren't in any big hurry to get here,' said Chenghu, standing up from a chair.

The four occupied a room resembling the main one at Caprock, and its copy on the planet below, as if this kind of dwelling space must be a requirement for them. Where the panoramic window had been at the first place, another window bulged out on vacuum, giving a magnificent view of the Geostation and the elevator. Yet they could look upon these objects through solid walls, so why the need for it? A human thing, he supposed, because it felt right to him. And it probably felt right to some smaller portion of the Fenris too. He studied them all.

Chenghu, Irene, Pranjab and Jane were present, and they no longer wore combat suits but a variety of favoured clothing. Seeing them directly with human eyes, he acknowledged his disappointment at not finding the others here too. They converged on him, and it surprised him to see the smiles and sense joy

621

through their network. He also noted their changes, for they all loomed large in their connection, and it seemed even Jane had stabilized. But he also felt a sense of separation. With a sudden relaxing of some internal tension, he realized their group hierarchy, with him at the top, must be breaking down. Chenghu grabbed his hand and pumped it. Pranjab came in and squeezed his shoulder. The two women held back, but once Chenghu had stepped back Jane came up and hugged him, kissing him meekly on the cheek, then moved back again beside Chenghu to take his hand. Irene, when she stepped up, was unexpected.

She moved quickly towards him and he tensed up, thinking she was just adhering to a brief social more, and what would follow would be pretence. But she paused, reached out, and touched his mutilated arm for a second. She looked pained, and did her eyes seem . . . watery? She then stepped forwards and flung her arms over his shoulders, pulling him in close and hugging him tightly. He looked over her head at Chenghu, and saw an unexpected look of amusement from the man. When he looked down at her she came up fast and kissed him hard. It wasn't in the least unpleasant. He ran with it for a while until uncomfortably aware of the attention of the others and then broke away.

'Why?' he asked, looking down at her.

She shrugged. 'I can analyse it and become cynical. I choose not to.'

'Perhaps that's the best way,' he said.

They finally parted, but she swung in beside him. He gazed at the others on every level and could see some other dynamic here. Between Chenghu and Jane he sensed a deeper empathetic connection. He also realized the hierarchy wasn't really breaking down, for there had been a shift, a rearrangement. It had taken the same format with them all as it had been, and still was, between him and Pranjab. He didn't dominate them. They chose to have him lead them. He could have analysed the relationship aspects here in more depth – like, for example, why Irene was going after him having lost her grip on Chenghu but, like Irene, decided not to take that further for now. Old biology was at play here, just that.

'The others?' he asked.

'They're all good,' said Irene, gazing at him intensely. 'They're continuing the grabs from Committee Earth. In fact, we were all doing that until the Fenris summoned us here. The population below has just exceeded a hundred thousand.'

'The army continues to grow,' said Ottanger flatly.

'It continues to grow,' Irene replied.

'And yet some defences have come down.'

'A tunnel is required for jaunts from the surface,' Chenghu interjected. 'The block in place down there is supposedly to keep jaunters from leaving, rather than the hive arriving.'

A short silence ensued as they all digested that.

'And the hive?' Ottanger asked.

'Jane told us what happened while you were there,' said Pranjab, 'since then we've had no information about it. Personally, I'd like to know a lot more.' He waved a hand at the others. 'They know my part in it, producing the flies.' His focus then switched back to where it had been before, as he studied Ottanger's arm stump. Ottanger grimaced, undid the patch at the end and pulled up his sleeve as far as it would go. He held out the stump to Pranjab, who immediately stepped forwards and took hold of it.

'So we don't know whether my—'

With a loud crump, and a steadily growing vibration, the ship detached from the engine and began to pull away. They all took on a slightly vacant look while they concentrated their senses

623

outside. Ottanger focused out there too, until a fuser drive came on, and he pulled his attention back in. He surveyed the ship, looking for anomalies that might hide something, while the engine retreated behind them. No sign of the Fenris – as he'd sensed the moment he stepped out of his cell. With nothing else changing, Pranjab returned his attention to Ottanger's stump in his hands. Ottanger could feel the intrusion and waves of iconic language advancing and retreating. Abruptly Pranjab released his hold and stepped back.

'The Fenris has often mentioned the long view – an almost historical perspective. It's difficult for us, with what we saw as limited lives, to understand that,' said the doctor. 'Maybe it will take time, but it's something we'll need to get used to and accept.'

'Your meaning?' asked Irene, turning sharply.

Pranjab gestured to Ottanger's stump. 'Limitless physical regeneration. Barring our major physical destruction, we are now immortal.'

Another thing to absorb. As he did so, Ottanger began applying it to his own thinking, and his assessment of the Fenris. He believed the creature had evaded responsibility and prepared for war because of a visceral, rather than logical, reaction to the hive. This had necessitated his own actions, to prevent what he saw as the inevitable devastation of that conflict. But could it be that he'd got all of that wrong, because his assessment had been within the narrow frame of a mortal? And could it even be the case that he'd been manipulated and done precisely as the Fenris wanted? He'd just been one brief snapshot of that long view? Something for further consideration.

'Looks like our destination is set,' Chenghu observed.

They all saw it in the multiverse view, though Ottanger accepted that the way their minds might interpret it could be wildly different to his own. He saw something like a tornado generating from the engine behind. And the mind-bending knowledge came to him that it was the same thing generating from all the engines simultaneously. The thing whipped out towards them, encompassed them, then speared on – the eye of an incursion shooting away and diminishing to a vanishing point. They were in a tunnel, but at present going nowhere.

'This ship took my blood,' said Ottanger. 'And it took yours too – I can feel it. This must be a joint effort.'

'You can't do it alone?' Irene enquired.

He noted her teasing expression and realized that, freed from the responsibility she'd burdened herself with, and her changes perhaps having enabled her to leave behind the terrible things that'd happened to her, a nicer and more playful character was revealing itself. He could get used to that. He reached out and took her hand. Pranjab grabbed his stump and reached out to Chenghu and the circle quickly completed.

'I could do it alone,' he replied. 'But sharing burdens perhaps leads to better decisions.'

Irene frowned at him.

The physical connection consolidated their network, which now, like threads from a central spore, tautened on the biotech laced throughout the ship around them. Ottanger initiated their jaunt, though in some sense it was with the agreement of them all. The ship sped down the tunnel, through the twisting multiverse, and it seemed more as if they were stationary and it was reforming around them. He hadn't said anything about the likely destination because there'd been no need to – they all knew where they were going. And why else would they have a vacuum-sealed ship?

The hive manifold loomed ahead, but much changed. It now seemed to consist of chunks of pipework anchored to the hive moon. It no longer extended to cover the world the moon orbited, and nor was it shadowed into parallels – Ottanger could see no connection to the split-away parallel Earth. It was as if a massive ceiling had been broken, and large portions of it had disappeared, while the remaining pieces kited on stretched strings. They next felt a disruption as they drew in closer and, since he didn't want to materialize the ship inside the moon, Ottanger pushed them out.

The ship slid into vacuum thousands of kilometres out in the system. The airless Earth and its large moon were distant bright dots. As if turning to and walking towards something, Ottanger manoeuvred the ship and set it on course to them. His wish for some kind of resolution then fired up the fuser engine to full power. He gave Irene a pull, and slid his hand from her grip as he headed over to the bulging window. They all followed him, which irritated him a little. They were deferring to him again, but did he really want to be their leader? Reaching the window, he gazed with human eyes at their destination.

'We can always take a closer look,' said Chenghu.

Ottanger nodded, pushed into the system, and confirmed access to a wide-spectrum telescope on the ship's hull. He could, if he wished, pull up magnified imagery in the window ahead, since it was no simple glass but consisted of fenris informational membranes. But he didn't want to know just yet.

'I'll use one of the cabins,' he said abruptly. 'I haven't washed in days.'

He turned and headed away, aware of the rooms they'd snared for themselves, and choosing an unused one for himself. At the exit he paused and looked back, taking in Irene's quizzical expression, then beckoned her after him. She hesitated briefly, and then seemed to relent, following. They had time before reaching the moon, he felt, for them to settle something between them.

★ ★ ★

'He's arrived,' said Irene.

Ottanger opened bleary eyes and resisted the impulse to tell her she was stating the obvious. She was lying next to him, naked and coiled in towards him, and he felt uncomfortable with the knowledge she'd been watching him while he slept. He pushed up on his elbows and surveyed the room. He'd called it a cabin, but it wasn't exactly of human design. Biotech webbed the walls of an oblate chamber. He'd showered in a cyst off to one side, below a spread hand spraying water from what looked like octopus cubs on its fingers. The hole beneath it, which captured the dirty water, seemed to serve as a toilet here too. No kitchen revealed itself, and no utensils for food preparation, just a tube to walk through to a small fenris garden. It seemed the needs of rugged bodies that could recycle and conserve were meagre. It was all, in its biotech way, quite Spartan.

'Clothing,' he said.

'You don't need any yet,' she replied, and abruptly pushed herself up to sling a leg over and sit astride him.

'You want to dominate me?' he enquired.

'Fuck you,' she snapped.

'Yes, you do that thing,' he shot back.

Clothing, when he finally came round to it, consisted of a membrane extruded between two spines summoned from the wall. It spread out over him, only pausing at his neck when he felt a second of panic about it flowing up over his face. Having found that control, he soon located the others too, and turned it into a facsimile of overalls. He then darkened those to black – despite his associates' ability to look through walls or anything else, he felt transparent clothing to be a step too far.

'Utile but boring,' said Irene.

She stood naked, holding a grey object like an ostrich egg, which she pressed against herself. The thing dissolved from her hand, spreading over her body, changing colour and texture as it did so. Below her waist, it transitioned into blue jeans, and below her knee into black boots, growing heels that pushed her up a few inches. Above the waist, it became a silky purple blouse. As this completed, she tilted her head one way then another, and the blouse stabbed up small stalks to her ears, depositing a gold ring in each.

'I'm just learning,' said Ottanger. 'What would you prefer? Some form of armour like our guest?' He stabbed a thumb towards the main room.

'No – in a way you're just right.'

They headed for the door and out, walking a short stretch of corridor whose floor resembled the back of a lizard. As they went, Ottanger played with his biotech connections and ran through the iconic language. The clothing was a living thing, and could even feed itself by running tendrils through his skin. But he wasn't inclined to let it do that yet. He made some adjustments, feeling it run down his ankles, enclose his feet and thicken there, and he stepped into the main room wearing army boots like those he had taken from a warlike world.

'You have come,' said the Fenris.

He was up at the bulbous window, looking out towards the airless Earth and its moon, which were now large enough to reveal some detail. The others sat down in the seats, looking pensive, and he could sense their puzzlement, as well as an underlying taint of fear. The Fenris turned from the window. Ottanger noticed a change to the armour he wore – it had transitioned back to how it'd been before, and didn't look so martial now. It also seemed to have lost its spines, and the weapons. But it was his face that attracted Ottanger's attention most, for this powerful creature looked grim and somewhat gaunter than before.

'So what has been the effect?' Ottanger asked, crossing the room with Irene still at his side, while the others rose out of their seats and moved hesitantly forwards.

He could feel tension knotting a fist inside. The Fenris sighed in a very human manner and beckoned them closer. They moved up onto the ledge in front of the window with the Fenris looming ahead, partially in silhouette against the moon.

'Some of you have looked already,' said the Fenris. 'But you have not, Ottanger. Why is that?'

'Perhaps I fear finding out I failed and what that might mean. Maybe some hints of a long view are kicking in, because I know I cannot avoid finding out – it will come eventually.'

'Well, it comes now.'

The Fenris raised a hand and made a gesture, as if reaching out to the moon and the Earth, and pulling them closer. They leapt into sharp focus. The Earth clearly revealed its geology in the form of mountain chains, deserts and the glint of shallow remaining oceans, all thinly veiled by streaks of cloud. The moon revealed its machine face, but had changed since the last time he'd viewed it. The thing possessed a smoky halo and fire gleamed down in some of those valleys between massive structures, and in deeper pits. He wondered what might be burning, and wasn't sure he wanted to know. At a gesture, the Fenris pulled back magnification a little, and now he could see that the halo extended in a ring around the Earth at the moon's orbit.

'What's burning?' he asked.

'Nothing much – the apparent fires you see are the result of power imbalances, which have turned many overground cables white hot. They glow in vacuum like old light-bulb filaments, until they blow out. The power then routes elsewhere and causes more cables to go.' The Fenris turned to look at him. 'A great deal is breaking down inside as well.'

'It's certainly thrown out a lot of smoke and debris,' said Ottanger. Even as he said this, he wondered if he was unconsciously in denial and trying not to see what was really there in front of him. He glanced at the others and saw the expressions on Chenghu and Irene's faces. They had seen this already.

'Actually, very little smoke and debris,' said the Fenris.

Now, as though pulling on a rope, he brought the images closer, focusing in on that ring around the planet. The smoke haze began to resolve into separate objects and, as the Fenris drew them closer, they grew arms and legs, and post and binocular heads. Ottanger swallowed drily as the perspective shifted along this ring.

The Fenris continued, 'At first, the hive mind tried to incorporate the jaunt technology. It then realized it was effectively losing its mind, as the cell components of that mind began randomly shifting to different locations, then growing a new perception of their surroundings and elements of free thought. You were correct on that aspect. But another analogy, concerning them becoming individuals, applies here. Cancer arises when cells start reverting to an earlier individual state.'

Ottanger was already extrapolating from that, sketching out numerous scenarios, but he decided not to usurp the Fenris. A point was being made here, albeit an obvious one.

'So what was the result of it?' he asked.

'The mind tried to excise all those cells that were causing problems. There are ancient bulkhead doors within the moon, and it sectioned off the volume nominally containing the cancer, then opened the surface doors above it. The explosive decompression threw some fifty billion of them out into vacuum.'

'There are more than fifty billion of them out there,' observed Ottanger succinctly, something dry and cold freezing him at that thought. The nominally two-and-a-half-million-kilometre ring of the moon's orbit was complete and flattening out into a disc, much like the rings of Saturn.

'The hive tried this method a number of times, and in the last few days finally ceased its efforts. It couldn't, and still cannot, effectively quarantine areas. Those of its creatures initially bitten, and almost immediately jumping, spread throughout the volume of the moon with inocular flies still biting them. The homing instinct also brought many the hive had ejected straight back into it.' The Fenris paused, perhaps winced. 'However, you are right. Of the three hundred billion hive humans out there, only half were ejected by the hive. The rest are those who either jaunted away, but were knocked straight out into vacuum by the disrupted manifold, or jumped out of the moon and simply drifted away. Some made it further, and are still moving off as the manifold breaks down. Fifty million or so are on, or in, the planet below too. Perhaps another eighty million have reached other worlds, and some of those have even survived.'

A long silence ensued while Ottanger absorbed all this. He was cold and exact in his extrapolations. Hive humans slung out to other worlds might cause some problems, but they wouldn't be self-propagating ones, since the creatures couldn't breed. Any that arrived on Committee Earth, or its near parallels, wouldn't last long at all.

'What about the split-away parallel?'

'I have been able to go to that world, since the manifold no longer blocks it. Some of the hive humans there are continuing allotted tasks, most are simply inactive – they're not even feeding themselves.'

'So the hive mind is done, and I succeeded?' Ottanger said flatly.

The Fenris quickly turned to him with the same anger in his expression that Ottanger had seen when he last returned from this place. 'That's yet to be determined.' He made one of those grasping gestures again, but this time swiping in from the window, towards Ottanger and the others. The force of the jaunt was undeniable, and it felt like being taken up in one of the cages. Ottanger knew he couldn't fight it even if he wanted to. In an instant, they were outside the ship and falling towards the moon.

Waves of disruption from the manifold crashed against them as they fell, and Ottanger could feel these trying to force them out into reality. He now understood viscerally why so few of the hive humans had made it beyond the orbit of the moon. However, the Fenris kept a firm grip on them, and he did see the ribs of a cage sphere revolving around them, as well as the hint of a tunnel spearing down. The moon's surface rose up, threads of conductor glowing in deep crevices, an open cap showing a well dropping deep down, bodies snowed across the buildings. Then they were in and down deep.

A confusion of tunnels and cysts slid by, until finally they snapped out into reality in a wide tube, which he estimated to be close to the centre of the moon. The Fenris just stepped out of the jaunt smoothly, but the others came out of it swirling around him, stumbling for balance, and in Chenghu's case falling into a roll. Ottanger staggered forwards too, tripping over something. He righted himself and looked back at the post-head sunk into the floor, with hands, knees and the top part of its head protruding. Their surroundings were like some medieval depiction of Hell, with hive humans imbedded in many surfaces. Expanded holosense showed the same scenes in surrounding tunnels. A continuous rumbling sounded, interspersed with crackling noises, like nearby and distant lightning. A warrior appeared fifty metres away, surveyed its surroundings, then disappeared with a snap. Similar jumps were occurring all around, and

Ottanger realized the perpetual air displacements were the source of the noise.

'It's as if they know what awaits beyond the surface. Like animals in a cage, they run back and forth to the walls,' said the Fenris.

'But surely they don't have the intelligence for that, individually,' said Chenghu.

'Perhaps some do – they are changing.'

Ottanger continued looking around, trying to understand what this situation reminded him of, then understood it to be a story Chenghu had told him. The man had shown Irene the riots she'd caused to try to dissuade her from further violent interventions on Committee Earth. This had repeated with the Fenris showing them the results of their assassination of world leaders. And it reflected his own knowledge of how rebel actions invariably failed. Now it was all circling round and coming back to land on him: consequences. Until that moment, he'd kept himself dry and factual, but now he imagined everything around him playing out through the entire massive volume of the moon. He imagined billions dying in vacuum, and his cold calculations of loss and gain bit him hard. Perhaps it was the fact they were changing that did it, but even if that wasn't the case, and individual hive humans were little more than animals, it didn't make them devoid of suffering.

'Ah fuck,' he said and stepped back, catching his ankle on a protruding hand. He fell slowly down onto his rear.

The Fenris studied him briefly, then turned to Jane. 'You know what I want.'

'I know,' she replied. 'And I've been trying since we arrived here.' She waved a hand at her head. 'Every time I open it, I do get communication, but it's millions of voices shouting nonsense, with no central contact establishing and no singular personality. The hive mind is gone.'

This was another, lesser blow. Ottanger thought about the hive humans he'd killed in self-defence and tried to equate that to what he'd done here. He couldn't do it, though, for some Rubicon had been crossed. An ironic thought about the inventor of the atomic bomb arose for his inspection – what that person had said when first seeing the weapon detonated. Was he himself Death, a destroyer of worlds? The misapplication throughout history of the word 'genocide' arose next – for in the precise definition of the word, it cannot have been committed unless an entire race is wiped out. He realized with horror that in both cases he was close to the real deal. He then looked up at the pale and sick faces all around him and knew that much of what he felt was spilling out into the others. He felt wretched.

'We cannot stay here for long,' said the Fenris. 'The chances of one of the hive humans rematerializing actually inside one of us are not negligible.' He stepped forwards to stand over Ottanger. 'Hurts, doesn't it?' he asked.

'Yes, it hurts.'

'Good, then at least you are redeemable, though I wonder if I am.'

Ottanger looked up, puzzled.

The Fenris continued, 'I have to apologize to you, Ottanger. I am very sorry.'

'For what?'

'For what I did and didn't do.' He looked around at them all, then focused back down on Ottanger. 'I saw your world and idealistically thought to change it by giving people there the powers and intelligence to free themselves. But it killed many and my idealism died. I then discovered a threat to us all, and to all we value.' He waved a claw at the surrounding hive. 'And I reneged on my responsibility to counter that threat properly.

Because, in the end, there was no way to avoid what you see all around you.'

'You were building an army,' said Chenghu.

'I was procrastinating. Circumventing the real, harsh solutions with pretence at action to salve my pride. And while I was doing so, the poisoned chalice was taken up by another. Do you forgive me, Ottanger?'

'Why do you assume it was your job to do anything?' Ottanger asked.

'Because I have great power, and power must be balanced by responsibility.' The Fenris held down a hand to him and he reached up, grasping it. 'We must live by principles or we do not really live.'

It eased the pain a little, and at least confirmed his choices – there had been no easy, non-lethal solution to dealing with the hive. Up on his feet, Ottanger released the Fenris's big hand and looked around, seeing hive humans flicking in and out of existence, running around in their cage.

'How many still survive?' he asked.

'I can only estimate,' said the Fenris. 'Maybe six hundred billion.'

'So their artificial environment is breaking down,' Ottanger surmised, 'and they cannot breed without artificial means. But nevertheless, they are humans, with steadily growing intelligence.'

'What's in your mind?'

'I think I have murdered enough of them.'

Epilogue

Chenghu

Chenghu steadily climbed the stairs up from their accommodation in City Slab One. Reaching the surface, he gazed out across the composite plain, past the nearest two landing pads, to a distant one currently full of more arrivals from Committee Earth. That was Irene bringing in another load, whereupon she'd undoubtedly soon seek out Ottanger. For she was constantly by his side, as though she feared he might evaporate. Which, with their abilities, he could do. But Ottanger had clearly developed beyond the first jaunters in their group, even though some of them had taken on their biotech before him. Chenghu often thought about Ottanger, but tended to avoid him now. The man no longer operated as he once did, and seemed to understand things right down to the nuts and bolts in psychology and biology. Humour, and the simple pleasures and interactions, seemed lost on him now, and he didn't appear quite human any more – less so, in fact, than the snatch patrol presently awaiting Chenghu. Perhaps that was what coming within a hair's breadth of committing genocide did to a person.

Walking at a leisurely pace, Chenghu watched Irene's people steadily disappearing below. They had this down to a fast routine now, but it still felt like trying to empty a lake with a cup. They weren't even a quarter of the way into removing all the mutated from Committee Earth. And in Chenghu's opinion, they'd never get to the point of being able to start taking normal human beings, as Ottanger had proposed. Funny that – all ideas of using their powers to bring down the Committee, and free their home world, had died in the calculated realities of the situation, while the lessons in that respect had all been learned. Simply pulling people out was the best, most humanitarian solution. And anyway, besides that lake they were emptying with a cup, there was an ocean they also had to deal with.

Beyond the landing pads, Chenghu finally came to the snatch vehicle. He could have used one of the fenris general-purpose vehicles, but had instead made this one almost in a fit of nostalgia. There was comfort in the familiar. The thing had balloon wheels, wasn't capable of flight, and resembled a big cargo hauler of his home world. He paused to gaze at it. His job right now was to sweep up all the stray arrivals, but this would be the last time. There'd be no more need for this with the system of the drains they'd put in operation. He shook his head, climbed the step to the door, pulled that open, and got inside to plunk himself down in the driver's seat.

'Are we all ready?' he enquired via his suit radio.

'Ready,' a voice replied, from a vocabulary that had just surpassed a hundred words at Chenghu's last count. He looked around.

The crew compartment behind him, and ahead of the main body of the vehicle, contained fifteen seats. In two to the fore sat warriors with stun rifles across their laps. They both dipped their binocular heads to him, then one turned to look out of the side window. The warriors, surgeons and a few other iterations of hive human were close to gaining independent intelligence now. Having been created for complex tasks, with some disconnection from the hive, they'd had more brain matter to begin with than others. The eight post-heads sitting behind, with their nets and stun pistols, were not so fortunate. It took all eight of them to form a coherent human being – a mini-hive, in essence. This was an advance on the first arrivals, though, who'd not been functional at all, and could only be welded into a single lucid mind after a month of being babied by fenris biotech. And even then it had taken nearly fifty of them. Feeding and waiting had also been required to allow the biotech to adjust their bodies to the higher gravity here.

He turned back and set the vehicle into motion, while checking a map screen for coordinates. He didn't much like having to, for he felt almost blind down here. But it was necessary to keep the world clamped down, with the engines preventing them from leaving. Too many of the newer arrivals, with their power and confidence growing, alongside their knowledge of what they could do, wanted to head straight back to Committee Earth to right some wrongs, or for payback. It was very human of them. And though many of the earlier ones were gaining maturity, there were still new arrivals coming in all the time.

With the vehicle in motion towards the coordinates, he mentally switched his radio from the hive frequency, which was broadcasting straight into the minds of those behind him, to another.

'They're still at the location?' he asked.

'Still there,' Ektian replied. 'Not a lot of movement, so probably post-heads.'

'But *some* movement.'

'Yeah, some.'

'Others?'

'Four thousand in the last day snatched up by biotech inside the city slabs. Over a hundred swimmers and eight hundred drowned. Estimates on the hard landings . . . maybe one and a half thousand – big drop-off now.'

Hard landings. So that's what they were now calling the hive humans who'd materialized inside solid objects, including the planet itself.

'I still think we should have waited for the drains before opening up that tunnel,' Ektian added.

'He told me it was a calculated risk. More would die inside the hive than here.'

'I think he let guilt overrule judgement.'

'Okay,' said Chenghu. He wasn't going to get into that, since the figures were marginal and highly debatable. When they'd opened a tunnel to the hive moon, so those hive humans jaunting within it would be drawn in to the Fenris world, the arrival rate here had been thousands every hour. During those arrivals, the losses had been in the region of ten per cent. But once they were safely here, that effectively ended. If left to jumping and jaunting without sufficient mental capacity to handle the process, the chances of them killing themselves just kept climbing. He guessed that focusing on such things was really tinkering at the edges for someone who'd triggered the extermination of hundreds of billions.

The plain of the city slab unrolled ahead of him. And out of it rose an apparent city of more conventional design, consisting of cooling vents, transmission towers and other paraphernalia the slab required for its function. He drove in along roads raised up out of deep crevasses of machinery, woven together in jungles of biotech. To his right, he saw a transport hub spilling out from below, with its tubes shooting away in every direction. Beyond it he could see further surface mechanisms, for the flat plain behind was just a rare clear area on top of this slab. He checked his map again, then looked up and ahead, slightly to the left.

And with better natural vision than he'd ever possessed before, he saw their prey.

The post-heads were clustered at the hexagonal junction of six surface roads. They were near the edge, which was inconvenient, though if any fell to the machinery below, they'd mostly be snatched up by the biotech before splattering themselves. Ranging out around them were six warriors. They'd fallen into a defensive patrol pattern, raised from their hard wiring, and were trudging painfully in the high gravity. But he could see it often breaking, some of them going back to the post-heads and just standing there, as if they wanted to ask questions. This was a lingering expression of the hive's system – individuals didn't make decisions but the overall majority did. Others were finding some detail in surrounding material to rivet their attention. How much they really felt or thought, he couldn't know. They'd been components of an intelligence and were now cut off. The bioradios in their skulls were still active, receiving the autonomous generalities they transmitted between each other. And perhaps with only that, they'd feel little at all. However, the biotech inside them was steadily raising the conscious function of their minds, so he guessed they must at least feel puzzled.

'Okay, let's pick them up,' he said.

He reached down beside his seat and took out his stun rifle. Just like the weapons of those behind, it was fenris tech, but pretty much followed the design of the ones the hive humans had used before. He climbed out and dropped to the ground. The others piled out of another door and rapidly spread out, following a protocol that they broadcast between each other. Two of the nearest warriors among the new arrivals swung towards them and squatted, and, picking up the threat broadcast, the other four did the same. Chenghu shouldered his weapon and fired. The shot was just a flash with no projectile visible, like the previous weapons. The targeted warrior shuddered, an electro-static haze appearing around it, then dissolving away as it keeled over. Other shots now sped in, dropping the warriors and then zeroing in on the post-heads. In less than a minute it was over.

'Load them up,' he said, while walking over to the prostrate post-heads.

His warriors moved in to pick up those of their own kind and sling them over a shoulder to carry them back. Post-heads picked up other warriors in nets and, being weaker, carried them back between them. He reached the fallen post-heads at the edge, and saw that none had gone over. Though one was hanging precariously, with its top half over the lip and legs pinned down by another of its kind. He went over to it, carefully took hold of an arm, and hauled it back. Next, hanging his weapon by its strap, he picked up two of them – one under each arm – and took them back to the vehicle. Here a warrior had lowered a ramp at the back, to open up the cargo space. He climbed up this and laid them carefully on the floor, beside the two warriors already inside, then went back to fetch more. Care had to be taken with what were light and flimsy creatures. But even so broken bones were unavoidable. All this was drudgery but necessary work.

With the hive humans all loaded up, and his crew back in place, he set the vehicle in motion, winding along roads. In an hour, they came in sight of some surface works being disassembled. Here big fenris robots, which reminded him of mantids, were hauling materials to wells and dropping them down. Massive biotech winches marked the edge of the drain, where a section of the surface structure for kilometres across had been dropped down. He drove along this edge, heading for the access road, and looked over. They'd named this the drain for very obvious reasons. The edge of it acted to contain the arrivals, while the hundreds of holes all across this area gave access to the hive-like structures below. Reaching the ramp road that led down, he stopped and took it all in.

Now, positioned just inside one of the tubes that branched out from the main incursion tube linked to the hive moon, Chenghu's holosense returned, and his grasp of what lay here expanded. The multiverse opened around him, like some vast crystalline mass, with versions of Earth seemingly dropped in at interfaces. He knew this conception was different from what the others perceived, while that of the tubes was the same for them all. In that vision, he looked up to see a rain of human life. Then he looked down and, in conventional view, saw clumps of post-heads, singular warriors, and other kinds snapping into existence on the surface, as well as down below. Meanwhile, hive human crews were constantly at work, down to a couple of kilometres deep in this volume. In some cases they used stunners, and in others simply guided the arrivals to where they needed to be – in most cases straight to the biotech feeders. The majority of drains all around the planet were like this, though four were designated for the large groups, which other jaunters were taking turns to bring over from the split-away parallel Earth. He drove down to add his small contribution to this flood.

The worry had been raised that maybe in collecting together so many hive humans, with their ability to jaunt suppressed, the hive intelligences might coalesce. This wasn't proving to be the case, however. It required work to form a singular, coherent intelligence like the one in the post-heads behind him. And as their biotech continued to make its changes, such groups tended to keep breaking apart rather than joining together. The final result would be individuals.

Chenghu saw this reflected in himself and his fellow jaunters too. What held them together now was a feeling of responsibility towards a task shared through their empathic connection. But once that task was done, well, he just didn't know. The Fenris had said that power must be balanced by responsibility, so perhaps it never went away. With one task completed, another would come along to keep them welded together. They were certainly not done with Committee Earth, and he could see that in the apparently endless multiverse there would be other places the same. He could extrapolate on all this and come to conclusions, and perhaps that was where Ottanger went in his mind, but he'd decided to limit speculation. He was alive, and endless possibilities had opened ahead.

But right now, he had a job to do.

About the Author

Neal Asher divides his time between Essex and Crete, mostly at a keyboard and mentally light years away. His full-length novels are as follows. First is the Agent Cormac series: *Gridlinked*, *The Line of Polity*, *Brass Man*, *Polity Agent* and *Line War*. Next comes the Spatterjay series: *The Skinner*, *The Voyage of the Sable Keech* and *Orbus*. Also set in the same world of the Polity are these standalone novels: *Prador Moon*, *Hilldiggers*, *Shadow of the Scorpion*, *The Technician*, *Jack Four*, *Weaponized*, *War Bodies* and *World Walkers*. The Transformation trilogy is also based in the Polity: *Dark Intelligence*, *War Factory* and *Infinity Engine*. Set in a dystopian future are *The Departure*, *Zero Point* and *Jupiter War*, while *Cowl* takes us across time. The Rise of the Jain trilogy, set in the Polity universe, too, comprises *The Soldier*, *The Warship* and *The Human*.

U.S. $24.95 • Science Fiction / Space Opera

PRAISE FOR NEAL ASHER

Neal Asher's books are like an adrenaline shot targeted directly for the brain.
—**John Scalzi, author of *Old Man's War***

Without a doubt the most entertaining science fiction author writing today.
—*SFF World*

He can jump between worlds. But can he save his own?

As a totalitarian Inspectorate tightens its grip, one man discovers the power to slip through the gaps and traverse alternate universes. *World Walkers* by Neal Asher is an exhilarating standalone novel set within the Owner Trilogy.

Ottanger is a rebel and mutant on an Earth governed by a ruthless Committee. But after its Inspectorate experiments on him, Ottanger realizes the mutation allows him to reach alternate worlds. The multiverse is revealed in all its glory and terror—and he understands that he can finally flee his timeline.

Then Ottanger meets the Fenris, an evolved human, visiting his Earth from the far future. He'd engineered the original world-walking mutation, so those altered could escape the Committee's nightmarish regime. Yet this only worked for a few, and millions continued to suffer. And Ottanger sees that that Committee will become unstoppable if not destroyed.

However, the Fenris has drawn yet another threat to Ottanger's Earth. With the power of its trillion linked minds, it craves world-walking biotech and will do anything to get it. As conflict looms at home, and war threatens the multiverse—the Fenris, Ottanger and his companions must prepare for a galaxy-altering battle . . .

An imprint of Start Science Fiction
Visit www.pyrsf.com

Cover design by Jennifer Do
Cover image © Shutterstock / Vezdehod
Cover design © Start Science Fiction

ISBN 978-1-64506-088-8   US $24.95

52495

9 781645 060888